About the Author

James Clavell, the son of a Royal Navy family, was educated in Portsmouth before, as a young artillery officer, he was captured by the Japanese at the Fall of Singapore. He spent the rest of World War II in the infamous Changi prison. It was on his experience in Changi that his bestselling novel KING RAT was based. The interest in Asia, its people and culture contined with TAI-PAN, a tale of Canton and Hong Kong in the mid-19th century and the founding of an Anglo-Chinese trading company, Struans. This was followed by the classic SHOGUN, the story of Japan during the period when Europe began to make an impact on the island people of the Rising Sun. NOBLE HOUSE, the fourth novel in the Asian saga published in 1981, continued the story of Struans, the Hong Kong trading company, as the winds of change blew through the Far East. WHIRLWIND, set in Iran, continued the saga. His last novel, GAI-JIN, is set in Japan in 1862, when the-Tai Pan of the Noble House seeks to profit from the decline of the Shogunate.

James Clavell lived for many years in Vancouver and Los Angeles, before settling in Switzerland, where he died in 1994.

TAI-PAN

is the second novel in the Asian Saga that consists of:

Other titles by James Clavell

Escape
The Children's Story
Thrump-O-moto
The Art of War by Sun Tzu
(edited by James Clavell)

Tai-Pan

James Clavell

FLAME
Hodder & Stoughton

Copyright © 1966 by James Clavell

The right of James Clavell to be identified as the Author
of the Work has been asserted by him in accordance with the
Copyright, Designs and Patents Act 1988.

First published in Great Britain in 1966
by Michael Joseph Limited

First published in paperback in 1975
by Hodder and Stoughton
A division of Hodder Headline PLC

A Flame Paperback

10 9 8 7 6

A CIP catalogue record for this title
is available from the British Library

ISBN 0 340 75069 3

Typeset by Hewer Text Ltd, Edinburgh
Printed and bound in Great Britain by
Mackays of Chatham plc, Chatham, Kent

Hodder and Stoughton
A division of Hodder Headline PLC
338 Euston Road
London NW1 3BH

For *Tai-tai*, for Holly,
and for Michaela

Author's Note

I would like to express my thanks to the people of Hong Kong who gave me so much of their time and knowledge and allowed me into their present and past. Of course, this is not a history but a novel. It is peopled with men and women created out of the author's imagination, and no reference to anyone, or to any company, that was – or is part – of Hong Kong is intended.

BOOK ONE

Dirk Struan *came up on the quarter deck of the flagship HMS* Vengeance, *and strode for the gangway. Surrounding her were the rest of the fleet's warships, the troop-ships of the expeditionary force, and the merchantmen and opium clippers of the China traders.*

It was dawn – a drab, chill Tuesday – January 26th, 1841.

As Struan walked among the main deck, he glanced at the shore and excitement swarmed over him. The war with China had gone as he had planned. Victory was as he had forecast. The prize of victory – the island – was something he had coveted for twenty years. And now he was going ashore to witness the formality of taking possession, to watch a Chinese island become a jewel in the crown of Her Britannic Majesty, Queen Victoria.

The island was Hong Kong. Thirty square miles of mountainous stone on the north lip of the huge Pearl River in south China. A thousand yards off the mainland. Inhospitable. Infertile. Uninhabited except for a tiny fishing village on the south side. Squarely in the path of the monstrous storms that yearly exploded from the Pacific. Bordered on the east and on the west by dangerous shoals and reefs. Useless to the mandarin – the name given to any official of the Chinese Emperor – in whose province it lay.

But Hong Kong contained the greatest harbour on earth. And it was Struan's stepping-stone into China.

'Belay there!' the young officer of the watch called to the scarlet-coated marine. 'Mr Struan's longboat to the midships gangway!'

'Yes, sirr!' The marine leaned over the side and echoed the order.

'Won't be a moment, sir,' the officer said, trying to contain his awe of the merchant prince who was a legend in the China seas.

'Nae hurry, lad.' Struan was a giant of a man, his face weathered by a thousand storms. His blue frock coat was silver-buttoned and his tight while trousers were tucked carelessly into seaboots. He was armed as usual – knife in the crease of his back and another in his right boot. He was forty-three, red-headed, and his eyes were emerald green.

'It's a bonny day,' he said.

'Yes, sir.'

Struan walked down the gangway, got into the prow of his longboat and smiled at his younger half-brother, Robb, who sat amidships.

'We're late,' Robb said with a grin.

'Aye. His Excellency and the admiral were longwinded.' Struan stared at the island for a moment. Then he motioned at the bosun. 'Cast off. Go ashore, Mr McKay!'

'Aye, aye, sorr!'

'At long last, eh, Tai-Pan?' Robb said. 'Tai-Pan' was Chinese for 'supreme leader'. In a company or army or fleet or nation there is only one such man – he who wields the real power.

'Aye,' Struan said.

He was Tai-Pan of the Noble House.

1

'A pox on this stinking island,' Brock said, staring around the beach and up at the mountains. 'The whole of China at our feets and all we takes be this barren, sodding rock.'

He was standing on the foreshore with two of his fellow China traders. Scattered about them were other clusters of traders, and officers from the expeditionary force. They were all waiting for the Royal Navy officer to begin the ceremony. An honour guard of twenty marines was drawn up in two neat lines beside the flagpole, the scarlet of their uniforms a sudden splash of colour. Near them were the untidy knots of sailors who had just fought the flagpole into the stony soil.

'Eight bells were time to raise the flag,' Brock said, his voice rasping with impatience. 'It be an hour past. Wot's godrotting delay for—'

'It's bad joss to curse on a Tuesday, Mr Brock,' Jeff Cooper said. He was a lean, hook-nosed American from Boston, his frock coat black and his felt top hat set at a jaunty angle. 'Very bad!'

Cooper's partner, Wilf Tillman, stiffened slightly, feeling the underlying edge to the younger man's nasal voice. He was thickset and ruddy, and came from Alabama.

'I'll tell thee right smartly, this whole godrotting flyspeck be bad joss!' Brock said. 'Joss' was a Chinese word that meant Luck and Fate and God and the Devil combined. 'Godrotting bad.'

'It better not be, sir,' Tillman said. 'The future of the China trade's here now – good joss or bad joss.'

Brock stared down at him. 'Hong Kong's got no future. It's open ports on the China mainland we be needing, and you knowed it, by God!'

'The harbour's the best in these waters,' Cooper said. 'Plenty of room to careen and refit all our ships. Plenty of room to build our homes and warehouses. And no Chinese interference at long last.'

'A colony's got to have arable land and peasants to work the land, Mr Cooper. An' revenue,' Brock said impatiently. 'I be walking all over

5

and so have you. Not a crop'll grow here. There be no fields or streams, no grazing land. So no meat and no spuds. Everything we be needing'll have to come by sea. Think of the cost. Why, even the fishing be rotten. An' who's to pay upkeep of Hong Kong, eh? Us and our trade, by God!'

'Oh, that's the sort of colony you want, Mr Brock?' Cooper said. 'I thought the British Empire' – he spat deftly to windward – 'had enough of that sort of colony.'

Brock's hand strayed near his knife. 'Be you spitting to clear yor throat, or spitting on the Empire?' Tyler Brock was nearing fifty, a big, one-eyed man as hard and as permanent as the iron he had been forced to peddle in Liverpool as a youth, and as strong and as dangerous as the fighting merchant ships he had escaped to and at length had come to rule as head of Brock and Sons. His clothes were rich and the knife at his belt was jewelled. His beard was greying like his hair.

'It's a cold day, Mr Brock,' Tillman said quickly, inwardly angry at his young partner's loose tongue. Brock was no man to bait, and they could not afford open enmity with him yet. 'Plenty of chill on the wind, eh, Jeff?'

Cooper nodded briefly. But he did not take his eyes off Brock. He had no knife, but there was a derringer in his pocket. He was of a height with Brock but slighter, and unafraid.

'I be givin' thee piece of advice, Mr Cooper,' Brock said. 'Best not spit too often after saying "British Empire". There be some wot baint be givin' thee benefit of doubt.'

'Thank you, Mr Brock, I'll remember,' Cooper replied easily. 'And I'll give you some advice: it's bad joss to curse on a Tuesday.'

Brock suppressed his temper. Eventually he would crush Cooper and Tillman and their company, the biggest of the American traders. But now he needed them as allies against Dirk and Robb Struan. Brock cursed joss. Joss had made Struan and Company the greatest house in Asia, and so rich and powerful that the other China traders had named it in awe and jealousy *The Noble House* – noble because it was first in riches, first in largess, first in trade, first in clippers, but mostly because Dirk Struan was Tai-Pan, *the* Tai-Pan among all the tai-pans of Asia. And joss had cost Brock an eye seventeen years ago, the year that Struan had founded his empire.

It had happened off Chushan Island. Chushan was just south of the huge port of Shanghai, near the mouth of the mighty Yangtse River. Brock had beaten up through the monsoon, with a huge cargo of opium – Dirk Struan a few days astern, also carrying opium. Brock had

6

reached Chushan first, sold his cargo and turned around, knowing happily that now Struan would have to go farther north and try a new coast with fresh risks. Brock had sped south for home – Macao – his coffers filled with bullion, the full wind astern. Then a great storm had suddenly swooped out of the China seas. The Chinese called these storms *tai-fung*, the Supreme Winds. The traders called them typhoons. They were terror incarnate.

The typhoon had battered Brock's ship mercilessly, and he had been pinned by the falling masts and spars. A shorn halyard, caught by the winds, had flailed him as he lay helpless. His men had cut him loose but not before the broken shackle-ended rope had gouged out his left eye. The ship had been on her beam ends and he helped them cut the rigging and spars adrift, and by some miracle she had righted herself. Then he had poured brandy into the bleeding socket; he could still remember the pain.

And he recalled how he had limped into port long after he had been given up for lost, his fine three-masted clipper no more than a hulk, the seams sprung, masts and guns and rigging gone. And by the time Brock had replaced spars and rigging and masts and cannon and powder and shot and men, and bought another cargo of opium, all the profits of this voyage had vanished.

Struan had run into the same typhoon in a small lorcha – a boat with a Chinese hull, English-rigged and used for coastal smuggling in fine weather. But Struan rode out the storm and elegant and untouched as usual, had been on the dock to greet Brock, his strange green eyes mocking him.

Dirk and his cursed joss, Brock thought. Joss be letting Dirk build that one stinking lorcha into a fleet of clippers and hundreds of lorchas, into warehouses and bullion to spare. Into godrotting Noble House. Joss pushed Brock and Sons into godrotting second place. Second. And, he thought, joss's given him ear of our godrotting, weak-gutted plenipotentiary, the Honourable Godrotting Longstaff, all these years. An' now, together, they've sold us out. 'A *pox* on Hong Kong and a *pox* on Struan!'

'If it weren't for Struan's plan, you'd never have won your war so easily,' Cooper said.

The war had begun at Canton two years before, when the Chinese emperor, determined to bring the Europeans to heel, tried to eliminate the opium smuggling which was essential to British trade. Viceroy Ling had surrounded the foreign settlement at Canton with troops, and demanded every case of opium in Asia to ransom the lives of the defenceless English traders. At length, twenty thousand cases of opium

7

had been given over and destroyed, and the British were allowed to retreat to Macao. But the British Empire could not take lightly either interference with its trade or threats to its nationals. Six months ago the British Expeditionary Force had arrived in the Orient and ostensibly had been placed under the jurisdiction of Longstaff, the Captain Superintendent of Trade.

But it was Struan who conceived the inspired plan to bypass Canton, where all the trouble had started, and instead send the expeditionary force north to Chushan. To take that island without loss would be simple, Struan had theorized, for the Chinese were unprepared and helpless against any modern European army or fleet. Leaving a small holding force at Chushan and a few ships to blockade the Yangtse, the expeditionary force could sail north to the mouth of the Pei Ho River and threaten Peking, the capital of China, which was only a hundred miles upstream. Struan knew that only so direct a threat would make the emperor immediately sue for peace. A superb conception. And it had worked brilliantly. The expeditionary force had arrived in the Orient last June. By July Chushan had been taken. By August it was moored at the Pei Ho. In two weeks the emperor had sent an official to negotiate peace – the first time in history that any Chinese emperor had officially acknowledged any European nation. And the war had ended with almost no loss to either side.

'Longstaff was very wise to follow the plan,' Cooper said.

'Any China trader knowed how to bring the Chinese to their knees,' Brock said, his voice rough. He pushed his top hat farther back on his forehead and eased his eye patch. 'But why did Longstaff and Struan agree to negotiate back at Canton, eh? Any fool knowed "negotiate" to a Chinese means to play for time. We should've stayed north at the Pei Ho till peace were signed. But no, we brung back the fleet and for the last six month we be waiting and waiting for the buggers to set pen to paper.' Brock spat. 'Stupid, crazy stupid. An' all that waste of time and money for this stinking rock. We should've kept Chushan. Now, there be island worth having.' Chushan was twenty miles long and ten wide and its land fertile and rich – good port and a big city. Tinghai. 'Space for a man to breathe in there, right enough. Why, from there three or four frigates can blockade the Yangtse at the drop of a topper. An' who controls that river controls the heart of China. That's where we should settle, by God.'

'You still have Chushan, Mr Brock.'

'Yus. But it baint deeded in godrotting treaty, so it baint our'n.' He stamped his feet against the growing chill wind.

'Perhaps you should mention it to Longstaff,' Cooper said. 'He's susceptible to advice.'

'Not to mine, he baint. As thee rightly knowed. But I'll tell thee, when Parliament hear about the treaty, there be hell to pay, I'll be bound.'

Cooper lit a cheroot. 'I'm inclined to agree. It is an astonishing piece of paper, Mr Brock. For this day and age. When every European power is land-grabbing and power-hungry.'

'And I suppose the United States baint?' Brock's face tightened. 'Wot about yore Indians? The Louisiana Purchase? Spanish Florida? You be havin' eyes on Mexico and Russian Alaska. The last mails told you be even trying to steal Canada. Eh?'

'Canada's American, not English. We're not going to war over Canada – she'll join us of her own free will,' Cooper said, hiding his worry. He tugged at his muttonchop whiskers and pulled his frock coat tighter around his shoulders against the sharpening wind. He knew that war with the British Empire would be disastrous at this time, and would ruin Cooper-Tillman. God damn wars. Even so, he knew that the States would have to go to war over Mexico and Canada unless there was a settlement. Just as Britain had had to go to war with China.

'There won't be a war,' Tillman said, trying to quiet Cooper diplomatically. He sighed and wished himself back in Alabama. A man can be a gentleman there, he thought. There you don't have to deal with the damned British every day, or with blasphemous, foulmouthed scum like Brock, or a devil incarnate like Struan – or even with an impetuous young man and senior partner like Jefferson Cooper, who thinks Boston the centre of the earth. 'And this war's over, for better or worse.'

'Mark my words, Mr Tillman,' Brock said. 'This godrotting treaty be no good for us'n and no good for they. We've to keep Chushan and open ports on mainland China. We be at war again in a few weeks. In June when the wind be ripe and the weather be ripe, the fleet'll have to sail north to Pei Ho again. An' if we be at war again, how we going to get season's teas and silks, eh? Last year almost no trade because of war – the year before no trade at all an' they stole all our opium to boot. Eight thousand cases from me alone. Two million taels of silver that cost me. Cash.'

'That money's not lost,' Tillman said. 'Longstaff ordered us to give it up. To ransom our lives. He gave us paper on the British Government. And there's a settlement in the treaty. Six million taels of silver to pay for it.'

Brock laughed harshly. 'Thee think Parliament be honouring Long-staff's paper. Why, any Government'd be throwed out of office the moment they asked for the brass to pay for opium. An' as to the six million – that be paying for the cost of the war. I knowed Parliament better'n you. Kiss yor half million taels goodbye be my advice to you both. So if we be at war again this year, there be no trade again. An' if we baint trading this year, we be all bankrupt. You, me, every China trader. An' even the godrotting Noble House.' He jerked out his watch. The ceremony was to have started an hour ago. Time be running out, he thought. Yus, but not on Brock and Sons, by God. Dirk's had seventeen-year run of good joss, and now be time for change.

Brock revelled in the thought of his second son, Morgan, who capably – and ruthlessly – controlled all their interests in England. He wondered if Morgan had been successful in undermining Struan's influence in Parliament and in banking circles. We be going to wreck thee, Dirk, he thought, and Hong Kong along with thee. 'Wot the hell be the delay for?' he said, hastening towards the naval officer who was striding up and down near the marines.

'What's the matter with you, Jeff? You know he's right about Hong Kong,' Tillman said. 'You ought to know better than to bait him.'

Cooper smiled his thin smile. 'Brock's so goddam sure of himself. I couldn't help it.'

'If Brock's right about the half million taels, we're ruined.'

'Yes. But Struan will lose ten times that if there's no payment. He'll get paid, never fear. So we'll get ours.' Cooper looked after Brock. 'Do you think he knows about our deal with Struan?'

Tillman shrugged. 'I don't know. But Brock's right about the treaty. It's stupid. It'll cost us a pretty penny.'

For the last three months Cooper-Tillman had been acting as secret agents for The Noble House. British warships had been blockading Canton and the Pearl River, and British traders were forbidden to trade. Longstaff – at Struan's bidding – had put the embargo on as another measure to force the peace treaty, knowing that the Canton warehouses were bulging with teas and silks. But since America had not declared war on China, American ships could go through the blockade freely and thumb their noses at the warships. So Cooper-Tillman had bought four million pounds of tea from Chen-tse Jin Arn – or Jin-qua, as he was nicknamed – the richest of the Chinese merchants, and shipped it to Manila, supposedly for Spanish merchants. The local Spanish official, for a considerable bribe, had issued the necessary import and export licences, and the tea was transferred – duty free –

into Struan's clippers and rushed to England. Payment to Jin-qua was a shipload of opium delivered secretly by Struan somewhere up the coast.

A perfect plan, Cooper thought. Everyone's richer and gets the trade goods he wants. But we would have made a fortune if our ships could have taken the teas direct to England. And he cursed the British Navigation Acts that forbade any but British ships to bring goods into English ports. Goddam them, they own the world.

'Jeff!'

Cooper followed his partner's glance. For a moment he could not pick out what Tillman wanted him to see in the crowded harbour. Then he saw the longboat pulling away from the flagship and in it the tall, redheaded Scotsman who was so powerful that he could twist Parliament to his purposes and put the greatest nation on earth to war.

'It would be too much to hope that Struan'd drown,' Tillman said.

Cooper laughed. 'You're wrong about him, Wilf. Anyway, the sea'd never dare.'

'Maybe it will, Jeff. It's time enough. By all that's holy.'

Dirk Struan stood in the prow of the longboat, riding the twist of the waves. And though he was already late for the ceremony, he did not hurry his oarsmen. He knew that there would be no starting until he arrived.

The longboat was three hundred yards offshore and the bosun's 'Steady as she goes' mixed nicely with the crisp northeast monsoon. Far aloft, the wind gathered strength and scudded cumulus off the mainland over the island and out to the ocean beyond.

The harbour was crowded with shipping, all British but for a few American and Portuguese vessels, merchantmen of every size. Before the war the merchantmen would have been anchored at Macao, the tiny Portuguese settlement on a tip of the mainland, forty miles southwest across the huge mouth of the Pearl River. Or off the island of Whampoa, thirteen miles south of Canton. This was the nearest that any European ship was allowed, by Chinese law, to approach Canton. By imperial decree all European trade was restricted to this city. Legend said that over a million Chinese lived within its walls. But no European knew for certain, for none had ever walked its streets.

Since antiquity the Chinese had had rigid laws excluding Europeans from their country. The inflexibility of these laws, the lack of freedom for Europeans to go where they pleased and trade as they pleased, had caused the war.

As the longboat passed near a merchantman, some children waved at

Struan and he waved back. It'll be good for the bairns to have their own homes at long last, on their own soil, he thought. When the war had begun, all British citizens had been evacuated on to the ships for safety. There were approximately a hundred and fifty men, sixty wives, eighty children. A few of the families had been aboard one ship or another for almost a year.

Surrounding the merchantmen were the warships of the British Expeditionary Force: ships of the line, 74-guns, 44's, 22's, brigs, frigates, a small part of the mightiest navy the world had ever known. And dozens of troopships with four thousand British and Indian soldiers aboard, part of the strongest army on earth.

And among these ships were the beautiful rake-masted opium clippers, the fleetest ships ever built.

Struan felt a glow of excitement as he studied the island with its dominating mountain that soared eighteen hundred feet almost sheer from the sea.

He had never set foot on the island even though he knew more about it than any man. He had sworn not to go ashore until it was British-owned. It pleased him to be so imperious. But this had not prevented him from sending his captains and his younger brother Robb ashore to survey the island. He knew the reefs and the rocks and the glens and hills, and he knew where he was going to build his warehouses and the Great House, and where the road would be.

He turned to look at his clipper, *China Cloud*, 22 guns. All of Struan and Company's clippers were surnamed 'Cloud' to honour his mother, a McCloud, who had died years ago. Seamen were painting and cleaning an already sparkling vessel. Guns were being examined and rigging tested. The Union Jack fluttered proudly aft and the company flag atop the mizen.

The flag of The Noble House was the royal red lion of Scotland entwined with the imperial green dragon of China. It flew on twenty armed clippers scattered over the oceans of the world, on a hundred swift-sailing armed lorchas that smuggled opium up the coast. It flew on three huge opium supply depot ships – converted hulks of merchantmen which were presently anchored in Hong Kong harbour. And it flew over *Resting Cloud*, his vast semi-stationary headquarters vessel that contained bullion strong rooms, offices, luxurious suites and dining-rooms.

You're a bonny flag, Struan thought proudly.

The first ship that had flown the flag had been an opium-laden pirate lorcha that he had taken by force. Pirates and corsairs infested the

12

coasts, and the Chinese and Portuguese authorities offered a silver bounty for pirates. When the winds had forbidden opium smuggling or when he had no opium to sell, he had scoured the China seas. The bullion he gained from the pirates he invested in opium.

Godrot opium, he thought. But he knew that his life was inexorably tied to opium – and that without it neither The Noble House nor the British Empire could exist.

The reason could be traced back to 1699, when the first British ship traded peacefully with China and brought back silks and, for the first time, the peerless herb called tea – which China alone on earth produced cheaply and in abundance. In exchange, the emperor would take only silver bullion. And this policy had persisted ever since.

Within fifty-odd years tea became the most popular drink of the Western world – particularly of Britain, the major trading nation on earth. In seventy years tea was the single major source of internal tax revenue for the British Government. Within a century the outpouring of wealth to China had critically depleted the British treasury and the unbalanced tea-bullion trade was a national catastrophe.

Over the century, the British East India Company – the gigantic semi-private, semi-public firm which possessed, by Act of Parliament, a total monopoly on Indian and Asian trade – had offered everything and anything with growing desperation – cotton goods, looms, even guns and ships – in place of bullion. But the emperors imperiously refused. They considered China self-sufficient, were contemptuous of 'barbarians', as they called all non-Chinese, and regarded all the nations of the earth as no better than vassal states of China.

And then, thirty years ago, a British merchantman, the *Vagrant Star*, had sailed up the Pearl River and anchored off Whampoa Island. Its secret cargo was opium, which British Bengal produced cheaply and in abundance. Although opium had been used in China for centuries – but only by the very rich and by those in Yunnan Province where the poppy also flourished – it was contraband. The East India Company had clandestinely licensed the captain of *Vagrant Star* to offer the opium. But only for bullion. The Chinese Guild of Merchants, which by imperial decree monopolized all Western Trade, bought the cargo and sold it secretly at a great profit. The captain of the *Vagrant Star* privately turned over the bullion to the Company's officers in Canton and took his profit in bank paper on London and rushed back to Calcutta for more opium.

Struan remembered the *Vagrant Star* well. He had been a cabin boy aboard her. It was in this vessel that he had become a man – and had

13

seen Asia. And had sworn to destroy Tyler Brock, who at the time was the *Vagrant Star*'s third mate. Struan was twelve, Brock eighteen and very strong. Brock had hated him on sight and delighted in finding fault, cutting his food ration, ordering him extra watches, sending him aloft in foul weather, baiting him, goading him. The slightest mistake and he had Struan tied to the rigging and lashed with the cat-o'-nine-tails.

Struan had stayed with the *Vagrant Star* for two years. Then one night she struck a reef in the Malacca Strait and went down. Struan had swum ashore and made his way to Singapore. Later he learned that Brock had survived too and this made him very happy. He wanted revenge, in his own way, in his own time.

Struan had joined another ship. By now the East India Company was secretly licensing many carefully selected independent captain-traders, and continuing to sell them exclusively Bengal opium at advantageous prices. The Company began to make huge profits and acquire vast quantities of silver bullion. The Chinese Guild of Merchants and the mandarins turned blind eyes to the illicit trade, for they too made huge profits. And these profits, being secret, were not subject to imperial squeeze.

Opium became the inbound staple of trade. The Company quickly monopolized the world supply of opium outside Yunnan Province and the Ottoman Empire. Within twenty years the bullion traded for smuggled opium equalled the bullion that was owed for teas and silks.

At last trade balanced. Then over balanced, for there were twenty times more Chinese customers than Western customers, and there began a staggering outpouring of bullion that even China could not afford. The Company offered other trade goods to stem the tide. But the emperor remained adamant: bullion for tea.

By the time Struan was twenty he was captain-owner of his own ship on the opium run. Brock was his chief rival. They competed ruthlessly with each other. Within six years Struan and Brock dominated the trade.

The opium smugglers became known as China traders. They were an intrepid, tough, vital group of individualistic owner-captains – English, Scots, and some Americans – who casually drove their tiny ships into unknown waters and unknown dangers as a way of life. They went to sea to trade peacefully: to make a profit, not to conquer. But if they met with a hostile sea or a hostile act, their ships became fighting ships. And if they did not fight well, their ships vanished and were soon forgotten.

14

The China traders soon realized that while they were taking all the risks, the Company was taking most of the profit. And, too, they were totally excluded from the legitimate – and hugely profitable – tea and silk trade. So although they continued to compete fiercely, at Struan's persuasion they began to agitate collectively against the Company to break its monopoly. Without the monopoly the traders could convert opium into bullion, bullion into tea, then ship the tea home and sell it directly to the markets of the world. The China traders would themselves control the world tea trade and their profits would become gigantic.

Parliament became their forum for agitation. Parliament had given the Company its exclusive monopoly two centuries ago, and only Parliament could take it away. So the China traders gambled heavily, buying votes, supporting members of Parliament who believed in free competition and free trade, writing to newspapers and to members of the Government. They were determined, and as their wealth increased so did their power. They were patient and tenacious and indomitable – as only men trained by the sea can be.

The Company was furious at the insurgents and reluctant to lose its monopoly. But it desperately needed the China traders to supply the bullion to pay for the teas, and by now it depended heavily on the huge revenue from the sale of Bengal opium. So it fought back carefully in Parliament. Parliament was equally trapped. It decried the sale of opium but needed the revenue from the teas and the Indian Empire. Parliament tried to listen to the China traders and to the Company, and satisfied neither.

Then the Company decided to make an example of Struan and Brock, its chief antagonists. It withdrew their opium licences and broke them.

Brock was left with his ship, Struan with nothing. Brock went into secret partnership with another China trader and continued to agitate. Struan and his crew fell on a pirate haven south of Macao, laid it waste, and took the fastest lorcha. Then he became a clandestine opium runner for other traders, and relentlessly took more pirate ships, and made more and more money. In consort with other China traders, he gambled ever more heavily, buying ever more votes and continuing to harass and exhort until Parliament was howling for the total destruction of the Company. Seven years earlier Parliament had passed the Act that eliminated the Company's monopoly on Asia and opened it to free trade. But it allowed the Company to retain the exclusive right to trade with British India – in the world monopoly of opium. Parliament deplored the sale of opium. The Company did not wish to trade with opium. The China traders themselves would have preferred another – though equally profitable – staple. But they all knew that without the tea-bullion-opium balance the Empire would be wrecked. It was a fact of life of world trade.

With freedom to trade, Struan and Brock became merchant princes. Their armed fleets expanded. And rivalry honed their enmity ever keener.

To replace the political vacuum left in Asia when the Company's control was nullified and trade freed, the British Government had appointed a diplomat, the Honourable William Longstaff, as Captain Superintendent of Trade to protect its interests. The interests of the Crown were an ever-expanding volume of trade – to gain more tax revenue – and the continued exclusion of all other European powers. Longstaff was responsible for the safety of trade and of British nationals, but his mandate was vague and he was given no real power to enforce a policy.

Poor little Willie, Struan thought without malice. Even with all my patient explanations over the last eight years, our 'exalted' Excellency, the Captain Superintendent of Trade, still canna see his hand afore his face.

Struan looked at the shore as the sun crested the mountains and bathed the men gathered there with sudden light: friends and enemies, all rivals. He turned to Robb. 'Would you no say they're a welcoming committee?' All his years away from Scotland had not completely erased his Scots brogue.

Robb Struan chuckled and set his felt hat at a crisper angle. 'I'd say they all hope we'll drown, Dirk.' He was thirty-three, dark-haired, clean-shaven, with deep-set eyes, thin nose, and heavy muttonchop whiskers. His clothes were black except for a green velvet cloak and white ruffled shirt and white cravat. His shirt and cuff buttons were rubies. 'Good God is that Captain Glessing?' he asked, peering at the shore.

'Aye,' Struan said. 'I thought it apt that he should be the one to read the proclamation.'

'What did Longstaff say when you suggested it?'

' " 'Pon me word, Dirk, all right, if you think it wise." ' He grinned. 'We've come a long way since we started, by God!'

'*You* have, Dirk. It was all done when I came out here.'

'You're the brains, Robb. I'm just the muscle.'

'Yes, Tai-Pan. Just the muscle.' Robb knew well that his stepbrother

16

was Tai-Pan of Struan and Company, and that in Asia Dirk Struan was *the* Tai-Pan. 'A beautiful day for the flag raising, isn't it?'

'Aye.'

Robb watched him as he turned back to the shore. He looked so huge, standing there in the prow, bigger than the mountains and just as hard. I wish I were like him, Robb thought.

Robb had gone opium smuggling only once, shortly after he arrived in the Orient. Their ship had been attacked by Chinese pirates and Robb had been terrified. He was still ashamed, even though Struan had said, 'Nae harm in that, laddie. The first time in battle is always bad.' But Robb knew that he was not a fighter, not brave. He served his half-brother in other ways. Buying teas and silks and opium. Arranging loans and watching the bullion. Understanding the ever more complicated modern procedures of international trading and financing. Guarding his brother and the company and their fleet and making them safe. Selling teas in England. Keeping the books and doing all the things that made a modern company function. Yes, Robb told himself, but without Dirk you're nothing.

Struan was studying the men on the beach. The longboat was still two hundred yards offshore. But he could see the faces clearly. Most of them were looking at the longboat. Struan smiled to himself.

Aye, he thought. We're all here on this day of destiny.

The naval officer, Captain Glessing, was waiting patiently to begin the flag-raising ceremony. He was twenty-six, a captain of a ship of the line, the son of a vice-admiral, and the Royal Navy was part of his bloodstream. It was getting lighter rapidly on the beach, and far to the east on the horizon the sky was threaded with clouds.

There'll be a storm in a few days, Glessing thought, tasting the wind. He took his eyes off Struan and automatically checked the lie of his ship, a 22-gun frigate. This was a monumental day in his life. It was not often that new lands were taken in the name of the queen, and for him to have the privilege of reading the proclamation was fortunate for his career. There were many captains in the fleet senior to him. But he knew that he had been chosen because he had been in these waters the longest, and his ship, HMS *Mermaid*, had been heavily involved in the whole campaign. Not a campaign at all, he thought with contempt. More of an incident. It could have been settled two years ago if that fool Longstaff had had any guts. Certainly, if I'd been allowed to take my frigate up to the gates of Canton. Dammit, I sank a whole bloody fleet of war junks, and the way was clear. I could have bombarded Canton and taken that heathen devil Viceroy Ling and hung him at the yardarm.

Glessing kicked the beach irritably. It's not that I mind the heathen stealing the damned opium. Quite right to want to stop smuggling. It's the insult to the flag. English lives ransomed by heathen devils! Longstaff should have allowed me to proceed forthwith. But no. He meekly retreated and evacuated everyone on to the merchant fleet and then hamstrung me. Me, by God, who had to protect the whole merchant fleet. Damn his eyes! And damn Struan, who leads him by the nose.

Well, he added to himself, even so you're lucky to be here. This is the only war we've got at the moment. At least, the only seaborne war. The others are mere incidents: the simple taking over of the heathen Indian states – by gad, they worship cows and burn widows and bow down before idols – and the Afghan wars. And he felt a surge of pride that he was part of the greatest fleet on earth. Thank God he had been born English!

Abruptly he noticed Brock approaching and was relieved to see him intercepted by a short, fat, neckless man in his thirties, with a huge belly that overflowed his trousers. This was Morley Skinner, proprietor of the *Oriental Times,* the most important of the English papers in the Orient. Glessing read every edition. It was well written. Important to have a good newspaper, he thought. Important to have campaigns well recorded to the glory of England. But Skinner's a revolting man. And all the rest of them. Well, not all of them. Not old Aristotle Quance.

He glanced at the ugly little man sitting alone on a bank overlooking the beach, on a stool in front of an easel, obviously painting away. Glessing chuckled to himself, remembering the good times he had had in Macao with the painter.

Apart from Quance, Glessing liked no one on the beach except Horatio Sinclair. Horatio was the same age as he, and Glessing had come to know him quite well in the two years he had been in the Orient. Horatio was also an aide to Longstaff, his interpreter and secretary – the only Englishman in the Orient who could speak and write fluent Chinese – and they had had to work together.

Glessing scanned the beach and saw, distastefully, that Horatio was down by the surf chatting with an Austrian, Wolfgang Mauss, a man whom he despised. The Reverend Mauss was the only other European in the Orient who could write and speak Chinese. He was a huge, black-bearded man – a renegade priest, Struan's interpreter and opium runner. There were pistols in his belt, and the tails of his frock coat were mildewed. His nose was red and bulbous and his long, black-grey hair matted and wild like his beard. His few remaining teeth were broken and brown, and his eyes dominated the grossness of his face.

18

Such a contrast to Horatio, Glessing thought. Horatio was fair and frail and clean as Nelson, for whom he had been named – because of Trafalgar and because of an uncle he had lost there.

Included in their conversation was a tall, lithe Eurasian, a young man that Glessing knew only by sight. Gordon Chen, Struan's bastard.

By gad, Glessing thought, how can Englishmen flaunt half-caste bastards so openly? And this one dressed like all the bloody heathens in a long robe with a damned queue hanging down his back. By gad! If it weren't for his blue eyes and his fair skin, you couldn't tell he had any English blood in him at all. Why the devil doesn't he cut his hair like a man? Disgusting!

Glessing turned away from them. I suppose the half-caste's all right, not his fault. But that damned Mauss is bad company. Bad for Horatio and bad for his sister, dear Mary. Now, there's a young lady worth knowing! She'd make a good wife, by gad.

He hesitated in his walk. This was the first time that he had actually considered Mary as a possible mate.

Why not? he asked himself. You've known her for two years. She's the toast of Macao. She runs the Sinclair house impeccably and treats Horatio as a prince. The food's the best in town and she rules servants beautifully. Plays the harpsichord like a dream and sings like an angel, by Jove. She obviously likes you – why else would you have an open invitation to dine whenever you and Horatio are in Macao? So why not as wife, eh? But she's never been home. She's spent all her life among heathens. She has no income. Parents are dead. But what does that matter, eh? The Reverend Sinclair was respected throughout Asia when he was alive, and Mary's beautiful and just twenty. My prospects are excellent. I've five hundred a year and I'll inherit the manor house and the lands eventually. By gad, she could be the one for me. We could get married in Macao at the English church and rent a house until this commission's up and then we'll go home. When the time's ripe I'll say to Horatio, 'Horatio, old boy, there's something I want to talk to . . .'

'Wot be all the delay, Cap'n Glessing?' Brock's rough voice shattered his reverie. 'Eight bells were time to raise the flag and it be an hour past.'

Glessing whirled around. He was not used to a belligerent tone of voice from anyone less than a vice-admiral. 'The flag gets raised, Mr Brock, when one of two things happens. Either when His Excellency comes ashore or when there's a signal cannon from the flagship.'

'An' when be that?'

'I notice that you're not fully represented yet.'

19

'You mean Struan?'

'Of course. Isn't he Tai-Pan of The Noble House?' Glessing said it deliberately, knowing it would irritate Brock. Then he added, 'I suggest you possess yourself with patience. No one ordered any of you tradesmen ashore.'

Brock reddened. 'You'd better be learning difference twixt merchants an' tradesmen.' He moved his tobacco quid in his cheek and spat on the stones beside Glessing's feet. A few flecks of spittle marred the polish of the silver-buckled shoe. 'Beg pardon,' Brock said with mock humility and strode away.

Glessing's face froze. But for the 'Beg pardon' he would have challenged him to a duel. Rotten low-class sod, he thought, filled with contempt.

'Beggin' yor pardon, sorr,' the master-at-arms said, saluting, 'signal from the flagship.'

Glessing squinted his eyes against the sharpening wind. The signal flags read: 'All captains to report aboard at four bells.' Glessing had been present last night at a private meeting of the admiral and Longstaff. The admiral had said that opium smuggling was the cause of all the trouble in Asia. 'Goddamme, sir, they've no sense of decency,' he had exploded. 'All they think of is money. Abolish opium and we'll have no more damned trouble with the damned heathen or with the damned tradesmen. The Royal Navy will enforce your order, by God!' And Longstaff had agreed, rightly. I suppose the order will be announced today, Glessing thought, hard put to contain his delight. Good. And about time. I wonder if Longstaff has just told Struan that he's issuing the order.

He glanced back at the longboat which was approaching leisurely. Struan fascinated him. He admired him and loathed him – the master mariner who had conned ships on every ocean in the world, who wrecked men and companies and ships to the glory of The Noble House. So different from Robb, Glessing thought; I like Robb.

He shuddered in spite of himself. Perhaps there was truth in the tales whispered by sailormen the China seas over, tales that Struan worshipped the Devil in secret, and that in return the Devil had given him power on earth. How else could a man of his age look so young and be so strong, with white teeth and all his hair and the reflexes of a youth, when most men would be infirm and used up and near death? Certainly the Chinese were terrified of Struan. 'Old Green-eyed Rat Devil' they had nicknamed him, and had put a reward on his head. All Europeans had rewards on their heads. But the Tai-Pan's was a hundred thousand taels of silver. Dead. For no one would catch him alive.

Glessing irritably tried to ease his toes in his buckled shoes. His feet hurt and he was uncomfortable in his gold-braided uniform. Damn the delay! Damn the island and the harbour and the waste of good ships and good men. He remembered his father's saying, 'Blasted civilians. All they think of is money or power. They've no sense of honour, none. Watch your backside, son, when there's a civilian in command. And don't forget that even Nelson had to put his telescope to his blind eye when there was an idiot in command.' How can a man like Longstaff be so stupid? The man's from a good family, well-bred – his father was a diplomat at the court of Spain. Or was it Portugal?

And why did Struan push Longstaff into stopping the war? Certainly we get a harbour that can anchor the fleets of the world. But what else?

Glessing studied the ships in the harbour. Struan's 22-gun ship, *China Cloud*. The *White Witch*, 22-guns pride of Brock's fleet. And the American Cooper-Tillman 20-guns brig, *Princess of Alabama*. Beauties, all of them. Now, they'd be worth fighting, he thought. I know I could sink the American. Brock? Hard, but I'm better than Brock. Struan?

Glessing pondered about a sea battle with Struan. Then he knew that he was afraid of Struan. And because of his fear he was filled with anger and sick of the pretence that Struan and Brock and Cooper and all the China traders were not pirates.

By God, he swore to himself, as soon as the order's official, I'll lead a flotilla that'll blast them all out of the water.

Aristotle Quance sat moodily in front of the half-finished painting on his easel. He was a tiny man with grey-black hair. His clothes, about which he was incredibly fastidious, were in the latest fashion: tight grey trousers and white silk socks and black bow-tied shoes. Pearl satin waistcoat and black wool frock coat. High collar and cravat and pearl pin. Half English and half Irish, he was, at fifty-eight, the oldest European in the Orient.

He took off his gold spectacles and began to clean them with an immaculate French lace kerchief. I'm sorry to see this day, he thought. Damn Dirk Struan. If it weren't for him there'd be no damned Hong Kong.

He knew that he was witness to the end of an era. Hong Kong will destroy Macao, he thought. It will steal away all the trade. All the English and American tai-pans will move their headquarters here. They will live here and build here. Then all the Portuguese clerks will come. And all the Chinese who live off Westerners and Western trade. Well, I'm never going to live here, he swore. I'll have to come to work from time to time to earn money, but Macao will always be my home.

Macao had been his home for more than thirty years. He alone, of all the Europeans, thought of the Orient as home. All the others came for a few years and then left. Only those who died stayed. Even then, if they could afford it, they would provide in their wills for their bodies to be shipped back 'home'.

I'll be buried in Macao, thank God, he told himself. Such good times I've had there, we all have. But that's finished. God damn the Emperor of China! Fool to wreck a structure so cleverly constructed a century ago.

Everything was working so well, Quance thought bitterly, but now it's over. Now we've taken Hong Kong. And now that the might of England is committed in the East and the traders have had a taste of power, they won't be content with just Hong Kong. 'Well,' he said involuntarily aloud, 'the emperor will reap what he has sown.'

'Why so glum, Mr Quance?'

Quance put on his spectacles. Morley Skinner was standing at the foot of the bank.

'Not glum, young man. Sad. Artists have a right – yes, an obligation – to be sad.' He put the unfinished painting aside and set a clean piece of paper on his easel.

'Quite agree, quite agree.' Skinner lumbered up the bank, his pale brown eyes looking like the dregs of ancient beer. 'Just wanted to ask you your opinion of the momentous day. Going to put out a special edition. Without a few words from our senior citizen the edition wouldn't be complete.'

'Quite correct, Mr Skinner. You may say, "Mr Aristotle Quance, our leading artist, bon vivant and beloved friend, declined to make a statement as he was in the process of creating another masterpiece." ' He took a pinch of snuff and sneezed hugely. Then with his kerchief he dusted the excess snuff off his frock coat and the flecks of sneeze off the paper. 'Good day to you sir.' Once more he concentrated on the paper. 'You are disturbing immortality.'

'Know exactly how you feel,' Skinner said with a pleasant nod. 'Exactly how you feel. Feel the same when I've something important to write.' He plodded away.

Quance did not trust Skinner. No one did. At least no one with a skeleton in his past, and everyone here had something he wanted to hide. Skinner enjoyed resurrecting the past.

The past. Quance thought about his wife and shivered. Great thunderballs of death! How could I have been so stupid to think that Irish monster could make a worthy mate? Thank God she's back in the loathsome Irish bog, never to darken my firmament again. Women are the cause of all man's tribulations. Well, he added cautiously, not all women. Not dear little Maria Tang. Ah, now, there's a luscious colleen if ever I saw one. And if anyone knows an impeccable cross of Portuguese and Chinese, you do, dear clever Quance. Damn, I've had a wonderful life.

And he realized that though he was witnessing the end of an era, he was also part of a new one. Now he had new history to eyewitness and record. New faces to draw. New ships to paint. A new city to perpetuate. And new girls to flirt with and new bottoms to pinch.

'Sad? Never!' he roared. 'Get to work, Aristotle, you old fart!'

Those on the beach who heard Quance chuckled one to another. He was hugely popular and his company sought after. And he was given to talking to himself.

'The day wouldn't be complete without dear old Aristotle,' Horatio Sinclair said with a smile.

'Yes.' Wolfgang Mauss scratched the lice in his beard. 'He's so ugly he's almost sweet-faced.'

'Mr Quance is a great artist,' Gordon Chen said. 'Therefore he is beautiful.'

Mauss shifted his bulk and stared at the Eurasian. 'The word is "handsome", boy. Did I teach you for years so that you still don't know the difference between "handsome" and "beautiful", *hein*? And he's not a great artist. His style is excellent and he is my friend, but he has not the magic of a great master.'

'I meant "beautiful" in an artistic sense, sir.'

Horatio had seen the momentary flash of irritation pass through Gordon Chen. Poor Gordon, he thought, pitying him. Of neither one world nor the other. Desperately trying to be English yet wearing Chinese robes and a queue. Though everyone knew he was the Tai-Pan's bastard by a Chinese whore, no one acknowledged him openly – not even his father. 'I think his painting wonderful,' Horatio said, his voice gentle. 'And him. Strange how everyone adores him, yet my father despised him.'

'Ah, your father,' Mauss said. 'He was a saint among men. He had high Christian principles, not like us poor sinners. May his soul rest in peace.'

No, Horatio thought. May his soul burn in hellfire for ever.

The Reverend Sinclair had been one of the first group of English missionaries to settle in Macao thirty-odd years ago. He had helped in the translating of the Bible into Chinese, and had been one of the teachers in the English school that the mission had founded. He had been honoured as an upstanding citizen all his life – except by the Tai-Pan – and when he had died seven years ago, he had been buried as a saintly man.

Horatio was able to forgive his father for driving his mother into an early grave, for the high principles that had given him a narrow, tyrannical approach to life, for the fanaticism of his worship of a terrifying God, for the obsessive single-mindedness of his missionary zeal, and for all the beatings he had inflicted on his son. But even after all this time he could never forgive him the beatings he had given Mary or the curses he had heaped on the Tai-Pan's head.

The Tai-Pan had been the one who had found little Mary when at the age of six she had run away in terror. He had soothed her and then taken her home to her father, warning him that if he ever laid a finger on her again he would tear him out of his pulpit and horsewhip him through the streets of Macao. Horatio had worshipped the Tai-Pan ever since. The beatings had stopped, but there had been other punishments. Poor Mary.

As he thought of Mary, his heart quickened and he looked out at the flagship where they had their temporary home. He knew that she would be watching the shore and that, like him, she would be counting the days until they were back safe in Macao. Only forty miles away, south, but so far. He had lived all his twenty-six years in Macao except for some schooling at home in England. He had hated school, both at home and in Macao. He had hated being taught by his father; he had tried desperately to satisfy him but never had been able to. Not like Gordon Chen, who had been the first Eurasian boy accepted in the Macao school. Gordon Chen was a brilliant scholar and had always been able to satisfy the Reverend Sinclair. But Horatio did not envy him: Mauss had been Gordon Chen's torturer. For every beating his father had given him, Mauss gave Gordon Chen three. Mauss was also a missionary; he had taught English, Latin and history.

Horatio eased the knot in his shoulders. He saw that Mauss and Gordon Chen were again staring fixedly at the longboat, and he wondered why Mauss had been so harsh with the young man at school – why he had demanded so much of him. He supposed it was because Wolfgang hated the Tai-Pan. Because the Tai-Pan saw through him and offered him money and the post of interpreter on opium-smuggling voyages up the coast. In return for allowing Wolfgang to distribute Chinese Bibles and tracts and to preach to the heathen wherever the ship stopped – but only after the opium trading was completed. He supposed Wolfgang despised himself for being a hypocrite and a party to such an evil. Because he was forced to pretend that the end justified the means when he knew it did not.

You're a weird man, Wolfgang, he thought. He remembered going to Chushan Island last year when it had been occupied. With Tai-Pan's approval, Longstaff had appointed Mauss temporary magistrate to enforce martial law and British justice.

Against custom, strict orders had been issued on Chushan forbidding sacking and looting. Mauss had given every looter – Chinese, Indian, English – a fair, open trial and then he had sentenced each of them to be hanged, using the same words: '*Gott im Himmel*, forgive this poor sinner. Hang him.' Soon the looting ceased.

Because Mauss was given to reminiscing freely in court between hangings, Horatio had discovered that he had been married three times, each time to an English girl; that the first two had died of the flux and his present one was poorly. That while Mauss was a devoted husband, the Devil still tempted him successfully with the whorehouse and gin cellars of Macao. That Mauss had learned Chinese from the heathen in Singapore where he had been sent as a young missionary. That he had lived twenty of his forty years in Asia and had never been home in all that time. That he carried pistols now because 'You can never tell, Horatio, when one of the heathen devils will want to kill you or heathen pirates will try to rob you'. That he considered all men sinners – himself above all. And that his one aim in life was to convert the heathen and make China a Christian nation.

'What's in your mind?' broke into Horatio's thoughts.

He saw Mauss studying him. 'Oh, nothing,' he said quickly. 'I was just . . . just thinking.'

Mauss scratched his beard thoughtfully. 'I also. This is a day to think, *hein*? Nothing in Asia will ever be the same again.'

'No, I suppose not. Will you move from Macao? Build here?'

'Yes. It will be good to own land, have our own soil away from the papist cesspool. My wife will like that. But me? Me, I do not know. I belong there,' Mauss added, filled with longing, and he waved a huge fist at the mainland.

Horatio saw the eyes of Mauss deepen as he looked into the distance. Why is China so fascinating? he asked himself.

He scanned the beach wearily, knowing that there was no answer. I wish I were rich. Not as rich as the Tai-Pan or Brock. But rich enough to build a fine house and entertain all the traders and take Mary on a luxurious trip home through Europe.

He enjoyed being interpreter to His Excellency, and his private secretary, but he needed more money. One had to have money in this world. Mary should have ball gowns and diamonds. Yes. But even so, he was glad he didn't have to earn their daily bread like the traders. The traders had to be ruthless, too ruthless, and the living was too precarious. Many who thought they were wealthy today would be broken in a month. A ship lost and you could be wiped out. Even The Noble House was hurt occasionally. Their ship *Scarlet Cloud* was already a month overdue, perhaps a battered hulk careening and refitting on some uncharted island between here and Van Diemen's Land two thousand miles off course. More likely at the bottom of the sea with half a million guineas' worth of opium in her gut.

And the things you had to do as a trader, to men and to friends, in order to survive, let alone prosper. Dreadful.

He saw Gordon Chen's fixed stare on the longboat and wondered what he was thinking. It must be terrible to be a half-caste, he thought. I suppose, if the truth were known, he hates the Tai-Pan too, even though he pretends otherwise. I would . . .

Gordon Chen's mind was on opium and he was blessing it. Without opium there would be no Hong Kong – and Hong Kong, he thought exultantly, is the most fantastic opportunity for money I could ever have and the most unbelievable stroke of joss for China.

If there had been no opium, he told himself, there would be no China trade. If there had been no China trade, then the Tai-Pan would never have had money to buy my mother from the brothel and I would never have been born. Opium paid for the house Father gave Mother years ago in Macao. Opium paid for our food and clothes. Opium paid for my schooling and English-speaking tutors and Chinese-speaking tutors, so that now, today, I am the best-educated youth in the Orient.

He glanced across at Horatio Sinclair, who was looking around the beach with a frown. He felt a shaft of envy that Horatio had been sent home to school. He had never been home.

But he pushed away his envy. Home will come later, he promised himself happily. In a few years.

He turned to watch the longboat again. He adored the Tai-Pan. He had never called Struan 'Father' and had never been called 'my son' by

26

him. In fact, he had spoken to him only twenty or thirty times in his life. But he tried to make his father very proud of him and he always thought of him secretly as 'Father'. He blessed him again for selling his mother to Chen Sheng as third wife. My joss has been huge, he thought.

Chen Sheng was comprador to The Noble House, and was almost a father to Gordon Chen. A comprador was the Chinese agent who bought and sold on behalf of a foreign establishment. Every item, large or small, would pass through the comprador's hands. By custom, on every item he would add a percentage. This became his personal profit. But his earnings depended on the success of his house, and he had to cover bad debts. So he had to be very cautious and clever to become rich.

Ah, Gordon Chen thought, to be as rich as Chen Sheng! Or better still as rich as Jin-qua, Chen Sheng's uncle. He smiled to himself, finding it amusing that the British had such difficulty with Chinese names. Jin-qua's real name was Chen-tse Jin Arn, but even the Tai-Pan, who had known Chen-tse Jin Arn for almost thirty years, still could not pronounce the name. So years ago the Tai-Pan had nicknamed him 'Jin'. The 'qua' was a bad pronunciation of the Chinese word that meant 'Mr'.

Gordon Chen knew that Chinese did not mind their nicknames. It only amused them, being another example, to them, of barbarian lack of culture. He remembered years ago as a child he had been watching Chen-tse Jin Arn and Chen Sheng secretly through a hole in the garden wall when they were smoking opium. He had heard them laughing together about His Excellency – how the mandarins in Canton had nicknamed Longstaff 'Obvious Penis', which was a joke on his name, and how the Chinese characters for the Cantonese translation had been used on official letters addressed to Longstaff for more than a year – until Mauss had told Longstaff about it and spoiled a wonderful jest.

He looked covertly at Mauss. He respected him for being a merciless teacher and was grateful to him for forcing him to be the best student in the school. But he despised him for his filth, for his stench and for his cruelty.

Gordon Chen had liked the mission school and liked learning and liked being one of the children. But one day he had discovered he was different from the other children. In front of them, Mauss had told him what 'bastard' and 'illegitimate' and 'half-caste' meant. Gordon Chen had fled home in horror. And he had seen his mother clearly for the first time and had despised her for being Chinese.

Then he had learned from her, through his tears, that it was good to

27

be even part Chinese, for the Chinese were the purest race on earth. And he had learned that the Tai-Pan was his father.

'But why do we live here, then? Why is Chen Sheng "Father"?'

'Barbarians have only one wife and they don't marry Chinese, my son,' Kai-sung explained.

'Why?'

'It is their custom. A stupid one. But that is the way they are.'

'I hate the Tai-Pan! I hate him! I hate him!' he had burst out.

His mother had hit him across the face, savagely. She had never struck him before. 'Get down on your knees and beg forgiveness!' she had said in rage. 'The Tai-Pan is your father. He gave you life. He is my god. He bought me for himself, then blessed me by selling me to Chen Sheng as *wife*. Why should Chen Sheng take a woman with an impure two-year-old son as *wife* when he could buy a thousand virgins if it wasn't because the Tai-Pan wanted it so? Why should the Tai-Pan give me property if he didn't love us? Why should the rent come to me and not to Chen Sheng if the Tai-Pan didn't order it so? Why should Chen Sheng treat me so well, even in old age, if it wasn't for the Tai-Pan's perpetual favour? Why does Chen Sheng treat you like a son, you ungrateful halfwit, if it wasn't for the Tai-Pan? Go to the temple and kowtow and beg forgiveness. The Tai-Pan gave you life. So love him and honour him and bless him like I do. And if you ever say that again, I'll turn my face from you for ever!'

Gordon Chen smiled to himself. How right Mother was, and how wrong and stupid I was. But not as stupid as the mandarins and the cursed emperor to try to stop the sale of opium. Any fool knows that without it there's no bullion for teas and silks.

Once he had asked his mother how it was made, but she did not know, nor did anyone in the house. The next day he had asked Mauss, who had told him that opium was the sap – the tears – of a ripened poppy seedpod. 'The opium farmer makes a delicate cut in the pod, and from this cut a tear of white liquid seeps, *hein*? The tear hardens in a few hours and changes from white to dark brown. Then you scrape off the tear and save it and make a new, delicate cut. Then scrape off the new tear and make a new cut. You collect the tears together and mould them into a ball – ten pounds is the usual weight. The best opium comes from Bengal in British India, *hein*? Or from Malwa. Where's Malwa, boy?'

'Portuguese India, sir!'

'It *was* Portuguese, but now it belongs to the East India Company. They took it to complete their world monopoly of all opium and thus ruin the Portuguese opium traders here in Macao. You make too many mistakes, boy, so get the whip, *hein?*'

Gordon Chen remembered how he had hated opium that day. But now he blessed it. And he thanked his joss for his father and for Hong Kong. Hong Kong was going to make him rich. Very rich.

'Fortunes are going to be made here,' he said to Horatio.

'Some of the traders will prosper,' Horatio said absently, staring at the approaching longboat. 'A few. Trading's a devilish tricky business.'

'Always thinking of money, Gordon, *hein?*' Mauss's voice was rough. 'Better you think of your immortal soul and salvation, boy. Money's not important.'

'Of course, sir.' Gordon Chen hid his amusement at the man's stupidity.

'The Tai-Pan looks like a mighty prince come to claim his kingdom,' Horatio said, almost to himself.

Mauss looked back at Struan. 'Isn't he, *hein?*'

The longboat was in the foreshore waves.

'Oars ho!' the bosun shouted, and the crew shipped the oars and slipped over the side and dragged the boat smartly above the surf.

Struan hesitated. Then he leaped off the prow. The moment his seaboots touched the shore he knew that the island was going to be the death of him.

'Good sweet Christ!'

Robb was beside him and saw the sudden pallor. 'What's amiss, Dirk?'

'Nothing,' Struan forced a smile. 'Nothing, laddie.' He brushed the sea spray off his forehead and strode up the beach towards the flagpole. By the blood of Christ, he thought, I've sweated and planned years to get you, Island, and you're not going to beat me now. No, by God.

Robb watched him and his slight limp. His foot must be paining him, he thought. He wondered what the ache of half a foot was like. It had happened on the only smuggling voyage Robb had made. In saving Robb's life when he had been helpless and paralysed with fear, Struan had been fallen on by the pirates. A musket ball had carried away the outside of his anklebone and two small toes. When the attack had been beaten off, the ship's doctor had cauterized the wounds and had poured molten pitch over them. Robb could still smell the stench of the burning flesh. But for me, he thought, it would never have happened.

He followed Struan up the beach, consumed with self-disgust.

'Morning, gentlemen,' Struan said as he joined some of the merchants near the flagpole. 'Beautiful morning, by God.'

'It be cold, Dirk,' Brock said. 'And it be right mannerly of thee to be so prompt.'

'I'm early. His Excellency's not ashore yet, and the signal gun's not been fired.'

'Yes, an' a hour an' a half late, an' all arranged twixt you and that weak-gutted lackey, I'll be bound.'

'I'll thank you, Mr Brock, not to refer to His Excellency in those terms,' Captain Glessing spluttered.

'An' I'll thank you to keep you opinion to yourself. I'm not in the navy and baint under you command.' Brock spat neatly. 'Better you think about the war yo're not fighting.'

Glessing's hand tightened on his sword. 'I never thought I'd see the day when the Royal Navy was called on to protect smugglers and pirates. That's what you are.' He looked across at Struan. 'All of you.'

There was a sudden hush and Struan laughed. 'His Excellency does na agree with you.'

'We've Acts of Parliament, by God, the Navigation Acts. One of them says, "Any unlicensed armed ship can be taken as prize by any nation's navy." Is your fleet licensed?'

'Lots of pirates in these waters, Captain Glessing. As you're aware,' Struan said easily. 'We've arms to protect oursel'. No more, no less.'

'Opium's against the law. How many thousand cases have you smuggled into China up the coast against the laws of China and humanity? Three thousand? Twenty thousand?'

'What we do here is well known in all the courts of England.'

'Your "trade" brings dishonour to the flag.'

'You'd better thank God for the trade, for without it England'll have no tea and no silk, but a universal poverty that'll tear her very heart out.'

'Right you are, Dirk,' Brock said. Then he turned on Glessing again. 'You'd better be getting it through thy head that without merchants there baint no British Empire and no taxes to buy warships and powder.' He looked at Glessing's immaculate uniform and white knee breeches and white stockings and buckled shoes and cocked hat. 'An' no brass to pay muckels to captain 'em!'

The marines winced and some of the sailors laughed, but very cautiously.

'You'd better thank God for the Royal Navy, by God. Without it there's no place to merchant in.'

30

A signal gun from the flagship boomed out. Abruptly, Glessing marched to the flagpole.

'Present arms!'

He took out the proclamation and a hush fell over the crowd. Then, when his anger had lessened a little, he began to read: 'By order of His Excellency the Honourable William Longstaff, Her Britannic Majesty Queen Victoria's Captain Superintendent of Trade in China. In accordance with the document known as the Treaty of Chuenpi, signed on January 20th, this year of Our Lord, by His Excellency on behalf of Her Majesty's Government, and by His Excellency Ti-sen, Plenipotentiary of His Majesty Tao Kuang, Emperor of China, I, Captain Glessing, RN, do hereby take possession of this Island of Hong Kong on behalf of Her Britannic Majesty, her heirs and assigns, in perpetuity without let or hindrance, on this day the 26th of January, year of Our Lord 1841. This island soil is now English soil. God Save the Queen!'

The Union Jack broke clear at the top of the flagpole, and the honour guard of marines fired a volley. Then the cannon roared throughout the fleet and the wind became thick with the tang of gunpowder. Those on the beach gave three cheers for the queen.

Now it's done, Struan thought. Now we're committed. Now we can begin. He left the group and went down to the surf, and for the first time he turned his back on the island and looked out into the great harbour at the land beyond: to mainland China, a thousand yards away.

The mainland peninsula was low-lying, with nine squat hills, and jutted into the harbour that hooped around it. It was named 'Kau-lung' – 'Kowloon' the traders pronounced it – 'Nine Dragons.' And to the north lay the limitless and unknown expanse of China.

Struan had read all the books ever written by the three Europeans who had been to China and returned. Marco Polo nearly six hundred years ago, and two Catholic priests who had been permitted in Peking two hundred years ago. The books had revealed almost nothing.

For two hundred years no Europeans had been permitted into China. Once – against the law – Struan had gone a mile inland from the coast up near Swatow when he was selling opium, but the Chinese were hostile and he was alone but for his first mate. It wasn't the hostility that had turned him back. Just the enormousness of their numbers and the limitlessness of the land.

God's blood! he thought. We know nothing about the most ancient and the most populated nation on earth. What's inside?

'Is Longstaff coming ashore?' Robb asked as he joined him.

31

'No, laddie. His Excellency has more important things to do.'

'What?'

'Things like reading and writing dispatches. And making private agreements with the admiral.'

'To do what?'

'To outlaw the opium trade.'

Robb laughed.

'I'm na joking. That's why he wanted to see me – with the admiral. He wanted to get my advice on when to issue the order. The admiral said the navy'd have no trouble in enforcing it.'

'Good God! Is Longstaff mad?'

'No. Just simple in the head.' Struan lit a cheroot. 'I told him to issue the order at four bells.'

'That's madness!' Robb burst out.

'It's very wise. The navy's not to enforce the order for a week: "to give the China traders time to dispose of their supplies".'

'But then what do we do? Without opium we're finished. China trade's finished. Finished.'

'How much cash do we have, Robb?'

Robb looked around to make sure there was no one near and lowered his voice. 'There's the bullion in Scotland. One million one hundred thousand pounds sterling in our bank in England. About a hundred thousand in silver bullion here. We're owed three million for the seized opium. We've two hundred thousand guineas of opium in *Scarlet Cloud* at present market price. There's—'

'Write off *Scarlet Cloud*, lad. She's lost.'

'There's still a chance, Dirk. We'll give her another month. There's about a hundred thousand guineas' worth of opium in the hulks. We owe nine hundred thousand in sight drafts.'

'What will it cost us to run for the next six months?'

'A hundred thousand guineas'll pay for ships and salaries and squeeze.'

Struan thought a moment. 'By tomorrow there'll be a panic among the traders. Na one of 'em – except Brock, perhaps – can sell their opium in a week. You'd better ship all our opium up the coast this afternoon. I think—'

'Longstaff's got to change the order,' Robb said with growing anxiety. 'He's got to. He'll ruin the exchequer and—'

'Will you na listen? When the panic's on, tomorrow, take every tael we've got and every tael you can borrow and buy opium. You should be able to buy at ten cents on the dollar.'

'We can't sell all of ours in a week, let alone more.'

Struan tapped the ash off his cheroot. 'A day before the order's to be enforced, Longstaff's going to cancel it.'

'I don't understand.'

'A matter of saving face, Robb. After the admiral had left, I explained to Longstaff that banning opium would destroy all trade. God's blood, how many times do I have to explain? Then I pointed out that he could na very well immediately cancel the order without losing face and making the admiral – who is well-meaning but knows nothing about trade – lose face. The only thing to do was to give the order, then, to save the admiral's face and job – *and his own* – to cancel it. I promised to explain "trade" to the admiral in the meantime. Also the order will look good to the Chinese and put them at a disadvantage. There's another meeting with Ti-sen in three days. Longstaff agreed completely and asked me to keep the matter private.'

Robb's face lit up. 'Ah, Tai-Pan, you're a man among men! But what's to guarantee Longstaff'll cancel the order?'

Struan had in his pocket a signed proclamation dated six days hence that cancelled the order. Longstaff had pressed it on him: 'Here, Dirk, take it now, then I can forget it. Damme! All this paper work, you know – dreadful. But better keep it private until the time.'

'Would you na cancel such a stupid order, Robbie?'

'Yes, of course.' Robb could have hugged his brother. 'If it's six days and no one else knows for certain, we'll make a fortune.'

'Aye.' Struan let his eyes drift to the harbour. He had found it twenty-odd years ago. The outer edge of the typhoon had caught him far out to sea, and though he had prepared for storm he could not escape and had been driven relentlessly into the mainland. His ship had been scudding under bare poles, taking the seas heavily, the day sky and horizon obliterated by the sheets of water the Supreme Winds clawed from the ocean and hurled before them. Then, close by shore in monstrous seas, the storm anchors had given way and Struan knew that the ship was lost. The seas took the ship and threw it at the shore. By some miracle a wind altered her course a fraction of a degree and drove her past the rocks into a narrow, uncharted channel, barely three hundred yards wide, that the eastern tip of Hong Kong formed with the mainland – and into the harbour beyond. Into safe waters.

The typhoon had wrecked much of the merchant fleet at Macao and sunk tens of thousands of junks up and down the coast. But Struan and the junks sheltering at Hong Kong weathered it comfortably. When the

33

storm had passed, Struan sailed around the island, charting it. Then he had stored the information in his mind and begun secretly to plan.

And now that you're ours, now I can leave, he thought, his excitement warming. Now Parliament.

For years Struan had known that the only means of protecting The Noble House and the new colony lay in London. The real seat of power on earth was Parliament. As a member of Parliament, supported by the power the huge wealth of The Noble House gave him, he would dominate Asian foreign policy as he had dominated Longstaff. Aye.

A few thousand pounds will put you in Parliament, he told himself. No more working through others. Now you'll be able to do it yoursel'. Aye, at long last, laddie. A few years and then a knighthood. Then into the Cabinet. And then, then, by God, you'll set a course for the Empire and Asia and The Noble House that will last a thousand years.

Robb was watching him. He knew that he had been forgotten but he did not mind. He liked watching his brother when his thoughts were far away. When the Tai-Pan's face lost its hardness and his eyes their chilling green, when his mind was swept with dreams he knew he could never share, Robb felt very close to him and very safe.

Struan broke the silence. 'In six months you take over as Tai-Pan.'

Robb's stomach tensed with panic. 'No. I'm not ready.'

'You're ready. Only in Parliament can I protect us and Hong Kong.'

'Yes,' Robb said; then he added, trying to keep his voice level, 'But that was to be sometime in the future – in two or three years. There's too much to be done here.'

'You can do it.'

'No.'

'You can. And there's no doubt in Sarah's mind, Robb.'

Robb looked at *Resting Cloud*, their depot ship, where his wife and children were living temporarily. He knew that Sarah was too ambitious for him. 'I don't want it yet. There's plenty of time.'

Struan thought about time. He did not regret the years spent in the Orient away from home. Away from his wife, Ronalda, and Culum and Ian and Lechie and Winifred, his children. He would have liked them to be with him, but Ronalda hated the Orient. They had been married in Scotland when he was twenty and Ronalda sixteen, and they had left immediately for Macao. But she had hated the voyage out and hated Macao. Their first son had died at birth, and the next year when their second son, Culum, was born, he too became sickly. So Struan had sent his family home. Every three or four years he had returned on leave. A

34

month or two in Glasgow with them and then he was back to the Orient, for there was much to do and a Noble House to be built.

I dinna regret a day, he told himself. Na a day. A man has to go out into the world to make what he can of it and himself. Is that na the purpose of life? Even though Ronalda's a bonny lass and I love my children, a man must do what he had to do. Is that na why we're born? If the laird of the Struans had not taken all the clan lands and fenced them and thrown us off – us, his kinsmen, us who had worked the lands for generations – then I might have been a crofter like my father before me. Aye, and content to be a crofter. But he sent us off into a stinking slum in Glasgow and took all the lands for himself to become Earl of Struan, and broke up the clan. So we almost starved and I went to sea and joss saved us and now the family's well-off. All of them. Because I went to sea. And because The Noble House came to pass.

Struan had learned very quickly that money was power. And he was going to use his power to destroy the Earl of Struan and buy back some of the clan lands. He regretted nothing in his life. He had found China, and China had given him what his homeland never could. Not just wealth – wealth for its own sake was an obscenity. But wealth and a purpose for wealth. He owed a debt to China.

And he knew that though he would go home and become a member of Parliament and a Cabinet minister and break the earl and cement Hong Kong as a jewel into the crown of Britain, he would always return. For his real purpose – secret from everyone, almost secret from himself most of the time – would take years to fulfil.

'There's never enough time.' He looked at the dominating mountain. 'We'll call it "the Peak",' he said absently, and again he had the strange sudden feeling that the island hated him and wanted him dead. He could feel the hatred surrounding him and he wondered, perplexed, Why?

'In six months you rule The Noble House,' he repeated, his voice harsh.

'I can't. Not alone.'

'A tai-pan is always alone. That's the joy of it and the hurt of it.' Over Robb's shoulder he saw the bosun approaching. 'Yes, Mr McKay?'

'Beggin' yor pardon, sorr. Permission to splice the main brace?' McKay was a squat, thickset man, his hair tied in a tarred, ratty pigtail.

'Aye. A double tot to all hands. Set things up as arranged.'

'Aye, aye, sorr.' McKay hurried away.

Struan turned back to Robb, and Robb was conscious only of the strange green eyes that seemed to pour light over him. 'I'll send Culum

35

out at the end of the year. He'll be through university by then. Ian and Lechie will go to sea, and they'll follow. By then your boy Roddy will be old enough. Thank God, we've enough sons to follow us. Choose one of them to succeed you. The Tai-Pan is always to choose who is to succeed him and when.' Then with finality he turned his back on mainland China and said, 'Six months!' He walked away.

Robb watched him go, suddenly hating him, hating himself and the island. He knew he would fail as Tai-Pan.

'Will you drink with us, gentlemen?' Struan was saying to a group of the merchants. 'A toast to our new home? There's brandy, rum, beer, dry sack, whisky and champagne.' He pointed to his longboat, where his men were unloading kegs and laying out tables. Others were staggering under loads of cold roast meat – chickens and haunches of pig and twenty suckling pigs and a side of beef – and loaves of bread and cold salt pork pies and bowls of cold cabbage cooked with ham fat and thirty or forty smoked hams and hands of Canton bananas and preserved fruit pies, and fine glass and pewter mugs, and even buckets of ice – which lorchas and clippers had brought from the north – for the bottles of champagne. 'There's breakfast for any that are hungry.'

There was a cheer of approval, and the merchants began to converge on the tables. When they all had their glasses or tankards, Struan raised his glass. 'A toast, gentlemen.'

'I be drinking with you, but not to this poxy rock. I be drinking to yor downfall,' Brock said, holding up a tankard of ale. 'On second thoughts, I be drinking to yor little rock as well. An' I give it a name: "Struan's Folly".'

'Aye, it's little enough,' Struan replied. 'But big enough for Struan's and the rest of the China traders. Whether it's big enough for both Struan's and Brock's – that's another question.'

'I be tellin' thee right smartly, Dirk, old lad: the whole of China baint.' Brock drained the mug and hurled it inland. Then he stalked to his longboat. Some of the merchants followed him.

'Pon me word, dreadful manners,' Quance said. Then he called out in the laughter, 'Come on, Tai-Pan, the toast! Mr Quance has an immortal thirst! Let history be made.'

'Excuse me, Mr Struan,' Horatio Sinclair said. 'Before the toast wouldn't it be fitting to thank God for the mercies He has shown us this day?'

'Of course, lad. Foolish of me to forget. Will you lead the prayer?'

'The Reverend Mauss is here, sir.'

Struan hesitated, caught off guard. He studied the young man, liking the deep humour that lurked behind the sky-grey eyes. Then he said loudly, 'Reve'n'd Mauss, where are you? Let's have a prayer.'

Mauss towered above the merchants. He haltingly moved in front of the table and set down his empty glass and pretended that it had always been empty. The men took off their hats and waited bareheaded in the cold wind.

Now it was quiet on the beach. Struan looked up at the foothills to an outcrop where the kirk would be. He could see the kirk in his mind's eye and the town and the quays and warehouses and homes and gardens. The Great House where the Tai-Pan would hold court over the generations. Other homes for the hierarchy of the house and their families. And their girls. He thought about his present mistress. T'chung Jen May-may. He had bought May-may five years ago when she was fifteen and untouched.

Ayeeee yah, he said, to himself happily, using one of her Cantonese expressions, which meant pleasure or anger or disgust or happiness or helplessness, depending on how it was said. Now, there's a wildcat if ever there was one.

'Sweet God of the wild winds and the surf and beauty of love, God of great ships and the North Star and the beauty of home, God and Father of the Christ child, look at us and pity us.' Mauss, his eyes closed, was lifting his hands. His voice was rich, and the depth of his longing swooped around them. 'We are the sons of men, and our fathers worried over us as You worried over your blessed Son Jesus. Saints are crucified on earth and sinners multiply. We look at the glory of a flower and see You not. We endure the Supreme Winds and know You not. We measure the mighty oceans and feel You not. We reap the earth and touch you not. We eat and drink, yet we taste You not. All these things. You are and more. You are life and death and success and failure. You are God and we are men . . .'

He paused, his face contorted, as he struggled with his agonized soul. Oh, God, forgive me my sins. Let me expiate my weakness by converting the heathen. Let me be a martyr to your Holy Cause. Change me from what I am to what I was once . . .

But Wolfgang Mauss knew that there was no turning back, that the moment he had begun to serve Struan, his peace had left him and the needs of his flesh had swamped him. Surely, oh God, what I did was right. There was no other way to go into China.

He opened his eyes and stared around helplessly. 'I'm sorry. Forgive me. I know not the words. I can see them – great words to make you know Him as once I knew Him – but I cannot the words say any more. Forgive me. Oh Lord, bless this island. Amen.'

Struan took a full glass of whisky and gave it to Mauss. 'I think you said it very well. A toast, gentlemen. The Queen!'

They drank, and when their glasses were drained, Struan ordered them refilled.

'With your permission, Captain Glessing, I'd like to offer your men a tot. And you, of course. A toast to the queen's newest possession. You've passed into history today.' He called out to the merchants, 'We should honour the captain. Let's name this beach "Glessing's Point".'

There was a roar of approval.

'Naming islands or a part of an island is the prerequisite of the senior officer,' Glessing said.

'I'll mention it to His Excellency.'

Glessing nodded curtly and snapped at the master-at-arms: 'Sailors one tot, compliments of Struan and Company. Marines none. Stand easy.'

In spite of his fury at Struan, Glessing could not help glorying in the knowledge that as long as there was a Colony of Hong Kong his name would be remembered. For Struan never said anything lightly.

There was a toast to Hong Kong, and three cheers. Then Struan nodded to the piper, and the skirl of the clan Struan filled the beach.

Robb drank nothing. Struan sipped a glass of brandy and ambled through the throng, greeting those he wished to greet and nodding to others.

'You're not drinking, Gordon?'

'No, thank you, Mr Struan.' Gordon Chen bowed in Chinese fashion, very proud to be noticed.

'How are things going with you?'

'Very well, thank you, sir.'

The lad's grown into a fine young man, Struan thought. How old is he now? Nineteen. Time goes so fast.

He remembered Kai-sung, the boy's mother, fondly. She had been his first mistress and most beautiful. Ayee yah, she taught you a lot.

'How's your mother?' he asked.

'She's very well.' Gordon Chen smiled. 'She would wish me to give you her prayers for your safety. Every month she burns joss sticks in your honour at the temple.'

Struan wondered how she looked now. He had not seen her for seventeen years. But he remembered her face clearly. 'Send her my best wishes.'

'You do her too much honour, Mr Struan.'

'Chen Sheng tells me you are working hard and are very useful to him.'

'He is too kind to me, sir.'

Chen Sheng was never kind to anyone who did no more than earn his keep. Chen Sheng's an old thief, Struan thought, but, by God, we'd be lost without him.

'Well,' Struan said, 'You couldna have a better teacher than Chen Sheng. There'll be lots to do in the next few months. Lots of squeeze to be made.'

'I hope to be of service to The Noble House, sir.'

Struan sensed that his son had something on his mind, but he merely nodded pleasantly and walked off, knowing that Gordon would find a way to tell him when the time was ripe.

Gordon Chen bowed and after a moment wandered down to one of the tables and waited politely in the background until there was space for him, conscious of the stares but not caring; he knew that as long as Struan was *the* Tai-Pan he was quite safe.

The merchants and sailors around the beach ripped chickens and suckling pigs to pieces with their hands and stuffed themselves with the meat, grease running down their chins. What a bunch of savages, Gordon Chen thought, and thanked his joss that he had been brought up as a Chinese and not a European.

Yes, he thought, my joss has been huge. Joss had brought him his secret Chinese Teacher a few years ago. He had told no one about the Teacher, not even his mother. From this man he had learned that not all that the Reverends Sinclair and Mauss had taught was necessarily true. He had learned about Buddha and about China and her past. And how to repay the gift of life and use it to the glory of his motherland. Then last year the Teacher had initiated him into the most powerful, most clandestine, most militant of the Chinese secret societies, the Hung Mun Tong, which was spread all over China and was committed by the most sacred oaths of blood brotherhood to overthrow the hated Manchus, the foreign Ch'ings, the ruling dynasty of China.

For two centuries under various guises and names the society had fostered insurrection. There had been revolts all over the Chinese Empire – from Tibet to Formosa, from Mongolia to Indochina. Wherever there was famine or oppression or discontent, the Hung Mun would band the peasants together against the Ch'ings and against their mandarins. All the insurrections had failed and had been put down savagely by the Ch'ings. But the society had survived.

Gordon Chen felt honoured that he, only part Chinese, had been considered worthy to be a Hung Mun. Death to the Ch'ings. He blessed his joss that he had been born in this era in history, in this part of China, with this father, for he knew that the time was almost ripe for all China to revolt.

And he blessed the Tai-Pan, for he had given the Hung Mun a pearl beyond price: Hong Kong. At long last the society had a base safe from the perpetual oppression of the mandarins. Hong Kong would be under barbarian control, and here on this little island he knew that the society would flourish. From Hong Kong, safe and secret, they would probe the mainland and harass the Ch'ings until the Day. And with joss, he thought, with joss I can use the power of The Noble House in the cause.

'Hop it, you bloody heathen!'

Gordon Chen looked up, startled. A squat, tough little sailor was glaring at him. He had a haunch of suckling pig in his hands and he was ripping at it with broken teeth.

'Hop it, or I'll twist yor pigtail around yor bleedin' neck!'

Bosun McKay hurried over and shoved the sailor aside. 'Hold yor tongue, Ramsey, you poxy sod,' he said. 'He don't mean no harm, Mr Chen.'

'Yes. Thank you, Mr McKay.'

'You want grub?' McKay stabbed a chicken with his knife and offered it.

Gordon Chen carefully broke off the end bone of the chicken wing, appalled by McKay's barbarian manners. 'Thank you.'

'That all you'll have?'

'Yes. It's the most delicate part.' Chen bowed. 'Thank you again.' He walked off.

McKay went over to the sailor. 'You all right, mate?'

'I oughta cut your bugger heart out. Is he yor Chinese doxy, McKay?'

'Keep your voice down, mon. That Chinee's to be left alone. If you want to pick on a heathen bastard, there's plenty others. But not him, by God. He's the Tai-Pan's bastard, that's what.'

'Then why don't he wear a bleedin' sign – or cut his bleedin' hair?' Ramsey dropped his voice and leered. 'I hear tell they's different – Chinese doxies. Built different.'

'I don't know. Never be'd near one of th' scum. There's enough of our own kind in Macao.'

* * *

40

Struan was watching a sampan anchored offshore. It was a small boat with a snug cabin fashioned from thin mats of woven rattan stretched over bamboo hoops. The fisherman and his family were Hoklos, boat people who lived all their lives afloat and rarely, if ever, went ashore. He could see that there were four adults and eight children in the sampan. Some of the infants were tied to the boat by ropes around their waists. These would be sons. Daughters were not tied, for they were of no value.

'When do you think we can return to Macao, Mr Struan?'

He turned around and smiled at Horatio. 'I imagine tomorrow, laddie. But I suppose His Excellency will need you for the meeting with Ti-sen. There'll be more documents to translate.'

'When's the meeting?'

'In three days, I believe.'

'If you have a ship going to Macao, would you give my sister passage? Poor Mary's been aboard two months.'

'Glad to.' Struan wondered what Horatio would do when he found out about Mary. Struan had learned the truth about her a little over three years ago . . .

He had been in a crowded marketplace at Macao, and a Chinese had suddenly pushed a piece of paper into his hand and darted away. It was a note written in Chinese. He had shown the paper to Wolfgang Mauss.

'They're directions to a house, Mr Struan. And a message: "The Tai-Pan of The Noble House needs special information for the sake of his house. Come secretly to the side entrance at the Hour of the Monkey." '

'When's the Hour of the Monkey?'

'Three o'clock in the afternoon.'

'Where's the house?'

Wolfgang told him and then added, 'Don't go. It's a trap, *hein*? Remember there's a hundred thousand taels' reward on your head.'

'The house is na in the Chinese quarter,' Struan had said. 'In daylight it'd na be a trap. Get my boat's crew together. If I'm na out safely in one hour come and find me.'

So he had gone, leaving Wolfgang and the armed boat's crew close by and ready if necessary. The house was joined to others in a row on a quiet, treelined street. Struan had entered through a door in the high wall and found himself in a garden. A Chinese woman servant was awaiting him. She was neatly dressed in black trousers and black coat, and her hair was arranged in a bun. She bowed and motioned him to be quiet and to follow her. She led the way through the garden and into the

41

house and up a flight of private stairs and into a room. He followed cautiously, ready for trouble.

The room was richly furnished and the panelled walls were hung with tapestries. There were chairs and a table and Chinese teak furniture. The room smelled strangely clean with the faintest suggestion of a subtle incense. There was one window which overlooked the garden.

The woman went to the far end of a side wall and carefully moved a strip of panelling. There was a tiny peephole in the wall. She peered through it, then motioned him to do the same. He knew that it was an old Chinese trick to dupe an enemy into putting his eye to such a hole in a wall while someone waited on the other side with a needle. So he kept his eye a few inches from the hole. Still he could see the other room clearly.

It was a bedroom. Wang Chu, the chief mandarin of Macao, was on the bed nude and corpulent and snoring. Mary was naked beside him. Her head was propped on her arms and she was staring at the ceiling.

Struan watched with fascinated horror. Mary languorously nudged Wang Chu and stroked him awake and laughed and talked with him. Struan had been unaware that she could speak Chinese, and he knew her as well as anyone – except her brother. She rang a small bell, and a maid came in and began to help the mandarin dress. Wang Chu could not dress himself for his nails were four inches long and protected with jewelled sheaths. Struan turned away filled with loathing.

There was a sudden chatter of singsong voices from the garden and he cautiously looked out the window. Wang's guards were assembling in the garden; they would block his exit. The servant woman motioned him not to worry but to wait. She went to the table and poured him tea; then she bowed and left.

In half an hour the men left the garden and Struan saw them form up in front of a sedan chair on the street. Wang Chu was helped into the sedan chair and carried away.

'Hello Tai-Pan.'

Struan spun around, drawing his knife. Mary was standing in a doorway which had been concealed in the wall. She wore a gossamer robe which hid none of her. She had long, fair hair and blue eyes and a dimpled chin; long legs and tiny waist and small, firm breasts. A priceless piece of carved jade hung from a gold chain around her neck. Mary was studying Struan with a curious, flat smile.

'You can put the knife away, Tai-Pan. You're in no danger.' Her voice was calm and mocking.

'You ought to be horsewhipped,' he said.

'I know all about whipping, don't you remember?' She motioned to the bedroom. 'We'll be more comfortable in here.' She went to a bureau and poured brandy into two glasses.

'What's the matter?' she said with the same perverse smile. 'Haven't you been in a girl's bedroom before?'

'You mean a whore's bedroom?'

She handed him a glass and he took it. 'We're both the same, Tai-Pan. We both prefer Chinese bedmates.'

'By God, you damned bitch, you—'

'Don't play the hypocrite; it doesn't suit you. You're married and you've children. Yet you've many other women. Chinese women. I know all about them. I've made it my business to find out.'

'It's impossible for you to be Mary Sinclair,' he said half to himself.

'Not impossible. Surprising, yes.' She sipped her brandy calmly. 'I sent for you because I wanted you to see me as I am.'

'Why?'

'First you'd better dismiss your men.'

'How do you know about them?'

'You're very careful. Like me. You wouldn't come here secretly without a bodyguard.' Her eyes were mocking him.

'What are you up to?'

'How long did you tell your men to wait?'

'An hour.'

'I need more of your time. Dismiss them.' She laughed. 'I'll wait.'

'You'd better. And put some clothes on.'

He left the house and told Wolfgang to wait for another two hours and then to come and find him. He told him about the secret door but not about Mary.

When he returned, Mary was lying on the bed. 'Please close the door, Tai-Pan,' she said.

'I told you to put some clothes on.'

'I told you to close the door.'

Angrily he slammed it. Mary took off the filmy robe and tossed it aside. 'Do you find me attractive?'

'No. You disgust me.'

'You don't disgust me, Tai-Pan. You're the only man I admire in the world.'

'Horatio should see you now.'

'Ah, Horatio,' she said cryptically. 'How long did you tell your men to wait this time?'

'Two hours.'

'You told them about the secret door. But not about me.'

'Why are you so sure?'

'I know you, Tai-Pan. That's why I trust you with my secret.' She toyed with the brandy glass, her eyes lowered. 'Had we finished when you looked through the peephole?'

'God's blood! You'd better—'

'Be patient with me, Tai-Pan,' she said. 'Had we?'

'Aye.'

'I'm glad. Glad and sorry. I wanted you to be sure.'

'I dinna understand.'

'I wanted you to be sure that Wang Chu was my lover.'

'Why?'

'Because I've information that you can use. You'd never believe me unless you'd seen that I was his woman.'

'What information?'

'I've lots of information you can use, Tai-Pan. I've many lovers. Chen Sheng comes here sometimes. Many of the mandarins from Canton. Old Jin-qua once.' Her eyes frosted and seemed to change colour. 'I don't disgust them. They like the colour of my skin and I please them. They please me. I have to tell you these things, Tai-Pan. I'm only repaying my debt to you.'

'What debt?'

'You stopped the beatings. You stopped them too late, but that wasn't your fault.' She got up from the bed and put on a heavy robe. 'I won't tease you any more. Please hear me out and then you can do what you like.'

'What do you want to tell me?'

'The emperor has appointed a new viceroy to Canton. This Viceroy Ling carries an imperial edict to stop opium smuggling. He will arrive in two weeks, and within three weeks he will surround the Settlement at Canton. No European will be let out of Canton until all the opium has been surrendered.'

Struan laughed contemptuously. 'I dinna believe it.'

'If the opium is given up and destroyed, anyone with cargoes of opium outside of Canton will make a fortune,' Many said.

'It will na be given up.'

'Say the whole Settlement was ransomed for opium. What could you do? There are no warships here. You're defenceless. Aren't you?'

'Aye.'

'Send a ship to Calcutta with orders to buy opium, all you can, two months after it arrives. If my information is false, that gives you plenty of time to cancel the order.'

44

'Wang told you this?'

'Only about the viceroy. The other was my idea. I wanted to repay my debt to you.'

'You owe me nothing.'

'You were never whipped.'

'Why did you na send someone to tell me secretly? Why bring me here? To see you like this? Why make me go through this – this horror?'

"I wanted to tell you. Myself. I wanted someone other than me to know what I was. You're the only man I trust,' she said with an unexpected, child-like innocence.

'You're mad. You should be locked up.'

'Because I like going to bed with Chinese?'

'By the Cross! Do you na understand what you are?'

'Yes. A disgrace to England.' Anger swept her face, hardening it, ageing it. 'You men do what you please, but we women can't. Good Christ, how can I go to bed with a European? They couldn't wait to tell others and shame me before all of you. This way no one's harmed. Except me, perhaps, and that happened a long time ago.'

'What did?'

'You'd better know a fact of life, Tai-pan. A woman needs men just as much as man needs women. Why should we be satisfied with one man? Why?'

'How long has this been going on?'

'Since I was fourteen. Don't be shocked! How old was May-may when you bought her?'

'That was different.'

'It's always different for a man.' Mary sat down at the table in front of the mirror and began to brush her hair. 'Brock is secretly negotiating with the Spaniards in Manila for the sugar crop. He's offered Carlos de Silvera ten per cent for the monopoly.'

Struan felt a surge of fury. If Brock could work that trick with sugar, he could dominate the whole Philippine market. 'How do you know?'

'His comprador, Sze-tsin, told me.'

'He's another of your – clients?'

'Yes.'

'Anything else you want to tell me?'

'You could make a hundred thousand taels of silver from what I've told you.'

'Have you finished?'

'Yes.'

Struan got up.

45

'What are you going to do?'

'Tell your brother. You'd better be sent back to England.'

'Leave me to my own life, Tai-Pan. I enjoy what I am and I'll never change. No Europeans – and few Chinese – know I speak Cantonese and Mandarin except Horatio and now you. But only you know the real me. I promise I will be very, very useful to you.'

'You're off home, out of Asia.'

'Asia is my home.' Her brow furrowed and her eyes seemed to soften. 'Please leave me as I am. Nothing has changed. Two days ago we met on the street and you were kind and gentle. I'm still the same Mary.'

'You're na the same. You call all this nothing?'

'We're all different people at the same time. This is one me, and the other girl – the sweet, innocent virgin nothing, who makes silly conversation and adores the Church and the harpsichord and singing and needlework – is also me. I don't know why, but that's true. You're Tai-Pan Struan – devil, smuggler, prince, murderer, husband, fornicator, saint and a hundred other people,. Which is the real you?'

'I'll na tell Horatio. You can just go home. I'll given you the money.'

'I've money enough for my own passage Tai-Pan. I earn my presents. I own this house and the one next door. And I'll go when I choose in the manner I choose. Please, leave me to my own joss, Tai-Pan. I am what I am, and nothing you can do will change it. Once you could have helped me. No, that's not honest either. No one could have helped me. I like what I am. I swear I will never change. I will be what I am: either secretly, and no one knowing except you and me – or openly. So why hurt others? Why hurt Horatio?'

Struan looked down at her. He knew that she meant what she said. 'Do you know the danger you're in?'

'Yes.'

'Say you have a child.'

'Danger adds spice to life, Tai-Pan.' She looked deeply at him, a shadow in her blue eyes. 'Only one thing I regret about bringing you here. Now I can never be your woman. I would like to have been your woman.'

Struan had left her to her joss. She had a right to love as she pleased, and exposing her to the community would solve nothing. Worse, it would destroy her devoted brother.

He had used her information to immense profit. Because of Mary, The Noble House had almost a total monopoly of all opium trade for a year, and more than made back the cost of their share of the opium –

twelve thousand cases – that had ransomed the Settlement. And Mary's information about Brock had been correct and Brock had been stopped. Struan had opened a secret account for Mary in England and paid into the account a proportion of the profit. She had thanked him but had never seemed interested in the money. From time to time she gave him more information. But she would never tell him how she started her double life, or why. Great God in Heaven, he thought, I'll never understand people . . .

And now, on the beach, he was wondering what Horatio would do when he found out. Impossible for Mary to keep her second life secret – she was sure to make a mistake.

'What's the matter, Mr Struan?' Horatio said.

'Nothing, lad. Just thinking.'

'Do you have a ship leaving today or tomorrow?'

'What?'

'Going to Macao,' Horatio said with a laugh. 'To take Mary to Macao.'

'Oh, yes. Mary.' Struan collected himself. 'Tomorrow, probably. I'll let you know, lad.'

He shoved his way through the merchants, heading for Robb, who was standing near one of the tables, staring out to sea.

'What's next, Mr Struan?' Skinner called out.

'Eh?'

'We've the island. What's the next move of The Noble House?'

'Build, of course. The first to build'll be the first to profit, Mr Skinner.' Struan nodded good-naturedly and continued his way. He wondered what the other merchants – even Robb – would say if they knew he was the owner of the *Oriental Times* and that Skinner was his employee.

'Na eating, Robb?'

'Later, Dirk. There's time enough.'

'Tea?'

'Thanks.'

Cooper wandered over to them and lifted his glass. 'To "Struan's Folly"?'

'If it is, Jeff,' Struan said, 'you'll all come down the sewer with us.'

'Aye,' Robb said. 'And it'll be an expensive sewer if Struan's has anything to do with it.'

'The Noble House does do things in style! Perfect whisky, brandy, champagne. And Venetian glass.' Cooper tapped the glass with his fingernail, and the note it made was pure. 'Beautiful.'

'Made in Birmingham. They've just discovered a new process. One factory's already turning them out a thousand a week. Within a year there'll be a dozen factories.' Struan paused a moment. 'I'll deliver any number you want in Boston. Ten cents American a glass.'

Cooper examined the glass more closely. 'Ten thousand. Six cents.'

'Ten cents. Brock'll charge you twelve.'

'Fifteen thousand at seven cents.'

'Done – with a guaranteed order for thirty thousand at the same price a year from today and a guarantee you'll only import through Struan's.'

'Done – if you'll freight a cargo of cotton by the same ship from New Orleans to Liverpool.'

'How many tons?'

'Three hundred. Usual terms.'

'Done – if you'll act as our agent in Canton for this season's tea. If necessary.'

Cooper was instantly on guard. 'But the war's over. Why should you need an agent?'

'Is it a deal?'

Cooper's mind was working like a keg of weevils. The Treaty of Chuenpi opened up Canton immediately to trade. On the morrow they were all going back to the Settlement in Canton to take up residence again. They would take over their factories – or hongs, as their business houses in the Orient were called – and stay in the Settlement as always until May when the season's business was over. But for The Noble House to need an agent now in Canton was as foolish as saying the United States of America needed a royal family.

'Is it a deal, Jeff?'

'Yes. You're expecting war again?'

'All life's trouble, eh? Is that na what Wolfgang was trying to say?'

'I don't know.'

'How soon will your new ship be ready?' Struan asked abruptly.

Cooper's eyes narrowed. 'How did you find out about that? No one knows outside our company.'

Robb laughed. 'It's our business to know, Jeff. She might be unfair competition. If she sails like Dirk thinks she'll sail, perhaps we'll buy her out from under you. Or build four more like her.'

'It'd be a change for the British to buy American ships,' Cooper said tensely.

'Oh, we would na buy them, Jeff,' Struan said. 'We've already a copy of her lines. We'd build where we've always built. Glasgow. If I were you, I'd rake her masts a notch more and add top ta' gallants to the main and mizzen. What're you going to call her?'

'*Independence*.'

'Then we'll call ours *Independent Cloud*. If she's worthy.'

'We'll sail you off the seas. We beat you twice in war, and now we'll beat you where it really hurts. We'll take away your trade.'

'You haven't a hope in hell.' Struan noticed that Tillman was leaving. Abruptly his voice hardened. 'An' never when half your country's based on slavery.'

'That'll change in time. Englishmen started it.'

'Scum started it!'

Yes, and madmen are continuing it, Cooper thought bitterly, remembering the violent private quarrels he was always having with his partner, who owned plantation slaves and trafficked in them. How could Wilf be so blind? 'You were in the trade up to eight years ago.'

'Struan's was never in human cargo, by God. And by the Lord God, I'll blow any ship out of the sea I catch doing it. In or out of British waters. We gave the lead to the world. Slavery's outlawed. God help us, it took till 1833 to do it, but it's done. Any ship, remember!'

'Then do another thing. Use your influence to let us buy opium from the goddam East India Company. Why should everyone but British traders be totally excluded from the auctions, eh? Why should we be forced to buy low-quality Turkish opium when there's more than enough from Bengal for all of us?'

'I've done more than my share to wreck the Company, as you well know. Spend some money, laddie. Gamble a little. Agitate in Washington. Push your partner's brother. Isn't he a senator from Alabama? Or is he too busy looking after four godrotting blackbirders and a couple of "markets" in Mobile?'

'You know my opinion on that, by God,' Cooper snapped. 'Open up the opium auctions and we'll trade you off the earth. I think you're all afraid to compete freely, if the truth was known. Why else keep the Navigation Acts in force? Why make it law that only English ships can carry goods into England? By what right do you monopolize the biggest consuming market on earth?'

'Na by divine right, laddie,' Struan said sharply, 'which seems to permeate American thinking and foreign policy.'

'In some things we're right and you're wrong. Let's compete freely. Goddam tariffs! Free trade and free seas – that's what's right!'

'Struan's is with you there. Do you na read the newspapers? I dinna mind telling you we buy ten thousand votes a year to support six members who'll vote free trade. We're trying hard enough.'

'One vote, one man. We don't buy votes.'

'You've your system and we've ours. And I'll tell you something else. The *British* were na for the American wars, either of them. Or for those godrotting Hanoverian kings. You did na win the wars, we lost 'em. Happily. Why should we war on kith and kin? But if the people of the Isles ever decide to war on the States, watch out, by God. Because you're finished.'

'I think a toast is in order,' Robb said.

The two men tore their eyes off each other and stared at him. To their astonishment he poured three glasses.

'You'll na drink, Robb,' Struan said, his voice a lash.

'I will. First time on Hong Kong. Last time.' Robb handed them glasses. The whisky was golden-brown and distilled exclusively for The Noble House at Loch Tannoch where they were born. Robb needed the drink; he needed the keg.

'You swore a holy oath!'

'I know. But it's bad luck to toast in water. And this toast's important.' Robb's hand shook as he raised his glass. 'Here's to our future. Here's to *Independence* and *Independent Cloud*. To freedom o' the seas. To freedom from any tyrants.'

He took a sip and held the liquor in his mouth, feeling it burn, his body twisting with the need of it. Then he spat it out and poured the remainder on the pebbles.

'If I ever do that again, knock it out of my hand.' He turned away, nauseated, and walked inland.

'That took more strength than I have,' Cooper said.

'Robb's sick in the head to tempt the Devil like that,' Struan said.

Robb had begun to drink to the point of insanity six years ago. The preceding year Sarah had come to Macao from Scotland with the children. For a time everything had been grand, but then she had found out about Robb's Chinese mistress of years, Ming Soo, and about their daughter. Struan remembered Sarah's rage and Robb's anguish, and he was sad for both of them. They should have been divorced years ago, he thought, and he damned the fact that a divorce could be obtained only by Act of Parliament. At length Sarah had agreed to forgive Robb, but only if he would swear by God immediately to rid himself for ever of his adored mistress and their daughter. Hating himself, Robb had agreed. He had secretly given Ming Soo four thousand taels of silver, and she and their daughter had left Macao. He had never seen them or heard of

50

them again. But though Sarah relented, she never forgot the beautiful girl and child and continued to salt the ever-open wound. Robb had begun drinking heavily. Soon the drink ruled him and he was besotted for months on end. Then one day he had disappeared. Eventually Struan had found him in one of the stinking gin cellars in Macao and had carried him home and sobered him; then he had given him a gun.

'Shoot yoursel' or swear by God you'll na touch drink again. It's poison to you, Robb. You've been drunk for almost a year. You've the children to think of. The poor bairns are terrified of you and rightly; and I'm tired of pulling you out of gutters. Look at yoursel', Robb! Go on!'

Struan had forced him to look into a mirror. Robb had sworn, and then Struan had sent him to sea for a month with orders that he was to be given no liquor. Robb had almost died. In time he had become himself again, and he had thanked his brother and lived with Sarah again and tried to make peace. But there was never peace again between them – or love. Poor Robb, Struan thought. Aye, and poor Sarah. Terrible to live like that, husband and wife.

'What the devil made Robbie do that?'

'I think he wanted break up a quarrel,' Cooper said. 'I was getting angry. Sorry.'

'Dinna apologize, Jeff. It was my fault. Well,' Struan added, 'let's na waste Robb's guts, eh? His toast?'

They drank silently. All around the shore the merchants and sailors were roistering.

'Hey, Tai-Pan! And you, you blasted colonial! Come over here!'

It was Quance, seated near the flagpole. He waved at them and shouted again. 'Blast it, come over here!' He took a pinch of snuff, sneezed twice and dusted himself impatiently with a French lace kerchief.

'By God, sir,' he said to Struan, peering up at him over rimless spectacles, 'how the blasted hell can a man work with all this din and tumult? You and your blasted liquor.'

'Did you try the brandy, Mr Quance?'

'Impeccable, my dear fellow. Like Miss Tillman's tits.' He took the painting off the easel and held it up. 'What do you think?'

'About Shevaun Tillman?'

'The painting. Great spheroids of balderdash, how can you think about a doxy's tail when you're in the presence of a masterpiece?' Quance took another pinch of snuff and choked, and gulped from his tankard of Napoleon brandy and sneezed.

The painting was a water colour of the day's ceremony. Delicate. Faithful. And a little more. It was easy to pick out Brock and Mauss, and Glessing was there, the proclamation in his hands.

'It's very good, Mr Quance,' Struan said.

'Fifty guineas.'

'I bought a painting last week.'

'Twenty guineas.'

'I'm na in it.'

'Fifty guineas and I'll paint you reading the proclamation.'

'No.'

'Mr Cooper. A masterpiece. Twenty guineas.'

'Outside of the Tai-Pan and Robb, I've the biggest Quance collection in the Far East.'

'Dammit, gentlemen, I've got to get some money from somewhere!'

'Sell it to Brock. You can see him right smartly,' Struan said.

'The pox on Brock!' Quance took a very large gulp of brandy and said, his voice hoarse. 'He turned me down, blast him!' and he dabbed furiously with his paintbrush and now Brock was gone. 'By God, why should I make him immortal? And a pox on both of you. I'll send it to the Royal Academy. On your next ship, Tai-Pan.'

'Who's going to pay the freight? And insurance?'

'I will, my boy.'

'With what?'

Quance contemplated the painting. He knew that even in old age he could still paint and improve; his talent would not deteriorate.

'With what, Mr Quance?'

He waved an imperious hand at Struan. 'Money. Taels. Brass. Dollars. Cash!'

'You've a new line of credit, Mr Quance?'

But Quance did not answer. He continued to admire his work, knowing he had hooked his prey.

'Come on, Aristotle, who is it?' Struan insisted.

Quance took an enormous gulp of brandy and more snuff and sneezed. He whispered conspiratorially, 'Sit down.' He looked to see there was no one else listening. 'A secret.' He held up the painting. 'Twenty guineas?'

'All right,' Struan said. 'But it better be worth it.'

'You're a prince among men, Tai-Pan. Snuff?'

'Get on with it!'

'It seems that a certain lady admires herself greatly. In a mirror. With no clothes on. I've been commissioned to paint her thus.'

'Great God Almighty! Who?'

'You both know her very well.' Then Quance added with mock sadness, 'I am sworn not to reveal her name. But I shall put her posterior into posterity. It's superb.' Another gulp of brandy. 'I er, insisted on seeing her all. Before I agreed to accept the commission.' He kissed his fingers in ecstasy. 'Impeccable, gentlemen, impeccable! And her tits! Good God on high, nearly gave me the vapours!' Another gulp of brandy.

'You can tell us. Come on, who?'

'First rule in nudes as in fornication. Never reveal the lady's name.' Quance finished the tankard regretfully. 'But not a man among you who wouldn't pay a thousand guineas to own it.' He got up and belched heartily and dusted himself down and closed his paint box and picked up his easel, enormously pleased with himself. 'Well, that's enough business for this week. I'll call on your comprador for thirty guineas.'

'Twenty guineas,' Struan said.

'A Quance original of the most important day in the history of the Orient,' Quance said scornfully, 'for hardly the price of a hogshead of Napoleon.' He returned to his longboat and danced a jig as he was cheered aboard.

'Good God Almighty, who?' Cooper said at length.

'Must be Shevaun,' Struan said, with a short laugh. 'Just the sort of thing that young lady would do.'

'Never. She's wild, yes, but not that wild.' Cooper glanced uneasily at the Cooper-Tillman depot ship where Shevaun Tillman was staying. She was his partner's niece, and she had come out to Asia a year ago from Washington. In that time she had become the toast of the continent. She was beautiful and nineteen and daring and eligible, and no man could trap her – into bed or into marriage. Every bachelor in Asia including Cooper had proposed to her. And they all had been refused but not refused: held on a rein, as she held all her suitors. But Cooper did not mind; he knew she was going to be his wife. She had been sent out under the guardianship of Wilf Tillman by her father, a senator from Alabama, in the hope that Cooper would favour her and she would favour him, to further cement the family business. And he had fallen in love with her the moment he had seen her.

'Then we'll announce the betrothal immediately,' Tillman had said delightedly a year ago.

'No, Wilf. There's no hurry. Let her get used to Asia and used to me.'

As Cooper turned back to Struan, he smiled to himself. A wildcat like that was worth waiting for. 'It must be one of Mrs Fortheringill's "young ladies".'

'Those rabbits'd do anything.'

'Sure. But they wouldn't *pay* Aristotle for that.'

'Old Horseface might. Good for business.'

'She's business enough now. Her clientele's the best in Asia. Can you imagine that hag giving money to Aristotle?' Cooper pulled impatiently at his muttonchop whiskers. 'Best she'd do is give it to him in trade. Perhaps he's joking with us?'

'He jokes about everything and anything. But never about painting.'

'One of the Portuguese?'

'Impossible. If she's married, her husband'd blow her head off. If she's a widow – that'd blow the top off the whole Catholic Church.' The weathered lines of Struan's face twisted into a grin. 'I'll put the whole power of The Noble House on finding out who. Bet you twenty guineas I find out first!'

'Done. I get the painting if I win.'

'Dammit, I've taken a fancy to it now that Brock's out.'

'The winner gets the painting and we'll ask Aristotle to paint the loser into it.'

'Done.' They shook hands.

A sudden cannon, and they looked seaward.

A ship was charging through the east channel under full sail. Her free-lifting square sails and gallants and royals and top-gallants were swelling to leeward, cut into rotund patterns by the buntlines and leach lines, her taut rigging straining and singing against the quickening wind. The rake-masted Clipper was on the lee tack on a broad reach and her bow wave flew upward, her gunnel awash, and above the froth of her wake – white against the green-blue ocean – sea-gulls cried their welcome.

Again the cannon barked, and a puff of smoke swung over her lee quarter, the Union Jack aft, the Lion and the Dragon atop the mizzen. Those on the beach who had won their wagers cheered mightily, for huge sums of money were gambled on which ship would be the first home and which ship would be the first back.

'Mr McKay!' Struan called, but the bosun was already hurrying over to him with the double telescope.

'Three days early an' record time, sorr,' Bosun McKay said with a toothless smile. 'Och aye, look at her fly. She'll cost Brock a barrel of silver!' He hurried inland.

The ship, *Thunder Cloud*, came barrelling out of the channel, and now that she was clear, she ran before the wind and gathered speed.

Struan put the short double telescope to his eyes and focused on the code flags he was seeking. The message read: 'Crisis not resolved. New treaty with Ottoman Empire against France. Talk of war.' Then Struan studied the ship; her paint was good, her rigging taut, her guns in place. And in one corner of her fore-royal sail was a small black patch, a code sign, used only in emergencies and meaning 'Important dispatches aboard.'

He lowered the binoculars and offered them to Cooper. 'Do you want to borrow them?'

'Thanks.'

'They're called bi-oculars, or binoculars. Two eyes. You focus with the central screw,' Struan said. 'I had them made specially.'

Cooper peered through them and saw the code flags. He knew that everyone on the fleet was trying to read their message and that all companies spent much time and money trying to break the code of The Noble House. The binoculars were more powerful than a telescope. 'Where can I get a gross of these?'

'A hundred guineas apiece. A year to deliver.'

Take it or leave it, Cooper thought bitterly, knowing the tone of voice. 'Done.' New code flags were raised, and Cooper handed the binoculars back.

The second message was a single word, 'Zenith', a code within the master code.

'If I were you,' Struan said to Cooper, 'I'd unload your season's cotton. In a hurry.'

'Why?'

Struan shrugged. 'Just trying to be of service. You'll excuse me?'

Cooper watched him leave to intercept Robb, who was approaching with the bosun. What's in those goddam flags? he asked himself. And what did he mean about our cotton? And why the hell hasn't the mail ship arrived?

This was what made trading so exciting. You bought and sold for a market four months ahead, knowing only the market position of four months ago. A mistake and the inside of a debtors' prison you'd see. A calculated gamble that came off and you could retire and never know the Orient again. A wave of pain swept up from his bowels. Pain of the Orient that was always with him – with most of them – and a way of life. Was it a friendly tip of the Tai-Pan's or a calculated ploy?

Captain Glessing, accompanied by Horatio, was eyeing *Thunder Cloud* enviously. And also impatiently. She was a prize worth taking, and as the first ship of the year to make the voyage out from England and from Calcutta, her holds would be crammed with opium. Glessing wondered what the flags had meant. And why there was a black patch on the foreroyal.

'Beautiful ship,' Horatio said.

'Yes, she is.'

'Even though she's a pirate?' Horatio asked ironically.

'Her cargo and owners make her a pirate. A ship's a ship, and that's one of the most gorgeous ladies who ever served man,' Glessing answered crisply, unamused by Horatio's wit. 'Speaking of ladies,' he said, trying not to be obvious, 'would you and Miss Sinclair care to sup with me tonight? I'd like to show you around my ship.'

'That's very nice of you, George. I would indeed. And I imagine Mary would be delighted. She's never been on a frigate before.'

Perhaps tonight, Glessing told himself there'll be an opportunity to determine how Mary feels about me. 'I'll send a longboat for you. Would three bells – the last dogwatch – be all right?'

'Better make it eight bells,' Horatio said nonchalantly, just to show that he knew that three bells in this watch would be seven-thirty, but eight o'clock would be eight bells.

'Very well,' Glessing said. 'Miss Sinclair will be the first lady I've entertained aboard.'

Good God, Horatio thought, could Glessing have more than a fleeting interest in Mary? Of course! The invitation was really for her, not me. What a nerve! Pompous ass! To think that Mary would even consider such a match. Or that I would allow her to marry yet!

A musket clattered to the stones and they glanced around. One of the marines had fainted and was lying on the beach.

'What the devil's the matter with him?' Glessing said.

The master-at-arms turned the young marine over. 'Don't know, sorr. It's Norden, sor. He's been acting strange like, for weeks. Perhaps he's the fever.'

'Well, leave him where he is. Round up the sailors, marines to the boats! When everyone's aboard, come back and fetch him.'

'Yes, sorr.' The master-at-arms picked up Norden's musket and threw it to another marine and marched the men away. When it was safe to move, Norden – who had only pretended to faint – slipped into the lee of some rocks and hid. Oh Lord Jesus, protect me till I can get to the Tai-Pan, he prayed desperately. I'll never get an opportunity like this again. Protect me, oh Blessed Jesus and help me get to him afore they come back for me.

* * *

56

Brock was standing on the quarterdeck of his ship, his telescope trained on the flags. He had broken Struan's code six months ago and understood the first message. Now, wot about 'Zenith'? Wot do that mean? he asked himself. And wot be so important about Ottoman treaty that Struan's'd risk telling about, open like, even in code, 'stead of in secret when they be aboard? Maybe they knowed I broke the code. Maybe they want me t'understand it and 'Zenith' means, private to them, the message be false. Crisis and war means price of tea and silk be going up. And cotton. Better buy heavily. *If* it be true. And perhaps put my head in Struan's trap. Where the hell be *Gray Witch*? Not right for her to be beat. Damn that Gorth! He costed me a thousand guineas.

Gorth was his eldest son and the *Gray Witch's* captain. A son to be proud of. As big as he, as rough, as strong, as fine a seaman as ever sailed the seas. Yes, a son to follow you an' worthy to be Tai-Pan in a year or two. Brock said a silent prayer for Gorth's safety, then damned him again for being second to *Thunder Cloud*.

He focused his telescope on the shore where Struan was meeting Robb, and wished that he could hear what they were saying.

'Excuse me, Mr Brock.' Nagrek Thumb was captain of the *White Witch*, a large, thickset Manxman with huge hands and a face the colour of pickled oak.

'Yes, Nagrek?'

'There's a rumour going around the fleet. I don't put much stock in it, but you never know. Rumour says that the navy's getting powers to stop us smuggling opium. That we can be took like pirates.'

Brock scoffed. 'That be a rare one.'

'I laughed too, Mr Brock. Until I heard that the order's to be give out at four bells. And until I heard that Struan said to Longstaff we should all have six days' grace to sell what stocks we have.'

'Be you sure?' Brock hardly had time to absorb the jolting news when he was distracted by a bustling on the gangway. Eliza Brock strode ponderously on to the deck. She was a big woman with thick arms and the power of a man; her iron-grey hair was worn in a loose bun. With her were their two daughters, Elizabeth and Tess.

'Morning, Mr Brock,' Liza said, setting her feet squarely on the deck, her arms crossed over the hugeness of her bosom. 'Tis a nice day, by gum!'

'Where you beed, luv? Morning, Tess. Hello, Lillibet luv,' Brock said, his adoration of his daughters overwhelming him.

Elizabeth Brock was six and brown-haired. She ran over to Brock and curtsied and almost fell down, then jumped into his arms and hugged him, and he laughed.

'We were over t'Mrs Blair,' Liza said. 'She be proper poorly.'

'Will she lose the baby?'

'No, the Lord willing,' Liza said. 'Morning, Nagrek.'

'Morning, ma'am,' Thumb said, taking his eyes off Tess who was standing at the gunnel looking towards the island. Tess Brock was sixteen, tall and curved, her waist fashionably narrow. Her features were sharp and she was not pretty. But her face was strong and the life in it made her attractive. And very desirable.

'I'll get some grub.' Liza made a note of the way Nagrek had looked at Tess. It's time she were wed, she thought. But not to Nagrek Thumb, by God. 'Come below, Tess. Get on with you, Lillibet,' she said as Elizabeth held out her arms to be carried.

'Please, please, please, Mumma. Please, please.'

'Use thy own legs, girl.' Even so, Liza swept her into her huge embrace and carried her below. Tess followed, and smiled at her father and self-consciously nodded to Nagrek.

'Are thee sure about Struan and Longstaff?' Brock asked again.

'Yes.' Nagrek turned to Brock, forcing his heated mind off the girl. 'A golden guinea in a man's hand makes his ears long. I've a bullyboy in the flagship.'

'Struan baint never agreeing to that. He couldn't. It'd wreck him with the rest of us.'

'Well, it were said right enough. This morning.'

'Wot else were said, Nagrek?'

'That's all the bullyboy heard.'

'Then it be trickery – more of his sodding devilment.'

'Yes. But what?'

Brock began churning possibilities. 'Send word to the lorchas. Get every case of opium up the coast. Meantime send a purse with twenty guineas to our bullyboy aboard *China Cloud*. Tell him there's twenty more if he finds out wot be aback of it. Be careful, now. We baint wantin' to lose him.'

'If Struan ever catched him he'd send us his tongue.'

'Along with his head. Fifty guineas says Struan's got a man aboard us'n.'

'A hundred says you're wrong,' Thumb said. 'Every man aboard's a trusty!'

'Better I never catched him alive afore thee, Nagrek.'

*　　*　　*

'But why should he fly "Zenith"?' Robb was saying. 'Of course we'd come aboard at once.'

'I dinna ken,' Struan said. Zenith meant 'Owner to come aboard – urgent.' He frowned at *Thunder Cloud*. Bosun McKay was out of earshot down the beach, waiting patiently.

'You go aboard, Robb. Give Isaac my compliments and tell him to come ashore at once. Bring him to the valley.'

'Why?'

'Too many ears aboard. It might be very important.' Then he called out, 'Bosun McKay!'

'Aye, aye, sorr.' McKay hurried up to him.

'Take Mr Struan to *Thunder Cloud*. Then go over to my ship. Get a tent and a bed and my things. I'll be staying ashore tonight.'

'Aye, aye, sorr! Beggin' yor pardon, sorr,' Bosun McKay said awkwardly. 'There's a young lad. Ramsey. In HMS *Mermaid*, Glessing's ship. The Ramseys're kin to the McKays. The first mate's got it in for the poor lad. Thirty lashes yesterday and more t'morrer. He was press-ganged out o' Glasgow.'

'So?' Struan asked impatiently.

'I heard, sorr,' the bosun said carefully, 'he'd like a berth somewheres.'

'God's blood, are you simple in the head? We take no deserters aboard our ships. If we take one knowingly, we could lose our ship – and rightly!'

'S'truth! I thought you might buy him out,' McKay said quickly, 'seeing as how Capt'n Glessing's a friend o' yorn. My prize money'll go to help, sorr. He's a gud lad and he'll jump ship if he's nothing ahead.'

'I'll think about it.'

'Thank you, sorr.' The bosun touched his forelock and scuttled away.

'Robb, if you were Tai-Pan, what would you do?'

'Pressed men are always dangerous and never to be trusted,' Robb said instantly. 'So I'd never buy him out. And now I'd watch McKay. Perhaps McKay's now Brock's man and put up to it. I'd put McKay to the test. I'd get intermediaries – probably McKay as part of the test, and also an enemy of McKay's – and string Ramsey along and never trust his information.'

'You've told me what I'd do,' Struan said with a glint of humour. 'I asked what you'd do.'

'I'm not Tai-Pan, so it's not my problem. If I was, I probably wouldn't tell you anyway. Or I might tell you and then do the opposite.

To test you.' Robb was glad that he could hate his brother from time to time. That made liking him so much greater.

'Why're you afraid, Robb?'

'I'll tell you in a year.' Robb walked after the bosun.

For a time Struan mused about his brother and the future of The Noble House; then he picked up a bottle of brandy and began to walk along the cleft of rocks towards the valley.

The ranks of the merchants were thinning and some were already leaving in their longboats. Others were still eating and drinking, and there were gusts of laughter at some who were dancing a drunken eightsome reel.

'Sir!'

Struan stopped and stared at the young marine. 'Aye?'

'I need your help, sir. Desperate,' Norden said, his eyes strange, his face grey.

'What help?' Struan was grimly conscious of the marine's side arm, a bayonet.

'I've the pox – woman sickness. You can help. Give me the cure, sir. Anything, I'll do anything.'

'I'm no doctor, lad,' Struan said, the hairs on his neck rising. 'Should you na be at your boat?'

'You've had the same, sir. But you had the cure. All I wants is the cure. I'll do anything.' Norden's voice was a croak, and his lips were flecked with foam.

'I've never had it, lad.' Struan noticed the master-at-arms starting towards them, calling out something that sounded like a name.

'You'd better get to your boat, lad. They're waiting for you.'

'The cure. Tell me how. I've me savings, sir.' Norden pulled out a filthy, knotted rag and offered it proudly, sweat streaking his face. 'I'm thrifty and there be – there be five whole shillin' an' fourpence, sir, and it be all I have in the world, sir, and then there's me pay, twenty shillin' a month you can have. You can have it all, sir, I swear by the blessed Lord Jesus, sir!'

'I've never had the woman sickness, lad. Never,' Struan said again, his heart grinding at the memory of his childhood when wealth was pennies and shillings and half shillings and not bullion in tens of thousands of taels. And living again the never-to-be-forgotten horror of all his youth – of no-money and no-hope and no-food and no-warmth and no-roof and the bloated heaving stomachs of the children. Good sweet Jesus, I can forget my own hunger, but never the children, never their cries on a starving wind in a cesspool of a street.

60

'I'll do anything, anything, sir. Here. I can pay. I don't want nuffink for nuffink. Here, sir.'

The master-at-arms was striding up the beach. 'Norden!' he shouted angrily. 'You'll get fifty lashes for breaking ranks, by God!'

'Is your name Norden?'

'Yes, sir. Bert Norden. Please. I only want the cure. Help me, sir. Here. Take the money. It's all yorn and there'll be more. In Jesus Christ's name, help me!'

'Norden!' the master-at-arms shouted from a hundred yards away, red with rage. 'God's blood, come here, you godrotting bastard!'

'Please, sir,' Norden said with growing desperation. 'I heard you got cured by the heathen. You bought the cure from the heathen!'

'Then you heard a lie. There's no Chinese cure that I know of. No cure. None. You'd better get back to your boat.'

'Course there's a cure!' Norden shrieked. He jerked out his bayonet. 'You tell me where to get it or I'll cut your sodding gizzard open!'

The master-at-arms broke into a horrified run. '*Norden!*'

A few on the beach turned around startled: Cooper and Horatio and another. They began to run towards them.

Then Norden's brain snapped, and gibbering and foaming, he hurled himself at Struan and slashed at him viciously, but Struan sidestepped and waited without fear, knowing that he could kill Norden at will.

It seemed to Norden that he was surrounded by devil-giants all with the same face, but he could never touch one of them. He felt the air explode from his lungs and the beach smash into his face, and he seemed to be suspended in painless agony. Then there was blackness.

The master-at-arms rolled off Norden's back and hacked down with his fist again. He grabbed Norden and shook him like a rag doll and threw him down again. 'What the devil happened to him?' he said, getting up, his face mottled with rage. 'You all right, Mr Struan?'

'Yes.'

Cooper and Horatio and some of the merchants hurried up. 'What's the matter?'

Struan carefully turned Norden over with his foot. 'The poor fool's got woman sickness.'

'Christ!' the master-at-arms said, nauseated.

'Better get away from him, Tai-Pan,' Cooper said. 'If you breathe his flux you can catch it.'

'The poor fool thought I'd had the disease and got cured. By the Cross, if I knew the cure for that I'd be the richest man on the earth.'

'I'll have the bugger put in irons, Mr Struan,' the master-at-arms said. 'Cap'n Glessing'll make him wisht he never been born.'

'Just get a spade,' Struan said. 'He's dead.'

Cooper broke the silence. 'First day, first blood. Bad joss.'

'Not according to Chinese custom,' Horatio said absently, sickened. 'Now his ghost will watch over his place.'

'Good omen or bad,' Struan said, 'the poor lad's dead.'

'Why does a corpse always look so obscene?' Horatio asked.

No one answered him.

'The Lord have mercy on his soul,' Struan said. Then he turned west along the foreshore towards the crest that came down from the mountain ridge and almost touched the sea. He was full of foreboding as he drank in the good clean air and smelled the tang of the spray. That's bad joss, he told himself. Very bad.

As he neared the crest, his premonition intensified, and when at last he stood in the floor of the valley where he had decided the town would be built, he felt for the third time a vastness of hate surround him.

'Good sweet Christ,' he said aloud. 'What's the matter with me?' He had never known such terror before. Trying to hold it in check, he squinted up at the knoll where the Great House would be, and, abruptly, he realized why the island was hostile. He laughed aloud.

'If I were you, Island, I'd hate me too. You hate the plan! Well, I tell you, Island, the plan's good, by God. Good, you hear? China needs the world and the world needs China. And you're the key to unlock the gates of China, and you know it and I know it, and that's what I'm going to do, and you're going to help!'

Stop it, he said to himself. You're acting like a madman. Aye, and they'd all think you mad if you told them that your secret purpose was not just to get rich on trade and to leave. But to use riches and power to open up China to the world and particularly to British culture and British law so that each could learn from the other and grow to the benefit of both. Aye. It's a dream of a madman.

But he was certain that China had something special to offer the world. What it was, he did not know. One day perhaps he would find out.

'And we've something special to offer as well,' Struan continued aloud, 'if you'll take it. And if it's na defiled in the giving. You're British soil for better or worse. We'll cherish you and make you the centre of Asia – which is the world. I commit The Noble House to the plan. If you turn your back on us you'll be what you are now – a nothing barren flyspeck of a stinking barren rock – and you'll die. And last, if The Noble House ever turns its back on you – destroy it with my blessing.'

He hiked up the knoll and, unsheathing his dirk, cut two long branches. He cleaved one and thrust it into the ground and with the other formed a crude cross. He doused the cross with brandy and lit it.

Those in the fleet who could see into the valley, and who noticed the smoke and the flame, found their telescopes and saw the burning cross and the Tai-Pan beside it, and they shuddered to themselves superstitiously and wondered what devilment he was up to. The Scots knew that the burning of a cross was a summons to the clan and to all the kinsmen of all kindred clans: a summons to rally to the cross for battle.

And the burning cross was raised only by the chief of the clan. By ancient law, once raised, the burning cross committed the clan to defend the land unto the end of the clan.

II

'Welcome aboard, Robb,' Captain Isaac Perry said. 'Tea?'

'Thank you, Isaac.' Robb sat back gratefully in the deep leather sea chair, smelling its tangy perfume, and waited. No one could hurry Perry, not even the Tai-Pan.

Perry poured the tea into porcelain cups.

He was thin but incredibly strong. His hair was the colour of old hemp, brown with threads of silver and black. His beard was grizzled and his face scarred, and he smelled of tarred hemp and salt spray.

'Good voyage?' Robb asked.

'Excellent.'

Robb was happy as always to be in the main cabin. It was large and luxurious like all the quarters. The fittings throughout the ship were brass and copper and mahogany, and the sails the finest canvas and the ropes always new. Cannon perfect. Best powder. It was the Tai-Pan's policy throughout his fleet to give his officers – and men – the finest quarters and the best food and a share of the profits, and there was always a doctor aboard. And flogging was outlawed. There was only one punishment for cowardice or disobedience, officer or seaman: to be put ashore at the first port and never given a second chance. So seamen and officers fought to be part of the fleet and there was never a berth empty.

The Tai-Pan had never forgotten his first ships and the fo'c'sles or his floggings. Or the men that had ordered them. Some of the men had died before he found them. Those that he found he broke. Only Brock he had not touched.

Robb did not know why his brother had spared Brock. He shuddered, knowing that whatever the reason, one day there would be a reckoning.

Perry ordered a spoonful of sugar and condensed milk. He handed Robb a cup, then sat behind the mahogany sea desk and peered out from eyes that were deep-set under shaggy brows. 'Mr Struan's in good health?'

'As always. You expected him to be sick?'

'No.'

There was a knock on the cabin door.

'Come in!'

The door opened and Robb gaped at the young man standing there. 'Great God, Culum lad, where'd you come from?' He got up excitedly, knocking his cup over: ' "Very important dispatches" indeed – and of course "Zenith"!' Culum Struan entered the cabin and shut the door. Robb held him affectionately by the shoulders, then noticed his pallor and sunken cheeks. 'What's amiss, lad?' he asked anxiously.

'I'm much better, thank you, Uncle,' Culum said, the voice too thin.

'Better from what, laddie?'

'The plague, the Bengal plague,' Culum said, puzzled.

Robb whirled on Perry. 'You've got plague aboard? In Christ's name, why aren't you flying the Yellow Jack?'

'Of course there's no plague aboard! It was in Scotland months ago.' Perry stopped. '*Scarlet Cloud!* She never arrived?'

'Four weeks overdue. No word, nothing. What's happened? Come on, man!'

'Shall I tell him, Culum lad, or do you want to?'

'Where's father?' Culum asked Robb.

'Ashore. He's waiting for you ashore. At the valley. For the love of God, what's happened, Culum?'

'Plague came to Glasgow in June,' Culum said dully. 'They say it came by ship again. From Bengal – India. First to Sutherland then Edinburgh, then it came to us in Glasgow. Mother's dead, Ian, Lechie, Grandma – Winifred's so weak she won't last. Grandpa's looking after her.' He made a helpless gesture and sat on the arm of the sea chair. 'Grandma's dead. Mother. Aunt Uthenia and the babies and her husband. Ten, twenty thousand died between June and September. Then the plague disappeared. It just disappeared.'

'Roddy? What about Roddy? My son's dead?' Robb said in anguish.

'No, Uncle. Roddy's fine. He wasn't touched.'

'You're certain, are you, Culum? My son's safe?'

'Yes, I saw him the day before I left. Very few at his school got the plague.'

'Thank God!' Robb shivered, remembering the first wave of the plague that had mysteriously swept Europe ten years ago. Fifty thousand deaths in England alone. A million in Europe. Thousands in New York and New Orleans. Some called this plague by a newer name – cholera.

'Your mother's dead?' Robb said, unbelieving. 'Ian, Lechie, Granny?'

'Yes. And Aunt Susan and Cousin Clair and Aunt Uthenia, Cousin Donald and little Stewart and . . .'

There was a monstrous silence.

Perry broke it nervously. 'When I berthed in Glasgow, well, Culum lad was on his own. I didn't know what to do, so I thought it best to bring him aboard. We sailed a month after *Scarlet Cloud*.'

'You did right, Isaac,' Robb heard himself say. How was he going to tell Dirk? 'I'd better go. I'll signal you to come ashore. You stay aboard.'

'No.' Culum said it aloud as though to himself, deep inside. 'No. I'll go ashore first. Alone. That's better. I'll see Father alone. I must tell him. I'll go ashore alone.' He got up and quietly walked to the door, the ship rocking smoothly and the sweet sound of the waves lapping, and he left. Then he remembered and came back into the cabin. 'I'll take the dispatches,' he said in his tiny voice. 'He'll want to see the dispatches.'

When the longboat pulled away from *Thunder Cloud*, Struan was on the knoll where the Great House would be. As soon as he saw his eldest son amidships, his heart turned over.

'Culummmm!' he roared exultantly from the top of the knoll. He ripped off his coat and waved it frantically like a man marooned six years who sees his first ship. 'Culummmm!' He tore headlong through the coarse brier towards the shore, careless of the thorns and forgetting the path that led from the shore over the crest to the fishing village and pirate nests on the south side of the island. He forgot everything except that here was his darling son on the first day. Faster. And now he was racing along the shore, ecstatic.

Culum saw him first. 'Over there. Put it over there.' He pointed at the nearest landing.

Bosun McKay swung the tiller over. 'Pull, my hearties,' he said, urging them shoreward. They all knew now, and word was flying through the fleet – and, in its wake, anxiety. Between Sutherland and Glasgow lived many a kin and in London Town most of the rest.

Culum got up and slipped over the side into the shallows. 'Leave us.' He began to splash ashore.

Struan ran into the surf that swept the beach, heading straight for his son, and he saw the tears and shouted, 'Culum laddie,' and Culum stopped for a moment, helpless, drowned in the abundance of his father's joy. Then he began running in the surf too, and finally he was

66

safe in his father's arms. And all the horror of the months burst like an abscess and he was weeping, holding on, holding on, and then Struan was gentling his son and carrying him ashore in his arms and murmuring, 'Culum laddie' and 'Dinna fash yoursel' and 'Oh ma bairn,' and Culum was sobbing. 'We're dead – we're all dead – Mumma, Ian, Lechie, Granny, aunts, Cousin Clair – we're all dead, Father. There's only me and Winifred, and she's dead by now.' He repeated the names again and again, and they were knives in Struan's guts.

In time Culum slept, spent, safe at last in the strength and warmth. His sleep was dreamless for the first time since the plague had come. He slept that day and the night and part of the next day, and Struan cradled him, rocking him gently.

Struan did not notice the passing of the time. Sometimes he would talk with his wife and children – Ronalda and Ian and Lechie and Winifred – as they sat on the shore beside him. Sometimes when they would go away he would call to them, softly lest he wake Culum, and later they would come back. Sometimes he would sing the gentle lullabies that Ronalda used to croon to their children. Or the Gaelic of his mother or Catherine, his second mother. Sometimes the mist covered his soul and he saw nothing.

When Culum awoke he felt at peace. 'Hello, Father.'

'You all right, laddie?'

'I'm all right now.' He stood up.

It was cold on the beach in the shadow of the rock, but in the sun it was warmer. The fleet was quietly at anchor, and tenders scurried back and forth. There were fewer ships than before.

'Is that where the Great House'll be?' Culum asked, pointing to the knoll.

'Aye. That's where we could live in the autumn till the spring. The climate's bonny then.'

'What's the valley called?'

'It has na a name.' Struan moved into the sun and tried to dominate the brooding aches in his shoulders and back.

'It should have a name.'

'Little Karen, your cousin Karen – Robb's youngest – wants to call it Happy Valley. We'd've been happy here.' Struan's voice grew leaden. 'Did they suffer much?'

'Yes.'

'Will you tell me about it?'

'Not now.'

'Little Winifred. She died before you left?'

'No. But she was very weak. The doctors said that being so weak . . . the doctors just shrugged and went away.'

'And Grandpa?'

'The plague never touched him. He came like the wind to us and then he took Winifred. I went to Aunt Uthenia's to help. But I didn't help.'

Struan was facing the harbour without seeing it. 'You told Uncle Robb?'

'Yes. Yes, I think I did.'

'Poor Robb. I'd better get aboard.' Struan reached down and picked up the dispatches, half buried in the sand. They were unopened. He wiped the sand off.

'I'm sorry,' Culum said. 'I forgot to give them to you.'

'Nay, lad. You gave them to me.' Struan saw a longboat making for shore. Isaac Perry was in the stern.

'Afternoon, Mr Struan,' Perry said cautiously. 'Sorry about your loss.'

'How's Robb?'

Perry did not answer. He stepped ashore and barked at the crew, 'Hurry it up!' and Struan wondered through the numbness of his torn mind why Perry was afraid of him. No reason to be afraid. None.

The men carried ashore a table and benches and food, tea and brandy and clothes.

'Hurry it up!' Perry repeated irritably. 'And stand off! Get to hell out of here and stand off.'

The oarsmen shoved the longboat off quickly and pulled out above the surf and waited, glad to be away.

Struan helped Culum into dry clothes and then put on a clean, ruffled shirt and warm reefer jacket. Perry helped him off with his soaking boots.

'Thanks,' Struan said.

'Does it hurt?' Culum asked, seeing the foot.

'No.'

'About Mr Robb, sir,' Perry said. 'After Culum left he went for the liquor. I told him no, but he wouldn't listen.' He continued haltingly, 'You'd given orders. So the cabin got a bit bent, but I got it away from him. When he came to, he was all right. I took him aboard *China Cloud* and put him into his wife's hands.'

'You did right, Isaac. Thank you.' Struan helped Culum to a dish of food – beef stew, dumplings, cold chicken, potatoes, hard-tack biscuits – and took a pewter mug of hot, sweet tea for himself.

68

'His Excellency sends his condolences. He'd like you to step aboard, at your convenience.'

Struan rubbed his face and felt the stubble of his beard, and he wondered why he always felt dirty when his face was unshaven and his teeth not brushed.

'Your razor's there,' Perry said, indicating a side table. He had anticipated Struan's need to spruce up. The Tai-Pan had a fanatical obsession with his personal cleanliness. There's hot water.'

'Thank you.' Struan soaked a towel in the water and wiped his face and head. Next he lathered his face and shaved deftly without a mirror. Then he dipped a small brush into his mug of tea and began to clean his teeth vigorously.

Must be another heathen superstition, Perry thought contemptuously. Teeth grow old and rot and fall out and that's all there is to it.

Struan rinsed his mouth with tea and threw the dregs away. He washed the mug with fresh tea and refilled it and drank, deeply. There was a small bottle of cologne with his shaving gear, and he poured a few drops on his hands and rubbed them into his face.

He sat down, refreshed. Culum was only toying with the food. 'You should eat, lad.'

'I'm not hungry, thank you.'

'Eat anyway.' The wind ruffled Struan's red-gold hair, which he wore long and uncurled, and he brushed it back. 'Is my tent set up, Isaac?'

'Of course. You gave orders. It's on a knoll above the flagstaff.'

'Tell Chen Sheng, in my name, to go to Macao and buy honey and fresh eggs. And to get Chinese herbs to cure distempers and the aftereffect of Bengal plague.'

'I'm all right, Father, thank you,' Culum protested weakly. 'I don't need any heathen witches' brews.'

'They're na witches as we know witches, lad,' Struan said. 'And they're Chinese, not heathen. Their herbs have saved me many a time. The Orient's not like Europe.'

'No need to worry about me, Father.'

'There is. The Orient's nae place for the weak. Isaac, order *China Cloud* to Macao with Chen Sheng, and if she's not back in record time, Captain Orlov and all the officers are beached. Call the longboat in.'

'Perhaps Culum should go with the ship to Macao, Mr Struan.'

'He's to stay in my sight till I think he's well.'

'He'd be well looked after in Macao. Aboard there's not—'

'God's blood, Isaac, will you na do as you're told? Get the longboat in!'

Perry stiffened momentarily and shouted the longboat ashore.

Struan, with Culum beside him, sat amidships, Perry behind them.

'Flagship!' Struan ordered, automatically checking the lie of his ships and the smell of the wind and studying the clouds, trying to read their weather message. The sea was calm. But he could smell trouble.

On the way to the flagship Struan read the dispatches. Profits on last year's teas, good. Perry had made a lucrative voyage, good. A copy of *Scarlet Cloud's* bill of lading that Perry had brought from Calcutta; bad: two hundred and ten thousand pounds sterling of opium lost. Thank God the ship was insured – though that would na replace the men and the time lost while another ship was abuilding. The cargo of opium was contraband and could not be insured. A year's profit gone. What had happened to her? Storm or piracy? Storm, more likely. Unless she'd run into one of the Spanish or French or American – aye, or English – privateers that infested the seas. Finally he broke the seal on his banker's letter. He read it and exploded with rage.

'What is it?' Culum asked, frightened.

'Just an old pain. Nothing. It's nothing.' Struan pretended to read the next dispatch while raging inwardly over the contents of the letter. Good sweet Christ! 'We regret to inform you that, inadvertently and momentarily, credit was over extended and there was a run on the bank, started by malicious rivals. Therefore we can no longer keep our doors open. The board of directors has advised we can pay sixpence on the pound. I have the honour to be, sir, your most obedient servant . . .' And we hold close to a million sterling of their paper. Twenty-five thousand sterling for a million, and our debts close to a million pounds. We're bankrupt. Great God, I warned Robb not to put all the money in one bank. Na with all the speculating that was going on in England, na when a bank could issue paper in any amount that it liked.

'But this bank's safe,' Robb had said, 'and we need the money in one block for collateral,' and Robb had gone on to explain the details of a complicated financial structure that involved Spanish and French and German bonds and National Debt bonds, and in the end gave Struan and Company an internationally safe banking position and a huge buying power for expanding the fleet that Struan wanted, and bought for The Noble House special privileges in the lucrative German, French and Spanish markets.

'All right, Robb,' he had said, not understanding the intricacies but trusting that what Robb said was wise.

Now we're broke. Bankrupt.

Sweet Christ!

He was still too stunned to think about a solution. He could only dwell on the awesomeness of the new Age. The complexity of it. The unbelievable speed of it. A new queen – Victoria – the first popular monarch in centuries. And her husband Albert – he did na ken about him yet, he was a bloody foreigner from Saxe-Coburg, but Parliament was strong now and in control, and that was a new development. Peace for twenty-six years and no major war imminent – unheard of for hundreds of years. Devil Bonaparte safely dead, and violent France safely bottled, and Britain world-dominant for the first time. Slavery out eight years ago. Canals, a new method of transport. Toll roads with unheard-of smooth and permanent surfaces, and factories and industry and looms and mass production and iron and coal and joint stock companies, and so many other new things within the past ten years: the penny post, first cheap post on earth, and the first police force in the world, and 'magnetism' – whatever the hell that was – and a steam hammer, and a first Factory Act, and Parliament at long last taken out of the hands of the few aristocratic rich landowners so that now, incredibly, every man in England who owned a house worth twenty pounds a year could vote, could actually vote, and any man could become Prime Minister. And the unbelievable Industrial Revolution and Britain fantastically wealthy and its riches beginning to spread. New ideas of government and humanity ripping through barriers of centuries. All British, all new. And now the locomotive!

'Now, there's an invention that'll rock the world,' he muttered.

'What did you say, Father?' Culum asked.

Struan came back into himself. 'I was just thinking about our first ride on a train,' he improvised.

'You been on a train, sorr?' McKay asked. 'What's it like? When was that?'

Culum said, 'We went on the maiden trip of Stephenson's engine, the *Rocket*. I was twelve.'

'No, lad,' Struan said, 'you were eleven. It was in 1830. Eleven years ago. It was the maiden run of the *Rocket*, on the first passenger train on earth. From Manchester to Liverpool. A day's run by stagecoach, but we made the journey in an hour and a half.' And once again Struan began to ponder the fate of The Noble House. Then he remembered his instructions to Robb to borrow all the money they could to corner the opium market. Let's see – we could make fifty, a hundred thousand pounds out of that. Aye – but a drop in the bucket for what we need. The three million we're owed for the stolen opium! Aye, but we canna

71

get that until the treaty's ratified – six to nine months – and we've to honour our drafts in three!

How to get cash? Our position's good – our standing good. Except there are jackals salivating at our heels. Brock for one. Cooper-Tillman for another. Did Brock start the run on the bank? Or was it his whelp Morgan? The Brocks have power enough and money enough. It's cash we need. Or a huge line of credit. Supported by cash, na paper. We're bankrupt. At least we're bankrupt if our creditors fall on us.

He felt his son's hand on his arm. 'What did you say, lad? The *Rocket*, you were saying?'

Culum was greatly unsettled by Struan's pallor and the piercing luminous green of his eyes. 'The flagship. We're here.'

Culum followed his father on deck. He had never been aboard a warship, let alone a capital ship. HMS *Titan* was one of the most powerful vessels afloat. She was huge – triple-masted – with 74 cannon mounted on three gundecks. But Culum was unimpressed. He did not care for ships, and loathed the sea. He was afraid of the violence and danger and enormousness of it, and he could not swim. He wondered how his father could love the sea.

There's so much I don't know about my father, he thought. But that's not strange. I've only seen him a few times in my life and the last time six years ago. Father hasn't changed. But I have. Now I know what I'm going to do with my life. And now that I'm alone . . . I like being alone, and hate it.

He followed his father down the gangway on to the main gun-deck. It was low-ceilinged and they had to stoop as they walked aft heading for the sentry-guarded cabin, and the whole ship smelled of gunpowder and tar and hemp and sweat.

'Day, sir,' the marine said to Struan, his musket pointing at him formally. 'Master-at-arms!'

The master-at-arms, scarlet uniformed, his white pipe-clay trimming resplendent, stamped out of the guard cabin. He was as hard as a cannon ball and his head as round. 'Day, Mr Struan. Just a moment, sirr.' He knocked deferentially on the oak cabin door. A voice said, 'Come in,' and he closed the door behind him.

Struan took out a cheroot and offered it to Culum. 'Are you smoking now, lad?'

'Yes. Thank you, Father.'

Struan lit Culum's cheroot and one for himself. He leaned against one of the twelve-foot-long cannon. The cannon balls were piled neatly, ever ready. Sixty-pound shot.

72

The cabin door opened. Longstaff, a slight, dapper man came out. His hair was dark and fashionably curled, his mutton-chop whiskers thick. He had a high forehead and dark eyes. The sentry presented arms and the master-at-arms returned to the guard cabin.

'Hello, Dirk, my dear fellow. How are you? I was so sad to hear.' Longstaff shook Struan's hand nervously, then smiled at Culum and offered his hand again. 'You must be Culum. I'm William Longstaff. Sorry that you came under these terrible circumstances.'

'Thank you, Your Excellency,' Culum said, astonished that the Captain Superintendent of Trade should be so young.

'Do you mind waiting a moment, Dirk? Admiral's conference and the captains. I'll be through in a few minutes,' Longstaff said with a yawn. 'I've a lot to talk to you about. If you're up to it.'

'Yes.'

Longstaff glanced anxiously at the gold jewelled fob watch which dangled from his brocade waistcoat. 'Almost eleven o'clock! Never seems to be enough time. Would you like to go down to the wardroom?'

'No. We'll wait here.'

'As you wish.' Longstaff briskly re-entered the cabin and shut the door.

'He's very young to be the plenipotentiary, isn't he?' Culum asked.

'Yes and no. He's thirty-six. Empires are built by young men, Culum. They're lost by old men.'

'He doesn't look English at all. Is he Welsh?'

'His mother's Spanish.' Which accounted for his cruel streak, Struan thought to himself. 'She was a countess. His father was a diplomat to the court of Spain. It was one of those "well-bred" marriages. His family's connected with the earls of Toth.'

If you're not born an aristocrat, Culum thought, however clever you are, you haven't a hope. Not a hope. Not without revolution. 'Things are very bad in England,' he told his father.

'How so, lad?' Struan said.

'The rich are too rich and the poor too poor. People pouring into the cities looking for work. More people than jobs, so the employers pay less and less. People starving. The Chartist leaders are still in prison.'

'A good thing, too. Those rabble-rousing scum should have been hung or transported, na just put in prison.'

'You don't approve of the Charter?' Culum was suddenly on his guard. The People's Charter had been written less than three years ago, and now had become the rallying symbol of liberty to all the dis-

73

contented of Britain. The Charter demanded a vote for every man, the abolition of the property qualification for members of Parliament, equal electoral districts, vote by secret ballot, annual Parliaments, and salaries for members of Parliament.

'I approve of it as a document of fair demands. But na of the Chartists or their leaders. The Charter's like a lot of basic good ideas – they fall into the hands of the wrong leaders.'

'It's not wrong to agitate for reform. Parliaments's got to make changes.'

'Agitate, yes. Talk, argue, write petitions, but don't incite violence and dinna lead revolutions. The Government was right to put down the troubles in Wales and the Midlands. Insurrection's no answer, by God. There's tales that the Chartists have na learned their lesson yet and that they're buying arms and having secret meetings. They should be stamped out, by God.'

'You won't stamp out the Charter. Too many want it and are prepared to die for it.'

'Then there'll be a lot of deaths, lad. If the Chartists dinna possess themselves with patience.'

'You don't know what the British Isles are like now, Father. You've been out here so long. Patience comes hard with an empty belly.'

'It's the same in China. Same all the world over. But revolt and insurrection's na the British way.'

It soon will be, Culum thought grimly, if there aren't changes. He was sorry now that he had left Glasgow for the Orient. Glasgow was the centre of the Scottish Chartists and he was leader of the undergraduates who had, in secret, committed themselves to work and sweat – and die if necessary – for the Chartist cause.

The cabin door opened again, and the sentry stiffened. The admiral, a heavyset man, strode out, his face taut and angry, and headed for the gangway, followed by his captains. Most of the captains were young but a few were grey-haired. All were dressed in sea uniform and wore cocked hats, and their swords clattered.

Captain Glessing was last. He stopped in front of Struan. 'Can I offer my condolences, Mr Struan? Very bad luck!'

'Aye.' Is it just bad luck, Struan wondered, to lose a bonny wife and three bonny children? Or does God – or the Devil – have a hand in joss? Or are they – God, Devil, luck, joss – just different names for the same thing?

'You were quite right to kill that damned marine,' Glessing said.

'I did na touch him.'

'Oh? I presumed you did. Couldn't see what happened from where I was. It's unimportant.'

'Did you bury him ashore?'

'No. No point in defiling the island with that sort of disease. Does the name Ramsey mean anything to you, Mr Struan?' Glessing asked, bluntly terminating the amenities.

'Ramsey's a common enough name.' Struan was on guard.

'True. But Scots stick together. Isn't that a key to the success of Scot-dominated enterprises?'

'It's hard to find trustworthy people, aye,' Struan said. 'Does the name Ramsey mean anything to you?'

'It's the name of a deserter from my ship,' Glessing said pointedly. 'He's a cousin to your bosun, Bosun McKay, I believe.'

'So?'

'Nothing. Just passing along information. As you know, of course, any merchantman, armed or otherwise, which harbours deserters can be taken as prize. By the Royal Navy.' Glessing smiled. 'Stupid to desert. Where can he go except on to another ship?'

'Nowhere.' Struan felt trapped. He was sure that Ramsey was aboard one of his ships and certain that Brock was involved and perhaps Glessing too.

'We're searching the fleet today. You've no objection, of course?'

'Of course. We're very careful who man our ships.'

'Very wise. The admiral thought The Noble House should have pride of place, so your ships will be searched immediately.'

In that case, Struan thought, there's nothing I can do. So he dismissed the problem from his mind.

'Captain, I'd like you to meet my eldest – my son, Culum. Culum, this is our famous Captain Glessing who won us the battle of Chuenpi.'

'Good day to you.' Glessing shook hands politely. Culum's hand felt soft and it was long-fingered and slightly feminine. Bit of a dandy, Glessing thought. Waisted frock coat, pale blue cravat and high collar. Must be an undergraduate. Curious to be shaking hands with someone who's had Bengal plague and lived. Wonder if I'd survive. 'That wasn't a battle.'

'Two small frigates against twenty junks of war and thirty or more fire ships? That's na a battle?'

'An engagement, Mr Struan. It could have been a battle . . .' If it hadn't been for that godrotting coward Longstaff, and you, you godrotting pirate, he itched to say.

'We merchants think of it, Culum, as a battle,' Struan said ironically.

75

'We dinna understand the difference between an engagement and a battle. We're just peaceful traders. But the first time the arms of England went out against the arms of China deserves the title "battle". It was just over a year ago. We fired first.'

'And what would you have done, Mr Struan? It was the correct tactical decision.'

'Of course.'

'The Captain Superintendent of Trade concurred completely with my actions.'

'Of course. There was little else he could do.'

'Fighting old battles, Captain Glessing?' Longstaff asked. He was standing at the door of the cabin and had been listening, unnoticed.

'No, Your Excellency, just rehashing an old engagement. Mr Struan and I have never seen eye to eye on Chuenpi, as you know.'

'And why should you? If Mr Struan had been in your command, his decision might have been the same as yours. If you had been in Mr Struan's place, then you might have been sure that they would not have attacked and you would have gambled.' Longstaff yawned and toyed with his watch fob. 'What would you have done, Culum?'

'I don't know, sir. I don't know the complications that existed.'

'Well said. "Complications" is a good word.' Longstaff chuckled. 'Would you care to join us, Captain? A glass of sack?'

'Thank you, sir, but I'd better get back to my ship.' Glessing saluted smartly and walked away.

Longstaff motioned the Struans into the conference room which presently served as the private quarters of the Captain Superintendent of Trade. It was spartan and functional, and the deep leather chairs and chart tables, chests of drawers and heavy oak table were all fastened tightly to the deck. The richly carved oak desk was backed by the semicircle of mullioned windows of the stern. The cabin smelled of tar and stale tobacco and sea and, inevitably, gunpowder.

'Steward!' Longstaff called out.

At once the cabin door opened. 'Yussir?'

Longstaff turned to Struan. 'Sack? Brandy? Port?'

'Dry sack, thank you.'

'The same, please, sir,' Culum said.

'I'll have port.' Longstaff yawned again.

'Yussir.' The steward took the bottles from the sideboard and poured the wines into fine crystal glasses.

'Is this your first trip abroad, Culum?' Longstaff asked.

'Yes, sir.'

'But I suppose you're well up-to-date on our recent "complications"?'

'No, Your Excellency. Father didn't write very much, and China isn't mentioned in the newspapers.'

'But it soon will be, eh, Dirk?'

The steward offered the glasses to Longstaff, and then to his guests. 'See that we're not disturbed.'

'Yussir.' The steward left the bottles within easy reach and went out.

'A toast,' Longstaff said, and Struan remembered Robb's toast and regretted that he had come first to the flagship. 'To a pleasant stay, Culum, and to a safe journey home.'

They drank. The dry sack was excellent.

'History's being made out here, Culum. And there's no one better equipped to tell you about it than your father.'

'There's an old Chinese saying, Culum: "Truth wears many faces",' Struan said.

'I don't understand.'

'Just that my version of "facts" is na necessarily the only one.' This reminded him of the previous viceroy, Ling, now in disgrace in Canton, because his policies had precipitated the open conflict with Britain, and presently under a death sentence. 'Is that devil Ling still in Canton?'

'I think so. His Excellency Ti-sen smiled when I asked him three days ago and said cryptically, "The Vermilion is the Son of Heaven. How can man know what Heaven wills?" The Chinese emperor is called the Son of Heaven,' Longstaff elaborated for Culum's sake. ' "The Vermilion" is another of his names because he always writes in vermilion-coloured ink.'

'Strange, strange people, the Chinese, Culum,' Struan said. 'For instance; only the emperor among three hundred millions is allowed to use vermilion ink. Imagine that. If Queen Victoria said, "From now on, only I am allowed to use vermilion," as much as we love her, forty thousand Britons would instantly forswear all ink but vermilion. I would myself.'

'And every China trader,' Longstaff said with an unconscious sneer, 'would instantly send her a barrel of the colour, cash on delivery, and tell Her Britannic Majesty they'd be glad to supply the Crown, at a price. And they'd write the letter in vermilion. Rightly so, I suppose. Where would we be without trade?'

There was a small silence and Culum wondered why his father had let the insult pass. Or was it an insult? Wasn't it just another fact of life –

that aristos always sneered at anyone who was not an aristo? Well, the Charter would solve aristos once and for all.

'You wanted to see me, Will?' Struan felt deathly tired. His foot ached, and so did his shoulders.

'Yes. A few minor things have happened since . . . in the last two days. Culum, would you excuse us for a moment? I want to talk to your father alone.'

'Certainly, sir.' Culum got up.

'No need for that, Will,' Struan said. But for Longstaff's sneer he would have let Culum go. 'Culum's a partner in Struan's now. One day he'll rule it as Tai-Pan. You can trust him as you'd trust me.'

Culum wanted to say, 'I'll never be part of this, never. I've other plans.' But he could say nothing.

'I must congratulate you, Culum,' Longstaff said. 'To be a partner in The Noble House – well, that's a prize beyond price.'

Na when you're bankrupt, Struan almost added. 'Sit down, Culum.'

Longstaff paced the room, and began: 'A meeting with the Chinese Plenipotentiary is arranged for tomorrow to discuss the treaty details.'

'Did he suggest the time and the place, or did you?'

'He did.'

'Perhaps you'd better change it. Pick another place and another time.'

'Why?'

'Because if you agree to his suggestion, he and all the mandarins will interpret it as weakness.'

'All right. If you think so. The day after tomorrow, what? At Canton?'

'Yes. Take Horatio and Mauss. I'll come with you if you like, and we must be four hours late.'

'But damme, Dirk, why go to such ridiculous extremes? Four hours? 'Pon me word!'

'It's not ridiculous. By acting like a superior to an inferior, you put them at a disadvantage.' Struan glanced at Culum. 'You have to play the Oriental game by Oriental rules. Little things become very important. His Excellency has a very difficult position here. One little mistake now, and the result will last fifty years. He has to make haste with extreme caution.'

'Yes. And no damned help!' Longstaff drained his glass and poured another. 'Why the devil they can't act like civilized people I'll never know. Never. Apart from your father there's no one who helps. The Cabinet at home doesn't know the problems I'm facing and doesn't care. I'm completely on my own here. They give me impossible instructions and expect me to deal with an impossible people. 'Pon me word, we have to be late four hours to prove we're "superior" when of course everyone knows we're superior!' He took some snuff irritably, and sneezed.

'When are you holding a land sale, Will?'

'Well, er, I thought when the Cabinet approves the treaty. There's plenty of time. Say in September.'

'Do you na remember your idea? I thought you wanted to start building in Hong Kong immediately.'

Longstaff tried to recollect. He seemed to remember talking about it to Struan. What was it? 'Well, of course, the ceding of Hong Kong isn't official until both governments approve the treaty – I mean, that's usual, isn't it, what?'

'Yes. But these are na usual circumstances.' Struan toyed with his glass. 'Hong Kong's ours. The sooner we start building the better, is that na what you said?'

'Well, of course it's ours.' What *was* that plan? Longstaff stifled another yawn.

'You said that all land was to belong to the queen. That until you were officially the first governor of Hong Kong, all government was to be in your hands as plenipotentiary. If you issue a special proclamation, then everything is as you planned. If I were you, I'd hold a land sale next month. Dinna forget, Will, that you'll need revenue for the colony. The Cabinet is sensitive about colonies that dinna pay for themselves.'

'Correct. Yes. Absolutely right. Of course. We should begin as soon as possible. We'll hold the first land sale next month. Let me see. Should it be freehold or on lease, or what?'

'Nine-hundred-and-ninety-nine-year leases. The usual Crown agreements.'

'Excellent.' Longstaff made a helpless gesture. 'As if we haven't enough to worry about, Culum! Now we have to act like damned tradesmen. How the devil do you go about building a colony, what? Got to have sewers and streets and buildings and God knows what else. A court and a prison, by Jove!' He paused in front of Culum. 'Have you any legal training?'

'No, Your Excellency,' Culum said. 'Just half a university degree in the arts.'

'No matter. I'll have to have a colonial secretary, an adjutant general, treasurer and God knows what else. There'll have to be a police force of some kind. Would you like to be in charge of the police?'

'No, thank you, sir.' Culum tried not to show the shock he felt.

'Well, I'm sure there's some place we can use you. Everyone'll have to pitch in. I can't take care of everything. Think about what you'd like to do and let me know. We'll need people we can trust.'

'Why not put him on your staff as a deputy?' Struan said. 'We'll lend him to you for six months.'

'Excellent.' Longstaff smiled at Culum. 'Good. You're deputy colonial secretary. Let's see. Make arrangements for the land sale. That's your first job.'

'But I don't know anything about land sales, sir. I don't know anything about—'

'You know as much as anyone, and your father can guide you. You'll be, er, deputy colonial secretary. Excellent. Now I can forget that problem. You find out what should be done and how, and let me know what's necessary to make it official. Have an auction. That's the fair way, I imagine.' Longstaff refilled his glass. 'Oh, by the way, Dirk, I ordered the evacuation of Chushan Island.'

Struan felt his stomach turn over. 'Why did you do that, Will?'

'I received a special letter from His Excellency Ti-sen two days ago asking that this be done as an act of good faith.'

'You could have waited.'

'He wanted an immediate answer, and there was, well – no way to reach you.'

'Immediate, Chinese style, means anything up to a century.' Oh Willie, you poor fool, he thought, how many times do I have to explain?

Longstaff felt Struan's eyes grinding into him. 'He was sending off a copy of the treaty to the emperor, and wanted to include the fact that we'd ordered the evacuation. We were going to hand it back anyway, what? That was the plan. Damme, what difference does it make, now or later?'

'Timing is very important to the Chinese. Has the order gone yet?'

'Yes. It went yesterday. Ti-sen was kind enough to offer us the use of the imperial horse relay. I sent the order by that.'

Damn your eyes, Struan thought. You impossible fool. 'Very bad to use their service for our orders. We've lost face and they've gained a point. Nae use in sending a ship now.' His voice was cold and hard. 'By the time it got to Chushan the evacuation'd be completed. Well, it's done, and that's that. But it was unwise. The Chinese will only interpret it as weakness.'

'I thought the act of good faith a splendid idea, splendid,' Longstaff went on, trying to overcome his nervousness. 'After all, we've everything we want. Their indemnity is light – only six million dollars, and that more than covers the cost of the opium they destroyed. Canton is open to trade again. And we have Hong Kong. At long last.' His eyes were sparkling now. 'Everything according to plan. Chushan Island's unimportant. You said to take it only as an expedient. But Hong Kong's ours. And Ti-sen said he'd appoint a mandarin for Hong Kong within the month and they'll—'

'He'll what?' Struan was aghast.

'He'll appoint a mandarin for Hong Kong. What's the matter?'

Hang on to your temper, Struan warned himself with a mighty effort. You've been patient all this time. This weak-brained incompetent's the most necessary tool you have. 'Will, if you allow him to do that, you're giving him power over Hong Kong.'

'Not at all, my dear, fellow, what? Hong Kong's British. The heathen'll be under our flag and under our Government. Someone's got to be in charge of the devils, what? There's got to be someone to pay the customs dues to. Where better than Hong Kong? They'll have their own customs house and buildings and—'

'They'll what?' the word slammed off the oak bulkheads. 'God's blood, you haven't agreed to this, I hope?'

'Well, I don't see anything wrong in it, Dirk, eh? 'Pon me word, it doesn't change anything, does it? It saves us a lot of trouble. We don't have to be in Canton. We can do everything from here.'

To stop himself from crushing Longstaff like a bedbug, Struan walked over to the bureau and poured himself a brandy. Hold on. Dinna wreck him now. The timing's wrong. You've got to use him. 'Have you agreed with Ti-sen that he *can* appoint a mandarin for Hong Kong?'

'Well, my dear fellow, I didn't exactly agree. It's not part of the treaty. I just said I agreed it seemed a good idea.'

'Did you do this in writing?'

'Yes. Yesterday.' Longstaff was bewildered by Struan's intensity. 'But isn't that what we've been trying to do for so long? To deal direct with the mandarins and not through the Chinese hong merchants?'

'Aye. But not on our island, by God!' Struan kept his voice level, but he was thinking. You godrotting apology for a leader, you stupid aristocratic indecisive wrong-decisioned dungheap. 'If we allow that, we sink Hong Kong. We lose everything.'

Longstaff tugged at the lobe of his ear, wilting under Struan's eyes.

'Why, Father?' Culum asked.

To Longstaff's relief, the eyes turned to Culum and he thought, Yes, why? Why do we lose everything, eh? I thought it a simply marvellous arrangement.

'Because they're Chinese.'

'I don't understand.'

'I know, laddie.' To put away the grief of the loss of his family that suddenly welled up inside him and to take his mind off his frantic worry over the loss of their wealth, he decided to explain – as much for Longstaff as for Culum. 'First thing to understand: for fifty centuries the Chinese have called China the Middle Kingdom – the land that the Gods have placed between heaven *above* and the earth *beneath*. By definition a Chinese is a uniquely superior being. They all believe that anyone else – anyone – is a barbarian and of no account. And that they alone have the God-given right, as the only really civilized nation, to rule the earth. As far as they're concerned, Queen Victoria is a barbarian vassal who should pay tribute. China has nae fleet, nae army, and we can do what we like with her – but they *believe* they are the most civilized, the most powerful, the richest – in this I think they're potentially right – nation on earth. Do you know about the Eight Regulations?'

Culum shook his head.

'Well, these were the terms under which the Emperor of China agreed to trade with "barbarians" a hundred and fifty years ago. The Regulations confined all "barbarian" trade to the single port of Canton. All tea and silk had to be paid for in silver, nae credit whatsoever allowed, and smuggling was forbidden. "Barbarians" were allowed to build warehouses and factories on a plot of land half a mile by two hundred yards at Canton; "barbarians" were totally confined to this walled-in area – the Canton Settlement – and could stay only for the winter shipping season – September until March – when they must leave and go to Macao. Nae "barbarian" families were allowed in the Settlement under any circumstances and all women forbidden. Nae arms whatsoever in the Settlement. Learning Chinese, boating for pleasure, sedan chairs, and mixing with Chinese were forbidden; "barbarian" warships were forbidden the Pearl River estuary. All "barbarian" merchant ships were to anchor at Whampoa, thirteen miles downstream, where cargoes were to be trans-shipped and export customs tax paid in silver. All "barbarian" business was to be conducted solely through a monopoly, a guild, of ten Chinese merchants which we call the Co-hong. The Co-hong were also the sole suppliers of food, the sole licenser of a set number of servants and boatmen and compradors. And finally, the one regulation that nailed us to the Cross

– and the one the treaty cancels – specified that the Co-hong were the only recipients of all "barbarian" petitions, requests and complaints, which would then, and solely by them, be forwarded to the mandarins.

'The whole point of the Regulations was to keep us at arm's length, to harass us, yet to squeeze every penny out of us. Remember another thing about the Chinese: they love money. But the "squeeze" benefited only the ruling Manchu class, not all Chinese. The Manchus think our ideas – Christianity, Parliament, voting, and above all, equality before the law and a jury system – are revolutionary and dangerous and evil. But they want our bullion.

'Under the Regulations we were defenceless, our trade was controlled and could be squeezed at will. Even so, we made money.' He smiled. 'We made a lot of money, and so did they. Most of the Regulations fell apart because of the greed of the officials. The important ones – nae warships, nae official contact other than through the Co-hong merchants, nae wives in Canton, nae staying beyond March or before September – remained in effect.

'And, typically Chinese, the poor Co-hong merchants were made responsible for us. Any "complication" and the wrath of the emperor fell on them. Which is again so completely Chinese. The Co-hong were squeezed and are being squeezed until they go bankrupt, most of them. We own six hundred thousand guineas of their worthless paper. Brock has about as much. In Chinese fashion, the Co-hong have to buy their positions from the emperor and they're expected continually to send huge "presents" to their superiors – fifty thousand taels of silver is the customary "gift" on the emperor's birthday from each of them.

'Above the Co-hong is the emperor's personal squeeze chief. We call him the Hoppo. He's responsible for squeezing the mandarins at Canton, the Co-hong, and anyone he can. The Hoppo also buys his position – he's the biggest trader of opium, by the way, and makes a fortune out of it.

'So if you allow one mandarin on Hong Kong, you allow the whole system. The mandarin will be a Hoppo. Every Chinese will be subject to him. Every Chinese trader who comes to trade will be "sold" licenses and squeezed, and in turn they'll squeeze us. The Hoppo will destroy those who will help us and help those who hate us. And they'll never give up until they drive us out.'

'Why?'

'Because they're Chinese.' Struan stretched to ease his shoulders, feeling the tiredness creeping over him, then walked over to the sideboard and poured another brandy. I wish I could be Chinese for an hour or so, he thought wearily. Then I'd be able to finesse a million taels from somewhere with nae trouble. If that's the answer, he told himself, then try to think like a Chinese. You're the Tai-Pan of the 'barbarians', the mandarin, with unlimited power. What's the point of power if you dinna use it to twist joss to help yoursel'? How can you use your power? Who has a million taels? Whom can you pressure to get it? Who owes you favours?

'What should we do, Dirk? I mean, I quite agree,' Longstaff said.

'You'd better send Ti-sen an immediate dispatch. Tell him . . . no, order him—'

Struan stopped abruptly as his brain cleared. His fatigue vanished. You're a stupid, blathering, half-witted gilly! Ti-sen! Ti-sen's your key. One mandarin. That's all you have to arrange. Two simple steps: first, cancel Longstaff's agreement as it must be cancelled anyway; second, in a week or two, make a secret offer to Ti-sen that in return for a million you'll make Longstaff reverse his stand and allow one mandarin into Hong Kong. Ti-sen will leap at the offer because he immediately gets back everything the war has forced him to concede; he'll squeeze the Co-hong for a million, and they'll be delighted to pay because they'll immediately add it on to the cost of the tea they're dying to sell us and we're dying to buy. Poor little Willie's nae problem and none of the other traders will object to one mandarin. We will na call the man 'mandarin', we'll invent a new name to throw the cleverest off the scent. 'Trade commissioner.' The traders will na object to the Chinese 'trade commissioner' because he'll assist trade and simplify the paying of customs. Now, who to make the secret offer? Obviously old Jin-qua. He's the richest and the most cunning of the Co-hong and your major supplier, and you've known him twenty years. He's the one, wi'out a doubt.

One mandarin will guarantee the future of The Noble House. Aye. But he will wreck Hong Kong. And destroy the plan. Do you gamble that you make the deal, knowing you'll have to outsmart them later? That's a terrible risk – you know one mandarin means the whole system. You canna leave that devil legacy for Robb or for Culum or for their children. But wi'out the bullion there's nae Noble House and nae future.

'You were saying, Dirk?'

'Order Ti-sen in the queen's name to forget a mandarin on Hong Kong.'

'My thought entirely.' Longstaff happily sat down at the desk and picked up the quill. 'What should I say?'

And what should I do, poor Willie, about the second step? Struan asked himself. Does the end justify the means? 'Write this: "To Ti-sen at Canton. A Special Proclamation: Only Her Britannic Majesty, Queen Victoria, has the authority to appoint officials in the British Island of Hong Kong. There will be no Chinese officials here and no customs houses whatsoever." ' He hesitated then continued deliberately, sensing that the timing was right, ' "And all Chinese residing in Her Majesty's colony of Hong Kong will henceforth be British subjects and subject only to the laws of England." '

'But that exceeds my authority!'

'It's custom for plenipotentiaries to exceed their authority. That's why they're so carefully selected, Will. That's why we've an Empire. Raffles, Hastings, Clive, Raleigh, Wellington. You have the plenipotentiary authority of Her Majesty's Government to arrange a treaty with China. What do they know or care about China at home? But you're an innovator, a maker of history, Will. You're ready to accept one tiny, barren, almost uninhabited island when it's a world custom to grab whole continents, when you could take all China if you wanted. You're so much smarter.'

Longstaff wavered and sucked the top of the quill. 'Yes, but I've already agreed that Chinese on Hong Kong would be subject to Chinese law, all forms of torture excepted.' A bead of sweat gathered on his chin. 'It was a clause in the treaty and I issued a special proclamation.'

'You've changed your mind, Will. Just as Ti-sen changed his. There was no clause to appoint a mandarin.'

'But it was understood.'

'Not in your mind. Or mine. He's trying to dupe you. As he did over Chushan.'

'Quite,' Longstaff agreed, happy to be convinced. 'You're right, Dirk. Absolutely. If we allow any control – you're right. They'll go back to their old devilment, what? Yes. And it's time the Chinese saw what justice really is. Law and order. Yes, You're right.'

'End the letter like the emperor would: "Fear this and tremblingly obey," and sign it with your full title,' Struan said and opened the cabin door.

'Master-at-arms!'

'Yes, sirr?'

'His Excellency wants his secretary, Mr Sinclair, on the double.'

'Yes, sirr.'

Longstaff finished writing. He re-read the letter. 'Isn't this a little

85

blunt, Dirk? I mean, none of his titles and finishing up like the emperor's edict?'

'That's the whole point. You'll want to publish it in the newspaper.'

'But it's a private document.'

'It's a historic document, Will. One you can be proud of. And one to make the admiral pleased with you. By the way, why was he angry?'

'Oh, the usual.' Longstaff mimicked the admiral: ' "God-damme, sir, we were sent out here to fight the heathen, and after two landings with no resistance to speak of, you've made a contemptible treaty which gets us far less than the demands the Foreign Secretary has ordered you to demand. Where are the open ports you were ordered to demand?" You're sure, Dirk, asking less is the correct procedure? I know you've said so before, but, well, the merchants seem to think it was a bad error. No open ports, I mean.'

'Hong Kong's more important, Will.'

'So long as you're sure. The admiral's also very irritated with some desertions and, too, with the delay in enforcing the order against smuggling. And, well, there's been a huge outcry by all the traders.'

'Headed by Brock?'

'Yes. Ill-mannered scum.'

Struan's heart sank. 'You told the merchants that you were cancelling the order?'

'Well, Dirk, I didn't exactly tell them. But I intimated that it would be cancelled.'

'And you intimated to the admiral that you were cancelling the order?'

'Well, I suggested that it was not advisable to proceed. He was most irritated and said that he was making his view known to the Admiralty.' Longstaff sighed and yawned. ' 'Pon me word, he has no conception of the problems. None. I'd be most grateful, Dirk, if you'd explain "trade" to him, what? I tried, but I couldn't get any sense into his head.'

And I canna get any into yours, Willie, Struan thought. If Robb's bought the opium, we're deeper in the mess. If he has na bought, we're still finished. Unless a trade – one cursed mandarin for one cursed million.

'I don't know what I'd do without your father's advice, Culum.' Longstaff took snuff from a jewelled snuff box. Damme, he thought, I'm a diplomat, not a warmonger. Governor of Hong Kong is just the ticket. Once governor of Hong Kong, then something worthwhile. Bengal, perhaps. Jamaica . . . now, there's a good place. Canada? No, too damned cold. Bengal or another of the Indian states. 'It's very complicated in Asia, Culum. Have to deal with so many different views and interests – the Crown's, the traders', the missionaries', the Royal Navy's, the Army's and the Chinese – all in conflict. And, damme, the Chinese are splintered into conflicting groups. The merchants, the mandarins and the Manchu overlords.' He filled both nostrils with snuff, sniffed deeply and sneezed 'I suppose you know the rulers of China aren't Chinese?'

'No, sir.'

'Half the damned trouble, so we're told. They're Manchus. From Manchuria. Wild barbarians from north of the Great Wall. They've ruled China for two hundred years, so we're told. They must think we're fools. We're told there's a huge wall – like Hadrian's Wall – a fortification all across the north of China to protect it from the wild tribes. It's supposed to be over three and a half thousand miles long, forty feet high and thirty feet thick, and wide enough at the top for eight horsemen to ride abreast. There are supposed to be watchtowers every three hundred yards. It's made of brick and granite, and it was built two thousand years ago.' He snorted. 'Ridiculous!'

'I believe it exists,' Struan said.

'Come now, Dirk,' Longstaff said. 'It was impossible to build such a fortification two thousand years ago.'

'The legend, Culum, is that every third man in China was conscripted to work on the wall. It was built in ten years. They say a million men died and are buried in the wall. Their spirits guard it, too.'

Culum grinned. 'If it's so huge, Father, the Manchus could never have breached it. It can't possibly exist.'

'The legend is that the Manchus broke through the wall by deceit. The Chinese general in charge of the wall sold out his own people.'

'That's more than likely,' Longstaff said disgustedly. 'No sense of honour these Orientals, what? The general thought he could usurp the throne by using the enemy. But the Manchus used them, then destroyed him. In any event, that's the story.'

Culum said, 'Quite a story, sir.'

Struan's eyes hardened. 'You'd better get used to many strange stories. And a new thought, Culum – the Chinese have had civilization for five thousand years. Books, printing presses, art, poets, government, silk, tea, gunpowder and a thousand other things. For thousands of years. We've been civilized for five hundred years. If you can call it that.'

There was a knock on the door. Horatio hurried in. 'You wanted me, Your Excellency?'

'Yes I want you to translate this immediately into Chinese, and send it off by special courier. And send a copy to Mr Skinner for publication.'

'Yes, sir.' Horatio took the paper and turned to Struan. 'I was so sorry to hear the terrible news, Mr Struan.

'Thank you. This is my son Culum. Horatio Sinclair.'

They shook hands, liking each other instantly.

Horatio read the letter. 'It will take me a little time to put it in the right court phrases, sir.'

'His Excellency wants it sent exactly like that,' Struan said. 'Exactly.'

Horatio's mouth dropped open. He nodded feebly. 'Yes, I'll, er, do it at once. But Ti-sen will never accept it, Mr Struan. Never, Your Excellency. He would lose too much face.'

Longstaff bristled. 'Face? I'll show that devious heathen some face, by God. Give the admiral my compliments and ask him to send the letter by a capital ship of the line to Whampoa, with orders to proceed immediately to Canton if it's not accepted forthwith!'

'Yes, sir.'

'Won't accept it, indeed!' Longstaff said after Horatio had gone. 'Damned insolence. They're all heathen barbarians. All of them. Chinese. Manchus. They've no justice, and their contempt for human life is unbelievable. They sell their daughters, sisters, brothers. Unbelievable.'

Culum suddenly thought of his mother and brothers, and how they died. The watery vomit and stools, and the stench and cramps and agony and sunken eyes and spasms. And the convulsions and more stench and then gasping death. And after death the sudden muscle spasms and his mother, dead an hour but suddenly twisting on the bed, dead eyes open, dead mouth open.

The old fear began to sicken him, and he groped for something to think about, anything to make him forget his terror. 'About the land sale, sir. First the land should be surveyed. Who's to do this sir?'

'We'll get someone, don't worry.'

'Perhaps Glessing,' Struan said. 'He's had charting experience.'

'Good idea. I'll talk to the admiral. Excellent.'

'You might consider naming the beach where the flag was raised "Glessing's Point".'

Longstaff was astonished. 'I'll never understand you. Why go out of your way to perpetuate the name of a man who hates you?'

Because good enemies are valuable, Struan thought. And I've a use for Glessing. He'll die to protect Glessing's Point, and that means Hong Kong.

'It would please the navy,' Struan said. 'Just an idea.'

'It's a good idea. I'm glad you suggested it.'

'Well, I think we'll get back aboard our ship,' Struan said. He was tired. And there was still much to do.

Isaac Perry was on the quarterdeck of *Thunder Cloud*, watching the marines search under tarpaulins and in the longboats and sail locker. He hated marines and naval officers; once he had been pressed into the navy. 'There're no deserters aboard,' he said again.

'Of course,' the young officer said.

'Please order your men not to make such a mess. It'll take a whole watch to clean up after them.'

'Your ship'll make a nice prize, Captain Perry. The ship and the cargo,' the officer sneered.

Perry glared at McKay who was by the gangplank, under armed guard. You're a dead man, McKay, Perry thought, if you've helped Ramsey aboard.

'Longboat on the aft gangway,' the third mate called out. 'Owner's coming aboard.'

Perry hurried to meet Struan.

'They think we've a deserter aboard, sir.'

'I know,' Struan said as he came on deck. 'Why is my bosun under guard?' he asked the arrogant young officer, a dangerous rasp to his voice.

'Just a precaution. He's a relation of Ramsey and—'

'A pox on precautions! He's innocent until proven guilty, by God,' Struan roared. 'You're here to search, not to harass and arrest my men.'

'I knowed nothin', sorr,' McKay burst out. 'Ramsey's not aboard by my doin'. He ain't.'

'God help you if he is,' Struan said. 'You're confined to the ship until I order otherwise. Get below!'

'Yes, sorr,' McKay said, and fled.

'God's blood, Isaac!' Struan raged on. 'You're supposed to be captain of this ship. What law says the navy can arrest a man without a warrant as a precaution?'

'None, sir.' Perry quailed and knew better than to argue.

'Get to hell off my ship. You're beached!'

Perry blanched. 'But, sir—'

'Be off my ship by sundown.' Struan moved towards the gangway that led to the bowels of the ship. 'Come on, Culum.'

Culum caught up with Struan in the passageway to the main cabin.

'That's not fair,' he said. 'It's not fair. Captain Perry's the best captain you have. You've said so.'

'He was, lad,' Struan said. 'But he did na watch the interests of his man. And he's afraid. What of, I dinna ken. But frightened men are dangerous and we've nae use for such.'

'McKay wasn't harmed.'

'The first law of a captain of mine is to protect his ship. The second, his men. Then they'll protect him. You can captain a ship alone, but you can't run her alone.'

'Perry did nothing wrong.'

'He allowed the navy to put McKay under guard against the law, by God,' Struan said sharply. 'A captain's got to know more than just how to sail a ship, by God! Isaac should have stood up to that young puppy. He was afraid, and he failed one of his men when it was important. Next time he might fail his ship. I'll na risk that.'

'But he's been with you for years. Doesn't that count?'

'Yes. It says we were lucky for years. Now I dinna trust him. So now he goes, and that's the end to it!' Struan opened the door of the cabin.

Robb was seated at the desk, staring out of the stern windows. Boxes and chests and children's clothes and playthings were strewn on the floor. Sarah, Robb's wife, was half curled in one of the sea chairs, dozing. She was a small woman, heavy with child, and in sleep her face was lined and tired. When Robb noticed Struan and Culum, he tried unsuccessfully to force a smile.

'Hello, Dirk, Culum.'

'Hello, Robb.' Struan thought, he's aged ten years in two days.

Sarah awoke with a start. 'Hello, Dirk,' She got up heavily and came over to the door. 'Hello, Culum.'

'How are you, Aunt Sarah?'

'Tired, dear. Very tired. And I hate being on a ship. Would you like some tea?'

'No, thank you.'

Robb watched Struan anxiously. 'What can I say?'

'Nothing, Robbie. They're dead and we're alive and that's the end of it.'

'Is it, Dirk?' Sarah's blue eyes were hard. She smoothed her auburn hair and straightened her long, green, bustled dress. 'Is it?'

'Aye. Would you excuse us, Sarah? I've got to talk to Robb.'

'Yes, of course.' She looked at her husband and despised the weakness of him. 'We're leaving Dirk. We're leaving the Orient for good. I've decided. I've given Struan and Company five years of my life and one baby. Now it's time to go.'

'I think you're wise, Sarah. The Orient is nae place for a family these days. In a year, when Hong Kong's built, well, then it'll be very good.'

'For some, perhaps, but not for us. Not for my Roddy or Karen or Naomi or Jamie. Not for me. We'll never live in Hong Kong.' She was gone.

'Did you buy opium, Robb?'

'I bought some. Spent all our cash and borrowed about a hundred thousand – I don't know exactly. Prices didn't come down much. Then, well, I lost interest.'

So we're deeper in the hole, Struan thought.

'Why our family? It's terrible, terrible,' Robb said, his voice tormented. 'Why all our family?'

'Joss.'

'Curse joss.' Robb stared at the cabin door. 'Brock wants to see you as soon as possible.'

'Why?'

'He didn't say.'

Struan sat and eased his boot off for a moment, and thought about Brock. Then he said, 'I've made Culum a partner.'

'Good,' Robb said. But his voice was flat. He was still staring at the door.

'Father,' Culum broke in, 'I want to talk to you about that.'

'Later, laddie. Robb, there's something else. We've bad trouble on our hands.'

'There's something I must say at once.' Robb tore his eyes off the door. 'Dirk, I'm leaving the Orient with Sarah and the children. By the next boat.'

'What?'

'I'll never be a tai-pan and I don't want to be.'

'You're leaving because Culum's a partner?'

'You know me better than that. You might have discussed it with me, yes, but that's unimportant. I want to leave.'

'Why?'

'The deaths at home made me think. Sarah's right. Life is too brief to sweat and die out here. I want some peace. And there's more than enough money. You can buy me out. I want to go on the next boat.'

'Why?'

'I'm tired. Tired!'

'You're just weak, Robb. Sarah's been on to you again, eh?'

'Yes, I'm weak, yes, she's been on to me again, but I've decided. Too many deaths. Too many.'

'I canna buy you out. We're bankrupt.' Struan handed him the bankers' letter.

Robb read the letter. His face aged even more. 'God curse them to hell!'

'Aye. But we're still bankrupt.' Struan pulled on his boot and stood up. 'Sorry, Culum, the partnership is worthless. There was a run on our bank.'

The air in the cabin seemed to thicken.

'We've a hundred thousand in Scotland,' Robb said. 'Let me have half of that and you take the rest.'

'Thanks, Robbie. Spoken like a man.'

Robb slammed the desk with his fist. 'It's not my fault the bank closed its doors!'

'Aye. So dinna ask for half our money when we'll need every penny!'

'*You* will, not me. You'll find the answer, you always have.'

'Fifty thousand pounds won't last Sarah five years.'

'That's my worry! The money's not on the books, so it's fairly ours. I'll take half. My share of the business's worth twenty times that!'

'We're bankrupt! Can you na get that through your head? *Bankrupt!*'

The cabin door opened and a little golden-haired girl came into the room. A straw doll was in her hands. She wore a frown. 'Hello, Daddy. Hello, Uncle Dirk.' She stared up at Struan. 'Are I ugly?'

With an effort Struan pulled his eyes off Robb. 'What, Karen lassie?'

'Are I ugly?'

'No. No. Of course not, Karen.' Struan lifted her up. 'Who's been saying such terrible things to you, lassie?'

'We was playing school on *Resting Cloud*. It were Lillibet.'

'Lillibet Brock?'

'Oh, no. She's my best friend. It were Lillibet Somebodyelse.'

'Well, you're na ugly. You tell Lillibet Somebodyelse that it's na nice to say such things. You're very pretty.'

'Oh, good!' Karen smiled hugely. 'My daddy always says I'm pretty, but I wanted to ask you 'cause you know. You know everything.' She gave him a big hug. 'Thank you, Uncle Dirk. Put me down now.' She danced to the door. 'I'm glad I aren't ugly.'

Robb slumped in his chair. At length he said, 'God damn the bankers. I'm sorry. It's my fault – and I'm sorry I said . . . sorry.'

'I'm sorry too, lad.'

Robb tried in vain to think. 'What can we do?'

'I dinna ken. Will you na do this, Robb? Give me a couple of months. We'll send Sarah and the children off by the first ship. The sooner the better, then they'll miss the typhoon season.'

'Maybe I can arrange a loan somehow. We've got to pay the sight drafts. We'll lose the ships – everything.' Robb forced his mind away from Sarah. 'But how in the little time we have?' His fingers twisted nervously. 'The mail packet came in yesterday. Nothing of importance for us. No news from home. Perhaps others know about the run on our bank. We bought a little stock in Brock's bank to keep an eye on it. Perhaps he knows about the run on ours. Is that why he wants to see you?'

'Perhaps. In any case he'll be on our necks right smartly, if he finds out. If he did na start it himsel'. He'll buy up our paper and ruin us.'

'Why?' Culum asked.

'Because I'll ruin him if I get half a chance.'

Culum wanted to ask why, and to tell them that he, too, was going home on the next ship. But his father looked so gaunt and Robb was so morose. Tomorrow he would tell them.

'I've got to get a few hours' sleep,' Struan said. 'I'm going ashore. You and Sarah go back to *Resting Cloud*, eh? Perry's ordered off by sundown. I beached him.'

'Who's going to take his place?'

'I dinna ken,' Struan said as he went out. 'Send word to Brock I'll see him ashore at sundown.'

III

Struan had slept little. The food on the table was untouched. He stared through the tent door at the ships riding at anchor. The sun was dying and a blurred moon was low on the horizon. Huge masses of cumulus dominated the sky. The wind brought the promise of storm.

Ti-sen, his mind kept repeating to him. Ti-sen. He's the only one to save you. Aye, but that's treachery to all you believe in, all you've worked for.

McKay came in with a lighted lantern and set it on the table. The tent was spacious and comfortable; there were carpets on the stony soil.

'Brock's longboat's coming ashore, sorr.'

'Take the men and move out of hearing, McKay.'

'Yes, sorr.'

'Has word come they've found Ramsey yet?'

'No, sorr.'

'Where is he?'

'I don't know, sorr.'

Struan nodded absently. 'Tomorrow put all our spies to work to find out where he is.'

'Beggin' you pardon, sorr, I already spread the word, sorr.' McKay tried to cover his anxiety. 'If he's aboard it's someone's devilment.' Then he added, 'I feel bad about Cap'n Perry, sorr.'

Struan's eyes were suddenly hard. 'I'll give you fifteen days to prove I was right about Isaac. Fifteen days, or you're beached with him.'

'Yes, sorr.' McKay felt a barb soar from his testicles into his guts and cursed himself for opening his mouth. Will you never learn, you stupid fool?

Brock's footsteps were heavy on the beach. He stood at the tent doorway. 'Permission to come aboard, Dirk?'

'Aye, Tyler.'

McKay went out. Brock sat at the table, and Struan poured him a large brandy.

94

'It were bad to lose yor family. I knowed how it feel. I lost two wives in childbirth, the kids too. Bad.'

'Aye.'

'Not much of a berth,' Brock said, taking in the tent.

'Hungry?' Struan indicated the food.

'Thank you kindly.' Brock took a chicken, ripped it in two and tore off half the white meat. He wore a big emerald, set in gold, on his little finger. 'Seems that the joss of The Noble House be runned out.'

' "Joss" is a big word.'

Brock laughed. 'Come now, Dirk. A company be havin' to have bullion to support its credit. Even Noble House.'

'Aye.'

'I spend a lot of time, Dirk, and a lot of brass, checking on thee.' Brock picked the other half of the breast off the chicken and devoured it. 'You've a good cook. Tell him I'll give him a job.'

'He likes the one he has.'

'No brass, no job, my fine muckel. No bank, no credit – no ships, no nothin!' Brock split another chicken. 'Be thee keepin' the champagne? This be special occasion, I'll be bound.'

Struan opened the bottle neatly and filled clean glasses for Brock and himself.

'Chilled just right, lad. Just right.' Brock smacked his lips. 'Twenty-five thousand be no much for a million, be it?'

Struan said nothing. His face was impassive.

'Sixpence on the pound, they sayed. I got a letter in the mail packet yesterday. I lost ten thousand nicker. Bad. Very bad of the bank to gamble with their customers' money.' Brock chuckled. 'I "happened" to run into that bugger Skinner. He thort it were bad too. He be writing a article – headlines, I'll be bound. An' quite right.'

He cut a piece of apple pie and ate with gusto. 'Oh, yes, by the way, I own eight hundred thousand of Struan and Company's sight drafts. I been buying the last six months against such a time. Leastways my son Morgan an' our agents in London Town has.'

'A good investment, Tyler. Very good.'

'Yes, Skinner thort so too, Dirk lad. He were mighty shocked at yor bad joss, but I tol' him I'd keep the names of yor ships. Bad joss to change names. But they'll improve under my flag.'

'You've got to get them first.'

'In thirty days I have them, lad. That's when the drafts be due. That be common knowledge too. So thee'll get no credit in the Orient. Thee be finished, lad.'

95

'Perhaps I'll wreck my ships before I let you take them.'

'Not you, Dirk. I know thee better. Others would, but not thee. We're both alike in that. Ships be special. Better'n any doxy.' He finished his champagne. Struan refilled the glass.

Brock belched. 'Beg pardon.' Then he sipped again. 'Champagne be proper belch water, baint it?'

'Did you start the run on the bank?'

'No. If I'd a thort of it I would've, long since. That be a right clever idea. Fancy thee getting caught with thy balls in the noose.'

'If it was deliberate I'll find out.'

'It were deliberate, lad.'

'Who was it?'

'Morgan,' Brock said. 'I've to hand it to him – the young nipper be growed up. Yes, My boy be the one, and I'm mortal proud.' He scratched contentedly at the lice that were a way of life. 'So thee be broke, Dirk. After all these years. Finished.'

'A lot can happen in thirty days.'

'Yes, it can. I heared yor son's in charge of the land sale.'

'Aye. But it'll be fair. The highest bidder gets the land. We dinna cheat, Tyler. Others do. We've nae need.'

'Damn yor eyes!' Brock bellowed. 'You be saying I cheat?'

'You cheat all the time,' Struan said, flaring. 'You cheat your men and cheat your ships and that's what'll destroy you. You can't build for ever wi' the lash.'

'I do no more than others, by God. Just because thee be having weak-gutted newfangled notions doan mean others be wrong. The lash keeps scum in line. Scum!'

'You live by the lash and you'll die by it.'

'Thee be wantin' to settle our score now? Lash against lash? Knife to knife? Now, by God! Or be thee still coward?'

'I told you once and I'll tell you a last time. One day I'll come after you with a lash – perhaps tonight, perhaps tomorrow, perhaps the next day. But, by God, one day I'll come after you. And I'll tell you another thing. If by chance you die before I'm ready, I'll go after Gorth and Morgan and I'll wreck your company.'

Brock's knife was out. 'Maybe, lad, I cut thy throat now.'

Struan poured more champagne. Now the bottle was empty. 'Open another bottle. There's plenty more.'

Brock laughed. 'Ah, Dirk lad, you be a rare 'un. You be busted an' you still pretends. You be finished, you hear, lad? Yor Noble House be on its uppers. An' you be coward!'

'Oh, I'm na coward, Tyler. You know that.'

'You knowed the hillock where yor Great House's to go?' Brock asked, his eye glittering.

'Aye.'

'It's mine, lad. I be buyin' it. Wotever you bid, I bid more.'

Struan felt the blood rush to his head, for he knew that he did not have the bullion to compete with Brock now. Na unless he made the deal with Ti-sen. Na unless he sold Hong Kong out. 'God rot you to hell!'

'It be mine, lad. An' all this stinking rock.' Brock drained his glass and belched again. 'After yor company's broked, I'm hounding you an' yors outa these seas.' He took out a purse and counted out twenty gold guineas. Then he tossed them on the floor of the tent. 'Buy thyself a coffin.'

He swaggered out.

'Beggin' yor pardon, sorr,' McKay said.

Struan came out of his reverie. 'Aye?'

'Mr Culum's ashore. He wants to see you.'

Struan was startled to see that the watery moon was high in the sky and the night deep.

'I'll see him.'

'Others came, sorr. That Chinee, Gordon Chen. Miss Sinclair. A couple I don't know. Old Quance. I said you'd see 'em tomorrer. Hope I did right not to let Mr Culum come without asking.' McKay saw the golden guineas on the floor, but said nothing.

'As long as you obey orders you're never wrong, McKay.'

Culum was at the tent door. 'Am I disturbing you, Father?'

'Nay, lad. Sit down.'

Culum saw the sovereigns on the floor and started to pick them up.

'Leave them where they are.'

'Why?'

'Because I want them left there.'

Culum sat down. 'I wanted to talk to you.'

'I'm na in a mood to talk, lad.'

'Were you serious about making me a partner?'

'Aye.'

'I don't want to be a partner. I don't want to stay in the Orient. I want to go home.'

'I know better than you, Culum. Give it time.'

'Time won't make any difference.'

97

'You're young, lad. There's plenty of time for you. Be patient with me. And with China. Did Robb tell you how to go about the land sale?'

'Yes.' Damn Uncle Robb, Culum thought. If only he hadn't exploded with Father and said that he was leaving. Damn, damn, damn. Blast that cursed bank. Ruined everything. Poor Father. 'I think I'll be able to do it.'

'You'll have nae trouble so long as it's run fairly. The highest bidder gets the land.'

'Yes, of course.' Culum stared at the guineas. 'Why do you want the coins left there?'

'They're my coffin-money.'

'I don't understand.'

Struan told him what had happened with Brock. 'Better you know about him, Culum. Watch your back because he'll come after you like I'm going after Gorth.'

'The sins of the father are not the fault of the son.'

'Gorth Brock's a pattern of his father.'

'Doesn't Christ teach forgiveness?'

'Aye, lad. But I canna forgive them. They're everything that's rotten on earth. They're tyrants and they believe the lash answers all questions. A fact of life, on earth: money is power – whether you're king or laird or chieftain or merchant or crofter. Without power you canna protect what you have nor improve the lot of others.'

'Then you're saying that the teachings of Christ are wrong?'

'Na wrong, lad. I'm saying that some men are saints. Some are happy being meek and humble and unambitious. Some men are born content to be second-best – I canna be. Nor Brock. Are you?'

'I don't know.'

'You'll be put to the test sometime. Then you'll know about yoursel'.'

'Then you mean that money is everything?'

'I'm saying that without power you canna be a saint in this day and age. Power for its own sake is a sin. Money for its own sake is a sin.'

'Is it so important to have money and power?'

'Nay, laddie,' Struan said with an ironic grin. 'The lack of money's what's important.'

'Why do you want power?'

'Why do you, Culum?'

'Perhaps I don't.'

'Aye. Perhaps. You'd like a drink, lad?'

'I'll have a little champagne.'

'Have you eaten?'

'Yes, thank you. I don't know very much about myself yet,' Culum said.

'There's time, laddie. I'm so glad you're here. Very glad.'

Culum looked back at the coins. 'It really doesn't matter, does it? About the partnership and everything. The company's finished. What are you going to do?'

'We're na finished for twenty-nine days. If joss is against us, this version of The Noble House dies. Then we start again.' Dinna fool yoursel', he thought, you can never start again.

'A never-ending battle?'

'What do you think life's supposed to be, lad?'

'Can I resign as a partner if it doesn't please me, or if I think I'm no good and not worth it? At my whim?'

'Aye. But na if you're ever Tai-Pan. The Tai-Pan can never resign until he's sure that the house is in good hands. He *must* be sure. That's his final responsibility.'

'If we're owed so much by the Chinese merchants, can't we collect it? Then we've the money to pay Brock.'

'They've na got it.' Devil take it, Struan told himself, you're trapped. Make up your mind. It's Ti-sen or nothing.

'What about His Excellency? Can't he give us an advance? From the ransom money?'

'It belongs to the Crown. Maybe Parliament'll honour his paper, maybe it'll repudiate it. The bullion will na pass hands for almost a year.'

'But we'll get it. Surely Brock'll take your surety?'

Struan's voice harshened. 'I've already told you the measure of Brock's charity. I'd na give him twenty guineas if I had him trapped equally. God damn him and his God-damned whelps.'

Culum shifted uneasily in his chair. His shoe moved one of the guineas and it glittered suddenly. 'His Excellency's not very – well, isn't he rather simple?'

'He's out of his depth in Asia – that's all. Wrong man for the job. I'd be lost in the courts of Europe. But he's plenipotentiary. That's all that counts. Aye, he's simple – but watch him too. Watch everyone.'

'Does he always do what you tell him to do?'

Struan looked out the tent door at the night. 'He takes my advice, most times. Provided I'm the last giver.'

Culum moved another guinea. 'There must be something – someone to turn to. You must have friends.'

99

Inexorably Struan's mind was filled with the name of the only person who could unspring the trap: Ti-sen. Brock'll take the ships right smartly, he thought, seething with impotent rage. Wi'out the ships you're lost, laddie. The house, Hong Kong, the plan. Aye, you can start again, but dinna fool yoursel'. You canna build and man such a fleet again. You'll never catch up with Brock again. Never. You'll be second-best. You'll be second-best for ever.

Struan felt the veins in his neck throbbing. His throat was parched. I'll na be the second-best. By the Lord God, I canna. I canna. I canna. To Brock or to anyone. 'Tomorrow, when *China Cloud* returns, I'm going to Canton. You'll come with me.'

'What about the land sale? Should I start that?'

'Devil take the land sale! We've the house to save first. Go aboard *Resting Cloud*, lad. We'll leave as soon as possible.'

'All right.' Culum stood up.

'Good night, laddie.'

The coins caught Culum's eyes, mesmerizing him. He began to pick them up.

'I told you to leave them alone!'

'I can't.' There were beads of sweat on Culum's forehead. The coins seemed to burn his fingers. 'I've . . . I've got to have them.'

'Why, for God's sake, eh?'

'I don't know. I – I just want them.' He put the coins in his pocket. 'They're mine now. Good night, Father.'

IV

Struan was eating dinner alone in the spacious dining-room of their stately factory in the Canton Settlement. The vast three-storey mansion had been built by the East India Company forty years ago. Struan had always coveted it as a perfect setting for The Noble House. Eight years ago he had bought it.

The dining-room was on the second floor facing the Pearl River. Below this floor was a labyrinth of offices and warehouses and storerooms. Above were living quarters, and the Tai-Pan's private rooms, carefully separate. There were courtyards and walks and suites and dormitories within and throughout its length. Forty to fifty Portuguese clerks lived and worked in the building, ten to fifteen Europeans. A hundred Chinese menservants. Women servants were not allowed by Chinese law.

Struan pushed his carved chair away from the table and irritably lit a cheroot. A huge fire warmed the marble that sheathed the walls and floor. The table could seat forty and the silver was Georgian, the chandelier crystal and bright with candles. He walked over to a window and looked down at the traders strolling in the garden below.

Beyond the garden was a square that ran the length of the Settlement and adjoined the wharf at the riverbank. The square was, as usual, teeming with Chinese hawkers, bystanders, sellers and buyers, soothsayers, letter writers, beggars and dogs. Outside their factories it was only in the English Garden, as it was called, that the merchants could move about in relative peace. Chinese, other than servants, were forbidden the garden and the factories. There were thirteen buildings in the colonnaded terrace that ran the length of the Settlement but for two narrow lanes – Hog Street and Old China Lane. Only Struan and Brock owned complete buildings. The other traders shared the remainder, taking space to suit their needs, and paid rent to the East India Company, which had built the Settlement a century ago.

On the north the Settlement was bounded by Thirteen Factory

Street. The walls of Canton City were a quarter of a mile away. Between the city walls and the Settlement was an anthill of houses and hovels. The river was congested with the inevitable floating towns of the boat people. And over all was the perpetual pulsating, singsong murmur suggesting an enormous beehive.

To one side of the garden Struan noticed Brock deep in conversation with Cooper and Tillman. He wondered if they were explaining the intricacies of the Spanish tea-opium sale to Brock. Good luck to them, he thought without rancour. All is fair in love and trade.

'Where the godrotting hell is Jin-qua?' he said out loud.

For twenty-four days Struan had tried to see Jin-qua, but each day his messenger returned to the Settlement with the same reply: 'Him no dooa back all same. You wait can. Tomollow he dooa back to Canton never mind.'

Culum had spent ten days in the Canton Settlement with him. On the eleventh day an urgent message had come from Longstaff asking Culum to return to Hong Kong: there were problems about the land sale.

Along with Longstaff's message was a letter from Robb. Robb wrote that Skinner's editorial about the Struan bankruptcy had provoked consternation among the traders, and most had sent immediate dispatches home spreading their money through various banks; that most were waiting for the thirtieth day; that no credit was to be had, and all the suggestions he had made to Brock's enemies were fruitless; that the navy had been incensed when Longstaff's official negation of the opium-smuggling order was made public, and the admiral had dispatched a frigate home with a request that the Government give him the permission he sought direct; and last, that Chen Sheng, their comprador, was inundated with creditors demanding payment on all the lesser debts that normally would wait their time.

Struan knew that he was beaten if he did not reach Jin-qua in the next six days, and he asked himself again if Jin-qua was avoiding him or if he was truly away from Canton. He's an old thief, Struan thought, but he'd never avoid me. And if you do see him, laddie, are you really going to make the offer to that devil Ti-sen?

There was the sound of angry singsong voices and the door burst open, admitting a filthy young Hoklo boat woman and a servant who was trying to restrain her. The woman wore the usual huge, conical sampan hat and grimy black trousers and blouse and over them a grimy padded jacket.

'No stop can this one piece cow chillo, Mass'er,' the servant said in pidgin English, holding on to the struggling girl. Only through pidgin could the traders converse with their servants, and they with them. 'Cow' meant 'woman'. 'Chillo' was a corruption of 'child'. 'Cow chillo' meant 'young woman'.

'Cow chillo out! Plenty quick-quick, savvy?' Struan said.

'You want cow chillo, heya? Cow chillo plenty good bed jig-jig. Two dollar never mind,' the girl called out.

The servant grabbed her and her hat fell off, and Struan saw her face clearly for the first time. She was barely recognizable because of the grime and he collapsed with laughter. The servant gaped at him as though he were mad and released the girl.

'This piece cow chillo,' Struan said through his laughter, 'stay can, never mind.'

The girl tidied her verminous clothes irately and shouted another torrent of invective at the departing servant.

'Cow chillo plenty good you see, Tai-Pan.'

'And you, May-may!' Struan stared down at her. 'What the hell're you doing here, and what the hell's the filth for?'

'Cow chillo think you dooa jig-jig with new cow chillo, heya?'

'God's blood, lassie, we're alone now! Stop using pidgin! I've spent enough time and money teaching you the queen's English!' Struan lifted her up at arm's length. 'Great God, May-may, you stink to high heaven.'

'You would too if you wear these smell clotheses.'

'*Had to* wear these *smelly clothes*,' he said, correcting her automatically. 'What are you doing here, and why the smell clotheses?'

'Put me down, Tai-Pan.' He did, and she bowed sadly. 'I arrive here in secret and in great sadness for you lost your Supreme Lady and all children by her but one son.' The tears streaked the grime on her face. 'Sorry, sorry.'

'Thank you, lass. Aye. But that's done now, and no grief can bring them back.' He patted her head and fondled her cheek, touched by her compassion.

'I do not know your custom. How long should I dress in mourning?'

'No mourning, May-may. They're gone. There's to be no weeping and no mourning.'

'I burned incense for their safe rebirth.'

'Thank you. Now, what are you doing here, and why did you leave Macao? I told you to stay there.'

'First bath, then change, then talk.'

'We've no clothes here, May-may.'

'My worthless amah, Ah Gip, is downstair. She carries clothes and my things, never mind. Where is bath?'

Struan pulled the bell cord and imediately the wide-eyed servant appeared.

'Cow chillo my bath, savvy? Amah can dooa. Get chow!' Then to May-may, 'You say what chow can.'

May-may chattered at the gaping servant imperiously, and left.

Her peculiar swaying gait never failed to move Struan. May-may had bound feet. They were only three inches long. When Struan had bought her five years ago he had cut off the bandages and been horrified at the deformity that ancient customs had decreed was a girl's essential sign of beauty – tiny feet. Only a girl with bound feet – *lotus feet* – could be a wife or concubine. Those with normal feet were peasants, servants, low-class prostitutes, amahs or workers, and despised.

May-may's feet were crippled. Without the binding tightness of the bandages her agony had been pitiful. So Struan had allowed the bandages to be replaced, and after a month the pain had lessened and May-may could walk again. Only in old age did bound feet become insensible to pain.

Struan had asked her then, using Gordon Chen as interpreter, how it was done. She had told him proudly that her mother had begun to bind her feet when she was six. 'The bindings were bandages two inches wide and twelve feet long and they were damp. My mother wrapped them tightly around my feet – around the heel and over the instep and under the foot, bending the four small toes under the sole of the foot and leaving the big toe free. As the bandages dried they tightened and the pain was terrible. Over the months and years the heel closes near to the toe and the instep arches. Once a week the bandages are taken off for a few minutes and the feet cleaned. After some years the little toes become shrivelled and dead and are removed. When I was almost twelve I could walk quite well, but my feet were still not small enough. It was then that my mother consulted a woman wise in the art of foot binding. On my twelfth birthday the wise woman came to our house with a sharp knife and ointments. She made a deep knife cut across the middle of the soles of my feet. This deep split allowed the heel to be squeezed closer to the toes, when the bandages were replaced.'

'What cruelty! Ask her how she stood the pain.'

Struan remembered her quizzical look as Chen translated the question and as she replied in charming singsong.

'She says, "For every pair of bound feet there is a lake of tears. But what are tears and pain? Now I am not ashamed to let anyone measure my feet." She wants you to measure them, Mr Struan.'

'I will na do such a thing!'

'Please, sir. It will make her very proud. They are perfect, in Chinese fashion. If you don't, she will feel that you're ashamed of her. She will lose face terribly in front of you.'

'Why?'

'She thinks you took the bandages off because you thought she was cheating you.'

'Why should I think that?'

'Because you're – well, she's never known a European. Please, sir. It is only your pride in her that repays all the tears.'

So he had measured her feet and expressed the joy that he did not feel, and she kowtowed three times to him. He hated to see men and women kowtowing, kneeling, their foreheads touching the floor. But ancient custom demanded this obeisance from an inferior to a superior and Struan could not forbid it. If he protested, May-may would be frightened again and she would lose face in front of Gordon Chen.

'Ask her if her feet hurt her now.'

'They will always hurt her, sir. But I assure you it would pain her much more if she had big, disgusting feet.'

May-may then had said something to Chen, and Struan recognized the word *fan-quai*, which meant 'devil barbarian'.

'She wants to know how to please a non-Chinese,' Gordon said.

'Tell her fan-quai are no different from Chinese.'

'Yes, sir.'

'And tell her that you are going to teach her English. Immediately. Tell her no one's to know you're teaching her. No one's to know she can speak English. In front of others she's to speak Chinese only, or pidgin, which you'll also teach her. Lastly, you will protect her with your life.'

'May I come in now?' May-may was standing in the doorway, bowing delicately.

'Please.'

Her face was oval, her eyes almond-shaped and her eyebrows perfect crescents. A perfume surrounded her now, and her long, flowing robe was of the finest blue silk brocade. Her hair was dressed in crescents on the top of her head and adorned with jade pins. She was tall for a Chinese and her skin so white as to be almost translucent. She was from the province of Soochow.

Though Struan had bought her from Jin-qua and had haggled many weeks over the price, he knew that actually T'chung May-may was Jin-qua's gift to him in return for many favours over the years; that Jin-qua could have sold her easily to the richest man in China, to a Manchu prince, even to the emperor, for her weight in jade – let alone the fifteen thousand taels of silver which they finally agreed on. She was unique, and priceless.

Struan lifted her up and kissed her gently. 'Now, tell me what's going on.' He sat in the deep chair and held her in his arms.

'First, I came disguised because of danger. Na only to me but to you. The reward still is on your head. And kidnapping for ransom is ancient custom.'

'Where did you leave the children?'

'With Elder Sister, of course,' she replied. Elder Sister was what May-may called Struan's ex-mistress Kai-sung, as was the custom, though they were not related. And now Kai-sung was the third wife of Struan's comprador. Yet between May-may and Kai-sung was intense affection, and Struan knew that the children would be safe and cherished as if they were her own.

'Good,' he said. 'How are they?'

'Duncan has the black eye. He tripped down, so I whipped his turtledung amah till my arm she fell off. Duncan has a bad temper from barbarian blood.'

'From you – na from me. Kate?'

'She has her second tooth. That was lucky. Before second birthday.' She nestled in his arms a moment. 'Then I read paper. That man Skinner. More bad joss, heya? That lump of dogmeat Brock is breaking you by huge monies owed. Is it true?'

'Part's true. Aye, unless there's a change in joss, we're broke. No more silk and perfumes and jades and houses,' he teased.

'Ayeeeee yah!' she said with a toss of her head. 'You're na the only man in China.'

He slapped her on the rump and she hacked at him with her long nails, and he caught her wrist neatly.

'Dinna say that again,' he said, and kissed her passionately.

'God's blood,' she said, trying to catch her breath. 'Now look wat you've done to my hair. That lazy whore Ah Gip spent one hour doing it, never mind.'

She knew that she pleased him greatly, and she was proud that she could now, at twenty, read and write English and Chinese, and speak English and Cantonese as well as her own dialect of Soochow, and also

Mandarin, the language of Peking and the court of the emperor; and also that she knew much of what Gordon Chen had learned at school for he had taught her well, and between them was great affection. May-may knew that she was unique in all China.

There was a discreet knock on the door.

'A European?' she whispered.

'Nay, lass. It's only a servant. They've orders to announce everyone. Aye?'

The servant was followed by two others and they all averted their eyes from Struan and the girl. But their curiosity was obvious, and they dawdled over laying out the dishes of Chinese food and chopsticks.

May-may assaulted them with a torrent of Cantonese and they bowed nervously and scuttled away.

'What did you say to them?' Struan asked.

'I just warned them, by God, if they told anyone I was here I'd personally slit their tongues and cut their ears off and then I'd persuade you to chain them in one of your ships and sink it in the ocean along with their godrotting wives and children and parents, and before that you'd put your Evil Eye on the godrotting scum and their godrotting scum offspring for ever.'

'Stop cursing, you bloodthirsty little devil! And stop joking about Evil Eye.'

'That's no joke. That's what you have, devil barbarian. To all but me. I know how to handle you.'

'Devil take you, May-may.' He intercepted her hands and the intimate caress. 'Eat while the food's hot and I'll deal with you later.' He picked her up and carried her over to the table.

She served him quick-fried shrimps and lean pork and mushrooms stewed delicately in soya and nutmeg and mustard and honey, then helped herself.

'God's death, I'm hungry,' she said.

'Will you na stop swearing!'

'You forgot the "by God", Tai-pan!' She beamed and began to eat with great relish.

He picked up the chopsticks and used them deftly. He found the food superb. It had taken him months to acquire the taste. None of the Europeans ate Chinese food. Struan, too, had once preferred the solid fare of old England, but May-may had taught him that it was healthier to eat as the Chinese did.

'How did you get here?' Struan asked.

May-may selected one of the large prawns that were fried and then stewed in soya-flavoured syrup and herbs, and daintily she decapitated it and began to peel off the skin. 'I bought passage on a lorcha. I buy fantastical cheap steerage ticket and dirtied myself for safety. You owe me fifty cash.'

'Pay it out of your allowance. I did na ask you here.'

'This cow chillo dooa cash easy can, never mind.'

'Stop it and behave yoursel'.'

She laughed and offered him the prawn and began to peel another.

'Thanks, no more for me.'

'Eat them. They're very good for you. I tell you many times they make you very healthy and very potent.'

'Give over, lass.'

'They do,' she said, very serious. 'Prawns are very good for your vigour. Very important to have plenty of vigour! A wife must look after her husband.' She cleaned her fingers on an embroidered napkin, then picked up one of the prawn heads with her chopsticks.

'Dammit, May-may, do you have to eat the heads?'

'Aye, by God, do you na ken they're the best part?' she said, mimicking him, and laughed so much she choked. He thumped her on the back, but gently, and then she drank some tea.

'That'll teach you,' he said.

'The heads are the best part, even so, never mind.'

'Even so, they look dreadful, never mind.'

She ate in silence a moment. 'It is bad with Brock?'

'Bad.'

'It is terrifical simple to solve this badness. Kill Brock. It is time now.'

'That's one way.'

'One way, another way, you will find a way.'

'What makes you so sure?'

'You do not want to lose me.'

'Why should I lose you?'

'I dinna enjoy second-best either. I belong to *the* Tai-Pan. I'm na a godrotting Hakka or boat woman or Cantonese whore. Tea?'

'Aye.'

'Drinking tea with food is very good for you. Then you will never get fat.' She poured the tea and offered him the cup gracefully. 'I like you when you're angry, Tai-Pan. But you dinna frighten me. I know I please you too much, as you please me too much. When I am second-best another will take my place, never mind. That is joss. For me. And also for you.'

'Perhaps you're second-best now, May-may.'

108

'No, Tai-Pan, not now. Later, yes, but not now.' She bent over him and kissed him and slid away as he tried to hold her.

'Ayee yah, I must not feed you so many prawns!' She ran from him laughing, but he caught her and she put her arms around his neck and kissed him. 'You owe me fifty cash!'

'Devil take you!' He kissed her, needing her, as much as she needed him.

'You taste so very good. First we play backgammon.'

'No.'

'First, I came disguise because of danger. Na only to me but plenty of time. I stay with you now. We play for one dolla point.'

'No.'

'One dolla point. Maybe I get headache, too tired.'

'Maybe I won't give you the New Year's present I was thinking about.'

'Wat present?'

'Never mind.'

'Please, Tai-Pan. I won't tease you any more. Wat present?'

'Never mind.'

'Please tell me. Please. Was it jade pin? Or gold bracelet? Or silks?'

'How's your headache?'

She slapped him crossly, then threw her arms tighter around his neck. 'You are so bad to me and I'm so good to you. Let's make love, then.'

'We'll play four games. A thousand dolla point.'

'But that is too much gamble!' She saw the mocking challenge in his face, and her eyes flashed. 'Four games. I beat you, by God.'

'Oh no, by God!'

So they played four games and she cursed and cheered and wept and laughed and gasped, consumed with excitement as her fortunes changed. She lost eighteen thousand dollars.

'God's death, I'm ruined, Tai-Pan. Ruined. Oh woe, woe, woe. All my savings and more. My house – One more game,' she begged. 'You must let me try to get back monies.'

'Tomorrow. Same stakes.'

'Never will I gamble again for such stakes. Never, never, never. Except one more time tomorrow.'

After they had made love, May-may got out of the four-poster bed and went to the fireplace. An iron kettle hissed softly on the little iron shelf near the flames.

She knelt down and poured the hot water from the kettle on the clean white towels. The flames danced over the purity of her body. Her feet were encased in tiny sleeping shoes and the bindings were neat around her ankles. Her legs were long and beautiful. She brushed the shiny blue-blackness of her hair behind her and came back to the bed.

Struan held out his hand for one of the towels.

'No,' May-may said. 'Let me. It gives me pleasure and it is my duty.'

When she had dried him she washed herself and then settled peacefully beside him under the quilts. A crisp wind rustled the damask curtains and made the flames in the grate hiss. Shadows danced on the walls and high ceiling.

'Look, there's a dragon,' May-may said.

'No. It's a ship. Are you warm enough?'

'Always, near you. There's a pagoda.'

'Aye.' He put an arm around her, glorying in the smooth coolness of her skin.

'Ah Gip is making tea.'

'Good. Tea will be very good.'

After the tea they were refreshed, and they lay back in the bed and he blew out the lamp. They watched the shadows again.

'Your custom is that you may only have one wife, heya?'

'Aye.'

'Chinese custom is better. *Tai-tai* is more wise.'

'What's that, lassie?'

' "Supreme of the Supreme." The husband is supreme in family, of course, but in the home, first wife is supreme of supreme. It is Chinese law. Many wives is also law but one Tai-tai.' She moved her long hair more comfortably. 'How soon will you marry? What is your custom?'

'I dinna think I'll marry again.'

'You should. A Scottish or English. But first you should marry me.'

'Aye,' Struan said. 'Perhaps I should.'

'Aye, perhaps you should. I am your Tai-tai,' and then she nestled closer to him and let herself slip into tranquil sleep.

Struan watched the shadows a long time. Then he slept.

Just after dawn he awoke, sensing danger. Taking his knife from under the pillow, he walked softly to the window and pulled the curtains aside. To his astonishment he saw that the square was deserted. Beyond the square, in the river, an uneasy silence seemed to hang over the floating villages.

Then he heard muffled footsteps padding towards the room. He glanced at May-may. She still slept peacefully. With his knife ready, Struan leaned against the wall behind the door and waited.

The footsteps ceased.

A gentle knock.

'Aye?'

The servant came softly into the room. He was frightened, and when he saw Struan naked, the knife in his hand, he gasped out, 'Mass'er! Hooknose Mass'er and Black Hair Mass'er dooa here. Say quick-quick plees can.'

'Say I quick-quick dooa.'

Struan dressed quickly. He dropped a hairbrush and May-may half awoke. 'Is too early to get up. Come back to bed,' she said sleepily, and curled deeper into the quilts and was instantly asleep again.

Struan opened the door. Ah Gip was squatting patiently in the corridor, where she had slept. Struan had given up trying to make her sleep elsewhere for Ah Gip would smile and nod and say, 'Yes, Mass'er,' and still sleep outside the door. She was short and square and a smile seemed to be permanently fixed on her round, pockmarked face. For three years she had been May-may's personal slave. Struan had paid three taels of silver for her.

He beckoned her into the room. 'Missee dooa sleep can. Waitee this piece room, savvy?'

'Savvy, Mass'er.'

He hurried downstairs.

Cooper and Wolfgang Mauss were waiting for him in the dining-room. Mauss was moodily checking his pistols.

'Sorry to disturb you, Tai-Pan. There's trouble,' Cooper said.

'What?'

'There's a rumour spreading that two thousand Manchu soldiers – bannermen – came into Canton last night.'

'Are you sure?'

'No,' Cooper said. 'But if it is true, there's going to be trouble.'

'How-qua sent for me this morning,' Mauss said heavily.

'Did he say if Jin-qua was back yet?'

'No, Tai-Pan. He still says his father's away. For myself, I do not think so, *hein*? How-qua was very afraid. He said that he'd been awoken early this morning. An imperial edict signed by the emperor was given him which said that all trade with us was to cease instantly. I read it. The seals were correct. The whole Co-hong's in an uproar.'

There was a clattering in the square. They hurried over to the window. Below them a company of mounted Manchu soldiers trotted

111

into the east end and dismounted. They were big men and heavily armed – muskets, long bows, swords and bannered lances. Some were bearded. They were called bannermen because they were imperial troops and carried the imperial banners. Chinese were not allowed into their regiments; they were the élite of the emperor's army.

'Well, there are certainly forty or fifty in Canton,' Struan said.

'And if there are two thousand?' Cooper asked.

'We'd better get ready to leave the Settlement.'

'Bannermen are a bad sign,' Mauss said. He did not want to leave the Settlement; he wished to stay with his Chinese converts and to continue the preaching to the heathen that took all of his time when he was not interpreting for Struan. '*Schrecklich* bad.'

Struan considered possibilities, then rang for a servant. 'Big chow quick-quick. Coffee – tea – eggs – meat – quick-quick!'

'Bannermen are in the square, and all you think of is having breakfast?' Cooper asked.

'No point in worrying on an empty stomach,' Struan said. 'I'm hungry this morning.'

Mauss laughed. He had heard the whispered rumour among the servants that the Tai-Pan's legendary mistress had arrived in secret. At Struan's suggestion, two years ago he had secretly taught May-may Christianity and had converted her. Yes, he thought proudly, the Tai-Pan trusts me. Because of him, oh Lord, one at least has been saved. Because of him, others are being saved for Thy divine mercy. 'Breakfast is a good idea.'

Standing beside the window, Cooper could see the traders scurrying through the garden and into their factories. The bannermen were grouped in an untidy mass, squatting and chattering. 'Maybe it'll be like the last time. The mandarins'll hold us for ransom,' Cooper said.

'Na this time, laddie. If they start anything, they'll try to cut us up first.'

'Why?'

'Why send bannermen to Canton? They're fighting men – na like the local Chinese army.'

Servants came in and began to lay the huge table. Later the food was brought. There were cold chickens and boiled eggs and loaves of bread and hot stew and dumplings and hot meat pies and butter, marmalade and jam.

Struan ate heartily and so did Mauss. But Cooper had no relish for his food.

'Mass'er?' a servant said.

112

'Aye?'

'One-Eye Mass'er dooa here. Can?'

'Can.'

Brock stalked into the room. His son Gorth was with him. 'Morning, gentlemen. Morning, Dirk lad.'

'Breakfast?'

'Thank you kindly.'

'You had a good voyage, Gorth?'

'Yes, thank you, Mr Struan.' Gorth was of a size with his father, a hard man, scarred and broken-nosed, with grizzled hair and beard. 'Next time I be beating *Thunder Cloud*.'

'Next time, lad,' Brock said with a laugh, 'you be captaining her.' He sat and began to gorge himself. 'Will thee pass the stew, Mr Cooper?' He jerked a bent thumb at the window. 'Them bastards doan mean no good.'

'Aye. What do you think, Brock?' Struan asked.

'The Co-hong be tearing their pigtails out. So trade be finished for the time. First time I seed poxy bannermen.'

'Evacuate the Settlement?'

'I baint bein' chased out by Chinee or by bannerman,' Brock helped himself to more stew. 'Course I may retreat a little. In me own time. Most of us'n be starting back tomorrer for the land sale. But we'd do good to call a council right smartly. You've arms here?'

'Na enough.'

'We've plenty for a siege. Gorth bringed 'em. This place be the best to defend. It be almost ourn anyway,' he added.

'How many bullyboys have you?'

'Twenty. Gorth's lads. They'll take on a hundred Chinese apiece.'

'I've thirty, counting the Portuguese.'

'Forget the Portuguese. Better us'n alone.' Brock wiped his mouth and broke a small loaf in two and smeared it with butter and marmalade.

'You can't defend the Settlement, Brock,' Cooper said.

'We can defend this factory, lad. Doan thee worry about us'n. You and the rest of the Americans hole up in yorn. They won't touch thee – it's us'n they want after.'

'Aye,' Struan said. 'And we'll need you to watch our trade if we have to leave.'

'That be another reason I come here, Dirk. Wanted to talk open about trade and Cooper-Tillman. I made a proposal which were accepted.'

113

'The proposal was accepted subject to Struan and Company's not being being able to fulfil prior arrangements,' Cooper said. 'We're giving you thirty days, Dirk. On top of the thirty days.'

'Thank you, Jeff. That's generous.'

'That be stupid, lad. But I doan mind the time, I be generous too with yor time. Five more days, Dirk, eh?'

Struan turned to Mauss. 'Go back to the Co-hong and find out what you can. Be careful and take one of my men.'

'I don't need a man with me.' Mauss heaved his girth out of the chair and left.

'We'll hold the council downstairs,' Struan said.

'Good. Perhaps we should all move in here. There be space enough.'

'That would give us away. Better to prepare and wait. It may just be a trick.'

'Right thee are, lad. We be safe enough till servants disappear. Come on, Gorth. Conference in an hour? Downstairs?'

'Aye.'

Brock and Gorth left. Cooper broke a silence. 'What does it all mean?'

'I think it's a ploy by Ti-sen to make us nervous. To prepare for some concessions he wants.' Struan laid a hand on Cooper's shoulder. 'Thanks for the thirty days, I will na forget.'

'Moses had forty days. I thought thirty'd be adequate for you.'

The conference was noisy and angry, but Brock and Struan dominated it.

All the traders – with the exception of the Americans – were in the huge state room that Struan used as his private office. Kegs of cognac, whisky, rum, and beer lined one wall. Tiers of books and ledgers lined another. Quance paintings hung on the walls – landscapes of Macao, portraits, and ships. Glassfronted chests with pewter mugs and silver tankards. And racks of cutlasses, and muskets; powder and shot.

'It's nothing, I tell you,' Masterson snorted. He was a red-faced, dewlapped man in his early thirties, head of the firm of Masterson, Roach and Roach. He was dressed like the other men – dark wool broadcloth frock coat, resplendent waistcoat and felt top hat. 'The Chinese have never molested the Settlement ever since there was one here, by God.'

'Aye. But that was before we went to war with them and won it.' Struan wished they would all agree and go. He held a perfumed handkerchief over his nose against the rancid stench of their bodies.

'I say toss the bloody bannermen out of the square right now,' Gorth said, refilling his tankard with beer.

'We be doing that if it be necessary.' Brock spat into the pewter spittoon. 'I be tired of all this talkin'. Now be we agreeing with Dirk's plan or baint we?'

He glared around the room.

Most of the traders glared back. There were forty of them – English and Scots, except for Eliksen the Dane, who factored for a London firm, and a corpulent Parsee dressed in flowing robes, Rumajee, from India. MacDonald, Kerney, Maltby from Glasgow and Messer, Vivien, Tobe, Smith of London were the chief traders, all tough, oak-hard men in their thirties.

'I sniff troubles, sir,' Rumajee said and pulled at his vast moustache. 'I counsel immediate retreat.'

'For God's sake, the whole point of the plan, Rumajee, is not to retreat,' Roach said caustically. 'To retreat only if necessary. I vote for the plan. And I agree with Mr Brock. Too much bloody talking and I'm tired.' Struan's plan was simple. They would all wait in their own factories; if trouble began, on a signal from Struan, they would converge on his factory under covering fire from his men if necessary. 'Retreat before the heathen? Never, by God!'

'May I suggest something, Mr Struan?' Eliksen asked.

Struan nodded at the tall, fair-haired, taciturn man. 'Of course.'

'Perhaps one of us should volunteer to take word to Whampoa. From there a fast lorcha could hare for the fleet at Hong Kong. Just in case they surround us and cut us off as before.'

'Good idea.' Vivien said. He was tall, pallid and very drunk. 'Let's all volunteer. Can I have another whisky? There's a good chap.'

Then all at once they were talking again and quarreling about who should volunteer, and at length Struan pacified them. 'It was Mr Eliksen's suggestion. If he's a mind to, why na let him have the honour?'

They trooped into the garden and watched as Struan and Brock escorted Eliksen across the square to the lorcha Struan had put at his disposal. The bannermen paid no attention to them, other than to point and jeer.

The lorcha headed downstream.

'Mayhaps we be never seeing him again,' Brock said.

'I dinna think they'll touch him or I'd never've let him go.'

Brock grunted. 'For a foreigner, he baint a bad 'un.' He went back with Gorth to his own factory. The other traders streamed to theirs.

When Struan was satisfied with the arrangement of the armed watch in the garden, and at the back door that let on to Hog Street, he returned to his suite.

May-may was gone. And Ah Gip.

'Where Missee?'

'Doan knowa, Mass'er. Cow chillo no see my.'

He searched the whole building, but they had vanished. It was almost as though they had never been there.

V

Struan was in the garden. It was just before midnight. There was an uneasy stillness in the air. He knew that most of the traders would be sleeping in their clothes, weapons beside them. He peered through the gate at the bannermen. Some were sleeping; others were jabbering over a fire that they had built in the square. The night was chill. There was scant movement on the river.

Struan left the gate and sauntered pensively around the garden. Where the devil was May-may? He knew that she would not casually leave the Settlement. Perhaps she had been enticed away. Perhaps – God's blood, that was nae way to think. But he knew that the richest warlord in China would not hesitate to take her – by force if necessary – once he had seen her.

A shadow jumped over the side wall and Struan's knife was instantly in his hand.

It was a Chinese who tremulously held out a piece of paper. He was a short, lithe man with broken teeth, his face stretched and opium-yellowed. Imprinted on the paper was Jin-qua's chop, a private seal used only on contracts and special documents.

'Mass'er,' the Chinese said softly. 'Dooa follow. Alone.'

Struan hesitated. It was dangerous to leave the protection of the Settlement and his men. Foolhardy. 'No can. Jin-qua here can.'

'No can. Dooa follow.' The Chinese pointed at the chop. 'Jin-qua wantshee, quick-quick.'

'Tomollow,' Struan said.

The Chinese shook his head. 'Now. Quick-quick, savvy?'

Struan realized that possibly Jin-qua's chop had fallen into other hands and that this could easily be a trap. But he dared not take Mauss or any of his men because the meeting must be very secret. And the sooner the better.

He studied the paper under the lantern and made absolutely sure that the chop was correct.

He nodded. 'Can.'

The Chinese led the way to the side wall and clambered over it. Struan followed, ready for treachery. The Chinese hurried along the side wall of the factory and turned into Hog Street. Incredibly, the street was deserted. But Struan could feel eyes watching him.

At the end of Hog Street the Chinese turned east. There were two curtained sedan chairs waiting. The sedan-chair coolies were terrified. Their fear intensified when they saw Struan.

Struan got into one sedan chair, the Chinese into the other. Immediately the coolies picked up the chairs and loped along Thirteen Factory Street. They turned south into narrow, deserted alleyways unfamiliar to Struan. Soon he had lost all sense of direction. He settled back and cursed his stupidity, at the same time exulting in the expectation of danger. At length the coolies stopped in a filthy, high-walled alley strewn with rotting offal. A festering dog was foraging.

The Chinese gave the coolies some money and when they had evaporated into the darkness, he knocked on a door. It opened, and he stepped aside for Struan to enter. Struan motioned him to go first, then warily followed him into a rancid stable where another Chinese was waiting with a lantern. This man turned and walked silently across the stable through another door and did not look behind him. Now they picked their way through a huge warehouse and up rickety steps and down more steps into another warehouse. Rats scurried in the darkness.

Struan knew they were somewhere near the river for he could hear water lapping and hawsers creaking. He was ready for an instant fight, the haft of his knife in his cupped hand, the blade concealed up his sleeve.

The man with the lantern ducked under a bridge of packing cases and led the way to another half-hidden door. He knocked and then opened the door.

'Halloa, Tai-Pan,' Jin-qua said. 'All same no seea longa time.'

Struan came into the room. It was another filth-strewn warehouse dimly lit with candles and cluttered with packing cases and mildewed fishing nets. 'Halloa, Jin-qua,' he said, relieved. 'No seea longa time.'

Jin-qua was ancient, fragile, tiny. His skin was like parchment. Thin wisps of greying beard fell to his chest. His robes were richly brocaded, and his hat jewelled. He wore thick-soled embroidered shoes and his queue was long and shiny. The nails of his little fingers were protected by jewelled sheaths.

Jin-qua nodded happily and shuffled to a corner of the warehouse and sat at a table set with food and tea.

Struan sat opposite him, his back to the wall. Jin-qua smiled. He had only three teeth. They were gold-capped. Jin-qua said something in Chinese to the man who had brought Struan, and the man left by another door.

'Tea-ah?' Jin-qua asked.

'Can.'

Jin-qua nodded to the servant who had carried the lantern, and he poured the tea and helped Jin-qua and Struan to some food. Then he moved to one side and watched Jin-qua. Struan noticed that the man was muscular and armed with a knife at his belt.

'Plees,' Jin-qua said, motioning Struan to eat.

'Thank you.'

Struan nibbled at his food and drank some tea and waited. It was necessary to let Jin-qua make the first opening.

After they had eaten in silence, Jin-qua said, 'You want see my?'

'Jin-qua dooa good trade out of Canton?'

'Bis'ness good bad all same, never mind.'

'Trade stoppee now?'

'Stoppee now. Hoppo very bad mandarin. Sodjers many, many. My payee big squeeze for sodjers. Ayee yah!'

'Bad.' Struan sipped his tea. Now or never, he told himself. And now that the right moment had at last arrived, he knew that he could never sell out Hong Kong. A pox on the mandarin! While I'm alive there'll be nae godrotting mandarin on Hong Kong. It'll have to be Brock. But murder's nae way to solve bankruptcy. So Brock's safe, because everyone expects me to remedy the problem that way. Or is he safe? Where the hell's May-may?

'Hear One-Eye Devil Brock have Tai-Pan by troat.'

'Hear Devil Hoppo have Co-hong by troat,' Struan said. Now that he had decided not to make a deal, he felt much better. 'Ayee yah!'

'All same. Mandarin Ti-sen anger-anger have got.'

'Why so?'

'Mass'er "Obvious Penis" writee werry bad-bad letter.'

'Tea-ah werry number-one good-ah,' Struan said.

'Mass'er "Obvious Penis" dooa what Tai-Pan say, heya?'

'Sometimes can.'

'Bad when Ti-sen anger have got.'

'Bad when Mass'er Longstaff anger have got.'

'Ayee yah.' Jin-qua fastidiously picked some food and ate it, his eyes narrowing even more. 'Savvy Kung Hay Fat Choy?'

'Chinese New Year? Savvy.'

'New year begin soon. Co-hong have got bad debts from old years. Good joss start new year when no debts. Tai-Pan have got plenty Co-hong paper.'

'Never mind. Can wait.' Jin-qua and the other Co-hong merchants owed Struan six hundred thousand.

'One-Eye Devil can wait?'

'Jin-qua paper can wait. Finish. Chow werry number-one good-ah.'

'Werry bad.' Jin-qua sipped his tea. 'Hear Tai-Pan Supreme Lady and chillo dead. Bad joss, solly.'

'Bad joss, plenty,' Struan said.

'Never mind. You plenty young, plenty new cow chillo. Your one piece cow chillo May-may. Why Tai-Pan have got only one bull chillo? Tai-Pan wantshee med'cine maybe. Have got.'

'When wantshee I ask,' Struan said affably. 'Hear Jin-qua have got new bull chillo. What number son this?'

'Ten and seven,' Jin-qua said, beaming.

Great God, Struan thought. Seventeen sons – and probably the same number of daughters, which Jin-qua does na count. He bowed his head and whistled in appreciation.

'Jin-qua laughed. 'How muchee tea-ah wantshee this season?'

'Trade stop. How can trade?'

Jin-qua winked. 'Can.'

'Doan knowa. You sell Brock. When I wantshee tea-ah I tell you, hey'a?'

'Must knowa two days.'

'No can.'

Jin-qua said something sharply to his servant, who went to one of the mildewed packing cases and removed the lid. It was full of silver bullion. Jin-qua motioned at the other packing case. 'Here forty lac dolla.'

A lac was approximately twenty-five thousand pounds sterling. Forty lacs was a million sterling.

Jin-qua's eyes slitted even more. 'I borrow. Werry hard. Werry expensee. You want? Jin-qua lend, maybe.'

Struan tried to conceal his shock. He knew there would be a hard deal attached to any loan. He knew that Jin-qua must have gambled his life and his soul and his house and his future and that of his friends and his sons to amass so much bullion secretly. The bullion had to be secret or the Hoppo would have stolen it and Jin-qua simply would have disappeared. If news leaked into the pirate and bandit nest that abounded in or near Canton that there were even a hundredth part of so much treasure close at hand, Jin-qua would have been obliterated.

'Many lac dolla,' Struan said. 'Man dooa fav'r must return fav'r.'

'Buy this your double tea-ah last year, same price last year. Can?'

'Can.'

'Sell double opium this year same price last year. Can?'

'Can.' Struan would pay over market price for the tea and would have to sell the opium at less than the present market price, but he would still make a vast profit. If the other conditions are possible, he reminded himself. Perhaps he was not finished after all. If Jin-qua did not want the mandarin. Struan said a silent prayer that a mandarin was not part of the deal. But he knew that if there was no mandarin on Hong Kong there could be no Co-hong. And if there was no Co-hong and no monopoly, Jin-qua and all the other merchants would be out of business. They had to have the system too.

'Only buy Jin-qua or Jin-qua son ten year. Can?'

Great God, Struan thought, if I give him a monopoly on the house, he can squeeze us at will. 'Can – when tea price, silk price all same other Co-hong.'

'Twenty year. Market price add ten p'cent.'

'Plus five p'cent – add five p'cent. Can.'

'Eight.'

'Five.'

'Seven.'

'Five.'

'Seven.'

'No can. No profit. Too plenty muchee,' Struan said.

'Ayee yah. Too much plenty profit. Seven!'

'Ten year six p'cent – ten year five p'cent.'

'Ayee yah,' Jin-qua replied hotly. 'Bad, plenty bad.' He waved a frail hand at the chests. 'Huge cost! Big interest. Werry muchee. Ten year six, ten year five, add new ten year five.'

Struan wondered if the anger was real or pretended. 'Suppose no Jin-qua, no Jin-qua son?'

'Plenty son – plenty son of son. Can?'

'New ten year add four p'cent.'

'Five.'

'Four.'

'Bad, bad. Werry high interest, werry. Five.'

121

Struan kept his eyes off the bullion but could feel it surrounding him. Dinna be a fool. Take it. Agree to anything. You're safe, laddie. You've everything.

'Mandarin Ti-sen say one mandarin Hong Kong,' Jin-qua said abruptly. 'Why you say no?'

'Jin-qua doan like mandarin, heya? What for I like mandarin, heya?' Struan replied, a knot in his stomach.

'Forty lac dolla, one mandarin. Can?'

'No can.'

'Plenty easy. Why for you say no can? Can.'

'No can.' Struan's eyes never wavered. 'Mandarin no can.'

'Forty lac dolla. One mandarin. Cheep.'

'Forty times ten lac dolla no can. Die first.' Struan decided to bring the bargaining to an end. 'Finish,' he said harshly. 'By my fathers, finish.' He got up and walked for the door.

'Why for goa?' Jin-qua asked.

'No mandarin – no dolla. Why talk, heya?'

To Struan's astonishment Jin-qua cackled and said, 'Ti-sen want mandarin. Jin-qua no lend money belong Ti-sen. Jin-qua lend Jin-qua money. Add new ten year five p'cent. Can?'

'Can.' Struan sat down again, his head dizzy.

'Five lac dolla buy Jin-qua land in Hong Kong. Can?'

Why? Struan asked himself helplessly. If Jin-qua lends me the money, he must know that the Co-hong's finished. Why should he destroy himself? Why buy land in Hong Kong?

'Can?' Jin-qua said again.

'Can.'

'Five lac dolla keep safe.' Jin-qua opened a small teak box and took out two chops. The chops were small square sticks of ivory two inches long. The old man deftly held them together and dipped the ends, which were intricately carved, into the solid ink and made a chop mark on a sheet of paper. Jin-qua gave Struan one of the chops and put the other back in the box. 'Man bring this piece chop, give land and dolla, five lac, savvy?'

'Savvy.'

'Nex' year I send one my bull chillo Hong Kong. You send all same your son school Lond'n. Can?'

'Can.'

'Your bull chillo, Gord'n Chen. Good? Bad maybe?'

'Good chillo. Chen Sheng say plenty good think-think.' Obviously Struan was supposed to do something with Gordon Chen. But why and how did Gordon fit into Jin-qua's machinations? 'I think-think give Gord'n maybe bigger job.'

'What for bigger job?' Jin-qua said contemptuously. 'Think you lend one lac dolla Chen bull chillo.'

'What inter'st?'

'Half profit.'

Profit on what? Struan felt that Jin-qua was playing him like a fish. But you're off the hook, laddie, he wanted to shout. You'll get the bullion wi'out the mandarin. 'Can.'

Jin-qua sighed and Struan assumed that the deal was concluded. But it was not. Jin-qua put his hand into his sleeve pocket and brought out eight coin halves and put them on the table. Each of four coins had been crudely broken in two. With one of his fingernail protectors Jin-qua pushed a half of each coin across the table. 'Last. Four fav'r. Man bring one thees, you grant fav'r.'

'What fav'r?'

Jin-qua leaned back in his chair. 'Doan knowa, Tai-Pan,' he said. 'Four fav'r sometime. Not my life maybe, son maybe. Doan knowa when, but ask four fav'r. One half coin one fav'r. Can?'

Sweat chilled Struan's shoulders. Agreeing to such a demand was an open invitation to disaster. But if he refused, the bullion was lost to him. You put your head into a devil trap, he told himself. Aye, but make up your mind. Do you want the future or na? You've known Jin-qua for twenty years. He's always been fair. Aye, and the shrewdest man in Canton. For twenty years he's helped you and guided you – and together you've grown in power and riches. So trust him; you can trust him. No, you canna trust any man, least of all Jin-qua. You've prospered with him only because you've always held the last card. Now you're asked to give Jin-qua four jokers in your pack of life and death.

Once more Struan was awed by the subtlety and diabolic cunning of a Chinese mind. The majesty of it. The ruthlessness of it. But then, Struan told himself, they were both gambling for huge stakes. Both gambling on each other's fairness, for there was nothing to guarantee that the favours would be granted. *Except that you will grant them and must grant them because a deal is a deal.*

'Can,' he said, holding out his hand. 'My custom, shake hand. Na Chinese custom, never mind.' He had never shaken hands with Jin-qua before, and he knew that the shaking of hands was considered barbaric.

Jin-qua said, 'Fav'r perhaps again' law. My, yours, savvy?'

'Savvy. You frien'. You or son no send coin ask bad fav'r.'

Jin-qua closed his eyes for a moment and thought about European barbarians. They were hairy and apelike. Their manners were repulsive and ugly. They stank beyond belief. They had no culture or manners or graces. Even the lowest coolie was ten thousand times better than the best European. And what applied to the men applied even more to the women.

He remembered his one visit to the Chinese-speaking English barbarian whore at Macao. He had visited her more for curiosity than for satisfaction, encouraged by his friends who said it would be an unforgettable experience for there was no refinement she would not diligently practise if encouraged.

He shuddered at the thought of her hairy arms and hairy armpits and hairy legs and cleft, the coarseness of her skin and face, and the stench of sweat mixed with the foul perfume.

And the foods that the barbarians ate – hideous. He had been to their dinners many times and had had to sit through the innumerable courses, almost faint with nausea and pretending not to be hungry. Watching appalled, at the stupendous quantities of half-raw meats they knifed into their mouths, blood gravy dripping down their chins. And the quantities of maddening spirits they swilled. And their revolting boiled, tasteless vegetables. And indigestible, solid pies. All in monstrous amounts. Like pigs – no, not like pigs: like sweating, gluttonous Gargantuan devils. Unbelievable!

They have no attributes to recommend them, he thought. None. Except their propensity to kill, and this they can do with incredible brutality although with no refinement. And their attribute for making money. At least, they are the medium for us to make money.

Barbarians are Evil personified. All except this man – this Dirk Struan. Once Struan was like other barbarians. Now he is partially Chinese. In the mind. The mind is important, for to be Chinese is partially a mental attitude. And he is clean and smells clean. And he has learned some of our ways. Still violent and barbarian and a killer. But a little changed. And if one barbarian can be changed into a civilized person, why not many?

Your plan is a wise one, Jin-qua told himself. He opened his eyes and reached across and delicately touched Struan's hand with his. 'Frien'.'

Jin-qua motioned for the servant to pour tea.

'Men my bring bullion your factory. Two days. Night. Werry secret,' Jin-qua said. 'Plenty danger, savvy? Werry plenty.'

'Savvy. I give paper and chop my for bullion. Send tomollow.'

'No chop, no paper. Word better, heya?'

Struan nodded. How would you explain it – say, to Culum – that Jin-qua'll give you one million in silver, will give you a fair deal knowing that he could ask any conditions, will give you everything you want on a handshake?

'Three times ten lac dolla pay Jin-qua, Co-hong debts. Now new year no debt. Good joss,' Jin-qua said proudly.

'Aye,' Struan said. 'Good joss for me.'

'Werry werry plenty danger, Tai-Pan. No can help.'

'Aye.'

'Werry plenty danger. Mustee wait two nights.'

'Ayee yah danger!' Struan said. He picked up the four half coins. 'Thank you, Chen-tse Jin Arn. Thank you very much.'

'No thanks, Dir'Str'n. Frien'.'

Suddenly the man who had guided Struan to Jin-qua burst in. He spoke urgently to Jin-qua, who turned to Struan, frightened. 'Servant dooa go! Gone Sett'ment. All gone!'

VI

Struan sat in the sedan chair and swayed easily to its motion as the bearer coolies trotted through the silent alleys. The inside of the curtained box was grimed and sweat-stained. From time to time he peered through the curtained side-window openings at the alleys. He could not see the sky, but he knew that dawn was near. The wind carried the stench of rotting fruit and faeces and offal and cooking and spices and, mixed with it, the smell of the sweat of the coolies.

He had worked out a safer plan with Jin-qua to get the bullion to Hong Kong. He had arranged for Jin-qua to load the bullion in its crates on to an armed lorcha. In two nights the lorcha was to be brought secretly to the Settlement wharf. At exactly midnight. If this was not possible, the lorcha was to be left near the south side of the wharf, one lantern on the foremast, another on the prow. To make sure that there was no mistake, Jin-qua had said that, as a sign, he would paint the near side eye of the lorcha red. Every lorcha had two eyes carved into the teak of their prows. The eyes were for joss and also to help the soul of the boat to see ahead. The Chinese knew that it was essential for a boat to have eyes to see with.

But why should Jin-qua let me have Hong Kong safe? he asked himself. Surely Jin-qua must realize the importance of a mandarin. And why should he want a son educated in London? Was Jin-qua, of all the Chinese he knew, so farsighted as to understand, at long last, that there was to be a permanent joining of the fortunes of China with the fortunes of Britain?

He heard dogs barking, and through the curtains saw them attack the legs of the front coolie. But the coolie who carried the lantern ahead of the sedan chair ran back and, with practised skill, hacked at the dogs with his iron-pointed staff. The dogs fled yelping into the darkness.

Then Struan noticed a cluster of bannermen foot soldiers – perhaps a hundred – seated at a far intersection. They were armed, and had lanterns. They were ominously quiet. Several of the men stood up and began to walk towards the chair. The coolies swerved into an alley, much to Struan's relief. Now all you have to do, laddie, he told himself, is to get the bullion safe to Hong Kong. Or safe to Whampoa, where you can trans-ship it into *China Cloud*. But until it's safe aboard, you're na safe, laddie.

The sedan chair lurched as a coolie almost stumbled into one of the potholes that pockmarked the roadbed. Struan craned around in the confining space, trying to get his bearings. Later he could see the masts of ships, half hidden by hovels. Ahead there was still nothing recognizable. The chair turned a corner, heading towards the river, then cut across this narrow alley into another. Finally ahead, over the roofs of huts, he could make out part of the Settlement buildings glinting in the moonlight.

Abruptly the sedan chair stopped and was grounded, throwing Struan to one side. He tore the curtains aside and leaped out, knife in his hand, just as three spears ripped through the thin sides of the chair.

The three spearmen desperately tried to pull their weapons free as Struan darted at the nearest one, shoved his knife into the man's side and spun as another charged him with a double-edged war axe. The axe blade scored his shoulder and he grimaced with pain but sidestepped and grappled with the man for possession of the axe. He tore it from the man's hand and the man screamed as a spear aimed for Struan impaled him. Struan backed against the wall. The remaining spearman circled him, panting and cursing. Struan feinted and hacked at him with the axe but missed and the man lunged. His spear pierced Struan's coat but Struan ripped free and buried his knife to the hilt in the man's stomach and twisted it, gutting him.

Struan jumped clear of the bodies, his back against the safety of the wall, and waited. The man that he had knifed was howling. Another was inert. The one he had gutted was holding his stomach and crawling away.

Struan waited an instant, gathering strength, and an arrow thudded into the wall above his head. He picked up one of the spears and raced down the alley towards the Settlement. He heard footsteps behind him and ran faster. As he rounded the corner, he saw that Thirteen Factory Street was just ahead. He dropped the spear and zigzagged across the street and into Hog Street, down Hog Street and across the square, which was filled with more bannermen than before.

Before the bannermen could intercept him, he was through the garden door. A musket slammed him in the stomach.

'Oh, it's thee, Dirk,' Brock said. 'Where the hell's thee beed?'

'Out,' Struan gulped for air. 'God's blood, I was jumped by stinking highwaymen.'

'Be that yor blood or theirs?'

Under the light of the lantern, Struan ripped the coat and shirt away from his wounded shoulder. The slice was clean and shallow across his shoulder muscle.

'A gnat's bite,' Brock scoffed. He found a bottle of rum and poured some into the wound and smiled when Struan winced. 'How many were they?'

'Three.'

'An' thee get cutted? Thee be getting old!' Brock poured two glasses of rum.

Struan drank, and felt better.

'I thort you was asleeping. Yor door were locked. Where thee beed?'

'What's going on here?'

'The servants vanished 'bout an hour ago. That's wot. I thort it best not to bringed everyone here till daybreak. Must be 'arf a hundred guns covered thee while thee ran.'

'Then why the devil shove a musket in my belly?'

'Just wanted to welcome thee rightly.' Brock gulped some rum. 'Just wanted thee to knowed we was awake.'

'Anyone know why the servants left?'

'No.' Brock walked over to the gate. The bannermen were settling back into sleep. A nervous dawn hesitated on the horizon. 'Looks godrotting bad,' he said, his face hard. 'Doan like this here a little bit. Them bastards doan do nothing but sit an' sometimes beat their drums. I think we better retreat while the retreating's good.'

'We're safe for a few days.'

Brock shook his head. 'I got a bad feeling. Something's right bad. We'd better goed.'

'It's a ploy, Brock.' Struan tore off a piece of his shirt and wiped the sweat from his face.

'Mayhaps. But I got this feeling, and when I gets this feeling it be time to move.' Brock jerked a thumb at the bannermen. 'We counted 'em. Hundred an' fifty. How-qua sayed there be more'n a thousand spread all round the Settlement.'

'I saw perhaps two or three hundred. To the east.'

'Where thee beed?'

'Out.' Struan was tempted to tell him. But that will na help, he thought. Brock'll do everything in his power to prevent the bullion from arriving safely. And without the bullion you're as dead as you ever were. 'There's a girl just around the corner,' he said flippantly.

'Pox on a girl! Thee baint so stupid to leave for any doxy.' Brock tugged his beard peevishly. 'Thee be taking over from me in a hour?'

'Aye.'

'At noon we pull out.'

'Nay.'

'I say at noon.'

'Nay.'

Brock frowned. 'Wot's to keep thee here?'

'If we leave before there's real trouble, we lose face badly.'

'Yus. I knowed. Doan please me to run. But somethin' tells me it be better.'

'We'll wait a couple of days.'

Brock was very suspicious. 'Thee knowed I never beed wrong about aknowing when to run. Why thee want to stay?'

'It's just Ti-sen up to his old tricks. This time you're wrong. I'll relieve you in an hour,' Struan said, and went inside.

Now wot be Dirk up to? Brock brooded. He hawked loudly, hating the danger stench that seemed to come from the dying night.

Struan climbed the marble staircase to his quarters. The walls were lined with Quance paintings and Chinese silk hangings. On the landings were giant Ming teak dragons and teak chests. The corridors leading off the first landing were lined with paintings of ships and sea battles, and on a pedestal was a scale model of HMS *Victory*.

Struan found his door locked.

'Open the door,' he said, and waited. Ah Gip let him inside.

'Where the hell've you been, May-may?' he said trying not to show his relief.

She was standing in the shadows near the window. She spoke to Ah Gip, then motioned her out.

Struan bolted the door. 'Where the hell've you been?'

She moved into the lantern light, and he was shocked by her pallor.

'What's amiss?'

'There's plenty of rumours, Tai-Pan. Word says all barbarians are going to be put to the sword.'

'Nothing new in that. Where've you been?'

'Bannermen are new. There's rumour that Ti-sen's in disgrace. That he's sentenced to death.'

'That's nonsense. He's cousin to the emperor, and the second-richest man in China.'

'Rumour says the emperor's so godrot angry Ti-sen make a treaty, Ti-sen is to suffer public torture.'

'That's madness.' Struan stood by the fire and stripped off his coat and shirt. 'Where've you been?'

'What happened to you?' she exclaimed, seeing the cut.

'Highwaymen jumped me.'

'Did you see Jin-qua?'

Struan was wonder-struck. 'How do you know about Jin-qua?'

'I went to kowtow and pay my respects to his Supreme Lady. She told me he just returned and sent for you.'

Struan had been unaware that May-may knew Jin-qua's first wife, but he was so furious that he dismissed this from his mind. 'Why the devil did you na tell me where you were going?'

'Because then you would have forbid me,' May-may snapped. 'I want to see her. Also to have my hair done and to consult the astrologer.'

'What?'

'There's a terrifical good hairdresser that Jin-qua's ladies use. Terrifical good for hair. This woman is famous in all Kwangtung. Very expensive. The astrologer said joss was good. Very good. But to watch building of houses.'

'You'd risk your life to talk to soothsayers and get your hair treated?' he erupted. 'What the hell's the matter with your hair? It's fine as it is!'

'You dinna ken these things, Tai-Pan,' she said coldly. 'That's where I hear rumours. At hairdresser's.' She took his hand and made him touch her hair. 'There, you see. It is much softer, no?'

'No! It is na! God's death, if you ever leave without first telling me where you're going, I'll whack you so hard you will no sit down for a week.'

'Just try, Tai-Pan, by God,' she said and glared back at him.

He grabbed her swiftly and carried her, struggling, to the bed and flung up her robe and petticoats and gave her a smack on her buttocks that stung his hand and tossed her on the bed. He had never struck her before. May-may flew off the bed at him and viciously raked his face with her long nails. A lantern crashed to the floor as Struan upended her again and resumed the spanking. She fought out of his grip, and her nails slashed at his eyes, missing by a fraction of an inch, and scoring his face. He caught her wrists and turned her over and tore off her robe and underclothes and smashed her bare buttocks with the flat of his

130

hand. She fought back fiercely, shoving an elbow in his groin and clawing at his face again. Mastering all his strength, he pinned her to the bed, but she slipped her head free and sank her teeth into his forearm. He gasped from the pain and slashed her buttocks again with the flat of his free hand. She bit harder.

'By God, you'll never bite me again,' he said through clenched teeth. Her teeth sank deeper, but he deliberately did not pull his arm away. The pain made his eyes water, but he smashed May-may harder and harder and harder, always on her buttocks, until his hand hurt. At last she released her teeth.

'Don't – no more – please – please,' she whimpered, and wept into the pillow, defenceless.

Struan caught his breath. 'Now say you're sorry for going out without permission.'

Her mottled, inflamed buttocks tightened and she flinched against the expected blow, but he had not raised his hand. He knew that the spirit of a thoroughbred must only be tamed, never broken. 'I'll give you three seconds.'

'I'm sorry – sorry. You hurt me, you hurt me,' she sobbed.

He got off the bed and, holding his forearm under the light examined the wound. May-may's teeth had bitten very deeply and blood seeped.

'Come over here,' he said quietly. She did not move but continued to weep. 'Come over here,' he repeated, but this time his voice was a lash and she jerked up. He did not look at her. She quickly pulled the remnants of her robe around her and began to get off the bed.

'I did na tell you to dress! I said come here.'

She hurried over to him, her eyes red and her face powder and eye makeup streaked.

He steadied his forearm against the table and daubed the seeping blood away and poured brandy into each wound. He lit a match and gave it to her. 'Stick the flame in the wounds, one by one.'

'No!'

'One by one,' he said. 'A human bite is as poisonous as a mad dog's. Hurry.'

It took three matches, and each time she wept a little more, nauseated by the smell of burning flesh, but she kept her hand steady. And each time the brandy ignited, Struan grit his teeth and said nothing.

When it was finished, he slopped more brandy over the blackened wounds and May-may found the chamber pot and was very sick. Struan quickly poured some hot water from the kettle over a towel and patted May-may's back gently, and when she had finished he wiped her face tenderly and made her rinse her mouth with some of the hot water. Then he picked her up and put her into the bed and would have left her. But she held on to him and began to weep, the deep inner weeping that cleans away the hatred.

Struan soothed her and gentled her until she slept. Then he left and took over the watch from Brock.

At noon there was another meeting. Many wished to leave immediately. But Struan dominated Brock and persuaded the merchants to wait until tomorrow. They agreed reluctantly and decided to move into the factory for mutual safety. Cooper and the Americans went to their own factory.

Struan returned to his suite.

May-may welcomed him passionately. Later they slept, at peace. Once they awoke together and she kissed him sleepily and whispered, 'You were right to beat me. I was wrong, Tai-Pan. But never beat me when I am na wrong. For sometime you must sleep and then I kill you.'

In the middle watch their peace was shattered. Wolfgang Mauss was pounding on the door. 'Tai-Pan! Tai-Pan!'

'Aye?'

'Quick! Downstairs! Hurry!'

Now they could hear the mob swarming into the square.

VII

'My Da' warned you all, God damn yor eyes!' Gorth said, turning away from the dining-room window and pushing through the traders.

'We've had mobs before,' Struan said sharply. 'And you know they're always controlled and only ordered out by the mandarins.'

'Yus, but not like this'n,' Brock said.

'There's got to be a special reason. Nothing to worry about yet.'

The square below was jammed with a heaving mass of Chinese. Some carried lanterns, others torches. A few were armed. And they were screaming in unison.

'Must beed two to three thousand of the buggers,' Brock said, then called out, 'Hey, Wolfgang! Wot be they heathen devils shouting?'

' "Death to the devil barbarians." '

'What rotten cheek!' Roach said. He was a small, sparrow-like man, his musket taller than himself.

Mauss looked back at the mob, his heart thumping uneasily, his flanks clammy with sweat. Is this Thy time, oh Lord? The time of Thy peerless martyrdom? 'I'll go and talk to them,' he said throatily, wanting the peace of such a sacrifice, yet terrified of it.

'An estimable idea, Mr Mauss,' Rumajee said agreeably, his black eyes twitching nervously from Mauss to the mob and back again. 'They're bound to listen to one of your persuasion, sir.'

Struan saw Mauss's beaded sweat and untoward pallor and he intercepted him near the door. 'You'll do nae such thing.'

'It's time, Tai-Pan.'

'You'll na buy salvation that easily.'

'Who are you to judge?' Mauss began to push past, but Struan stood in his way.

'I meant that salvation's a long and hurt-filled process,' he said kindly. Twice before he had seen the same strangeness in Mauss. Each time it had been before a battle with pirates, and later, during the battle,

133

Mauss had dropped his weapons and gone towards the enemy in a religious ecstasy, seeking death. 'It's a long process.'

'The – Lord's peace is . . . is hard to find,' Mauss muttered, his throat choking him, glad to be stopped and hating himself for being glad. 'I just wanted . . .'

'Quite right. Know all about salvation meself,' Masterson butted in. He steepled his hands and his manner was pious. 'Lord preserve us from the godrotting heathen! Couldn't agree more, Tai-Pan. Damn all this noise, what?'

Mauss collected himself with an effort, feeling naked before Struan, who once again had seen into the depths of his soul. 'You're . . . you're right. Yes. Right.'

'After all, if we lose you, who's left to preach the Word?' Struan said, and decided to watch Mauss if there was real trouble.

'Quite right,' Masterson said, blowing his nose with his fingers. 'What's the point of throwing a valuable Christian to the wolves? That damned bunch of scallawags is whipped to a frenzy and in no mood to be preached at. Lord protect us! Goddamme, Tai-Pan, I told you there'd be an attack.'

'The hell you did!' Roach called from across the room.

'Who the devil asked your opinion, by God? Having a quiet talk to the Tai-Pan and Reverend Mauss,' Masterson shouted back. Then to Mauss, 'Why not say a prayer for us, eh? After all, we're the Christians, by God!' He bustled over to the window. 'Can't a fellow see what's going on, eh?'

Mauss wiped the sweat off his brow. Oh Lord God and sweet Jesus, Thine only begotten Son, give me Thy peace. Send me disciples and missionaries so that I may lay down Thy burden. And I bless Thee for sending me the Tai-Pan who is my conscience and who sees me as I am. 'Thank you, Tai-Pan.'

The door was flung open and more traders poured into the room. All were armed. 'What the devil's going on? What's amiss?'

'Nobody knows,' Roach said. 'One moment it was peaceful; the next, they started to arrive.'

'I bet we never see poor old Eliksen again. Poor devil's probably had his throat cut already.' Masterson said, malevolently priming his musket. 'We'll die in our beds tonight.'

'Oh, shut up, for the love of God,' Roach said.

'You're a harbinger of sweetness and comfort, ain't you?' Vivien, a bull-like trader, glowered down on Masterson. 'Why don't you pee in your hat?'

134

The other traders roared, and then Gorth shouldered his way to the door. 'I'll take my bullyboys and blow 'em to hell!'

'No!' Struan's voice was a lash. A hush fell. 'They're doing us nae harm yet. What's the matter, Gorth? Are you frightened of a few men cursing you?'

Gorth reddened and started towards Struan, but Brock moved in the way. 'Get thee below,' he ordered. 'Stand guard in the garden, and the first Chinese wot come in, blow his bloody head off!'

Gorth controlled his rage with an effort and walked out. Everyone started talking again.

'Baint proper to bait the lad, Dirk.' Brock poured a tankard of ale and drank it thirstily. 'He might be handing thee thy head.'

'He might. And he might be taught a few manners.'

'Excuse me, Mr Struan,' Rumajee interrupted, his nervousness overcoming his politeness. 'Are there guards at the back entrance?'

'Aye. Three of my men. They can hold that against an army of this rabble.'

There was a burst of arguing among the traders and then Roach said, 'I'm with Gorth. I say we should fight our way out instantly.'

'We will. If necessary,' Struan said.

'Yus,' Brock said. 'Askin' for trouble to do it now. We waits and keeps our guard up till light. Mayhaps they be gone by then.'

'And if they're not? Eh? That's what I'd like to know!'

'Then we spill a lot of blood. I snuck three of my men on to our lorcha and put her in midstream. There be a ten-pounder aboard.'

Struan laughed. 'I think Mr Brock deserves a vote of confidence.'

'By God, Mr Brock, you're right smart,' Masterson said. 'Three cheers for Mr Brock!'

They cheered and Brock grinned. 'Thank'ee kindly, lads. Now, best to get some sleep. We be safe enough.'

'*Gott im Himmel!* Look!' Mauss was pointing out of the window, his eyes bulging.

A lanterned procession with gongs and drums was pouring out of Hog Street into the square. Bannermen with flails preceded it, hacking a path through the mob. At the head of the procession was a man of vast girth. His clothes were rich but he was barefoot and hatless, and he staggered under the weight of chains.

'God's death!' Struan said. 'That's Ti-sen!'

The procession wound into the centre of the square and halted. All the Co-hong merchants except Jin-qua were in the procession. All had their ceremonial rank buttons removed from their hats, and they stood quaking. The mob began to jeer and hiss. Then the chief bannerman, a tall, black-bearded warrior, banged a huge gong and the mob fell silent once more.

An open sedan chair with mounted bannermen in front and behind was carried into the square. Seated on the chair, in full ceremonial grey-and-scarlet dress, was Hi'pia-kho, the imperial Hoppo. He was a squat, obese Manchu mandarin, almost neckless, and in his hand was the imperial fan of his office. The fan was ivory and studded with jade.

The Hoppo's chair was put down in the centre of the square and the chief bannerman screamed out an order. Everyone in the square kowtowed three times and then got up again.

The Hoppo unrolled a paper and, under the light of a lantern held by a guard, began to read in a high-pitched voice.

'Wot's he asaying?' Brock asked Mauss.

'Look, there's old How-qua,' Masterson said with a chuckle. 'He's bloody well shaking in—'

'Please. Quiet. I can't hear, *hein*?' Mauss said. He craned out the window. They all listened.

'It's an emperor's edict,' Mauss said quickly. ' "And the traitor Ti-sen, our late cousin, shall immediately be put in chains and sent to our capital under sentence of death and . . ." – I can't hear *hein*? Wait a moment – "and the contemptible treaty called the Convention of Chuenpi, that he signed without our authority, is revoked. The barbarians are ordered out of our kingdom and out of Canton and out of Hong Kong under pain of immediate and lingering death and—" '

'I don't believe it,' Roach scoffed.

'Shut thy face! How can Wolfgang be hearing?'

Mauss listened intently to the eerie high-pitched voice cutting the brooding silence. 'We're ordered out,' he said. 'And we've to pay an indemnity for all the trouble we've caused. No trade except under the Eight Regulations. Queen Victoria's ordered to present herself at Canton in mourning – something about . . . it sounded like rewards are on our heads and – "as a symbol of our displeasure, the criminal Ti-sen will be scourged publicly and all his property is forfeit. Fear this and tremblingly obey!" '

The chief bannerman approached Ti-sen and gestured at the ground with his flail. Ti-sen, chalk-white, knelt down and the chief bannerman raised his flail and brought it crashing down on Ti-sen's back. Again and again and again. There was no sound in the square but for the slash of the whip. Ti-sen fell forward on his face and the bannerman continued to scourge him.

'I don't believe it,' Masterson said.

'It's impossible,' Mauss said.

'If they'll do this to Ti-sen – by the Cross, they'll kill us all.'

'Nonsense! We can take the whole of China – any time.'

Brock started guffawing.

'What's so funny, *hein*?' Mauss asked impatiently.

'This mean war again,' Brock said. 'Good, says I.' He glanced at Struan, mocking him. 'I told thee, lad. This be wot thee gets for making a soft treaty with the scum.'

'It's a ruse of some kind,' Struan said calmly. But inwardly he was stunned by what was happening. 'Ti-sen's the richest man in China. The emperor's got a whipping boy, a scapegoat. And all Ti-sen's wealth. It's a matter of face. The emperor's saving face.'

'Thee and thy face, lad,' Brock said, no longer amused. "Tis thy face that be red. Treaty be finished, trade finished, Hong Kong finished, thee be finished, and all thee talks about be face.'

'You're so wrong, Tyler. Hong Kong's just begun,' Struan said. 'A lot of things have just begun.'

'Yus. War, by God.'

'And if there's war, where's the base for the fleet, eh? Macao's as useless as it always has been – it's part of the mainland and the Chinese can fall on that at whim. But na our island, by God. Na with the fleet protecting it. I'll agree that wi'out Hong Kong we're finished. That wi'out it we canna launch a campaign north again. Never. Nor protect whatever mainland ports or settlements we get in the future. You hear, Tyler? Hong Kong's the key to China. Hong Kong's got you by the short and curlies.'

'I knowed all about havin' a island fortress, by God,' Brock blustered above the chorus of agreement. 'Hong Kong baint the only place, I be saying. Chushan be better.'

'You can na protect Chushan like Hong Kong,' Struan said exultantly, knowing that Brock was committed as they were all committed. 'That "barren, sodding rock", as you call it, is your whole godrotting future.'

'Maybe, maybe not,' Brock said sourly. 'We be seeing about that. But thee baint be enjoying Hong Kong nohow. I be having the knoll, and thee be finished.'

'Dinna be too sure.' Struan watched the square again. The lash still rose and fell. He pitied Ti-sen, who had been caught in a trap not of his own choosing. He had not sought the job as Chinese Plenipotentiary – he was ordered to take it. He was trapped by the era in which he lived.

Just as Struan himself, and Longstaff and Brock and the Hoppo and all of them were trapped now that the first move had been made. The result would be as inexorable as the flail. There would be a move against Canton just as before. First take the forts at the approaches to Canton and then only threaten the city. There would be no need to capture it, for Canton would pay ransom first. Then, when the winds were ripe in the summer, north once more to the Pei Ho River mouth and landings, and once more the emperor, trapped like everyone else, would immediately sue for peace. The treaty would stand because it was fair. Then, over the years, the Chinese would gradually open up their ports willingly – seeing that the British had much to offer: law, justice, the sanctity of property, freedom.

For the ordinary Chinese want what we want, he thought, and there's nae difference between us. We can work together for the benefit of all. Perhaps we'll help the Chinese to throw out the barbaric Manchus. That's what will happen so long as there's a reasonable treaty now, and we're patient, and we play the Chinese game with Chinese rules, in Chinese time. Time measured not in a day or year, but in generations. And so long as we can trade while we're waiting. Without trade the world will become what it was once – a hell where only the strongest arm and the heaviest lash was law. The meek will never inherit the earth. Aye, but at least they can be protected by law to live out their lives as they wish.

When Ti-sen had had a hundred blows, the bannermen picked him up. Blood was streaming from his face and neck, and the back of his robe was shredded and bloody. The mob jeered and hooted. A bannerman banged the gong but the mob paid no attention and the bannermen cut into them, slashing and chopping. There were screams, and the mob backed away and fell silent again.

The Hoppo waved an imperious hand towards the garden. The sedan chair was lifted and the bannermen moved ahead of it, wielding their flails to clear the way towards the traders.

'Come on,' Struan said to Mauss and Brock. 'The rest of you get ready in case there's an attack.' He dashed out into the garden. Brock and Mauss close behind.

'Be thee sick in the head?' Brock said.

'No.'

They watched tensely as the mob parted and the bannermen appeared at the garden gate. The Hoppo stayed in his chair, but he called out to them imperiously.

'He orders you to take a copy of the edict, Mr Struan,' Mauss said.

'Tell him that we are not dressed in ceremonial clothes. Such an important matter needs great ceremony to give it the dignity it merits.'

The Hoppo seemed puzzled. After a moment he spoke again.

'He says, "Barbarians have no ceremony and are beyond contempt. However, the Son of Heaven has urged clemency on all those who fear him. A deputation will come to my palace in the morning, at the Hour of the Snake." '

'When the hell be that?' Brock asked.

'Seven a.m.,' Mauss said.

'We baint about to put our heads in his godrotting trap. Tell him to dung himself.'

'Tell him,' Struan said, 'according to the Eight Regulations we're na allowed to meet personally with the exalted Hoppo but must receive documents through the Co-hong here in the Settlement. The Hour of the Snake gives us na enough time.' He looked up; dawn was streaking the sky. 'When's eleven o'clock at night?'

'The Hour of the Rat,' Mauss said.

'Then tell him that we will receive the document from the Co-hong here with "due ceremony" at the Hour of the Rat. *Tomorrow* night.'

' "Due ceremony" be clever, Dirk,' Brock said. 'That be plenty of time to prepare a bleeding welcome!'

Mauss listened to the Hoppo. 'He says that the Co-hong will deliver the edict at the Hour of the Snake – that's nine a.m. – today. And all British barbarians are to leave the Settlement by the Hour of the Sheep – that's one p.m. – today.'

'Tell him that one p.m. today gives us na enough time. At the Hour of the Sheep tomorrow.'

'He says we must evacuate the Settlement at three p.m. today – the Hour of the Monkey – that our lives are spared until that time and that we can leave without harm.'

'Tell him: the Hour of the Monkey tomorrow.'

The Hoppo replied to Mauss, and barked an order. His chair was lifted and the procession began to form again.

'He said we must leave today. At the Hour of the Monkey. Three o'clock this afternoon.'

'Curse him to hell!' Struan said, enraged. The procession was heading for Hog Street. One of the bannermen shoved Ti-sen behind the sedan chair and flailed him as he stumbled after it; more began to close on the mob, which coursed out of the square. The bannermen who remained split into two groups. One moved closer to the factory, cutting it off from Hog Street; the other was posted to the west. The factory was surrounded.

'Why was you pressing for delay?' Brock said.

'Just normal negotiation.'

'Thee knowed right well; be more'n the Hoppo's life be worth to delay after wot happened to Ti-sen! Wot be so important to stay another night, eh? Most of us was leaving today, anyway. For the land sale.'

Good sweet Christ! Struan thought, knowing that Brock was right. How can I wait for the bullion?

'Eh?' Brock repeated.

'No reason.'

'There be a reason,' Brock said, and entered the factory.

Promptly at the Hour of the Snake the full complement of Co-hong merchants came into the square, escorted by fifty bannermen with gongs and drums sounding. The guard bannermen let them through and then closed ranks again. Again Jin-qua was absent. But his son How-qua, the leading Co-hong merchant, was there. How-qua, a middle-aged, roly-poly man, always smiled. But today he was sombre and sweating, so terrified that he almost dropped the neatly rolled imperial edict, bound with vermilion ribbon. His fellow merchants were equally panic-stricken.

Struan and Brock were waiting to receive them in the garden, dressed in their best frock coats and white cravats and top hats. Struan was freshly shaved and Brock had had his beard combed. Both wore ostentatious flowers in their buttonholes. They knew that ceremony gained them much face and made the Hoppo lose face.

'Right you are,' Brock had said with a hoarse laugh. 'Struan an' me'll take the godrotting edict, an' if we baint acting proper like they, then mayhaps they be burning us up like rats in a trap an' not waiting the time they give us. Now, do exactly as Struan sayed.'

The party halted at the gate. Mauss opened it and Struan and Brock went to the threshold. The bannerman glowered at them. Struan and Brock were grimly aware of the rewards that were still on their heads, but they showed no fear, for they were covered by unseen guns in the windows behind them and by the cannon on Brock's lorcha anchored in mid-stream.

The chief bannerman spoke heatedly, gesticulating with his flail.

'He says come out and get the edict,' Mauss interpreted.

Struan merely raised his hat and held out his hand and planted his

140

feet firmly. 'The Hoppo said the edict was to be delivered. Deliver it.' He kept his hand out.

Mauss translated what he had said and then after a nervous moment the bannerman cursed at How-qua and How-qua hurried forward and gave Struan the rolled paper.

Struan and Brock and Mauss immediately doffed their top hats, and shouted at the top of their voices, 'God save the Queen.' At this signal Gorth put a taper to the firecrackers and tossed them into the garden. The Co-hong merchants leaped back, and the bannermen drew their bows and swords, but Struan and Brock, their faces solemn, stood perfectly still, holding their hats in the air.

The exploding firecrackers filled the garden with smoke. When the explosions ceased, to the Co-hong's horror Mauss, Struan and Brock shouted, 'God rot all Manchus!' and from inside the factory there were three resounding cheers.

The chief bannerman strode forward belligerently and harangued Mauss.

'He asks what this is all about, Tai-Pan.'

'Tell him, just like I told you.' Struan caught How-qua's eye and winked covertly, knowing his hatred of the Manchus.

Mauss said in loud, ringing, perfect Mandarin, 'This is our custom on a very important occasion. Not every day are we privileged to receive so estimable a document.'

The bannerman cursed him for a moment, then ordered the Co-hong away. The Co-hong went, but now they were emboldened.

Brock started laughing. And laughter spread through the factory and was echoed from the far end of the square where the American factory was situated. A Union Jack appeared from one of its windows and waved bravely.

'We'd best be getting ready t'move,' Brock said. 'That were very good.'

Struan did not answer. He tossed the edict to Mauss. 'Give me an accurate translation, Wolfgang,' he said, and went back to his suite.

Ah Gip bowed him in and went back to her cooking pots. May-may was dressed but she was lying on the bed.

'What's the matter, May-may?'

She glared at him and turned her back, pulling up her robe and revealing her bruise-tinted buttocks.

'That's wat's matter!' she said, with mock rage. 'Look what you've done, you brute barbarian fan quai. I must either stand or lying on my belly.'

'Must lie on,' he said, and slumped moodily in a chair.

May-may pulled down her robe and gingerly got off the bed. 'Why do you na laugh? I thought that would make you laugh.'

'Sorry, lass. I should have. But I've got a lot to think about.'

'Wat?'

He motioned to Ah Gip. 'You dooa out, heya, savvy?' and bolted the door after her. May-may knelt beside the pot and stirred it with a chopstick.

'We've got to leave at three o'clock,' Struan said. 'Say you wanted to stay in the Settlement until tomorrow, what would you do?'

'Hide,' she said immediately. 'In a – how you say – a small up room near the roof.'

'Attic?'

'Yes. Attic. Why you want to stay?'

'Do you think they'll search the factory when we've left?'

'Why stay? Very unwise to stay.'

'Do you think the bannermen will count us as we leave?'

'Those godrotting scum canna count.' She hawked noisily and spat in the fire.

'Will you na spit!'

'I tell you many times, Tai-Pan, it is important, wise Chinese custom,' she answered. 'There is poisons in the throat always. You become very sick if you dinna expectorate it. It is very wise to expectorate it. The louder the hawk, the more the spit-poison god is frightened.'

'That's nonsense, and it's a disgusting habit.'

'Ayee, yah,' she said impatiently. 'Do you na understand English? Sometimes I wonder why I trouble to explain all so many civilizationed Chinese wisdoms to you. Wat for should we hide here? It is dangerous na to go with the others. It will be dangerous badly if the bannermen see me. We will need protections. Why should we hide?'

He told her about the lorcha. And about the bullion.

'You must trust me very much,' she said very seriously.

'Aye.'

'What must you give Jin-qua in returns?'

'Business concessions.'

'Of course. But what else?'

'Just business concessions.'

There was a silence.

'Jin-qua is a clever man. He would na want just business concessions,' she mused. 'Wat concessions I would ask if I am Jin-qua! To anything you must agree. Anything.'

'What would you want?'

She stared at the flames and wondered what Struan would say if he knew that she was Jin-qua's granddaughter – second daughter of his eldest son How-qua's fifth wife. And she wondered why she had been forbidden to tell Struan – on pain of the removal of her name from the ancestral scrolls for ever. Strange, she told herself, and shuddered at the thought of being cast out of the family, for it meant that not only she but her offspring and their offspring and theirs for ever would be lost from the mainstream, and therefore deprived of the protective mutual help that was the single rock of Chinese society. A perpetual rock. The only real thing of value that five thousand years of civilization and experimenting had taught was safe and worthwhile. The family.

And she wondered why, in truth, she had been given to Struan.

'Second daughter of fifth mother,' her father had said on her fifteenth birthday. 'My illustrious father has conceived a great honour for you. You are to be given to the Tai-Pan of the barbarians.'

She had been terrified. She had never seen a barbarian and believed them to be unclean, loathsome cannibals. She had wept and begged for mercy, and then, secretly, she had been shown Struan when he was with Jin-qua. The giant Struan had frightened her but she had seen that he was not an ape. Even so, she had still begged to be married to a Chinese.

But her father had been adamant and had given her a choice: 'Obey, or leave this house and be cast out for ever.'

So she had gone to Macao and into Struan's house with instructions to please him. To learn the barbarian tongue. And to teach Struan things Chinese without his knowing he was being taught.

Once a year Jin-qua and her father would send someone to her to learn her progress and to bring news of the family.

Very strange, May-may thought. Certainly I wasn't sent as spy, but to be Struan's concubine. And certainly neither Father nor Grandfather would do such a thing lightly – not with their own bloodline. Was I not Jin-qua's favourite granddaughter?

'So much bullion,' she said, avoiding his question. 'So much is terrifical big temptation. Huge. All in one place – just one risk, attack, or theft, and twenty, forty generations would be safe.' How foolish I was to be afraid of the Tai-Pan. He is a man like any other and my lord. Very much man. And I will be Tai-tai soon. At long last. And I will have face at long last.

She bowed deeply. 'I'm honoured you trust me. I will bless your joss,

Tai-Pan, for ever. You do me huge honour and give me so much face. For anyone would consider how to steal it. Anyone.'

'How would you go about that?'

'Send Ah Gip to the Hoppo,' she said at once and went back to stirring the pot. 'For a guarantee fifty per cent he disregard even the emperor. He would allow you to stay, secretly if you wish, until lorcha arrived. When he made sure it was right lorcha, he would let you go aboard secretly and intercept downriver. And cut your throat. But then he would cheat me out of my share and I'd have to be his woman. Dirty turtledung! Na for all the tea in China, na that pig fornicator. He has dirty tricks. You know that he's almost impotent?'

'What?' Struan said, not really listening to her.

'It's common knowledge,' she said. She tasted the stew daintily and added a little soya sauce. 'He has to have two girls at the same time. One has to play with him while the other works. Then, too, he's so small that he fits things on himself, enormous things. Then, too, he likes to sleep with ducks.'

'Will you na talk such drivel!'

'What's "drivel" mean?' May-may asked.

'Nonsense.'

'Huh, that's na nonsense. Everyone knows.' She tossed her head prettily and the long plume of hair danced. 'I dinna understand you at all, Tai-Pan. You are shock when I tell you about ordinary things. Many people use things to improve sex. Very important to improve if you can. Eat right food, use right medicines. If you're small, ayee yah, not bad to improve your joss and give your girl more pleasure. But na like that dirty pig! He does it just to hurt.'

'Will you na stop it, woman!'

She stopped stirring and looked at him. A tiny frown crossed her face. 'Are all European like you, Tai-Pan? Na like to talk open about man-woman things, heya?'

'Certain things you dinna talk about, and that's the end of it.'

She shook her head. 'That's wrong. It's good to talk. How else can one improve? Man is man and woman woman. You dinna get shock about food! Why so crazy, eh? Sex is food, never mind.' Her eyes crinkled mischievously, and she looked him up and down. 'Heya, all Mass'er dooa jig-jig like youa all same can, heya?'

'Are all Chinese girls like you, heya?'

'Yes,' she said calmly. 'Most. Like me but na so good. I hope.' She laughed. 'I think you must be very special. I'm special too.'

'And modest.'

'A pox on that sort of modest. I'm honest, Tai-Pan. Chinese are honest. Why for should I not appreciate me? And you. I enjoy you, like you me. Stupid to pretend na.' She peered into the pot, and took a piece of meat with the chopsticks and tasted it. Then she took the pot off the fire and put it near enough to the flames to keep it warm. She opened the door and whispered to Ah Gip. Ah Gip plodded away. May-may went back to the fire.

'Where's she gone?'

'To find us place to hide.'

'I'll do that.'

'In this she would be better. First we eat, then you decide about Brock.'

'What about him?'

'He will na let you hide and stay easily, heya?'

'I've already decided what to do about him.' Struan's face crinkled with the breadth of his smile. 'You're very, very special, May-may.'

'Special enough for you to make me Tai-tai? Your Supreme Lady, according to your custom?'

'I'll decide about that after I've accomplished three things.'

'Wat three things?'

'The first is to get the bullion safe into *China Cloud*.'

'Next?'

'The second is to make Hong Kong absolutely safe.'

'The last?'

'I'm na sure. You'll have to be patient on that one.'

'I will help you with the first two. The last I dinna ken. I am Chinese. The Chinese are very patient. But I am also a woman.'

'Aye,' he said, after a long moment.

VIII

Struan was in his private office on the ground floor, writing a dispatch to Robb. It was almost two o'clock. Outside the traders and their clerks and coolies and servants were carrying possessions from their factories to their lorchas. The Hoppo had relaxed the order withdrawing all the servants. Servants and coolies were to be allowed until the Hour of the Monkey – three o'clock – the time by which the Settlement was to be abandoned. Bannermen were still in the square preventing access to the American factory.

Struan finished the letter, affixed his special chop and sealed it with wax and signet ring. He had told Robb not to worry, that he would bring good news to Hong Kong, and that if he was late Robb should go to the land sale and buy all the land they had long ago decided upon. And buy the knoll, whatever the cost. Whatever Brock bid, Robb was to bid one dollar more.

Now Struan sat back and rubbed the fatigue out of his eyes and began to recheck his plan, trying to find the holes in it. Like all plans that involved the reactions of others, there always had to be a measure of joss. But he felt that the weathervane of his joss had backed to the old quarter, where he was always guarded and things happened as he wanted them to happen.

The tall grandfather clock chimed twice. Struan got up from the carved teak desk and joined the servants, who were streaming in and out of the factory under the supervision of the Portuguese clerks.

'We're almost finished, Mr Struan,' Manoel de Vargas said. He was an elderly, grey-haired, sallow Portuguese of great dignity. He had been with The Noble House for eleven years and was chief clerk. Before this he had had his own company with its headquarters in Macao, but he had been unable to compete with the British and American traders. He bore them no grudge. It is the will of God, he had said without rancour, and had gathered his wife and his children around him and had gone to Mass and had thanked the Madonna for all their blessings. He was like

146

the vast majority of Portuguese – faithful, calm, content and unhurried. 'We can go as soon as you say,' he said tiredly.

'Are you feeling all right, Vargas?'

'A little agued, senhor. But once we get settled, I will be well once more.' Vargas shook his head. 'Bad to move and to move and to move.' He spoke sharply in Cantonese to a coolie staggering past under the weight of ledgers, and pointed to a lorcha.

'That's the last of the books, Mr Struan.'

'Good.'

'This is a sad day, sad. Many bad rumours. Some stupid.'

'What?'

'That we will all be intercepted on our way and killed. That Macao is to be terminated, and we're to be thrown out of the Orient once and for all. And the usual rumours that we'll be back in a month and trade will be better than ever. There's even a rumour that there's forty lacs of bullion in Canton.'

Struan kept the smile on his face. 'There are na that many lacs in Kwangtung Province!'

'Of course. Stupid, but it is amusing to relate. The bullion's supposed to have been collected by the Co-hong as a gift to placate the emperor.'

'Drivel.'

'Of course, drivel. No one would dare to have so much in one place. All the bandits in China would fall on it.'

'Take this letter and deliver it into Mr Robb's hands. As soon as possible,' Struan said. 'Then go immediately to Macao. I want you to organize teams of building workmen. I want them on Hong Kong Island two weeks from today. Five hundred men.'

'Yes, senhor.' Vargas sighed and wondered how long he would have to keep up the pretence. We all know The Noble House is finished. Five hundred men? Why do we need men when there is no money to buy land? 'It will be difficult, senhor.'

'In two weeks,' Struan repeated.

'It will be difficult to find good workmen,' Vargas said, politely. 'All the traders will be competing for their services – and the emperor's edict has revoked the treaty. Perhaps they will not agree to work on Hong Kong.'

'Good wages will change their minds. I want five hundred men. The best. Pay double wages if necessary.'

'Yes, senhor.'

'If we've nae money to pay for them,' Struan added with a grim smile, 'Brock will pay you well. There's nae need to worry.'

'I am not worried about my own labours,' Vargas said with great dignity, 'but I am worried about the safety of the house. I would not wish The Noble House to cease.'

'Aye, I know. You've served me well, Vargas, and I appreciate it. You take all the clerks with you now. I'll go with Mauss and my men.'

'Shall I lock up, or will you, senhor?'

'You do that when all your clerks are aboard.'

'Very well. Go with God, senhor.'

'And you, Vargas.'

Struan walked across the square. Around him men were hurrying to make last-minute additions to the cargoes of the heavily laden lorchas that lay the length of the wharf. Farther up the wharf he saw Brock and Gorth profanely exhorting their sailors and clerks. Some of the traders had already left, and he waved cheerily to a lorcha as it headed downstream. Across the river, the boat people were watching the exodus, clamouring to offer their sampans for tows to midstream, since the direction of the wind made departure from the dock awkward.

Struan's lorcha was two-masted, forty feet long, and commodious. Mauss was already on the poop.

'All squared away, Tai-Pan. There's a rumour that the Hoppo seized Ti-sen's house. Fifty lacs of silver bullion was in it.'

'So?'

'Nothing, Tai-Pan. A rumour, *hein*?' Mauss looked tired. 'All my converts have disappeared.'

'They'll be back, dinna worry. And there'll be plenty to convert on Hong Kong,' Struan said, feeling sorry for him.

'Hong Kong is our only hope, isn't it?'

'Aye.' Struan headed up the wharf. He saw a tall coolie emerge from the American factory and join the throng in the square. He changed direction.

'Heya, wat you Yankee dooa can?' he called out to the coolie.

'Damn you, Tai-Pan,' Cooper said from under the coolie hat. 'Is my disguise so bad?'

'It's your height, laddie.'

'Just wanted to wish you Godspeed. Don't know when I'll see you again. You've the thirty days, of course.'

'But you dinna think they're of value?'

'I'll find that out in thirty-odd days, won't I?'

'In the meantime, buy eight million pounds of tea for us.'

'With what, Tai-Pan?'

148

'What do you usually pay for tea with?'

'We're your agents, certainly. For the next thirty days. But I can't buy for you without bullion.'

'Did you sell all your cotton?'

'Not yet.'

'You better sell fast, lad.'

'Why?'

'Perhaps the bottom's out of the market.'

'If it is, there goes *Independence*.'

'That'd be a pity, would it na?'

'I hope you settle with Brock somehow. And build your *Independent Cloud*. I want the satisfaction of beating you myself.'

'Stand in the line, lad,' Struan said good-naturedly. 'Be prepared to buy heavily and fast. I'll send word.'

'It won't be the same without you, Tai-Pan. If you go, we'll all lose a little.'

'Perhaps I won't go after all.'

'Half of me wants you out. You, more than any, have had a too huge slice of the market, too long. It's time for free seas.'

'Free for American ships?'

'And others. But not on British terms.'

'We'll always rule the seas, lad. We have to. You're an agricultural country. We're industrialists. We need the seas.'

'One day we'll take the seas.'

'By that time perhaps we will na need the seas because we'll rule the skies.'

Cooper chuckled. 'Don't forget about our bet.'

'That reminds me. I got a letter from Aristotle a few days ago. He asked for a loan to tide him over because "that delectable commission has to wait till summer because she suffers from goose pimples." We've plenty of time to run her to earth – or would it be to bed?'

'Can't be Shevaun. She's got ice for blood.'

'Did she say nay to you again?'

'Yes. Put in a good word for me, huh?'

'I'll na get in the middle of that negotiation!'

Over Struan's shoulder Cooper could see Brock and Gorth approaching. 'If the Brocks never reached Hong Kong, you'd get the time you need. Wouldn't you?'

'Are you suggestin' a wee bit o' murder?'

'That wouldn't be a little. That would be very much, Tai-Pan. Afternoon, Mr Brock.'

'I thort it were thee, Mr Cooper,' Brock said breezily. 'Nice of thee to see us'n off.' Then, to Struan, 'Thee be off now?'

'Aye. I'll show Gorth the stern of my ship all the way to Whampoa. Then, in *China Cloud*, all the way to Hong Kong. As usual.'

'The only stern you'll show is yors in four days when you be tossed into debtors' prison, where you belong,' Gorth said thickly.

'All the way to Hong Kong, Gorth. But there's nae point in having a race with you. As a seaman you're na fit to row a boat.'

'I be better'n you, by God.'

'If it were na for your father, you'd be the laughingstock of Asia.'

'By God, you son of—'

'Hold yor tongue!' Brock barked. He knew Struan would be delighted to be called son of a bitch publicly by Gorth, for then he could challenge him to a duel. 'Why bait the lad, eh?'

'Na baiting him, Tyler. Just stating a fact. You better teach him some manners as well as seamanship.'

Brock held himself in check. Gorth was no match for Struan yet. Yet. In a year or two, when he be more cunning, that be different. But not now, by God. An' it baint the English way to kick yor enemy in the gut when he be lying on his back, helpless. Like godrotting Struan. 'Friendly wager. A hundred guineas says my boy can beat thee. First to touch the flagpole at Hong Kong.'

'Twenty thousand guineas. His money, not yours,' Struan said, his eyes taunting Gorth.

'How you going to pay, Tai-Pan?' Gorth said contemptuously, and Brock boiled at his son's stupidity.

'He doan mean that other'n as a joke, Dirk,' Brock said quickly. 'Twenty thousand it is.'

'Aye, a joke it is. If you say so, Tyler.' Struan was outwardly cold but inwardly jubilant. They had swallowed the bait! Now Gorth and Brock would hurry to Hong Kong – twenty thousand guineas was a tidy fortune, but nothing against forty lacs safe in *China Cloud*. Brock was safely out of the way. A dangerous game though. Gorth nearly went too far and then blood would have been spilled. Too easy to kill Gorth.

He put out his hand to Cooper. 'I'm holding you to the thirty days.' They shook. Then Struan glanced at Gorth. 'The flagpole at Hong Kong! Good voyage, Tyler!' and he hared for his lorcha, which had already cast off and was being nosed into midstream.

He leaped on to the gunnel and turned back and waved mockingly. Then he disappeared belowdecks.

'Excuse us'n, eh, Mr Cooper?' Brock said, taking Gorth by the arm. 'We be in touch!'

He shoved Gorth towards their lorcha. On the poop deck he pushed him violently against the gunnel. 'You cursed halfwit poxwobbled scupper rat! You want your godrotting troat cut from godrotting ear to ear? You call a man son of a bitch in these waters, you got to fight. You call him that, he's the right to kill thee!' He backhanded Gorth across the face, and blood trickled from Gorth's mouth. 'I tell thee fifty times to watch that devil. If I watch he, by God, thee better!'

'I can kill him, Da', I know I can!'

'I tell thee fifty times, act perlite to him. He be waiting to cut thee up, fool. An' he can. You baint fighting that devil but once! Understand?'

'Yes.' Gorth felt the blood in his mouth, and the taste increased his rage.

'Next time I let thee get deaded, fool. An' another thing. Never challenge a man like 'im on a gamblin' debt. Nor kick him in the groin when he be beat an' helpless. That not be the code!'

'Pox on the code!'

Brock backhanded him again. 'The Brocks live by the code. Open. Man t'man. Go again' it, and thee be out of Brock and Sons!'

Gorth wiped the blood off his mouth.

'Doan hit me again, Da'!'

Brock felt the violent edge to his son's voice, and his face tightened.

'Doan do it, Da'. By the Lord Jesus Christ, I'll hit you back,' Gorth said, his weight on both legs, fists like granite. 'You hit me a last time. You hit me again and I won't stop. By the Lord Jesus, you hit me a last time!'

The veins in Brock's throat were black and throbbing as he squared up to his son, no longer a son but an enemy. No, not an enemy. Only a son who was no longer a youth. A son who had challenged his father as all sons challenge all fathers. Brock knew and Gorth knew that if they fought, blood would be spilled and there would be a casting out. Neither wanted a casting out, but if it came, both father and son knew they would be blood enemies.

Brock hated Gorth for making him feel his age. And loved him for standing up to him when he knew, beyond doubt, that he was more cunning in the art of death fighting than Gorth would ever be.

'Thee best get to Hong Kong.'

Gorth unclenched his fists with an effort. 'Yes,' he said hoarsely. 'But thee'd best settle with that bastard right smartly, if thee've a mind – or next time I do it my own way.' He glared at the bosun. 'What the hell're you scum waiting for? Get under way!'

He wiped the blood off his chin and spat overboard. But his heart was still pumping heavily and he was sorry that there had not been a third blow. I were ready, by God, an' I could've beat him – like I can beat that green-eyed son of a bitch. I know I can.

'Which course should we follow, Da'?' he asked, for there were many different ways to go. The approaches to Canton on the river were a maze of islands large and small, and multitudinous waterways.

'Thee got thyself into this mess. Chart thy own course.' Brock walked to the port gunnel. He felt old and very tired. He was remembering his own father who was an ironworker, and how as a boy he had had to take the beatings and guidance and watch his temper and do what he was told until the day he was fifteen and the blood filled his eyes. And when his sight had cleared, he saw that he was standing over his father's inert body.

Lord above, he thought, that were near. I be glad I doan have to fight him proper. I doan want to lose my son.

'Doan thee take after Dirk Struan, Gorth,' he said, his voice not unkind.

Gorth said nothing. Brock rubbed the socket of his eye and replaced the patch. He watched Struan's lorcha. It was already in midstream, Struan nowhere in sight. The sampan shoved the bow around, then scuttled neatly to the other side. A tangle of Struan's men leaned on the ropes and chanteyed the sails aloft. The sampan poled back towards Vargas' lorcha.

Baint like Dirk to leave so fast, Brock reflected. Baint right at all. He glanced back at the wharf and saw that Vargas and all Struan's clerks were still there, their lorcha still tied up. Now, that baint like Dirk. To leave afore his clerks. Dirk be strange about things like that. Yus.

Struan was hiding in the cabin of the sampan. As the boat nosed around the bow of Vargas' lorcha, Struan rammed the coolie hat low on his head and pulled the padded Chinese jacket tighter around him. The sampan owner and his family did not appear to notice him. They had been well paid not to hear or to see.

The plan he had made with Mauss was the safest under the circumstances. He had told Mauss to hurry to *China Cloud*, which lay at anchor off Whampoa Island thirteen miles away; to take the shorter northern passage there and then order Captain Orlov to cram on all sail and rush downstream to the end of the island; to change course there and cut around it and head back upstream by the south channel towards Canton again; he had warned that it was of paramount importance that this manoeuvre not be observed by Brock. Struan, meanwhile, would wait for the bullion lorcha and then take the long route and sneak by devious waterways to the south side of the island where they would rendezvous. By the Marble Pagoda. The pagoda was two hundred feet high and easily seen.

'But why, Tai-Pan?' Mauss had said. 'It's dangerous. Why all the risk, *hein*?'

'Just be there, Wolfgang,' he had said.

When the sampan reached the wharf, Struan picked up some panniers that he had had prepared, and hurried through the throng to the garden gate. No one paid any attention to him. Once inside, he tossed the panniers aside, raced to the dining-room window and peered carefully through the curtains.

His lorcha was well away. Brock was in mid-channel, gaining way, the sails billowing as the breeze caught them. Gorth stood on the poop and Struan could faintly hear his obscenities. Brock was at the port gunnel, staring downstream. Vargas had just finished checking the clerks and was walking back towards the garden.

Struan ducked out of the dining-room and ran quietly upstairs. From the landing he saw Vargas come into the foyer, make a final check and leave. Struan heard the key turn in the door. He relaxed, and climbed a narrow staircase to the loft. He eased his way past old packing cases and walked cautiously towards the front of the building.

'Hello, Tai-Pan,' May-may said. She was dressed in her verminous Hoklo trousers and padded jacket, but she had not dirtied her face. She was kneeling on a cushion behind some packing cases. Ah Gip got up and bowed and then squatted down again near the small bundle of clothes and cooking utensils. May-may indicated another cushion that was opposite her, and the backgammon board that was set up. 'We play, same stakes, heya?'

'Just a moment, lassie.'

There was a skylight in the loft and another in the front wall. Struan could scan the whole square clearly and safely. People were still milling and cursing and making last-minute changes. 'Did you notice me?'

'Oh yes, very,' she said. 'But we watch from top of you. Down level perhaps no one saw. Wat for did Brock hit his son, heya?'

'I did na know he did.'

'Yes. Two times. Wat for such blows! We laughed till we choke. The son almost hit back. I hope they fight – kill each other – then no money to pay back. I still think you fantastical crazy na just to pay pirate to assassination him.' She sat on the cushion, then knelt again with an oath.

'What's the matter?'

'My bum, she is still sore.'

'*It* is still sore,' he said.

'She. That was joke. Ayee yah, this time I beat you to hell and make back all my dolla.' She added innocently, 'How much I owe? Fourteen thousand?'

'You remember very well.'

He sat down and picked up the dice cup. 'Four games. Then sleep. We've a long night ahead.' He threw the dice and she cursed.

'Wat joss you have! Double six, double six, a pox on double six!' She threw the dice and equalled him and slammed the cup down and whooped, 'Good dear sweet double six!'

'Keep you voice down, or we will na play.'

'We're safe, Tai-Pan. Throw. My joss is good today!'

'Let's hope it's very good,' he said. 'And tomorrow.'

'Ayee yah tomorrow, Tai-Pan! Today. Today is what counts.' She threw again. Another double six. 'Dear sweet dice I adore you.' Then she frowned. 'What for does "adore" mean?'

'Love.'

'And "love"?'

Struan's eyes crinkled and he shook a finger at her. 'I'm na going to get into that argument again.' Once he had tried to explain what love meant. But there was no Chinese word for the European concept of love.

The grandfather clock began to sound eleven. Struan shifted wearily at his post beside the wall skylight. May-may was curled up asleep. Ah Gip slumped against a mildewed packing case. A few hours ago he had dropped off to sleep for a moment, but his dreams were bizarre and mixed with reality. He had been aboard *China Cloud*, lying crushed under a weight of bullion. Jin-qua had come into the room and eased the bullion off him, and had taken it all in exchange for a coffin and twenty golden guineas, and then he was no longer on his ship but ashore in the Great House on the knoll. Winifred brought him three eggs and he was eating breakfast and May-may had said, behind him, 'God's blood, how can you eat the unborn children of a hen?' He had turned around and seen that she was wearing no clothes and she was achingly beautiful. Winifred had said, 'Was Mother as beautiful without clothes on?' and he had replied, 'Yes, but in a different way,' and he had awakened suddenly.

Dreaming of his family had saddened him. I'll have to go home soon, he had thought. I dinna ken even where they're buried.

He stretched and watched the movement on the river, and thought about Ronalda and May-may. They're different, very different – were different. I loved them both equally. Ronalda would have enjoyed London and a fine mansion there and taking the waters in the season at Brighton or Bath. She'd have been a perfect hostess for all the dinners and balls. But now I'm alone.

Will I take May-may home with me? Perhaps. As Tai-tai? Impossible. Because that would cast me out from those I must use.

He stopped musing and concentrated on the square. It was deserted. Just before nightfall the bannermen had left. Now there was only the dull moonlight and blurred shadows, and this emptiness felt eerie and cruel to Struan.

He wanted to sleep. You canna sleep now, he told himself. Aye, but I'm tired.

He stood and stretched, and settled himself once more. The chimes rang the quarter-hour and then the half, and he decided to wake May-may and Ah Gip in a quarter of an hour. There's nae hurry, he thought. He did not allow himself to speculate about what would happen if the lorcha from Jin-qua did not arrive. His fingers were touching the four half coins in his pocket and he wondered again about Jin-qua. What favours and when?

He partially understood Jin-qua's motives now. Ti-sen's disgrace had clarified them. Obviously there would be war. Obviously the British would win it. Obviously trade would begin again. But never under the Eight Regulations. So the Co-hong would lose its monopoly and it would be every man for himself. Hence the thirty-year trade span: Jin-qua simply had been cementing his business relationship for the next three decades. That was the Chinese way, he thought: na to worry about immediate profit, but profit over years and years.

Aye, but what's really in Jin-qua's mind? Why buy land in Hong Kong? Why train a son in 'barbarian' ways and to what calculated end? And what will the four favours be? And now that you've agreed and promised, how are you going to implement them? How can you ensure that Robb and Culum fulfil the bargain?

Struan began to contemplate that. He mulled a dozen possibilities before arriving at an answer. He hated what he knew he had to do. Then, having decided, he turned his thoughts to other problems.

What to do about Brock? And Gorth? For a moment on the wharf he

155

had been ready to go after Gorth. One more word, and he would have had to challenge him openly. Honour would have forced – and allowed – him to humble Gorth. By a knife in the gut. Or by the lash.

And Culum. What's he been up to? Why hasn't he written? Aye, and Robb, too. And what mischief's Longstaff done?

The chimes sounded eleven o'clock. Struan awakened May-may. She yawned and stretched luxuriously, like a cat. Ah Gip had been up the instant Struan had moved, and she was already collecting the bundles.

'The lorcha is come?' May-may asked.

'Nay. But we can move downstairs and be ready.'

May-may whispered to Ah Gip, who unpinned May-may's hair and brushed it vigorously. May-may closed her eyes and enjoyed it. Then Ah Gip braided the hair as a Hoklo would, and bound it with a piece of red ribbon and let it fall down her back.

May-may rubbed her hands in the dust and dirtied her face. 'Wat I do for you, Tai-Pan! This filth dirt will destroy the perfection of beauty skin. I will need much bullion to repair. How much, heya?'

'Get along with you!'

He led the way carefully downstairs into the dining-room and motioning them to sit patiently, went to the window. The square was still deserted. There were oil lights in the massed sampans of the floating villages. Dogs barked from time to time and fire-crackers sounded and quarrelling voices were raised and hushed, and sometimes there were happy voices – and the ever-present *clack-clack* of mahjongg tiles being banged on to a deck or a table and the chattering singsong. Smoke rose from cooking fires. Junks and lorchas and sampans filled the estuary. Everything – the sounds and the smells and sights – seemed normal to Struan. Except the emptiness of the square – he had presumed that the square would be populated. Now they had to cross a deserted expanse, and in the moonlight they could be seen for hundreds of yards.

The clock chimed midnight.

He waited and watched and waited.

The minutes became long and after an eternity the chimes sounded the quarter-hour. Then the half-hour.

'May be the lorcha is south,' May-may said, stifling a yawn.

'Aye. We'll wait another half an hour, then we'll look.'

Almost at the hour he saw the two lanterns of a lorcha coming downstream. The boat was too far away for him to see the red-painted eye and he held his breath and waited. The lorcha was sailing gently but was sluggish and low in the water. This was a favourable sign to him because the bullion would weigh many tons. After the boat passed the north end of the Settlement, it changed course and crept into the wharf. Two of the Chinese crew jumped ashore with hawsers and tied up. To his relief, another Chinese went to the lantern on the prow, blew it out and lit it again according to the prearranged signal.

Struan searched the half-darkness for peril. He sensed none. He checked the priming of his pistols and stuck them in his belt. 'Follow me, quickly now!'

Silently he went to the front door and unlocked it and guided them cautiously through the garden. He opened the gate and they hastened across the square. Struan felt as though all Canton was watching them. Reaching the lorcha, he saw the red-painted eye and recognized on the poop the man who had led him to Jin-qua. He helped May-may aboard. Ah Gip leaped aboard easily.

'Wat for two cow chillo, heya? No can!' the man said.

'Your name wat can?' Struan asked.

'Wung, heya!'

'Cow chillo my. Cast off, Wung!'

Wung noticed May-may's tiny feet and his eyes narrowed. He could not see May-may's face, for she kept the sampan hat low over her forehead. Struan did not like the way Wung hesitated or the way he looked at May-may. 'Cast off!' he said curtly, and bunched a fist. Wung rapped an order. The hawsers were cast off and the lorcha slipped away from the wharf. Struan took May-may and Ah Gip down the gangway to the lower deck. He turned aft where the main cabin would be and opened the door. Inside were five Chinese. He motioned them out. Reluctantly they got up and left, looking May-may up and down. They too, noticed her feet.

The cabin was tiny with four bunks and a crude table and benches. It smelled of hemp and rotting fish. Wung was standing at the door of the cabin scrutinizing May-may.

'Wat for cow chillo? No can.'

Struan paid no attention to him. 'May-may – you locka doora, heya? Only open doora my knock, savvy?'

'Savvy, Mass'er.'

Struan went to the door and beckoned Wung outside. He heard the bolt lock behind them, and he said, 'Go hold!'

Wung took him into the hold. The forty crates were stacked in two neat rows against the sides of the ship, with a wide passage-way between them.

'Wat in box, heya?' Struan asked.

157

Wung seemed perplexed. 'Wat for you, saya, heya? All same Mass'er Jin-qua say.'

'How muchee men knowa?'

'My only! All knowa, ayee yah!' Wung said, drawing his finger across his throat.

Struan grunted. 'Guard doora.' He selected a crate at random and opened it with a crowbar. He stared down at the bullion, then lifted one of the silver bricks from the top layer. He sensed Wung's tension and it heightened his own. He replaced the brick and the top of the crate.

'Wat for cow chillo, heya?' Wung said.

'Cow chillo my. Finish.' Struan made sure the lid was tight again. Wung stuck his thumbs in the belt of his ragged pants. 'Chow? Can?'

'Can.'

Struan went on deck and checked the rigging and the sails. A four-pound cannon was in the bow and another in the stern. He made sure that both were loaded and primed, and that the powder keg was full and the powder dry. Grape and shot were ready at hand. He ordered Wung to assemble the crew and picked up a belaying pin. There were eight men aboard.

'You saya,' he said to Wung, 'all knives, all boom-boom, on deck plenty quick-quick.'

'Ayee yah, no can,' Wung protested. 'Plenty pirate in river. Plenty—'

Struan's fist caught him in the throat and slammed him against the gunnel. The crew chattered angrily and prepared to rush Struan, but the raised belaying pin discouraged them.

'All knives, all boom-boom on deck, plenty quick,' Struan repeated, his voice steely.

Wung hauled himself up weakly and muttered something in Cantonese. After an ominous silence he threw his knife on the deck, and, grudgingly, the others followed suit. Struan told him to gather up the knives and tie them in a piece of sacking that was on the deck. Next he made the crew turn around and he began to search them. He found a small pistol on the third man, and with the butt end smashed the man across the side of the head. Four more knives clattered to the deck from other men, and out of the corner of his eye Struan saw Wung drop a small fighting hatchet overboard.

After he had searched the men, he ordered them to stay on deck and taking the weapons with him, he carefully searched the rest of the ship. There was no one concealed below decks. He found a cache of four muskets, six swords, four bows and arrows and three fighting irons, behind some crates, and carried them into the cabin.

158

'Heya, May-may, youa heara what topside can?' he whispered.

'Yes,' she said, as softly. 'You say we can talk English in front of Ah Gip safely. You dinna want to now?'

'I forgot. Habit. Nay, lass, it's all right.'

'Why hit Wung? He's Jin-qua's trusted, no?'

'The cargo's the lodestone of this voyage.'

' "Lodestone"?'

'Magnet. Compass needle.'

'Oh, I understand.' May-may sat on the bunk, her nostrils quivering from the stench of rotting fish. 'I be very sick if I stay here. Can I be on deck?'

'Wait till we're clear of Canton. You're safer here. Much safer.'

'How long before we meet *China Cloud*?'

'A little after first light – if Wolfgang makes no mistakes on the rendezvous.'

'Is that possible?'

'With this cargo, anything's possible.' Struan picked up one of the muskets. 'Do you know how to use this?'

'Wat for should I shoot gunses? Me, I am a civilizationed fright-filled old woman – of great beauty I agree, but na gunses.'

He showed her. 'If anyone but me comes into the cabin, kill him.' He went back on deck, carrying another musket.

The lorcha was in mid-channel now, under a soaring moon, ponderous and low in the water and making about four knots. They were still passing the suburbs of Canton, and both sides of the river were thickly lined with floating villages. From time to time they passed boats and sampans and junks beating upstream. The river here was half a mile wide, and there were boats of all sizes ahead and astern going downstream.

The sky told Struan that the weather would be fair, but the tang on the wind felt smooth and dry and dewless, without body. He knew that this wind would lessen and further reduce their speed. But he was not worried; he had made the journey so many times that he knew the shoals and the rivers and tributaries and checkpoints intimately.

The approach to Canton was a maze of waterways and islands, large and small, covering an area of five miles by twenty miles. There were many different ways to come upstream. And to go downstream.

Struan was happy to be afloat again. And happy that their journey to the Marble Pagoda had begun. He swayed easily to the motion of the lorcha. Wung was near the helmsman, and the crew was scattered around the deck, malevolent and sullen. Struan saw that the prow lookout was in place.

Ahead, half a mile, the river forked around an island. At the approaches to the fork was a shoal to be avoided. Struan said nothing and waited. He heard Wung speak to the helmsman, who put his tiller over and swerved the lorcha safely away from the shoal. Good, Struan thought. At least Wung knew part of the waterways. He was anxious to see what route Wung would take around the island. Both routes were good but the north was better than the south. The lorcha held its course and headed into the north channel. Struan turned and shook his head and pointed to the south channel just in case Wung had arranged an ambush.

The helmsman glanced at Wung for confirmation. Struan made only the slightest movement towards the helmsman. The helm was swung over quickly and the sails flapped momentarily and the lorcha came about on to the new course.

'Wat for go that way, heya? Wat for hit my? Plenty bad. Plenty.' Wung moved over to the gunnel and glared into the night.

The wind freshened slightly, and the lorcha increased speed as they moved into the south channel. At the limit of their tack, Struan motioned the helmsman to put his tiller over. The boat came about slowly, and then, on the new tack, the wind caught the flapping sails. The booms creaked across the deck and the boat lurched slightly and began to gain way once more.

He ordered the sails trimmed and they sailed smoothly for half an hour, part of the river traffic. Then out of the corner of his eye Struan saw a big lorcha bearing down on them swiftly from the windward. Brock was standing in the bow. Struan crouched and scurried over to the tiller and shoved the man aside. Wung and the helmsman were startled and began chattering excitedly, and all the crew watched Struan.

He swung the tiller hard to starboard and prayed that the lorcha would answer the helm quickly. He heard Brock's voice faintly – 'Starboard yor helm, right smartly!' – and he felt the wind scud from his sails. Struan slammed the tiller over to jib and reverse direction; but the lorcha did not respond, and Brock's lorcha drew alongside. He saw the grappling hooks catch and hold fast. He levelled a musket.

'Oh, it's thee, Dirk, by God!' Brock called out, feigning astonishment. He was leaning on the gunnel, a broad smile on his face.

'Grapples are an act of piracy, Brock!' Struan tossed his knife, haft first, to Wung. 'Chop grapples quick-quick!'

'Right you are, lad. Beg pardon for the grapples,' Brock said. 'I thort you be lorcha in need of a tow. Doan see thy flag aloft. Thee be ashamed of it maybe?'

Struan saw that Brock's crew was armed and at action stations. Gorth was on the poop deck beside a small swivel gun, and although the gun was not pointing at him, he knew it would be primed and ready to fire. 'Next time you grapple a ship of mine, I'll presume you're pirates and blow your head off.'

'Permission to come aboard, Dirk?'

'Aye.'

Brock slipped through the rigging of his ship and leaped aboard. Three men jumped up on the gunnel to follow him, but Struan levelled the musket and shouted, 'Hold there! Any of you come aboard without permission, I'll blow you to hell.'

The men stopped in their tracks.

'Quite right,' Brock said sardonically. 'That be the law of the sea. A captain invites who he likes and who he doan. Stay where thee be!'

Struan shoved Wung forward. 'Chop grapples!'

The frightened Chinese rushed forward and began to hack the ropes. Gorth swung the swivel gun and Struan aimed at him.

'Stand off, Gorth!' Brock said sharply.

The law of the sea was on Struan's side: grappling was an act of piracy. And coming aboard armed, without permission, was piracy, and of all the laws of England none was so zealously guarded or enforced as the laws of ships at sea and the powers of a captain afloat. For piracy there was only one punishment: hanging.

Wung cut the last of the lines and the boats began to drift apart. When Brock's lorcha was thirty feet away, Struan put down the musket and shouted. 'You come within fifty feet of me without permission, by God, I'll charge you with piracy!' Then he leaned against the gunnel. 'What's all this about, Tyler?'

'I could ask thee the same thing, Dirk,' Brock said easily. 'I seed thee snuck down in that there sampan yesterday.' His eye glittered in the light of the lantern. 'Then I seed thee, dressed right proper curious like a coolie and, glory be to God, thee went back into factory. Strange, says I. Maybe old Dirk's gone sick in the head. Or maybe old Dirk be needin' a hand to get safe out of Canton. So we sails downstream aways and then snuck back and anchors north o' the Settlement. Then we seed thee board this stinking craft. Thee an' two doxies.'

'What I do's my own affair.'

'Yus, that it be.'

Struan's mind was churning. He knew that Brock's lorcha was far swifter than his, that the crew was dangerous and well armed, and that he was no match for them alone. He cursed himself for being so confident and for not keeping watch.

But then you could na have seen Brock sneak upstream. How to put Brock to your advantage? Must be some way. He can easily run you down in the night, and even if you survive, there'd be little you could prove. Brock'd claim that it was an accident. Then, too. May-may can na swim.

'This old tub be low in water. Leaking, maybe? Or be it the weight of cargo?'

'What's on your mind, Tyler?'

'Rumours, lad. There was rumours all yester' morning. Afore we left. Rumours about Ti-sen's bullion. Did thee hear it?'

'There were dozens of rumours.'

'Yus. But they all sayed that there was a king's ransome o' bullion in Canton. I baint thinking about it. Till I seed thee go back. An' I thort that were very interestin'. After the twenty-thousand-guinea bet. Very interestin'. Then thee gets on a heavy lorcha like a thief in the night, an' head south by the wrong channel.' Brock stretched, then scratched his head vigorously. 'Old Jin-qua baint about, were he?'

'He's out of Canton, yes.'

'Old Jin-qua's yor dog. Leastways,' Brock said with a leer, 'he be yor man, eh?'

'Come to the point.'

'There be no rush, lad. No, by God!' He glanced at the prow of his lorcha. 'She be light in the nose, baint she?' Brock was alluding to the foot-square iron spike that jutted six feet out from the prow, just below the waterline. Struan had invented the ram many years ago as a simple method of gouging and sinking a ship. Brock and many of the China traders had adopted it.

'Aye. And we're heavy. But we're armed well enough.'

'So I seed. Aft cannon and bow cannon, but no swivels.' A taut silence. 'Five days an' thy notes be due. Right?'

'Aye.'

'Be thee ameeting them?'

'In five days you'll find out.'

'Forty or fifty lacs o' bullion be many tons o' silver.'

'I imagine they would.'

'I ask't Gorth. Now, wot would old Dirk do if he'd some bad joss? Gorth sayed, he'd try to change it. Yus, says I, but how? Borrow, says he. Ah, says I, borrow it is. But where? Then, Dirk lad, I thort of Jin-qua and Ti-sen. Ti-sen be finished, so it be Jin-qua.' He ruminated a moment. 'There be two women aboard. I be glad to give 'em passage to Whampoa or Macao. Wherever thee says.'

'They've passage already.'

'Yus. But this old wreck might sink. I doan like the thort of women drowning when it baint necessary.'

'We will na sink, Tyler.'

Brock stretched again and shouted to his lorcha for a long-boat. Then he shook his head sadly. 'Well, lad, I just wanted to offer the women passage. An' thee, of course. This tub feel very unseaworthy. Uncommon unseaworthy.'

'Plenty of pirates in these waters. If any ship comes too close, I'll use my cannon.'

'That be wise, Dirk. But if in the blackness o' night I suddenly be seein' a ship ahead and was taking avoiding action, an' that ship were so impertinent as to fire a cannon at me, well, lad, thee would do wot I would do. Presume they be pirate and blow her out of the water. Right?'

'If you were still alive after the first shot.'

'Yus. 'Tis a cruel world we be livin' in. Baint wise to fire cannon.'

The longboat pulled alongside.

'Thank'ee kindly, Dirk. Better fly thy flag while thee has one. Then godrotting mistakes be not happening. Beg pardon for the grapples. See thee in Hong Kong.'

Brock slipped over the side of the lorcha and stood in the longboat. He waved derisively and was rowed smartly away.

'Wat for One-Eye Mass'er wantshee?' Wung asked shakily. The crew was horror-struck by Brock's lorcha.

'Wat you think, heya? You dooa all same I say, not deaded can,' Struan said curtly. 'All sail, plenty quick-quick. Kill see-fire, heya!'

Taking heart, they doused the lanterns and fled before the wind.

When Brock swung aboard his own lorcha, he glared into the darkness. He could not pick Struan's lorcha out of the many that sailed, ghost-like, south downstream.

'You see her?' he asked Gorth.

'Yes, Da'.'

'I be going below. If thee happen to ram a lorcha, that be bad. Terrible bad.'

'The bullion's aboard?'

'Bullion, Gorth?' Brock said, with mock surprise. 'I doan know wot thee mean.' He lowered his voice. 'If thee needs help, call me. But no cannons, mind, not less he fires at us'n. We baint going to pirate him. We've plenty of enemies who'd be happy to mark us's pirates.'

'Sleep well, Da',' Gorth said.

For three hours Struan wove in and out of the river traffic, backing, then changing course, skirting the sandbanks dangerously, always making certain that there were boats between him and Brock's lorcha, which dogged his heels relentlessly. Now they were coming out of the south channel looping around the small island, into the main river once more. He knew that there would be more room to manoeuvre, but that would help Brock more than him.

Once in the south channel, Brock could bear off to windward nicely, then assault him when he was on the lee tack. Struan would have no wind to swing with and would be struck amidships. A direct or a glancing blow with the iron probe would gut him and sink him like a stone. Since his cannon were set solid into the prow and stern, he could not shift them amidships to protect himself. If he had his own crew it would be different; he would heave to until light, certain that his men could use their weapons to thwart any attempt to get close. But he was dubious about the Chinese crew, and about the ancient Chinese muskets which were likely to blow up in your face when you pulled the trigger. And Brock was right too. If he fired first in the darkness, Brock had the right to fire back. One deft broadside would blow them sky-high.

He looked up at the sky for the thousandth time. He desperately needed a sudden storm and rain, or clouds that would hide the moon. But there were no signs of storm or rain or cloud.

He peered aft and saw the lorcha gaining on them. It was a hundred yards astern and reaching to windward, tacking nearer to the wind than they, gaining way.

Struan ransacked his brains for a feasible plan. He knew he could escape easily if he lightened the ship by throwing the bullion overboard. Half a mile ahead the river was going to fork again, around Whampoa Island. If he took the north channel he would be safer, for most of the river traffic used that channel and he might be able to avoid a ram. But then he would never be able to escape long enough to sail the length of Whampoa and then around it to rendezvous with *China Cloud* far up the south side. He was forced to use the south channel.

He could see no way out of the trap. Dawn would come in two or three hours, and he would be lost. Somehow he had to escape in darkness and hide, and then slip down to his rendezvous. But how?

In the darkness ahead he could see the river fork, glinting silver, around Whampoa Island. Then he noticed Ah Gip at the gangway. She beckoned to him. Astern, Brock's lorcha was well away, still bearing up to windward, readying to run before the wind if he took the south channel, or still be to windward of him if he took the north channel.

He pointed at a small pagoda on the south bank, giving the helmsman a bearing. 'Savvy?'

'Savvy, Mass'er!'

'Savvy plenty good!' Struan drew his finger across his throat. He hastened below.

May-may was very sick. The stench of fish and the closeness of the cabin and the heeling of the boat had made her almost helpless with nausea. But she still held on to the musket. Struan picked her up and began to carry her on deck.

'No,' May-may said weakly. 'I ask for you because of Ah Gip.'

'What about her?'

'I send her forward, secret. To listen to crew.' May-may retched and held on. When her spasm had passed she said, 'She heard a man talking to another. They talked about the bullion. I think they all know.'

'Aye,' Struan said. 'I'm sure they do.' He patted Ah Gip's shoulder. 'You plenty big pay soon can.'

'Ayee yah,' Ah Gip said. 'Wat for pay, heya?'

'Brock is still on our heels?' May-may asked.

'Aye.'

'Maybe lightning bolt will strike him.'

'Aye maybe. Ah Gip, make chow Misse can! Soup. Savvy? Soup.'

Ah Gip nodded. 'Doan soup. Tea-ah gooda!'

'Soup!'

'Tea-ah.'

'Oh, never mind,' Struan said irritably, knowing that it would be tea however many times he said soup.

He carried May-may on deck and set her on the keg of powder. Wung and the helmsman and the crew did not look at her. But Struan knew they were acutely conscious of her, and she added to the tension on the deck. Then he remembered what she had said about a lightning bolt and this triggered a plan. His worry left him and he laughed aloud.

'Wat for ha-ha, hey'a?' May-may said, breathing the sea air deeply, her stomach beginning to settle.

'Think good way to chop One-Eye Mass'er,' Struan said. 'Heya,

Wung! You come my.' Struan gave May-may one of his pistols. 'Man near, kill, savvy?'

'Savvy, Mass'er!'

Struan motioned Wung to follow him, and went forward. As he walked easily along the deck the Chinese crew moved out of his way. He stopped at the fo'c'sle for a last check to make sure that Brock's lorcha was well clear and he hurried below, Wung close behind him. The crew's quarters consisted of a single large cabin the width of the boat, with bunks lining each side. There was a crude fireplace made of bricks, under an open hatch grill. A kettle swung over the wood coals that glowed dully. Bunches of herbs and dried mushrooms and dried and fresh fish and fresh vegetables and a sack of rice were nearby, and large and small earthenware jars.

He took the tops off the jars and sniffed the contents.

'Mass'er want chowa? Can.'

Struan shook his head. The first jar was soya. The next, ginger in syrup. Then ginseng root in vinegar and spices. There were cooking oils: one jar each of peanut oil and corn oil. Struan threw a few drops from both jars on the fire. The corn oil burned longer than the peanut oil.

'Wung, you fetch upside,' he said, pointing to the jar of corn oil.

'Wat for, heya?'

Struan hurried back on deck. The lorcha was nearing the point in the fork where they would have to turn for the north or the south channel. Struan pointed south.

'Wat for longa way, heya?' Wung asked, putting down the jar.

Struan looked at him and Wung backed a little. The helmsman had already swung the tiller over. They headed into the south fork. Brock's lorcha followed swiftly on the same tack. There were still many boats between the two lorchas and Struan was safe for a while.

'You stay,' he said to Wung. 'Heya, cow chillo. You stay. Use boom-boom all same.'

'Savvy, Mass'er,' May-may said. She was feeling much better.

Struan went into the main cabin and collected all the weapons and brought them back to the poop. He selected a musket, the two bows and arrows and a fighting iron, and threw the rest of the weapons overboard.

'Pirate can, no hav got boom-boom.' Wung muttered sullenly.

Struan picked up the fighting iron and swung it aimlessly. It was a linked iron whip, a deadly weapon at close-range – three foot-long iron shafts linked together, and at the very end a barbed iron ball. The short

166

iron haft fitted neatly into the hand and a protective leather thong slipped over the wrist.

'Pirate come, plenty dead-dead have got,' Struan said harshly.

Wung pointed furiously at Brock's lorcha. 'Him no stop can, heya?' He pointed at the nearest shore. 'There. We run shore – we safe!'

'Ayee-yah!' Struan turned his back contemptuously. He sat on the deck, the thong of the fighting iron attached to his wrist. The frightened crew watched, astonished, as Struan ripped the sleeve off his padded coolie jacket and tore it into strips and soaked the strips in the oil. He took one of the strips and carefully bound it round the head of an iron-tipped arrow. They backed away from him as he fitted the arrow to the bow, sighted along the deck at the mast and let fly. The arrow missed the mast, but buried itself in the fo'c'sle teak door. He pulled the arrow out with difficulty.

He went back and unbound the strip of padding and dunked it into the oil. Next he carefully sprinkled it with gunpowder, rebound it around the arrowhead and wrapped a second strip around the outside.

'Hola!' the stern lookout shouted. Brock's lorcha was gaining on them ominously.

Struan took the helm and conned the ship for a while. He slipped dangerously behind a ponderous junk and changed direction adroitly, so that when he was clear he was scudding on the opposite tack. Brock's lorcha turned quickly to intercept, but had to detour to avoid a convoy of junks heading north. Struan gave the helm to one of the crew and finished four arrows. Wung could contain himself no longer. 'Heya, Mass'er, wat can?'

'Get see-fire, heya?'

Muttering obscenities, Wung left and came back with a lantern. 'See-fire!'

Struan pantomimed dipping the arrow in the lantern flame and shooting the blazing shaft at the mainsail of Brock's lorcha.

'Plenty fire, heya? They stop, we go, heya?'

Wung's mouth dropped open. Then he burst into laughter. When he could talk he explained to the crew and they beamed at Struan. 'Youa plenty – plenty Tai-Pan! Ayeeeeyah!' Wung said.

'Plenty fantastical youa,' May-may said, joining in the laughter. 'Jig-jig One-Eye Mass'er plenty!'

'Hola!' the lookout called.

Brock's lorcha had negotiated the detour and was gaining on them. Struan took the tiller and began weaving and twisting through the traffic deeper and deeper into the south channel. Brock's lorcha closed in inexorably, always staying to windward. Struan knew that Brock was waiting for the traffic to clear before making his fatal stab. Struan was slightly more confident now. If the arrow hits the sail, he told himself, and if it does na go through, and if it stays alight while in flight and if the mains'l is dry enough to catch fire, and if they'll only wait for four miles before they make the first pass, and if my joss is good, then I can lose them. 'A pox on Brock!' he said.

The river traffic was thinning appreciably. Struan moved the tiller and beat to windward to get as near to the south side of the river as possible so that, when he turned again, the wind would be abaft the beam and he could run before it.

The south side of the river was shoal-ridden and hazardous. Tacking so far to windward left Struan dangerously open. Brock's lorcha was waiting to pounce. But Struan wanted him to attack now. It was time. He long ago had learned a basic law of survival: bring your enemy to battle only on your terms, never on his.

'Heya, May-may, go downside!'

'Watchee my. Can, never mind.'

Struan picked up the second musket and gave it to Ah Gip. 'Go downside, now!'

Both women went below.

'Wung-ah, get see-fire two.'

Wung brought a second lantern and Struan lit them both. He put the arrows ready and the two bows. Now we're committed, he told himself.

Brock's lorcha was two hundred yards away to windward. Gradually the river traffic disappeared. The two ships were alone. Instantly Brock's lorcha heeled over and hurled at him. Struan's crew scattered and ran to the far gunnel. They hung on to the rigging and prepared to jump overboard. Only Wung remained with Struan on the poop.

Struan could see Gorth clearly now, conning the lorcha, his crew at action stations. He searched the deck for Brock but could not see him and wondered what devilment he was up to. When the lorchas were fifty yards apart, Struan swung the tiller over and lumbered before the wind, shoving his stern at Gorth. Gorth was gaining rapidly, staying windward, and Struan knew that Gorth was much too smart to make the pass at his lee quarter. He motioned to Wung to take the tiller and hold the course. He readied the bow and arrows and ducked under the gunnel. He could see the masts of the lorcha bearing down on him swiftly. He stuck an arrowhead into the lantern's flame. The oil-soaked padding flared immediately, and he stood up and aimed. The lorcha was thirty yards away. The arrow travelled in a flaming arc amid warning shouts and hit the mainsail squarely. But the force of the impact extinguished the flame.

Gorth shouted to his crew and still bore down as a second arrow came at him. This one smashed into the mainsail, and held, showering sparks on the deck. The gunpowder that was inside the padding caught and exploded in flames. Involuntarily Gorth shoved the helm over and the boat peeled away, shuddering under the violence of the turn.

Struan had a third arrow ready, and as the lorcha went scudding past he fired it and saw it smash into the huge foresail. Flames began to lick the canvas. He gleefully swung the tiller over and bore away to windward and saw Brock charge up from belowdecks and shove Gorth aside, grab the tiller, and veer the boat around. Then Brock jerked the helm hard over and flung the boat at Struan's starboard amidships, cutting off his escape.

Struan had anticipated Brock's move, but his lorcha did not respond to the rudder and he knew that he was finished. He lit the last arrow and waited, his weight pressed against the tiller, praying for the lorcha to come around. Brock was standing on the poop, shouting at the crew who were desperately trying to douse the fire. A cluster of burning rigging fell near Brock but he paid it no attention, concentrating only on the point amidships starboard that he had selected for impact.

Struan aimed carefully and when the lorcha was fifteen yards away he shot. The arrow tore into the bulkhead beside Brock's head but Brock's lorcha held her course. Struan's boat started to come around, but it was too late. Struan felt a shuddering impact and heard the sickening crunch of splintered timber as the barb on Brock's lorcha sliced along the larboard side. Struan's boat reeled over and almost capsized, throwing Struan to the deck.

Showered with sparks of burning rigging and sails, Struan climbed to his feet. There were shrieks from the panic-stricken Chinese and raucous cries from Brock's men as both crews fought out of the fiery tangle. Amid the uproar Struan heard Brock shout, 'Beg thy pardon,' and the two boats separated, Brock's lorcha moving ahead, its sails aflame. Struan's boat righted herself, heeled drunkenly to starboard, rolled back and hung upright, listing dangerously to port.

Struan seized the tiller and shoved it over with all his might. The lorcha obeyed sluggishly, and when the wind caught the sails, Struan headed for shore, hoping frantically that he could beach her before she sank.

He could see that both of Brock's sails were on fire. He knew that they would have to be cut adrift and then replaced. Suddenly he noticed that his deck was angled ten degrees to port – to the *opposite* side of impact. He struggled up the sloping deck and stared over the side at the huge gash that had been ripped open. The bottom of the gash was only an inch under the waterline and Struan realized that the shock of impact had shifted the bullion crates across the hold. The weight of the bullion was keeping the boat at this permanent list.

He yelled at Wung to man the tiller and hold it on the same course.

Then he picked up the fighting iron and scrambled forward and, whirling the fighting iron, herded several of the crew below. En route to the hold he glimpsed May-may and Ah Gip, unhurt but shaken, in the wreck of the main cabin.

'Go upside! Hold boom-boom!'

The hold was a shambles. The crates were shattered and silver bricks were strewn everywhere. The unbroken crates were jammed against the port side. Water was pouring in through the gash. The crew turned, at bay, but he drove them deeper into the hold and made them douse the small fires created by the scattered coals.

Swearing and gesturing, he showed them that he wanted the crates shoved and stacked farther to port. Ankle deep in water, the Chinese were terrified of drowning but more terrified of the slashing iron whip, and they did as Struan ordered. The lorcha heeled perilously, scream-ing, and the gash inched out of the water. Struan fetched the spare mizzen and began to cram the canvas into the torn side of the vessel, using a few of the silver bricks as wedges.

'God's blood!' he roared. 'Quick-quick!'

The crew leaped to help, and soon the gash was sealed against the water. Struan motioned the crew to pick up the spare mainsail, and drove them back on deck.

May-may and Ah Gip were shaken but unharmed. May-may still grasped the pistol, Ah Gip the musket. Wung, paralysed with fright, was holding the course. Struan goaded the men forward and with their help passed the canvas mainsail under the prow of the boat, under the hull, then lashed it tightly over the rip. The suction from the water tightened the sail over the gash as the boat wallowed helplessly, near capsizing.

Once more he forced the men below and after wedging the caulking canvas tighter, had them rearrange the rest of the crates to maintain a less dangerous list to port.

He went back on deck and inspected the mainsail lashings. When he ascertained they were firm and tight and holding, he began to breathe freely again.

'You all right, May-may?'

'Wat ah?' she said.

'Hurt youah?'

'Can.' She pointed to her wrist. It was torn and bleeding. He examined it carefully. Though it pained her, it did not seem to be broken. He poured rum over the wounds and then drank deeply and looked aft. Brock's lorcha was drifting, the mainsail and foresails rigging burning furiously. He watched the crew cut away the rigging and the sails fell overboard. They burned for a moment in the water. Then there was blackness. A few junks and sampans were nearby, but none of them had gone to the assistance of the burning lorcha.

Struan peered ahead. Six Rock Channel – a little-known waterway – was on the lee quarter. He tried the tiller cautiously and the ship eased off a few points. The wind pressed the sails and the boat listed sharply, submerging the gash. There was a warning shout from the crew and Struan corrected the list. Dangerous to sail like this, he thought. I dare na tack to starboard. A slight sea'll rip the covering off and we'll sink like a stone. If I go through Six Rock Channel, Brock'll never find me, but I canna tack to manœuvre. So I have to stay in the river. Scud down before the wind, as straight as possible.

He checked his position. The Marble Pagoda was eight or nine miles downstream.

With the protective sail around her keel acting like a storm anchor, the lorcha was making only two or three knots. Having to stay close to the wind to avoid tacking would further cut down her speed. Ahead the river curled and twisted. With joss I will na have to tack to starboard. I'll down sails and let her drift and raise sail again when I'm in position.

He gave the tiller to Wung and went below and rechecked the caulking canvas. It will hold for a time – with joss, he thought. He picked up some teacups and went on deck.

The crew was grouped to one side, holding on grimly. There were only six men.

'Heya! Six bull only. Where two-ah?'

Wung pointed over the side and laughed. 'Crash-bang, fall!' Then he waved astern, and shrugged. 'Never mind.'

'God's blood, wat for na save, heya?'

'Wat for save, heya?'

Struan knew that it was pointless to try to explain. According to the Chinese, it was joss that the men had fallen overboard. It was just joss – their joss – to drown, and also it was the will of the gods. Very unwise to interfere with the will of the gods. Save a man from dying, then you yourself are responsible for him for the rest of the man's life. That's fair. Because if you interfere with the will of the gods, you must be prepared to assume their responsibility.

Struan poured a cup of rum and gave it to May-may. He offered each of the crew a tot in turn, expecting no thanks and receiving none. Strange, he told himself, but Chinese. Why should they thank me for saving their lives? It was joss that we did not sink.

Thank you, God, for my joss. Thank you.

'Hola!' one of the crew called out anxiously, looking over the side.

The canvas caulking was coming adrift. Struan rushed below. He slipped off the fighting iron and pushed the water-logged sail deeper into the ship's wound. Water three feet deep sloshed around in the bilges. He levered a crate tighter against the canvas and wedged more silver bricks into the crevices.

'It'll hold,' he said aloud. 'Aye, maybe.'

He picked up the fighting iron and went into the main cabin. It was a shambles. He looked at the bunk longingly, picked up a grass-filled palliasse and climbed the gangway.

He froze at the top of the steps. Wung was pointing the pistol at him. A second Chinese held the musket, Ah Gip inert at his feet. One of the crew had an armlock on May-may, and was holding a hand over her mouth. Wung pulled the trigger as Struan instinctively lifted up the palliasse and hurtled to one side of the gangway. He felt the ball crease his neck and he lunged up on deck, his face stung by the gunpowder, the palliasse a pathetic shield. The second Chinese fired point-blank, but the musket exploded and blew his hands off, and he stared at the stumps of his arms, astonished, and screamed.

Struan whirled the fighting iron as Wung and the crew attacked. The barbed ball caught Wung flush on the side of the face, tearing off half his mouth, and he reeled away. Struan flailed and another man fell and another jumped on his back and tried to throttle him, using his own queue as a garrotte, but Struan shook him off. The man holding May-may leaped forward and Struan shoved the fighting iron's haft into his face and then, when the man shrieked and fell, Struan trampled him. The two men who were unhurt fled to the bow. Gasping for breath, Struan instantly rushed after them. They jumped overboard. There was a scream from the poop. Wung, grotesque, the blood gushing from half a face, was groping blindly for May-may. She slid out of his grasp and hobbled for cover.

Struan walked back and killed him.

The man with no hands was screaming hideously. Struan killed him quickly and painlessly.

172

There was silence on the deck.

May-may stared down at a dismembered hand and was violently sick. Struan kicked the hand overboard. When he had regained his strength, he threw all but one of the bodies overboard. He examined Ah Gip. She was breathing through her mouth, the blood trickling from her nose.

'I think she'll be all right,' he said, and was astonished at the thickness of his voice. He felt his face. The pain was coming in violent waves. He slumped beside May-may. 'What happened?'

'I dinna ken,' she said, beyond tears. 'One moment I was with pistol, the next, they had hand over my mouth and they fired at you. Why aren't you deaded?'

'I feel like I am,' he said. The left side of his face was badly scorched. His hair was singed and half an eyebrow was missing. The pain in his chest was lessening.

'What for they – Wung and they – do this? What for? He's Jin-qua's trusted,' she said.

'You said yoursel' that any'd try to steal the bullion. Aye. Any. I dinna blame them. I was a fool to go below.'

He checked the course ahead. They were still limping in the right direction.

May-may saw the sear on his neck. 'Another inch, half an inch,' she whispered. 'Praise the gods for joss. I will make huge gift.'

Struan was smelling the sweet blood stench, and now that he was safe, his stomach turned over and he groped for the side and retched. Afterwards he found a wooden pail and cleaned the deck. Then he cleaned the fighting iron.

'What for do you leave that man?' May-may asked.

'He's na dead.'

'Throw him overboard.'

'When he's dead. Or when he wakes, if he does, he can jump.' Struan breathed the air deeply and his nausea left him. His legs aching with fatigue, he went over to Ah Gip and lifted her on to the main housing. 'Did you see where she got hit?'

'No.'

Struan undid her padded coat and examined her carefully. Her chest and back were unmarked but there was a trace of blood at the base of her queue. He wrapped her again and settled her as well as he could. Her face looked grey and mottled; her breathing was choked. 'She does na look good.'

'How far must we go now?' May-may said.

'Two or three hours.' He took the helm. 'I dinna ken. Maybe more.'

May-may lay back and let the wind and chill air clear her head.

Struan saw the broken bottle of rum rolling in the scuppers. 'Go below. See if there's another bottle of rum, will you? I think there were two, eh?'

'Sorry, Tai-Pan. I almost kill us with my own stupid.'

'Nay, lass. It was the bullion. Check the hold.'

She picked her way below. She was gone a long time.

When she returned she was carrying a teapot and two cups.

'I make tea,' she said proudly. 'I make fire and I make tea. The rum bottle, she was broke. So we have tea.'

'I didn't know you could even make tea, let alone light a fire,' he said, teasing her.

'When I'm old and toothless I become amah.' She noticed absently that the last of the Chinese seamen was no longer on deck. She poured the tea and offered him a cup, smiling wanly.

'Thanks.'

Ah Gip regained consciousness. She vomited, then collapsed again. 'I dinna like the look of her at all,' Struan said.

'She's a fine slave.'

He drank the tea gratefully. 'How much water's in the hold?'

'The floor is washed with water.' May-may sipped her tea. 'I think it would be wise to – to – how you say? – "buy" sea god on our side.'

'Petition? Aye, petition.'

She nodded. 'Aye. Wise if I petition sea god.'

'How do you do that?'

'There is much bullion downstairs. One bar would be very good.'

'It would be very bad. A big waste of silver. We've been through this a thousand times. There are nae gods but God.'

'True. But please. Please, Tai-Pan. Please.' Her eyes were begging him. 'We need fantastical plenty help. I counsel asking immediate for sea god's particular blessings.'

Struan had given up trying to make her understand that there was only one God, that Jesus was the Son of God, that Christianity was the only true religion. Two years ago he had tried to explain Christianity to her.

'You want me to be Christian? Then I'm Christian,' she had said cheerfully.

'But it's na so easy as that, May-may. You have to believe.'

'Of course. I believe wat you want me to believe. There is one God. The Christian barbarian God. The new God.'

'It's na a barbarian God, and na a new God. It's—'

'Your Lord Jesus was na Chinese, heya? Then he is a barbarian. And wat for you tell me this Jesus God is na new, when only he was na even born two thousand years ago, heya? That is plenty werry new. Ayee yah, our gods are five, ten thousand years old.'

Struan had been out of his depth, for though he was a Christian and would go to kirk and sometimes pray and knew the Bible as well as most men, ordinary men, he had not the learning or the skill to teach her. So he had had Wolfgang Mauss explain the Gospel to her in Mandarin. But after Mauss had taught her and had baptized her, Struan had discovered that she still went to the Chinese temple.

'But why go there? That's being a heathen again. You're bowing down before idols.'

'But wat for is the wood carving of the Lord Jesus on the Cross in the church but idol? Or Cross itself? Is that na all same an idol?'

'It's na the same.'

'The Buddha is only symbol of Buddha. I dinna worship idol, laddie. I'm Chinese. Chinese dinna worship idols, only the idea of statue. We Chinese are na stupid. We're terrifical clever about these god things. And how for do I know the Lord Jesus, who was barbarian, likes Chinese, heya?'

'Will you na say such things? That's blasphemy. Wolfgang's explained the whole Gospel to you these last months. Of course Jesus loves all people the same way.'

'Then why for do the Christian men priests who wear long skirts and dinna have womens say other Christian priests who dress like men and spawn many children are for crazy, heya? Mass'er Mauss says previously there were many wars and many killings. Ayee yah, the longskirt devils burn men and women on fires.' She shook her head firmly. 'Better we change right now, Tai-Pan. Let's be the longskirt Christian; then if we lose to them we'll na be burned. Your kind Christians dinna burn people, do they, heya?'

'You dinna just change like that, for that reason. Catholics are wrong. They've—'

'I tell you, Tai-Pan. I think we should be longskirt Christians. And I think also, you look after your new Jesus God very careful, and I look after the Jesus God as best I can, and at the same time I watch our proper Chinese gods for us too, very careful.' She had nodded very firmly, then smiled marvellously. 'Then whosoever is the strongest god will look after us.'

'You canna do such a thing. There is only one God. One!'

'Prove it,' she had said.

'I canna do that.'

'There, you see. How can mortal man prove God, any god? But I am a Christian like you. But, fortunate, also Chinese, and in these god things better think a little Chinese. Werry wise to keep a werry open mind. Werry. It's joss for you that I'm Chinese; then also on our behalf I can petition Chinese gods.' She had added hastily, 'Who, of course, dinna exist.' She had smiled. 'Isn't that fine?'

'No.'

'Of course, if I had choice – which I dinna, because there is only one God – I'd prefer Chinese god. They dinna want their devoters to slaughter other gods or dead all people who dinna kowtow.' Again she had run on hastily, 'But the Christian barbarian God, who is alone and only God, seems to me, as a poor, simple woman, werry bloodthirst and difficult to get along with, but of course I believe in Him. There,' she had finished emphatically.

' "There" nothing.'

'I think your heaven is one hell of strange place, Tai-Pan. Everyone flying around like birds and everyone with beards. Do you make love in heaven?'

'I dinna ken.'

'If we canna make love, I'm na going to your heaven. Oh no, absolutely. True God or no true God. That'd be a werry bad place. I must find out before go there. Yes, indeed. And another thing, Tai-Pan. Wat for should the only true God, who is therefore fantastical clever, say only one wife, heya, which is terrifical stupid? And if you are Christian, wat for we as husband and wife, when you already got wife? Adulteratiousness, eh? Werry bad. Wat for you break so many of the Ten Commands, heya, yet still werry all right call yourself a Christian?'

'Well, May-may, some of us are sinners and weak. The Lord Jesus will forgive us, some of us. He promised to forgive us if we repent.'

'I wouldna,' she had said, very firmly. 'Na if I was the Most One God. No, indeed. And another thing, Tai-Pan. How can God be "Trinity" yet have number-one Son who is also God who was born of real woman, without help of real man, who then becomes Mother of God? That's wat I dinna understand. But dinna mistake me, Tai-Pan, I'm Christian as any, by God. Heya?'

They had had many such talks, and each time he had found himself locked into an argument that had no end and no beginning, except that he knew there was only one God, the true God, and knew also that May-may would never understand. He hoped that perhaps in His time He would make Himself clear to her . . .

'Please, Tai-Pan,' May-may said again. 'One little pretend will na harm anything. I said a prayer already to One God. Dinna forget that we're in China and it is a Chinese river.'

'But it does nae good at all.'

'I know. Oh yes, Tai-Pan, I know absolutely. But I'm only a two-year Christian, so you and God must be patient with me. He will forgive me,' she ended triumphantly.

'All right,' Struan said.

She went below. When she came back she had washed her face and her hands, and her hair was braided. In her hands was a silver brick wrapped in paper. The paper was covered with Chinese characters.

'Did you write the characters?'

'Yes. I found writing pen and ink. I wrote a prayer to the sea god.'

'What does it say?'

' "Oh Great Wise and Powerful Sea God, in return for this enormous gift which is almost hundred taels of silver, please bring us safe to a barbarian ship called *China Cloud* belonging to my barbarian, and thence to the island Hong Kong wat the barbarians have stolen from us." '

'I dinna think much of that prayer,' he said. 'After all, lass, it's my silver, and I dinna like being called a barbarian.'

'It's a polite prayer, and it tells the truth. It's a Chinese sea god. To a Chinese you're barbarian. It's most important to tell the truth in prayer.' She walked gingerly down the listing side of the ship, and with great difficulty held the heavy, paper-covered silver brick at arm's length, and closed her eyes and intoned the prayer that she had written. Then, her eyes still closed, she neatly unwrapped the silver brick and let the paper fall into the water and tucked the brick quickly into the folds of her jacket. She opened her eyes and watched the paper being sucked down into the river by the wash of the boat.

She clambered back joyfully, the silver safe in her arms.

'There. Now we can rest.'

'That's a cheat, by God,' Struan said, exploding.

'Wat?'

'You did na drop the silver overboard.'

'Shusssssssssh! Na so loud! You spoil everything!' Then she whispered, 'Of course na. Do you think I'm a fool?'

177

'I thought you wanted to make an offering.'

'I've just make it,' she whispered, perplexed. 'You dinna think I'd really throw all that silver in the river, do you? God's blood, am I a lump of dog meat? Am I mad?'

'Then why go through—'

'Shussssssh!' May-may said urgently. 'Na so loud! The sea god may hear you.'

'Why pretend to drop the silver overboard? That's no offering.'

'I swear to God, Tai-Pan, I dinna understand you at all. Wat for do gods need real silver, heya? Wat for should they use real silver? To buy real clothes and real food? Gods are gods and Chinese are Chinese. I've made the offering and saved your silver. I swear to God, barbarians are strange people.'

And she went below, muttering to herself in Soochow dialect, 'As if I'd destroy so much silver! Am I an empress that I can throw silver away? Ayeee yah,' she said, negotiating the corridor into the hold. 'Even the devil empress would not be so foolish!' She put the silver in the bilge where she had found it and went back on deck.

Struan heard her returning, still mumbling irritably in Chinese.

'What are you saying?' he demanded.

'Am I so mad as to waste so much hard-earned cash? Am I a barbarian? Am I a waster—'

'All right. But I still dinna understand why you think the sea god'll answer your prayers when he's been so obviously duped. The whole matter is fantastical stupid.'

'Will you na say such things so loudly,' she said. 'He's got offering. Now he'll protect us. It's na real silver a god want, merely idea. That's what he got.' She tossed her head. 'Gods are like people. They believe anything if you tell them right way.' Then she added. 'Maybe the god is out and will na help us anyway and we'll sink, never mind.'

'Another thing,' Struan said dourly. 'Why should we whisper, eh? It's a Chinese sea god. How the hell can he understand English, heya?'

This confounded May-may. She frowned, thinking hard. Then she shrugged. 'A god is a god. Perhaps they speak the barbarian tongue. Would you like more tea?'

'Thanks.'

She poured it into his cup and hers. Then she clasped her hands around her knees and settled herself on a hatchway and hummed a little song.

The lorcha wallowed in the river current. Dawn was breaking.

'You're quite a woman, May-may,' Struan said.

'I like you, too.' She nestled against him. 'How many men are there like you, in your country?'

'About twenty million, men, women and children.'

'There are, they say, three hundreds of millions of Chinese.'

'That would mean that every fourth person on earth is Chinese.'

'I worry for my people if all barbarians are like you. You kill so many, so easily.'

'I killed them because they were trying to kill me. And we're na barbarians.'

'I'm glad I saw you at your killing,' she said weirdly, her eyes luminous, her head framed by the growing light of dawn. 'And I'm werry glad you were na deaded.'

'One day I'll be dead.'

Of course. But I'm glad I saw you at your killing. Our son Duncan will be worthy of you.'

'By the time he's grown it will na be necessary to kill.'

'By the time his children's children's children are grown there will still be killing. Man is killer beast, Most all men. We Chinese know. But barbarians are worse than us. Worse.'

'You think that because you're Chinese. You've many more barbaric customs than we have. People change, May-may.'

Then she said simply, 'Learn from us, from the lessons of China, Dirk Struan. People never change.'

'Learn from us, from the lessons of England, lass. The world can grow into an ordered place where all are equal before the law. And the law is just. Honest. Without graft.'

'Is that so important if you are starving?'

He thought about that a long time.

The lorcha plodded downstream. Other craft passed, upstream and downstream, and the crews stared at the lorcha curiously but said nothing. Ahead the river curled and Struan eased the lorcha into the channel. The canvas patch seemed to be holding.

'I think so,' he finally answered. 'Aye. I think that's very important. Oh yes, I wanted to ask you something. You said you went to see Jinqua's Supreme Lady. Where did you meet her?'

'I was slave in her house,' May-may said calmly. 'Just before Jinqua sold me to you.' She looked into his eyes. 'You bought me, didn't you?'

'I acquired you according to your custom, aye. But you're no slave. You can leave or stay, freely. I told you that the first day.'

'I did na believe you. I believe you now, Tai-Pan.' She watched the

179

shore and the boats passing. 'I've never seen a killing before. I dinna like killing. Is that because I am woman?'

'Aye. And nay. I dinna ken.'

'Do you like killing?'

'Nay.'

'It is a pity your arrow miss Brock.'

'I did na aim at him. I was na trying to kill him, just to make him swerve.'

She was astonished. 'I swear to God, Tai-Pan, you're peculiar fantastical.'

'I swear to God, May-may,' he said, his eyes crinkled into a smile, 'you're peculiar fantastical.'

She lay on her side, watching him, cherishing him. Then she slept.

When she awoke the sun was up. The land beside the river was low and ran back to misted horizons. An abundant land, patterned with numberless paddy fields, green and waving with winter rice. Clouded hills afar off.

The Marble Pagoda was just ahead. Beneath it was *China Cloud*.

BOOK TWO

IX

Four days later *China Cloud* was secretly at anchor in Deepwater Bay, on the south side of Hong Kong Island. It was a cold morning with a sky cloud-locked, the sea grey.

Struan was standing by the diamond-shaped windows in the main cabin, looking at the island. The barren mountains fell steeply into the sea around the bay, their peaks cloud-shrouded. There was a small sand beach at the bay's apex and then the land climbed quickly once more to the clouds, rugged and lonely. Sea gulls cawed. Waves lapped the hull of the ship sweetly and the ship's bell sounded six times.

'Aye?' Struan said in answer to a knock.

'Cutter's returned,' Captain Orlov said wearily. He was a vast-shouldered hunchback, barely five feet tall with massive arms and huge head. A fighting iron was thonged to his wrist. Since the bullion had come aboard he had worn the fighting iron night and day and had even slept with it. 'By the beard of Odin, our cargo's worse'n the black plague.'

'More trouble?'

'Trouble, you say? Never on a ship o' mine, by Jesus Christ's mother's head!' The tiny, misshapen man, cackled with malevolent glee. 'Least not while I'm awake, eh, Green Eyes?'

Struan had found Orlov wandering the docks of Glasgow many years ago. He was a Norseman who had been shipwrecked in the dangerous Orkneys and could not find a new ship. Though seamen knew no nationality, no owner would trust a ship to so strange a man who would call no one 'sir' or 'mister', who would serve only as captain – nothing less.

'I'm best in world,' Orlov would shout, his mottled, beaknosed face shaking with fury. 'I've served my time before the mast – never again! Test me, and I'll prove it, by the blood of Thor!'

Struan had tested Orlov's knowledge of sea and wind, and tested his strength and courage, and had found nothing wanting. Orlov could

183

speak English, French, Russian, Finnish and Norwegian. His mind was brilliant and his memory astonishing. And though he looked like a goblin and could kill like a shark if need be, he was fair, and completely trustworthy. Struan had given him a small ship and then a bigger one. Then a clipper. Last year he had made him captain of *China Cloud* and he knew that Orlov was everything he claimed.

Struan poured more tea, hot and sweet and spiced with rum. 'As soon as Mr Robb and Culum are aboard, make course for Hong Kong harbour.'

'Sooner the better, eh?'

'Where's Wolfgang?'

'In his cabin. Do you want him?'

'Nay. And see that we're na disturbed.'

Orlov shifted his damp sea clothes irritably as he left. 'Sooner we get ride of this plague-besotted cargo the better. Terriblest I've ever had.'

Struan did not reply. He was exhausted but his brain was alert. Almost home, he told himself. A few more hours and you'll be safe in harbour. Thank God for the Royal Navy. Alongside one of the frigates you can rest.

The main cabin was luxurious and spacious. But now it was cluttered with muskets and knives and fighting irons and swords and cutlasses. He had disarmed all his crew before bringing the bullion aboard. Now only he and Captain Orlov carried weapons. Struan could feel the violent tension that pervaded the ship. The bullion had infected everyone. Aye, he thought, it'll leave no man untouched. Even Robb. Even Culum. Maybe even Orlov.

On the voyage from the Marble Pagoda Ah Gip had sunk into a coma and had died. Struan had wanted to bury her at sea; but May-may had asked him not to.

'Ah Gip was a faithful slave,' she had said. 'It would be bad joss na to return her to her parents and bury her as a Chinese, oh, absolutely very bad terrifical, Tai-Pan.'

So Struan had changed course and gone to Macao. There, with Mauss's help, he had bought Ah Gip a fine coffin and had given it to her parents. He had also given them ten taels of silver for her funeral. Her parents were Hoklo boat people, and they had thanked him and had pressed him to take Ah Gip's younger sister, Ah Sam, in her place. Ah Sam was fifteen, a merry, round-faced girl, who could also speak pidgin and, most unusual for a Hoklo, had bound feet. May-may had known Ah Sam and approved of her, so Struan had agreed. The parents had asked three hundred taels of silver for Ah Sam. Struan would have given them the money but May-may had said that he and she would lose great face if they paid the first price asked. So she had bargained with the parents and knocked down the price to one hundred and sixteen taels.

Struan had gone through the formality of buying the girl because it was customary. But then, when the sale was complete and he, according to Chinese law, owned a slave, he had torn up the document in front of Ah Sam and had told her that she was not a slave but a servant. Ah Sam had not understood. Struan knew that later she would ask May-may why he had torn up the paper and May-may would say that some of the ways of the barbarian were strange. Ah Sam would agree with her and her fear of him would increase.

While *China Cloud* was at Macao, Struan had confined his crew aboard – except Wolfgang Mauss. He was afraid that word of the bullion would leak out, and though he ordinarily trusted his crew he did not trust them when there was so much wealth ready just for the taking. He expected to be pirated either from within or from without. At Macao there had almost been a mutiny, and for the first time he and his officers had had to use the lash indiscriminately and put guards on the quarterdeck and anchor far out in the shallow harbour. All sampans had been forbidden to come within a hundred yards of *China Cloud*.

He had sent his mate, Cudahy, ahead to Hong Kong in the cutter to fetch Robb and Culum to the secret rendezvous at Deepwater Bay with strict instructions to say nothing about the bullion. He had known that this was an added danger, but he knew he had to take the risk. With the bullion safe in *China Cloud* he had had time to think about Jin-qua and about The Noble House and Robb and Culum and what to do about the future. He knew that now it was time to set the future pattern of the company. With or without Robb and Culum. At all costs.

He had left May-may in Macao in the house that he had given her. Before he had sailed he and May-may had gone to the house of Chen Sheng.

Duncan, his three-year-old son, had begun to kowtow but he had lifted him up and told him that he must never do that again, to any man. Duncan had said, 'Yes, Tai-Pan,' and had hugged him and May-may.

Kate, the baby, had been as cherished as Duncan, and Chen Sheng fussed like an old hen. Food and tea were brought, and then Chen Sheng had asked Struan's permission to present Kai-Sung, who wished to kowtow to the Tai-Pan.

Kai-sung was now thirty-six. She was dressed beautifully in robes of gold and crimson with jade and silver pins in her jet hair. It was almost as though the seventeen years had never been. Her face was like alabaster and her eyes as deep as in her youth.

But there were tears running down her cheeks and she whispered in Cantonese and May-may translated cheerfully. 'Elder Sister's so sorry your Tai-tai is deaded, Tai-Pan. Elder Sister says anytimes you want for the children to be here they are like hers. And she thanks you for being kind to her and her son.'

'Tell her she looks very pretty, and thank her.'

May-may did so and then wept a little with Kai-sung and then they were happy. Kai-sung kowtowed again and departed.

Chen Sheng had drawn Struan aside. 'Hear maybe you good joss have got, Tai-Pan.' His huge face was a total smile.

'Maybe.'

'I buy mens build Hong Kong werry cheep 'gainst good joss!' Chen Sheng held his vast stomach and roared with laughter. 'Heya, Tai-Pan! Have wirgin slave. You want? I buy you, heya? Cheep-cheep.'

'Ayee yah, wirgin! Troubles 'nuff hav got!'

Struan and May-may had taken their children and they went back to their home. The money May-may had lost to him was more than the value of the house. She formally gave him the deed of the house with great ceremony and simultaneously offered him a pack of cards. 'Double or nothings, Tai-Pan, on debts.'

He had picked a jack and she had wailed and torn her hair. 'Woe, woe, woe! I am for a lump of dogmeat-whore-strumpet! I wat for open my oily mouth?'

In utter agony she had closed her eyes and picked a card and cringed and half opened her eyes. It was a queen and she shrieked with happiness and flung herself into his arms.

He had arranged with May-may that he would come back quickly from Hong Kong or send *China Cloud* for her, and then he had sailed for Deepwater Bay.

The cabin door opened.

'Hello, Father,' Culum said.

'Hello, Dirk,' Robb said.

'Welcome aboard. Did you have a good voyage?'

'Good enough.' Robb dropped into a chair. There were dark rings under his eyes.

'You looked exhausted, Robb.'

'I am. I've tried everything, everything.' He eased out of his heavy, steaming topcoat. 'No one'll give us credit. We're lost. What good news could you bring, Dirk?' He felt in the pocket of his reefer jacket and pulled out a letter. 'Afraid I don't bring good tidings either. This came for you in yesterday's mail packet. From Father.'

All of Struan's excitement and happiness at what he had achieved, disappeared. Winifred, he thought, it's got to be about her. He took the letter. The seal was intact. He recognized his father's spidery writing. 'What's the news from home?' He said, trying to level his voice.

'That's all that came, Dirk. I got nothing. Sorry. How is it with you? What's the matter with your face? Have you burned it? Sorry I've been so little help.'

Struan put the letter on the desk. 'Did you buy the land?'

'No. The land sale's been postponed.' Robb tried to keep his eyes off the letter.

'It's tomorrow, Father. There wasn't enough time to get the lots surveyed. So it was postponed.' Culum lurched unsteadily as the ship heeled under a press of canvas. He steadied himself against the desk. 'Shall I open the letter for you?'

'Nay, thanks. Have you seen Brock?'

'The *White Witch* came back from Whampoa two days ago,' Robb said. 'Haven't seen him myself. We're really at war again?'

'Aye,' Struan said. 'Is the fleet still at Hong Kong?'

'Yes. But when Eliksen came with the news, it deployed into war positions. Patrols were sent to guard the east and west entrances. Will they attack Hong Kong?'

'Dinna be ridiculous, Robbie.'

Robb watched the wake of the ship. Dirk looks different, he thought. Then he noticed the clutter of the cabin. 'Why are there so many weapons here, Dirk? What's amiss?'

'What's Longstaff been up to, Culum?' Struan asked.

'I don't know,' Culum said. 'I've only seen him but once, and that was to get his approval for the postponement.'

'I haven't seen him either. Dirk. After the piece about us in the paper I've had great difficulty in seeing a lot of people. Especially Longstaff.'

'Oh? What happened?'

'I saw him the next day. He said. " 'Pon me word, is it true?" and when I told him "Yes" he took a pinch of snuff and said, "Pity. Well, I'm very busy, Robb. Good day", and took another glass of port.'

'What did you expect?'

'I don't know, Dirk. I suppose I expected sympathy. Or some help.'

'Longstaff did na sack Culum. That's in his favour.'

'He wanted me back only because there's no one else at the moment to do this for him,' Culum said. He had started to fill out in the last two weeks and was losing his plague pallor. 'I think he enjoys the fact that we're broken. At least,' Culum added quickly, 'I'm unimportant. I mean that The Noble House is broken.'

'If it's na us, it's another company, Culum.'

'Yes, I know, Father. What I meant was . . . well, I think you were very special with Longstaff. He kowtowed to your knowledge because of your wealth. But without wealth you've no breeding. Without breeding you cannot be equal. Without equality you can't have knowledge. None. I think that's rather sad.'

'Where'd you learn "kowtow"?'

'Wait till you see Hong Kong.'

'What does that mean, lad?'

'We'll be there in a few hours. You can see for yourself.' Then Culum's voice sharpened. 'Please open the letter, Father.'

'The news'll keep. Winifred was failing when you left. Do you expect a miracle?'

'I hope for one, yes. I've prayed for one, yes.'

'Come below,' Struan said.

The neat stacks of silver bricks glinted eerily under the swaying lantern in the hold. The air was close and the sick-sweet smell of raw opium permeated it. Cockroaches swarmed.

'It's impossible,' Robb whispered, touching the bullion.

'I didn't know there was this much silver in one place on earth,' Culum said, as stunned.

'It's here, right enough,' Struan said.

Robb picked up one of the bricks to reassure himself, his hand trembling. 'Unbelievable.'

Struan told them how he obtained the bullion. He related all that Jinqua had said, except about the chop and about the four half coins and about the five lacs to be put into Hong Kong land, and the five lacs to be kept safe and the one lac to Gordon Chen. He described the sea battle with Brock. But he made no mention of May-may.

'That bloody pirate!' Culum stormed. 'Longstaff will have Brock and Gorth hanged when he hears about it.'

'Why?' Struan asked. 'Brock did nae more than I'd've done. He simply happened to collide with me.'

'But that's a lie. You can prove that he—'

188

'I can and will prove nothing. Brock tried and failed, that's all. It's our business, no one else's.'

'I don't like that,' Culum said. 'That's not a lawful way of looking at a deliberate piracy.'

'There'll be a reckoning. In my own time.'

'God help us, we're saved,' Robb said, his voice weak. 'Now all the international money plans will go through. We'll be the richest company in the Orient. Bless you, Dirk. You're incredible.' Now the future's assured, Robb inwardly exulted. Now there'll be enough for even Sarah's extravagant tastes. Now I can go home immediately. Perhaps Dirk will change his mind and never leave, will never go home, will forget Parliament. No more worries. Now I can buy a castle and live like a laird in peace. The children will marry and live well and there'll be enough for their children's children. Roddy can finish university and go into banking and never worry about the Orient. 'Bless you, Dirk!'

Culum, too, was ecstatic. His brain shrieked. This isn't bullion, but power. Power to buy guns, or to buy votes to dominate Parliament. Here is the answer for the Charter and the Chartists. As Tai-Pan I can use the power of all this wealth – and more – to a good end. I thank Thee, oh Lord, he prayed fervently, for helping us in our hour of need.

Culum saw his father very differently now. In the past weeks he had thought greatly about what his father had said concerning wealth and power and the uses thereof. Being close to Glessing and on the edge of Longstaff's power, and feeling the covert smirks and open amusement at the death of The Noble House, he had realized that a man alone, without birthright or power, was defenceless.

Struan could feel Robb's and Culum's avarice. Aye, he told himself. But be honest. It's what the bullion'd do to any. Look at yoursel'. You've killed eight, ten men to protect it. Aye, and you'll kill a hundred more. Look what it's forcing you to do to your son and to your brother.

'There's something I want to make clear to you both,' he said. 'This bullion's been loaned to me. On my word. I'm responsible to Jin-qua for it. *I* am. Na The Noble House.'

'I don't understand, Dirk,' Robb said.

'What did you say, Father?'

Struan took out a Bible. 'First swear on the Holy Book that what I say will be secret among the three of us.'

'Is it necessary to swear?' Robb said. 'Of course I would never tell anyone.'

'Will you swear, Robb?'

189

'Of course.'

He and Culum swore secrecy.

Struan placed the Bible on the silver. 'This bullion will be used to salvage The Noble House only with the proviso that when and if either of you become Tai-Pan you agree, first, to commit the company totally to the support of Hong Kong and to China trade; second, to head-quarter the company permanently in Hong Kong; third, to take over my responsibility and my word to Jin-qua and to his successors; fourth, to guarantee that the successor you choose as Tai-Pan does the same; last' – Struan pointed at the Bible – 'agree now that only a Christian, a kinsman, can ever be Tai-Pan. Swear on the Holy Book, as you agree to swear your successor on the Holy Book to the conditions before passing over control.'

There was a silence. Then Robb said, knowing how his brother's mind worked, 'Do we know all the conditions that Jin-qua imposed?'

'Nay.'

'What are the rest?'

'I'll tell you after you've sworn. You can trust me or na, just as you like.'

'That's not very fair.'

'This bullion is na very fair, Robb. I have to be sure. This is nae game for children. And I'm na thinking of either of you as kin at this moment. We're playing with a hundred years. Two hundred years.' Struan's eyes were a luminous green in the half-light of the swaying lantern. 'I'm committing The Noble House to Chinese time. With or without the both of you.'

The air seemed to thicken perceptibly. Robb felt the wetness on his shoulders and neck. Culum stared at his father, astounded.

Robb said, 'What does "commit the company totally to the support of Hong Kong" mean to you?'

'To back it, guard it, make it a permanent base for trade. And trade means to open up China. All China. To bring China into the family of nations.'

'That's impossible,' Robb said. 'Impossible!'

'Aye, maybe. But that's what The Noble House is going to try to do.'

'You mean, help China become a world power?' Culum asked.

'Aye.'

'That's dangerous!' Robb snapped. 'That's madness! There's enough trouble on earth without helping that heathen mass of humanity! They'll swamp us. All of us. All Europe!'

'Every fourth person on earth's Chinese now, Robb. We've the great chance to help them now. To learn our ways. British ways. Law and order and justice. Christianity. They'll swarm out one day, on their own. I say we've got to show them our way.'

'It's impossible. You'll never change them. Never. It's futile.'

'Those are the conditions. In five months you're Tai-Pan. Culum follows you in time – if he's worthy.'

'Christ in heaven!' Robb exploded. 'Is this what you've been striving for all these years?'

'Aye.'

'I've always known you had dreams, Dirk. But this – this is too much. I don't know whether it's monstrous or marvellous. It's beyond me.'

'Maybe,' Struan said, his voice hard. 'But it's a condition for your survival, Robbie, and your family's and their future. You're Tai-Pan in five months. For at least one year.'

'I've told you before, I think that's another unwise decision,' Robb flared, his face contorted. 'I've not the knowledge or the cunning to deal with Longstaff or to keep The Noble House at the forefront of all this war intrigue. Or to cope with the Chinese.'

'I know. And I know the risk I take. But Hong Kong's ours now. The war will be over as quickly as the last one.' Struan waved a hand at the bullion. 'All this is a rock which canna be dissipated easily. From now on it's a matter of trade. You're a good trader.'

'It's not just trading. There're ships to be sailed, pirates to be fought, Brock to be dealt with, and a thousand other things.'

'Five months will clean up the important ones. The rest are your problem.'

'Are they?'

'Aye. Because of all this bullion we're worth more than three million. When I leave I take one. And twenty per cent of the profit for my lifetime. You do the same.' He glanced at Culum. 'At the end of your term we will be worth ten million because I'll protect you and The Noble House from Parliament and make her rich beyond your dreams. We'll nae longer have to rely on Sir Charles Crosse, Donald MacDonald, McFee, Smythe, Ross or all the others we support to do our bidding – I'll do it mysel'. And I'll come back and forth to Hong Kong, so both of you have nae need to worry.'

'I want only enough wealth to let me dream quietly and wake up peacefully,' Robb said, 'in Scotland. Not in the Orient. I don't want to die here. I'm off by the next boat.'

'A year and five months is na much to ask.'

'It's a demand, not an ask, Dirk.'

'I'm forcing nothing on you. A month ago, Robb, you were prepared to accept fifty thousand and leave. Very well. That offer still holds. If you want what is rightfully yours – more than a million – you'll get it within two years.' Struan turned to Culum. 'From you, lad, I want two years of your life. If you become Tai-Pan, a further three years. Five years in all.'

'If I don't agree to the conditions, then I have to leave?' Culum asked, his mouth parched, heart hurting.

'Nay. You're still a partner, albeit a junior one. But you'll never be Tai-Pan. Never. I'll have to find and train someone else. A year's as much as it's fair to ask – to demand – from Robb. He's already been eleven years abuilding.' He picked up one of the bricks. 'You'll have to prove yoursel', Culum, even if you agree now. You'll be heir apparent, that's all. You'll na wax fat on my sweat, or Robb's. That's clan law and a good law of life. Every man has to stand on his own feet. Of course I'll help you all I can – as long as I'm alive – but it's up to you to prove your worth. Only a real man has the right to stand at the pinnacle.'

Culum flushed.

Robb was staring at Struan, detesting him. 'You don't want a Tai-Pan in five months, Dirk. Just a nursemaid for a year, isn't that it?'

'Guarantee to take over for five years and you choose whom you wish.'

'I can eliminate Culum right now, in return for a promise of five years?'

'Aye,' Struan said at once. 'I think it would be a waste, but that'd be your decision. Aye.'

'You see what power does to a man, Culum?' Robb said, his voice strained.

'This version of The Noble House is dead without this bullion,' Struan said without rancour. 'I've told you my conditions. Make up your own minds.'

'I understand why you're hated throughout these seas,' Culum said.

'Do you, lad?'

'Yes.'

'You'll never know that, truly know that, until your five years are up.'

'Then I've no option, Father. It's five years or nothing?'

'It's nothing or everything, Culum. If you're prepared to be second-

192

best, go topside now. What I'm trying to make you understand is that to be *the* Tai-Pan of The Noble House you have to be prepared to exist alone, to be hated, to have some aim of immortal value, and to be ready to sacrifice anyone you're na sure of. Because you're my son I'm offering you today, untried, a chance at supreme power in Asia. Thus a power to do almost anything on earth. I dinna offer that lightly, I *know* what it means to be *the* Tai-Pan. Choose, by God!'

Culum's eyes were transfixed by the Bible. And the bullion. I don't want to be second-best, he told himself. I know that now. Second-best can never do worthwhile things. There's all the time in the world to worry about conditions and Jin-qua and the Chinese and about the problems of the world. Perhaps I won't ever have to worry about being Tai-Pan; perhaps Robb won't think I'm good enough. Oh God, let me prove myself to become Tai-Pan so that I can use the power for good. Let this be a means to Thy ends. The Charter must come to pass. It is the only way.

Sweat pocked his forehead. He picked up the Bible. 'I swear by the Lord God to abide by these conditions. If and when I become Tai-Pan. So help me God.' His fingers were trembling as he replaced the Bible.

'Robb?' Struan said, not looking up.

'Five years as Tai-Pan and I can send Culum back to Scotland? Now? Change anything and everything I like?'

'Aye, by God. Do I have to repeat mysel'? In five months you do what you like. If you agree to the other conditions. Aye.'

There was a vast silence in the hold, but for the constant scurry of the rats in the darkness.

'Why should you want me out, Uncle?' Culum said.

'To hurt your father. You're the last of his line.'

'Aye, Robb. That he is.'

'That's a terrible thing to say! Terrible.' Culum was aghast. 'We're kin. Kin.'

'Yes,' Robb said, anguished. 'But we've been talking truths. Your father will sacrifice me, you, my children, to his ends. Why shouldn't I do the same?'

'Maybe you will, Robb. Maybe you will,' Struan said.

'You know I'd do nothing to hurt you. Lord God on high, what's happening to us? We've acquired some bullion and all of a sudden we're stinking with greed and God knows what else. Please let me go. In five months. Please, Dirk.'

'I *must* leave. Only in Parliament can I really control Longstaff and his successors – as you'll do when you leave Asia. That's where we can put the plan into effect. But Culum must be trained. A year as Tai-Pan and you leave.'

'How can he be trained in such a short time?'

'I'll know in five months if he can be Tai-Pan. If na, I'll make other arrangements.'

'What arrangements?'

'Are you ready to agree to the conditions, Robb? If so, swear on the Book and let's go aloft.'

'What arrangements?'

'God's death! Do you agree, Robb, or do you na? Is it one year or five? Or none?'

Robb shifted his weight on his legs as the ship heeled under a thickening wind. His whole being was warning him not to take the oath. But he had to. For his family's sake he had to. He took the Bible and it was heavy. 'Even though I loathe the Orient and everything it stands for, I swear by God to abide by the conditions to the best of my abilities, so help me God.' He handed the Bible to Struan. 'I think you'll regret making me stay as Tai-Pan – for one year.'

'I may. Hong Kong will na.' Struan opened the Bible and showed them the four half coins that he had stuck on the inside cover with sealing wax. He listed all Jin-qua's conditions – except the one lac to Gordon Chen. That's my business, Struan told himself, and he wondered briefly what Culum would think of his half brother – and of May-may – when he heard about them. Robb knew about May-may though he had never met her. Struan wondered if his enemies had already told Culum about Gordon and about May-may.

'I think you were right to swear us, Dirk,' Robb said. 'God alone knows what devilment these coins mean.'

When they returned to the cabin, Struan went to the desk and broke the seal on the letter. He read the first paragraph and shouted with joy. 'She's alive! Winifred's alive, by God. She got well!'

Robb grabbed the letter. Struan was beside himself and hugged Culum and began to dance a jig and the jig became a reel and Struan linked arms with Culum and they pulled Robb with them and all at once their hatred and distrust vanished.

Then Struan held them still with the hugeness of his strength. 'Now, together! One, two, three,' and they shouted the Latin battle cry of the clan at the top of their voices.

'*Feri*.' Strike home!

Then he hugged them again and roared, 'Steward!'

The seaman came running. 'Aye, aye, sorr?'

'A double tot for all hands. Order the piper to the quarterdeck! Bring a bottle of champagne and another pot of tea, by God!'

'Aye, aye, sorr!'

So the three men made peace with each other. But they all knew in the secret depths of their minds that everything had changed between them. Too much had been said. Soon they would go their separate ways. Alone.

'Thank God you opened the letter afterwards, Dirk,' Robb said. 'Thank God for the letter. I was feeling terrible. Terrible.'

'And I,' Culum said. 'Read it out, Father.'

Struan settled himself in the deep leather sea chair and read the letter to them. It was in Gaelic, dated four months ago, a month after Culum had sailed from Glasgow.

Parlan Struan wrote that Winifred's life had hung in the balance for two weeks and then she had begun to mend. The doctors could give no reason, other than to shrug their shoulders and say, 'The will of God.' She was living with him in the little croft that Struan had bought for him many years ago.

'She'll be happy there,' Culum said. 'But there are only gillies and goats to talk to. Where's she going to go to school?'

'First let her get very well. Then we can worry about that,' Robb said. 'Go on, Dirk.'

Then the letter gave news of the family. Parlan Struan had had two brothers and three sisters and they had all married, and now their children were married and they had children. And too, his own children, Dirk and Flora by his first marriage, and Robb, Uthenia and Susan by his second, had families.

Many of his descendants had emigrated: to the Canadian colonies, to the United States of America. A few were scattered over the Indies and Spanish South America.

Parlan Struan wrote that Alastair McCloud, who had married Robb's sister Susan, had come back from London with his son Hector to live again in Scotland – the loss of Susan and his daughter Clair from the cholera weighed heavily on him and had almost broken him; that he had received a letter from the Kerns – Flora, Dirk's sister, had married Farran Kern and last year they had sailed for Norfolk, Virginia. They had arrived safely and the voyage had been good, and they and their three children were fit and happy.

The letter continued: 'Tell Robb Roddy went off to university yesterday. I put him on the stagecoach for Edinburgh with six shillings in his pocket and food for four days. Your cousin Dougall Struan has written that he will take him in in his holidays and be his guardian until Robb comes home. I took the liberty of sending a sight draft in Robb's name for fifty guineas to pay for a year's room and board and a shilling a week for pocket money. I also gave him a Bible and warned him against loose women and drunkenness and gambling and read out the piece of Will Shakespeare's *Hamlet* about "neither a borrower nor a lender be" and made the lad write it down and put it on the cover of the Good Book. He writes with a good hand.

'Your dear Ronalda and the children are buried in one of the plague pits. I am sorry, Dirk laddie, but the law said that all that died had to be buried thus with burning and then with quicklime for the safety of the living. But the burial was consecrated according to our faith and the land set aside as hallowed ground. God rest their souls.

'Do not worry about Winnie. The lassie is truly bonny now and here by Loch Lomond where the foot of God has lain, she will grow into a fine, Godfearing woman. Take heed now: do not let the barbarian heathen in Indian Cathay take your soul awa' and lock your door carefully against the evil that breeds in those devil lands. Will you not come home soon? My health is very fine and the good Lord has blessed me. Only seven more years for my three score and ten which the Lord promised but one in four hundred sees these evil days. I am very well. There were bad riots in Glasgow and in Birmingham and Edinburgh, so the papers say. More Chartists' riots. The factory workers are demanding more money for their labours. There was a good hanging two days ago in Glasgow for sheep stealing. Damn the English! What a world we are living in when a good Scotsman's hanged for just stealing an English sheep, by a Scots judge. Terrible. At the same assize hundreds were transported to Australian Van Diemen's land for rioting and striking, and for burning down a factory. Culum's friend, Bartholomew Angus, was sentenced to ten years' transportation, to New South Wales, for leading a Chartist riot in Edinburgh. Folk are . . .'

'Oh my God!' Culum said.

'Who's Bartholomew, Culum?' Struan said.

'We shared chambers at university. Poor old Bart.'

Struan said sharply. 'Did you know he was a Chartist?'

'Of course.' Culum went to the window and gazed at the wake of the ship.

'Are you a Chartist, Culum?'

'You said yourself that the Charter was good.'

'Aye. But I also gave you my views on insurrection. Are you an active Chartist?'

'If I were home I would be. Most university students are in favour of the Charter.'

'Then it's a good thing you're out here, by God. If Bartholomew led a riot then he deserved ten years. We've good laws and the finest parliamentary system on earth. Insurrection, rioting and striking are na the ways to get changes made.'

'What else does the letter say, Father?'

Struan watched his son's back for a moment, hearing an echo of Ronalda's tone of voice. He made a mental note to look more carefully into Chartist affairs in the future. Then he began to read again: 'Folk are still arriving daily in Glasgow from the Highlands where the lairds are still enclosing the clan lands and taking away the clansmen's birthright. That blackhearted fiend, the Earl of Struan, may the Lord strike him dead, is raising a regiment to fight in the Indian colonies. Men are flocking to his banner sucked in by promises of loot and land. There's a rumour that we will have to go to war again with the cursed Americans over the Canadian colonies, and there are stories that war has broken out between those devils the French and the Russians over the Ottoman Turks. Those cursed Frenchmen. As if we haven't suffered enough over that archfiend Bonaparte.

'It is a sorry state we live in, laddie. Oh, I forgot to mention that plans have been laid for a railway to join Glasgow and Edinburgh within five years. Will that not be grand? Then mayhaps we Scots can band together and throw out the devil English and have our own king. I embrace you and your brother and hug Culum for me. Your respectful father, Parlan Struan.'

Struan looked up with a wry smile. 'Still as bloodthirsty as ever.'

'If the earl raises a regiment for India, it may come out here,' Robb said.

'Aye. I had the same thought. Well, lad, if he ever reaches the domain of The Noble House, that regiment will go home headless, so help me God.'

'So help me God,' Culum echoed.

There was a knock on the door and the steward hurried in with the champagne and glasses and tea. 'Cap'n Orlov thanks you on behalf of the crew, sorr.'

'Ask him and Wolfgang to join us at the end of the watch.'

'Aye, aye, sorr.'

After the wine and tea had been poured, Struan raised his glass. 'A toast. To Winifred, who has returned from the dead!'

They drank and Robb said, 'Another toast. Here's to The Noble House. Maybe we'll never think evil or do evil to one another ever again.'

'Aye.'

They drank again.

'Robb, when we get to Hong Kong, write to our agents. Tell them to find out who the directors of our bank were and who was responsible for over-extending credit.'

'All right, Dirk.'

'And then, Father?' Culum asked.

'Then we'll destroy those responsible,' Struan said. 'And their families.'

Culum felt chilled by the implacable finality of the sentence. 'Why their families?'

'What did their greed do to ours? To us? To our future? We've to pay for years for their greed. So they'll pay in like measure. All of them.'

Culum got up and walked for the door.

'What do you want, laddie?'

'The latrine. I mean the "head".'

The door closed after him.

'Sorry about what I said.' Struan sighed. 'It had to be done that way.'

'I know. I'm sorry too. But you're right about Parliament. More and more power will pass to Parliament, and that's where the big trading deals will be settled. I'll watch the financing and we can both watch Culum and help him. Isn't it wonderful about Winifred?'

'Aye.'

'Culum's got very definite ideas about some things, hasn't he?'

'He's very young. Ronalda brought them up – well, she took the Scriptures literally, as you well know. Culum'll have to grow up sometime.'

'What are you going to do about Gordon Chen?'

'You mean about him and Culum?' Struan watched the sea gulls mewing. 'That has to be dealt with as soon as we get back to Hong Kong.'

'Poor Culum. Growing up's not easy, is it?'

Struan shook his head. 'It's never easy.'

After a moment Robb said, 'Remember my lassie, Ming Soo?'

'Aye.'

'I often wonder what happened to her and the bairn.'

'The money you gave her would set her up like a princess and find her a wonderful husband, Robb. She's a mandarin's wife somewhere. No need to worry about them.'

'Little Isabel would be ten now.' Robb let himself drift back into the ever-pleasant memory of her laughter, and the gratification Ming Soo had given him. So much, he thought. She had given him more love and kindness and gentleness and compassion in one day than Sarah had given him in all their marriage. 'You should marry again, Dirk.'

'There's time to think about that.' Struan absently checked the barometer. It read 30.1 inches, fair weather. 'Ride Culum very hard, Robb, when you're Tai-Pan.'

'I will,' Robb said.

As Culum came on deck, *China Cloud* heeled over and broke out of the channel that the small offshore island of Tung Ku Chau formed with Hong Kong. The ship came swiftly out of the neck of the mountain-dominated passageway into open sea and turned southwest. Another larger island, Pokliu Chau, was two miles to port. A stiff northeast monsoon flecked the waves, and above was the dull blanket of clouds.

Culum picked his way forward, carefully avoiding the neat circles of ropes and hawsers. He skirted the gleaming rows of cannon and marvelled at the cleanliness of everything. He had been aboard other merchantmen in Hong Kong harbour and they were all squalid.

The port head was occupied by two seamen, so he clambered over the side into the starboard one. He hung on to the lifelines and, with great difficulty, pulled down his trousers and squatted precariously on the netting.

A young, redheaded sailor wandered up and swung neatly over the gunnel into the head, and took down his pants. He was barefoot and did not hold on to the ropes as he squatted.

'Top o' the morning, sorr,' the sailor said.

'And to you,' Culum said, holding grimly on to the lines.

The sailor was done quickly. He leaned forward to the gunnel and took a square of newspaper from a box and wiped himself, then carefully tossed the paper below and retied his pants around his waist.

'What're you doing?' Culum asked.

'Eh? Oh, the paper, sorr? God rot me if I knows, sorr. It be the Tai-Pan's orders. Wipe yor arse wiv paper or lose two month pay and ten days in the bleedin' brig.' The sailor laughed. 'The Tai-Pan be a right one, beggin' yor pardon. But she be 'is ship, so you wipes yor bleedin' arse.' He leaped aboard easily and dunked his hands in a pail of seawater and slopped it over his feet. 'Wash yor bleeding 'ands too, by God, then yor feets, or in the bleedin' brig you goes! Right proper strange. Stark raving . . . beggin' yor pardon, sorr. But wot wiv wiping yor bleedin' 'ands an' wiping yor bleedin' arse an' bathin' once a bleedin' week an' fresh clothes once a bleedin' week, life's a proper bleeder.'

'Bleeder nuffink,' another sailor said, leaning on the gunnel, chomping on a tobacco quid. 'Pay in good silver? When it be bleedin' due, by God! Grub like a bleeder prince? Prize money to boot. Wot more you want, Charlie?' Then to Culum, 'I ain't about to know 'ows the Tai-Pan do it, sorr, but 'is ships got less pox an' less scurvy'n any on the 'igh seas.' He spat tobacco juice to windward. 'So I wipes me arse and 'appy to do it. Beggin' yor pardon, sorr, if I wuz you, sorr, I'd do the same. The Tai-Pan be terrible fond o' 'aving 'is orders obeyed!'

'Reef tops'ls and top ta'gallants,' Captain Orlov shouted from the quarterdeck, his voice huge for so small a man.

The sailors touched their forelocks to Culum and joined the men who were climbing into the shrouds.

Culum used the paper and washed his hands and went below and waited for the opportunity to break into their conversation.

'What's the point of using paper?'

'Eh?' Struan said.

'In the head. Use paper or ten days in the brig.'

'Oh. I forgot to tell you, laddie. The Chinese think there's some connection between dung and disease.'

'That's ridiculous,' Culum scoffed.

'The Chinese dinna think so. Neither do I.' Struan turned to Robb. 'I've tried it for three months on *China Cloud*. Sickness is down.'

'Even compared with *Thunder Cloud*?' Robb asked.

'Aye.'

'It's a coincidence,' Culum said.

Robb grunted. 'You'll find a lot of coincidences in our ships, Culum. It's only fifty-odd years since Captain Cook found that limes and fresh vegetables cured scurvy. Maybe dung does have something to do with disease.'

'When did you last bathe, Culum?' Struan said.

'I don't know – a month – no, I remember. Captain Perry insisted that I bathe with the crew once a week in *Thunder Cloud*. Nearly caught my death of cold. Why?'

'When did you last wash your clothes?'

Culum blinked at his father and looked down at his heavy brown woollen trousers and frock coat. 'They've never been washed! Why should they be washed?'

Struan's eyes glinted. 'From now on, ashore or afloat, you bathe your whole body once a week. You use paper and wash your hands. You have your clothes washed once a week. You drink nae water, only tea. And you brush your teeth daily.'

'Why? No water? That's madness. Wash my clothes? Why, that'll make them shrink and spoil the cut and goodness knows what!'

'That's what you'll do. This is the Orient. I want you alive. And well. And healthy.'

'I will not. I'm not a child or one of your seamen!'

'You'd better do as your father says,' Robb said. 'I fought him too. Every new idea he tried. Until he proved that these things worked. Why, no one knows. But where people have died like flies, we're fit.'

'You're not at all,' Culum said. 'You told me you're sick all the time.'

'Yes. But that goes back years. I never believed your father about water, so I kept drinking it. Now my guts bleed and they'll always bleed. It's too late for me, but, by God, I wish I'd tried. *Perhaps* I'd be without gutrot. Dirk never drinks water. Only tea.'

'That's what the Chinese do, lad.'

'I don't believe it.'

'Well, while you're finding out the truth or na,' Struan snapped, 'you'll obey those orders. Those *are* orders.'

Culum's chin jutted. 'Just because of some heathen Chinese customs, I have to change my whole way of life. Is that what you're saying?'

'I'm prepared to learn from them. Aye, I'll try anything to keep my health, and so will you, by God.' Struan let out a bellow. 'Steward!'

The door opened. 'Aye, aye, sorr.'

'Get a bath ready for Mr Culum. In my cabin. And fresh clothes.'

'Aye, aye, sorr.'

Struan walked across the cabin, towering over Culum. He examined his son's head. 'You've lice in your hair.'

'I don't understand you at all!' Culum burst out. 'Everyone's got lice. Lice are with us whether we like it or not. You scratch a little and that's an end to it.'

'I dinna have lice, nor does Robb.'

'Then you're peculiar. Unique.' Culum took an irritable swallow of champagne, 'Bathing is a stupid risk to health, as everyone knows.'

'You stink, Culum.'

'So does everyone,' Culum said impatiently. 'Why else do we always carry pomades? Stinking is a way of life, too. Lice are a curse of people, and that's the end of it.'

'I dinna stink, nor does Robb and his family, nor do my men, and our health's the best in the Orient. You'll do as you're told. Lice are na necessary and neither is stink.'

'Best you go to London, Father. That's the biggest stink in the world. If people hear you go on about lice and stink, they'll think you mad.'

Father and son glared at each other. 'You'll obey orders. You'll clean yoursel', by God, or I'll get the bosun to do it for you. On deck!'

'Do it, Culum,' Robb interceded. He could feel Culum's resentment and Struan's inflexibility. 'What does it matter? Compromise. Try it for five months, eh? If you don't feel better yourself by that time, then go back to the usual way.'

'And if I refuse?'

Struan glowered down at him implacably. 'I cherish you, Culum, beyond my own life. But certain things you'll do. Else I'll treat you like a disobedient seaman.'

'How's that?'

'I'll tow you behind the ship for ten minutes and wash you that way.'

'Instead of giving orders,' Culum burst out indignantly, 'why don't you just say "please" occasionally?'

Struan laughed outright. 'By God, you're right, lad.' He thumped Culum on the back. 'Will you please do what I ask? By God, you're right. I'll say "please" more often. And dinna worry about clothes. We'll get you the best tailor in Asia. You need more clothes, anyway.' Struan glanced at Robb. 'Your tailor, Robb?'

'Yes. As soon as we're settled in Hong Kong.'

'We'll send for him tomorrow to come from Macao, with his staff. Unless he's already in Hong Kong. For five months, lad?'

'All right. But I still think it's peculiar.'

Struan refilled their glasses.

'Now. I think we should celebrate the rebirth of The Noble House.'

'How, Dirk?' Robb asked.

'We'll give a ball.'

'What?' Culum looked up excitedly, his indignation forgotten.

'Aye, a ball. For the whole European population. In princely style. A month from today.'

'That'll set a hawk among the pigeons!' Robb said.

'What do you mean, Uncle?'

'There'll be the biggest panic among the ladies you've ever seen. They'll vie with each other for the honour of being the best-dressed – in the latest fashion! They'll hound their husbands and try to steal each other's dressmakers! My God, a ball is a marvellous idea. I wonder what Shevaun will wear.'

202

'Nothing – if it pleases her!' Struan's eyes glowed. 'Aye, a ball. We'll give a prize for the best-dressed lady. I think the prize—'

'Have you not heard of the judgment of Paris?' Robb said aghast.

'Aye. But Aristotle'll be the judge.'

'He's much too clever to take that position.'

'We'll see.' Struan reflected a moment. 'The prize has to be worthy. A thousand guineas.'

'You must be joking!' Culum said.

'A thousand guineas.'

Culum was overwhelmed by the idea of such extravagance. It was obscene. Criminal. A thousand guineas in England today and you could live like a king, for five or ten years. The wage of a factory man who worked from sunup to sundown and deep into the night, six days a week, for all the weeks of the year, was fifteen to twenty pounds a year – and on this a home was made and children brought up and a wife kept, rent, food, clothing, coal. My father's mad, he thought, money-mad. Think of the twenty thousand guineas he peed – yes, peed away – on the stupid bet with Brock and Gorth. But that was a gamble to dispose of Brock. A worthwhile gamble if it had come off, and in a way it has – the bullion is in *China Cloud* and we're rich again. Rich.

Now Culum knew that to be rich was no longer to be poor. He knew that his father was right – it wasn't money that was important. Only the lack of it.

'It's too much, too much,' Robb was saying, shocked.

'Aye. In one way it is.' Struan lit a cheroot. 'But it's the duty of The Noble House to be princely. The news will flood like no news before. And the story of it will last for a hundred years.' He put his hand on Culum's shoulder. 'Never forget another rule, laddie: when you're gambling for high stakes you must risk high. If you're na prepared to risk high, you dinna belong in the game.'

'Such a – a huge amount will make, may make, some people risk more money than they can afford. That's not good, is it?'

'The point of money is to use it. I'd say this is going to be money well spent.'

'But what are the stakes you gain?'

'Face, lad.' Struan turned to Robb. 'Who's the winner?'

Robb shook his head helplessly. 'I don't know. Beauty – Shevaun. But best-dressed? There're some who'd risk a fortune to get the honour, let alone the prize.'

'Have you met Shevaun yet, Culum?'

'No, Father. I saw her once taking a promenade on the road that

George – George Glessing – has laid out from Glessing's Point to Happy Valley. Miss Tillman's beautiful. But I think Miss Sinclair's much more attractive. So charming. George and I spent some time in her company.'

'Did you, now?' Struan held down his sudden interest.

'Yes,' Culum replied ingenuously. 'We had a farewell dinner with Miss Sinclair and Horatio on George's ship. Poor George has had his ship taken away from him. He was most upset. We're really going to have a ball?'

'Why has Glessing lost his ship?'

'Longstaff appointed him harbour master and chief surveyor, and the admiral ordered him to accept the position. Miss Sinclair agreed with me that it was a good opportunity for him – but he didn't think so.'

'Do you like him?'

'Oh, yes. He was very nice to me.' Culum almost added, even though I'm the son of the Tai-Pan. He thanked his luck that Glessing and he had a shared interest. Both were fine cricket players – Culum had captained the university team, and last year had played for his country.

'By Jove,' Glessing had said, 'you must be damned good. Only fielded for the navy myself. What bat did you play?'

'First wicket down.'

'By Gad – best I've made was second. Damme, Culum old chap, perhaps we should set aside a place for a cricket ground, eh? Get a bit of practice in, eh?'

Culum smiled to himself, very glad he was a cricketer. Without that he knew Glessing would have dismissed him; then he would not have had the pleasure of being near Mary. He wondered if he could escort her to the ball. 'Miss Sinclair and Horatio like you very much, Father.'

'I thought Mary was in Macao.'

'She was, Father. But she came back to Hong Kong for a few days, a week or so ago. A lovely lady, isn't she?'

There was a sudden clanging of the ship's bell and the scurry of feet, and the cry 'All hands on deck!' Struan bolted out of the cabin.

Robb started to follow, but stopped at the cabin door. 'Two things quickly while we're alone, Culum. First, do what your father says and be patient with him. He's a strange man, with strange ideas, but most of them work. Second, I'll help you all I can to become Tai-Pan.' Then he rushed out of the cabin, with Culum trailing behind.

When Struan burst on to the quarterdeck, the crew was already at action stations and opening the gunports, and aloft men were swarming the rigging.

Directly ahead, spread against the horizon, was a menacing fleet of war junks.

'By Thor's left buttock, it's a bloody fleet!' Captain Orlov said. 'I've counted more than a hundred, Tai-Pan. Turn and run?'

'Hold your course, Captain. We've the speed of them. Clear decks! We'll go closer and have a look. Set royals and fore-royals!'

Orlov bellowed aloft, 'Set royals and fore-royals! All sails ho!' The officers took up the shouts and the men raced into the shrouds and unfurled the sails, and *China Cloud* picked up speed and sliced through the water.

The ship was in the channel between the big island of Pokliu Chau, two miles to port, and the smaller island of Ap Li Chau half a mile to starboard. Ap Li Chau was a quarter of a mile off the coast of Hong Kong Island and formed a fine bay that had been named Aberdeen. On the shore at Aberdeen was a small fishing village. Struan observed more sampans and fishing junks than had been there a month ago.

Robb and Culum came up on to the quarterdeck. Robb saw the junks and his scalp prickled. 'Who are they, Dirk?'

'Dinna ken, lad. Keep clear there!'

Culum and Robb jumped out of the way as a bevy of sailors clambered down the rigging and chanteyed the hawsers tight, then raced aft to their action stations. Struan passed the binoculars to Mauss, who had lumbered up beside him. 'Can you make out the flag, Wolfgang?'

'No, not yet, Tai-Pan.' Wolfgang was peering dry-mouthed at a huge ponderous war junk in the lead, one of the biggest he had ever seen – over two hundred feet long and about five hundred tons, the dominating stern heeling slowly under the press of the three vast sails. '*Gott im Himmel*, too many for a pirate fleet. Would they be an invasion armada? Surely they wouldn't dare attack Hong Kong with our fleet so near.'

'We'll soon find out,' Struan said. 'Two points to starboard!'

'Two points to starboard,' the helmsman called.

'Steady as she goes!' Struan checked the lie of the sails. The throbbing of the wind and the straining rigging filled him with excitement.

'Look!' Captain Orlov cried out, pointing astern.

Another flotilla of junks was swooping out from behind the southern tip of Pokliu Chau, readying to cut off their retreat.

'It's an ambush! Ready to go about . . .'

'Avast there, Captain! I'm on the quarterdeck!'

Captain Orlov walked sourly over to the helmsman and stood by the binnacle, damning the rule which provided that when the Tai-Pan was on the quarterdeck of any ship of The Noble House he was captain.

Well, Orlov thought, good luck, Tai-Pan. If we don't go about and run, those gallows-baited junks will cut us off and the others ahead'll swamp us, and my beautiful ship will be no more. The devil she will! We'll blow thirty of them to the fire pits of Valhalla and sail through them like a Valkyrie.

And for the first time in four days, he forgot the bullion and gleefully thought only of the coming fight.

The ship's bell sounded eight bells.

'Permission to go below, Captain!' Orlov said.

'Aye. Take Mr Culum and show him what to do.'

Orlov preceded Culum nimbly into the depths of the ship. 'At eight bells in the forenoon watch – that's noon, shore time – it's the duty of the captain to wind the chronometer,' he said, relieved to be off the quarterdeck now that Struan had usurped command. But then, he told himself, if you were Tai-Pan you'd do the same. You'd never allow anyone to have the most beautiful job on earth when you were there.

His small blue eyes were studying Culum. He had seen Culum's immediate distaste and the covert looks at his back and tiny legs. Even after forty years of such looks he still hated to be thought a freak. 'I was birthed in a blizzard on an ice floe. My mother said I was so beautiful the evil spirit Vorg mashed me with his hoofs an hour after my birth.'

Culum moved uneasily in the half-darkness. 'Oh?'

'Vorg has cloven hoofs.' Orlov chuckled. 'Do you believe in spirits?'

'No. No, I don't think so.'

'But you believe in the Devil? Like all good Christians?'

'Yes.' Culum tried to keep his fear off his face. 'What has to be done to the chronometer?'

'It has to be wound.' Again Orlov chuckled. 'If you'd been born as I was, mayhaps you'd be Culum the Hunchback instead of Culum the Tall and Fair, eh? You look at things differently from here.'

'I'm sorry – it must be very hard for you.'

'Not hard – your Shakespeare had better words. But don't worry, Culum the Strong. I can kill a man twice my size so easily. Would you like me to teach you to kill? You couldn't have a better teacher. Except the Tai-Pan.'

'No. No, thank you.'

'Wise to learn. Very wise. Ask your father. One day you'll need such knowledge. Aye, soon. Did you know I had second sight?'

Culum shuddered. 'No.'

Orlov's eyes glittered and his smile made him more gnome-like and evil. 'You've a lot to learn. You want to be Tai-Pan, don't you?'

'Yes. I hope to be. One day.'

'There'll be blood on your hands that day.'

Culum tried to control his sudden start. 'What do you mean by that?'

'You've ears. You'll have blood on your hands that day. Yes. And soon you'll need someone you can trust for many a day. So long as Norstedt Stride Orlov, the hunchback, is captain of one of your ships, you can trust him.'

'I'll remember, Captain Orlov,' Culum said, and promised himself that when he did become Tai-Pan Orlov would never be one of his captains. Then, as he looked back into the man's face, he had the weird feeling that Orlov had seen into his heart.

'What's the matter, Captain?'

'Ask yourself that.' Orlov unlocked the housing of the chronometer. To do this he had to stand on a rung of the ladder. Then he began to wind the clock carefully with a large key. 'You wind this clock thirty-three times.'

'Why do you do it? Not one of the officers?' Culum asked, not really caring.

'It's the captain's job. One of them. Navigation's one of the secret things. If all aboard knew how to do it, there'd be mutiny after mutiny. Best that only the captain and a few of the officers know. Then, without them, the seamen are lost and helpless. We keep the chronometer locked and here for safety. Isn't it beautiful? The workmanship? Made by good English brains and good English hands. It tells London time exactly.'

Culum felt the closeness of the passageway and nausea building inside of him – overlaid by fear of Orlov and of the coming battle. But he caught hold of himself and was determined that he would not allow Orlov to bait him into losing his temper, and tried to close his nostrils against the pervading sour smell from the bilges. There'll be a reckoning later, he swore. 'Is a chronometer so very important?'

'You've been to university and you ask that? Without this beauty we'd be lost. You've heard of Captain Cook? He used the first one, and proved it, sixty years ago. Until that time we could never find our longitude. But now, with exact London time and the sextant, we know where we are to a mile.' Orlov relocked the housing and shot an abrupt glance at Culum. 'Can you use a sextant?'

'No.'

'When we sink the junks, I'll show you. You think you can be Tai-Pan of The Noble House ashore? Eh?'

There was the sound of scurrying feet on deck and they felt *China Cloud* surge even faster through the waves. Here, below, the whole ship seemed to pulsate with life.

Culum licked his dry lips. 'Can we sink so many and escape?'

'If we don't, we'll be swimming.' The little man beamed up at Culum. 'Ever been shipwrecked or sunk?'

'No. And I can't swim.'

'If you're a sailor, best not know how to swim. Swimming only prolongs the inevitable – if the seas wants you and your time has come.' Orlov pulled the chain to make certain the lock was secure. 'Thirty years I've been to sea an' I can't swim. I've been sunk upwards of ten times, from the China seas to the Bering Straits, but I've always found a spar or a boat. One day the sea'll get me. In her own time.' He eased the fighting iron on his wrist. 'I'll be glad to be back in port.'

Culum thankfully followed him up the gangway. 'You don't trust the men aboard?'

'A captain trusts his ship, only his ship. And himself alone.'

'You trust my father?'

'He's the captain.'

'I don't understand.'

Orlov made no reply. Once on the quarterdeck, he checked the sails and frowned. Too much sail, too close to shore. Too many unknown reefs and the smell of a squall somewhere. The line of encroaching junks was two miles ahead: implacable, silent, closing in on them.

The ship had full sails set, the mainsails still reefed, the whole ship throbbing with joy. This joy permeated the crew. When Struan ordered the reefs let go, they sprang to the rigging and sang the sails into place and forgot about the bullion that had infected them. The wind freshened and the sails crackled. The ship heeled over and gathered speed, the seawater frothing like yeast in the scuppers.

'Mr Cudahy! Take a watch below and brings arms aloft!'

'Aye, aye, sorr!' Cudahy, the first mate, was a black-haired Irishman with dancing eyes, and he wore a golden ear-ring.

'Steady as she goes! Deck watch! Prepare cannon! Load grape!'

The men flung themselves at the cannons, wheeled them out of their ports, charged them with grape and wheeled them back again.

'Number-three gun crew an extra tot of rum! Number eighteen to clean out the bilges!'

There were cheers and curses.

It was a custom Struan had started many years ago. When going into a fight the first gun crew ready was rewarded and the last was given the dirtiest job on the ship.

Struan scanned the sky and the tautness of the sails and turned the binoculars on the huge war junk. It had many cannon ports and a dragon for a figurehead and a flag which at this distance was still indistinct. Struan could see dozens of Chinese thronging the decks and torches burning.

'Get the water barrels ready!' Orlov shouted.

'What're the water barrels for, Father?' Culum said.

'To douse fires, lad. The junks have torches burning. They'll be well stocked with fire rockets and stink bombs. Stink bombs're made from pitch and sulphur. They can make havoc of a clipper if you're na prepared.' He looked aft. The other flotilla of junks was surging into the channel behind them.

'We're cut off, aren't we?' Culum said, his stomach turning over.

'Aye. But only a fool'd go that way. Look at the wind, lad. That way we'd have to beat up against it, and something tells me it'll shift farther against us soon. But for'ard we've the wind and the speed of any junk. See how ponderous they are, laddie! Like cart horses against us – a greyhound. We've ten times the firepower, ship to ship.'

One of the halyards at the top of the mainmast parted abruptly and the spar screamed, smashing itself against the mast, the sail flapping free.

'Port watch aloft!' Struan roared. 'Send up the royal lift line!'

Culum watched the seamen claw out on to the spar almost at the top of the mainmast, the wind ripping at them, hanging on with nails and toes, knowing he could never do that. He felt the fear bile in his stomach and could not forget what Orlov had said: blood on your hands. Whose blood? He lurched for the gunnel and vomited.

'Here, laddie,' Struan said, offering the water bag that hung from a belaying pin.

Culum pushed it away, hating his father for noticing that he had been sick.

'Clean your mouth out, by God!' Struan's voice was harsh.

Culum obeyed miserably and did not notice that the water actually was cold tea. He drank some of it and it made him sick again. Then he rinsed out his mouth and sipped sparingly, feeling dreadful.

'First time I went into battle I was sick as a drunk gillie – sicker than you can imagine. And frightened to death.'

'I don't believe it,' Culum replied weakly. 'You've never been afraid or sick in your life.'

Struan grunted. 'Well, you can believe it. It was at Trafalgar.'

'I didn't know you were there!' In his astonishment Culum momentarily forgot his nausea.

'I was a powder monkey. The navy uses children on the capital ships to carry powder from the magazine to the gundecks. The passageway has to be as small as possible to lessen the chance of fire and the whole ship exploding.' Struan remembered the roaring guns and the screams of the wounded, limbs scattered on the deck, slippery with blood – and stench of blood and redness of the scuppers. Smell of vomit in the never-ending black little tunnel, slimy with vomit. Groping up to the exploding guns with kegs of powder, then groping down another time into the horrifying darkness, lungs on fire, heart a violent machine, terror tears streaming – hour after hour. 'I was frightened to death.'

'You were really at Trafalgar?'

'Aye. I was seven. I was the oldest of my group but the most afraid.' Struan clapped his son warmly on the shoulder. 'So dinna worry. Nae anything wrong in that.'

'I'm not afraid now, Father. It's just the stench of the hold.'

'Dinna fool yoursel'. It's the stench of the blood you think you smell – and the fear it'll be your own.'

Culum quickly hung over the side of the ship as he retched again. Though the wind was brisk, it would not blow the sick sweet smell out of his head or the words of Orlov from his brain.

Struan went over to the brandy keg and drew a tot and handed it to Culum and watched while he drank it.

'Beggin' yor pardon, sirr,' the steward said. 'The bath wot was ordered be ready, sirr.'

'Thank you.' Struan waited until the steward had joined his gun crew, then he said to Culum. 'Go below, lad.'

Culum felt the humiliation well in him. 'No. I'm fine here.'

'Go below!' Though it was an order, it was given gently, and Culum knew that he was being allowed the chance to go below and save face.

'Please, Father,' he said near tears. 'Let me stay. I'm sorry.'

'No need to be sorry. I've been in this sort of danger a thousand times, so it's easy for me. I know what to expect. Go below, lad. There's time enough to bathe and come back on deck. And be part of a fight, if fight it is. Please go below.'

Despondently, Culum obeyed.

Struan turned his attention to Robb, who was leaning on the gunnel, grey-faced. Struan thought for a moment, then walked over to him. 'Would you do me a favour, Robb? Keep the lad company? He's na feeling well at all.'

Robb forced a smile. 'Thanks, Dirk. But this time I need to stay. Sick or not. Is it an invasion armada?'

'Nay, lad. But dinna worry. We can blast a way through them if need be.'

'I know I know.'

'How's Sarah? She's very near her time, is she na? Sorry, I forgot to ask.'

'She's as well as most women feel with a few weeks to go. I'll be glad when the waiting's over.'

'Aye.' Struan turned away and adjusted the course a shade.

Robb forced his mind off the junks that seemed to fill the sea ahead. I hope it's another girl, he thought. Girls are so much easier to raise than boys. I hope she's like Karen. Dear little Karen!

Robb hated himself again for shouting at her this morning – was it only this morning that they had all been together in *Thunder Cloud*? Karen had disappeared, and Sarah and he had thought she had fallen overboard. They were frantic and when the search had begun, Karen had come blithely on deck from the hold where she had been playing. And Robb had been so relieved that he had shouted at her, and Karen had fled sobbing into her mother's arms. Robb had cursed his wife for not looking after Karen more carefully, knowing that it was not Sarah's fault, but being unable to stop himself. Then in a few minutes little Karen was like any child, in easy laughter, everything forgotten. And he and Sarah were like any parents, still sick with mutual anger, everything not forgotten . . .

Fore and aft, the junk fleets were blocking *China Cloud*'s avenues of escape. Robb saw his brother leaning against the binnacle, casually lighting a cheroot from a smouldering cannon taper, and wished that he could be so calm.

Oh God, give me strength to endure five months and another twelve months and the voyage home, and please make Sarah's time easy.

He leaned over the rail and was very sick.

'Two points to port,' Struan said, watching the shore of Hong Kong carefully. He was almost close enough to the finger of rocks off the starboard bow and well to windward of the line of junks. A few minutes more and he would turn and hurtle at the junk he had already marked for death, and he would smash through the line safely – if there were no fire ships and if the wind did not slacken and if no hidden reef or bank mutilated him.

211

The sky was darkening to the north. The monsoon was holding true, but Struan knew that in these waters the wind could shift a quarter or more with alarming suddenness, or a violent squall could sweep out of the seas. With the ship carrying so much sail he would be in great danger, for the wind could rip away his sails before he could reef them, or tear away his masts. Then too, there could be many reefs and shoals waiting to tear his ship's belly open. There were no charts of these waters. But Struan knew that only speed would carry them to safety. And joss.

'*Gott im Himmel!*' Mauss was peering through the binoculars. 'It's the Lotus! The Silver Lotus!'

Struan grabbed the binoculars and focused on the flag that flew atop the huge junk: a silver flower on a red background. No mistake. It was the Silver Lotus, the flag of Wu Fang Choi, the pirate king, whose sadism was legendary, whose countless fleets ravaged and ruled the coasts of all south China and exacted tribute a thousand miles north and south. Supposedly, his base was in Formosa.

'What's Wu Fang Choi doing in these waters?' Mauss asked. Again he felt the weird hope-fear welling in him. Thy will be done, oh Lord.

'The bullion,' Struan said. 'It must be the bullion. Otherwise Wu Fang Choi would never risk coming here, na with our fleet so close.'

For years the Portuguese and all the traders had paid tribute to Wu Fang Choi for the safe-conduct of their ships. Tribute was cheaper than the loss of the merchantmen, and his junks kept the south China seas rid of other pirates – most of the time. But with the coming of the expeditionary force last year, the British traders had ceased paying for this safe passage, and one of Wu Fang's pirate fleets had begun to plunder the sea-lanes and the coast near Macao. Four Royal Navy frigates had sought out and destroyed most of the pirate junks, and followed those that fled into Bias Bay – a pirate haven on the coast, forty miles north of Hong Kong. There the frigates had laid waste the pirate junks and sampans, and had fired two pirate villages. Since that time the flag of Wu Fang Choi had never ventured near.

A cannon boomed from the pirate flagship, and astonishingly all the junks except one turned into the wind and downed mainsails, leaving only their short sails aft to give them leeway. A small junk detached itself from the fleet and headed the mile towards *China Cloud*.

'Helm alee!' Struan ordered, and *China Cloud* was turned into the wind. The sails flapped anxiously and the ship lost way and almost stopped. 'Keep her head t'wind!'

'Aye, aye, sorr!'

Struan was looking through the binoculars at the small junk. Waving from the masthead was a white flag. 'God's death! What're they playing at? Chinese never use a flag o' truce!' The ship came closer and Struan was even more dumbfounded at the sight of a huge black-bearded European dressed in heavy seafaring clothes, cutlass at his belt, conning the junk. Beside the man was a young Chinese boy, richly dressed in green brocade gown and pants and soft black boots. Struan saw the European train his long telescope on *China Cloud*. After a moment the man put the telescope down, laughed uproariously and waved.

Struan passed the binoculars to Mauss. 'What do you make of that man?' He leaned across to Captain Orlov, who had a telescope trained on the junk. 'Cap'n?'

'Pirate, that's certain.' Orlov handed his telescope to Robb. 'Another rumour is confirmed – that Wu Fang Choi has Europeans in his fleet.'

'But why would they all down sails, Dirk?' Robb said incredulously.

'The emissary'll tell us.' Struan walked to the edge of the quarterdeck. 'Mister,' he called out to Cudahy, 'ready to put a shot across his bows!'

'Aye, aye, sorr.' Cudahy jumped for the first cannon and trained it.

'Cap'n Orlov! Get the longboat ready. You lead the boarding party. If we dinna sink her first.'

'Why board her, Dirk?' Robb said, approaching Struan.

'No pirate junk's coming within fifty yards. It may be a fire ship or full of powder. In times like these it's better to be ready for devilment.'

Culum self-consciously appeared in the companionway dressed in a seaman's clothes – heavy woollen shirt and woollen jacket and wide-legged trousers and rope shoes.

'Hello, lad,' Struan said.

'What's going on?'

Struan told him, and added, 'The clothes suit you, lad. You're looking better.'

'I am much better,' Culum said, feeling uncomfortable and alien.

When the pirate junk was a hundred yards away, *China Cloud* put a shot across her bows and Struan picked up a horn. 'Heave to!' he shouted. 'Or I'll blow you out of the water!'

Obediently the junk swung into the wind and dropped her sails and began to drift with the strength of the tide.

'Ahoy, *China Cloud*! Permission to come aboard,' the black-bearded man shouted.

'Why, and who are you?'

'Cap'n Scragger, late o' London Town,' the man called back and guffawed. 'A word in yor ear, M'Lord Struan, privy like!'

'Come aboard alone. Unarmed!'

'Flag o' truce, matey?'

'Aye!' Struan walked to the quarterdeck rail. 'Keep the junk covered, Mr Cudahy!'

'He be covered, sorr!'

A small dinghy was lowered over the side of the junk, and Scragger climbed into it nimbly and began rowing towards *China Cloud*. As he approached he began singing in a rich, lilting voice. It was a sea chanty, 'Blow The Man Down'.

'Cocky sod,' Struan said, amused in spite of himself.

'Scragger's an uncommon name,' Robb said. 'Didn't Great-Aunt Ethel marry a Scragger of London?'

'Aye. I thought the same, lad.' Struan grinned. 'Mayhaps we've a relation who's a pirate.'

'Aren't we all pirates?'

Struan's grin broadened. 'The Noble House'll be safe in your hands, Robb. You're a wise man – wiser than you give yoursel' credit for.' He looked back at the dinghy. 'Cocky sod!'

Scragger appeared to be in his thirties. His long unkempt hair and his beard were raven-black. His eyes were pale blue and small, and his hands like hams. Golden rings hung from his ears and a jagged scar puckered the left side of his face.

He tied his dinghy up and scaled the boarding net with practised ease. As he jumped on to the deck he touched his forelock with mock deference to the quarterdeck and made an elaborate bow. 'Morning, Yor Honours!' Then to the seamen who were gaping at him. 'Morning, mateys! Me guv', Wu Fang Choi wishes you a safe journey 'ome!' He laughed and showed broken teeth, then came to the quarterdeck and stopped in front of Struan. He was shorter than Struan but thicker. 'Let's go below!'

'Mr Cudahy, search him!'

'Now, it be a flag o' truce and I ain't armed, that be the truth. You've me oath, so help me!' Scragger said, the picture of innocence.

'So you'll be searched anyway!'

Scragger submitted to the search. 'Be you satisfied, Tai-Pan?'

'For the moment.'

'Then let's below. Alone. Like I asked.'

Struan checked the priming of his pistol and motioned Scragger down the gangway. 'Rest of you stay on deck.'

To Struan's amazement, scragger proceeded through the ship with the familiarity of one who had been aboard before. Reaching the cabin, he plopped to the sea chair and stretched out his legs contentedly. 'I'd like to wet me whistle afore I starts, if it please you. Rowin' be thirsty work.'

'Rum?'

'Brandy. Ah, brandy! An' if you've a keg to spare, I'll be mighty favourable inclined.'

'To do what?'

'To be patient.' Scragger's eyes were steely. 'You be like wot I thort you be like.'

'You said you were late o' London Town?'

'Yus, that I did. A long time ago. Ah, thankee,' Scragger said, accepting the tankard of fine brandy. He sniffed it lovingly, then gulped it down and sighed and brushed his greasy whiskers. 'Ah brandy, brandy! Only thing wrong with me present post be the lack of brandy. Does me heart good.'

Struan refilled the tankard.

'Thankee, Tai-Pan.'

Struan toyed with his pistol. 'What part of London are you from?'

'Shoreditch, matey. That were where I were brung up.'

'What's your Christian name?'

'Dick. Why?'

Struan shrugged. 'Now get to the point,' he said. He planned to write by the next mail to find out if Dick Scragger was the name of a descendant of his great-aunt.

'That I will, Tai-Pan, that I will. Wu Fang Choi wants to talk to you. Alone. Now.'

'What about?'

'I didn't askt him and 'ee didn't tell me. "Go get the Tai-Pan," says he. So here I am.' He emptied the tankard, then smirked. 'You've bullion aboard, so the rumour says. Eh?'

'Tell him I'll see him here. He can come aboard alone and unarmed.'

Scragger roared with laughter and scratched unconsciously at the lice that infested him. 'Now, you know he baint about t'do that, Tai-Pan, any more'n you'd go aboard alone his ship wivout protection like. You seed the boy aboard my junk?'

'Aye.'

'It be his youngest son. He be hostage. You're to go aboard, armed if you likes, an' the boy stays here.'

'And the boy turns out to be just a dressed-up coolie's son and I get chopped!'

215

'Oh no,' Scragger said, pained. 'You've me oath, by God, and 'is. We baint a scallawag bunch o' pirates. We've three thousand ships in our fleets and rule these coasts as you rightly knowed. You've me oath, by God. And 'is.'

Struan noticed the white scars on Scragger's wrists and knew there would be more on his ankles. 'Why're you, an Englishman, with him?'

'Why indeed, matey? Why indeed?' Scragger replied, rising. 'Can I helps meself to more grog? Thank you kindly.' He brought the bottle back to the desk and settled himself again. 'There be upwards of fifty of us Limeys through 'is fleet. And fifteen or so others, Americans mostly, an' one Frenchy. Captains, cannon makers, gunners, mates. I were a bosun's mate by trade,' he continued expansively, inspired by the brandy. 'Ten year or more ago I were shipwrecked on some islands north. The dirty little heathen bastards catched me for slave, Japaners they were. They sold me to some other heathen bastards, but I escaped and fell in with Wu Fang. He offer me a berth when he knowed I were a bosun's mate and could do most things aboard.' He drained the tankard, belched, and refilled it. 'Now, do we go or doan we?'

'Why do you na stay aboard now? I can blow a path through Wu Fang right smartly.'

'Thank you, matey, but I likes it where I be.'

'How long were you a convict?'

Scragger's tankard stopped in midair and his expression became guarded. 'Long enough, matey.' He looked at the wrist scars. 'The iron marks, hey? Aye, the marks be still with me after twelve year.'

'Where'd you escape from? Botany Bay?'

'Aye, Botany Bay it were,' Scragger said, amiable once more. 'Fifteen year transportation I got when just a lad, leastways when I were younger. Twenty-five abouts. How old be you?'

'Old enough.'

'I've never knowed for sure. Maybe I'm thirty-four or forty-five. Yus. Fifteen year for striking a muck-pissed mate on a muck-pissed frigate.'

'You were lucky you were na hanged.'

'Yus, that I were.' Scragger happily belched again. 'I likes talking to you, Tai-Pan. It be a change from me mates. Yus, transported from Blighty I were. Nine month at sea chained along o' four hundred other poor devils an' the same of women or thereabouts. Chained belowdecks we were. Nine months or more. Water an' hardtack an' no beef. That's no way to treat a man, no way at all. A hundred of us lived to reach port. We mutinied in the port o' Sydney and broke our chains. Killed all the muck-ficked jailers. Then into the bush for a year, then I found me a ship. A merchantman.' Scragger chuckled malevolently. 'Leastways, we fed on merchantmen.' He gazed into the depths of his tankard and his smile disappeared. 'Yus, gallows bait, that what we all be, God curse all piss-arsed peelers,' he snarled. For a moment he fell silent, lost in his memories. 'But I were shipwrecked like I said, and the rest.'

Struan lit a cheroot. 'Why serve a mad-dog pirate scum like Wu Fang?'

'I'll tell you, matey. I'm free like the wind. I got three wives an' all the food I can eat, an' pay, an' I be captain of a ship. He treats me better'n my God-cursed kin. God-cursed kin! Yus, I be gallows bait to they. But to Wu Fang I baint, an' where else and how else could the likes o' me have wives an' food and loot and no peelers an' no gallows, eh? Course I be wiv him – or any wot gives me that.' He got up. 'Now be you acomin' like he asked or do we have to board you?'

'Board me, Captain Scragger. But first finish your brandy. It'll be the last you taste on this earth.'

'We be having more'n a hundred ships again' you.'

'You must think me a right proper fool. Wu Fang'd never venture personally into these waters. Never. Na with our warships just the other side of Hong Kong. Wu Fang's na wi' your fleet.'

'You be right proper smart, Tai-Pan,' Scragger cackled. 'I were warned. Yus. Wu Fang baint with us but his chief admiral be. Wu Kwok, his eldest son. An' the boy be 'is. That be the truth.'

'Truth wears many faces, Scragger,' Struan said. 'Now get to hell off my ship. The flag o' truce is for your vessel only. I'll show you what I think of your godrotting pirate fleet.'

'That you will, Tai-Pan, given 'arf a chance. Oh yus, I forgot,' he said and pulled out a small leather bag that was thonged around his neck. He took out a folded piece of paper and pushed it across the desk. 'I were to give you this' he said, his face twisting derisively.

Struan unfolded the paper. It bore Jin-qua's chop. And it contained one of the coin halves.

X

Struan was standing easily in the prow of his longboat, his hands deep in the pockets of his heavy sea coat, a fighting iron thonged to his wrist, pistols in his belt. His men were rowing tensely, heavily armed. Scragger was sitting amidships boozily singing a sea chanty. A hundred yards ahead was the pirate flagship. By prearrangement with Scragger – at Struan's insistence – the flagship had detached itself from the protective junk fleet and had moved closer to shore, a few hundred yards to leeward of *China Cloud*. There, with only the small aft sail aloft to give her leeway, the flagship was under *China Cloud's* guns and at her mercy. But the remainder of the junk armada was still in blockade positions surrounding the two ships.

Struan knew that it was dangerous to board the pirate ship alone, but the broken coin left him no choice. He would have taken Mauss along – an interpreter was necessary and Mauss was also a demon in a fight. But Scragger had refused: 'Alone, Tai-Pan. There be they aboard wot talks the heathen and talks the English. Alone. Armed if you likes but alone. That be the askt.'

Before leaving *China Cloud*, Struan had given final orders in front of Scragger.

'If the flagship raises sail, blow her out of the water. If I've na left in one hour, blow her out of the water.'

'Now, Tai-Pan,' Scragger had said uncomfortably, forcing a laugh, 'that not be the way of alooking at 'is invitation like. No way at all, at all. The flag o' truce, matey.'

'Blow her out of the water. But first hang the boy from the yardarm.'

'Don't worry,' Orlov said malevolently. 'The boy's dead, and by the blood of Jesus Christ I'll never leave this water while one junk's afloat.'

'Oars ho!' Struan ordered as the cutter came alongside the junk. A hundred Chinese pirates lined the sides, chattering, jeering. Struan noted the firing ports. Twenty a side. Forty guns.

He mounted the boarding ladder, and once on deck he observed that the cannons were in good order; that powder kegs were scattered carelessly, and stink bombs and fire bombs numerous; that the pirate ship was heavily manned. Filth everywhere but no sign of disease or scurvy. Sails in good condition, rigging tight. Hard – if not impossible – to take, hand to hand. But no trouble for *China Cloud* to sink – with joss.

He followed Scragger below to the main cabin under the poop deck, unconsciously marking gangways and hazards in case retreat was necessary. They came to a filthy anteroom jammed with men. Scragger pushed through them to a door at the far end, guarded by a truculent Chinese who pointed to Struan's weapons and reviled Scragger. But Scragger shouted back in Cantonese and, contemptuously shoving the guard aside with one hand, opened the door.

The cabin was enormous. Dirty cushions littered a raised dais which was dominated by a low, scarlet-lacquered table. The room, like the ship, stank of sweat and decayed fish and blood. Behind the dais aft was a latticed wall, deck to bulkhead. It was richly carved, and curtained from the other side, where the warlord slept. Impossible to see through from this side, Struan thought, but easy to shoot or stick a sword through. He noted the four barred portholes, and six oil lanterns swinging from the rafter beams.

A door in the latticed wall opened.

Wu Kwok was short and burly and middle-aged. His face was round and cruel, his queue long and greasy. The rich green silk gown tied around his protruding belly was grease-stained. He wore fine leather seaboots, and his wrists were encircled with many priceless jade bracelets.

He appraised Struan for a while, then motioned him to the dais and sat down on one side of the table. Struan sat opposite him. Scragger leaned against the closed door, scratching absently, a sardonic smile on his face.

Struan and Wu Kwok stared at each other unwaveringly, motionless. At length Wu Kwok raised his hand slightly and a servant brought chopsticks and cups of tea and moon cakes – tiny delicate rice-flour cakes stuffed with almond custard – and a plate of assorted *dim sum*.

Dim sum were small delicate rice-dough pastries filled with shrimp or fried pork or chicken or vegetables, or fish. Some were steamed, others deep-fried.

The servant poured the tea.

Wu Kwok lifted his cup and motioned Struan to do the same. They drank silently, their eyes locked. Then the pirate picked up his chopsticks and selected a dim sum. He placed it on the small dish in front of Struan and motioned him to eat. Struan knew that although he had been provided with chopsticks, Wu Kwok expected him to eat with his hands like a barbarian and lose face.

Up you, you flyblown offal, he thought, and thanked his joss for May-may. He picked up the chopsticks deftly and carried the dim sum to his mouth and replaced the chopsticks on their porcelain bed and chewed with enjoyment and was further pleased to sense the pirate's astonishment – that a barbarian could eat like a civilized person!

Struan picked up his chopsticks again and meticulously chose another dim sum from the plate: the smallest and the most delicate, the most difficult to hold. It was one of the steamed, shrimp-filled doughs, the white pastry so thin as to be almost translucent. He lifted it quickly and effortlessly, praying to himself that he wouldn't drop it. He held it out at arm's length, offering it to Wu Kwok.

Wu Kwok's chopsticks snaked out and he took the dim sum and carried it to his small dish. But a tiny piece of shrimp fell on to the table. Though Wu Kwok remained impassive, Struan knew that he was enraged, for he had lost face.

Struan delivered the *coup de grâce*. Leaning over, he picked up the morsel of shrimp and put it on his plate, and selected another tiny dim sum. Again he offered it. Wu Kwok took it. He did not drop any part of it.

He offered one to Struan, and Struan took it casuálly in mid-air and ate with relish but refused the next one offered. It was the height of Chinese decorum to pretend to the host that the food was so good that one could eat no more, even though both host and guest knew they would continue to eat ravenously.

'You take more grub, matey! There be plenty o' the likes o' this,' Wu Kwok said suddenly, pressing him as a host should.

The shock of hearing the harsh Cockney accent coming from Wu Kwok lessened Struan's pleasure with the face he had gained by making Wu Kwok speak first.

'Thank you. I'm glad you speak English. That makes things easier,' Struan said. 'A lot easier.'

'Yus, that it do.' Wu Kwok was very proud that he could talk barbarian.

'Where did you learn English?' Struan leaned down and scratched his ankle. The deck and cushions were flea-infested.

'Where'd the likes o' you learn t' eat like'n *China* man, hey?'

Struan selected another pastry. 'I've tried to learn Cantonese, many times. But I'm na a good student and my tongue canna get the sounds right.' He ate the pastry delicately and drank some tea. 'The tea is excellent. From Soo-chow?'

Wu Kwok shook his head, 'Lin Tin. You like Soo-chow tea?'

'Lin Tin is better.'

'I learned English from Scragger'n others. Over years.' He ate for a moment and again pressed on Struan more of the delicious food. 'Have more grub, mate. You be a queer'n. I be right proper glad t' meet a man o' the likes of you. You baint natural, I'll be bound. You'd take many a day to die, many a day.'

Struan's eyes became greener and more luminous. 'You'd die very quickly. My methods are different from yours. One moment alive, the next dead.' He snapped his fingers. 'That's best – for friend or enemy. Or mad dog!'

'Why you talks so strange, eh?' Wu Kwok asked after a dangerous pause.

'What?'

'You doan talks like me. You be hard to un'erstand. Sounds different like.'

'There are many dialects – kinds – of English,' Struan said calmly, giving Wu Kwok face.

'He be a toff, Wu Kwok, like I sayed,' Scragger explained. 'Toffs talk different. They go t' school like I tol' you.'

'Do that gallows bait Scragger talk true, matey? My English baint proper?'

'Who talks more correct Cantonese – a peasant or a schoolmaster? The peasant's is correct for the fields an' the schoolmaster's for the school.'

Wu Kwok leaned back on the cushions and sipped his tea. He broke the silence. 'We heard you've bullion aboard. Forty lac.'

'How'd you get this?' Struan unbunched his fist and put the half coin on the table.

'One 'arf a coin, one favour, right, matey?'

'Aye,' Struan said, furious at himself for falling into Jin-qua's trap. 'How'd you get it?'

'From me dad.'

'How'd he get it?'

'Where'd you think that old highwayman Jin-qua laid his dirty mitts fast on forty lac o' bullion, matey? Eh? From his old shipmates, o' course. You've ten lac o' me dad's aboard.' Wu Kwok's belly shook with laughter. 'Pour 'is Honour some grog, Scragger. He be needin' it.'

221

'Wu Fang Choi and Jin-qua are shipmates?' Struan asked, shaken.

'In a manner o' speakin', matey. We be protecting his sea trade from muck-pissed pirate. We be keepers o' the sea. It be fair do's to pay for service, eh? An' a wise man invest his money to profit, hey? So we invests with him occasional. Tea, silk, opium. Loans.' Wu Kwok held his belly, and tears of laughter seeped from his slitted eyes. 'So now we be partners like, us'n Noble House. Wot better invest be there, eh, matey?'

'What's your "favour", Wu Kwok?'

'We be drinking to the bullion and yor joss, Tai-Pan. Then we talks.'

'He sayed t' hang the boy if he was aboard more'n an hour,' Scragger said, filling three tankards with rum. 'An' if you raised sail, to blow us'n out o' the sea and hang the lad.'

'How long be'n hour, mate?'

'Long enough.'

Wu Kwok ate for a moment. 'You'd hang th' lad?'

'Would you?' Struan took out his timepiece and laid it on the table. 'You've used up half your time.'

Wu Kwok accepted a tankard from Scragger and drank slowly. Struan felt the hair on his neck prickle with the tension. He could hear the muted sounds of babbling Chinese and straining hawsers and creaking timbers.

There was the faint patter of rain on the deck above. Wu Kwok picked up a toothpick and cleaned his teeth, one hand politely covering his mouth. The rain intensified.

'Th' favour of Wu Fang Choi,' Wu Kwok began. 'Yor fleet be twenty clippers, right?'

'Nineteen.'

'Nineteen. On each we puts one o' our lads. You train they as cap'ns. Officers. Nineteen men. You train 'em good. Howsomever you wants as proper cap'ns. Lash 'em, keelhaul 'em, wot you wishes – if they baint obeying – but no killing. For five year they be yorn, then they come back 'ome. Next: In a year'n a day we wants a clipper. Like *China Cloud*. We pay bullion wot she costed. You give us'n bills an' the like, an' we pays bullion. Cannoned an' rigged an' sailed like *China Cloud*. Ten o' our men to go to Blighty to watch her builded, then come home with her. Where an' how we takes the ship come later – right, Scragger?'

'Yus.'

'Last, we gi' you a nipper – three nippers – to train. Three boys to train like toffs. Best school in Lon'on,' Wu Kwok said. 'Wot ever it costed.'

222

'Best clotheses an' carriages an' lodgings an' grub,' Scragger added. 'Like bleeding toffs they t' be brung up. Treated proper. Oxford or Cambridge University. Yus. Through t' unyversity and then 'ome.'

'That's na one favour,' Struan said. 'That's many.'

'Many – few – they be favour,' Wu Kwok said viciously. 'By God, they be the askt. Maybe I takes the ten lac back an' the thirty as well. Then buy ship. If money, buy anything, right, matey? Yus, I take lacs maybe and make deal with One-Eye Devil. Wot's 'is name?'

'Brock,' Scragger said.

'Aye, Brock. Make deal with Brock or other. Deal is deal. Just train men. One ship. Fair ask. You say yes or no.'

'I'll make a new deal with you. Take back the coin, and, with or without me aboard *China Cloud*, just try to take all the bullion, by God.'

'There be two hundred ship over the horizon. I lose hundred, two hundred ships, never mind. I take lac, Tai-Pan. I take lac.'

Struan picked up his half coin and stood up. 'Agreed?'

'No agree. Favour – you agree favour. Has Tai-Pan of Noble House no face, heya? Yes, no?'

'In one month bring a hundred men, none of whom are wanted by the mandarins for any crime, all of whom can read and write. Of these I pick nineteen to be captains. And ten men to watch the building. Bring the three boys then.'

'Too dangerous, matey,' Wu Kwok said, 'so many men. Right, Scragger?'

'Not if we brunged' em, say, t' Aberdeen. To pick be fair, no harm in that. Eh? Secret like?'

Wu Kwok pondered a moment. 'Agree. One month. Aberdeen.'

'I'll hand the clipper over to you personally – or to Wu Fang Choi – only,' Struan said. 'No one else.'

'To any I sends.'

'No.'

'Or to me, matey?' Scragger said.

'No. To Wu Kwok or to Wu Fang Choi. In open seas.'

'Why?' Wu Kwok said. 'Eh, why? Wot muckstink devilment be in yor head, matey?'

'She'll be your ship. I'm nae passing over such a beauty to anyone else. Where's your face, eh?'

'Agree,' Wu Kwok said at last. 'No treachery, by God, or you'll pay.'

Struan contemptuously started for the door, but Scragger blocked his path. 'Yor holy oath, Tai-Pan?'

'Jin-qua's already had it, Scragger. You know the value of my oath, by God!'

Scragger nodded to Wu Kwok and stepped aside. 'Thankee, Tai-Pan.'

'Seeing as how you agrees, so nice and friendly like, Tai-Pan,' Wu Kwok said, 'me dad's sended a gift for you and a message.' He waved a hand at Scragger who opened a sea chest, brought out a bundle, handed it to Struan.

The bundle contained a flag – the entwined Lion and Dragon. And a ship's log book: the log of the lost *Scarlet Cloud*.

Struan opened the book and turned to the last page: 'Nov. 16th. Noon. N 11° 23' 11" E 114° 9' 8". Storms continuing, gale force. At three bells in the middle watch last night storm sails were carried away and the masts. Our ship was thrust helpless here on to Tizard Reefs where, by Divine Mercy, she came to rest, her keel torn away and hull holed.

'Nov. 18th. Four o'clock. Four junks sighted northeast by east. Final preparing for abandoning ship done.

'Nov. 18th. Five o'clock. The four junks have changed course and are heading for us. I issued muskets. I have tried to prepare a cannon but the list of the ship forbade us. Prepared ourselves as best we can. In case they're pirates.

'Nov. 18th. Eight o'clock. Overrun. Pirates. Killed the first wave but they're . . .'

Struan closed the book. 'You killed them all?'

'The junks was not part of our regular fleets, mate. Leastways not mostly.'

'You killed them all?'

'They deaded 'emselves, Tai-Pan, I wasn't there.'

'You knowed how some of them scallawags is, Tai-Pan,' Scragger said. 'If the men'd be Wu Fang Choi's – why'd he give you the log, eh? Word were brought to Wu Fang Choi. He sent me to have a look. There weren't no men aboard when I were there. Or bodies. None.'

'You looted her?'

'You knowed the laws o' the seas, Tai-Pan. She were shipwrecked an' abandoned. Half yor cargo were salvaged. Sixteen cannon and a mess of powder'n shot.'

'Where's the chronometer?'

Scragger's eyebrows soared. 'Why, aboard me junk, o' course, not that I can use one. Yet. Finders keepers, eh? Fair do's, eh? But you knowed, Tai-Pan, you knowed what them God-cursed scallawags

224

done? They let her stop. Imagine that? Gawd's truth. They let it run down. Took us'n weeks to find a merchantman with London time. An American, the *Boston Skylark*.' He guffawed, remembering, then added. 'Four o' her boys elected to go along with us'n.

'And the rest?'

'They were set adrift, off the Philippines. Near t' shore. You've me oath. Three, four weeks ago.'

Wu Kwok shifted on the cushions, scratching leisurely. 'Last, Tai-Pan, me dad sayed, "Ten taels a ship ain't much for safe passage. Ten taels a ship an' the English flag be protected by Wu Fang Choi." You've a new berth now, here at Hong Kong, so we feared. Put it to your mandarin.'

'I might put one tael to him.'

'Six be the lowest. The lowest. That be wot my dad sayed, knowing you be a hard trader. Six.'

'One.'

'Sit. We drinks more grog an' there be other grub coming,' Wu Kwok said.

'In five minutes this ship's blown out of the water and the hostage hangs.'

Wu Kwok belched. 'You baint hanging my son, matey.'

'O' course,' Struan said disdainfully, 'only some poor dressed-up lad.'

Wu Kwok smirked and drank deeply. 'You be proper smart, Tai-Pan. Two taels a ship it is. Put it to your mandarin, eh? And tell you wot, keep the lad – hang him, throw him in the sea – he be yorn. Put him aboard us and I'll hang him for you.'

'Wot?' Scragger exploded. 'The lad baint your son?'

'O' course, Scragger. You think I'm a fool?' Struan said harshly. 'I know the value of the oath of scum.' He stalked out.

'But it were yor oath an' mine,' Scragger said, appalled, to Wu Kwok. 'We giv him our oath. You sayed he were yor son. You tol' me, by God.'

'The Tai-Pan'd never put his son aboard us'n – why should I put mine aboard his'n?'

'But I give 'im me oath, by God. That be cheat!'

Wu Kwok got up very slowly. 'You call me cheat, matey?'

'No, Guv', no,' Scragger said quickly, keeping his blinding rage away from his face. 'It were just me oath. We keeps our oaths. That not be proper wiv us'n, what were done, not proper. That be all.'

Wu Kwok shook his head wearily as he retired to his sleeping quarters. 'Barbarians is right proper strange, matey. Right proper strange indeed.' The latticed door closed behind him.

Scragger went on deck. By God, he thought, almost weeping with rage, by God, that do it. I'll fix that sodding, duck-fornicating heathen, by God, see if I don't. But not till after the men be picked. Oh no, not till then. Daren't afore that, no, by God, 'cause that'd spoil everything.

But after that, by God, after that . . .

XI

China Cloud cut through the driving rain, heading up the south coast of
Hong Kong Island for the main harbour on the north side.

The Struans were having dinner in the main cabin: oyster stew,
smoked sausages, kippers, boiled cabbage and bacon fat, cold fried
chickens, sea biscuits, dishes of apple pie and preserved fruit pies. Sea-
chilled dry white wine and champagne. And tea.

'Forty lacs – four coins,' Robb said, toying with his food. 'One to Wu
Fang Choi. Who has the other three?'

'Jin-qua kept one, certainly. Perhaps two,' Struan said. He reached
across the table and helped himself to another fried kippered herring.

'We're committed to an immense favour,' Robb said. 'That's worth
ten lacs to those devils. With a clipper like *China Cloud* in their hands,
why, even frigates could be ravaged. The Asian sea-lanes of the whole
Empire could be cut. One ship – and ten men trained to build more.
Nineteen men trained as captains – to train more! We're trapped and
our future's trapped. Terrible.'

'Jin-qua cheated you. He cheated you,' Culum said.

'No. Outsmarted me, yes, but even that's na correct. I was na smart
enough. Me, lad! Na him. When you sit down at a table to make a deal,
each side is obligated to make the best deal possible. It's very simple.
Aye, I was weaker than he, that's all. But even if I'd thought that the
coins would be split among other men – I still must make the deal as he
wanted it. We'd nae option, nae option at all.'

'If you get outsmarted, Dirk, what chance is there for me? For
Culum?'

'None. Unless you're ready to think for yoursel' and learn by the
mistakes of others. And na treat the Chinese like one of us. They're
different.'

'Yes, they are,' Culum said. 'Ugly, repulsive, heathen. And impossible to tell apart.'

'I dinna agree. I meant they think differently,' Struan said.

'Then what's the answer to them, Father?'

'If I knew that, I'd be right every time. They've just had five thousand years practice, that's all. Now pass the stew please, there's a good laddie.'

Culum handed him the dish and Struan helped himself to a third portion.

'You don't seem perturbed, Dirk,' Robb said. 'This could ruin us. Ruin Asian trade.'

'You're na eating, Robb. And you, Culum. Eat.' Struan tore off a chicken leg and put it on his plate. 'The situation's na quite so dismal as all that. First the nineteen men: aye, they'll be spies for Wu Fang Choi and his scum. But for us to teach 'em they have to learn English, eh? And if we can *speak* to them, why can we na change them? From pirate to useful citizen? Perhaps even to Christian, eh? Nineteen chances to bring them to our side. Good odds, I'd say. And if they're on our side – even one of them – we'll know the pirate lairs. Then we control them and destroy them at will. Second, the clipper: in a year and a day I've a sea battle to look forward to, that's all. I'll hand the ship over, then sink it. I made nae promise na to sink it.'

'Why not hand it over with kegs of powder in the hold and a slow taper to them?' Robb said.

'Wu Kwok's too smart for that.'

'Is there no way you could hang mines on the outside of the hull, below sea level?'

'That'd be possible, perhaps. That might pass their scrutiny. But even when you're trapped you have to try to work your way out, you canna break a holy oath. Nae trick, Robb. We'd lose face for a hundred years. I'm going to kill Wu Kwok.'

'Why?'

'To teach him the value of an oath. And to protect oursel' for the next generation.'

There was a silence. 'I thought you were going home in five months,' Robb said.

'I am. I'll sail the new ship back when she's ready. We'll call her *Lotus Cloud*.' Struan wiped his mouth with a napkin. 'The men and the ship I can understand. But why train three boys as "toffs"? I dinna understand that. The boys worry me and I dinna know why.'

'They'd be Wu Kwok's sons?'

'Sons or nephews, aye, certainly. But why? What do they gain?'

'Everything English. All our secrets,' Culum said.

'No, lad. The same applies to the boys as to the men. More so. Boys will be easier to convert to our ways. Wu Fang and Wu Kwok must have thought of that. Why would they be prepared to lose three sons? Why as "toffs" – not as captains or soldiers or boat builders or armourers or anything useful? Why "toffs"?'

They could not answer him.

When *China Cloud* broke through the west entrance into Hong Kong harbour, Struan was coming on to the quarterdeck to join Culum and Robb. The rain had ceased and the wind was brisk. Dusk was gathering. Struan felt greatly refreshed, and serene. But as soon as he stepped on deck, his serenity was shattered.

'Great God Almighty!'

The harbour was packed with the merchant shipping of Asia, and with the Royal Naval Fleet. And the beach was crowded with the tents which quartered the four thousand soldiers of the expeditionary force.

What really jolted Struan, however, were the hundreds of Chinese sampans clustered to the north of Glessing's Point. Swarms of junks and sampans were leaving and arriving. Thousands of tiny hovels had sprung up like obscene mushrooms on the slopes of one of the hills.

'Chinese've been pouring in ever since I got back from Canton,' Culum said. 'God alone knows how many. At least four or five thousand. They're swamping us. They arrive by sampan or junk loads and stream ashore. Then they get swallowed up in that mess. By night those devils sneak out and steal anything that's movable.'

'Great God Almighty!'

'At first they were spreading over all the island. Then I got Longstaff to allocate them that hillside temporarily. They call it Tai Ping Shan, something like that.'

'Why did you na tell me?'

'We wanted you to see for yourself, Uncle and I. A few hours wouldn't make any difference. The European population – apart from soldiers – is about a hundred and fifty. Longstaff is tearing out what little hair he has left. We've been picking up ten or fifteen Chinese bodies a night in the harbour. Murdered or drowned.'

'You've got to see the squalor up there to believe it,' Robb said. 'The way they live! There was space enough, but they keep coming with every tide.'

'Well,' Struan said, 'we will na suffer for lack of coolies and help.' He turned to Orlov. 'Salute the flagship and send a signal in your name:

"Permission to moor within eight cables." All hands on deck, and come aft!'

Orlov nodded.

China Cloud's cannon boomed and there was an answering gun. Permission was granted. The crew was assembled. Then Struan walked to the quarterdeck rail. 'Everyone's confined to the ship till noon tomorrow. And no one's to come aboard until noon tomorrow. Nae word of our cargo. Or that I'm aboard. I'll keelhaul any that spills a word. A double month's pay to all hands, paid in silver tomorrow at dusk. Officers will mount armed guard by the watch on the quarterdeck. Dismissed.'

There were three cheers for the Tai-Pan, and the men dispersed.

'What time's the land sale, Culum?'

'Three o'clock, Father, tomorrow. In Happy Valley.'

'Robb, make sure we've the correct lot numbers well in advance.'

'Yes. We brought a list. We buy the knoll?'

'Of course.'

Robb thought a moment. 'If Brock's as inflexible as you, we may have to put our whole future on that damned hill.'

'Aye,' Struan beckoned Orlov. 'At two bells in the forenoon watch, send a signal to Brock in Robb's name, asking him to come aboard at four bells. Wake me at two bells. Until that time I'm na to be disturbed. You're in command now.'

'Good,' Orlov said.

'I'm going to get some sleep. Robb, you and Culum do the same. We've a long day tomorrow. Oh yes, and, Culum, perhaps you'd like to think about the ball. Where and how. In thirty-one days.' He went below.

When *China Cloud* was nearing the flagship, Culum walked over to Orlov. 'Please bring the longboat alongside as soon as we're anchored.'

'The Tai-Pan said everyone's confined aboard. There's no longboat without his permission.'

'That obviously didn't apply to us, to Mr Struan and me,' Culum said sharply.

Orlov chuckled. 'You don't know your father, Culum the Strong. He said "everyone". And that's the way it'll be.'

Culum turned for the hatch, but Orlov stopped him, the fighting iron easy in his hand. 'He's not to be disturbed. That's his orders.'

'Get out of my way!'

'He never gives an order without meaning it. Ask your uncle. No one

230

goes ashore while I'm captain o' *China Cloud*! If he wanted you ashore, he'da said so.'

'We're aboard till noon, Culum,' Robb said.

Through his fury Culum asked himself if he would be obeyed with such finality when he was Tai-Pan. He knew that such obedience was not paid automatically to the title. It had to be earned. 'Very well, Captain.' He went and stood beside Robb at the gunnel. Silently they watched the island grow nearer. Soon they could see the knoll.

'That's going to break us,' Robb said.

'Now we've the bullion, Brock won't compete.'

'He'll bid and bid and bid, knowing that Dirk'll have it, whatever the cost. Brock'll stop bidding when the price is astronomic. Dirk's committed to the knoll like we're committed to The Noble House. Now it's a matter of face, godrotting face! Their godrotting hatred for one another will destroy both of them eventually.'

'Father said he'd deal with him, in five months, didn't he?'

'Yes, lad. He has to. I canna. Nor can you.'

Culum riveted his eyes on the knoll and Hong Kong. Like it or not, he told himself, his stomach twisting, there's your kingdom. If you've the strength. And the guts to take it.

Suddenly he was very frightened.

At dawn Orlov turned out all hands and had the immaculate ship holystoned and cleaned. At two bells he sent the signal and went below.

'Morning. Two bells,' Orlov said to the bolted door.

'Morning, Cap'n,' Struan said, opening the door. 'Come in.' He wore a green silk brocade dressing-gown, and nothing underneath. Cold or hot, Struan slept naked. 'Order breakfast for me. And ask Mr Robb and Culum to join me in half an hour.'

'It's ordered.'

'Where's Wolfgang?'

'Aloft.'

'And the Chinese lad?'

'With him. Following him around like a dog.' Orlov handed Struan a neatly written list. 'These boats came alongside last night or this morning, asking for you. Your brother's wife sent a boat to ask for him to go aboard as soon as possible. Captain Glessing asked for your son – Sinclair and his sister asked for him too. She asked for you, so she's on your list. There were a signal from the flagship. "Your son to go aboard the soonest." Cap'n Glessing cursed like a gutter rat when I sent him away.'

'Thank you.'

There was a knock on the door.

'Aye?'

'Morning, sorr!' the seaman said. 'Signal from the *White Witch*: "With pleasure." '

'Thank you, signalman.'

The man hurried away. Struan handed Orlov a bank draft for one thousand guineas. 'With our compliments, Captain.'

Orlov read the amount. He blinked and read it again. 'That's princely. Princely.' He handed it back. 'I was only doing my job.'

'Na with that amount of bullion. Take it. You've earned it.'

Orlov hesitated, then put it in his pocket. He unthonged the fighting iron and thoughtfully placed it in the rack with the others. 'Your son,' he said at length, 'best watch him. There's bad trouble ahead for him.'

'Eh?' Struan's eyes snapped away from the list.

'Yes.' Orlov rubbed the stubble of his beard.

'What's this. More of your devil witchcraft?'

'More of my second sight, yes.'

'What trouble?' Struan knew from long experience that Orlov did not forecast lightly. Too many times the strange little man had been right.

'I don't know.' A sudden smile lit his face. 'When he's Tai-Pan he thinks he's going to take away my ship.'

'Then you'll have to earn his respect, change his mind, else you lose her.'

Orlov grinned. 'Yes. And I will, never fear.' Then the smile faded. 'But he'll take over on a bad day. There'll be blood on his hands.'

After a pause Struan said, 'Whose? Mine?'

Orlov shrugged. 'I don't know. But he'll be much trouble to you. Of that I'm sure.'

'What son is na?'

'You're right there.' Orlov thought of his family in Narvik, of his own two sons, fine strapping men of twenty. Both of them hated him, despised him, even though he adored them and adored his wife Leka, a Laplander. They had been very happy until the sons turned against him. 'Yes,' he said, feeling very tired, 'you're right. As usual.'

'Best get some sleep,' Struan said. 'I'll need you at eight bells.'

Orlov left.

For a long time Struan stared into space. What trouble? Whose blood? Why a 'bad day'? Then he turned his mind away from the unanswerable, content to think about today, perhaps tomorrow. 'You're becoming more Chinese every day,' he said aloud. He smiled to himself and perused the list again. Gorth Brock. Miss Tillman. Quance. Gordon Chen. Skinner. Bosun McKay. McKay?

'Steward!' he called out.

'Yus, sorr.' The steward set the hot water on the cabinet beside the shaving gear.

'Send word to Mr Cudahy. If Bosun McKay comes alongside, bring him aboard.'

'Yus, sorr.' The steward vanished.

Struan stood by the cabin windows. He could see the pulsating mass that was the Chinese settlement of Tai Ping Shan. But his mind was elsewhere: Why did Shevaun Tillman come alongside? Now, there's a beddable queen if ever there was one. I wonder if she's a virgin. Surely she is! Has to be. Would you bed her if you knew she was? Without marrying her? Nay. I would na bed her then. A man needs virginity but twice in his life. Once with his wife. And once in the prime of life with a young mistress chosen with great care. When the man has learned the knowledge of patience, and compassion, and can painlessly transmute girl into woman.

Of course Shevaun's a virgin; you're thinking like a fool. But the sparkle behind her eyes and the waggle of her buttocks promise well for her husband, eh? She'd make an interesting mistress. Do you want to marry Shevaun? Or just bed her?

If you were Chinese, you could have many wives openly. And they'd all live in peace under the same roof. Struan chuckled. I'd like to see Shevaun and May-may together under the same roof. Who'd win that battle? For battle it would be, hellcats both of them.

'Hello, Father.' Culum stood in the doorway.

'You sleep well, laddie?'

'All right, thank you.' Culum had had bad dreams: Orlov mixed with the knoll and prophesying poverty again. Oh God, don't let us lose again. Help me to do that which I must do. 'By the way, if we're to be hosts at the ball, should we invite a partner?'

'Mary Sinclair?'

Culum tried unsuccessfully to be offhand. 'Yes.'

Struan told himself that he had better find a girl for his son and quickly. 'Perhaps, as we're hosts, it would be better if we just welcomed everyone without favour. There's twenty-odd young ladies for you to cast your eye on.'

'Orlov said there was a message from the flagship. For me to come aboard. Can I leave now? I want to see Longstaff about the final details of the land sale. I'd like this job to be well done.'

'Aye,' Struan said after a pause. 'I would na' fire Orlov if I was you.'

Culum flushed. 'Oh, he told you, did he? I don't like him. He makes my flesh crawl.'

'Accept him as the finest captain afloat – be patient with him. He could be a valuable ally.'

'He says he has second sight.'

'He has. Sometimes. Many people have. "Blood on your hands" could mean anything or nothing. Dinna worry, laddie.'

'I won't, Father. Can I go aboard the flagship now?'

'Aye. As soon as Brock's left.'

'You don't think I can keep a still tongue in my head?'

'Some men have a knack of extracting information just by looking at a face. Orlov for one. Brock for another. You've changed since you saw the bullion.'

'No I haven't.'

Struan picked up his shaving brush. 'Breakfast'll be served in twenty minutes or so.'

'How have I changed?'

'There's a great difference between a young lad who knows he's bankrupt and a young lad who knows he's not. You've a wind under your tail, lad, and you can see it from four cables.' Struan began lathering his face. 'Have you ever had a mistress, Culum?'

'No,' Culum answered uneasily. 'I've been to a whorehouse, if that's what you mean. Why?'

'Most men out here have mistresses.'

'Chinee?'

'*Chinese*. Or Eurasian.'

'Have you?'

'Of course.' Struan picked up his razor. 'There are whorehouses in Macao. Oriental and European. But very few are safe, most diseased. So the custom – do you know about "woman disease", the French pox or Spanish pox, call it what you will?'

'Yes. Of course. Yes.'

Struan began to shave. 'They say that it was first introduced into Europe by Columbus and his seamen, who caught it from the American West Indians. It's ironic that we call it the French or Spanish pox, the French call it the Spanish pox or English pox, the Spanish call it the French pox. When we're all to blame. I'm told it's been in India and Asia for ever. You know there's nae cure for it?'

'Yes.'

'Then you'll know the only way to catch it is from a woman?'

234

'Yes.'

'Do you know about "protections"?'

'Yes – yes, of course.'

'Nothing to be shy about. I'm sorry that I was away so much. I would have liked to tell you about – about life – myself. Perhaps you know, perhaps you're just shy. So I'll tell you anyway. It's very necessary to wear a sheath. The best are made of silk – they come from France. There's a new type made out of some sort of fishskin. I'll see you get a supply.'

'I don't think I'll need—'

'I agree,' Struan interrupted. 'But there's nae harm in having them. In case. I'm na trying to interfere in your life or to suggest you become a rake. I just want to be sure you know certain ordinary things – and that you're safe. A sheath will prevent the pox. And prevent the girl getting with child, thus avoiding trouble for her and embarrassment for you.'

'That's against all the laws of God, isn't it? I mean, using – well, it's a sin, isn't it? Doesn't it destroy the whole point of love-making? The whole reason is to have children.'

'The Catholics think so, aye, and the very religious Protestants, aye.'

'You question the Holy Book?' Culum was appalled.

'Nay, lad. Only some of the – what's the word? – interpretations.'

'I thought I was an advanced thinker, but you – well, what you say is heresy.'

'To some men. But the House of God is very important to me – it has precedence over me, you, everyone, even The Noble House.' Struan continued to shave. 'It's custom out here to have your own girl. For yoursel' alone. You keep her, pay her bills, provide her with food and clothes, a servant and so on. When you nae longer want her, you give her some money and dismiss her.'

'Isn't that pretty callous?'

'Yes – if it's done without face. Usually the little money, on our standards, you give her is more than enough to provide the girl with a dowry and find her a fine husband. The selecting of the girl is done very gracefully. You do it through a "broker" – a matchmaker – and it's all according to ancient Chinese custom.'

'Isn't that slavery? Of the worst kind?'

'If your idea is to buy a slave, aye, and you treat her like a slave. What do you do when you indenture a servant? Pay some money and buy them for a number of years. It's the same thing.' Struan felt his chin and then began to relather the patches that were still rough. 'We'll go to Macao. I'll arrange it for you, if you wish.'

'Thank you, Father, but' – he was going to say, but buying a woman, whore or slave or mistress, is disgusting and a sin – 'I; well, thank you, but it's not necessary.'

'If you change your mind, tell me, lad. Dinna be shy about it. I think it's quite normal to have "appetites" and nae sin. But beware of houses. Never go to one drunk. Never bed a girl unprotected. Never be forward out here with the wife or daughter of a European – particularly a Portuguese – or you'll end up very dead, very quickly, and rightly so. Never call a man a son of a bitch, unless you're prepared to back the words with steel or a bullet. And never, never go to a house that is na recommended by a man you can trust. If you dinna want to ask me or Robb, ask Aristotle. You can trust him.'

Very unsettled, Culum watched his father as he finished shaving with firm, definite strokes. He seems so sure of everything, Culum thought. But he's wrong – about many things. Wrong. The Scriptures are quite clear – the lusts of the flesh are devil-sent. Love is God-sent, and lovemaking without wanting the child is lust. And a sin. I wish I had a wife. And could forget lust. Or a mistress. But that's unlawful and against the Holy Word.

'You bought your mistress?' he asked.

'Aye.'

'How much did you pay for her?'

'I'd say that was none of your business, lad,' Struan said gently.

'I'm sorry. I didn't mean to be rude – to be inquisitive or . . .' Culum flushed.

'I know. But that's nae the question to ask another man.'

'Yes. I meant what does a woman cost? To buy?'

'That'd depend on your taste. From as little as a tael to anything.' Struan was not sorry he had begun this line of talk. Better you do it yoursel', he told himself, than let others do it for you. 'By the way, Culum. We've never settled your salary. You start at fifty guineas a month. That'll be almost pocket money, for everything will be found.'

'That's very, very generous,' Culum burst out. 'Thank you.'

'In five months we'll considerably improve the amount. As soon as we own the land, we'll begin to build. Warehouses, the Great House – and a house for you.'

'That'd be wonderful. I've never had a house – I mean I've never had even rooms of my very own. Not even at university.'

'A man should have a place of his own, however small. Privacy is very important to a clear head.'

'Fifty guineas a month is a lot of money,' Culum said.

'You'll earn it.'

That's enough to marry on, Culum was thinking. Easily. No whore-houses or stinking natives for him. He remembered with repugnance the three occasions he had gone to the house that the university students favoured and could afford. He had had to be half grogged to act like a man and enter the stink-filled room. A shilling to tumble in a sweat-rancid bed with a cowlike hag twice his age. To get rid of the aches, devil-sent, that plague a man. And always the weeks of terror afterwards, waiting for the pox to arrive. God guard me from sinning again, he thought.

'You feeling all right, Culum?'

'Yes, thank you. Well, I think I'll shave before breakfast. I'm sorry. I didn't mean to, well – I didn't mean to be rude.'

'I know.'

'Brock be alongside, sorr,' the seaman said.

'Guide him below,' Struan said. He did not look up from the catalogue of lots that Robb had given him.

Culum and Robb felt the tension in the cabin mount as they waited.

Brock stamped in. He smiled broadly. 'Ah, it be thee right enough, Dirk. I thought thee be aboard!'

'Grog?'

'Thankee. Morning, Robb. Morning, Culum.'

'Morning,' Culum said, hating the fear that seized him.

'Them clotheses suit thee right proper. Be you becomin' a seafaring man now? Like your da'?'

'No.'

Brock sat in the sea chair. 'Last time I seed yor da', Culum, he were listing terrible. Sinking he were. Terrible indeed. That be a horrid occurrence – the accident.' He accepted a mug of rum from Struan. 'Thankee. By the time I'd doused that godrotting fire wot sprung out of the night like a bolt from the deep and were ready to help him, why, he'd vanished. Spent all night and best part of next day asearching.'

'That was considerate of you, Tyler,' Struan told him.

'I send Gorth last night to inquire after thee. Right proper strange, eh, Culum?'

'What's strange, Mr Brock?'

'Why, that that devil midget doan knowed yor da's aboard. An no one be allowed aboard till noon, so I hears. An' anchoring under the guns o' flagship – right proper strange.'

'Did Gorth touch the flagpole?' Struan asked.

'Aye. He were proper sad. He sayed it were like putting another nail in yor coffin. He were turrible reluctant.'

Struan passed over a banker's order – twenty thousand guineas.

'Thankee, Dirk,' Brock said without touching it or looking at it. 'But it baint mine. Mayhaps thee'd best give it to Gorth. Or send it aboard. It baint payment to me.'

'As you wish, Tyler. He'll be at the land sale?'

'Oh, yes.'

Struan picked up the catalogue. 'The choice marine lots are 7 and 8 to the west of the valley, 16 and 17 in the centre, 22 and 13 to the east. Which do you want?'

'You be giving me a free pick, Dirk?'

'There's enough for both of us. You choose which you want. We'll na bid against you. Nor you against us.'

'I'd the same thort. That be fair. An' wise. 16 and 17 of the marine lots and 6 and 7 of the suburban lots.'

'We'll take marine lots 7 and 8. Suburban lots 3 and 4.'

'Done. And that leave the knoll. You be planning on bidding, eh?'

'Aye.'

Brock swallowed some rum. He could sense Culum's unease. 'The fleet be leaving tomorrow, Dirk. Did thee hear?'

'No. Leaving for where?'

'North. To fight the war,' Brock said sardonically.

'I'd forgotten about the war,' Struan said with a short laugh. 'To stab at Peking again? In winter?'

'Yes. Our leader be ordering 'em north. Yor lackey's cannon balls in his head. I heard the admiral screamed, but Longstaff just ranted, "North, by God, you be ordered north! We'll teach the heathen treaty-breaking scum! Teach 'em a proper lesson!" '

'They will na go north.'

'With thee back, mayhaps not. It be a sorry state when the likes o' Longstaff's Tai-Pan. Ridikilus. An' when the likes o' you've his god-rotting ear. When we've to rely on thee t' save our fleet.' He cleared his throat noisily, then sniffed the air. 'There be a right proper strange smell aboard.'

'Oh?'

'Smells like bullion. Aye, bullion to be sure.' Brock shot a glance at Culum. 'So you baint bankrupt, be you, lad?'

Culum said nothing, but the blood soared into his face.

Brock grunted. 'I smelled it when thee anchored, Dirk. Why, even when thee come into harbour. So thee doan sink and thee've brass to pay and I be beat again.'

'When are the notes due?'

'Today, as thee well knowed.'

'Do you want to extend the time?'

'Weren't for the lad's face, an' all aboard, I'd ask meself if you was bluffing. That mayhaps the bullion weren't in yor hold. But I knowed better. It be writ in every face on board 'cepting yourn – and Robb's. I'll take yor banker's draft today, by God. No credit.'

'After the land sale, we'll settle.'

'Before. Aye, before. Thee'd better be clean o' debts afore you bid,' he said, his eye glittering, his anger surfaced. 'Thee beat me again. God curse you and the devil you serve to hell! But the knoll be mine. It be mine.'

'It belongs to The Noble House. Na to the second-best.'

Brock got up, his fists clenched. 'I'll spit on yor grave yet, by God.'

'I'll spit on your house from my knoll, by God, before sunset!'

'Mayhaps there bain't enough treasure in Asia to pay the price, by God! Good day to you.'

Brock stormed off, the sound of his seaboots clattering up the gangway.

Culum wiped the sweat off his hands.

'The knoll's trapped you, Dirk. He'll stop bidding and ruin us,' Robb said.

'Yes, Father. I know he will.'

Struan opened the cabin door. 'Steward!'

'Yus, sorr!'

'Mr Cudahy on the double!'

'Yus, sorr.'

'Listen, Dirk,' Robb said. 'Here's your chance. Do to him what he'll do to you. Stop bidding suddenly. Leave him holding the mess. Then he's ruined. *He is*! Not *us*!'

Struan said nothing. There was a knock and Cudahy hurried in.

'Yes, sirr?'

'Get the cutter alongside. Tell the bosun to take Mr Robb and Mr Culum to *Thunder Cloud*. Wait for Mr Culum and take him to the flagship. Then report back here. All hands on deck and aft!'

Cudahy closed the door again.

'Father, Uncle's right. For the love of God, don't you see that that damn pirate has you trapped?'

'Then we'll have to see if the love of God will get us out of the trap. It's a matter of face!'

'Dirk,' Robb pleaded, 'will you not listen to reason?'

'Sarah wants you aboard. Nae word of the bullion yet. And, Culum, lad, if Longstaff asks about me, just say I'm aboard. Nothing more.'

'Dirk, here's your one chance—'

'You'd better hurry, Robb. Give my best wishes to Sarah and the children.' He returned to the pile of papers on his desk.

Robb knew it was useless to argue further and left without another word. Culum followed, sick at heart. He knew that nothing would change his father – or Brock; that The Noble House was committed to a worthless hillock on a worthless rock. Stupid, he shouted to himself. Why is Father so damned stupid?

XII

That afternoon Struan was standing beside the large tent that he had had set up on the foreshore of Happy Valley. He was watching Captain Orlov supervise the seamen as they hauled barrels from the longboat and stacked them neatly inside the tent. He was so engrossed that he did not hear Mary Sinclair come up behind him.

Her face was framed by a bonnet which tied under her chin. Her maroon broadcloth gown swept the sand, tight at the waist to make a fashionable hour-glass figure. But the cloth was of poor quality and the cut old-fashioned. She carried a ragged muff, and around her shoulders was a grey shawl that matched her eyes. She appeared neat and plain and poor, demure, ladylike.

'Hello, Tai-Pan,' she said.

Struan came out of his reverie. 'Oh, hello, Mary. You look very pretty.'

'Thank you, kind sir,' Mary said with a fleeting smile. She curtsied gracefully. 'That's praise indeed.'

The beach and valley were filling up with traders and their wives and children, festive and in their best clothes, greeting one another and conversing volubly. Groups of soldiers and sailors, their officers resplendent, were dotted about. Longboats were bringing other families and officers ashore. Close to the shore were clusters of sampans fishing, and to the west a mass of noisy, curious Chinese, cordoned off from the valley by soldiers.

The auctioneer's dais had been placed on a small rise fifty yards away, and Struan noticed Gordon Chen standing nearby. His son bowed immediately. It was obvious to Struan that the youth wanted to talk to him and must have been waiting patiently for an unobtrusive opportunity.

'Afternoon, Gordon. I'll see you in a minute,' he called out.

'Thank you, sir,' Gordon Chen called back, and he bowed again.

Struan saw Robb strolling with Sarah who was heavy with child, her face strained. Karen was romping beside them. Struan looked for Culum but couldn't find him and presumed he was still on the flagship; then he saw him, deep in conversation with Glessing. He found it odd that Culum had not sought him out as soon as he had come ashore.

'Excuse me, Tai-Pan, Miss Sinclair,' Orlov said. 'That's all of them.'

'I should hope so, Captain Orlov,' Mary said teasingly. 'I hear you've been bringing barrels ashore for the last two hours. Do you want the whole European population inebriated, Mr Struan?'

Struan laughed shortly. 'No. Thank you, Cap'n.'

Orlov touched his forelock to Mary and entered the tent with some of the seamen. Others collected around it, while a few sat on the shore and began to shoot dice.

'You're early, Mary. The bidding does na start for an hour yet.'

'Captain Glessing was kind enough to offer me escort,' she said. 'Let's walk a little, shall we?'

'Surely,' Struan replied as he detected an edge to her voice. They began to stroll inland.

The bed of the valley was damp, and the rain of yesterday was lying in quiet pools. A stream snaked placidly from the small waterfall. Flies and dragonflies and bees and gnats sang an undercurrent to the breakers. The sun carried the promise of spring.

When they were well removed from the crowd, Mary stopped. 'First, I wanted to tell you how sorry I was over your loss.'

'Thank you, Mary.'

'I tried to see you before you left for Canton.'

'I remember. That was kind of you.'

'Last night I tried to come aboard. I wanted to see how you were. That was bad joss.'

'Aye. But it's over. Past.'

'Yes. But I can read the hurt in your face. Others won't, but I can see it.'

'How are things with you?' he asked, staggered, as always, that Mary could seem so ordinary – sweet, gentle, everything she should be – but was not. I should na like her, he thought, but I do.

'Life amuses me. For a time.' Mary glanced back at the beach. Brock, Gorth and Nagrek Thumb, Eliza Brock and her daughters were getting out of their longboat. 'I'm glad you've beaten Brock again. So very glad.'

'Have I?'

Mary's eyes crinkled. 'Forty lacs of bullion? Four coins?'

'How do you know about that?'

'Have you forgotten, Tai-Pan? I have friends in high places.' She said it conversationally. But when she was with the Tai-Pan she despised these 'friends'.

'Who has – who have the other half coins?'

'Would you like me to find out?'

'Maybe I think you already know.'

'Ah, Tai-Pan, you are a man among men.' Her warmth deepened. 'I know where two are. When I know about the other two, I'll tell you.'

'Who have the two?'

'If you arranged such a huge loan, how many would you keep?'

'All of them. Aye, by God, all of them. Jin-qua has two?'

'One.' She toyed with her shawl and arranged it more neatly. 'There are four thousand bannermen in Canton now. And a big armada of fire ships. There's to be an attack on our fleet if it tries to force the Bogue forts. Another fleet's waiting fifty miles north. Does the name Wu Kwok mean anything?'

Struan pretended to think, but inside he was reeling. Before the meeting with Scragger he had never heard of Wu Kwok – of Wu Fang Choi, the father, of course, but not the son. Mauss had not been told what had transpired on the junk or what Scragger had said. Only Robb and Culum knew. Impossible for Mary to have heard about Wu Kwok from them. So it must have come from Wu Kwok – or from Jin-qua. But how? 'That's an ordinary enough name,' he said. 'Why?'

'He's Wu Fang Choi's eldest son.'

'The pirate warlord? The White Lotus?' Struan feigned astonishment.

'I adore shocking you,' she said gaily. 'Well, the emperor has secretly offered mandarinates to Wu Kwok and Wu Fang Choi through the Hoppo at Canton. And the governor-generalships of Fukien Province – and Formosa – in return for an attack on the shipping in Hong Kong harbour. Their entire fleet.'

'When's the attack?' His shock was authentic.

'They haven't accepted yet. As the Chinese say, "negotiations are proceeding".'

Could the favours Wu Kwok requested be a blind? Struan asked himself. A devilish play within a play to put him at ease and trap him? Why, then, the coin? Would they risk their entire fleet? Four thousand junks manned by those pirate scum could finish us – perhaps!

'Would you know if they accept – if there's to be an attack?'

'I'm not sure – but I think so. But that's not all, Tai-Pan. You should know that the reward on your head is doubled. There's a reward on

243

Culum now, too. Ten thousand dollars. On all the English. George Glessing, Longstaff, Brock.' Her voice flattened. 'And on May-may, Duncan and Kate. If kidnapped alive.'

'What?'

'I heard three days ago. You weren't here, so I caught the first boat I could for Macao, but you'd just left. So I went to see May-may. I told her I'd been sent by you, that you'd heard she and the children were in danger. Then I went to your comprador and told him, in your name, to take May-may and the children into his house; that if anything happened to them before you got back you'd hang him and his children and his children's children.'

'What did Chen Sheng say?'

'He said to tell you that you need have no fear. I saw May-may, and the children into his house, then came back to Hong Kong. I think they're safe for the time being.'

'Does he know about the bullion?'

'Of course. Part of it, a small part of it, is his. What better investment could he make?'

'Who else put up the bullion?'

'I know about Chen Sheng, Jin-qua, the Co-hong merchants – they all have a share. That made about fifteen lacs. The rest I'm not sure. Probably the Manchu mandarins.'

'Ti-sen?'

'No. He's in complete disgrace. All his wealth is forfeit. The Co-hong estimate that to be about two thousand lacs. Gold.'

'Chen Sheng said he'd look after them?'

'Yes. Now that you're rich again, he'll guard them with his mother's life. For the time, anyway.'

'Wait here, Mary.' Struan turned for the beach. He picked out Wolfgang and shouted to him, beckoning, and hurried towards him.

'Wolfgang, get Orlov and take *China Cloud* to Macao. Get May-may and the children and bring them and the amah back. Full sail. Leave Cudahy in charge of the tent.'

'Bring them here?'

'Aye. Be back by tomorrow. They're at Chen Sheng's.'

'Bring them here? Openly?'

'Aye, by God! Leave immediately.'

'I won't do it, Tai-Pan. Not openly. You'd destroy yourself. You know you'd be ostracized.'

'The mandarins have put a ransom on their heads. Hurry!'

'*Gott im Himmel!*' Mauss tugged at his beard nervously. 'I'll bring them aboard secretly and swear Orlov to secrecy. *Gott im Himmel,* forgive this poor sinner.'

Struan walked back to Mary. 'Who told you about the kidnapping, Mary?'

'No one you know.'

'You put yoursel' in great danger, lassie. Getting information, then acting on it yoursel'.'

'I'm very careful.'

'Leave Macao once and for all. Take yoursel' out of that life while you have your life. Your joss will na last for ever.'

'Let's talk about you, Tai-Pan. You can't flaunt your Chinese mistress here.'

'She and the children be safe aboard, and that's all that counts.'

'Not in our society, by God, and you know it. They'll break you, Tai-Pan – even you – if you go against their godrotting code. They have to. She's Chinese.'

'The pox on them!'

'Yes. But it'll be a lonely curse, and you've your house to think of. So long as May-may's kept private, she's no threat to them – what's not seen does not exist. It's not my place to advise you – you know that better than anyone – but I beg you, keep her private.'

'I do, and I will – unless they're in danger. I owe you a favour, Mary.'

'Yes.' Her eyes lit with a curious flame. 'I would like a favour.'

'Name it.'

'Anything I ask?'

'Name it.'

'Not now. When I want my favour, I'll ask it. Yes. One day I'll want a favour.' Then she added lightly, 'You should be more cautious, Tai-Pan. I'm a woman, and a woman's mind works very differently from a man's.'

'Aye,' he said, and grinned.

'You've such a nice smile, Tai-Pan.'

'Thank you, kind lady,' he said. He bowed elegantly. 'That's praise indeed!' He put his arm in hers and they began to walk back to the beach. 'Who told you about May-may and the children?'

'We agreed, two years ago, that the sources of my information were sacrosanct.'

'Will you na use those long words?'

'I'm glad I met May-may at long last. She's so beautiful. And the children.' She was feeling warmed by his touch.

'Is there a chance the information was incorrect?'

'No. Kidnapping for ransom is an ancient Chinese art.'

'It's filthy. To touch women and children.' Struan was silent a moment. 'How long are you staying here?'

'A few days. Horatio – Horatio gets a little lost when he's alone. By the way, Chen Sheng knows I speak Cantonese, of course. Now May-may knows. I asked her to keep it secret. She will, won't she?'

'Aye. Nae fear of that. But I'll remind her.' He forced his mind off May-may and the children and Wu Kwok and the fire ships and the remaining three half coins. 'One secret deserves another. The Noble House is giving a ball in thirty-odd days. Of course you're invited.'

'What a marvellous idea!'

'We're giving a prize. A thousand guineas for the best-dressed lady.'

'Good God, Tai-Pan, you'll have your eyes scratched out!'

'Aristotle's going to be the judge.'

'You'll still have your eyes scratched out.' Her eyes seemed to change colour. 'You'd best remember. Now you're the most eligible man in Asia.'

'What?'

Her laugh was half mocking. 'Best choose a wife while you've the time. There'll be many a doxy shaking her drawers at you and many a mother pimping her daughters into your bed.'

'Will you na say such things!'

'Don't say you weren't warned, my lad. A thousand guineas? I think I'd like to win that prize.' Abruptly her mood changed. 'I've the money to buy such a dress, as you well know – but if I did, it would, well, it would spoil the Mary Sinclair people know. Everyone knows we're as poor as coolies.'

'But nothing says I canna give you a dress. At least, there's nothing that says I canna make the offer through Horatio. Is there?'

'God's blood, Tai-Pan, would you really? I'll give you back the money.'

'If you'll stop Gods-blooding, aye. But a gift is a gift.' He studied her thoughtfully. 'Have you ever thought of your great aunt Wilhelmina?'

'Who?'

'Your mother's second cousin once removed. In Holland.'

'Who?'

'The heiress – the one who could leave you a lot of money.'

'I've no relations in Holland.'

'Perhaps your mother forgot to tell you. Perhaps a solicitor in Amsterdam could write that you've come into an inheritance.' He lit a cheroot. 'As an heiress you could spend money openly. Could you na?'

'But – but . . .' Her voice became brittle. 'What about Horatio?'

'Aunt Wilhelmina could leave him two thousand guineas. The bulk to you. She only really liked female offspring. Your mother was her favourite – strange no one told you or Horatio about her. Poor Aunt Wilhelmina. She died yesterday.'

Mary's eyes were huge with excitement. 'Could you, Tai-Pan? Would you?'

'It will take three months for a letter to get to London. A month to make the arrangements in Holland. Three months back. In seven months you're an heiress. But you'd better act the part of a church mouse for that time. And be surprised when it happens.'

'Yes. Sorry, I'm . . . I'm overwhelmed by . . . Don't worry. Don't worry. If I go a little mad and break into tears or scream – I worship you, Tai-Pan.'

His smile faded. 'Will you na say such a thing!'

'I've never said it before, and perhaps I'll never say it again. But to me you're God.' She turned and walked inland alone.

Struan watched her for a moment, then headed for Gordon Chen. He looks more Chinese every day, Struan thought. Out to sea, the longboat with Orlov and Mauss aboard was still well away from *China Cloud*. Hurry it up, by God!'

Skinner intercepted him anxiously. 'Afternoon, Mr Struan.'

'Oh, hello, Mr Skinner.'

'Great day in the Orient, isn't it?'

'Aye. If you'll excuse me, I have to—'

'Won't keep you a moment, Mr Struan. I tried to see you last night.' Skinner dropped his voice. He was sweating more than usual and smelling foul as always. 'The notes of The Noble House're due today, I seem to recall.'

'Do you, now?'

'Are they going to be met?'

'Had you ever any doubt, Mr Skinner?'

'There are rumours. About bullion.'

'So I've heard.'

'I hope they're true. I wouldn't like a change in the ownership of the *Oriental Times*.'

'Nor would I. This evening I'll give you an item of interest. Now, if you'll excuse me?'

Skinner watched Struan approach Gordon Chen and wished he could be privy to that conversation. Then he noticed Brock and his family chatting with Nagrek Thumb. This *is* a great day, he

247

thought gleefully, as he lumbered towards them. Who'll get the knoll?

'I was sorry to hear about your loss, sir,' Gordon Chen was saying. 'I tried to see you but failed in my duty. I offered a prayer.'

'Thank you.'

'My mother asked me to tell you she would observe the usual hundred days of mourning.'

'Please tell her that's na necessary,' Struan said, knowing that she would do so anyway. 'Now, what's been going on with you since I last saw you?'

'Nothing very much. I tried to help Chen Sheng find the house some credit, sir. But I'm afraid we were not successful.' The wind tugged at his queue, shaking it.

'Credit is very hard to come by,' Struan said.

'Yes, it is indeed. I'm sorry.' Gordon Chen thought about the vast quantity of bullion in *China Cloud*'s hold and was filled with admiration for his father. He had heard the rumours this morning, and they had confirmed others that had filtered into Tai Ping Shan: that the Tai-Pan had smuggled the bullion out of Canton from under the noses of the hated Manchus. But he said nothing about the rebirth of The Noble House, for that would be impolite.

'Perhaps it's time that you had a little credit. I might be able to arrange it. Say, one lac of silver.'

Gordon Shen's eyes flickered, and he gasped, 'That is a huge amount of credit, sir.'

'You take one-fourth of the profit, I take three.'

'That would be very fair, sir,' Gordon Chen said, collecting his shattered wits quickly. 'Generous. In such hard times as these, most fair. But if I were to have two-thirds and you one-third, that would assist me to increase your profit considerably. Very considerably.'

'I expect the profit to be considerable.' Struan threw his cheroot away. 'We'll be partners. You take one half; I one half. This is a private arrangement between us. To be secret. You will keep books and accounts monthly. Agreed?'

'Agreed. You are more than a little generous, sir. Thank you.'

'See me this evening and I'll give you the necessary paper. I'll be aboard *Resting Cloud*.'

Gordon Chen was so happy that he wanted to jump and shout with joy. He could not fathom why his father was so generous. But he knew that the one lac was very safe and that it would increase a thousandfold. With joss, he added quickly. Then he remembered the Hung Mun Tong

248

and wondered if loyalty to the tong would conflict with loyalty to his father. And if it did, which would dominate. 'I can't thank you enough, sir. Can this agreement begin at once?'

'Aye, I suppose you'll want to bid on some land.'

'I had thought –' Gordon Chen stopped.

Culum was approaching them, his face set.

'Hello, Culum,' Struan said.

'Hello, Father.'

'This is Gordon Chen. My son, Culum,' Struan said, conscious of the stares and the silence of the crowd on the beach.

Gordon Chen bowed. 'I'm honoured to meet you, sir.'

'Gordon's your half-brother, Culum,' Struan said.

'I know.' Culum stuck out his hand. 'I'm pleased to meet you.'

Still dumbfounded from hearing Struan acknowledge him as son, Gordon weakly shook the hand. 'Thank you. Thank you very much.'

'How old are you, Gordon?' Culum asked.

'Twenty, sir.'

'Half brothers should call each other by their Christian names shouldn't they?'

'If it pleases you.'

'We must get to know each other.' Culum turned to Struan, who was rocked by his son's acknowledgement of Gordon. 'Sorry to disturb you, Father. I just wanted to meet Gordon,' he said, and left.

Struan felt the silence break as the still-life beach came alive again. And he was astonished to see tears streaming down Gordon's face.

'I'm sorry – I'm – I've waited all my life, Mr Struan. Thank you. Thank you. Thank you,' Gordon said brokenly.

'Most people call me "Tai-Pan", lad. We'll forget the "Mr Struan".'

As Struan started to go after Culum, he saw Longstaff's cutter beach. The admiral and a group of naval officers were with him. Horatio as well.

Good, Struan thought. Now Brock.

He waved to Robb and motioned at Brock. Robb nodded and left Sarah and overtook Culum. Together they joined Struan.

'Do you have the papers, Robb?'

'Yes.'

'Come on, then. Let's get our notes back.' Struan glanced at Culum. 'Nothing to be nervous about, lad.'

'Yes.'

They walked away and Struan said, 'I'm glad you met Gordon, Culum. Thank you.'

'I – I wanted to meet him today. With you. Well – publicly.'

'Why?'

'Isn't that giving you the face you say is so important?'

'Who told you about Gordon?'

'I heard rumours when I came back from Canton. People are ever ready to spread bad news.' He remembered the sardonic amusement of most of the traders and their wives whom he had met. 'So sorry, lad, you came at such a bad time. Pity the house is dead. Won't be the same without The Noble House,' they would say in various ways. But Culum knew they were all gloating, glad to see the house humbled. Aunt Sarah had really been the one to open his eyes to his naïvety. They had been walking along Queen's Road and had passed some Eurasians, the first he had seen, a boy and a girl, and he had asked her what nationality they were, and where they came from.

'Here,' she had said. 'They're half-castes, half-English half-heathen. Many of the traders have bastards from heathen mistresses. It's all very secret, of course, but everyone knows. Your Uncle Robb has one.'

'What?'

'I sent her and her whelp packing years ago. It wouldn't have been so bad, I suppose, if the woman had been Christian and pretty. I could have understood that. But her – no.'

'Has – has Father – other children?'

'Children I don't know, Culum. He has a son who works for his comprador, called Gordon Chen. Your father has a curious sense of humour, giving him a clan Christian name. I hear he's been baptized a Christian. I suppose that's something. Perhaps I shouldn't have told you, Culum. But someone has to, and perhaps it's better for you to learn the truth from your kin and not overhear it snickered behind your back. Oh, yes. You've at least one half brother in Asia.'

That night he had been unable to sleep. The next day he had gone ashore despairingly. Some naval officers, Glessing among them, were playing cricket, and he had been asked to make up the team. When it was his turn to bat, he took all his anger out on the ball, smashing it, wanting to kill it, and with it, his shame. He had played brilliantly but had got no pleasure from the game. Later Glessing had drawn him aside and asked him what was the matter. He had blurted it out.

'I don't approve of your father – as you no doubt know,' Glessing had said. 'But that has nothing to do with his private life. Have the same problem as you, myself. At least, I know my father's got a mistress in Maida Vale. Two sons and a daughter. He's never men-

250

tioned it to me, though I expect he knows I know. Damned difficult, but what's a man to do? Probably when I'm that old I'll do the same. Have to wait and see. Course, I agree it's damned uncomfortable knowing you've a half-caste brother.'

'Do you know him?'

'I've seen him. Never talked to him, though I hear he's a good chap. Take some advice – don't let what your father does in his private life get under your skin. He's the only father you'll have.'

'You disapprove of him, yet you're taking his side. Why?'

Glessing had shrugged. 'Perhaps because I've learned that the "sins" of the father are the father's problem, not the son's. Perhaps because the Tai-Pan's a better seaman than I'll ever be and runs the best fleet of the most beautiful ships on earth – treats his seamen like they should be treated, good food, pay and quarters – when we've to work with what the damned Parliament gives us; no cursed money, and pressed men and gallows bait as crew. Perhaps because of Glessing's Point – or because he's *the* Tai-Pan. Perhaps because the Sinclairs admire him. I don't know. I don't mind telling you that if I ever get an order to go after him, I'll do it to the limit of the law. Even so, I hope to God he manages to outsmart that uncouth bugger Brock again. Couldn't stand that sod as *the* Tai-Pan.'

From that day Culum had seen a lot of Glessing. Between them a friendship had ripened . . .

'Today,' Culum continued to Struan, very uncomfortably, 'well, when I saw you and Gordon Chen together, I asked George Glessing. He was honest enough to tell me.'

Struan stopped. 'You mean it was dishonest of me na to tell you?'

'No. You don't have to justify anything you do. To me. A father doesn't have to justify anything to a son, does he?'

'Gordon's a nice lad,' Robb said uneasily.

'Why did you want to know how old he was?' Struan asked.

'He's the same age as me, isn't he?'

'So?'

'It's not important, Father.'

'It is. To you. Why?'

'I'd rather not—'

'Why?'

'A matter of ethics, I suppose. If we're the same age, his mother was – isn't the word "concurrent"? – with mine.'

'Aye. Concurrent would be the right word.'

' "Adultery" would be another right word, wouldn't it?'

251

'One of the truths of man is that adultery's as inevitable as death and sunrise.'

'Not according of the Commandments of God.' Culum avoided his father's eyes. 'The sale should start – now that Longstaff's here,' he said.

'Is that why you're so nervous? Meeting Gordon and applying Commandments to me?'

'You don't need me, do you, Father, with Brock? I think I'll – if you don't mind, I'll see everything's ready.'

'Please yoursel', lad. I think you should be with us. This is a rare occasion. But please yoursel'.' Struan resumed his course along the road. Culum hesitated, then caught up with him.

Queen's Road ran due west from the valley along the shore. A mile away it passed the tents of the marines who guarded the growing number of naval stores. Beyond them a mile were the tented rows of the soldiers near Glessing's Point, the terminus of Queen's Road.

And above Glessing's Point was Tai Ping Shan, connected to the shore by a quivering, never-ending line of Chinese, bowed by the weight of their possessions. The line was perpetually moving and constantly replenished from the incessant arrival of junks and sampans.

'Good day, Your Excellency,' Struan said, raising his hat as they met Longstaff and his party.

'Oh, afternoon, Dirk. Day, Robb.' Longstaff did not stop. 'Aren't you ready to begin, Culum?'

'In just a moment, Excellency.'

'Well, hurry it up. I've got to get on board, what?' And he added to Struan, as an insulting afterthought, 'Good to have you back, Dirk.' He continued his stroll, greeting others.

'He'll change in about three minutes,' Struan said.

'Stupid, contemptible, pox-ridden fool.' Culum's voice was raw and soft. 'Thank God this is the last day I serve him.'

Struan shook his head. 'If I were you, I'd use "Deputy Colonial Secretary" to my advantage.'

'How?'

'We have our power back. But it's still his hand that signs paper into law. And his hand still has to be guided, eh?'

'I suppose so – I suppose so,' Culum replied.

As the Struans approached the Brocks, a silence fell over the beach and excitement quickened.

Gorth and Nagrek Thumb were ranged alongside Brock and Liza and the girls.

252

Skinner began whistling tonelessly and moved closer.

Aristotle Quance hesitated in the middle of a brush stroke.

Only the very young did not feel the excitement, and were not watching and listening.

'Afternoon, ladies, gentlemen,' Struan said, doffing his hat.

'Day, Mr Struan,' Liza Brock said blandly. 'Thee knowed Tess and Lillibet, doan thee?'

'Of course. Day, ladies,' Struan said as the girls curtsied, noticing that Tess had grown considerably since he had last seen her. 'Can we settle our business?' he said to Brock.

'Now's as good a time as may be. Liza, you'n the girls, back to the ship. And, Lillibet, you be akeeping thy hands outa the sea or thee'll catch thy death. And doan fall overboard. And thee, Tess luv, thee watch thyself and Lillibet. Run along now, and be adoing wot yor ma tells thee.'

They curtsied hastily and ran ahead of their mother, glad to be dismissed.

'Children an' shipboard just doan mix, do they?' Brock said. 'Never watch where they be agoin'. Enough to drive you barmy.'

'Aye.' Struan handed the banker's draft to Gorth. 'We're even now, Gorth.'

'Thank you,' Gorth said. He examined it deliberately.

'Perhaps you'd like to double it.'

'How?'

'A further twenty thousand says one of our ships will beat you home.'

'Thankee. But they sayed a fool'n his money is soon split. I baint fool – or a betting man.' He looked at the draft. 'This'll come in right handy. Maybe I can buy a bitty of the knoll from me da'.'

The colour of Struan's eyes deepened. 'Let's go over to the tent,' he said, and began to lead the way.

Robb and Culum followed, and Robb was very glad that his brother was Tai-Pan of The Noble House. His old fear returned. How am I going to deal with Brock? How?

Struan stopped outside the tent and nodded to Cudahy.

'Come on, lads,' Cudahy said to the small group of waiting seamen. 'On the double.'

To everyone's astonishment the men collapsed the tent.

'Our sight drafts, if you please, Tyler.'

Brock warily took the notes out of his pocket. 'Eight hundred and twenty-four thousand nicker.'

Struan gave the notes to Robb, who checked them carefully against the duplicates.

'Thank you,' Struan said. 'Would you sign this?'

'Wot be this?'

'A receipt.'

'An' where's thy banker's draft?' Brock said suspiciously.

'We decided to pay cash,' Struan said.

The seamen dragged the collapsed tent away. Almost concealing the bulk of empty barrels were neat walls of silver bricks. Hundreds upon hundreds of silver bricks, glinting under the bleak sun. Brock stared of them transfixed, and there was a monstrous silence over Hong Kong.

'The Noble House decided to pay cash,' Struan said offhandedly. He lit a match and put it to the roll of sight drafts. He took out three cheroots, offered one to Robb and to Culum, and lit them with the burning paper. 'It's all been weighed. But there's scale if you wish to check the amount.'

The blood rushed to Brock's face. 'God rot you to hell!'

Struan dropped the charred paper and ground it into the sand. 'Thank you, Mr Cudahy. Take the men aboard *Thunder Cloud*.'

'Aye, aye, sorr.' Cudahy and the men took a last, sweating look at the bullion and dashed to their boats.

'Well, that's finished,' Struan said to Robb and Culum. 'Now we can deal with the land.'

'A rare occasion indeed, Dirk,' Robb said. 'That was a masterly idea.'

Culum scanned the beach. He saw the greed and envy, and the eyes that watched them covertly. Thank you, oh God, he said silently, for letting me be part of The Noble House. Thank you for letting me be Thy instrument.

Brock came out of his shock. 'Gorth, get thy bullyboys ashore and on the double.'

'What?'

'On godrotting double,' he said, his voice low and violent. 'Armed. We be having every heathen pirate in Asia on our necks inside minutes.'

Gorth took to his heels.

Brock pulled out his pistols and gave them to Nagrek. 'If any comes within five yards, blow their heads off.' He stamped over to Longstaff. 'Can I borrow them sodjers, Yor Excellency? Else we be havin' a passel of trouble on our hands.'

'Eh? Soldiers? Soldiers?' Longstaff blinked at the bullion. 'Goddamme, is that all real silver? All of it? Goddamme, eight hundred thousand pounds' worth, did you say?'

'A little more,' Brock said impatiently. 'Them sodjers. Marines, sailors. Any wot is armed. To guard it, by God!'

'Oh, armed! Of course. Admiral, would you arrange it, please?'

'Belay, there!' the admiral shouted, whipped into fury by the avarice on every face, including officers of the Royal Navy. Marines and soldiers and sailors came on the double. 'Form a circle fifty paces from this treasure. No one's allowed near. Understand?' He glared at Brock. 'I'll be responsible for its safety for one hour. Then I leave it where it is.'

'Thankee kindly, Admiral,' Brock said, repressing an oath. He glanced seaward. Gorth's cutter was pulling strongly for the *White Witch*. An hour be enough, he thought, cursing Struan and the bullion. How in the name of God can I unload so much bullion? Whose paper dare I takes? With war acoming and maybe no trade, eh? If there be trade, then it'd pay for all the season's tea. But unless trade be guaranteed, why, all the companies' paper be worthless. Except the godrotting Noble House.

No bank an' no vault and no safety until it be off'n yor hands. Yor life's on rack. You should've thort, by God. You should've thort this were wot that belly-fornicating-bugger'd do. He trap you right proper.

Brock tore his mind off the bullion and looked at Struan. He saw the mocking smile, and rage rose in him. 'The day's not over yet, by God.'

'Quite right, Tyler,' Struan answered. 'One more thing to settle.'

'Yus, by God.' Brock shoved through the silent crowd towards the dais.

Abruptly Culum's anxiety returned, more excruciating than before. 'Listen, Father,' he said in a rush, his voice held down, 'Uncle Robb's right. Brock'll leave you when the bidding's reached—'

'Na again, laddie, for the love of God. The knoll belongs to The Noble House.'

Culum stared at his father helplessly. Then he walked away.

'What the devil's the matter with him?' Struan asked Robb.

'I don't know. He's been as nervous as a bitch in heat all day.'

Then Struan noticed Sarah standing on the edge of the crowd – Karen beside her – white-faced, statuelike. He took Robb's arm and began to guide him towards them. 'You've na told Sarah yet, have you, Robb? About staying?'

'No.'

'Now's a good time. Now that you're rich again.'

They came up to Sarah but she did not notice them.

'Hello, Uncle Dirk,' Karen said. 'Can I play with your pretty bricks?'

'Are they truly real, Dirk?' Sarah asked.

'Yes, Sarah,' Robb answered.

'God only knows how you did it, Dirk, but thank you.' She winced as the child kicked in her womb, and took out her smelling salts. 'This means – this means we're saved, doesn't it?'

'Aye,' Struan said.

'Can I play with one of those, Mummy?' Karen said shrilly.

'No, dear. Run along and play,' Sarah said. She went up to Struan and kissed him, her tears streaming. 'Thank you.'

'Dinna thank me, Sarah. The price of so much metal comes high.' Struan touched his hat and left them.

'What did he mean, Robb?'

Robb told her.

'I'm still leaving,' she said. 'As soon as I can. Soon as the baby's born.'

'Yes. It's best.'

'I pray you never find *her*.'

'Oh, don't start that again, Sarah. Please. It's a beautiful day. We're rich again. You can have everything in the world you want.'

'Perhaps I just want a man for a husband,' Sarah walked heavily towards the longboat, and when Robb began to follow, she snapped, 'Thank you, but I can get aboard myself. Come along, Karen dear.'

'Just as you wish,' Robb said, and he stalked up the beach again. He couldn't see Struan among the crowd for a while. Then, as he neared the dais, he noticed him chatting with Aristotle Quance. He joined them.

'Hello, Robb, my dear fellow,' Quance said expansively. 'Marvellous gesture, I was just saying to the Tai-Pan. Marvellous. Worthy of The Noble House.' Then to Struan, his ugly face dancing with joy, 'By the way, you owe me fifty guineas.'

'I dinna such thing!'

'The portrait of Culum. It's ready for delivery. Surely you didn't forget?'

'It was thirty guineas, and I gave you ten in advance, by God!'

'You did? I'll be damned! Are you sure?'

'Where's Shevaun?'

'She has the flux, so I hear, poor lady.' Quance took some snuff. 'Princely, that's what you are, my lad. Can I have a loan? It's in a good cause.'

'What sort of flux?'

Quance looked around and dropped his voice, 'Lovesick.'

'Who?'

256

Quance hesitated. 'You, lad.'

'Oh, go to hell, Aristotle!' Struan said sourly.

'Believe it or believe it not. I can tell. She's asked after you several times.'

'During sittings?'

'What sittings?' Quance said innocently.

'You know what sittings.'

'Lovesick, my lad.' The little man laughed. 'And now that you're rich again, expect to be swept off your feet and into the hay! Immortal testicles of Jove! She'd surely be magnificent. Only fifty guineas, and I won't bother you for a month.'

'What's the "good cause"?'

'Me, dear boy, I need a cure. I've been poorly.'

'Aye, and I know what your problem is. You're feeling your oats. Disgusting for a man your age!'

'You should be so lucky, dear lad. Must admit I'm marvellous. Fifty's not much for an impoverished immortal.'

'You'll get your twenty guineas when I get the painting.' Struan bent down and whispered significantly, 'Aristotle, do you want a commission? Say a hundred pounds? Gold?'

Immediately Quance stuck out his hand. 'I'm your man. My hand on it. Who do I have to kill?'

Struan laughed and told him about the ball and the judgeship.

'Great balls of fire, never, by God!' Quance exploded. 'Am I a bloody fool? Do you want me detesticled? In an early grave? Hounded by every doxy in Asia? Ostracized? Never!'

'Only a man of your knowledge, your stature, your—'

'Never, by God! You, my erstwhile friend – for a miserable hundred pounds you put me in mortal danger. Yes, by God! Mortal danger! To be devilled, hated, ruined, dead before my time . . . make it two hundred?'

'Done!' Struan said.

Quance threw his hat in the air and danced a jig and hugged his stomach. Then he adjusted his purple silk waistcoat and picked up his hat and set it rakishly on his head. 'Tai-Pan, you're a prince. Who but I, Aristotle Quance, would dare to do such a thing? Who but I would be the perfect choice? Perfect! Oh, marvellous Quance! Prince of painters! Two hundred. In advance.'

'After the judging.'

'Don't you trust me?'

'No. You might leave. Or have the vapours.'

'I'd get off my deathbed to judge this contest. In fact, I'd have volunteered. Yes, by the blood of Rembrandt, I'd willingly pay – I'd pay a hundred guineas, if I had to crawl to Brock to borrow it, to have that privilege.'

'What?'

Quance threw his hat into the air again. 'Oh happy, happy day! Oh, perfect Quance, immortal Quance. You've got your place in history. Immortal, perfect Quance.'

'I don't understand you at all, Aristotle,' Robb said. 'You really want the job?'

Quance picked up his hat and brushed the sand off it, his eyes dancing. 'Have you considered the advantages such a position gives me? Eh. Why, every doxy in Asia will be – how shall I put it? – will be ready to sway the judge, eh? In advance.'

'And you'll be ready to be swayed!' Struan said.

'Of course. But it will be an honest choice. The perfect choice. I know the winner now.'

'Who?'

'Another hundred pounds? Today?'

'What do you do with all the money, eh? Between Robb, Cooper and myself we give you a fortune!'

'Give? Huh! Give? It's your privilege to support immorality. Privilege, by Lucifer's hind tit! By the way, is there any brandy in those barrels? I've an immortal thirst.'

'There's none. None at all.'

'How uncivilized! Disgusting.' Quance took some more snuff, and saw Longstaff bearing down. 'Well, I'll be off. Good day, lads.' He walked off whistling, and as he passed Longstaff he raised his hat gravely.

'Oh, Dirk,' Longstaff said, a broad smile on his face. 'Why is Aristotle in such a good humour?'

'He's just glad, like you, that we're still The Noble House.'

'And quite right, too, what?' Longstaff was jovial and full of respect. 'I didn't know there was that much bullion in Asia. Magnificent to pay like that. By the way, would you have dinner this evening? There are some matters I'd like your opinion on.'

'Afraid I'm busy this evening, Will. Tomorrow? Why not come aboard our headquarters, *Resting Cloud*? At noon.'

'Noon would be perfect. Perfect. I'm so glad—'

'Oh, by the way, Will. Why do you na cancel the fleet's order sending them north?'

Longstaff frowned. 'But those devils repudiated our treaty, what?'

'The Manchu emperor has, yes. But this is typhoon weather. Better to keep the fleet in one piece. And under your thumb.'

Longstaff took a pinch of snuff, and dusted the ruffles of his resplendent waistcoat. 'The admiral's not concerned about weather. But if you say so.' He sneezed. 'If we don't go north, what do we do, eh?'

'Let's talk about it tomorrow, shall we?'

'Very wise. Sleep on it. That's the ticket, what? I'll be glad to have your counsel again. Well, looks like we're ready to begin. Delighted, by the way, with your other gesture.' Longstaff departed happily.

'What did he mean by that?' Robb asked.

'I dinna ken. The bullion, I suppose. Listen, Robb, tomorrow you welcome him,' Struan said. 'Tell him what to do.'

'What's that?' Robb's face crinkled into a smile.

'Take the Bogue forts. Then stab at Canton. At once. Ransom Canton. Six million taels of silver. Then when the wind's right, north. Just as before.'

'But he wants to talk to you.'

'You can twist him around your finger now. He's seen the bullion.'

'He won't trust me like he trusts you.'

'In five-odd months he'll have to. How did Sarah take it?'

'As you expected. She'll leave anyway.' Robb looked at the dais as there was a rustle of excitement. Longstaff was mounting the steps. 'You're so nice to his face, Dirk, even after he was so insulting. Yet I know you'll put your mark on him now. Won't you?'

'He's the first governor of Hong Kong. Governors last for four years. There's time and to spare for Longstaff.'

'What about the knoll?'

'That's already been decided on.'

'You're going to leave Brock holding it?'

'Nay.'

'Gentlemen,' Longstaff said to the assembled traders, 'before we begin, I wish to confirm the principles of land ownership and disposal that have been recommended by me to Her Majesty's Government.' He began reading from an official document. 'All land is vested in Her Majesty. Allotments are to be made at a public auction to the highest bidder of an annual ground rent – the annual rent to be the subject of the bidding. Nine-hundred-and-ninety-nine-year leases. A building of a minimum value of one thousand dollars is to be erected within one year, the rate being fixed at four shillings and fourpence to the dollar. Otherwise the allotment is forfeit. A deposit of half the amount bid is to be paid in specie at once.' He looked up. 'Originally we planned to offer one hundred lots today, but it has not been possible to survey them all. Approximately fifty are offered and the rest as soon as practicable. I have also recommended that purchasers be allowed to buy their lots in freehold, subject to Her Majesty's pleasure. Oh yes, and purchasers of "marine lots" may also choose "suburban" or "country" lots. Marine lots are fixed at one hundred feet wide, fronting on Queen's Road and stretching to the sea.' He looked up and smiled pleasantly. 'With the offering of land for sale, today we can presume the foundations of the town to be laid. Land has been set aside for the courthouse, government offices, governor's mansion, jail, a cricket ground, market square and for the Orientals. I formally have called our town-to-be Queen's Town!'

There were cheers.

'This is the first opportunity I've had for many a day of addressing you all. I would say that we have hard times ahead. But let us not falter. We must all pull together. We must put our backs to the plough and then, with God's good help, we'll conquer the heathen to the glory of her Britannic Majesty and the glory of the Colony of Hong Kong.'

There were three cheers for the queen and three cheers for the colony and three cheers for Longstaff. And the Chinese onlookers chattered and watched and laughed.

'Now, if Mr Brock will kindly take his mind off the loose change of The Noble House, I will declare the auction open!'

Brock and Gorth smouldered as the laughter swooped over them.

Longstaff stepped off the platform and Glessing moved closer.'

'I must reiterate, Your Excellency,' Glessing said, 'that due to the lack of time not all the lots have been accurately surveyed.'

'Details. Details, my dear fellow. What do a few feet matter? There's land enough for all. Please carry on, Culum, my dear chap. Good day to you.' Longstaff walked off towards his cutter, and as he passed Struan he smiled and raised his hat. 'Tomorrow at noon, Dirk.'

Culum wiped the sweat off his face and glanced at the little man beside him. 'Mr Hibbs?'

Henry Hardy Hibbs drew himself up to his full five and a half feet and mounted the platform. 'Day, gents,' he said with an unctuous smile. ' 'Enry 'Ardy 'Ibbs. Of London Town, late o' the firm of 'Ibbs, 'Ibbs and 'Ibbs, Auctioneers and Estate Agents, official auctioneers to 'Is Hexcellence, the Right 'Onourable Longstaff. At yor service.' He was an untidy, verminous gnome with a bald head and fawning manner. 'Lot Number One. Now, wot'm I bid?'

'Where the devil did you find him, Culum?' Struan asked.

'Off one of the merchantmen,' Culum heard himself say, wishing the day over. 'He'd worked his passage from Singapore. He had had his pocket picked there and all his money stolen.'

Struan listened as Hibbs efficiently and dexterously wheedled the price upwards and upwards. He scrutinized the crowd, and frowned.

'What's the matter, Dirk?' Robb asked.

'I was looking for Gordon. Have you seen him?'

'Last I saw of him he was walking towards Glessing's Point. Why?'

'Nae matter,' Struan said, thinking it very strange Gordon was not here. 'I would have thought he'd be bidding for land himself. What better investment could there be?'

The bidding for the lots was brisk. All the traders knew that a colony meant permanence. Permanence meant land values would skyrocket. Especially in an island colony where level building land was in short supply. Land meant safety; land could never be lost. Fortunes would be made.

As the sale continued, Struan felt his excitement rising. Across the press of men Brock was waiting, equally on edge. Gorth was near him, his eyes darting from Struan to his men who were surrounding the bullion. Struan and Brock bought the lots they had agreed on. But the prices were higher than they had expected, for the bidding was hotly competitive. They bid against each other for some minor lots. A few Struan bought – on some he withdrew. The tension among the traders grew.

The last of the marine lots were offered and bought. Then the suburban and country lots were offered and they too were bought expensively. Only the knoll remained. It was the largest piece of land, and the best.

'Well, gents, that's it,' Hibbs said, his voice hoarse from auction-eering. 'Them wot has bought has to pay 'arf the nicker now. Receipts from the deputy colonial secretary. If you please!'

An astonished hush fell over the crowd.

'The sale's not complete yet.' Struan's voice split the air.

'Yus, by God!' Brock said.

'Eh, gents?' Hibbs said cautiously, sensing trouble.

'What about the knoll?'

'Wot knoll, Yor 'Onours?'

Struan pointed a blunt finger. 'That knoll!'

'It, er, ain't on the list, Guv. Nuffink to do wiv me, Guv,' Hibbs said hastily, and prepared to run. He glanced at Culum who was standing stock-still. 'Is it Yor 'Onour?'

'No.' Culum forced himself to look at his father, the silence choking him.

'Why is it na on the list, by God?'

'Because – because, well it's already been purchased.' The hairs on the nape of Culum's neck crawled as he saw – as though in a dream – his father walk over to him, and all the carefully worked-out words vanished from his head. The reasons. How he had said to Longstaff this morning, in desperation, that it was his father's thought to put a church there. For the benefit of all Hong Kong. It was the only way, Culum wanted to shout. Don't you see? You'd've destroyed us all. If I'd told you, you'd never have listened. Don't you see?'

'Purchased by whom?'

'By me. For the Church,' Culum stuttered. 'One pound a year. The knoll belongs to the Church.'

'*You took my knoll?*' The words were soft-spoken but barbed, and Culum felt their cruelty.

'For the Church. Yes,' he croaked. 'The . . . deed . . . the deed was signed this morning. I . . . His Excellency signed the deed. In perpetuity.'

'*You knew I wanted that land?*'

'Yes.' All Culum saw was the blinding light that seemed to stream from his father's eyes, consuming him, taking his soul. 'Yes. Yes. But I decided it was for the Church. I did. The knoll belongs to the House of God.'

'*Then you've dared to cross me?*'

There was a frantic silence. Even Brock was appalled by the power that seemed to pour out of Struan and surround them all.

Culum waited for the blow that he knew was coming – that they all knew was coming.

But Struan's fists unlocked and he whirled around and walked out of the valley.

Brock's bellow of laughter shattered the sickening quietness, and everyone flinched involuntarily.

'Shut up, Brock,' Quance said. 'Shut up.'

'That I will, Aristotle,' Brock said. 'That I will.'

The traders splintered into whispering pockets and Hibbs called out tremulously. 'If them wot has bought will kindly step this way. If you please, gents.'

Brock was studying Culum, almost compassionately. 'I'd say thy days were numbered, lad,' he said. 'Thee doan knowed that devil like I knowed him. Watch thy back.' He went up to Hibbs to pay for his land.

Culum was trembling. He could feel people watching him. He could feel their awe. Or was it horror?

'For the love of God, why didn't you ask him?' Robb said, hardly over his shock. 'Eh? Before you did it?'

'He wouldn't have agreed, would he?'

'I don't know. I don't know. He might have. Or he might have left Brock holding –' He stopped weakly. 'And don't pay any attention to what Brock said. He's just trying to frighten you. There's no need to worry. None.'

'I think Father is the Devil.'

An involuntary shudder ran through Robb. 'That's stupid, lad. Stupid. You're just overwrought. We all are. The bullion and – well, the excitement of the moment. Nothing to worry about. Of course he'll understand when . . .' Robb's words trailed off. Then he hurried after his brother.

Culum was finding it was difficult to focus. Sounds seemed to be stronger than before, but voices more distant, colours and people bizarre. His eyes saw Mary Sinclair and her brother in the distance. Suddenly they were talking to him.

'Sorry,' he said. 'I didn't hear you.'

'I just said that it will be a fine place for the church.' Horatio forced a smile. 'A perfect place.'

'Yes.'

'Your father's always wanted that knoll. Ever since he saw Hong Kong,' Mary said.

'Yes. But now it belongs to the House of God.'

'Yes,' she said sadly. 'But at what cost?'

Then they no longer were talking to him and he was looking at Hibbs.

'Yes?'

'Beggin' yor pardon, sirr, but it's the receipts. For them wot has bought land,' Hibbs said uneasily.

'Receipts?'

'Yus. Land receipts. You've t' sign 'em.'

Culum watched himself as he followed Hibbs to the stand. Mechanically he signed his name.

Robb was hurrying along Queen's Road, careless of the appalled looks that followed him, his chest aching from the exertion of the chase. 'Dirk, Dirk,' he called out.

Struan stopped momentarily. 'Tell him I'll see him on *his* knoll at dawn.'

'But, Dirk, Culum was only—'

'Tell him to come alone.'

'But, Dirk, listen a moment. Don't go. Wait. The poor lad was only—'

'*Tell him to come alone.*'

XIII

That night in the middle watch the wind veered from east-northeast to east and fell off a knot. The humidity increased and the temperature rose a degree and the captains of the fleet stirred in their sleep and awoke momentarily, knowing that another monsoon had blown its course. Now the wind would blow wet-warm from the east for three months until May and then would veer as suddenly southward gathering heat and wetness. Then in the fall to east-northeast again, dry and cool, until the spring of next year, when it would once more veer to the east and fall off a knot.

The captains fell asleep again, but they slumbered less easily. The east wind heralded the time of the typhoons.

Brock shifted irritably in his bunk and scratched.

'What's with thee, Tyler?' Liza said, awake and clearheaded instantly as a woman is when a mate is troubled or her child ill. She was in the bunk across the fetid cabin.

'Nothing, Liza. The wind be changed, that be all. Get thy rest.' He adjusted his flannel nightcap and yawned heavily.

Liza got up ponderously and plodded across the cabin.

'Wot be thee doing?'

'Opening porthole, lad. Go to sleep.'

Brock turned over and closed his eyes, but he knew that sleep had left him. He felt the tang of the wind sweep into the cabin. 'There be fog soon,' he said.

Liza got back into her bunk, and the straw-filled mattress creaked. She lay comfortably under the covers. 'It be the bullion that be worryin' thee, baint it?'

'Yus.'

'Doan worry thy head now. Tomorrow's the time for that.'

She yawned and scratched at the bite of a bedbug. 'It'll be grand to be ashore again. Will it take long to build a house?'

'Not long,' he said, and turned over.

'This ball wot Struan be giving,' she said, choosing the words with great care. 'That be a smack in thy face.'

'Ridikilus. Go to sleep.' Brock was instantly on his guard.

'Course, if we was dressed proper, that'd be a smack right back, eh, Tyler?'

Brock groaned but was careful not to let Liza hear. The news of the ball had swept the fleet the moment Struan had told Skinner. Every husband in Asia had denounced the Tai-Pan, for they knew that he had stolen their peace. And every man's blood had quickened. The betting had begun. Shevaun Tillman was odds-on favourite. 'Thee means spike his guns with finery?' he said. 'Good idea, Liza. Thee look proper smart in that red silk dress wot I—'

'That old rag?' Liza said with a contemptuous sniff. 'Thee must be joking!'

' "Old," thee says? Why, thee's only worn it but three or four time. I think thee looks—'

'Three year I be wearing that. An' thee be needin' new dress, coat and breechers and fancy waistcoat and wot not.'

'I enjoys the ones I got,' he said. 'I thinks—'

'It be time I went shopping. Afore every decent bolt of silk in Asia be buyed up – and every seamstress be booked. Tomorrow I be going to Macao. In *Gray Witch*.'

'But, Liza! For a flipperty ball wot Dirk—'

'I be leavin' on the noon tide.'

'Yus, Liza,' Brock said, recognizing that special tone in her voice, knowing that no amount of arguing would take the bit out of her teeth. The pox on Struan! But in spite of his fury, the thought of the prize and the judging stirred him. That be a marv'lous idea! Marv'lous! Now, why baint I athinking o' that? The pox on Struan!

Liza adjusted her pillow and continued to ruminate about the ball. She had already decided that Tess was going to win the prize. And the honour. Whatever the cost. Yes, she told herself, whatever it costed. But how to persuade Tyler to let Tess go t'ball? He be right pigheaded 'bout her.

'It be time to think about our Tess,' she said.

'Wot about her?'

'It be time thee be thinking about a mate for her.'

'Wot?' Brock sat upright in the bunk. 'Be thee outa thy head? Tess be hardly outa nappies. She's bare sixteen.'

'How old were I when thee married me?'

'That be different, by God! Thee were old for thy age, by God. Times is changed. Time enough and plenty for that flibberty folderol, by God! A mate for Tess? Thee be sick in thy head, woman! And wot a thing to say in't middle of night! Now, doan be mentioning that again or I be takin' my belt to thy back.' He turned his back on her furiously and slammed the pillow and closed his eyes.

'Yes, Tyler,' Liza said, smiling. She did not condemn him for the beatings he had given her. They had been few – and never with violence or in a drunken rage. And were a long time ago. For twenty years she had lived with him and she was content with her man.

'Liza, girl,' Brock said tentatively, his face still to the wall, 'do Tess know about – well, about "things"?'

'Course not,' she said, shocked. 'She be brought up proper!'

'Well, by God, it's about time thee took her aside an' tells her,' he fumed, sitting up again. 'An' thee better watch her careful like. By the Cross, if I catch any sniffing around our Tess . . . wot makes thee think she be old enough? Has the girl sayed anything? Be she acting different?'

'Course she be watched. Ridikilus to think not. Ridikilus!' Liza snorted. 'You men be all the same. Huh! "Do this an' do that," and threats and wot not when the girl's just agrowing and readying to be wed! And I'll thank thee not to swear so much, Mr Brock. It baint nice and baint proper!'

'Thee'll say no more about it, by God, and that be an end to it, by God!'

Liza smiled complacently to herself. Now, who's it to be? Not that Nagrek Thumb, by God. Who? Young Sinclair? No brass, and too hoity-toity and churchy. But sound as a bell and a future, no doubt, and in the counsel of godrotting Longstaff. Nothing like a Reverend's son in a family. Possible. The American, Jefferson Cooper? Better. Rich enough. Powerful enough. But a bleedin' foreigner wot hates us English. Even so, Brock and Cooper-Tillman joined together be making a nice knife in the gut of the Noble House. Gorth'd be good, but he be her half brother so he be out. Pity.

Her mind ranged over the many that would make good husbands. The man had to have money and power and potential. And an iron will and a strong arm to control her. Yes, Liza thought. That girl'll be needin' a good belting on her buttocks from time to time. She be as wilful as they come. And not an easy one to tame. Longstaff would be perfect. But he be married, though I heard his wife be sickly and in London, so mayhaps we should wait.

The list whittled to two. But which?

'Tyler?'

'For the luv of God, won't thee let a man sleep? Wot is it now?'

'Wot'll that devil do to Culum Struan?'

'Doan know. Kill him, mayhaps. I doan know. He'll be doing something terrible, that be certain.'

'Culum be a gutty young spark to stand up like that'n.'

Brock laughed. 'I wisht thee'd seed Dirk's face. That bastard were rocked solid. Rocked solid he were.'

'The boy were right smart to give the land to the Church. He saved his da' from danger. An' thee.'

'Ridikilus, woman. Not me, by God. Dirk be awantin' that hillock desperate. He'da bid and bid and I'da stopped when he were strangled by the price. Weren't for that whippersnapper. Dirk'd be on his knees right now. Busted.'

'Or Struan's let thee strangle. Likewise.

'No. He be wanting that hillock.'

'He be wanting thee wrecked more.'

'No. Thee be wrong. Go t'sleep.'

'Wot'll he do to Culum?'

'Doan know. He be a vengeful man. They two've hatred between 'em now. I never seed Dirk so riled. A feud 'tween him and the boy could work nice for us'n.'

For a moment fear swarmed through Liza. Fear for her man. Fear of the violence between him and Struan. Enmity that would end only in the death of one. Or both. Dear Lord above, she prayed for the millionth time, let there be peace between them. Then the fear left her and she said to herself as she had always said, 'Wot's t' be is t' be.' And this reminded her of *Hamlet*, and of Will Shakespeare who was her passion.

'Why not build a playhouse, Tyler? On Hong Kong. We be staying here now, baint we?'

'Yus.' Brock brightened, his mind taken away from Struan. 'That be a good idea, Liza. Right good. Afore that sod think of it. Yus, I be talking to Skinner tomorrow. I'll start the fund. An' we be sending for a group of players. We be putting on a play for Christmas. You think wot it'll be.'

Liza held her tongue. She would have said *Romeo and Juliet*, but that would have been stupid for she knew that her husband would see instantly through her purpose. Yes. Tess be the key to the Brocks and the Struans. But the match be not ending in tragedy. Not like them Montagues and Capulets.

'If Gorth had done that to thee, taken thy knoll, wot would thee have done?'

'Doan know, luv. I'm glad it weren't Gorth. Go t'sleep now.'

Liza Brock let her mind wander. Now, which of the two'd be best? Best for us'n and best for Tess? Culum Struan or Dirk Struan?

The fog crept down on the ships at calm anchor. With the tendrils came a shadowed sampan. It nudged the anchoring fore hawser of the *White Witch* momentarily. Hands held the hawser briefly, an axe rose and fell, and the sampan vanished as silently as it had appeared.

Those on deck, the armed seamen and Nagrek, officer of the watch, noticed nothing untoward. In fog, without a shore or other ships to judge by, a faint wind and a calm sea and a gentle tide would give no hint of movement. The *White Witch* drifted shoreward.

The bosun sounded eight bells, and Nagrek was filled with panic at the risk he was about to take. You cursed fool, he thought. You put yourself in mortal danger making tryst with Tess like this'n. Doan go! Stay on deck – or go to your bunk and sleep. But doan go to her. Forget her and forget today and forget last night. For months Nagrek had been conscious of her, but last night, during his watch, he had peeked through the porthole of the cabin she shared with her sister. He had seen her in her shift, on her knees beside the bunk like an angel, saying her prayers. The buttons of the shift were undone, her nipples taut against the grasp of white silk. After she had finished her prayers she had opened her eyes, and for an instant he had thought she had seen him. But she had turned her eyes away from the porthole and had gathered the nightgown into a bustle, moulding it to herself. Then she had moved her hands over herself. Caressingly. Languorously. Breasts, thighs, loins. Then she had slipped out of the shift and stood in front of the mirror. A tremble had run through her and then she had slowly dressed herself again, and sighed, and blown out the lantern and slipped into bed.

And then today, watching her run down the beach, her skirts flying, watching her legs and wishing himself between them, he had made up his mind to have her. This afternoon on board, helpless with terror and longing, he had whispered to her and seen the blush and heard her whisper back, 'Yes, Nagrek, tonight at eight bells.'

The new watch came on deck.

'Get thee below, Nagrek,' Gorth said, stamping up to the poop. He relieved himself in the scuppers, then yawned and took his place on the quarterdeck by the binnacle and shook himself almost like a dog.

'The wind veered to the east.'

'I felt it.' Gorth irritably poured himself a tot of rum. 'Cursed fog!'

Nagrek went to his cabin. He took off his shoes and sat on the bunk, the sweat chilling him. Choked by his stupidity but unable to control it, he slipped out of his cabin and noiselessly tip-toed aft down the corridor. He stopped outside the cabin. His hand was wet as he tried the handle. Hardly breathing, he entered the cabin and closed the door behind him.

'Tess?' he whispered, half praying that she would not hear him.

'Hist,' she answered,' or you'll wake Lillibet.'

His dread increased – his mind shouting 'Leave!' – his ache forcing him to stay.

'This be terrible dangerous,' he said. He felt her hand come out of the darkness and take his and guide him to the bunk.

'You wanted to talk to me? What did you want?' she said, fired by the darkness and the secrecy and Nagrek's presence, terrified by the fire, loving it.

'Now be not the time, luv.'

'But you wanted to talk secret. How else can it be secret?' She sat up in the bunk and pulled the clothes tighter around her, and let her hand rest in his, her limbs liquid.

He sat on the bunk, choked with desire. His hand reached out and he touched her hair, and then her neck. 'Don't,' she murmured, and shivered as he fondled her breasts.

'I want to marry thee, luv.'

'Oh yes, oh yes.'

Their lips touched. Nagrek's hand moulded her, travelled her. And in the wake of his touch came the frantic terror-heat. Centring. Centring.

Gorth turned away from the fog as the bosun sounded one bell and wandered over to the binnacle. He looked down at it, the screened lantern flickering, and couldn't believe what he saw. He shook his head to clear it and looked again.

'It be impossible!'

'What amiss, sorr?' the bosun said, startled.

'The wind, by God. It be west! West!'

The bosun ran to the binnacle, but Gorth was already charging along the deck scattering the seamen.

He leaned over the bow and spotted the severed hawser. 'Belay there! We be adrift!' he shouted in sudden panic, and pandemonium swept the deck. 'Let go the aft anchor! Godrot you, hurry.'

As the seamen rushed for the aft hawser, the keel scraped the rock bottom and the ship shuddered and cried out.

The cry swept through the timbers and into the furnace of the cabin, and Nagrek and the girl were paralyzed for an instant. Then he left her clinging warmth and was out in the corridor and charging for the deck. Brock ripped open his cabin door and half saw Nagrek racing up the gangway, and he half noticed that the girls' cabin door was open but forgot it in his blind rush aloft. Liza hurried out of the main cabin and across the corridor and through the open door.

As Brock came on to the quarterdeck, the anchor was let go, but too late. The *White Witch* gave a final scream, heeled slightly to port, and grounded heavily. At that moment sampans swarmed out of the fog and fell on her with grapples, and pirates began to scramble aboard.

The pirates were armed with muskets, knives and cutlasses, and the first on deck was Scragger. Then the men of the *White Witch* were fighting for their lives.

Gorth sidestepped a Chinese who lunged at him and, catching the man by the throat, broke his neck. Nagrek picked up a fighting iron and slashed at the encroaching horde, noticing Scragger and other Europeans among the Chinese. He maimed a man and rushed towards Brock, who was covering the gangway into the quarters below. And to the bullion in the hold.

Scragger cut down a man and backed off, and watched his men attacking. 'Below, by God!' he shouted, and he led the rush at Brock. Others swept forward and decimated the first of the watch that was pouring from below decks.

Brock blew the face off a European, ground the useless pistol into the groin of another and slashed a berserk swath with his cutlass. He lunged at Scragger, who sidestepped and pulled the trigger of his levelled pistol, but at the second Nagrek crashed into him and the ball whined harmlessly into the fog. Scragger whirled, snarling, and hacked at Nagrek with his cutlass, wounding him slightly, then turned in the mêlée and hurled himself at Brock again. His cutlass sliced through a seaman; then Brock had him by the neck and they fell, flailing with fists and knees. Brock gasped as Scragger's cutlass crunched into his face. He picked himself up and flung Scragger aside and cut at him. Scragger rolled away just in time, and the cutlass fractured as it smashed into the deck. Brock buried the broken cutlass in a Chinese who jumped at his throat, and Scragger darted to safety behind a screen of his men.

Gorth was charging into the main-deck maelstrom, cutting, hacking, when a knife ripped into his side and he gasped and fell. Brock saw his son drop, but he stayed at the gangway fighting and killing.

Below, Liza Brock herded Tess and Lillibet into the main cabin. 'Now, doan thee fret, girls,' she said, slamming the door from the outside.

She planted herself in the corridor, a pistol in each hand and two spare pistols in her pocket. If the enemy came down the gangway before the fight was over, it would mean that her man was dead of unconscious. But four pirates would die before they passed her.

Led by Scragger, the pirates slammed into Brock's crew and were again repulsed. More seamen fought their way out of the fo'c'sle. Three of them joined Brock near the gangway and they flew at the pirates, driving them back.

A belaying pin smashed into Scragger's back and he knew the fight was lost. Immediately he shouted something in Chinese and his men broke off battle, shinned like rats down the side into the sampans, and fled. Scragger leaped off the prow and vanished into the water. Brock grabbed a musket from one of his men and rushed to the side. When Scragger's head broke the surface for an instant, Brock fired but missed and the head disappeared. Brock swore, then hurled the empty musket into the darkness.

His men began firing at the sampans, which quickly dissolved into the fog. When there were no more escaping pirates to kill, Brock ordered the enemy dead and wounded to be cast overboard and turned his attention to Gorth.

Blood was oozing out of the wound that Gorth covered with a clenched fist. Brock pried his son's hand away. The knife had cut deeply under his arm and towards his back. 'Have thee coughed blood, lad?'

'No, Da'.'

'Good.' Brock wiped the sweat off his face and stood up. 'Get pitch. And grog. Hurry, by God! Them wot's cutted, come aft. The rest get to the boats and pull us'n off. Tide's full. Hurry!'

Nagrek tried to clear the agony from his head as he got the boats lowered. Blood streamed from his shoulder wound.

Brock gave Gorth a tankard of rum, and as soon as the pitch was bubbling on the brazier, he dipped a belaying pin into it and worked the pitch into the wound. Gorth's face contorted but he made no sound. Then Brock doctored the others with rum and pitch.

'Me, sorr, you forgot me,' one of the seamen moaned. He was holding his chest. There was blood on his lips, and air sucked and hissed from the wound in his chest.

'Thee's dead. Best make thy peace with thy Maker,' Brock said.

'*No!* No, by God! Give me the pitch, sorr. Come on, by God!' And he began screaming. Brock knocked him out and he lay where he fell, the air hissing and bubbling.

Brock helped Gorth up. Once erect, Gorth stood on his own feet. 'I be all right, by God!'

Brock left him and checked aft. The boats were pulling strongly. It was slack water.

'Put yor backs into it!' he shouted. 'Ready a fore anchor, Nagrek!'

They hauled the ship to safety, the leadsman calling the soundings, and when Brock was sure that they were safe, he ordered the anchor let go. The ship swung with the ebb tide and settled herself.

'Sailmaker!'

'Aye, aye, sirr,' the old man said.

'Sew shrouds for they,' he said, pointing at the seven bodies. 'Use the old mains'l. A chain at their feets and over the side at sunup. I be sayin' the service like always.'

'Aye, aye, sirr.'

Brock turned his attention to Gorth. 'How long after thee came on watch were we grounded?'

'Naught but a few minutes. No. It were just one bell. I remember distinct.'

Brock thought a moment. 'We couldn't be drifting from our moorings to shore in one bell. Nohow. Then we been cut adrift in watch before.' Brock looked at Nagrek and he flinched. 'Thy watch. Twenty lashes at sunup for them wot was on deck.'

'Yes, sir,' Nagrek said, terrified.

'But for thee I beed deaded from the God-cursed pirate's pistol, so I be thinking about thee, Nagrek.'

Then he went below.

'All's well, luv,' he said. Liza was stationed like a rock in front of the children's cabin.

'Thank you, Tyler,' she said and put down the pistols. 'Were it bad?'

'Passing bad. It be the bullion. Pirated in harbour! In harbour! There beed English among pirates. I killed one, but the leader, godrot him, he slipped away. The kids all right?'

'Yes. They be inside. Asleep now.' Liza hesitated. 'I think I'd better talk to thee.'

'We be talkin', baint we?'

She walked down the corridor gravely, into the main cabin. He followed her, and she closed the door.

At three bells Brock came on deck again. The fog had lessened but the wind had fallen off. He sniffed and tasted it and knew that soon the wind would freshen again and by morning the fog would vanish. 'Gorth, let's below and check the cargo.'

'None of those gallows-fornicating bait got below, Da'!'

'We be looking anyways. You come too, Nagrek.'

Brock picked up a lantern and they went to the hold.

'There! The door be still bolted,' Gorth said, his wound racking him.

Brock unlocked the door and they went inside. He set the lantern on the bullion and relocked the door.

'Have thee lost thy senses, Da'?' Gorth said.

Brock was looking at Nagrek.

'What's amiss, Mr Brock?' Nagrek was petrified.

'Seems that Nagrek's been fingering thy sister, Gorth. Tess.'

'I didn't – I didn't, by God,' Nagrek burst out. 'I didn't at all.'

Brock picked up the cat-o'-nine-tails that hung on the wall of the hold. 'Seems he went to her cabin while she slept and then woked her and played with her.'

'I didn't touch her I didn't harm her I didn't by God,' Nagrek cried. 'She askt me into her cabin. She askt me. This afternoon she askt me. She did, by God.'

'So you was in her cabin!'

Gorth lunged for Nagrek and cursed with pain as the pitch over the wound in his side parted. Nagrek fled for the door, but Brock shoved him back.

'Yo're a dead man, Nagrek!'

'I didn't harm her I swear to God I swear to—'

'You put yor stinking hands under her shift!'

The cat clawed Nagrek again and again as Brock drove him deeper into the hold. 'You did, by God, didn't you?'

'I swear to God I didn't touch her. Doan, Mr Brock. Please. It were no harm done – I'm sorry – I only touched here – there were nothing more – nothing more.'

Brock stopped, his breathing spasmodic. 'So it were true. You heared, Gorth?' Both men sprang at Nagrek, but Brock was faster and his fist smashed Nagrek unconscious. He pushed Gorth away. 'Wait!'

'But, Da' – that scum . . .'

'Wait! Yor ma said the poor lass was afeared to say anything at first. Tess be thinking because he touched her there now she be going to have child. But Liza sayed Tess still be virgin. He only touched her, praise be to God!'

When Brock had caught his breath, he stripped Nagrek and waited until he was conscious. Then he cut away his manhood. And beat him to death.

XIV

'You wanted to see me, Father?' Culum's face was stark. Struan was standing on the top of the knoll, the binoculars around his neck, knife in his belt, a bunched fighting iron on the ground. He had watched Culum come ashore and walk into the valley and climb the knoll. The wind had broomed the sky clean and the sun on the horizon brought the promise of a fine day.

Straun gestured below. 'The view's good from here, eh?'

Culum said nothing. His knees were jelly under the flame of his father's eyes.

'Do you na agree?'

'The church will – everyone will be—'

'I know all about the church,' Struan interrupted. 'Did you hear about Brock?' The voice was too soft, too calm.

'What about him?'

'He was pirated in the night. Pirates cut his cable and he drifted ashore. Then they boarded him. Did you na hear the shooting?'

'Yes.' Culum was oppressed and spent. Sleepless nights, and then realizing that he alone could save them, then deciding and tricking Longstaff. 'But I didn't know it was that.'

'Aye. Pirated in Hong Kong harbour. Soon as the fog had cleared I went alongside. Brock said he'd lost seven men and the captain.'

'Gorth?'

'Nay. Nagrek Thumb. Poor man died of his wounds. Gorth was cut but not badly.' Struan's face seemed to harden. 'The captain died defending his ship. That's the way to die.'

Culum bit his lip and looked around the knoll, his heart pounding. 'You mean that this is my Calvary?'

'I dinna follow you.'

'Captains dying defending their ships? This is my ship – this knoll – isn't that what you mean? Are you asking me if I want to die defending this?'

276

'Do you?'

'I'm not afraid of you.' The words rasped out of Culum's parched throat. 'There are laws against murder. I can't fight you, and you can kill me, but you'll hang for it. I'm unarmed.'

'You think I'd kill you?'

'If I got in your way, yes, and I have got in your way, haven't I?'

'Have you?'

'You used to be God to me. But in the thirty days I've been here I've come to know you for what you are. Killer. Murderer. Pirate. Opium smuggler. Adulterer. You buy and sell people. You've sired bastards and you're proud of them and your name stinks in the nostrils of decent people.'

'What decent people?'

'You wanted to see me. I'm here. Tell me what you want and let's have done with it. I'm tired of playing mouse to your cat.'

Struan picked up his haversack and set it on one shoulder. 'Come on.'

'Why?'

'I want you in private.'

'We're alone now.'

Struan motioned with his head at the ships at anchor. 'There're eyes there. I can feel them watching us.' He pointed at the foreshore dotted with Chinese and Europeans. Traders were pacing out their lots. Children were already at play. 'We're being watched everywhere.' He pointed to a hilltop in the west. 'That's where we're going.'

The hill was almost a mountain. It rose to thirteen hundred feet, rocky and sparse and brooding.

'No.'

'It is too far for you?' Struan saw the hatred in Culum's face and waited for an answer. There was none. 'I thought you were na afraid.'

He turned away and walked down the knoll and on to the rising shoulder of the mountain. Culum hesitated, fear consuming him. Then he began to follow, dominated by Struan's will.

As Struan climbed, he knew that he was playing another dangerous game. He did not stop or look back until he had gained the crest of the mountain. It was windswept and gaunt. He looked back and saw Culum struggling far below.

He turned his back on his son.

The panorama was vast. Awesomely beautiful. The sun high in the blue sky and the Pacific sea a blue-green carpet. Brown-green mountains of the islands were jutting from the sea carpet, Pokliu Chau to the southwest; Lan Tao, the huge island, bigger than Hong Kong, fifteen miles westward; and the hundreds of small, barren islands and bleak rocks that surrounded the Hong Kong archipelago. The ships in harbour were clear in his binoculars, and north was mainland China. He could see fleets of junks and sampans tacking up the Lan Tao channel heading for Hong Kong's western approaches. More were sailing back into the Pearl River estuary. North and south and east and west there was sea traffic; frigates on patrol, fishing junks, sampans, but no merchantmen. Well, he thought, a few weeks and the end of the second war and then the merchantmen will dominate the sea.

Culum was fighting his way up the track made by Struan. He was almost exhausted and only his dogged will kept his feet moving. His clothes were torn and his face scratched from the clawing weeds. But still he climbed.

At length he came to the crest, his chest heaving, the wind tugging at him.

Struan was sitting on the ground a few feet below in the lee of the wind. A tablecloth was spread and there was food and a bottle of wine.

'Here, lad,' Struan said, and offered a half glass of wine.

Still panting, Culum took the wine and tried to drink but most of it dribbled down his chin. He wiped it off and gulped for air.

'Sit down,' Struan said.

To Culum's astonishment, Struan was smiling benignly.

'Come on, laddie. Sit down. Please sit down.'

'I – I don't understand.'

'The view's better from here, isn't it?'

'One moment, you're the Devil,' Culum said, his lungs burning from the exertion, 'and now – now – I just don't understand . . .'

'I brought chicken and bread,' Struan said. 'And another bottle of wine. Does that suit you?'

Culum sank down, spent. 'Chicken?'

'Well, you did na have breakfast, did you? You must be starving.'

'About the knoll. I—'

'Catch your breath, rest, then eat. Please. You'll na have slept these two nights. It's nae good to talk on an empty stomach. Eat sparingly, or you'll be sick. It was a strong climb up here. I'm tired mysel'.'

Culum lay back against a rock and closed his eyes and gathered his strength, his body crying out for rest. He forced his eyes open, expecting this to be a dream. But there was his father, studying the south sea through binoculars.

'About the knoll. I was—'

278

'Eat,' Struan interrupted, and offered him some chicken.

Culum took a drumstick. 'I can't eat. Not before I've said it. I had to do it. *I had to*. You'd never have agreed and it was the only way. Brock would have destroyed you. He would have stopped bidding. I know he would. If he didn't hate you so much and you him, then you'd have the knoll. *You* forced the issue. You did. It's your fault. The knoll's the Church's and that's right. You forced it.'

'Aye,' Struan said. 'Of course. I'm very proud of you. It took great courage. Robb would never have done it, or even if he'd thought of it he'd never have been able to carry it through.'

Culum was dumbfounded. 'You – you wanted me to do that?'

'Of course, laddie. It was the only solution to an impossible situation.'

'You – you planned me to do that?'

'I'd gambled that you'd do it, aye. I hinted that you should do it. When you were so nervous about seeing Longstaff – and when you avoided me at Happy Valley – I thought you'd arranged it. Then I was put off by your reaction to Gordon. But Longstaff later said, "Your *other* gesture, marvellous!" and then I knew you'd worked out the only possible solution. I'm very proud of you, lad. Brock would certainly have slaughtered us. I could do nothing to prevent it. The knoll was a matter of face.'

'You – you pushed me – pushed me for two days and two nights into hell – knowing there was a simple answer?'

'Was it so simple?'

'For you it was!' Culum shouted. He jumped to his feet.

'Aye,' Struan said, suddenly harsh. 'For me. But na for you. But you made the decision and you're better for it. Now you're a man. If I'd suggested the "House of God" to you, you'd na have been able to carry it through. Never. You'd've given yoursel' awa'. You had to believe in what you were doing. If Brock had thought for an instant that I planned it with you, he'd've made us the laughing-stock of Asia. We'd've lost face for ever.'

'You'd sacrifice me for face?' Culum screamed. 'Your godrotting face?'

'Ours, Culum,' Struan said. 'And it's good to hear you swear at long last. It improves you, lad!'

'Then all the anger, your anger – it was pretence?'

'Of course, lad,' Struan said. 'That was for the benefit of Brock. And the others.'

'Even Robb?'

'Robb more than any. Eat some food.'

'The pox on food! You're the Devil! You'll pull us all into hell with you. By the Lord God, I swear I'll—'

Struan bounded up and grabbed Culum by the shoulders. 'Before you say something you may regret, you'll listen. I gambled you had the guts to decide, and you did. By yoursel'. Wi'out help from me. And I blessed you. Now you're Culum Struan, the man that dared to cross the Tai-Pan. The man that took his cherished knoll away. You're unique. You've gained more face in one day than you could acquire in twenty years. How in God's name do you think you control men and lead them by the nose? By the strength of your arm only? No. But by your brain. And by magic.' He let go of Culum.

'Magic!' Culum choked out. 'But that's black magic!'

Laughing softly, Struan sat down and poured himself a glass of wine. 'Those with brains will see how wise you are. "That Culum's clever. He gives the knoll to the Church. And thus stops that devil Struan from destroying The Noble House by placing their wealth on a worthless knoll. But Culum's saved the Tai-Pan's face at the same time – that devil canna kill Culum Struan for giving the land to the Church." ' Struan sipped the wine. 'Even Brock's got to be impressed, whether he thinks it's a secret deal or na – because you carried it off. The religious will bless you for giving the "best" to the Church. The fools like Longstaff will fear you and ask your counsel. The cynics will be awed by the smartness of your solution and loathe you and say, "Culum's got the devil of his father in him. Best watch out." I'd say you've gained stature, lad.'

'But – but if I've – then you, you've lost face?'

'Aye. But I've enough and to spare. For you and for Robb. And na much time to cement you into place. You watch, laddie. They'll all be thinking, "Culum got away with it once, but will he try again?" And they'll hope we'll hate each other so much that we'll destroy each other. And that's exactly what we're going to try to do. Openly. In public.'

'What?'

'Certainly. Cold hostility whenever we meet. And before long, Brock'll try to seduce you to his side. Cooper will – and Tillman. They'll feed you lies – or twisted truths – hoping you'll become so full of hatred that you'll ruin me and yoursel' in the bargain. And The Noble House. For all the traders want that prize. But now, now they'll never get it. You've proved yoursel', by God.'

'I'll have nothing to do with this,' Culum said quietly.

'You'll have everything to do with it. For five months and five years. You made a holy oath.'

'You'd hold me to that? Now?'

'You'll hold yoursel' to it. Your salary's trebled.'

'You think money's important in a thing like this?'

'It's small payment for two days of hell.'

'I don't want any money. And I won't do it. I can't.'

Struan selected a drumstick reflectively. 'I considered you very carefully. I was tempted na to tell you at all. To let you act a role unknowingly. But then I weighed you. I decided you could do it, knowing. It'll be more enjoyable for both of us now that you know.'

'You'd let me live my life and end my life hating you? Just to further The Noble House?'

'You know the answer to that.'

'You're unholy.'

'I agree. In some ways,' he said, munching the chicken, 'I'm all the things you said, and more. I break many of the Commandments but na all. I know what I do and I'm ready to answer for what I do. But I'm the only man on earth you can completely trust – providing you dinna, with calculation, go against the house. I'm *the* Tai-Pan. With suffering and devilment you'll be the *same*.'

'It's not worth the hypocrisy. Or the evil.'

'Ah, lad, you do my heart good,' Struan said, throwing away the chicken bone. 'You're so young. I envy you your years ahead. Na worth it? To be the best? To rule Brock and the others by the skill of your presence? Longstaff, and through him the Crown? The Emperor of China? And through him three hundred millions of Chinese?' Struan drank some wine. 'It's worth it. Much hatred and a little playacting is a small price to pay.'

Culum leaned back into the cradle of the rock, his mind raging with the relentless words and questions and implacable answers. Is this the will of God? he asked himself. The strongest survive at the expense of the weak? For God made all things and the pattern thereof. But Jesus said, 'The meek shall inherit the earth.' Did He mean the earth – or the Kingdom of God?

Meekness would not have obtained the bullion, or protected it. Meekness would not have saved The Noble House this time over the knoll. Meekness will never make progress, never overcome the cruel and the greedy. If I'm Tai-Pan, the Charter will go forward. Wealth with a purpose – an immortal purpose, *he* said. 'Very well.'

Culum Struan's hatred of his father vanished. And with the hatred, his love. All that remained was respect.

'Why did you come up here?' Culum asked.

Struan knew that he had lost his son. He was saddened as a father, but not as a man. He had brought his enemy to battle on his own terms and in his own time. So he had done his duty as a father.

'To tire you so I could talk and make you understand,' he said. 'And to show you that though the view from the knoll is fine, from here it is grand.'

Culum saw the view for the first time. 'Yes. Yes, it is.' Then he leaned forward and chose a piece of chicken and began to eat.

Struan kept the pain off his face. The lad's smile will come back, he told himself. Give the lad time. It's raw growing up so fast. Give the lad time.

He felt very tired. He leaned against a rock and turned his binoculars south, seeking *China Cloud*. But it was nowhere in sight. Idly he scanned the horizon. Then his eyes fixed.

'Look, lad. There's *Blue Cloud*!'

Culum took the binoculars and saw the clipper. She was a sister to *Thunder Cloud*, 18 guns, as fleet, as beautiful. Beautiful even to Culum, who loathed ships and the sea.

'She'll have a hundred thousand guineas' worth of opium aboard her,' Struan said. 'Now what should you do? We've three ships here and sixteen more due within the month.'

'Send them north? To sell their cargoes?'

'Aye.' A shadow crossed Struan's face. 'That reminds me. You remember Isaac Perry?'

'Yes. It seems a century ago.'

'I beached him, remember? Because he failed McKay, and because he was afraid of me and I didn't know why. I gave McKay fifteen days to find out the answer to that riddle, but he never came back to Canton. Last night I saw McKay. He's got a shore berth now – a deputy magistrate and peeler.' He lit a cheroot, cupping his hand against the wind, and passed it over to Culum and lit another. 'Well, it seems that Perry has a berth with Cooper-Tillman now. On their Virginia-Africa run. Slaving.'

'I don't believe it.'

'Wilf Tillman told me. Last night. He shrugged and said that Perry had na wanted the China run any more. So he had offered Perry a blackbirder. Perry took it. He left a week ago. Just before Perry left, McKay tricked him. They got drunk together. McKay said he'd been sacked by me – as he had – and cursed me, asked for a berth on Perry's new ship, swearing to revenge himself on me. Drink makes any tongue wag and Perry's wagged. He told McKay that he'd sold a copy of our secret trading places up the coast – latitudes and longitudes – and names of our opium dealers to Morgan Brock. The last time he was in London.'

'Then Brock knows all the secret places?'

'The ones Perry's used. Ten years of trading. That covers most.'

'What can we do?'

'Find new places and new men to trust. So you see, lad, you canna put too much faith in anyone.'

'That's terrible.'

'That's a law of survival. Rest for an hour, then we'll be off.'

'Where to?'

'Aberdeen. We're going to have a look quietly. Against the picking of Wu Kwok's men.' He opened the haversack and passed over a pistol. 'Can you use one of these?'

'Not very well.'

'It might be as well for you to practise.'

'All right.' Culum examined it. He had used duelling pistols once in a foolish university squabble, and both he and his adversary had been so terrified that the bullets had missed by yards.

'We can go now,' Culum said. 'I'm not tired any more.'

Struan shook his head. 'I want to wait until *China Cloud* heaves over the horizon.'

'Where's she been?'

'Macao.'

'Why?'

'I sent here there.' Struan brushed crumbs off his jacket. 'A reward's just been put on the head of my mistress. And my son and daughter by her, if they're captured alive. I sent Mauss and *China Cloud* to bring them both here. They'll be safe aboard.'

'But Gordon's already here. I saw him yesterday.'

'This lass is not his mother.'

Culum found it curious that now he was not hurt by the knowledge that his father had two – no, three – families. Three, counting himself and Winifred. 'Kidnapping's a terrible thing. Terrible,' he said.

'There's a reward on your head now. Ten thousand dollars.'

'Am I worth that? I wonder.'

'If a Chinese offers ten, you can bet that you're worth a hundred.' Struan again focused the binoculars on *Blue Cloud*. 'I think a hundred thousand would be more correct. For you.'

Culum shaded his eyes from the sun and understood his father's compliment. But he let it pass unacknowledged. He was thinking about the other mistress and wondered what she was like and what Gordon's mother was like. His mind was working coldly, dispassionately, without rancour, but with contempt for the weakness and promiscuousness of his father. Culum found it strange that his mind was so very calm.

'What's Brock going to do about the bullion? He'll be pirated and pirated so long as he has it.'

'He'll have to ask us to take some back. For paper. We'll do this immediately. And then at less than the usual interest. Tell Robb to arrange it.'

'Then we'll be pirated.'

'Perhaps.' Struan was watching *Blue Cloud* slowly beating up against the wind in the passage between Lan Tao and Hong Kong. 'As soon as *China Cloud* returns, I'm leaving. I'll go with the expeditionary force and I'll na be back to Hong Kong until the day before the ball.'

'Why?'

'To give you time to get used to our "enmity". You'll need practice. You and Robb are to start the buildings. The plans are already settled. Except for the Great House. I'll decide about that later. Begin to build a church on the knoll. Get Aristotle to design it. Pay him a tenth of what he asks in his first breath. You and Robb are to do everything.'

'Yes, Tai-Pan,' Culum said. Tai-Pan. Not Father. Both men heard its finality. And accepted it.

'Build my cottage on suburban lot seventeen. Robb has the plan. It's to be up in three weeks, the garden planted, and a ten-foot wall around it.'

'That's impossible.'

'Whatever it costs. Put a hundred, two hundred men abuilding it if necessary. Furnished, landscaped as the plan says. And I want all our buildings finished in three months.'

'There's at least ten months of building there. A year or more.'

'Aye. So we use more men. More money. Then we'll finish earlier.'

'Why hurry?'

'Why na?'

Culum looked out to sea. 'What about the ball?'

'You arrange everything. With Robb and Chen Sheng, our comprador.'

'And Robb? He's not to know that our enmity is a masquerade?'

'I'll let you decide that. You can tell him the night of the ball. If you want.'

China Cloud crested the horizon.

'We can go now,' Struan said.

'Good.'

Struan put the glasses and the remains of the food back into the haversack. 'Send some men up here secretly to keep a permanent watch during daylight.'

'What for?'

'Ships. From here we'd have four or five hours' advance notice of arrivals. Especially the mail packets. Then we send a fast cutter and intercept her and get our mail before the others.'

'And then?'

'We've the jump on everyone. In four hours you can do a lot of buying and selling. Knowing four hours ahead of others could be the difference between life and death.'

Culum's respect increased. Very clever, he thought. He was staring idly westward at the big island of Lan Tao. 'Look!' he cried suddenly, pointing just south of it. 'There's smoke. A ship's on fire!'

'You've sharp eyes, lad,' Struan said, swinging the binoculars over. 'God's death, it's a steamer!'

The ship was black and lean and ugly and sharp-nosed. Smoke poured from her squat funnel. She was two-masted and rigged for sails, but she wore no sails now and steamed male-volently into wind, the red ensign fluttering aft.

'Look at that belly-gutted, stinking fornication of a Royal Navy ship!'

Culum was rocked by the vehemence. 'What's the matter?'

'That bloody iron-festering whore – that's what's the matter! Look at her steam!'

Culum stared through the glasses. The ship looked harmless to him. He had seen a few paddle ships like her before. The Irish mail packets had been steamers for ten years. He could see the two giant paddle wheels, amidships port and starboard, and the billowing smoke and the frothing wake. There were cannon aboard. Many.

'I can't see anything wrong with her.'

'Look at her wake! And her heading! Into wind, by God! She's steering due east. Into wind. Look at her! She's overhauling our ship as though *Blue Cloud's* a pig-rotten brig in the hands of godroting apes – instead of one of the best crews on earth!'

'But what's wrong with that?'

'Everything. Now a steamer's in the Orient. She's done the impossible. That rusty, iron-hulked, machine-powered, Stephenson-invented pus-ridden harlot has sailed from England to here, against all the sea's disgust and the wind's contempt. If one does it, a thousand can. There's progress. And the beginning of a new era!' Struan picked up the empty wine bottle and hurled it against a rock. 'That's what we'll have to use in twenty or thirty years. Those bitch-fornicating abortions of a ship, by God!'

'It is ugly, when you compare it to a sail ship. To *Blue Cloud*. But being able to sail into wind – to forget the wind – means that it'll be faster and more economic and—'

'Never! Na faster, na with the wind abaft the beam, and na as seaworthy. And na in a storm. Those smellpots'll turn turtle and sink like a stone. And na as economic. They have to have wood for the boilers, or coal. And they'll be nae good for the tea trade. Tea's sensitive and it'll spoil in that stink. Sail'll have to carry tea, thank God.'

Culum was amused but didn't show it. 'Yes. But in time they'll improve, certainly. And if one can sail out here, as you say, a thousand others can. I think we should buy steamers.'

'*You* can, and you'll be right. But damned if I'll buy one of those stench-filled monstrosities. Damned if the Lion and Dragon'll fly on one of them while I'm alive!'

'Do all seamen feel as you do?' Culum asked the question carelessly, warmed inside.

'That's a right stupid question! What's on your mind, Culum?' Struan said tartly.

'Just thinking about progress, Tai-Pan.' Culum looked back at the ship. 'I wonder what her name is.'

Struan was studying Culum suspiciously, knowing that the man's mind was working but unaware of what it was planning. That's odd, he told himself. That's the first time you've thought of Culum as a man and na as your son and na as 'Culum' or 'lad' or 'laddie'. 'Thank God I won't live to see the death of sail. But that whore heralds the death of the China clipper. The most beautiful ships that have ever sailed the seas.'

He led the way down the mountain towards Aberdeen. Later the steamer passed close enough for them to read her name. It was *Nemesis*. HMS *Nemesis*.

BOOK THREE

The two frigates poured broadside after broadside into the first of the forts athwart the Bogue, the ten-mile neck of water that guarded the approach to Canton. The Bogue was heavily fortified with dominating forts and dangerously narrow at its mouth, and the frigates appeared to be at a suicidal disadvantage. There was scant room to manoeuvre, and the cannon in the forts could hold the attackers easily at point-blank range as they tacked back and forth, groping upstream. But the cannon were set firm in their beds and could not traverse, and centuries of corrupt administration had allowed the fortifications to languish. Thus the token cannon balls of the forts passed harmlessly to port or to starboard of the frigates.

Cutters left the frigates, and the marines stormed ashore. The forts were taken easily and without loss, for the defenders, knowing themselves to be helpless, had wisely retreated. The marines spiked the cannon and a few stayed to occupy the forts. The rest went aboard again, and the frigates moved north a mile and poured broadside after broadside into the next forts, subduing them as easily.

Later the fleet of junks and fire ships was sent against them but the fleet was sunk.

The two frigates could decimate so many junks so easily because of superior firepower, and because their rigging and sails gave them speed to all points of the compass, wherever the wind blew. Junks could not tack as a frigate could tack, or beat to windward. Junks were designed for Chinese waters and monsoon winds, the frigates for the howling misery of the English Channel or North Sea or Atlantic where storm was commonplace and tempest a way of life.

XV

'Like potting sitting ducks,' the admiral said disgustedly.

'Aye,' Struan said. 'But their losses are slight and ours negligible.'

'A decisive victory, that's the ticket,' Longstaff said. 'That's what we want. Horatio, remind me to ask Aristotle to record today's storming of the Bogue.'

'Yes, Your Excellency.'

They were on the quarterdeck of the flagship HMS *Vengeance*, a mile aft of the path-blazing frigates. Astern was the main body of the expeditionary force, *China Cloud* in the van – May-may and the children secretly aboard.

'We're falling behind, Admiral,' Longstaff said. 'Can't you catch up with the frigates, what?'

The admiral controlled his temper, hard put to be polite to Longstaff. Months of being held in check, months of orders and counter-orders and a contemptible war had sickened him. 'We're making way nicely, sir.'

'We're not. We're tacking back and forth, back and forth. Complete waste of time. Send a signal to *Nemesis*. She can tow us upstream.'

'Tow my flagship?' the admiral bellowed, his face and neck purple. 'That sow-gutted sausage-maker? Tow my 74-gun ship of the line? Tow it, did you say?'

'Yes, tow it, my dear fellow,' Longstaff said, 'and we'll be in Canton all the sooner!'

'Never, by God!'

'Then I'll transfer my headquarters to her! Put a cutter alongside. Ridiculous, all this jealousy. A ship is a ship, sail or steam, and there's a war to be won. You can come aboard at your convenience. I'd be glad if you'd accompany me, Dirk. Come along, Horatio.' Longstaff stamped off, exasperated by the admiral and his insane attitudes, by the feuding between the army and navy: feuding over who was in command, whose counsel was the more worthy, who had first choice of careening or

290

barrack space on Hong Kong, and whether the war was a sea war or a land war and who had preference over whom. And he was still privately angry at that cunning little devil Culum for tricking him into signing away the Tai-Pan's knoll – into believing that the Tai-Pan had already approved the idea – and for jeopardizing the nice relationship he had built so carefully with the dangerous Tai-Pan over so many years, moulding him to his purposes.

And Longstaff was sick of trying to set up a colony, and sick of being pleaded with and railed at, trapped in the squalid competition between traders. And he was furious with the Chinese for daring to repudiate the wonderful treaty that he and he alone had magnanimously given them. Goddamme, he thought, here am I, carrying the weight of all Asia on my shoulders, making all the decisions, keeping them all from each other's throats, fighting a war for the glory of England, saving her trade, by God, and what thanks do I get? I should have been knighted years ago! Then his wrath abated, for he knew that soon Asia would be stabilized and from the safety of the Colony of Hong Kong the threads of British power would spin out. At the dominating whim of the governor. Governors are knighted. Sir William Longstaff – now, that had a nice ring to it. And as colonial governors were commanders-in-chief of all colonial forces, lawmakers officially and by law – and the direct representatives of the queen – then he could deal with popinjay admirals and generals arbitrarily and at leisure. The pox on every one of them, he thought, and he felt happier.

So Longstaff went aboard *Nemesis*.

Struan joined him. Steamship or not, he would be first in Canton.

In five days the fleet was at anchor at Whampoa, the river behind them subdued and safe. A deputation of the Co-hong merchants, sent by the new viceroy, Ching-so, arrived immediately to negotiate. But at Struan's suggestion the deputation was sent away unseen, and the next day the Settlement was reoccupied.

When the traders came ashore at the Settlement, all their old servants were waiting beside the front doors of their factories. It was as though the Settlement had never been left. Nothing had been touched in their absence. Nothing was missing.

The square was given over to the tents of a detachment of the military, and Longstaff made his headquarters in the factory of The Noble House. Another deputation of Co-hong merchants arrived and was again sent away as before, and laborious and elaborate preparations were openly begun to invest Canton.

By day and by night Hog Street and Thirteen Factory Street were a booming, seething mass of buying and selling and fighting and thieving. The brothels and the gin shops thrived. Many men died of drink and some had their throats cut and others simply vanished. Shopkeepers fought for space and prices rose or fell but were always as much as the market would bear.

Again a deputation sought audience with Longstaff, and again Struan dominated Longstaff and had them sent away. The ships of the line settled themselves athwart the Pearl River and the *Nemesis* steamed calmly back and forth, leaving horror in her wake. But the junks and the sampans continued to ply their trade, upstream and downstream. The teas and silks of the season came down from the hinterland and overflowed the Co-hong warehouses that lined the banks of the river.

Then Jin-qua arrived, by night. In secret.

'Hola, Tai-Pan,' he said as he entered Struan's private dining-room, leaning on the arms of his personal slaves. 'Good you see my. Wat for you no come see my, heya?' The slaves helped him sit, bowed and then left. The old man seemed older than ever, his skin more lined. But his eyes were young and very wise. He was wearing a long, silk gown of pale blue and blue silk trousers and soft slippers on his tiny feet. A light silk jacket of green, padded with down, protected him from the damp and chills of the spring night. And on his head was a hat of many colours.

'Hola, Jin-qua. Mandarin Longstaff plenty mad hav got. No want this piece Tai-Pan see frien'. Ayee yah! Tea?' Struan had deliberately received him in his shirt-sleeves, for he wanted Jin-qua to know at once that he was very angry because of Wu Fang Choi's coin. Tea was poured and servants appeared carrying trays of delicacies that Struan had especially ordered.

Struan helped Jin-qua and himself to some dim sum.

'Chow plenty werry good,' Jin-qua said, sitting very straight in his chair.

'Chow werry bad,' Struan said apologetically, knowing it was the best in Canton. A servant came in with coal and put it on the fire, adding a few sticks of fragrant wood. The delectable perfume of the wood filled the small room.

Jin-qua ate the dim sum fastidiously and sipped the Chinese wine, which was heated – as were all Chinese wines – to just the correct temperature. He was warmed by the wine and even more by the knowledge that his protégé Struan was behaving perfectly, as a subtle Chinese adversary would. By serving dim sum at night, when tradition dictated that it be eaten only in the early afternoon, Struan was not only further indicating his displeasure, but was testing him to see how much he knew about Struan's encounter with Wu Kwok.

And though Jin-qua was delighted that his training – or rather the training performed by his granddaughter, T'chung May-may – was bearing such delicate fruit, he was beset with vague misgivings. That's the infinite risk you take, he told himself, when you train a barbarian into civilized ways. The student may learn too well, and before you know it, the student will rule the teacher. Be cautious.

So Jin-qua did not do what he had intended to do: select the smallest of the shrimp-filled steamed doughs and offer it in midair, repeating what Struan had done on the ship of Wu Kwok, which would have indicated with exquisite subtlety that he knew all that had happened in Wu Kwok's cabin. Instead, he picked one of the deep-fried doughs and put it on his own plate and ate it placidly. He knew that it was much wiser, for the present, to hide the knowledge. Later, if he wished, he could help the Tai-Pan avoid the danger he was in and show him how he could extricate himself from disaster.

And as he munched the dim sum he reflected on the utter stupidity of the mandarins and the Manchus. Fools! Contemptible, dung-eating, motherless fools! May their penises shrivel and their bowels fill with worms!

Everything had been planned and executed so ingeniously, he thought. We manoeuvred the barbarians into a war – at a time and place of our own choosing – which solved their economic problems, but in defeat we conceded nothing of importance. Trade continued as before, through Canton only, and thus the Middle Kingdom was still protected from the encroaching European barbarians. And we yielded only a fly-blown malodorous island which, with the first coolie to set foot on shore, we had already begun to retrieve.

And Jin-qua considered the perfection of the scheme which had exploited the emperor's greed and his fear that Ti-sen was a threat to the throne, and had made the emperor himself destroy his own kinsman. A divine jest! Ti-sen had been so beautifully trapped, and so cleverly selected so far in advance. The ideal tool to save the emperor's and China's face. But after years of planning and patience and a complete victory over the enemies of the Middle Kingdom, that greed-infected, harlot-sniffing lump of dogmeat – the emperor – had had the fantastic and incredible stupidity to repudiate the perfect treaty!

Now the barbarian British are angry, rightly so. They have lost face before their devil queen and her besotted intimates. And now we'll have to begin all over again, and the ancient purpose of the Middle Kingdom – to civilize the barbarian earth, to bring it out of the Darkness into the Light, one world under one government and one emperor – is delayed.

Jin-qua did not mind beginning again, for he knew that time was centuries. He was only a little irritated that the time had been put back unnecessarily, and a superb opportunity wasted.

First Canton, he told himself. First our beloved Canton must be ransomed. How little can I settle for? How little? . . .

Struan was seething. He had expected Jin-qua to pick one of the shrimp-filled doughs and offer it to him in midair. Does that mean he does na yet know that Wu Kwok passed the first coin? Surely he realizes that significance of the dim sum? Watch your step, laddie.

'Plenty boom-boom ship, heya!' Jin-qua said at length.

'Plenty more Longstaff hav, never mind. Werry bad when mandarin mad hav.'

'Ayee yah,' Jin-qua said. 'Mandarin Ching-so werry mad hav. Emperor say all same Ti-sen.' He drew his finger across his throat and laughed, '*Phfft!* Wen L'ngst'ff no go away, hav war – no hav trade.'

'Hav war, take trade. Longstaff plenty mad hav.'

'How muchee tael help plenty mad, heya?' Jin-qua put his hands into the sleeves of his green silk coat, leaned back and waited patiently.

'Doan knowa. Maybe hundred lac.'

Jin-qua knew that a hundred could be settled amicably at fifty. And fifty lacs for Canton was not unreasonable when she was helpless. Even so he feigned horror. Then he heard Struan say, 'Add hundred lac. Tax.'

'Add hundred wat?' he said, his horror real.

'Tax my,' Struan said bluntly. 'No like tax on head cow chillo slave my, chillo little my. Mandarin Ching-so werry plenty bad.'

'Tax on head chillo? Ayee yah! Plenty werry bad godrottee mandarin, werry!' Jin-qua said, pretending astonishment. He thanked his joss that he had heard about the reward and had already settled that matter quickly and adroitly, and had sent word through an intermediary to the English whore – and thus to Struan – just in case someone had attempted to collect the reward for May-may and the children before they were in safety.

'Jin-qua fix! Doan worry, heya? Jin-qua fix for frien' in few days. Werry godrottee mandarin Ching-so. Bad, bad, bad.'

'Plenty bad,' Struan said. 'Hard fix maybe, cost many lac. So no add one hundred lac. Add two hundred!'

'Jin-qua fix for frien',' Jin-qua said soothingly. 'No add one, no add two! Fix plenty quick-quick.' He smiled happily at the perfect solution he had already instigated. 'Werry easy. Put other name on Ching-so list. One-Eye Mass'er cow chillo, and two cow chillo little.'

'What?' Struan exploded.

'Wat bad, heya?' What in the world is the matter? Jin-qua wondered. He had arranged a simple exchange – a worthless barbarian woman and two worthless girl children belonging to the man committed to Struan's destruction in return for the safety of his own family. What's wrong with that? How is it possible to understand the barbarian mind?

In God's name, Struan was thinking, how can you understand these heathen devils? 'No like list,' he said. 'Na chillo my na chillo One-Eye Devil, na chillo any. Werry godrottee bad.'

Kidnapping certainly is very, very terrible, Jin-qua thought in agreement, for he was in constant fear that he or his children or his children's children would be kidnapped and held for ransom. But some names have to go on the list in replacement. Whose? 'Jin-qua not put cow chillo on list, never mind. I fix. No worry, heya?'

Struan said, 'Add two hundred tax my, never mind.'

Jin-qua sipped his tea. 'Tomollow Co-hung talkee L'ngst'ff, can?'

'Ching-so can.'

'Ching-so add Co-hong, heya?'

'Tomollow Ching-so can. Next day Co-hong can. Talkee how muchee tael. While talkee, we buy sell tea all same.'

'Finish talkee, trade can.'

'Talkee trade all same.'

Jin-qua argued and begged and tore his hair and eventually conceded. He had already obtained Ching-so's agreement to begin trade immediately and had handed over half the agreed amount of squeeze – the other half to be due in six months. And he had already suggested the face-saving device that Ching-so would use to protect himself from the wrath of the emperor for disobeying orders: that the negotiations were to be protracted until the last ship was filled with tea and the last tael of bullion paid, at which time Ching-so would fall on the Settlement and burn and loot it and send fire ships against the barbarian merchantmen and drive them out of the Pearl River. Trading would lull the barbarians into a false sense of security and give time for the obviously necessary Chinese reinforcements to arrive. Thus the barbarians would be defenceless and Ching-so would win a great victory.

Jin-qua marvelled at the beauty of the plan. For he knew that the barbarians would not be helpless. And that looting and burning the

Settlement would infuriate them. And that they would instantly sail north from Canton and stab at the Pei Ho gate to Peking again. And that the instant the fleet appeared at the Pei Ho, the emperor would again sue for peace and the treaty would be in force again. The perfect treaty. It would be so because the Tai-Pan wanted the 'perfect' treaty and 'Obvious Penis' was only the Tai-Pan's dog.

And thus I avoid having to ransom our beloved Canton now, and avoid paying the other half of the squeeze, for of course Ching-so and his family are finessed into coffins underground where they belong – may that odious Fukienese usurer be impotent for the last few months that remain to him on earth! The 'ransom' that will have to be found to placate the emperor now and the barbarians later will come from the profit on this season's tea and silk and opium. And leave plenty of profit besides. How glorious and exciting life is!

'No worry chillo, heya? Jin-qua fix.'

Struan got up. 'Add two hundred, tax my.' And he added sweetly, 'Jin-qua say Ching-so: "Touch one hair cow chillo my, Tai-Pan bring fire-breathing sea dragon my. Eat Canton, never mind"!'

Jin-qua smiled but shivered at the threat. He cursed all the way home. Now I'll have to employ more spies and guards and send more money to protect Struan's children, not only against obvious duck-fornicating kidnappers but also against any jail offal who stupidly thinks he can make an easy dollar. Woe, woe, woe!

And once in the safety of his home, he kicked his favourite concubine and had thumbscrews put on two female slaves and then he felt much better. Later he slipped out of his house and went to a secret meeting place where he put on the scarlet ceremonial robes of his office. He was the Tai Shan Chu – the Supreme Leader of the Hung Mun Tong in South China. With lesser tong leaders, he heard the first report from the newly formed Hong Kong lodge. And confirmed Gordon Chen as its leader.

So, to the ecstatic delight and relief of the Chinese merchants and the traders, trade began. All the soldiers, except a token force of fifty men, were sent back to Hong Kong. The fleet returned to home harbour in Hong Kong. But HMS *Nemesis* continued to patrol the river, surveying the approaches to Canton and charting all the waterways it found.

And the Settlement and the sea roads at Whampoa exploded with frantic competition day and night. The merchantmen had to be prepared for the delicate teas: the holds repainted and the bilges cleaned and made wholesome. Stores for the homeward voyage had to be found. Allocation of cargo space had to be settled.

The traders who owned no ships of their own – and there were many – descended on the shipowners and fought for choice cargo space on the best ships. Exorbitant freight rates were charged and gladly paid.

The Noble House and Brock and Sons had always bought teas and silks and spices on their own account. But being canny, the Struans and Brocks also carried cargo for others and acted not only as shippers but as brokers and bankers and commission agents, both inbound to England and outbound. Outbound they would carry cargo for others – cotton goods, cotton yarn and spirits, mostly, but anything and everything that the industrial might of England produced, and anything that a trader thought would be marketable. Sometimes ships from other English companies would be consigned to them and they would accept the responsibility for selling the cargo, whatever it was, in Asia on commission, and finding an inbound cargo on commission. Outward bound the only cargo the Struans and Brocks bought was opium, cannon, gunpowder, and shot.

Bullion began to change hands, and Struan and Brock made small fortunes by providing the cash for other traders and taking bank paper on London. But the cash was to be delivered only when a ship and its cargo had passed the Bogue safely and was a day out into open sea.

This year Struan overrode Robb and kept all the cargo space of the *Blue Cloud* for The Noble House alone, and all the teas and the silks for the house alone. Four hundred and fifty-nine thousand pounds of tea, gently crated in fifty-pound cedar-lined boxes, and five and a half thousand bales of silks began to fill the hold of the *Blue Cloud*, around the clock: six hundred thousand pounds sterling if delivered safely in London Town, if she was first; one hundred and sixty thousand pounds of profit, if she was first.

And this year Brock kept the whole cargo of *Gray Witch*. She was to carry half a million pounds of tea and four thousand bales of silk. Like Struan, Brock knew that he would not sleep easily until the mail packet, six months ahead, brought the news of her safe arrival – and safe sale.

Longstaff was flushed with pride that he, and he alone, had reopened trade so easily and brought the Viceroy Ching-so personally to the bargaining table. 'But my dear Admiral, why else did I send away the three deputations, what? Matter of face. Got to understand face and heathen mentality. Negotiations and trade almost without firing a shot! And trade, my dear sir, trade is the lifeblood of England.'

He cancelled the investing of Canton, which further infuriated the army and the navy. And he repeated what Struan reminded him: that he, Longstaff, had said in the past; 'We must be magnanimous, gentlemen, to the defeated. And protect the meek. The trade of England can't swim on the blood of the helpless, what? Negotiations will be concluded in a few days and Asia stabilized once and for all.'

But the negotiations were not concluded. Struan knew that there could be no conclusion at Canton. Only at Peking, or at the gate of Peking. And he wanted no conclusion yet. Only trade. The vital thing was to get the season's teas and silks and dispose of the season's opium. With the profit of the year's trading all the merchant houses would recoup their losses. Profit would encourage them to hold on for another year and to expand. The only place to expand was Hong Kong. Profit and trade would buy vital time. Time to build warehouses and wharves and homes in their island haven. Time until the summer winds made the stab north again possible. Time to weather any storm until the next trading season next year. Time and the money to make Hong Kong safe – and the stepping-stone into Asia.

So Struan soothed away Longstaff's impatience and kept the negotiations simmering and slammed into competition with Brock for the best of the teas and the silks, and the best of the shipping business. Eighteen clippers had to be filled and dispatched. Eighteen crews and captains had to be dealt with.

Brock got the *Gray Witch* away first and she tore downstream, her holds bulging. The final hatch of *Blue Cloud* was battened down half a day later and she charged in pursuit. The race was on.

Gorth ranted and raved because his ship had gone with a new captain, but Brock was inflexible. 'It be no good with thy wound and thee be needed here.' So Gorth planned against the time that he would be Tai-Pan. The Tai-Pan, by God. He went back aboard *Nemesis*. Since the ship had steamed into harbour he had spent every spare moment in her, learning how to sail her, how to fight her, what she would do and what she would not do. For he knew, and his father knew, that *Nemesis* meant the death of sail – and, with joss, the death of The Noble House. Both knew of Struan's abhorrence of steamers, and though they realized that the transition from sail to steam would be hazardous, they decided to gamble heavily on the future. The same wind and the same tide that *Nemesis* had beaten coming into Hong Kong harbour later carried the mail packet back to England. In the ship was a letter from Brock to his son Morgan. The letter cancelled two of the clippers he had ordered and substituted the first two keels of Brock and Sons' new steamship line. The Orient Queen Line.

*   *   *

'Tai-Pan,' May-may said in the darkness of their bedroom and in the comfort of their bed, 'can I go back to Macao? For few days? I take the children with me.'

'Are you tired of the Settlement?'

'No. But difficult here without all clotheses and children's toys. Just for few days, heya?'

'I've already told you about the rewards, and I—'

She stopped his words with a kiss and moved closer into his warmth. 'You smell so nice.'

'And you.'

'That Ma-ree Sin-clair. I liked her.'

'She's – she's got a lot of courage.'

'It was strange you sent woman. Na like you.'

'There was nae time to send anyone else.'

'Her Cantonese and Mandarin is fantastical good.'

'That's a secret. You must na tell anyone.'

'Of course, Tai-Pan.'

The darkness thickened for both of them and they were lost in their own thoughts.

'Have you always slept without clotheses?' she asked.

'Aye.'

'How for do you na get chills?'

'I dinna ken. The Highlands are colder than here. As a bairn I was very poor.'

'What's a bairn?'

'Child.'

She smiled. 'I like to think of you as child. But you're na poor now. And two of the three things are done. Aren't they?'

'What things?' he asked, conscious of the perfume of her, and the touch of the silk that enclosed her.

'The first was to get the bullion, remember? The second to get Hong Kong safe. What was third?'

She turned on to her side and moved one of her legs over his and he lay motionless. But he felt the touch of her leg through the silk and waited, his throat parched. 'Hong Kong's na safe yet,' he said.

Her hand began to move over him. 'With trade this year it is, isn't it? So the second will soon be done.'

'With joss.'

His hand loosened her sleeping gown without haste and his hand began to move over her. He helped her out of her sleeping gown and lit the candle and moved the silk sheets aside. He looked at her, filled with the wonder of her – the smooth lucency of her, like molten porcelain.

'It's exciting – you looking at me, knowing I please you,' she said.

And then they loved, without haste.

Later she said, 'When do you return to Hong Kong?'

'In ten days.' Ten days, he thought. Then the picking of Wu Kwok's men at Aberdeen, and the next night the ball.

'Shall I go with you?'

'Aye.'

'Will the new house be ready then?'

'Aye. You'll be safe there.' His arm was resting across her loins and he ran the tip of his tongue over her cheek and on to her throat.

'It will be good to live on Hong Kong. Then I will be able to see more of my teacher. It's months since I had good talk with Gordon. Perhaps we could have weekly lessons again? I need to learn more and better words. How is he?'

'Fine. I saw him just before I left.'

After a pause she said gently, 'It's na good to have fight with your number-one son.'

'I know.'

'I burn three candles that your anger flies to Java and you forgive him. When you forgive him I would like to meet him.'

'You will. In time.'

'Can I go to Macao before Hong Kong? Please. I would be very careful. I would leave the children here. They would be safe here.'

'Why's Macao so important?'

'I need things and – it's secret, a nice one, a surprise secret. Only few days? Please. You could send Mauss and some of the men if you wish.'

'It's too dangerous.'

'Na dangerous now,' May-may said, knowing that their names were off the list, and filled with astonishment again that Struan had not clapped his hands with delight – as she had – when he had told her of Jin-qua's solution to the list. Ayeee yah, she thought, Europeans are very strange. Very. 'Nae danger now. Even so I would be very careful.'

'What's so important? What secret?'

'Surprise secret. I tell you very soon. But secret now.'

'I'll think about it. Now sleep.'

May-may relaxed contentedly, knowing that in a few days she would be going to Macao, knowing that there are many ways for a woman to get her way with her man – good or bad, clever or stupid, strong or

300

weak. My ball gown will be the bestest, the very bestest, she told herself excitedly. My Tai-Pan will be proud of me. So very proud. Proud enough to marry me and make me his Supreme Lady.

And her last thought before sweet sleep took her was of the child that was budding in her womb. Only a few weeks agrowing. My child will be a son, she promised herself. A son for him to be proud of. Two wonderful surprise secrets for him to be proud of.

'I dinna ken, Vargas,' Struan said peevishly. 'You'd better take this up with Robb. He knows the figures better than I.'

They were in Struan's private office, poring over the ledger. The windows of the office were open to the hum of Canton, and the flies were swarming. It was a warm spring day and already the stench had grown appreciably from its winter low.

'Jin-qua is very anxious to have our final order, senhor, and—'

'I know that. But until he gives us his final order of opium we canna do that accurately. We're offering the best price on tea and the best on opium, so what's the delay?'

'I don't know, senhor,' Vargas said. He did not ask, as he would have liked to, why The Noble House was paying ten per cent more for Jin-qua's teas than other traders, and selling the best Indian Padwa opium to Jin-qua at ten per cent under the current market price.

'Devil take it!' Struan said, and poured some tea. He wished he hadn't allowed May-may to go to Macao. He had sent Ah Sam with her, and Mauss and some of his men to watch over them. She had been due to return yesterday but was still not back. Of course that was not unusual – the passage from Macao to the Canton Settlement could never be judged exactly. No sea voyage could. Na when you have to depend on the wind, he thought sardonically. If she was in a stinkpot steamer, that would be different. Steamers can hit schedules and forget winds and forget tides, godrot them.

'Aye?' he snapped harshly at a knock on the door.

'Excuse me, Mr Struan,' Horatio said, opening the door. 'His Excellency would like you to wait on him.'

'What's amiss?'

'Perhaps His Excellency should tell you, sir. He's in his quarters.'

Struan closed the ledger. 'We'll take this up with Robb as soon as we get back, Vargas. You're coming to the ball?'

'I'd get no peace for the next ten years, senhor, if my lady, my son and my eldest daughter weren't there.'

'Are you fetching them from Macao?'

'No, senhor. They're being escorted to Hong Kong by friends. I'll go direct from here.'

'As soon as Mauss returns, send me word.' Struan walked out and Horatio fell into step.

'I can't thank you enough, Mr Struan, for Mary's gift.'

'What?'

'The ball gown, sir.'

'Oh. Have you seen what she's had made?'

'Oh no, sir. She left for Macao the day after the land sale. I got a letter from her yesterday. She sends her best to you.' Horatio knew that the gift of the gown gave Mary a very good chance to win the prize. Except for Shevaun. If only Shevaun would get sick! Nothing serious, just enough to eliminate her on *the* day. Then Mary would win the thousand guineas. With that they could do marvellous things! Go home for the season. Live in splendour. Oh God, let her win the prize! I'm glad she's away from Hong Kong while I'm here, he told himself. Then she's out of Glessing's reach. Damned man. I wonder if he'll really ask for her hand. What cheek! He and Culum . . . ah, Culum . . . poor Culum.

Horatio was a step behind Struan as they climbed the stairs so he did not have to hide his disquiet. Poor, brave Culum. He remembered how strange Culum had been the day after the land sale. He and Mary had sought Culum out and had found him aboard *Resting Cloud*. Culum had asked them to stay to dinner, and every time they tried to bring the conversation around to the Tai-Pan, hoping to make peace between them, Culum had changed the subject. Then finally Culum had said, 'Let's forget my father, shall we? I have.'

'You mustn't, Culum,' Mary had said. 'He's a wonderful man.'

'We're enemies now, Mary, like it or not. I don't think he'll change, and until he does, I won't.'

Poor, brave Culum, Horatio thought. I know what it's like to hate a father.

'Tai-Pan,' he said as they reached the landing, 'Mary and I were terribly sorry about what happened over the knoll. But even sorrier about what's happened between you and Culum. Culum's, well, become quite a friend, and—'

'Thank you for the thought, Horatio, but I'd be glad if you'd na mention it again.'

Horatio and Struan crossed the landing in silence and went into Longstaff's anteroom. It was large and rich. A huge candelabrum dominated the ornate ceiling and the gleaming conference table underneath it. Longstaff sat at the head of the table, the admiral and General Lord Rutledge-Cornhill flanking him.

'Day, gentlemen.'

'Good of you to join us, Dirk,' Longstaff said. 'Take a seat, my dear fellow. I thought your advice would be valuable.'

'What's amiss, Your Excellency?'

'Well, er, I asked Mr Brock to join us too. It can wait till he comes, then I don't have to repeat myself, what? Sherry?'

'Thank you.'

The door opened and Brock strode in. His caution increased when he saw Struan and the resplendent officers.

'You be wanting me, Yor Excellency?'

'Yes. Please take a seat.'

Brock nodded at Struan. 'Day, Dirk. Day, gents,' he added, knowing it would infuriate the general. He was grimly amused by the cold nods he received in return.

'I asked you two to join us,' Longstaff began, 'well, apart from the fact that you're the leaders of the traders, what? – well, your counsel would be valuable. It seems that a group of anarchists has settled on Hong Kong.'

'What?' the general erupted.

' 'S truth!' Brock said, equally surprised.

'Contemptible anarchists, can you imagine that? Seems that even the heathen are infected by those devils. Yes, if we don't watch out, Hong Kong will become a hotbed. Blasted nuisance, what?'

'What sort of anarchists?' Struan asked. Anarchists meant trouble. Trouble interfered with trade.

'This, er, what was the word, Horatio? "Tang"? "Tung"?'

' "Tong", sir.'

'Well, this tong's already operating under our very noses. Dreadful.'

'Operating in what way?' Struan asked impatiently.

'Perhaps you'd better start from the beginning, sir,' the admiral said.

'Good idea. At the meeting today the Viceroy Ching-so was most upset. He said the Chinese authorities had just learned that these anarchists, a secret society, have set up their headquarters in that festering eyesore, Tai Ping Shan. The anarchists have many, many names and they're – well, you'd better tell them, Horatio.'

'Ching-so said that this was a group of revolutionary fanatics who are committed to overthrow the emperor.' Horatio began. 'He gave His Excellency half a hundred names that the society went under – Red Party, Red Brotherhood, Heaven and Earth Society, and so on – it's almost impossible to translate some of the names into English. Some call it just the "Hung Mun" or "Hung Tong" – "tong" meaning a "secret brotherhood".' He collected his thoughts. 'In any event, these men are anarchists of the worst order. Thieves, pirates, revolutionaries. For centuries the authorities have tried to stamp them out, without success. There are supposed to be a million members in South China. They're organized in lodges and their initiation ceremonies are barbaric. They foster rebellion under any pretext and feed on the fear of their brothers. They demand "protection money". Every prostitute, merchant, peasant, landowner, coolie – everyone is subject to paying them squeeze. If no squeeze is forthcoming, then death or mutilation follows quickly. Every member pays dues – rather like a trade union. Wherever there's discontent, the tong whips the discontented into rebellion. They're fanatics. They rape, torture and spread like a plague.'

'Have you ever heard of Chinese secret societies?' Struan asked. 'Before Ching-so mentioned it?'

'No, sir.'

'Anarchists be devils, right enough,' Brock said worriedly. 'That be the sort of devilment the Chinee'd go for.'

Longstaff pushed a small, red triangular banner across the table. There were two Chinese characters on it. 'The viceroy said that the triangle is always their symbol. The characters on this flag mean "Hong Kong". In any event we've trouble on our hands, that's certain. Ching-so wants to send bannermen and mandarins into Tai Ping Shan and go through it with a sword.'

'You did na agree?' Struan said.

'Good God, no. We're having no interference on our island, by Jove. I told him we'd have no truck with anarchists under our flag and we'd deal with them promptly, in our own way. Now, what should we do?'

'Throw every man jack Oriental off Hong Kong and be done with it,' the admiral said.

'That's impossible, sir,' Struan said. 'And na to our advantage.'

'Yus,' Brock said. 'We've to have labourers and coolies and servants. We needs 'em right enough.'

'There's a simple answer,' the general said, taking a pinch of snuff. He was a red-faced, grey-haired bull of a man with a well-used face. 'Issue an order that anyone belonging to this – what did you call it, tong? – will be hanged.' He sneezed. 'I'll see the order's carried out.'

'You canna hang a Chinese, M'Lord, just for wanting to throw out a foreign dynasty. That's against English law,' Struan said.

'Foreign dynasty or not,' the admiral said, 'fostering insurrection against the emperor of a "friendly power" – and he'll be friendly soon enough, by God, if we're allowed to fulfil the function we were ordered here by the Government for – is against international law. And English law. Look at those scallawag Chartists, by God.'

'We dinna hang them for being Chartists. Only when they're caught rebelling or breaking the law, and that's right!' Struan glowered at the admiral. 'English law says man has a right to free speech. And free political association.'

'But not associations that promote rebellion!' the general said. 'You approve of rebelling against legal authority?'

'That's so ridiculous I'll na give it the courtesy of an answer!'

'Gentlemen, gentlemen,' Longstaff said. 'Of course we can't hang anyone who is a – whatever it is. But equally we can't have Hong Kong festering with anarchists, what? Or poxy trade-unionist ideas.'

'It could be a ploy of Ching-so's to throw us off guard.' Struan looked across at Brock. 'Have you ever heard of the tongs?'

'No. But I be thinking that if the Triangs squeeze all, then they be squeezing trade an' soon they be squeezing us'n.'

The general petulantly flicked some non-existent dust off his immaculate scarlet uniform tunic. 'This obviously comes under the province of the military, Your Excellency. Why not issue a proclamation outlawing them? And we'll do the rest. Namely, apply the rules we've learned in India. Offer a reward for information. Natives are always ready to sell out rival factions at the toss of a guinea. We make an example of the first dozen and then you have no more trouble.'

'You canna apply Indian rules here,' Struan said.

'You've no experience in administration, my dear sir, so you can hardly express an opinion. Natives are natives and that's the end to it.' The general glanced at Longstaff. 'This is a simple matter for the military, sir. As Hong Kong will soon be stabilized as a military cantonment, it will be in our sphere. Issue a proclamation outlawing them and we'll see justice done.'

The admiral snorted. 'I've said a thousand times that Hong Kong should come under the jurisdiction of the senior service. If we don't command the sea-lanes, Hong Kong's dead. Therefore the navy's position is paramount. This would come under our jurisdiction.'

'Armies settle wars, Admiral – as I've mentioned repeatedly. Land battles finish wars. Certainly the navy slaughtered Bonaparte's fleets and starved France. But we still had to finish the conflict once and for all. As we did at Waterloo.'

'Without Trafalgar there'd have been no Waterloo.'

'A moot point, my dear Admiral. But take Asia. Soon we'll have the French and Dutch and Spanish and Russians on our necks encroaching our rightful leadership of this area. Yes, you can dominate the sealanes, and thank God you do, but unless Hong Kong is militarily impregnable, then England has no base either to protect her fleets or to jump off from against the enemy.'

'The prime function of Hong Kong, M'Lord, is as a trade emporium for Asia,' Struan said.

'Oh, I understand the importance of trade, my good man,' the general said testily. 'This is an argument about strategy and hardly concerns you.'

'Weren't for trade,' Brock said, his face reddening, 'there'd be no reason for armies and fleets.'

'Poppycock, my good man. I'll have you know—'

'Strategy or no,' Struan said loudly, 'Hong Kong is a colony and comes under the Foreign Secretary, and this will be decided by the Crown. His Excellency has acted wisely in this matter and I'm sure he feels that both the Royal Navy and the queen's armies have a vital place in Hong Kong's future. As a Royal Naval dockyard and military base and trade emporium' – he kicked Brock surreptitiously under the table – 'and as a free port its future is assured.'

Brock covered a wince and added quickly, 'Oh yus indeed! A free port'll mean huge brass for the Crown, that it will. An' revenue for the best dockyards and barracks in the world. His Excellency's got all thy interests at heart, gents. The army be very important and the Royal Navy. And open port'll work to all thy advantage. Most of all the queen's, God bless her.'

'Quite right, Mr Brock,' Longstaff said. 'Of course we need both the navy and the army. Trade's the lifeblood of England and free trade the coming thing. It's to all our interests to have Hong Kong prosperous.'

'His Excellency wants to open up Asia to all civilized nations without favour,' Struan said, choosing the words carefully. 'How better than from a free port? Guarded by the élite forces of the Crown.'

'I disapprove of letting foreigners grow fat off our backs,' the admiral said curtly, and Struan smiled to himself as the bait was taken. 'We fight the wars and win them and have to fight more because the peace is always fouled in civilian conference. The pox on foreigners, I say.'

'A noteworthy sentiment, Admiral,' Longstaff said as curtly, 'but not a very practical one. And as to "civilian conference", it's more than a little fortunate that diplomats take the long-term point of view. War, after all, is only the long arm of diplomacy. When all else fails.'

'And "diplomacy" has failed here,' the general said, 'so the sooner we land in force in China and implant English law and order throughout the land, the better.'

'Diplomacy has not failed, my dear General. Negotiations proceed cautiously and well. Oh, by the way, there are three hundred millions of Chinese in China.'

'One English bayonet, sir, is worth a thousand native spears. Goddamme, we control India with a handful of men and we can do the same here – and look what a benefit our rule in India has brought those savages, eh? Show the flag in strength, that's what should be done. At once.'

'China is one nation, M'Lord,' Struan said. 'Not dozens like you have in India. The same rules canna apply.'

'Without safe sea-lanes the army couldn't hold India for a week,' the admiral said.

'Ridiculous! Why, we could—'

'Gentlemen, gentlemen,' Longstaff said wearily, 'we're discussing the anarchists. What's your counsel, Admiral?'

'Throw every Oriental off the island. If you want workers, then select a thousand, or two thousand – however many you need on the island – and exclude all others.'

'M'Lord?'

'I've already given my opinion, sir.'

'Oh yes. Mr Brock?'

'I thinks with thee, Excellency, that Hong Kong be a free port and we needs the Chinese an' should deal with Triangs ourselves. I thinks with the general: hang any of these Triangs wot be caught inciting rebellion. An' with the admiral: that we doan want any anti-emperor secret treason on the island. Outlaw 'em, yus. An' I thinks with thee, Dirk, that it baint lawful to hang 'em if they be acting peaceable. But any wot bats an eyeball and be caught as a Triang – lash 'em, brand 'em and toss 'em out for ever.'

'Dirk?' Longstaff asked.

'I agree with Mr Brock. But no lashing and no branding. Those belong in the Dark Ages.'

'From what I've seen of these heathens,' the general said distastefully, 'they're still in the Dark Ages. Of course they have to be punished if they belong to an outlawed group. The lash is an ordinary punishment. Set it at fifty lashes. And branding on the cheek is correct English legal punishment for certain felonies. Brand them too. But better hang the first dozen we catch and they'll evaporate like dervishes.'

'Mark them permanently,' Struan flared, 'and you never give them a chance to become good citizens again.'

'Good citizens don't band into secret anarchistic societies, my good sir,' the general said. 'But then, only a gentleman would appreciate the value of that advice.'

Struan felt the blood soar to his face. 'The next time you make a remark like that, M'Lord, I'll send some seconds to call on you and you'll find a bullet between your eyes.'

There was an aghast silence. White with shock, Longstaff rapped the table. 'I forbid either of you to proceed with this line of talk. It is forbidden.' He took out his lace kerchief and wiped away the sudden sweat on his forehead. His mouth tasted dry and sour.

'I quite agree, Your Excellency,' the general said. 'And I suggest further that this problem is solely one for the *authorities* to decide: you, in conjunction with the admiral and myself, should decide this sort of matter. It's not in the – in the domain of tradespeople.'

'Thee's so full of wind, M'Lord General,' Brock said, 'that if thee farted here in Canton, it'd blow the gate off'n Tower of London!'

'Mr Brock!' Longstaff began. 'You will not—'

The general slammed to his feet. 'I'll thank you, my good sir, to keep that sort of remark to yourself.'

'I baint yor good sir. I be a China trader, by God, and the sooner thee knows it the better. The time be gone for ever when the like of me's to suck thy arse 'cause of a poxy title which like as not were gifted first to a king's whore, a king's bastard, or buyed by knife in a king's back.'

'By God, I demand satisfaction. My seconds will call on you today!'

'They will do no such thing, M'Lord,' Longstaff said, crashing the flat of his hand on to the table. 'If there is any trouble between either of you I'll send you both home under guard and impeach you before the Privy Council. I'm Her Majesty's plenipotentiary in Asia and I am the law. Goddamme, it's most unseemly. You will each apologize to the other! I order you to. Immediately.'

The admiral hid his grim amusement. Horatio looked from face to face with disbelief. Brock was aware that Longstaff had the power to hurt him and he wanted no duel with the general. And, too, he was furious for allowing himself to be drawn into open hostility. 'I apologize, M'Lord. For calling thee a bagful of fart.'

'And I apologize because I'm ordered to do so.'

'I think we'll close this meeting for the present,' Longstaff said, greatly relieved. 'Yes. Thank you for your advice, gentlemen. We'll postpone a decision. Give us all time to think, what?'

The general put on his bearskin helmet, saluted, and made for the door, spurs and sword clinking.

'Oh, General, by the way,' Struan said casually, 'I hear that the navy's challenged the army to a prizefight.'

The general stopped in his tracks, his hand on the doorknob, and bristled as he remembered the remarks the admiral purportedly had been making about his soldiers. 'Yes. I'm afraid it won't be much of a match though.'

'Why, General?' the admiral said irately, remembering the remarks that the general purportedly had been making about his jolly jacktars.

'Because I'd say our man'll win, M'Lord. Without too much of an effort.'

'Why na have the match the day of the ball?' Struan suggested. 'We would deem it an honour and we'd be glad to put up a purse. Say fifty guineas.'

'That's very generous, Struan, but I don't think the army'll be ready by then.'

'The day of the ball, by God,' the general said, purple. 'A hundred guineas on our man!'

'Done,' said the admiral and Brock simultaneously.

'A hundred to both of you!' The general turned on his heel and stalked out.

Longstaff poured himself some sherry. 'Admiral?'

'No, thank you, sir. I think I'll get back to my ship.' The admiral picked up his sword, nodded to Struan and Brock, saluted and left.

'Sherry, gentlemen? Horatio, perhaps you'd do the honours?'

'Certainly, Your Excellency,' Horatio said, glad to have something to do.

'Thankee.' Brock emptied the glass and held it out to be refilled. 'That be tasting good. You've a excellent palate, Your Excellency. Eh, Dirk lad?'

'I really must remonstrate with you, Mr Brock. Unforgivable to say such things. Lord—'

'Yus, sir,' Brock said, acting the penitent. 'You was right. I were in the wrong. We be lucky to have thee in charge. When be thee issuing the proclamation about the free port?'

'Well, er, there's no hurry. These damned anarchists have to be dealt with.'

'Why not deal with them both together?' Struan said. 'As soon as you get back to Hong Kong. Why not give our Chinese British subjects the benefit of the doubt? Deport them, but no flogging and no branding to begin with. That's fair, eh, Tyler?'

'If thee says so and His Excellency agrees,' Brock replied expansively. Trade had been huge. *Gray Witch* was well away and in the lead. Buildings were going up at Happy Valley. There was open hostility between Struan and Culum. And now Hong Kong was to be a free port. Aye, Dirk, lad, he told himself ecstatically, you be having your uses still. You be smart as a whip. Free port be making up for all thy devilment. An' in two year our steamships be driving thee into bankruptcy. 'Yus,' he added, 'if thee both agrees. But soon you'll be having to flog and brand.'

'I certainly hope not,' Longstaff said. 'Disgusting business. Still, the law must be enforced and felons dealt with. An excellent solution, gentlemen, to the – what did you call them, Mr Brock? Ah, yes, Triads. We'll call them Triads in future. Horatio, make a list in characters of the tong names His Excellency Ching-so gave us and we'll post it with the proclamation. Take this down while I think of it: "All the above tongs are outlawed and will be known in future under the general name of 'Triads'. The penalty for being a Triad is instant deportation and handing over to the Chinese authorities. The penalty for inciting overt rebellion against Her Britannic Majesty's Government – or against His Highness, the Emperor of the Chinese – is hanging." '

XVI

The village of Aberdeen lay dark and humid and silent under the full moon. The streets were deserted and the doors of the huts barred tight. Hundreds of sampans were moored in the still, muddy waters. And though they were as jam-packed as the huts, there was neither sound nor movement aboard.

Struan was standing at the prearranged place, at the fork in the path just outside the village, beside the well. The well was rock-lipped and Struan had hung three lanterns on it. He was alone and his gold fob watch told him it was almost time. He wondered if Wu Kwok and his men would come from the village or from the sampans or from the desolate hills. Or from the sea.

He studied the sea. Nothing moved but the waves. Somewhere out in the darkness, sailing close-hauled, was *China Cloud*, her men at action stations. Too far for those aboard to observe him closely, but near enough to see the light of the lanterns. Struan's orders were that if the lanterns were abruptly extinguished, the men were to take to the boats and come ashore with musket and cutlass.

The muted voices of a handful of men he had brought along wafted up faintly from the beach. They were waiting beside the two cutters, armed and ready, also watching the lanterns' light. He listened intently but could not distinguish what they were saying. I'd be safer to be completely alone, he told himself. I want no prying eyes in this. But to be ashore alone wi'out guards'd be foolish. Worse, it'd be testing my joss. Aye.

He stiffened as a dog snarled in the quiet of the village. He listened intently and watched for moving shadows. But he saw none and knew that the dog was only scavenging. He leaned back against the well and began to relax, content to be back on the island. Content that May-may and the children were safe in the house that had been built for them in Happy Valley.

Robb and Culum had handled expertly all that had had to be done while he was away. The small house, with surrounding walls and strong gates, had been completed. Two hundred and fifty men had worked on it day and night.

There were still many details to be finished and all of the garden yet to be planted, but the house itself was habitable and mostly furnished. It was built of bricks and had a fireplace and wooden roof. The rooms were beamed. Many of the walls were paper-covered, but a few were painted, and all had glass windows.

The house faced the sea and contained a master suite and dining-room and large living-room. And, to the west, a latticed haven around a garden, private from the rest of the house. Here were May-may's quarters and the children's rooms, and beyond them the servants' quarters.

Struan had brought May-may and the children and Ah Sam, the amah, with him into the house the day before yesterday and had settled them there. A trusted cook boy named Lim Din and a wash amah and makee-learnee – as apprentice scullion maids were called – had come back with him from Canton.

And though no Europeans had seen May-may, most of them were sure that the Tai-Pan had brought his mistress into the first permanent habitation on Hong Kong. They chuckled among themselves, or denounced him through their jealousy. But they said nothing to their wives. In due course they would want to bring their own mistresses and the less said the better. The wives who suspected held their peace. There was nothing they could do.

Struan had been very pleased with his house and with the progress on the warehouses and factory. And also with the results of his public coldness towards Culum. Culum had told him covertly that already he had had the first tentative probe from Brock, and that Wilf Tillman had invited him aboard Cooper-Tillman's expansive opium hulk and had entertained him lavishly.

Culum had said that trade was discussed – how the future of Asia depended vitally on co-operation, particularly between the Anglo-Saxon races. He had said that Shevaun had been at dinner and that she had been very beautiful and vivacious.

A fish leaped out of the water, hung for a moment in the air, and fell back again. Struan watched for a moment, listening. Then he relaxed again and let his mind roam.

Shevaun'd make a good match for Culum, Struan thought dispassionately. Or for yoursel'. Aye. She'd make a fine hostess and an interesting addition to the banquets you'll be giving in London. To the lords and ladies and members of Parliament. And Cabinet ministers. Will you buy yoursel' a baronetcy? You could afford to ten times over. If *Blue Cloud's* home first. Or second, even third – so long as she's safe. If the season's trade is safely concluded, then you can buy yoursel' an earldom.

Shevaun's young enough. She'd bring a useful dowry and interesting political connections. What about Jeff Cooper? He's head over heels in love with her. If she says no to him, that's his problem.

What about May-may? Would a Chinese wife bar you from the inner sanctum? Certainly. She would weigh the dice heavily against you. Out of the question.

Wi'out the right sort of wife English social life will be impossible. Diplomacy is mostly settled in private drawing-rooms, in luxury. Perhaps the daughter of a lord, or earl or Cabinet minister? Wait till you're home, eh? There's plenty of time.

Is there?

A dog barked shrilly among the sampans and then shrieked as others fell on it. The sounds of the death battle rose and fell, then ceased. Silence again but for the furtive growling, scuffling, ripping in the darkness as the victors began to feed.

Struan was watching the sampans, his back to the lanterns. He saw a shadow move, and another, and soon a silent press of Chinese was leaving the floating village and grouping on the shore. He saw Scragger.

Struan held his pistol loosely and waited calmly, searching the darkness for Wu Kwok. The men came up the path noiselessly, Scragger cautiously in the middle. They stopped near the well and stared at Struan. All were young, in their early twenties, all dressed in black tunics and black trousers, thonged sandals on their feet, large coolie hats masking their faces.

'Top of the evening, Tai-Pan,' Scragger said softly, on guard and readying for instant retreat.

'Where's Wu Kwok?'

'He asks your pardon, like, but he be powerful busy. Here be the 'undred. Take the pick and let's be off, hey?'

'Tell them to split themsel' into tens and to strip.'

'Strip, did y'say?'

'Aye. Strip, by God!'

Scragger blinked at Struan. Then he shrugged and went back to the men and spoke in soft singsong. The Chinese chattered quietly, then sorted themselves into separate tens and took off their clothes.

Struan beckoned to the first ten and they walked into the light. From some of the groups he picked one, from others two or three, from a few, none. He chose with utmost care. He knew he was assembling a task force which would spearhead his advance into the heart of China. If he could bend them to his will. The men who would not meet his eye he excluded immediately. Those whose queues were ratty and unkempt he passed over. Those with weak physiques were not considered. Those whose faces were dotted with smallpox marks had a point in their favour – for Struan knew that smallpox ravaged ships in all the seas, and that a man who had had the disease and had recovered was a man immune and strong and one who knew the value of life. Those with well-healed knife wounds he favoured. Those who bore their nakedness carelessly he approved. Those who bore their nakedness with hostility he scrutinized painstakingly, knowing that violence and the sea are shipmates. Some he picked for the hatred in their eyes and some only because of a hunch he had when he looked into their faces.

Scragger watched the selecting with growing impatience. He drew his knife and repeatedly threw it into the dirt.

At last Struan had finished. 'These are the men I want. They can all dress now.'

Scragger barked an order and the men dressed. Struan took out a sheaf of papers and handed one to Scragger.

'You can read this out to them.'

'Wot be it?'

'A regulation indenture. Rates of pay and terms of five years' service. They're all to sign one.'

'I doan read. An' wot's paper for, eh? Wu Fang Choi's tol' them they be yorn for five years.'

Struan gave him another sheet covered with Chinese characters. 'Give this to someone who can read. They'll each sign or I will na accept them and the deal is off.'

'Doings things right proper, baint you?' Scragger took the paper and called out to a short, pockmarked Chinese who had been selected. The man came forward, and taking the paper, studied it under the lantern's light. Scragger jerked a thumb at those who had been rejected and they disappeared into the sampans.

The man began to read.

'What's his name?'

'Fong.'

'Fong what?'

'Fong wot you likes. Who's t'know wot name these monkeys run under?'

The Chinese were listening intently to Fong. At one point a muted, nervous gust of laughter wafted from them. 'Wot's funny?' Scragger asked in Cantonese. Fong took a long time to explain.

Scragger turned to Struan. 'Wot's all this about, eh? They's to promise not to fornicate and not to marry for the five year? That baint proper. Wot d'you think they be?'

'That's just the normal clause, Scragger. All indentures have the same.'

'Not seamen's papers, by God.'

'They're to be captains and officers, so they must have indenture papers. To make it legal.'

'Very unproper, if you asks me. You mean they can't bed a doxy for five year?'

'It's only a formality. But they canna marry.'

Scragger turned and made a short speech. Again there was laughter. 'I sayed they's to obey you like God all-bloody-mighty. 'Cepting in fornication.' He wiped the sweat off his face. 'Wu Fang's tol' 'em they be yors for five year. So there be no need to worry.'

'Why're you so nervous, eh?'

'Nothing. Nothing, I tells you.'

Fong continued to read. There was a hush and someone asked for a clause to be repeated. Scragger's interest increased. It was about their pay. Potential captains were to be paid fifty pounds for the first year, seventy the second and the third, a hundred when they had a first mate's ticket and a hundred and fifty with their master's. A sixtieth share of profits for any ships they captained. A bonus of twenty pounds if they learned English in three months.

'A hundred and fifty nicker be more'n they be earning in ten years,' Scragger said.

'You want a job?'

'I be happy with me present employ, thankee kindly.' He screwed up his face as a thought struck him. 'Wu Fang won't be paying all that nicker,' he said cagily.

'He will na be asked. These men'll earn every penny, you can be sure of that. Or they'll be beached.'

'So long as me guv's not to pay, you pays 'em wot you likes and wastes yor own money.'

After Fong had finished reading the document, Struan made each man write his name in characters on a copy. Every man could write. And he made each man daub his left palm with chop ink and imprint the palm on the back of the paper.

'Wot be that for?'

'Every hand palm's different. Now I know each man – whatever his name. Where're the boys?'

'You want the men t' the boats?'

'Aye.' Struan gave Fong a lantern and motioned him to the beach. The other men followed silently.

'The picking and papering were clever, Tai-Pan. Yo're right smart.' Scragger sucked the end of his knife pensively. 'I heared you one-upped Brock right proper. Over the bullion too.'

Struan glanced back at Scragger, abruptly suspicious. 'There were Europeans in that attack, so Brock said. Were you one of them?'

'If I'd been ordered in by Wu Fang, Tai-Pan, there beed no failure. Wu Fang Choi doan like failure. Musta beed some poxy locals. Terrible.' Scragger peered around the darkness. When he'd made sure they were quite alone, he spoke conspiratorially. 'Wu Kwok be Fukienese. He come from Quemoy, up the coast, eh? You know the island?'

'Aye.'

'Midsummer Night there be a festival. Wu Kwok be there for sure. Something to do with his ancestors.' Scragger's eyes took on a malevolent glitter. 'If a frigate or two was cruising there, why, he'd be caught like a poxy gutter rat in a barrel.'

Struan smiled scornfully. 'That he would!'

'It be th' truth I tells you, by God. You've me oath, by God. That bugger tricked me into giving you me oath when it were lie and I'll not forgive that. Scragger's oath be as good as yorn!'

'Aye. Of course. Do you think I'd trust a man who'd sell his master like a rat?'

'He baint my master. Wu Fang Choi's me guv, no one else. I swore 'legiance to him, no other. You've me oath.'

Struan contemplated Scragger. 'I'll think about Midsummer Night.'

'You've me oath. I want him deaded, by God. A man's oath be all he's got twixt hisself and damnation. That swine took mine, God curse him, so I wants him deaded to pay.'

'Where're the boys?'

'They's to be toffs, like you sayed?'

'Hurry it up, I want to be off.'

Scragger turned and whistled into the darkness. Three small shadows moved out of the sampans. The boys walked cautiously down the rickety gangplank on to the ground and hurried up the path. Struan's eyes widened as the boys came into the light. One was Chinese. One was

316

Eurasian. And the last was a grubby little English urchin. The Chinese boy was richly gowned, his queue thick and well plaited. He carried a bag. The other two were pathetically dressed in grimy pseudo-English boys' clothes – their frock coats homespun, their little top hats battered, and their trousers and shoes home-made and crudely stitched. Over the shoulders each carried a stick with a bundle dangling from the end.

All the boys tried desperately – and unsucessfully – to cover their anxiety.

'This be Wu Pak Chuk,' Scragger said. The Chinese boy bowed nervously. 'He be Wu Fang Choi's grandson. One of 'em, but not from Wu Kwok. And these be me own lads.' He pointed proudly at the little urchin, who flinched involuntarily. 'This be Fred. He be six. And this'n's Bert, seven.'

He made a slight motion and both boys doffed their hats and bowed and mumbled something through their panic and looked back at their father to see if they had done it right. Bert, the Eurasian boy, had had his queue coiled under his hat, but now, from all the fidgeting, the queue hung down his back. The urchin's hair was filthy and, like his father's, tied with a piece of tarred hemp at the nape of his neck.

'Come over here, lads,' Struan said compassionately.

The urchin took his half brother's hand and the two came slowly forward. They stopped, barely breathing. The English boy wiped a dribble of mucus from his nose with the back of his hand.

'You're Fred?'

'Yus, Yor Worship,' he whispered, scarcely audible.

'Speak up, lad,' Scragger said, and the boy blurted out, 'Yus, Yor Worship, I be Fred.'

'I be Bert, Yor Worship.' The Eurasian quailed as Struan looked at him. He was a tall, handsome lad with beautiful teeth and golden skin. He was the tallest of the three.

Struan glanced at Wu Pak. The boy lowered his eyes and scuffed at the earth.

'He does na speak English?'

'No. But Bert here speaks his tongue. An' Fred some words. Bert's ma be Fukienese.' Scragger's discomfort worsened.

'Where's your mother, Fred?'

'Dead, Yor Worship,' the urchin choked out. 'She be dead, sirr.'

'She be deaded two year back. Scurvy got her,' Scragger said.

'You've English women with your fleet?'

'Some has. Back over there, lads,' he said, and his sons fled to where he was pointing and stood rock-still, out of hearing. Wu Pak hesitated, then ran back and stood close beside them.

Scragger dropped his voice. 'Fred's ma were convict. Transported ten year for stealing coal in the depth of winter. We was married by a priest in Australia but he were renegade so maybe it weren't proper. We was married anyways. I give her me oath afore she deaded to do right by the lad.'

Struan took out more papers. 'These give me guardianship of the boys. Until they're twenty-one. You can sign for your sons but what about Wu Pak? Should be a relation.'

'I'll put me mark on all. You got one for me to show Wu Fang? Wot I signeed?'

'Aye. You can take one.'

Struan began to fill in the names, but Scragger stopped him. 'Tai-Pan, doan put Scragger on the boys. Put another name. Any you likes – no, doan tell me wot,' he added quickly. 'Any name. You think of a good one.' The sweat was beading his forehead. His fingers trembled as he took the pencil and made his mark. 'Fred's to forget me. An' his ma. Do yor best with Bert, eh? His ma's still me woman and she baint bad, for a heathen. Do yor best for 'em and you've a friend for life. Me oath on't. They both beed taught to say their prayers proper.' He blew his nose in his fingers and wiped them on his trousers. 'Wu Pak's got to write once a month to Jin-qua. Oh yus, and yor t'bill Jin-qua for the schooling and wot. Once a year. They's all to go to the same school and vittle together.'

He beckoned to the Chinese boy. Wu Pak came forward reluctantly. Scragger jerked a thumb towards the boats and the boy left obediently. Then he beckoned his sons.

'I be off now, lads.'

The boys ran to him and clung to him and begged him not to send them away, their tears streaming and terror overwhelming them. But he pushed them off and forced his voice hard. 'Be off with you now. Obey the Tai-Pan here. He's t'be like a dad to yer.'

'Doan send us'n off, Dad,' Fred said piteously. 'I beed a good boy. Bert'n me be good boys, Dad, doan send us'n off.'

They stood in the enormousness of their grief, their shoulders heaving.

Scragger cleared his throat noisily and spat. After a second's hesitation, he jerked out his knife and seized Bert's queue. The Eurasian squealed with horror and tried to fight free. But Scragger chopped off the queue and cuffed the hysterical boy hard enough to bring him out of shock, but no harder.

'Oh, Dad,' Fred said tremulously in his little piping voice, 'you knowed Bert promised his mum to keep his hair proper.'

'Better I do's it, Fred, afore another,' Scragger said, his voice breaking. 'Bert doan need it now. He's t'be toff like you.'

'I doan want to be toff. I want t'stay home.'

Scragger tousled Bert's head a last time. And Fred's.

'Bye, my sons,' he said. He rushed away and the night swallowed him.

XVII

'Why go so early, Tai-Pan?' May-may asked, stifling a yawn. 'Two hours' sleep last night for you is na enough. You will lose your vigour.'

'Get on with you, lass! And I told you na to wait up.' Struan pushed his breakfast plate away and May-may poured him more tea. It was a glorious morning. The sun beamed through the latticed windows and cast delicate patterns on the floor.

May-may tried to close her ears to the pounding and sawing from the building that was going on all over the foreshore of Happy Valley, but she could not. The noise had been permanent and overpowering day and night since they had arrived three days ago.

'There's lot to be done, and I want to be sure all's well for the ball,' Struan said. 'It's to start an hour after sundown.'

May-may shivered with delight as she remembered her secret gown and the beauty of it. 'Breakfast at dawn is barbarisms.'

' "Barbaric," ' he said. 'And it's not dawn. It's nine o'clock.'

'It feels like dawn.' She arranged her pale yellow silk robe more comfortably, feeling her nipples hard against its texture. 'How long are horriblitious noises going on?'

'It'll settle down in a month or so. No work on Sundays of course,' he said, half listening to her, thinking about all he had to accomplish today.

'It's too much noises,' she said. 'And something's bad with this house.'

'What?' he said absently, not listening.

'It feels bad, terrifical bad. Are you sure the *fêng shui* is correct, heya?'

'Fêng what?' He looked up, startled, and gave her his full attention. May-may was appalled. 'You did not have a fêng-shui gentlemans?'

'Who's he?'

'God's blood, Tai-Pan!' she said, exasperated. 'You build house and dinna consult fêng shui! How crazy mad! Ayee yah! I deal with that today.'

320

'What does the fêng-shui gentleman do,' Struan asked sourly, 'apart from costing money?'

'He makes sure that the fêng shui is correct, of course.'

'And what, for the love of God, is fêng shui?'

'If the fêng shui is bad, the devil spirits come into the house and you'll have terrifical bad joss and terrible sickness. If the fêng shui is good, then no devil spirits come in. Everyone knows about fêng shui.'

'You're a good Christian and you dinna believe in evil spirits and mumbo jumbo.'

'I absolute agree, Tai-Pan, but in houses fêng shui is fantastical vital. Dinna forget this is China and in China there's—'

'All right, May-may,' he said resignedly. 'Get a fêng-shui gentleman to cast a spell if you must.'

'He does na cast spells,' she said importantly. 'He makes sure the house is positioned right for the Heaven-Earth-Air currents. And that it's na built on a dragon's neck.'

'Eh?'

'Good sweet God, as you say sometimes! That'd be horrifical, for then the dragon that sleeps in the earth would no longer be able to sleep peaceful. God's blood, I hope we're na on his neck! Or head! Could you sleep with a house on your neck, or head? Of course na! If the dragon's sleep is disturbed, of course fantastical worst things happen. We'd have to move instantaneous!'

'Ridiculous!'

'Fantastical ridiculous, but we still move. Me, I protect us. Oh yes. It's very important that one protects her man and her family. If we're builded on a dragon, we move.'

'Then you'd better tell the fêng-shui gentleman that he'd better not find any dragons around here, by God!'

Her chin jutted. 'The fêng-shui gentlemans will na learn you to sail a ship – why for'll you learn him about dragons, heya? It's very gracious hard to be a fêng-shui gentlemans.'

Struan was happy that May-may was beginning to be her old self. He had noticed that since she returned to Canton from Macao, and during the journey to Hong Kong, she had seemed piqued and distracted. Particularly the last few days. And she was right, the noise was very bad.

'Well, I'll be off.'

'Is all right I invite Ma-ree Sin-clair today?'

'Aye. But I dinna ken where she is – or if she's arrived yet.'

'She's on flagship. She arrive yesterday with her amah, Ah Tat, and

321

her ball gown. It's black and very pretty. It's going to cost you two hundred dolla. Ayeee yah, if you'd let me arrange the dress, I'd save you sixty, seventy dolla, never mind. Her cabin's next to her brother's.'

'How do you know all that?'

'Her amah is Ah Sam's mother's sister's fourth daughter. Wat for is the use of a mealy mouth slave like Ah Sam if she does na keep her mother inform and have connections?'

'How did Ah Sam's mother tell her?'

'Oh, Tai-Pan, you are so funny,' May-may cried. 'Na Ah Sam's mother, *me*. All Chinese slaves call their mistress "Mother". Just as she calls you "Father" .'

'She does?'

'All slaves call the master of the house "Father". It's ancient custom and very polite. So Ah Tat, Ma-ree's slave, told Ah Sam. Ah Sam, who is a good-for-nothing lazy maggot and needs a whipping, told her "mother". Me. It's really very simple. Oh yes, and to be absolutal correct, if you could speak a Chinese language, you'd call Ah Sam "Daughter" .'

'Why do you want to see Mary?'

'It's lonely na to talk. I'll only talk Cantonese, dinna worry. She knows I'm here.'

'How?'

'Ah Sam told Ah Tat,' she said as though explaining to a child. 'Naturally such an interesting piece of news Ah Tat told her mother – told Ma-ree. That old whore Ah Tat's a jade mine of secrets.'

'Ah Tat's a whore?'

'God's blood, Tai-Pan, that's only a figured speech. You really should go back to bed. You're very simple this morning.'

He finished his tea and pushed his plate away. 'And I've nae wonder, listening to all this nonsense. I'm lunching with Longstaff, so I'll send word to Mary. What time shall I say?'

'Thank you, Tai-Pan, never mind. Ah Sam will be better. Then no one knows except the servants and they know all anyways, never mind.'

Lim Din opened the door. He was Struan's personal servant as well as cook boy, a small squat man in his middle fifties, neat in black trousers and white tunic. He had a round, happy face and darting, cunning eyes. 'Mass'er. Missee and Mass'er come see my. Can?'

'Mass'er wat?' Struan was astonished that anyone would be so impolite as to come uninvited.

Lim Din shrugged. 'Mass'er and Missee. Wantshee wat Mass'er, wat Missee?'

'Oh, never mind,' Struan said and got up from the table.

'You expect guest?' May-may said.

'No.' Struan walked out of the room and into the small ante-room. He opened the far door and closed it behind him. Now he was in the corridor that led to a hallway and to the separate quarters in the front of the house. And the moment he was in the corridor he knew that one caller was Shevaun. Her fragrance, a special Turkish perfume that only she used, had delicately changed the quality of the air.

His heart quickened and his anger lessened as he strode down the corridor, his soft leather half boots clicking on the stone floor, and turned into the living-room.

'Hello, Tai-Pan,' Shevaun said.

Shevaun was twenty and graceful as a gazelle. She wore her dark red hair, darker than Struan's, in long ringlets. Her full breasts, under the discreetly décolleté green velvet dress, sailed over an eighteen-inch waist. Her delicate ankles and feet peeped from beneath a dozen petticoats. Her bonnet was green, her sunshade a startling orange.

Aye, Struan thought, she gets prettier every day.

'Morning, Shevaun, Wilf.'

'Morning. Sorry to arrive uninvited.' Wilf Tillman was exceedingly uncomfortable.

'Oh, come now, Uncle,' Shevaun said blithely, 'it's a good old American custom to wish a house well.'

'We're not in America, dear.' Tillman wished he were, today. And that Shevaun was safely married to Jeff Cooper and no longer his responsibility. Damn Shevaun. And damn Jeff, he thought. I wish to God the man'd formally press his suit. Then I could simply announce the marriage and that would be that. But all this shilly-shallying around is ridiculous. 'Give her time. There's plenty of time,' Jeff is always saying. But I damn well know there's very little time left, now that Struan's wifeless. I'm absolutely sure Shevaun's set her cap for the Tai-Pan. Why else insist on coming here this morning? Why else keep asking questions about him?

All the way to Struan's house he had been pondering the wisdom of a match between Struan and Shevaun. Naturally there would be definite financial advantages, but Struan was totally opposed to their way of life in America; he just simply wouldn't understand.

He would certainly turn Shevaun against us, Tillman thought. He'd force the issue through her. Jeff would be furious over losing her and he'd probably break up Cooper-Tillman. Nothing I could do to stop that. If that company goes on the rocks, there's no money for brother

John to entertain so lavishly in Washington. Politics is expensive, and without political pull life for the family will be very hard, and we need every bit of help against the blasted Northern states. No, by Heaven. Shevaun's going to marry Jeff and not the Tai-Pan, and that's that.

'Sorry to arrive uninvited,' he repeated.

'You're both very welcome.' Struan motioned Lim Din to the decanter and glasses. 'Sherry?'

'Well, thank you, but I think we ought to be going,' Tillman said.

Shevaun laughed and her tilted nose wrinkled prettily. 'But we've just arrived. I wanted to be the first to welcome you to your house, Tai-Pan,' she said.

'And you are. Sit down. It's good to see you.'

'We brought some gifts for the house.' She opened her carrying bag and took out a small loaf of bread and a tiny container of salt and a bottle of wine. 'It's an old custom to bring the house good luck. I would have arrived by myself, but Uncle said that would be in the worst possible taste. It's not his fault at all.'

'I'm glad you came.' Struan picked up the bread. It was gold-brown and crisp and fragrant.

'I baked it last night.'

Struan broke off a piece and tasted it. 'It's excellent!'

'You're not really supposed to eat it. At least, well, it's just the idea.' She laughed again and picked up her carrying bag and sunshade.' And now that I've done my duty, we'll be off.'

'My first guests will do no such thing. I insist, at least a sherry.'

Lim Din offered the glasses. Shevaun took one and settled herself comfortably while Wilf Tillman scowled. Lim Din padded away.

'You really cooked it yoursel'? All by yoursel'?' Struan asked.

'It's very important for a girl to know how to cook,' she said and stared back at him, eyes challenging.

Tillman sipped the sherry. 'Shevaun's a good cook.'

'I'll take a loaf a day,' Struan said. He sat in the big leather chair and lifted his glass. 'Long life!'

'And to you.'

'Your house is lovely, Tai-Pan.'

'Thank you. When it's finished I'd like to show you over it.' Struan knew that she was curious to find out whether the rumour about May-may was true. 'Aristotle said you were poorly the last time I saw him.'

'It was just a chill,' she said.

'Are you having another portrait done?'

'I'm considering it,' she said unruffled. 'Dear Mr Quance, I admire his paintings so much. Uncle and I are trying to persuade him to try a second in Washington. I think he'd make a fortune.'

'In that case I'd say you'll have a visitor.' Struan wondered if the innocence in her face was assumed or real. He glanced at Tillman. 'How's business?'

'Excellent, thank you. Jeff's coming back from Canton this afternoon. Things are booming in the Settlement. Will you be going back there?'

'In a few days.'

'I hear *Blue Cloud* and *Gray Witch* are neck and neck. One of our ships, beating up from Singapore, passed them two days out, going at full speed. Best of luck.'

While the two of them chatted politely about business matters, neither really interested in the other's opinion, Shevaun sipped her sherry and studied Struan. He was dressed in a light woollen suit, well-tailored and elegant.

You're quite a man, she thought; you may not know it, Dirk Struan, but I'm going to marry you. I wonder what your Oriental mistress is like; I feel her presence in the house. Mistress or not, I'm the girl for you. And when I'm your wife you won't need to stray for a long time. A very long time.

'Well, I think we'll be going,' Tillman said, and got up. 'Again, sorry to arrive uninvited.'

'You're always welcome.'

'Oh, by the way, Tai-Pan,' Shevaun said. 'I understand ladies aren't invited to the prizefight this afternoon. Would you put a guinea on the navy man for me?'

'Good God, Shevaun,' Tillman said, shocked. 'You mustn't say such things. Most unladylike!'

'And you're most dishonest,' she said, 'and old-fashioned. You men enjoy a prizefight, why shouldn't we? You men enjoy a gamble, why shouldn't we?'

'A good question, Shevaun.' Struan was amused by Tillman's discomfort.

'After all, it's an Oriental custom.' She looked innocently at Struan. 'I hear the Chinese gamble all the time, particularly the women.'

Struan blandly ignored the remark.

'Gambling's a bad habit,' Tillman said.

'I quite agree, Uncle. How much have you wagered?'

'That has nothing to do with it.'

Struan laughed. 'With your permission, Wilf, we'll indulge her. A guinea on the navy?'

'Thank you, Tai-Pan,' she said before Tillman could answer, and she held out her gloved hand to Struan. 'It's just the principle. You're most understanding.'

He let her hand rest in his a moment longer than necessary, then kissed it, fascinated by the thought of taming her, and escorted them to the door. 'See you both this evening.'

'If I don't win that prize, I'll be livid. And also in debtor's prison.'

'You won't, Shevaun, but your poor long-suffering father and uncle may be,' Tillman said.

When they had gone, Struan returned to May-may's quarters.

She stared at him coldly.

'What's amiss?'

'That mealymouthed godrotting doxy's after you. That's wat's amiss.'

'Will you na be so foolish and will you na swear! How'd you see her, anyway?'

'Huh! Have I no eyes? No nose? Wat for should I pore over plans of house, eh, hour after godrot hour? So it's to be planned so I can see who comes here and who passes by without seen. Huh! That maggoty-drawers dung-heap doxy's after you to marriage.'

'To marry,' he corrected.

'Kiss the hand, huh? Wat for you no kiss my hand, eh?' She slammed the teapot down. 'Wat for you linger with cow eyes, hey? Ayeee yah!'

'You ayeee yah yoursel'. And one more remark like that and I'll paddle you. You want to be paddled?'

'Mens!' She tossed her head. 'Mens!'

' "Men" – not "mens". How many times do I have to tell you?'

'Men!' May-may shakily poured herself some tea, then slammed the cup down and got up. ' "I hear Chinese mens gamble hugely, partikilly the womens," ' She said, mimicking Shevaun, lifting her breasts to give them size and waggling her backside. 'And you sats there and eat up her busums. Wat for my busums you no stare at, heya?'

Struan quietly put down his teacup and rose. May-may retreated to the other side of the table.

'I na say nothing, never mind,' she said hastily.

'That's what I thought.' He calmly finished his tea and she watched him without moving, but ready to run.

He set down the cup. 'Come over here.'

'Huh! I for no trust you when your eyes speak green fire.'

'*Come over here*. Please,' he added as sweetly.

She was almost cross-eyed with rage, and she seemed to him like one

326

of the Siamese cats that he had seen in Bangkok. And just as spiteful, he thought.

She cautiously came over to him, ever ready to retreat or hack with her nails. He gently patted her cheek, and turned for the door. 'There's a good girl.'

'Tai-Pan!' May-may imperiously held out her hand to be kissed.

Restraining a smile, he walked back and gallantly kissed her hand. Then he spun her around before she knew what was happening and slapped her smartly on the backside. She gasped and fought out of his hands and jumped for the safety of the table. Once safe, she hurled a cup at him. It shattered against the wall near his ear and she picked up another.

'Dinna throw it!'

She put it down.

'That's a good lass. One is fine. Two extravagant.' He turned for the door.

'I only say you to protect you,' she shouted. 'Protect from mealy-mouthed, ugly, old cow-busumed doxy!'

'Thank you, May-may,' he said, closing the door after him. He pretended to walk down the corridor, then listened in the silence, trying not to laugh. The cup crashed against the other side of the door. The sound was followed by a stream of curses and Ah Sam's name and more curses.

Struan cheerfully tiptoed away.

The whole of Happy Valley was pulsating with activity, and as Struan walked down the slight rise from his house towards the foreshore, he felt not a little pride. There were the beginnings of many buildings. The biggest two were the huge three-storey factories of The Noble House and Brock and Sons that fronted on Queen's Road – the vast buildings containing warehouses, offices and living quarters, favoured by the China traders and similar to those in the Canton Settlement. At present they were just shells of peripheral bamboo scaffoldings soaring skywards, hundreds of Chinese labourers swarming them. And around these dominating structures were dozens of other buildings, dwellings and wharves.

In the distance, halfway to Glessing's Point, Struan could see that work had already begun on the dockyard; a never-ending stream of coolies was dumping stones and rocks to form the first of the deep-water wharves. Opposite the harbour master's small house, complete but for its roof, were the stone walls of the jail, three-quarters finished.

And beyond the dockyard was the first of the army's barracks and its scaffoldings.

Struan turned west to the series of large tents that housed their temporary headquarters. They had been set up on the outskirts of the valley. The church was not yet under construction, though Struan could see men surveying the top of the knoll.

'Morning, Robb,' he said, going into the tent.

'Welcome back.' Robb was unshaven and there were dark smudges under his eyes. 'You dealt with Aberdeen?'

'Aye. How are things here?'

'Good and bad. Can't walk along Queen's Road without a stinking swarm of beggars falling on you. And worse than that, we're bringing in ten thousand Macao bricks a day by sampan and junk, and upwards of two thousand vanish by next morning.' He tossed up his hands violently. 'And not only bricks – timber, desks, cement, quills, paper – they steal everything. At this rate our building costs will double.' He tossed over a list of figures. 'A present for you: the figures on your house – so far. Three times as much as Vargas estimated.'

'Why so much?'

'Well, you wanted it up in three weeks.'

'For a thousand pounds I can damn nearly buy a fifth of a clipper.'

'If the *Blue Cloud* does na reach London, we're in terrible trouble. Again.'

'She'll get there.'

'I wish I was so confident,' Robb slammed back.

Struan sat down at his desk. 'What's the real matter, lad?'

'Oh, I don't know. The thieving and the begging – and there's too much to do. And this constant, confounded noise. I'm tired, I suppose. No, that's not true. Two things. First, Sarah. She's two weeks overdue and you've no idea how irritable a woman is then, and the poor lass is frightened she's going to die. Rightly. Nothing you can do to help, except say everything'll be all right. Then too, there's the business of me staying on. We've had nothing but terrible rows. She's absolutely set on leaving within a month or so – as soon as she's fit again.'

'Would you like me to talk to her?'

'No. Nothing'll help. She's made up her mind, and that – with Sarah – is that. Of course she's delighted that we're rich again but she's still going home. The ball hasn't helped – she's furious that she's with child and "fat and ugly", as she calls herself. Nothing you say makes any difference.'

'That's "first". What's second?'

'Culum. You and Culum.'

Struan glanced out the tent door at the harbour and at the many ships neatly at anchor. 'He seems well enough.'

'That's not what I meant.'

'Let that rest for the time being.'

'It's a very bad situation. Bad for the two of you and bad for the house.'

'Let it rest, Robb.'

'I'm asking you. Please forgive him. Please.'

'Give it time, Robb.' Struan turned back. 'A little time.'

'All right, Dirk.' Robb shoved his hands in his pockets. 'What happened last night at Aberdeen?'

Struan told him, and gave him the indenture and guardianship papers. But he said nothing about Wu Kwok and Quemoy and Midsummer Night. Midsummer Night would come while he was still Tai-Pan, and what to do about it was the Tai-Pan's decision – and his alone.

Robb was concerned. 'Where are the boys now?'

'Aboard *Resting Cloud.* I put them in Wolfgang's charge. The men're aboard *China Cloud.*'

'We'd better get the boys home as soon as possible. If it becomes common knowledge we're connected with those pirate scum – well, God knows what trouble we'll have on our hands.'

'*Thunder Cloud*'s almost full of cargo. She'll be ready to sail in four or five days. They'll go by her.'

'I'll send them to Whampoa today.'

'Nay, lad. I'll take 'em mysel' tomorrow. Safer. Too much is at stake in Canton, so I'd better go straight back. Do you want to come?'

'I can't, Dirk. Not with Sarah so near her time. Why not take Culum?'

'There's plenty to do here.'

'There's plenty to teach him about teas and silks and shipping. Four months only to go.'

'All right.'

'What's your plan for the men?'

'Wolfgang and Gordon to teach them English first. In three months we'll put them in the clippers. Never more than one to a ship. Put that canny mind of yours on to how we're to bend them to our side.'

'I'll try. I wonder what devilment Wu Kwok and Scragger are up to. I dinna trust them a little bitty.'

'Aye.' Struan thought, I wonder what you'd do, Robb, about

329

Midsummer Night – if you knew. You'd send frigates, I'm sure. And perhaps be sending them into a trap. Will I? I dinna ken yet.

Robb looked out the tent door at the building activity. 'If God's on our side this season, we'll be far ahead of Brock.'

'Aye.' But what to do about him? And Gorth?

'I think we should reclaim part of the land from the sea and extend the wharves into deep water,' Robb said. 'Might as well do it now as next year.'

'Good idea, lad.'

'Excuse me, sir,' Cudahy said hurying up, 'but you sayed t' report immediately.'

'Come in, Mr Cudahy,' Robb said. 'How did it go?'

'Like a bloody breeze, sir. The mail packet were there like you sayed. I got a list of passengers like you wanted. We intercepted her off Pokliu Chau. She'll be in harbour in three hours.' Cudahy smiled and put down a small mail sack. 'Er, beggin' yor pardon, sir, but how'd you know the mail packet was acomin'? She be a day early.'

'Just a hunch, Mr Cudahy,' Robb said. 'Wait outside, will you please?' And he began to glance at their mail. Cudahy touched his forelock and left.

'Brilliant idea of yours,' Robb said, 'to put a lookout on the mountain.'

'Culum remembered, did he?' Struan was pleased and docketed the information, and was further pleased that Robb and Culum had put the plan into effect secretly. 'How'd you signal?'

'We assigned one of the clerks, old Vargas' nephew, Jesús de Vargas, to look at the mountaintop every quarter of an hour. Telescope of course, secretly of course. Culum worked out a system of flag codes. Now we can tell if a ship's a mail packet, one of ours, or one of Brock's or Cooper-Tillman's.'

They went through the mail. The three months of newspapers and periodicals they set aside to be enjoyed at leisure. Books, music sheets, plays, fashion books for Sarah, shipping improvements for Struan, financial papers for Robb.

First, business.

The London market price of spices – ginger, nutmeg, pepper, cinnamon – had risen appreciably. On molasses it had declined. The buying price on tea, due to short supply, was up fifty per cent which meant, if *Blue Cloud* was first, that their profit would be over two hundred and forty thousand pounds. Serious Chartist riots had hurt the capacity of the Lancashire cotton mills and Welsh coal mines, which meant that the cost of coal oil for lamps would go up and the price for cotton cloth would be higher than expected. The Calcutta price on opium had come down because there was a bumper crop. So Struan changed the orders of *Sea Cloud*, one of his clippers in the Hong Kong roads, and sent her urgently to Manila to load spices instead of Whampoa to load teas, and ordered her home to England with all speed via the Cape of Good Hope. Robb instructed Vargas to buy up every available yard of cotton cloth, yarn and sewing cottons, to unload all their stocks of molasses and to step up their order of opium to be bought at Calcutta, and unload their present stocks as soon as possible.

And before the mail packet was at rest in harbout, *Sea Cloud* had sailed for Manila and their three hours of dealing had made them potentially forty thousand guineas richer. For in three hours they had cornered the market on available imported supplies of lamp oil, cotton goods, yarn, sewing cottons, and spices, and had booked up in advance all the available cargo space on all available American and English ships – outside of Brock and Sons. They knew that as soon as the packet anchored and the news was spread, buyers would be rushing to their doors to buy cottons and spices, and to charter ships to rush for home. No one would know, outside the brothers, that *Sea Cloud* had the bit between her teeth, at least a day's start, and would take the cream off the London market.

'Pity that it will take us at least two days to fill all our customers' orders and get the Manila ships away,' Robb said gleefully.

'Sad, Robb, very sad.'

'I'd say that we've done a fine morning's work.'

They were standing at the door of the tent watching the mail ship let go her anchors. Swarms of cutters surrounded her, packed with men anxious for their mail. Struan glanced over the incoming passenger list. 'Good God, look at this!' He shoved over the paper.

Robb's eyes fled down the list of names. They fixed HRH Archduke Zergeyev. 'What's a Russian grandee doing in Asia, eh?'

'Nay, na him, lad, though he's curious, right enough. Finish the list.'

Robb read on. Wives of merchants, three returning merchants, names of men who meant nothing to him. Finally he came to it. 'Maureen Quance and family?' He laughed up-roariously.

'Dammit, it's no laughing matter,' Struan said. 'What about the judging?'

'Oh my God!'

Six years ago Aristotle's wife had furiously boarded a ship in Macao

331

for home, believing – as they all had – that Aristotle, who lived in mortal terror of her, had escaped to England. But instead of fleeing he had been hiding in Mrs Fortheringill's Establishment for Refined Young Ladies – the 'F and E', or, as the locals called the whorehouse, the 'Fornicating Eels'. Aristotle had come out of hiding a week after Maureen had sailed, and it had taken him months to become his old self again and overcome the 'vapours'. The traders ascribed his 'vapours' to an overtaxing of his welcome in the house. He had denied it vehemently: 'When one finds oneself in such an extremity, by God, one hardly has an inclination to partake of what – for want of a better word – I can only describe as quent. Delectable, to be sure, but quent. No, my dear misguided friends, terror and quent are not bedfellows.' No one believed him.

'What'll we do?' Robb asked.

'If Aristotle hears, he's sure to vanish. He'll go up to Canton and then we're sunk. We've got to find him first and keep him out of the way until tonight.'

'Where is he?'

'I dinna ken. Send out search parties. Every man. Take him aboard *Thunder Cloud* – any pretext – and keep him there until we're ready for the judging. Send Cudahy aboard the packet at once. Tell Maureen that she and the family are our guests – put them aboard the small hulk. Perhaps we can keep her busy until tomorrow.'

'You'll never do it. She has a nose for Aristotle.'

'We have to try. Are you prepared to be the judge?'

'What about the prizefight? He won't miss that!'

'For a portrait of Sarah, or one of the children, he will.'

Robb rushed out.

Struan glanced at his watch. He was not due aboard the flagship for an hour. He sent for Gordon Chen and asked him to recruit thirty Chinese to be watchmen.

'I think it would be wise, Tai-Pan, as an added precaution to have watchmen on your house too,' Gordon said. 'I'd feel happier if you did.'

'Good idea, Gordon. Increase the men to thirty-five.'

'I'm afraid most of the Chinese who have come into Tai Ping Shan are very bad people. Most are wanted for crimes in Kwangtung and, well, here in Hong Kong they're beyond the reach of the mandarins.' He produced a parchment scroll from the deep sleeve of his robe. 'Oh, by the way, I made an arrangement with the King of the Beggars for your ball tonight.' He put the scroll on the desk. 'Here's his receipt. Perhaps I can be reimbursed by the comprador?'

'Receipt? For what?'

'Three taels. This modest squeeze insures that none of your guests will be harassed tonight. I also made a most reasonable monthly arrangement with him – three taels – on your behalf, for beggars to stay away from the confines of your home and The Noble House.'

'I'll na pay it,' Struan exploded. 'I dinna care if Macao has its Beggar King, or every town in China likewise. We're na starting that on Hong Kong, by God.'

'But he's already here and organized,' Gordon Chen said, his voice calm. 'Who else will license beggars? Who else will be responsible? Who else can one pay squeeze to to ensure special treatment due to people of wealth and position like ourselves? I beg you to reconsider, Tai-Pan. I would most strongly advise it. I assure you it will be money well spent. At least try it for a month. That's not too much to ask. Then you'll see the wisdom of the custom. Certainly, too, it will protect your property, for the beggars will inform on thieves. It's very necessary, believe me.'

'Very well,' Struan said at length, 'but one month, no more.' He initialled the receipt, knowing that there would be a permanent fee to the Beggar King. There was no way to fight the custom – except by excluding all Chinese from Hong Kong.

'You can get this from Chen Sheng tomorrow.'

'Thank you.'

'What gives this particular man the right to be King of the Beggars, eh?'

'I suppose the others trust him, Tai-Pan.' Gordon Chen made a mental note to talk to the man this afternoon to make certain all went as planned for the next month. He was very pleased, not only with the very low rate of squeeze that he had negotiated on Struan's account – two taels for tonight and two taels a month, the balance of one tael to be his own rightful squeeze – but also with his own foresight in asking Jin-qua to provide a 'King' from Canton. This man was the younger brother of the Beggar King of Canton, which meant he was a professional, a man well versed in the methods of extracting the most with the least effort. And this man had, of course, been inducted as a lesser Hung Mun official into the Hong Kong lodge. A perfect arrangement, Gordon told himself. The squeeze from the beggars would be a valuable and permanent part of the tong's revenues. Then he heard his father ask the question he had been waiting for.

'Have you heard of the Triads, Gordon?'

'I read the proclamation, of course,' Gordon said calmly. 'Why?'

'Do you know anything about them?'

'Well, Tai-Pan, I've heard that, historically, secret societies have always been a form of defence against foreign intruders. That they have many names.'

'Keep your ears open and keep me informed, privately, about their doings, if any. Another thing, I've twenty Chinese recruits for my fleet. I'm going to try to train them as mates. You're to work with Mr Mauss to teach them English. And ten others are to go to England to train as shipbuilders.'

'Yes, sir.' Gordon beamed. Thirty men. Of course, thirty new Triads. Yes, the name Triads had a nice sound to it, better than Hung Mun. And twenty such men, strategically placed in the ships of The Noble House, would be an enormously valuable addition to the power of the lodge. He felt enormously pleased with himself. Recruitment had been going very well. All Triad servants had been placed under his control – for of course, ever since the barbarian had been in Asia, the servants had been hand-picked Triad members. Next, Gordon was going to form a guild of ships' coolies, all of whom would be Triads. The Labourers' Guild was already well under way. Soon all labour and all Chinese on Hong Kong would be paying members – for the glory of their country and to the common good. Yes, he told himself excitedly, here in Hong Kong, free from fear of the mandarins, we will become the most powerful lodge in China. And when we throw out the Manchus, the leadership of the lodge will be in the forecourt of those in the new emperor's debt. Death to the Ch'ings – hurry the time of the rightful rulers, our previous Chinese dynasty, the Mings. 'When can I start?'

'Tomorrow.'

'Excellent. You can be sure of my interest.' He bowed slightly. 'Perhaps, at your convenience, I might be allowed to kowtow and pay my respects to the Lady T'chung. And the children. I haven't seen them for many months.'

'Of course, Gordon,' Struan said. 'Come tomorrow at noon. Why not start weekly lessons again? I think it would be good for her.'

'I would enjoy that. And talking with the children.' Gordon withdrew two more scrolls from his sleeve. 'I have the accounts for last month on our private arrangement. Would you like to go over the figures?'

'Aye.'

Gordon opened the scrolls. One was written in characters, the other in English. 'I'm happy to report, Tai-Pan, that based on an initial investment of ten thousand dollars we have a joint profit of six thousand and fifty-eight dollars and forty-two cents.'

Struan's eyes widened. 'That's quite a profit for one month's trading.'

'I am rather proud too. Our investments in land are excellent, also. They promise great profit.'

'But you did na buy any land.'

'Not at your land sale. But, er, I've been buying parcels in the Tai Ping Shan settlement. They were approved by the, er, Land Office last week. And we own substantial lots around the village of Aberdeen and Deepwater Bay.'

'But they have na been offered for sale yet.'

'These are, er, locally held lands, Tai-Pan. Ancient rights. I've bought up all the deeds that exist, at least all that I've found to exist this far.'

'But they're na legal, lad. All land's invested in the Crown.'

'Yes. But of course some arrangement would have to be made to, er, compensate the local village. It's been here for years, and, well, the Crown is magnanimous.' His eyes were guileless. 'Mr Culum seemed to think that His Excellency would look favourably on deeds that are, er, "validated" I think is the word, by the village elders.'

I wonder how much of the 'deeded' land does na belong to village or man and never has, Struan asked himself. 'All "our" deeds are "validated" ?'

'Oh absolutely, Tai-Pan. Very carefully. Otherwise they would be quite valueless, wouldn't they?' Gordon smiled. 'Our holdings are in the names of, er, our various "appointees", and we do not, naturally, hold any land openly. Only the prime deed. The other subdeed and sub-sub- and sub-sub-subdeeds can be subject to the closest scrutiny. I have been suitably cautious.'

'I'd say there's a great future for you in business, Gordon.' He went through the balance sheet thoroughly. 'What's this item? Two thousand nine hundred and seventy-eight dollars?'

'Rents from our property in Tai Ping Shan.'

'You've made a mistake. According to your dates, this account covers a rent period of two months and you've only owned the land for one month.'

'Well, Tai-Pan, as soon as the Chinese began to settle on our land in Tai Ping Shan, I began to charge them a service rent. That we didn't actually acquire the land for one month afterwards is not their worry. Is it?'

'Nay. Except that that's fraud.'

'Oh no, sir. Not according to the facts. The incoming tenant of

335

course wanted the best land available to rent. We took a down payment – giving him the use of the land in advance in good faith. He was happy because he was paying "rent", for of course everyone has to pay rent. This amount is really a charge for service. I went to a great deal of risk to perform the service for them. If I hadn't managed to buy the lot and thus give them the benefit of a long lease, why, surely they would have fallen into the hands of usurers, thieves and brigands.'

Struan grunted. 'What do you plan to do with the rest of the money?'

'If I may ask your patience, I would like to leave that to next month. I will continue to draw on the credit you were kind enough to arrange for me, but with great caution.'

Struan rolled up the scroll and handed it back.

'Oh no, Tai-Pan. That's your copy.'

'Very well.'

Struan thought a moment; then he said delicately, 'I've heard that Chinese are accustomed to borrowing monies at very high rates of interest. I trust that none of our investments will be so used.' His eyes fixed on Gordon's. There was a long silence. 'Usury is bad business.'

'The lending of money is very important business.'

'At reasonable rates of interest.'

Gordon toyed with the end of his queue. 'One per cent under the usual?'

'Two.'

'One and a half would be very, very fair.'

'Aye. Very fair. You're a clever businessman, Gordon. Perhaps next year I might improve the limit of credit.'

'I will endeavour to make a superb profit against your decision.'

'I'd wager you will too, Gordon,' Struan said. He glanced out the tent door and was surprised to see that the marine master-at-arms was hurrying towards them.

'Mr Struan?' The master-at-arms saluted crisply. 'His Excellency's compliments, will you join him on the flagship right smartly.'

Struan looked at his watch. He was not late, but he said nothing other than 'Of course'.

XVIII

Longstaff had his back to the door and was staring out the main cabin windows at the mail packet. Struan noticed that the dining-table was set for four. On the desk were many official dispatches. 'Morning, Will.'

'Hello, Dirk.' Longstaff turned and stuck out his hand, and Struan saw that he looked younger than he had for months. 'Well, this is curious, isn't it?'

'What?' Struan asked, knowing that it must be the Russian. But he let Longstaff have the pleasure of telling him. Too, he wanted to hear Longstaff's evaluation, for though Longstaff was out of his depth in Asia and useless as Captain Superintendent of Trade, Struan knew Longstaff's views on European diplomatic affairs to be incisive and extremely knowledgeable.

Ever since Struan had settled the immediate problem of Aristotle and had seen Robb take him aboard safely, he had puzzled over the reason for the Russian's arrival. He found it strangely unsettling but did not know why.

'You won't have heard yet, but we've an uninvited guest.'

'Oh, who?'

'An archduke, no less. A Russian archduke, Alexi Zergeyev. He came on the mail packet.'

Struan was suitably impressed. 'Why should we be "honoured" here in Asia?'

'Why, indeed?' Longstaff rubbed his hands together happily. 'He's joining us for lunch. Clive's escorting him.'

Clive Monsey was Longstaff's deputy captain superintendent of trade, a civil servant by profession and, like Longstaff, a Foreign Office appointee. Normally Monsey's duties kept him at Macao, where Longstaff maintained his permanent headquarters.

'There are some interesting dispatches too,' Longstaff was saying, and Struan's interest heightened. He knew that none would contain the

337

formal approval of the Treaty of Chuenpi and the appointment of Longstaff as the first governor of the Colony of Hong Kong, because the news of the successful conclusion of the war would just be reaching England.

Struan accepted the sherry. 'The Middle East?' he asked and held his breath.

'Yes. The crisis is over, thank God! France accepted the Foreign Secretary's settlement, and there's no longer any fear of general war. The Turkish sultan's so grateful for our support that he's signed a commercial treaty with us cancelling all Turkish trade monopolies, throwing open the whole Ottoman Empire to British trade.'

Struan let out a yell. 'By all that's holy! That's the best news we've had in many a long day!'

'I thought you'd be pleased,' Longstaff said.

The longstanding crisis had to do with the Dardanelles, the strait that was controlled by the Turkish Ottoman Empire. It was the key to Mediterranean Europe and a perpetual *casus belli* among the Great Powers – Britain, France, Russia, Austria-Hungary, and Prussia – because the Dardanelles was a shortcut for Russian warships to enter the vital Mediterranean, and also for warships of other nations to enter the Black Sea and threaten the weak underbelly of Russia. Eight years ago Russia had compelled Turkey to sign a treaty which gave Russia joint suzerainty over the Dardanelles, and international tension had been acute ever since. Then, three years ago, Mehemet Ali, the French-supported upstart soldier-pasha of Egypt, had launched an attack on Constantinople, proclaiming himself Caliph of the Ottoman Empire. France openly and delightedly had supported him against the sultan. But a French ally athwart the Dardanelles would imperil the interests of the remaining Great Powers, and the whole of Europe promised to be immediately involved in open conflict again.

The British Foreign Secretary, Lord Cunnington, had persuaded the Great Powers – other than France, and without consulting her – to use their influence on the side of the sultan against Mehemet Ali. France was furious and had threatened war. The settlement proposed was that Mehemet Ali was to withdraw to Egypt; that he would be given suzerainty over Syria for his lifetime; that he was confirmed as the independent ruler of Egypt; that he should pay only a nominal annual tribute to the Turkish sultan; and that, most important, the ancient rule of the Dardanelles strait was to be guaranteed by all Powers once and for all: that while Turkey was at peace the strait was forbidden to *all* warships of *all* nations.

That France had accepted the proposed settlement and the withdrawal of her Egyptian ally meant riches to The Noble House. Now the complex financial arrangements on which Robb and Struan had gambled so heavily for two years would be cemented. Their commercial power would extend through financial tentacles into the hearts of all the Great Powers, thus giving them the safety to weather continuous international crises and to open huge new tea and silk markets. Furthermore, if British interest now dominated the Ottoman Empire, perhaps its opium production would be stopped. Without Turkish opium to balance their outpouring of bullion, the American companies would have to increase trade with Britain, and the closer ties that Struan wanted with America would come to pass. Aye, Struan told himself happily, this is a very good day. He was mystified that Longstaff had received the official news before he had; Struan's informants in Parliament usually advised him of important disclosures like this well in advance. 'That's excellent,' he said.

'There'll be peace for a long time now. So long as France doesn't try any more tricks.'

'Or Austria-Hungary. Or Prussia. Or Russia.'

'Yes. Which brings us to Zergeyev. Why should a very important Russian come to Asia at this time? And how is it we had no official or unofficial warning, eh? When we control all sea-lanes east of Africa?'

'Perhaps he's just making a state visit to Russian Alaska, and came out via the Cape of Good Hope.'

'I'll wager a hundred guineas that's what he says,' Longstaff said. He settled himself comfortably in a chair and put his feet on the table. 'Zergeyev is an important name in St Petersburg. I lived there for five years when I was a boy – my father was a diplomat to the court of the tsars. Tyrants, all of them. The present one, Nicholas I, is typical.'

'Zergeyev is important in what way?' Struan asked, surprised that Longstaff had never mentioned St Petersburg in all the years he had known him.

'Huge landowners. Related to the tsar. They "own" tens of thousands of serfs and hundreds of villages, so I seem to remember. I recall my father saying that Prince Zergeyev – it must be the same family – was privy to the inner court of the tsar and one of the most powerful men in the Russias. Curious to find one here of all places, what?'

'You think Russia's going to try to interfere in Asia?'

'I'd say this man's too convenient to be a coincidence. Now that the *status quo* is restored in the Middle East, and the Dardanelles settled, up pops an archduke!'

'You think there's a connection?'

Longstaff laughed gently. 'Well, the Middle East settlement neatly stops Russian advances westward, but she can afford to sit back and wait. France is spoiling for a fight and so is Prussia. That Austro-Hungarian devil Metternich is in trouble dominating their Italian possessions, and furious with France and Britain for assisting the Belgians to form their own nation at the expense of the Dutch. There's going to be big trouble between Britain and France over the Spanish succession – the Spanish queen's twelve, and soon she'll be given in marriage. Louis Philippe wants his appointee as her husband, but we can't afford a joining of the thrones of France and Spain. Prussia wants to extend its domination of Europe, which historically France has always considered her exclusive and divine right. Oh yes,' he added with a smile, 'Russia can afford to wait. When the Ottoman Empire breaks up, she'll calmly take all the Balkans – Romania, Bulgaria, Bessarabia, Serbia – and as much of the Austro-Hungarian Empire as she can gobble up as well. Of course we can't let her, so there'll be a general war, unless she accepts a reasonable settlement. So, from Russia's point of view, Europe is no danger at present. Russia's been blocked effectively, but that doesn't matter. Her historical policy has always been to conquer by guile – to bribe the leaders of a country, and the leaders of the opposition, if any. To extend by "sphere of influence" and not by war, then to obliterate the leaders and digest the people. When there's no threat from the west, I'd think her eyes would turn eastward. For she too believes she has a divine position on earth, that she too – like France and Prussia – has a God-given mission to rule the world. Eastward no Great Power stands between her and the Pacific.'

'Except China.'

'And we know, you and I, that China is weak and helpless. That's not to our advantage, is it? To have China weak and Russia very strong, perhaps controlling China?'

'No,' Struan said. 'Then she could strangle us at will. And India.'

The two men fell silent, each lost in his own thoughts.

'But why send an important man here?' Struan asked.

'To test us. The answer's clear historically. Russia's a sower of seeds of discontent, and she always will be until she finds what, in her opinion, are her natural borders. She borders Turkey – there's trouble in Turkey. She borders India – there's trouble there. She borders China – at least, so far as we know – so there has to be trouble there. Zergeyev's here to probe our success. The weaker he thinks China is, the more reason for them to hurry their expansion eastward. So we

340

have to try to neutralize him, throw him off the scent, make him think that China is very strong. I'll need all the help you can give me. Could we invite him to the ball this evening?'

'Of course.'

'We've got to indicate, in any event, that China is Her Majesty's private sphere of influence – that Her Majesty's Government will brook no interference here.'

Struan's mind jumped ahead rapidly. The more the Crown was involved in Asia, the more it helped the basic plan – to bring China into the family of nations as a Great Power. The stronger China was, English-trained and assisted, the better for the world in general. Aye. And we canna afford despotic Russian interference when we're on the threshold of success.

There was a knock on the door, and Clive Monsey appeared in the doorway. He was a thin man in his middle forties, quiet, unassuming, with scant hair and a huge bulbous nose.

'Your Excellency,' he said, 'may I present His Highness Archduke Alexi Zergeyev?'

Longstaff and Struan rose. Longstaff went towards the archduke and said, in perfect Russian, 'I'm delighted to meet you, Your Highness. Please come in and sit down. Did you have a pleasant voyage?'

'Perfect, Your Excellency,' Zergeyev replied, unsurprised, and he shook the extended hand, bowing slightly with perfect grace. 'It's kind of you to invite me to lunch when I've not had the good manners to acquaint you of my arrival. And particularly as my visit is unofficial and unplanned.'

'It's our good fortune, Your Highness.'

'I was hoping that you would be the son of the esteemed friend of Russia, Sir Robert. This is a most fortunate coincidence.'

'Yes, indeed,' Longstaff said dryly. 'And how is your father the prince?' he asked, gambling on a hunch.

'In good health, I'm pleased to say. And yours?'

'He died a few years ago.'

'Oh, I'm sorry. But your mother, the Lady Longstaff?'

'In perfect health, I'm happy to say.'

Struan was inspecting the Russian. Zergeyev was a fine, tall man impeccably and richly dressed. He was broad-shouldered and narrow hipped. High cheekbones and curious, slightly slanting blue eyes gave his face an exotic cast. The dress sword at his belt under his opened frock coat seemed to belong there. Around his neck, below his pure white cravat, was a discreet decoration of some order on a thin scarlet ribbon. No man to pick a quarrel with, Struan thought. I'd wager he's a devil with a sword and a demon if his 'honour' is touched.

'May I present Mr Dirk Struan?' Longstaff said in English.

The archduke put out his hand, smiled and added in English with only the trace of an accent, 'Ah, Mr Struan, it is my pleasure.'

Struan shook hands and found Zergeyev's grip like steel. 'You have me at a disadvantage, Your Highness,' he said, deliberately being blunt and undiplomatic. 'I get the distinct impression that you know a lot about me, but I know nothing about you.'

Zergeyev laughed. 'The Tai-Pan of The Noble House has a reputation that reaches out even to St Petersburg. I had hoped I would have the privilege of meeting you. And I look forward to chatting and telling you about myself, if it interests you.' He smiled at Longstaff. 'You're too kind to me, Your Excellency. I assure you that I will inform His Highness the Tsar that Her Britannic Majesty's plenipotentiary is more than a little hospitable. Now that I have had the pleasure of meeting you, I will withdraw and let you get on with affairs of state.'

'Oh no, Your Highness, please, we expect you for lunch.' Longstaff warmed to the task that he had been trained for and understood. 'We would be most disappointed. And it's quite informal, as you can see.'

'Well, thank you. I'd consider it an honour.'

The door opened and a steward came in with iced champagne and glasses. He offered the tray to Zergeyev, then to Longstaff and to Struan and to Monsey.

'To a safe journey home,' Longstaff said.

They drank.

'Superb champagne, Your Excellency. Superb.'

'Please sit down.'

The lunch was served with flawless protocol, Zergeyev sitting on Longstaff's right hand and Struan on his left. Stewards brought smoked sausages and oysters, Yorkshire hams, a bubbling stew of fresh-killed beef, a roast haunch of lamb, boiled potatoes and pickled cabbage.

'I'm sorry we have no caviar,' Longstaff said.

'I would be glad to give you some, Your Excellency, as soon as my ship arrives. We had the misfortune to run into a storm in the Sundra Strait. We sprang a leak and put into your port of Singapore. The mail packet was leaving by the same tide, so I booked passage here.'

And thus avoided giving us advance notice, Longstaff thought. Sundra Strait meant a voyage via the Cape of Good Hope. What the devil was he up to?

'I've heard that the Singapore climate's intemperate, Mr Struan, at this time of the year,' Zergeyev was saying.

'Aye, it is,' Struan said. 'Is this your first voyage to Asia, Your Highness?'

'Yes.'

'Well, perhaps we can make your stay pleasant. I'm giving a ball this evening. I'd be honoured if you would come. It would give you an opportunity to meet everyone.'

'You are too kind.'

'How long do you plan to stay?'

'Only until my ship arrives. I'm making an informal visit to our Alaskan possessions.'

'Was the ship damaged badly?'

'I don't really know, Mr Struan. I'm not too experienced in these things. She'll follow here as soon as possible.'

'Then you'll need accommodations,' Struan said, suspecting that Zergeyev knew a great deal about 'these things', and that the 'unseaworthiness' of his ship would be a convenient way to vary, at his pleasure, the length of his stay. Struan also had a hunch that Singapore was the first port of call, outward bound from St Petersburg. 'We'll be glad to offer you a suite aboard one of our stationary vessels. It will na be luxurious, but we'll endeavour to make you comfortable.'

'That's exceedingly kind of you. There's just myself and four servants. They can sleep anywhere.'

'I'll see they're well berthed. Ah, thank you,' Struan said to the steward as his glass was refilled. 'Is she a four-masted brig?'

'Three.'

'I prefer three-masters mysel'. Much handier in a high sea. Sails are easier to reef. You carry royals and top ta'gallants?'

'There seems to be an adquate number of sails, Mr Struan. Whatever their names.'

Struan had caught the imperceptible hesitation, and he knew that Zergeyev was a seaman. Now, why would he wish to hide that?

'I hear the Middle East crisis has been solved?' Zergeyev said.

'Yes,' Longstaff replied. 'The news came by the mail packet.'

'Most fortunate. France was more than a little wise to withdraw from her militant position.'

'The importance of the Dardanelles to Britain is obvious,' Longstaff said. 'It's to the advantage of all of us to keep the peace.'

'It's a pity that France and Prussia seem to feel the opposite. And the Hapsburgs. Britain and Russia are hereditary allies and their interests are similar. It's a happy thought that we'll be working more closely together in the future.'

'Yes,' Longstaff said blandly. 'Of course Paris is very close to London.'

'Isn't it a pity that the glorious city should always seem to find the most curious leaders?' Zergeyev said. 'A beautiful people, beautiful. Yet their leaders are always puffed with vanity and seemingly determined to pull the world apart.'

'The great problem of the world, Your Highness. Europe, and how to curb the vanity of princes. Of course, in Britain we're fortunate to have a Parliament, and the might of Britain no longer goes to war on a single man's whim.'

'Yes. It's a great and glorious experiment, one fit for the splendid attributes of your country, sir. But it's not suitable for all nations. Wasn't it the ancient Greeks who came to the conclusion that the most perfect form of government was a benevolent dictatorship? The rule of one man?'

'Benevolent, yes. But elected. Not a ruler by divine right.'

'Who can say, with absolute surety, that divine right does not exist?'

'Ah, Your Highness,' Longstaff said, 'no one questions the existence of God. Only the right of a king to do what he likes, when he likes, without consulting the people. We've had a long line of English "divine" kings whom we've found to be fallible. Fallibility in a leader is very trying. Isn't it? They spill so much of other people's blood.'

Zergeyev chuckled. 'I love the humour of the English.' He glanced at Struan. 'You're Scots, Mr Struan?'

'Aye. British. There's nae difference between Scots and English nowadays.' He sipped his wine. 'We tired of stealing their cattle. We thought it'd be better to steal the whole country, so we left Scotland and moved south.'

They all laughed and drank more wine.

Longstaff was amused to note that Monsey had remained silent throughout the meal, agitated by Struan's bluffness.

'What do you think, Mr Struan?' Zergeyev said. 'Could you run The Noble House with a "Parliament" to contend with?'

'No, Your Highness. But I only commit a *company* into conflict – into competition – with other traders. I risk only myself and my company. Na the lives of others.'

'Yet there is a war now with China. Because the heathen had the temerity to interfere with your trade. Isn't that correct?'

'Partially. Of course, the decision for war was hardly mine.'

'Of course. My point was that you have sole right to operate a vast trading concern and that is the most efficient way. One man's rule. Right for a company, a fleet, a nation.'

'Aye. Provided you're successful,' Struan said, making a joke. Then he added seriously, 'Perhaps, for the present, a parliamentary system is not suitable for Russia – and some other countries – but I'm convinced this earth will never be at peace until all nations have the English parliamentary system, and all the people have a right to vote, and no single man ever controls the destiny of any nation, either by divine right or by right of stupid votes of a stupid electorate.'

'I agree,' Zergeyev said. 'Your hypothesis is correct. But it has one vast flaw. You presume an enlightened world population – all equally educated, all equally prosperous – which is of course impossible, isn't it? You should travel in Russia to see how impossible that is. And you make no allowances for nationalism or for differences in faith. If you added "until all nations are Christian", then perhaps you would be correct. But how can you imagine French Catholics will agree with Protestant English? Or the Russian Orthodox Church with Spanish Jesuits? Or all of those with the masses of infidel Mohammedans and they with the miserable Jews and they with the idolators and heathen?'

Struan took a deep breath. 'I'm glad you asked that question,' he said and stopped with finality.

'I can see we will be having many interesting discussions,' Longstaff said easily. 'Tea, Your Highness? There's a prize-fight in an hour. If you're not too tired, perhaps you'd care to witness it. It promises to be quite a match. The navy versus the army.'

'I'd be delighted, Excellency. Which do you pick? I'll take the opposition.'

'A guinea on the navy.'

'Done.'

After lunch they had tea and cigars, and at length Monsey escorted the archduke back to the mail packet. Longstaff dismissed the stewards.

'I think a frigate should instantly "happen" to take a visit to Singapore,' he said to Struan.

'I had the same thought, Will. He's a seaman, I'm sure.'

'Yes. That was very clever, Dirk.' Longstaff played with his teacup. 'And he's a most astute man. Such a man would probably be most careful with official documents.'

'I had the same thought.'

'I enjoyed my stay in St Petersburg. Except for the long hours at school. I had to learn to read and write Russian, as well as French, of course. Russian's a very difficult language.'

Struan poured some tea. 'You never did like prizefights, did you, Will?'

'No. I think I'll just escort him ashore and then come back aboard. Take a nap in private.' Longstaff laughed dryly. 'Prepare for tonight's festivities, what?'

Struan got up. 'Aye. And I'd better think of a few seeds of discontent to sow mysel'.'

As the stewards cleared the table, Longstaff stared idly at the leaves in his cup. 'No,' he said, retaining it and the teapot. 'And see that I'm not disturbed. Call me in an hour.'

'Yes, sirr.'

He stifled a yawn, his mind drifting pleasantly in the quiet of the cabin. 'Pon my word, I'm delighted Zergeyev's here. Now we can enjoy life a little. Parry and thrust diplomatically. Probe his mind, that's the ticket. Forget the incessant irritations of the colony, and the damned traders and the cursed emperor of the cursed heathen, damn bunch of thieves.

He opened the door to his private cabin and lay comfortably on the bunk, his hands behind his head. What was it Dirk said? he asked himself. Ah yes, seeds of discontent. That's a good way of putting it. What seeds can *we* plant? Grim hints about China's power? The hugeness of her population? That Her Majesty's Government may annex the whole country if *any* power intrudes? The complications of the trade in opium? Tea?

He heard the clatter of feet aloft as the watch changed and the marine band began practising. He yawned again and closed his eyes contentedly. Nothing like a nap after lunch, he told himself. Thank God I'm a gentleman – don't have to plant real seeds like a smelly peasant or filthy farmer. Damn, fancy working with your hands all day! Sowing seeds. Growing things. All the muck spreading. Horrifying thought. Sowing diplomatic seeds is much more important and the work of a gentleman. Now, where was I? Ah yes. Tea. Life must have been terrible before we had tea. Absolutely. Can't understand how people existed without tea. Pity it doesn't grow in England. That would save a lot of trouble.

'Great God in Heaven!' he burst out and sat upright. 'Tea! Of course tea! It's been under your nose for years and you've never seen it! You're a genius!' He was so excited with his idea that he jumped off the bed and danced a jig. Then he relieved himself in the chamber pot and went into the main cabin and sat at his desk, his heart pounding. You know how to solve the Britain-China nightmare of the tea-bullion-opium imbalance. *You know*, he told himself, astonished and awed by the brilliance and simplicity of the idea that Struan's final sally had triggered. 'Good God, Dirk,' he chortled aloud, 'if you only knew! You've cut your own throat, and all the China traders along with you. To the glory of Britain and the immortality of me!'

Yes, absolutely. So you'd better keep your mouth shut, he cautioned himself. Walls have ears.

The idea was so simple: destroy China's tea monopoly. Buy or beg or steal – in great secrecy – a ton of the seeds of the tea plant. Transport the seeds surreptitiously to India. There must be dozens of areas in which tea could flourish. Dozens. And in my lifetime plantations could be flourishing – growing our own teas, on our soil. With our own tea, we'll no longer need bullion or *opium* to pay for China teas. Profit on Indian tea sales will soon equal, double, triple the sale of opium, so that's not a problem. We'll grow the teas of the world and we'll sell to the world. The Crown gains in fantastically increased tea revenues, for of course we will grow it cheaper and better and the price will be below China teas. British brains and all that! And we'll gain in moral grandeur for ceasing opium trading. The cursed opium smugglers are put out of business, for without the lever of opium they serve no useful function, so we can outlaw opium. India gains hugely. China gains, for there'll be no more opium smuggling, and she consumes her own tea anyway.

And you, William Longstaff – the only man who can implement such a plan – you will gain in monumental prestige. With modest luck, a dukedom offered by a grateful Parliament, for you and you alone will have solved the unsolvable.

But whom can I trust to get the tea seeds? And how to persuade the Chinese to sell them? Of course they'll discern the consequences immediately. And whom to trust to transport the seeds safely? Can't use one of the traders – they'd sabotage me at once if they had the slightest inkling! And how to get the Viceroy of India on your side now, so that he won't steal the credit for the idea?

XIX

As the two men and their seconds climbed into the ring that had been
erected near the flag at Glessing's Point, a breathless silence settled on
the massed spectators.

Each was a burly hard-faced six-footer in his early twenties. Each had
his head shaven to protect him from the other's grip. And when they took
off their rough shirts each had the same rippling steel of knotted muscles
and bore on his back ancient ruts from the cat-o'-nine-tails.

The fighters were beautifully matched and everyone knew that much
was at stake. The admiral and the general had personally approved the
selection of the fighters, and had exhorted them to win. The honour of
the whole Service was on their shoulders, the wealth of the savings of
their mates. The future would be sweet for the victor. For the vanquished there would be no future.

Henry Hardy Hibbs climbed through the single rope and stood in the
centre of the ring where the yard-square mark had been chalked. 'Yor
Hexcellency, Yor 'Ighness, M'Lords and Yor 'Onours,' he began. 'A
fight to the finish, between, in this corner, Bosun Jem Grum o' the
Royal Navy—'

There was a huge cheer from the mob of sailors to the east and jeers
and obscenities from the packed ranks of English and Indian soldiers to
the west. Longstaff, the archduke, the admiral and the general were
seated in the place of honour on the north ringside, an honour guard of
impassive marines surrounding them. Behind the archduke were his
two liveried bodyguards, armed and vigilant. Struan, Brock, Cooper,
Tillman, Robb, Gorth and all the tai-pans had seats on the south side,
and behind them were the lesser traders and naval and army officers, all
elbowing for a better view. And on the periphery was the ever-growing
crush of Chinese who poured down from the hovels of Tai Ping Shan,
chattering, giggling, waiting.

'And in this corner, representing the Royal Army, Sergeant Bill
Tinker—'

And again raucous cheers interrupted him. Hibbs held up his arms, and his verminous frock coat lifted away from his ball-like paunch. When the cheers and jeers died away, he called out, 'London prize-ring rules: each round to end with a fall. There be thirty seconds 'twixt rounds, and when the bell be rung, eight seconds be allowed for the man to come up to the scratch and toe the line. No kickin' an' no buttin' an' no hittin' below the belt and no gougin'. Him wot doan come out of corner, or him wot's seconds throw in the towel, be the loser.'

He motioned importantly to the seconds, who examined the fists of each other's fighter to see that they were pickled in walnut juice, as was customary, and held no stone, and inspected the fighting boots to see that the soles had only the regulation three spikes.

'Now shakes 'ands an' may the best man win!'

The fighters came to the centre of the ring, their shoulder muscles quivering with pent-up excitement, their belly muscles tight, nostrils flaring as they smelled the dank sour sweat of each other.

They toed the line, and touched hands. Then they bunched their rocklike fists and waited, their reflexes hair-triggered.

Hibbs and the seconds ducked under the ropes and out of the way.

'Your Highness?' Longstaff said, giving Zergeyev the honour.

The archduke got up and walked to the ship's bell that was near the ring. He slammed it with the striker and a wild frenzy swept the foreshore.

The instant the bell sounded, the fighters lashed out at each other, their legs planted like oaks and as strong, toes firm on the line. Grum's knuckles rocked into Tinker's face and left a bloody weal in their wake, and Tinker's fist sank violently into Grum's belly. They mauled each other incessantly, driven by the tumult and their anger and hatred. There was no science to their fighting, no attempt at avoiding blows.

After eight minutes their bodies were scarlet-splotched, their faces bloody. Both men had broken noses, and their knuckles were raw and slippery with sweat and blood. Both were gasping for breath, their chests heaving like mighty bellows, and both had blood in their mouths. And then in the ninth minute Tinker smashed a right hook that caught Grum in the throat and felled him. The army cheered and the navy cursed. Grum got up, beside himself with rage and pain, and rushed at his enemy, forgetting that the first round was over, forgetting everything except that he had to kill this devil. He caught Tinker around the throat and they were hacking and gouging and the army screamed 'Foul!' The seconds swarmed into the ring and tried to drag the fighters apart, and there was almost a riot among the soldiers and the sailors and their officers.

'By the Lord Harry,' Glessing shouted to no one in particular. 'That bastard gouged our man!'

'And who started the mêlée, by God? The round was over!' Major Turnbull said, his temper rising, hand on his sword. He was a taut man of thirty-five and chief magistrate of Hong Kong. 'Just because you've been appointed harbour master, you think that gives you the right to mask a foul?'

'No, by God! But don't try to bring the full majesty of *your* appointment into a social affair.' Glessing turned his back on him, and shoved forward in the crowd.

'Hello, Culum!'

'Hello, George. Good fight, isn't it?'

'Did you see that bastard gouge our man?'

'I think he got gouged back, didn't he?'

'That's not the point, by God!'

And then the half minute was up and the fighters rushed at each other.

The second and third rounds were almost as long as the first, and the spectators knew that no man could stand such punishment for long. In the fourth round a sailing left hook caught the soldier under the ear and he crashed to the canvas. The bell sounded and the seconds grabbed their man. After the cruelly brief half-minute respite the soldier charged to the line, pummelled the sailor, then grabbed him around the chest and savagely hurled him down. Then back into the corner again and thirty seconds and fight once more.

Round after round. Ahead on falls, behind on falls.

In the fifteenth round Tinker's fist connected with Grum's broken nose. Fire burst in Grum's head, blinding him; he screamed and flailed wildly in panic. His left fist hit home and his eyes cleared a moment and he saw that the enemy was open and tottering and heard a hugeness of screaming and cheering close by, yet far away. Grum hurled his right fist, clenching it as he had never clenched it before. He saw it crush into the soldier's belly. His left crossed and smashed his enemy on the side of the face and he felt a small bone in his hand shatter and then he was alone. There was once more that god-hating bell and hands grabbed him, and someone shoved the liquor bottle into his broken mouth and he drank deeply and vomited the blood-streaked liquor and croaked, 'What round, mate?' and someone said, 'Nineteenth', and he was up to scratch once more and there was the enemy again, hurting him, killing him, and he had to stay and conquer or die.

'Good fight, eh, Dirk?' Brock bellowed above the excitement.

'Aye.'

'You wants to change yor mind and wager?'

'No thanks, Tyler,' Struan told him, awed by the bravery of the fighters. Both were at the limit of their strength, fiercely beaten. Grum's right hand was almost useless, Tinker's eyes barely open. 'I would na like to take on one of them in a ring, by God!'

'They be gutty as any alive!' Brock laughed, showing his brown and broken teeth. 'Who's t' win?'

'Take your pick. But I'll wager they'll never give up, and no towel for either of them.'

'That be truth, by God!'

Hibbs intoned, 'Twenty-fourth round,' and the fighters lumbered heavily into the centre of the ring, their limbs leaden, and smashed at each other. They kept on their feet only by the strength of their wills. Tinker hurled a monstrous left that would have felled an ox, but the blow slid off Grum's shoulder and he slipped and fell. The navy cheered and the army roared as the seconds carried the soldier to his corner. When the half minute was up, the army watched breathlessly as Tinker gripped the ropes and pulled himself up. The veins on his neck contorted with the effort, but he rose on both feet and staggered back to the line.

Struan felt someone watching him, and upon turning, saw the archduke beckoning. He pushed his way around the ring and wondered tensely if Orlov, whom he had sent to 'assist' the archduke's transfer to the hulk, had out-smarted the servants and if he had found any documents of value.

'Have you picked the winner, Mr Struan?' Zergeyev asked.

'No, Your Highness.' Struan glanced at the admiral and the general. 'Both men are a credit to your services, gentlemen.'

'The navy man's full of guts, by God, remarkable,' the general said jovially, 'but I think our man's got the wind to stay.'

'No. Our man will be the lad to toe the line. But, by God, your man's good, M'Lord. A credit to any service.'

'Why don't you join us, Mr Struan?' Zergeyev said, indicating the empty chair. 'Perhaps you'd explain the finer points of prize-fighting?'

'With your permission, gentlemen,' Struan said politely, sitting. 'Where's His Excellency?'

'Left early, by God,' the general said. 'Something about dispatches.'

The bell sounded again.

Zergeyev shifted restlessly in his chair. 'What's the largest number of rounds that a fight has had?'

'Saw the Burke-Byrne fight in '38,' the admiral said shortly. 'Ninety-nine rounds. By the blood of Christ, that was a battle royal. Fantastic courage! Byrne died of the beating he took. But he never gave up.'

'Neither of these two will give up either – they've beaten each other senseless,' Struan said. 'It'd be a waste of time to kill one – or both – of them, eh, gentlemen?'

'Stop the fight?' the archduke asked incredulously.

'The point of a match is a test of strength and courage, man to man,' Struan said. 'They're equally matched and equally brave. I'd say they've both proved their worth.'

'But then you have no winner. Surely that's unfair, weak, and proves nothing.'

'It's unfair to kill a courageous man, aye,' Struan said calmly. 'Only courage is keeping them on their feet.' He turned to the others. 'After all, they're both Englishmen. Save them for a real enemy.'

A sudden burst of cheering distracted the admiral and the general but not Zergeyev.

'That almost sounds like a challenge, Mr Struan,' he said with a dead-calm smile.

'Nay, Your Highness,' Struan said graciously, 'only a fact. We honour courage, but in a case like this, winning is secondary to the preservation of their dignity as men.'

'What do you say, Admiral?' the general said. 'Struan has a point, eh? What's the round? Thirty-five?'

'Thirty-six,' Struan said.

'Say we limit the bout to fifty. One's got to go before that – impossible to stay on their feet till then. But if they can both toe the line on the fifty-first round, we throw in the towel together, eh? Declare it a draw. Hibbs can make the announcement.'

'I agree. But your man won't last.'

'Another hundred guineas says he will, by God!'

'Done!'

'A wager, Mr Struan?' the archduke said, as the admiral and general grimly turned away and signalled to Hibbs. 'You name the stakes and pick a man.'

'You're our guest, Your Highness, so it's your privilege to pick – if the stakes please you: one question – answered by the loser in private, tonight. Before God.'

352

'What sort of question?' Zergeyev asked slowly.

'Anything that the winner wants to know.'

The archduke was tempted, yet filled with huge misgivings. It was a monumental gamble but a worthy one. There was much he would like to learn from the Tai-Pan of The Noble House. 'Done!'

'Who's your man?'

Zergeyev pointed instantly at Bosun Grum. 'I'll put my honour on him!' And he immediately roared at the sailor, 'Kill him, by God!'

The rounds mounted. Forty-three. Forty-four. Forty-five, forty-six. Forty-seven, forty-eight, forty-nine. And now the spectators were almost as exhausted as the fighters.

Finally the soldier fell. He dropped like a dead oak and the noise of his falling resounded around the beach. The sailor, drunk with pain, still flailed blindly at the air, impotently seeking the enemy. Then he too fell, equally inert. The seconds carried the men to their corners and the half minute expired and the army screamed at their man to get up and the general was pounding the ring floor, his face flushed, imploring Tinker, 'Get up, get up for God's sake, lad!' And the admiral was purple as Grum forced himself to his feet and stood reeling in his corner. 'Toe the line, lad, toe the line!' And Struan was exhorting the soldier, and the archduke was shouting a paroxysm of Russian-French-English encouragement to the sailor to get to the line.

Each fighter knew that the other was beaten. Both tottered to the line and swayed, their arms and legs dead and helpless. Each lifted his arms and tried to hit. But all the strength had vanished. Both fell.

Last round.

The crowd went wild, for it was obviously impossible for either fighter to leave his corner in half a minute and walk back to the line.

The bell sounded and again there was an unearthly silence. The fighters groped to their feet and hung on to the ropes and stayed reeling in their corners. The sailor whimpered and made the first agonized step with one foot towards the line. Then, after a breathless eternity, another. The soldier still was in his corner shivering and swaying and almost falling. Then his foot arched forward pathetically and there was a maniac screaming – urging, willing, begging, praying, cursing, blending into a final roar of impossible excitement as both men tottered ahead inch by inch. Suddenly the soldier weaved helplessly and almost slipped, and the general nearly collapsed. Then the sailor lurched drunkenly, and the admiral closed his eyes, sweat streaming his face, and prayed.

There was pandemonium as both men toed the line and the towels flew over the ropes, and only when the ring was a welter of men jumping up and down did the fighters know for truth that the brawl was over. And only then did they allow themselves to vanish into nightmare pain, not knowing if they were victor or vanquished – or awake or dead or dreaming or alive – only knowing they had done their best.

'By St Peter's beard,' the archduke said, his voice hoarse and painful, his clothes soaked with sweat, 'that was a fight of fights.'

Struan, also sweat-stained and exhausted, pulled out a hip flask and offered it. Zergeyev tilted it and drank deeply of the rum. Struan drank and passed it to the admiral, who gave it to the general, and they finished the flask together.

'God's blood,' Struan croaked. 'God's Blood.'

XX

The sun had already dipped below the mountains, but the harbour was still bathed with gold. Ah Sam took the binoculars from her eyes and scuttled anxiously away from the spy hole in the garden wall. She ran through the piles of rocks and earth that would soon be a real garden and hurried through a door into the living-room.

'Mother! Father's boat's near the shore,' she said. 'Oh-ko, he looks very angry indeed.'

May-may stopped sewing the petticoat. 'Did he come from *China Cloud* or *Resting Cloud*?'

'*Resting Cloud*. You'd better look for yourself.'

May-may snatched the binoculars and ran out into the garden and stood behind the tiny latticed window and searched the foreshore waves. She focused on Struan. He was sitting amidships in the long-boat, the Lion and Dragon fluttering aft. Ah Sam was right. He looked very angry indeed.

She closed and barred the cover to the spy window and ran back. 'Tidy all this up, and make sure it's well hidden.' And when Ah Sam carelessly scooped up the ball gown and petticoats, she pinched her cheek sharply. 'Don't crush them, you mealy-mouthed whore. They're worth a fortune. Lim Din!' she shrieked. 'Pour Father's bath quickly, and make sure his clothes are laid out properly and nothing's forgotten. Oh yes, and make sure the bath's hot if you know what's good for you. Put out the new cake of perfumed soap.'

'Yes, Mother.'

'And watch yourself. It looks as if Father's anger's in front of him!'

'Oh-ko!'

'Oh-ko indeed! Everything better be ready for Father or you'll both get a whipping. And if anything interferes with my plan, you'll both get thumbscrews and I'll whip you till your eyeballs fall out. Go on with you!'

Ah Sam and Lim Din scurried away. May-may went into her

bedroom and made sure that there were no signs of the ball gown. She put perfume behind her ears and composed herself. Oh dear, she thought. I don't want him in a bad mood tonight.

Struan strode irascibly towards the gate in the high wall.

He reached for the gate handle but the door was flung open by a beaming, bowing Lim Din.

'Nice piece sunfall, heya, Mass'er?'

Struan answered with a sullen grunt.

Lim Din locked the door and bustled for the front door, where he beamed more hugely and bowed lower.

Struan automatically checked the ship's barometer that hung on the wall in the hallway. It was set in gimbals, and the thin, glass-encased column of mercury read a comfortable fair-weather 29.8 inches.

Lim Din closed the door softly and scampered ahead of Struan, down the corridor, and opened the bedroom door. Struan went in and kicked the door shut and bolted it. Lim Din's eyes turned upwards. He took a moment to compose himself, then he evaporated into the kitchen. 'Someone's going to get a whipping,' he whispered apprehensively to Ah Sam. 'As certain as death and squeeze.'

'Don't worry about our devil barbarian father,' Ah Sam whispered back. 'I'll bet you next week's salary Mother will have him like a turtledove in one hour.'

'Done!'

May-may stood at the door. 'What are you two lumps of dog-meat motherless slaves whispering about?' she hissed.

'Just praying that Father won't be cross with our poor dear beautiful Mother,' Ah Sam said, her eyes fluttering.

'Then hurry up, you oily-mouthed whore. For every cross word he says to me, you get a pinch!'

Struan was standing in the centre of the bedroom staring at the bulky, grubby, knotted handkerchief that he had taken out of his pocket. Goddammit to hell, what do I do now? he asked himself.

After the fight he had escorted the archduke to his new quarters on *Resting Cloud*. He had been relieved when Orlov had told him privately that he had had no trouble in rifling the archduke's luggage.

'But there weren't any papers,' Orlov had said. 'There was a small strongbox, but you said not to break anything, so I left it as it was. I'd plenty of time – the men kept the servants busy.'

'Thank you. No word of this, now.'

'Do you take me for a fool?' Orlov had said, his dignity offended. 'By the way, Mrs Quance and the five children are settled on the small hulk. I said Quance was in Macao and due to arrive on the noon tide tomorrow. Had a job avoiding her cursed questions. She'd pester an answer out of a barnacle.'

Struan had left Orlov and had gone to the boys' cabin. They were clean now and had new clothes. Wolfgang was still with them and they were not afraid of him. Struan had told them that tomorrow they would be going with him to Canton, where he would put them on a ship for England.

'Yor 'Onour,' the little English boy had said as he had turned to go, 'could I be a seeing you? Privy like?'

'Aye,' Struan had said, and he had taken the boy into another cabin.

'Me dad said I were to give you this'n, Yor Worship, an' not t'tell nobody, not Mr Wu Pak or'n even Bert.' Fred's fingers trembled as he undid the cloth bundle that was still attached to the stick and laid the cloth open. It contained a small knife and a rag dog and a bulky knotted kerchief. He passed over the kerchief nervously and, to Struan's astonishment, turned his back and closed his eyes.

'What're you doing, Fred?'

'Me dad sayed I weren't t'look and to turn me back, Yor Worship. An' not to see,' Fred replied, his eyes tight shut.

Struan untied the kerchief, and gawked at the contents: ruby earrings, diamond pendants, rings studded with diamonds, a big emerald brooch and many broken, twisted gold belt buckles, heavy with diamonds and sapphires. Forty to fifty thousand pounds' worth. Pirate loot. 'What did he want me to do with this?'

'Can I open my eyes, Yor Worship? I be not to see.'

Struan knotted the kerchief and put it into his frock-coat pocket. 'Aye. Now, what did your dad want me to do with it?'

'He sayed it were me – I forgits the word. It were, it were somethin' like "mittance" or "ritance".' Fred's eyes filled with tears. 'I beed a good boy, Yor Worship, but I forgits.'

Struan squatted down and held him firmly and gently. 'No need to cry, lad. Let's think. Was it "inheritance"?'

The boy stared up at Struan as though he was a magician. 'Yus. "Ritance". How'd yer knowed?'

'No need to cry. You're a man. Men dinna cry.'

'What's a "ritance"?'

'It's a gift, usually money, from a father to a son.'

Fred mulled that a long time. Then he said, 'Why'd me dad sayed not to tell bruvver Bert?'

'I dinna ken.'

'Wot, Yor Worship?'

'Perhaps because he wanted you to have it and not Bert.'

'Can a "ritance" be for lots of sons?'

'Aye.'

'Can me bruvver Bert an' me share a "ritance" if we gets one?'

'Aye. If you have one.'

'Oh good,' the boy said, drying his tears. 'Bruvver Bert's me best friend.'

'Where did you and your dad live?' Struan asked.

'In a house. Wiv Bert's mum.'

'Where was the house, lad?'

'Near the sea. Near the ships.'

'Did the place ever have a name?'

'Oh yus, it were called "Port". We was livin' at a house in Port,' the boy said proudly. 'Me dad sayed I were to tell you everythin', truthful.'

'Let's go back now, eh? Unless there's anything else.'

'Oh yus.' Fred quickly tied up the bundle. 'Me dad sayed to tie it up like before. Secret like. And not to tell. I be ready, Yor Worship.'

Struan opened the kerchief again. God's death, what do I do with this treasure? Throw it away? I canna do that. Find the owners? How? They might be Spanish, French, American or English. An' how do I explain how I got the jewels?

He went over to the huge four-poster bed and pushed it away from the wall. He noticed that his new evening clothes were laid out meticulously. He knelt down beside the bed. An iron strong-box was cemented into the floor. He unlocked the box and deposited the bundle with his private papers. The Bible that contained the other three half coins caught his eye and he swore. He relocked the box and moved the bed back in place and walked to the door.

'Lim Din!'

Lim Din appeared immediately, glassy-eyed and beaming.

'Bath plenty quick!'

'Bath all ready, Mass'er! Never mind!'

'Tea!'

Lim Din vanished. Struan crossed the bedroom to the special room that had been set aside solely for the bath and for the toilet. Robb had laughed when he had seen the plans. Even so, Struan had insisted that the innovation be built exactly as he had planned it.

The high copper bath was set on a low platform, and a drain led from it through the wall and into a deep rock-filled pit that had been dug in the garden. Above the bath a holed iron bucket was suspended from the beams. A pipe led into the bucket from the freshwater tank on the roof. There was a cock on the pipe. The toilet was an enclosed cabinet with a movable lid and removable bucket for the night soil.

The bath was already filled with hot water. Struan stripped off his sweat-sour clothes and stepped into the bath gratefully. He lay back and soaked.

The bedroom door opened and May-may came in. Ah Sam followed her, carrying a tray with tea and hot dim sum, Lim Din close behind. They all walked into the bathroom and Struan closed his eyes in quiet exasperation; no amount of explaining and chastizing had made Ah Sam understand that she could not come into the bathroom while he was having a bath.

'Hello, Tai-Pan,' May-may said with a glorious smile. All his irritation faded. 'We're having tea together,' she added.

'Good,' he said.

Lim Din picked up the soiled clothes and vanished. Ah Sam set down the tray merrily, for she knew she had won her bet. She said something to May-may in Cantonese, which caused May-may to laugh, and Ah Sam giggled and ran out of the bathroom and closed the door.

'What the devil did she say?'

'Woman's talk!'

He lifted up the sponge to throw it, and May-may said hurriedly, 'She said you were a mighty built of a mans.'

'Why, for the love of God, will Ah Sam na understand a bath is a private matter?'

'Ah Sam's very private, never mind. Wat for you're shy, hey? She's lots of pride in you. You've nothing to be shy of.' She took off her robe and stepped into the bath and sat at the other end. Then she poured the tea and offered it.

'Thanks.' He drank the tea and then reached over and ate one of the dim sum.

'The fight was good?' she asked. She noticed the well-healed scars that her teeth had made in his forearm, and hid a smile.

'Excellent.'

'Why were you angry?'

'Nae reason. These are good,' he said, eating another of the pastries. Then he smiled at her. 'You're beautiful and I canna think of a nicer way to have tea.'

'You're beautiful too.'

'Is the house fêng-shuied?'

'When is the dress judging?'

'Midnight. Why?'

She shrugged. 'Half before midnight, will you come back?'

'Why?'

'I like to see my man. Take him away from the cow-busumed weevil mouth.' Her foot slid under the water. Struan recoiled at the intimate attack and almost dropped his tea. 'Will you na do that and be careful, by God.' He intercepted her hand and laughed. 'Now be a good girl.'

'Yes, Tai-Pan. If you're likewise careful.' May-may smiled sweetly and let her hand rest quiet in his. 'You dinna stare at me like you did at that devil womans, even though I've no clotheses on. What's wrong with my busums?'

'They're perfect. You're all perfect. Of course you are. Now stop teasing.'

'So you will come back, half an hour before?'

'Anything for peace.' Struan drank some more tea. 'Oh, yes. You did na answer me. Has the house been fêng-shuied?'

'Aye.' She picked up the soap and began to lather herself. But she said nothing more.

'Well, has it or has it na?'

'Aye.' Again she was silent, a beautiful infuriating sweetness about her.

'Well what happened?'

'I'm horrified sorry, Tai-Pan, but we're right square on the dragon's eyeball and we've to move.'

'We will na move and that's an end to it.'

She hummed a little song as she finished using the soap. She washed off the lather and looked at him, wide-eyed and gentle. 'Turn around, I'll soap your back,' she said.

'We'll na move,' he said suspiciously.

'Ma-ree came over this afternoon and we had a nice talk.'

'We'll na move! And that's the end to it.'

'Really, Tai-Pan, I'm na deaf. I heard you fantastical well the first time. Do you want your back scrubbed or do you na?'

He turned his back and she began to soap him. 'We're going to move and that's the end to it. Because your old mother's decided,' she said in Cantonese.

'What?' he said, moving his neck a little, glorying in her probing touch as her hands exquisitely massaged his shoulder muscles.

360

'An old Cantonese proverb: "When swallows nest, the sunrise smiles." '

'What's that supposed to mean?'

'What it says.' She felt very pleased with herself. 'It's just a happy thought, that's all.' She scooped some water and rinsed away the soap. 'Ah Sam, ahhhh!'

Ah Sam ran in carrying huge towels. May-may got up and Ah Sam wrapped one around her and held the other for Struan.

'Tell her I'll do it myself, by God!' he said.

May-may translated and Ah Sam put down the towel, giggled and ran out.

Struan emerged from the bath and May-may swathed him in the towel. To his surprise he found it was heated.

'I tell Ah Sam in future to cook the towels a little,' May-may said. 'It's good for health.'

'It feels splendid,' he said, and rubbed himself dry. He opened the door and found that the bed had been turned down and his new clothes put on the bureau.

'You have time for short rest,' May-may said, and when he started to argue, she added imperiously, 'You will rest!'

Struan glanced at his watch. There's plenty of time, he thought, so he climbed into bed and stretched out luxuriously.

May-may beckoned to Ah Sam, who went into the bathroom and closed the door. Kneeling, Ah Sam unbound May-may's feet and dried them. She powdered the feet and replaced the bandages with clean dry ones and put new embroidered slippers on them. 'They are so beautiful, Mother,' she said.

'Thank you, Ah Sam.' May-may pinched Ah Sam's cheek tenderly. 'But please don't make so many remarks about Father's appendages.'

'I was only being polite, and they are more than a little worthy of respect.' Ah Sam unpinned May-may's hair and began brushing it. 'Normally a father would be very happy to be complimented. Really I don't understand our barbarian father a little bit. He hasn't taken me to bed once. Am I so disgusting?'

'I keep telling you that barbarian fathers don't bed all the women of the house,' May-may said wearily. 'He just won't do it. It's against his religion.'

'It's really very bad joss,' Ah Sam sniffed, 'to have such a father, so endowed, and for it to be against his religion.'

May-may laughed, and gave her the towel. 'Run along little oily mouth. Bring some tea in one hour, and if you're late I'll give you a good whipping!'

Ah Sam fled.

May-may put perfume on herself and, thinking excitedly about the ball gown and her other surprise, she went into the bedroom.

Liza Brock opened the cabin door and went to the bunk. She could feel cold sweat running from her armpits. She knew it was now or never for Tess. 'Come on, luv,' she said, shaking Brock again. 'Time to get up.'

'Leave me be.' Brock turned over again, rocked gently by the tide nudging the hull of the *White Witch*. 'I be dressing in good time.'

'Thee's been asaying that for half an hour or more. Get thee up or thee be late.'

Brock yawned and stretched and lifted himself in the bunk. 'Baint even sundown yet,' he said blearily, staring out of the porthole.

'Gorth be arriving soon and thee wanted to be ready early. Then there be books to go through with comprador. Thee ask'd me to wake thee.'

'All right, doan carry on, Liza.' He yawned again and looked at Liza. She was wearing a new dress, dark red silk brocade with a large bustle, and the dress showed many petticoats. Her hair was tight in a bun. 'Thee look right smart,' he said automatically and stretched again.

Liza played with the huge feathered hat that was in her hands, then put it down. 'I'll help thee dress,' she said.

'Wot be this! I told thee my old suit were nice,' he exploded as he saw the new clothes on the chair. 'Dost think brass be so easy to come by that thee can spend it like salt water?'

'No luv, thee needed new dress clothes and thee's to look thy best.' She offered the small corset that fashion decreed a man must wear to give him a neat waist. Brock cursed and got out of bed. After tightening the corset over his long woollen underwear, he grudgingly allowed himself to be helped into his clothes.

But looking at himself in the mirror, he was most pleased. The new ruffled shirt billowed on his chest, and the maroon velvet frock coat with gold-embroidered lapels fitted perfectly: huge on the shoulders and snug at the waist. His tight white trousers were held into a smooth line by thongs under polished soft black evening boots. Orange-embroidered waistcoat, gold chain and fob seal.

'By gum, thee looks like King of England, luv!'

He brushed his beard and it jutted violently. 'Well,' he said gruffly, trying to hide his pleasure, 'mayhaps thee was right.' He turned to

362

profile and smoothed the velvet closer against his chest. 'Mayhaps it could be tighter to me chest, eh?'

Liza laughed. 'Get on with thee, lad,' she said, less afraid now. 'I think the ruby pin in thy cravat'd be better'n the diamond.'

He changed the pin and continued to admire himself. Then he laughed and caught her around the waist and hummed a waltz and forced her into a dance. 'Thee's the belle of the ball, luv,' he said.

Liza tried to be gay for the moment, but Brock could tell from her eyes that something was amiss. 'Wot be the matter?'

She took out a handkerchief and wiped the perspiration off her forehead and sat down. 'It's well, it be Tess.'

'She be sickly?'

'No. It's well – we be taking her to the ball!'

'Are thee out of head?'

'I've a dress done for her – oh, it be proper lovely – and done her hair and she be ready for thy approval afore—'

'Then tell her to get to bed, by God! She baint goin' to no ball, by God! Thee knowed my mind on that! Thee's made her a dress, have thee?' and he lifted his hand to strike her.

'Listen a moment,' Liza said, her strength dominating her fear. 'First listen. Nagrek – and her.'

The blow stopped in midair. 'Wot about Nagrek?'

'It be lucky he died that night. Tess, well, Tess she –' The tears welled. 'I baint wanting to worry thee, but she—'

'She's with child?'

'No. I be terrored this past month since thee beed in Canton. In case I were wrong. But her monthly start last week, bless the Lord, so that fear's away.'

'But she baint virgin?' he asked horror-stuck.

'She be virgin still.' The tears ran down her face.

'Then for the love of God, if she still be virgin, then wot the devil's thy worry? There, there, Liza,' he said patting her cheek.

Liza knew that she could never tell him that Tess was truly not a virgin. But she blessed the Lord for letting her convince the girl that it had been mostly her imagination and that she was still as pure as a girl must be.

'This past month be terrible,' she said. 'Terrible. But it be a warning to us'n, Tyler. I be worried about thee and thy not seeing that she be growed up, and I'm afeared. Thee won't see wot's afore thy eyes.' He started to speak but she rushed on.

'Please, Tyler. I'm beggin' thee. Just look at her and if thee agrees she be growd up, then we takes her. If thee thinks otherwise, she doan go. I told her it were thy decision.'

'Where be Tess now?'

'In the main cabin.'

'Thee wait here.'

'Yes, luv.'

XXI

When night had firmly settled over Hong Kong, Culum walked to the edge of *Thunder Cloud's* poop deck and gave the signal. The cannon boomed and there was a moment's hush around the fleet. He stared nervously towards the shore of Happy Valley. His excitement mounted as he saw a flicker of light, then another and soon the whole of marine lot 8 was a sea of dancing lights.

The servants on the foreshore were hurrying to light the remaining lanterns. Hundreds had been placed around the huge circle of smoothed boards that formed the dance floor, and their light was warm and enticing. Tables and chairs were set in attractive groups, a lamp and flowers from Macao on each table. More lamps were strung on ropes between slender bamboos near the trestle tables and their weight of food. Others were draped over the barrels of Portuguese and French wines and rum and brandy and whisky and sack and beer. Forty cases of champagne were on ice and ready at hand.

Servants scurried everywhere, all neatly uniformed in black trousers and white tunics, their queues dancing. They were under the imperious supervision of Chen Sheng, comprador of the Noble House. He was a man of immense girth, his robes rich and his hat jewel-studded. A priceless piece of pure white jade formed his belt buckle, and his feet were encased in black silk boots with white soles. He sat like a huge spider on a seat in the centre of the dance floor and played with the long hairs that sprouted from a small wart on his chin. A personal slave fanned him against the gentle night.

When all was ready to his satisfaction, he stood up ponderously and lifted his hand. The servants rushed for their positions and stood like graven images while he made a last inspection. Another wave of his hand and a servant hurried out of the circle of light into the foreshore darkness, a taper in his hand.

There was a monstrous cannonade of firecrackers which lasted for several minutes, and everyone in the fleet and on shore rushed to look.

365

Next were fireballs and coloured lights and more noise and smoke and thundering, and more firecrackers. And fire wheels and volcanoes of coloured fire. The thundering continued for several minutes more, and there was a sound like a fleet's broadside and a hundred rockets exploded into the sky. Their trails soared and vanished. After a moment's silence the whole sky burst into feathers of scarlet and green and white and gold. The feathers dipped majestically and fell into the sea.

The servant lit the final taper and raced away. Red and green fire snaked up the huge bamboo scaffolding which soon was aflame with the Lion and the Dragon. The flag blazed for minutes, and died with a vast explosion, as suddenly as it had begun.

There was blackness for a moment, broken only by a mighty cheer that reverberated around the enclosing hills. As eyes adjusted to the darkness, the inviting lights of the dance floor glowed once more. And an expectant joy settled over Hong Kong.

Shevaun was whimpering with agony. 'No more,' she begged.

Her maidservant took a firmer grip on the corset laces and put her knee into Shevaun's rump. 'Let your breath out,' she ordered. And as Shevaun obeyed, she gave the laces a final pull and knotted them. Shevaun gasped.

'There, me darlin',' the bonneted maid said. 'That's done.' She was a small, neat Irishwoman with wrists of steel, and her name was Kathleen O'Rourke. She had been nurse and maid-servant to Shevaun ever since Shevaun had been in swaddling clothes and she adored her. Her dark brown hair framed a nice face with laughing eyes and dimpled chin. She was thirty-eight.

Shevaun steadied herself against a chair in the cabin and groaned, hardly able to breathe. 'I'll faint before the evening's over.'

Kathleen found the tape and measured Shevaun's waist. 'Seventeen and a half inches, by the Blessed St Mary! And when you faint, me darlin', be sure you're as graceful as a cloud and that everyone's watching.'

Shevaun was dressed in frilled pantaloons, her legs encased in silk stockings. The whaleboned corset gripped her hips, violently squeezed her waist and rose to cushion her breasts and force them up. 'I've got to sit down for a moment,' she said weakly.

Kathleen found the smelling salts and brandished them under Shevaun's nose. 'There, me darlin' heart. As soon as those doxies see you, you won't feel faint at all at all. By the Blessed St Mary, Mother and Joseph, you'll be the belle of the ball.

There was a sharp knock on the door. 'Aren't you ready yet, Shevaun?' Tillman called out.

'No, Uncle. I won't be long.'

'Well, hurry it up, dear. We've got to be there before His Excellency!' He stamped away.

Kathleen chuckled softly. 'Silly man, me darlin' heart. He doesn't realize a body's got to make an entrance.'

Quance put his paints away. 'There!'

'Excellent, Aristotle,' Robb said, and he held little Karen up to look at her portrait. 'Isn't it, Karen?'

'Do I look like that?' Karen said disappointedly. 'It's awful.'

'It's immortal, Karen,' Quance said, shocked. He took her out of Robb's arms and held her tight. 'Look at the superb glow to your cheeks, the light to your beautiful eyes, the happiness that surrounds you like a halo. By the beard of Alcazabedabra, it's marvellous good like you are.'

'Oh, good.' She gave him a hug and he set her down and she looked at the painting again. 'Who's Alcaza – who you sayed?'

'A friend of mine,' Quance said gravely. 'A bearded friend who watches over painters and beautiful children.'

'It's very, very pretty,' Sarah said, her face stretched. 'Run along, now, it's past your bedtime.'

'It's early,' Karen said with a pout. 'And you promised I could stay up till Daddy goes.'

Quance smiled and cleaned his fingers with turpentine and took off his smock. 'I'll pick up my paints tomorrow, Robb.'

'Of course.'

'Well, we'd better be off.' Quance smoothed the startling purple-embroidered waistcoat and put on his gold silk frock coat. 'I like you, Mr Quance,' Karen said. 'You're very pretty even though the painting's awful.'

He laughed and gave her a hug and put on his top hat. 'I'll wait in the longboat, Robb.'

'Why don't you show Mr Quance the way, Karen?' Robb said.

'Oh yes,' she replied and danced to the door. Quance followed her out like a peacock.

'Are you feeling all right, Sarah?' Robb asked solicitously.

'No,' Sarah said coldly. 'But that doesn't matter. You'd better go. You'll be late.'

'I'll stay if it'll help,' Robb said tautly.

'The only thing that'll help is the coming of the baby, and the ship to home.' Sarah peevishly brushed a lank strand of hair out of her eyes. 'And away from this accursed island!'

'Oh, don't be ridiculous!' he said unable to stop himself, his anger swamping his resolve not to quarrel. 'Nothing to do with Hong Kong!'

'Ever since we had it, there's been nothing but trouble,' she said. 'You've changed, Dirk's changed, Culum, me. For the love of God, what's going on? We'd finally decided to leave – then we're bankrupt. We're frightened to death and quarrelling hideously and poor Ronalda and Dirk's family dead. Then the bullion saves us, but oh no, Dirk grinds you into a corner and you're too weak to get out, so you swear you'll stay. Culum hates Dirk and Dirk hates Culum and you're stupidly in the middle, without the courage to take what's ours by right and leave to enjoy it at home. I've never been late with a bairn before but now I'm late. I've never felt poorly before but now I feel like death. If you want a date for all our troubles starting, it's the 26th of January, 1841!'

'That's stupid nonsense,' he retorted, furious that she articulated what long had been simmering in his mind, and realizing that he had equally cursed that day in the brooding watches of the night. 'Superstitious nonsense,' he added, more to convince himself than her. 'The plague happened last year. The run on the bank was last year. We just didn't get the news till we were in Hong Kong. And I'm not stupid. We've got to have money, lots of money, and a year is neither here nor there. I'm thinking of you and the children and their children. I've got to stay. It's all settled.'

'Have you booked our passage home yet?'

'No.'

'Then I'll be glad if you'll do that immediately. I'm not going to change my mind, if that's what you think!'

'No, Sarah,' Robb said icily, 'I don't think you'll change your mind. I was waiting to see how you felt. We've plenty of ships available. As you well know.'

'A month from today I'll be fit enough and—'

'You won't and going so quickly's dangerous. Both for you and the child!'

'Then perhaps you'd better escort us home.'

'I can't.'

'Of course not. You've more important things to do.' Sarah's temper snapped. 'Perhaps you've another heathen whore ready and waiting.'

'Oh shut up, for God's sake. I've told you a thousand times—'

'Dirk's got one on the island already. Why should you be different?'

'Has he?'

'Hasn't he?'

They stared at each other, hating each other.

'You'd better go,' she said, and turned away.

The door opened and Karen danced into the room. She jumped into her father's arms, then ran to Sarah and embraced her.

'Daddy's arranging our ship home, darling,' Sarah said, feeling the baby kicking violently in her womb. Her time was very near at last, and she was stabbed with untoward fear. 'We'll have Christmas at home this year. Won't that be wonderful? There'll be snow and carol singing and wonderful presents. And Father Christmas.'

'Oh good, I love Father Christmas. What's snow?'

'It's all white – the trees and the houses – its rain that's become ice. It's very pretty, and the shops will be full of toys and wonderful things.' Sarah's voice trembled and Robb felt the knife of her torment. 'It'll be so nice to be in a real city again. Not a – not a wilderness.'

'I'll be off now.' Robb said, consumed with grief. He kissed Sarah briefly and she imperceptibly turned her face away, infuriating him once more. He hugged Karen and walked out.

Mary Sinclair put the finishing touches to her coiffure and pinned into place the tiny coronet of wildflowers that Glessing had sent.

Her dress – jet-black Shantung silk, bustled and flowing – was worn over many petticoats that rustled as she moved. It was cut fashionably to reveal bare smooth shoulders and swelling breasts.

She studied her reflection dispassionately.

The face that looked back at her from the mirror was strange. There was an untoward loveliness in the eyes, no colour in the cheeks. The lips were deep red and glistening.

Mary knew that she had never looked lovelier.

She sighed and took up the calendar. But she knew that there was no need to re-count the days again. The total would always be the same, and the discovery that had shrieked to her this morning would be the same: you're with child.

Oh God oh God oh God.

XXII

Culum bowed politely. 'Evening,' he said automatically, and another guest dissolved into the festive throng. For almost an hour he had been standing beside his father and uncle, formally receiving their guests, and he was impatient for the ritual to end.

He surveyed the dance floor. Amid the bare shoulders and multi-coloured gowns and resplendent uniforms and constantly quivering fans he spied Mary Sinclair. For a moment he was annoyed to see that she was chatting with Glessing. But then, he thought, you shouldn't be jealous. Mary's obviously the most beautiful woman in the room and George is quite right to be with her. Don't blame him a bit.

Two bandstands had been erected on either side of the circle, one for the navy band and one for the army. When the general had heard that the admiral had agreed to lend his band for the evening, he had done the same.

The soldiers, scarlet-uniformed, were playing now. Everyone was anxious to begin dancing, but had to wait until Longstaff arrived. And he was late, which was his prerogative.

Culum bowed to another guest and another and he noticed with relief that the line was thinning. He glanced shoreward, where a ribbon of lanterns guided the guests from their boats, and saw Longstaff's cutter hit the beach. Longstaff, the archduke and the admiral were assisted ashore. Good, Culum thought. Not long now. Again his eyes strayed around the floor and this time came to rest on Manoelita de Vargas. She was watching him over the top of her fan. She was very beautiful – stark-white skin, dark eyes, a mantilla in her black hair. Culum smiled and made a slight bow. Manoelita's eyes crinkled and she fluttered her fan and then turned away. Culum promised himself that he would have at least one dance with her.

He brushed some dust off his lapels, conscious that he was dressed in the latest English fashion, well in advance of most of the men tonight. His coat was sky-blue, with dark-blue silk lapels, tight at the waist and flaring over his hips. Pale blue skin-tight trousers were tucked into soft black half boots. Hair curled over his ears and over his high, starched collar. Robb's tailor had done a very good job, he thought. And so cheap! Why, on a hundred and fifty a month he could afford dozens of superb suits and boots. Life was wonderful.

He bowed as another group of guests passed by, leaving in their wake the dankness of ancient sweat overlaid with perfume. Strange, he thought. Now he could smell other people and they did stink. He was amazed that he hadn't noticed it before. Certainly he felt better, much better, since he had been having a daily bath and change of clothes, the Tai-Pan was right.

He looked at his father, who was deep in conversation with Morley Skinner. Culum was aware that people were watching him, and that his expression was antagonistic. As far as the guests were concerned, there was no sign that the hostility between father and son had lessened. In fact, it had deepened into cold politeness. Since the game had started, Culum had found it increasingly easier to carry out the deception in public. Be honest, Culum, he said to himself. You no longer idolize him. You still respect him – but he's a heretic, adulterer, and dangerous influence. So you're not pretending – you are cold. Cold and cautious.

'Come on, Culum laddie,' Robb whispered uneasily.

'What, Uncle?'

'Oh, nothing. Just that tonight's a night to celebrate.'

'Yes, it is.' Culum read the troubled expression in Robb's eyes but said nothing and turned back to greet other guests and to watch Mary and occasionally Manoelita. He decided he would not tell Robb what had happened between the Tai-Pan and himself on the mountaintop.

'You haven't met my nephew Culum,' he heard Robb say. 'Culum, this is Miss Tess Brock.'

Culum turned. His heart twisted, and he fell in love.

Tess was curtsying. The skirt of her dress was huge and billowing, white silk brocade over cascading petticoats that broke like froth from beneath the hem. Her waist seemed incredibly small below the swelling low-cut bodice. Her fair hair fell in soft ringlets on her bare shoulders. Culum saw that her eyes were blue, her lips inviting. And she was looking at him as he was looking at her.

'I'm honoured to meet you,' he heard himself say in an unreal voice. 'Perhaps you'd honour me with the first dance.'

'Thank you, Mr Struan,' he heard her say, her voice bell-like, and she was gone.

Liza had been watching carefully. She had seen Culum's expression

371

and Tess's response. Oh Lord, let it happen, make it happen, she thought as she followed Brock across the floor.

'I did na recognize little Tess, did you?' Struan was saying to Robb. He too had noticed the exchange between his son and the Brock girl, and his mind was churning with the advantages and dangers inherent in a Culum-Tess match. Good sweet Christ!

'No. Look at Brock. He's bursting with pride.'

'Aye.'

'And look at Mary. I'd never have thought that she could be so – so stunning either.'

'Aye.' Struan watched Mary a moment. The black dress enhanced the ethereal luminous pallor of her skin. Then he scrutinized Manoelita. Then Tess again. She was smiling at Culum, who was smiling back, as obliviously. Good God, he thought, Culum Struan and Tess Brock.

'Damn Shakespeare,' he said involuntarily.

'Er, Dirk?'

'Nothing. I'd say Mary is in the race for the prize right enough.'

'She's not in the same class, by God,' Quance said as he strolled past and winked. 'Not with Manoelita de Vargas.'

'Or Shevaun, I'll wager,' Struan said, 'when she deigns to honour us with her presence.'

'Ah the delectable Miss Tillman. I hear she's only wearing pantaloons and gossamer. Nothing else! Great spheroids of Jupiter, eh?'

'Ah Aristotle,' Jeff Cooper said, coming up to them. 'Can I have a word with you? It's about a painting commission.'

'God bless my beautiful soul! I really don't understand what's come over everyone,' Quance said suspiciously. 'Nothing but commissions all day long.'

'We've suddenly realized the perfection of your work,' Cooper said quickly.

'And it's about time, by God, and that's the immortal truth. Me price is up. Fifty guineas.'

'Let's discuss it over a champagne, eh?' Cooper winked surreptitiously to Struan over Quance's head and steered the little man away.

Struan chuckled. He had spread the word to keep Quance occupied and away from wagging tongues – until the judging. And he had effectively marooned Maureen Quance aboard the small hulk by withdrawing all the longboats.

At that moment Longstaff and the archduke and the admiral came into the light.

There was a roll of drums and everyone stood as the bands played

372

'God Save the Queen'. Next they played, haltingly, the Russian national anthem, and finally 'Rule Britannia'. There was a round of applause.

'That was most thoughtful of you, Mr Struan,' Zergeyev said.

'It's our pleasure, Your Highness. We want you to feel at home.' Struan knew that all eyes were on the two of them, and he knew that he had chosen his clothes wisely. In contrast to everyone else, he wore black, except for a small green ribbon which tied his long hair at the nape of his neck. 'Perhaps you'd care to lead the first dance?'

'I would be honoured. But I'm afraid I don't know any ladies.' Zergeyev was wearing a brilliant Cossack uniform, the tunic draped elegantly on one shoulder, a dress sword at his jewelled belt. Two liveried servants were obsequiously in attendance.

'That's easily remedied,' Struan said breezily. 'Perhaps you'd care to choose. I'd be glad to make the formal introduction.'

'That would be very impolite of me. Perhaps you'd decide who might care to honour me.'

'And get my eyes scratched out? Very well.' He turned and began to cross the floor. Manoelita would be the best choice. That would greatly honour and please the Portuguese society on whom The Noble House and all the traders relied completely to supply clerks, book-keepers, storesmen – all those who made the companies function. Mary Sinclair would be almost as good a choice, for she was strangely intriguing tonight and the most beautiful woman in the room. But nothing would be gained by choosing her, except Glessing's support. Struan had noticed how Glessing was close in attendance on her. Since he had become harbour master his position of influence had increased. And he would be a very useful ally.

Struan saw Manoelita's eyes widen and Mary Sinclair catch her breath as he headed in their direction. But he stopped in front of Brock.

'With your permission, Tyler, perhaps Tess could lead the first dance with the archduke?' Struan was pleased with the rustle of astonishment he could feel.

Brock nodded, flushed with pride. Liza was ecstatic. Tess blushed and almost fainted. And Culum cursed and hated his father and blessed him for giving the honour to Tess. And all the traders wondered if the Tai-Pan was making peace with Brock. And if so, why?

'I don't believe it,' Glessing said.

'Yes,' Cooper agreed worriedly, knowing a peace between Brock and Struan would not work to his benefit. 'Doesn't make sense.'

'It makes very good sense,' Mary said. 'She's the youngest and she should have the honour.'

'More to it than that, Miss Sinclair,' Glessing said. 'The Tai-Pan never does anything lightly. Perhaps he hopes she'll fall down and break a leg or something. He hates Brock.'

'I think that's a very unkind thought, Captain Glessing,' Mary said sharply.

'Yes it is, and I apologize for saying aloud what everyone's thinking.' Glessing regretted his stupidity; he should have realized that such exquisite innocence would defend that devil. 'I'm irritated only because you're the most beautiful lady present and you undoubtedly should have the honour.'

'You're very kind. But you mustn't think that Tai-Pan does things maliciously. He doesn't.'

'You're right and I'm wrong,' Glessing said. 'Perhaps I can have the first dance – and take you in to dinner. Then I'll know I'm forgiven.'

For more than a year she had been considering George Glessing as a possible husband. She liked him but did not love him. But now everything was ruined, she thought.

'Thank you,' she said. She lowered her eyes and fluttered her fan. 'If you promise to be more – more gentle.'

'Done,' Glessing said happily.

Struan was leading Tess across the floor. 'Can you waltz, lass?'

She nodded, and tried to keep her eyes from the Tai-Pan's son.

'May I present Miss Tess Brock, Your Highness? Archduke Alexi Zergeyev.'

Tess stood paralyzed, her knees trembling. But the thought of Culum, and the way he'd looked at her, bolstered her confidence and restored her poise.

'I'm honoured, Your Highness,' she said curtsying.

The archduke bowed and gallantly kissed her hand. 'It's my honour, Miss Brock.'

'Did you have a pleasant voyage?' she asked, fanning herself.

'Yes, thank you.' He glanced at Struan. 'Are all English young ladies so beautiful?'

No sooner had he spoken that Shevaun swept into the light on Tillman's arm. Her dress was a mist of green gossamer, its skirt huge and bell-like. The outer dress was knee-length to dramatize the tiers of a dozen cascading emerald petticoats. She wore long green gloves, and there were birds-of-paradise feathers in her red hair. Incredibly, her bodice was without supporting sleeves.

'I'm sorry we're late, Your Excellency, Mr Struan,' she said, with a curtsy in the silence. 'But I broke a shoe buckle just as we were leaving.'

Longstaff pried his eyes off the décolletage and wondered, with all of them, how the devil the dress was supported and if it would come down. 'Your timing is always perfect, Shevaun.' He turned to Zergeyev. 'May I present Miss Shevaun Tillman from America. Oh, and Mr Tillman. His Highness, Archduke Alexi Zergeyev.'

Standing there forgotten, Tess watched as Shevaun curtsied again, and hated her for taking away her moment of glory. It was the first time she had been jealous of another woman. And it was the first time she had thought of herself as a woman, not a girl.

'What a beautiful dress, Miss Tillman,' she said sweetly. 'Did you make it yourself?'

Shevaun's eyes blazed, but she replied as sweetly, 'Oh no, dear, I haven't your talent, I'm afraid.' You gutternosed-whore-bitch.

'Perhaps I may have the honour of the first dance, Shevaun?' Longstaff said.

'Delighted, Your Excellency.' She was exhilarated by the envy and jealousy that she had provoked. 'Everything looks so beautiful, Tai-Pan.' She smiled at Struan.

'Er, thank you,' Struan said. He turned and motioned to the navy bandleader.

The baton fell and then the first exciting bars of a Viennese waltz began. Although waltzes were frowned on, they were the most popular of all dances.

The archduke led Tess into the centre of the floor and Shevaun prayed that Tess would trip and fall, or even better, dance like a cow. But Tess floated like a leaf. Longstaff led Shevaun out. As she spun with marvellous grace, she noticed Struan heading for a dark-eyed Portuguese beauty whom she had never seen before, and she was furious. But when she had spun again, she saw that Struan had led Liza Brock on to the floor, and she thought, Ah, Tai-Pan, you're a smart man. I love you for that. Then her eyes saw Tess and the archduke holding the centre of the floor and she guided Longstaff, who danced very well, into the centre of the floor without his knowing that he had been guided.

Culum stood on the sidelines and watched. He took a glass of champagne and drank it without tasting it, and then he was bowing in front of Tess and asking for the second dance.

He did not notice Brock's frown or Liza hurriedly distracting Brock. Or Gorth's sudden curiosity.

There were waltzes and polkas and reels and gallops. Shevaun was surrounded at the end of every dance, and so was Manoelita – but more cautiously. Culum danced with Tess a third time, and four times in an evening was all that convention would allow.

The last dance before supper Struan pushed through the crush encircling Shevaun. 'Gentlemen,' he said with calm finality, 'I'm sorry, but this dance is the prerogative of the host.' The men groaned and let him take her. He did not wait for the music but began to lead her out on to the floor.

Jeff Cooper watched jealously. It had been his dance.

'They look well together,' he said to Tillman.

'Yes. Why don't you press your suit? You know my views. And my brother's.'

'There's time.'

'Not now that Struan's unmarried.'

Cooper's eyes narrowed. 'You'd encourage such a match?'

'Of course not. But it's quite apparent to me that Shevaun's infatuated with the man.' Then Tillman added testily, 'It's time she settled down. I've had nothing but trouble ever since she arrived and I'm tired of being a watchdog. I know your mind, so formally ask for her hand and let's be done with it.'

'Not until I'm sure she's ready to accept me – and happy about it – of her own free will. She's not a chattel to be bought and sold.'

'I agree. But she's still a female, a minor, and will do what her father and I consider in her best interests. I must confess I do not approve of your attitude, Jeff. Asking for trouble.'

Cooper made no reply. He gazed at Shevaun, his loins aching.

'They make a perfect couple,' Mary said, desperately wanting to be Shevaun. And at that moment, she suddenly felt unclean: because of her secret life, and the child, and Glessing. He had been so tender tonight, tender and masculine and very English and very clean. And she almost wept from the pain of her futile love for the Tai-Pan.

'They do,' Glessing said. 'But if there's any justice, you'll win the prize, Miss Sinclair.'

She managed a smile, and again tried to think who the father of the child would be – not that that mattered, for the father was Chinese. To have a Chinese bastard! I'll die before that, she told herself. Two or three months and then it'll begin to show. But I'll not live to see the horror and reproach on their faces. Tears filled her eyes.

'There, there, Mary,' Glessing said, touching her arm affectionately. 'You mustn't cry because I paid you a compliment. You really are the most beautiful person here – the most beautiful that I've ever seen. That's the truth.'

She brushed the tears away behind her fan. And through the mist of terror she remembered May-may. Perhaps May-may could help? Perhaps the Chinese have medicines to abort a child. But that's murder. Murder. No, it's my body and there's no God and if I have the child I'm damned. 'Sorry, George dear,' she said, more at peace with herself now that she'd made the decision. 'I felt faint for a moment.'

'You're sure you're all right now?'

'Oh, yes.'

Glessing was brimming with protective love. Poor, frail little girl, he thought. She needs someone to look after her, and that's me. Only me.

Struan stopped in the dead centre of the floor.

'I was wondering when I would be honoured, Tai-Pan.' Shevaun radiated devilment.

'This dance is in your honour, Shevaun,' he said blandly.

The first bar of the most electrifying music on earth began. The Kankana. A wild, hilarious, rowdy, high-stepping dance that had rushed into vogue in Paris in the 'thirties and had taken the capitals of Europe by storm, but was forbidden as outrageous in the best circles.

'Tai-Pan!' she said, dumbfounded.

'I bribed the bandleader,' Struan whispered.

She hesitated, but feeling all the scandalized eyes on her, she casually took Struan's arms, the beat of the music whipping her.

'Nothing will fall down, I trust?' Struan said.

'If it does, you'll protect me, I trust?'

And then they were high-stepping. Shevaun broke from Struan's arms and lifted her skirts and kicked high and showed her pantaloons. There was a jubilant shout as the men rushed for partners. Now everyone was dancing and kicking, possessed by the infectious, abandoned rhythm.

The music ravaged them. All of them.

When it ended, there was wild applause and continuing shouts for an encore, and the band struck up again. Mary forgot the child, and Glessing decided that tonight he would ask – demand, by God – that Horatio bless the marriage. The dancers continued their twirling, kicking, cheering, gasping, and then it was done. The young people swarmed Struan and Shevaun, and thanked him and congratulated her. She held his arm possessively and fanned herself, vastly pleased with herself. He wiped the perspiration off his forehead and was very glad that his two gambles had paid off: Tess and the Kankana.

All returned to their seats and servants began carrying trays of food to the tables. Smoked salmon and smoked hams and fish and oysters and clams and sausages. Fresh fruit that Chen Sheng had wheedled out of a lorcha which had made the perilous journey from Manila. Sides of fresh-killed beef purchased from the navy, barbecued over open fires. Suckling pigs. Pickled hog's feet in sweet jelly.

'By my life,' Zergeyev said, 'I've never seen so much food, or had such a wonderful time in years, Mr Struan.'

'La, Your Highness,' Shevaun said, raising an eyebrow, 'this is positively ordinary for The Noble House.'

Struan laughed with the others and sat down at the head of a table. Zergeyev was on his right and Longstaff at his left, Shevaun beside the archduke and Mary Sinclair beside Longstaff, Glessing close in attendance next to her. At the same table were Horatio, Aristotle, Manoelita and the admiral. Then Brock and Liza and Jeff Cooper. Robb and Culum were hosts at tables of their own.

Struan glanced at Aristotle and wondered how he had managed to persuade Vargas to allow Manoelita to be Aristotle's dinner partner. Great God, he thought, is Manoelita the one who's posing for the picture?'

'The Kankana,' Longstaff was saying, ''pon me word. A devilish, dangerous gamble, Tai-Pan.'

'Na for so many modern people, Excellency. Everyone seemed to enjoy it vastly.'

'But if Miss Tillman hadn't taken the initiative,' Zergeyev said, 'I doubt if one of us would have had the courage.'

'What else could a body do, Your Highness?' Shevaun said. 'Honour was at stake.' She turned to Struan. 'That was a very naughty thing to do, Tai-Pan.'

'Aye,' he said. 'If you'll excuse me a moment, I have to see my guests are taken care of.'

He walked among the tables, greeting everyone. When he came to Culum's table, there was a slight hush and Culum looked up. 'Hello,' he said.

'Is everything all right, Culum?'

'Yes, thank you.' Culum was perfectly polite but there was no warmth. Gorth, who was sitting opposite Tess at Culum's table, laughed inside. Struan walked away.

When dinner was over, the ladies retired to the large tent that had been set aside for them. The men grouped at the tables and smoked and sipped port, delighted to be alone for a while. They relaxed and talked about the rising sale price of spices, and Robb and Struan made profitable deals on spices and cargo space. Everyone decided Shevaun was the winner, but Aristotle did not seem convinced.

'If you don't give her the prize,' Robb said, 'she'll kill you.'

'Ah, Robb, dear innocent!' Aristotle said. 'You're all transfixed by her tits – true, they're impeccable – but the contest is for the best-dressed, not the most undressed!'

'But her dress is marvellous. The best, easily.'

'You poor man, you haven't got a painter's eye – or the responsibility of an immortal choice.'

So the odds lengthened on Shevaun. Mary was favoured. Manoelita had her backers.

'Whom do you favour, Culum?' Horatio asked.

'Miss Sinclair, of course,' Culum said gallantly, though as far as he was concerned there was only one lady worthy of the honour.

'You're very kind,' Horatio said. He turned away as Mauss called to him. 'Excuse me a moment.'

Culum sat at one of the tables, content to be alone with his thoughts. Tess Brock. What a lovely name! How beautiful she was! What a lovely lady. He saw Gorth bearing down on him.

'A word in your ear, Struan?' Gorth said.

'Of course. Won't you sit down?' Culum tried to cover his unease.

'Thankee.' Gorth sat. He put his huge hands on the table. 'Best I be blunt. That's the only way I know how. It be about your da' and mine. They be enemies and that be fact. Nout we can do about that'n, you'n me. But just 'cause they be enemies, baint necessary for us'n to do likewise. Least that be my thort. China's big enough for you and me. Least, that be my thort. I'm mortal sick of they two acting stupid. Like over the knoll – why each'll risk the house at the drop of a topper over *face*. If we baint careful, we'll be drug down into enmity, you an' me, without having anything to hate about. What do you say? Let's us'n judge for ourselves. What my da' thinks or your da' thinks – well, that be their own affair. Let's you and me start fair. Open. Maybe we could be friends, who knows? But think it be unchristian for us'n to hate just because of our da'. What do you say?'

'I agree,' Culum said, bewildered by the offer of friendship.

'I baint saying my da's wrong and yours be right. All I be saying is that we've to try, as men, to live our own lives, best we can.' Gorth's craggy face broke into a smile. 'You look right proper shocked, lad.'

'I'm sorry. It's just that – well, yes, I'd like to be friends. I never expected that – well, that you'd have an open mind.'

'There, you see? That be my whole point, by God. We baint never said more'n four words in our whole lives, yet you've been thinking I hate thy guts. Ridikulus.'

'Yes.'

'It baint easy, what we be atrying. Doan forget, we come from different lives. My school were a ship. I was afore the mast at ten. So you've to go easy with my manners and talk. Even so, I knowed more about the China trade than most, and I'm the best seaman in these waters. 'Cepting my da'– an' that bastard Orlov.'

'Is Orlov that good?'

'Yes. That bugger were sired by a shark and whelped by a mermaid.' Gorth picked up some salt that had been spilled and superstitiously threw it over his shoulder. 'That bugger give me the creeps.'

'Me too,' Culum agreed.

Gorth was silent for a moment and then he said, 'Our da's baint liking it a bit if we be friends.'

'Yes. I know.'

'I be straight with you, Struan. It were Tess what sayed tonight were a good time to talk privy with you. Weren't my idea first off. To talk open tonight. But I be right glad it be sayed. What do you say? Let's give it a try, eh? Here's my hand on't.'

Culum shook the proffered hand gladly.

Glessing was irritably drinking brandy across the floor, waiting impatiently. He had been on the verge of interrupting Horatio and Culum when Mauss had called him over. What are you so damned nervous about? he asked himself. I'm not. Just anxious to have it said. By Jove, Mary looks stunning. Absolutely stunning.

'Excuse me, Captain Glessing,' Major Turnbull said crisply, coming up to him. He was a grey-eyed, meticulously neat man, who took his appointment as chief magistrate of Hong Kong very seriously. 'Good party, what?'

'Yes.'

'I think now's the time, if you've a mind. His Excellency's free. We'd better catch him while we've the opportunity.'

'All right.' Glessing automatically adjusted his sword belt and followed Turnbull through the tables until they intercepted Longstaff.

'Could we have a moment, Your Excellency?' Turnbull said.

'Certainly.'

'Sorry to bring up official matters at a social affair, but it's somewhat

380

important. One of our patrol frigates has captured a bunch of scalla-wag pirates.'

'Excellent. Open-and-shut case?'

'Yes, Your Excellency. The navy caught the buggers on the south side, off Aberdeen. They were pirating a junk. Murdered the crew.'

'Damned swine,' Longstaff said. 'Have you tried them yet?'

'That's the problem.' Turnbull said. 'Captain Glessing thinks it should be an Admiralty court – I think it's a civil trial. But my authority doesn't cover anything but minor crimes and certainly not capital crimes of any sort. This case should have a proper judge, jury, and rightly belong in an assize.'

'True. But we can't have a judge till we're officially a colony. That'll take months yet. We can't leave anyone accused of any crime in jail without a quick, fair trial – that's illegal.' Longstaff thought a moment. 'I'd say it's a civilian matter. If the jury convicts, send me the papers and I'll confirm the sentence. You'd better erect the gibbet outside the jail.'

'I can't do that, Your Excellency. It wouldn't be legal. The law's very clear – only a proper judge can try such a case.'

'Well, we can't have men accused of crimes locked up indefinitely without giving them an open and fair trial. What do you suggest?'

'I don't know, sir.'

'Damned annoying!' Longstaff said. 'You're right, of course.'

'Perhaps we should hand them over to the Chinese authorities to deal with,' Glessing said, eager to have the matter settled so that he could talk to Horatio.

'I disapprove of that,' Turnbull said sharply. The crime was com-mitted in British waters.'

'I quite agree,' Longstaff said. 'For the moment hold all such accused, and I'll send an urgent dispatch to the Foreign Office and ask for a ruling.'

'Yes, Your Excellency.' Turnbull paused. 'Then I'd like to draw funds to extend the jail. I've dozens of cases of robbery with violence and one breaking and entering with a deadly weapon.'

'Very well,' Longstaff said languidly. 'Let's discuss it tomorrow.'

'Perhaps I could have an appointment tomorrow, Your Excellency,' Glessing said. 'I've got to have some money to hire pilots, and we should settle harbour dues and wharfage, and I want authority to requisition some fast pirate hunters. There're strong rumours that that devil Wu Fang Choi's got a fleet north. Also I'll need authority to extend jurisdiction over all the Hong Kong waters. There's an urgent need to standardize port clearances and allied matters.'

'Very well, Captain,' Longstaff said. 'At noon.' And then to Turnbull, 'Nine o'clock?'

'Thank you, Your Excellency.'

To Glessing's chagrin, Longstaff turned away and walked towards Horatio. Good Lord, he thought, I'll never get him alone tonight.

Struan was watching the ships at anchor, and checking the sky. Good weather, he told himself.

'A beautiful harbour, Mr Struan,' Zergeyev said amiably, wandering up to him.

'Aye. It's good to have our own waters at long last.' Struan was on guard, but his manner was relaxed. 'Hong Kong will be a perfect jewel in the queen's crown, eventually.'

'Let's walk a little, shall we?'

Struan fell into step as the archduke strolled down towards the surf.

'I understand you've only had the island a little over two months.' The archduke waved a hand at the beginnings of buildings all over Happy Valley. 'Yet you've almost a town. Your energy and industry are astounding.'

'Well, Your Highness, if there's something to be done, there's nae use waiting, is there?'

'No. But I find it curious, with China so weak that you take only a barren rock. There must be many more important prizes.'

'We're na after prizes in China. Just a small base where we can careen and refit our ships. I'd say a nation of three hundred millions is hardly weak.'

'Then with the war unfinished, I presume you're expecting substantial reinforcements. Armies, not a few thousand men. Fleets – not thirty or so ships.'

'His Excellency would know more about that than I. But I'd say that any Power that takes on China would have a very long struggle on its hands. Without the necessary plans and the necessary men.' Struan motioned at the mainland across the harbour. 'The land's limitless.'

'Russia's limitless,' Zergeyev said. 'But only in symbolic terms. Actually, even Russia is bounded. By the Arctic and the Himalayas. By the Baltic and the Pacific.'

'You've taken lands north?' Struan tried to keep the astonishment out of his voice. Where, for the love of God? North of Manchuria? Manchuria? Or China, my China?

'Mother Russia stretches from sea to sea. Under God, Tai-Pan,' Zergeyev said simply. 'You should see the earth of Mother Russia to

382

understand what I mean. It is black and rich and filled with life. Yet we laid waste fifteen hundred miles of it to contain Bonaparte and his *Grande Armée*. You belong to the sea. But I belong to the land. I bequeath you the sea, Tai-Pan.' Zergeyev's eyes seemed to cloud over. 'That was a great battle this afternoon. And an interesting wager. Most interesting.'

The lines on Struan's cheeks deepened with his smile. 'A pity it was a draw. Now we'll never know – will we, Your Highness? – who was the better man.'

'I like you, Mr Struan. I would like to be your friend. We could be of great service to each other.'

'I'd be honoured to assist in any way.'

Zergeyev laughed, his teeth brilliant white. 'There's time enough. One advantage Asia has over Europe is its appreciation of time. My family comes from Karaganda. That's this side of the Urals, so perhaps, in part, I am Asian. We are Kazaki. Some people call us "Cossacks".'

'I dinna understand. The Urals?'

'A mountain chain that runs from the Arctic to the Caspian Sea. It splits Russia into east and west.'

'I know so little about Russia – or Europe, for that matter,' Struan said.

'You should come to Russia. Give me six months of your time and let me be your host. There is much to see, cities – and seas of grass. It could be a very profitable experience. Huge markets for tea and for silk and all manner of trade goods.' His eyes twinkled. 'And the women are most beautiful.'

'I'm a little busy this week, but perhaps next?'

'Now, let us not joke but be a little serious. Please consider it. Next year, the year after. I think it's very important. For you and your country and the future. Russia and Britain have never warred on each other. For centuries we've been allies, and we're both at odds with France, our hereditary enemy. Russia has huge land resources and millions of people, strong people. You're land-poor, so you need your Empire and we favour that. You rule the seas and we favour that. You have your astounding industrial power and the wealth it brings. We are greatly pleased. You have trade goods and the means to deliver them and we have markets. But we also have trade goods *you* can use: the raw materials that you need to feed your incredible machines, and food for your astonishing people. Together we're unbeatable. Together we can dominate France. And the Holy Roman Empire, Prussia and the infidel Turk. Together we can keep the peace. And grow and prosper to the benefit of all.'

'Aye,' Struan said, as seriously. 'I'm for that. But you're talking on a national level. From a historical point of view. That's na practical. And I dinna think you can blame Frenchmen for the ambition of her kings. Or justify changing Turks into Christians by the use of the sword. I had my say at lunch. On an international level, without some form of control over kings – and queens – we'll always have wars. His Excellency said it very well. Kings – and any form of leader – spill other people's blood. To be practical, there's little I can do. I dinna operate on a national level – and I've no real power in Parliament, as you well know.'

'But about Asia your opinion is carefully listened to. And I have great power in St Petersburg.'

Struan took a long pull on his cigar and then he exhaled.

'What do you want in Asia?'

'What do you want in China?'

'Trade,' Struan said immediately, but very much on guard and careful not to reveal his true aim. There's a devil of a difference, he said to himself, between Asia and China.

'I could, perhaps, see the Noble House was granted an exclusive tea-import licence for the market for all the Russias. And outward bound, all the fur exports and grain of all the Russias.'

'In return for what?' Struan said, overwhelmed by the enormousness of the offer. Such a monopoly would mean millions. And such a position of power would stand him in good stead in English political circles and give him enormous face.

'Friendship,' Zergeyev said.

'That word covers a multitude of meanings, Your Highness.'

'It has only one meaning, Mr Struan. Of course there are many ways a friend may help a friend.'

'What specific help would you specifically want in return for a specific trade agreement with my company?'

Zergeyev laughed. 'Those are too many specifics for one evening, Mr Struan. But it is worth thinking about and worth considering. And discussing at a specific time, eh?' He gazed over the harbour and past the ships to the mainland. 'You should come to Russia,' he repeated.

'When did you want it translated, Your Excellency?' Horatio looked up from the paper which Longstaff had handed him.

'Anytime, my dear fellow. In the next few days, what? But put the Chinese characters over the English words, eh?'

'Yes, sir. Should it be sent to someone?'

'No. Just give it back to me. Of course, it's a private matter.' Longstaff walked off, pleased with the way his scheme was progressing. The letter had said: 'His Excellency the English Captain Superintendent of Trade wishes to buy fifty pounds' weight of mulberry seeds or a thousand saplings, to be delivered as soon as possible.' All he had to do when Horatio returned it translated was substitute 'tea' for 'mulberry'. He could manage this himself; the Chinese character for tea was written on every box exported. Then he would wait until he had decided who could be trusted enough to receive it.

Standing alone, Horatio reread the letter. Now, why would Longstaff want mulberries? There were tens of thousands of mulberry trees, and their silkworms, in the south of France, and it would be simple to get seeds from there. But not simple to get them from China. Is Longstaff planning to plant a grove of trees here? But why fifty pounds? That's a fantastic quantity of seeds and he's no gardener. And why say pointedly, 'Of course it's a private matter'?

'Horatio?'

'Oh hello, George. How are you?'

'Fine, thank you.'

Horatio noticed that Glessing was perspiring and ill at ease. 'What's the matter?'

'Nothing. It's just that, well, there comes a time in every man's life . . . when he should . . . well, you meet someone who – I'm not putting it right. It's Mary. I want to marry her and I want your blessing.'

Horatio calmed himself with an effort and said what he had previously decided to say. He had been very conscious of Glessing's attention to Mary tonight and had remembered the look on his face on that first day. He loathed Glessing for daring to complicate his and Mary's life, and daring to have the impertinence to think that Mary would consider him for an instant. 'I'm most flattered, George. And Mary will be too. But she's, well, I don't think she's ready for marriage yet.'

'But of course she is. And I've fine prospects and my grandfather's going to leave me the manor. I'll be quite well-off and my service prospects are damned fine and I've—'

'Slow down, George. We must consider things very carefully. Have you discussed this with Mary?'

'Good Lord, no. Wanted to have your feeling first. Of course.'

'Well, why don't you leave it with me? I had no idea your intentions were serious. I'm afraid you must be patient with me – I've always thought of Mary as much younger than she is. She is, of course, under the age of consent,' he added carelessly.

'Then you approve in a general way?'

'Oh yes – but it never occurred to me that . . . well, in due time, when she's of age, I'm sure she'd welcome and be honoured by your suit.'

'You feel I should wait until she's twenty-one?'

'Well, I have only her interests at heart. She's my only sister and, well, we're very close to each other. Since Father died I've brought her up.'

'Yes,' Glessing said, feeling flattered. 'Damn fine job you did too. Damned decent of you to consider me at all; she's so – well, I think she's wonderful.'

'Still, it's best to be patient. Marriage is such a final step. Particularly for someone like Mary.'

'Yes. Quite right. Well, let's have a drink to the future, eh? I'm in no hurry to – well, but I'd like a formal answer. Plans must be made, mustn't they?'

'Of course. Let's drink to the future.'

'Devil take it,' Brock said as Gorth came up to him. 'Struan's be having every godrotting foot of cargo space outside of our ships. How'd they be doing that? This morning? Baint reasonable!'

'It be almost like he'd advance news – but that be impossible.'

'Well, no matter, by God,' Brock said, smug with the knowledge that he had a ship speeding for Manila but unaware that Struan's ship was hours ahead. 'That were a dance all right, weren't it?'

'Culum be fair taken with our Tess, Da'.'

'Yus – I marked that too. It be time she went home.'

'Not afore the judging.' Gorth's eyes burned into his father's. 'A match 'twixt they two'd be right good for us.'

'Never, by God,' Brock said tightly, his face reddening.

'I say yes, by God. I heard a rumour – from one of our'n Portuguese clerks, who hav' it from one of the Struans – that the Tai-Pan be goin' home in half a year.'

'Wot?'

'Leaving for good.'

'I doan believe it.'

'With that devil out, who's Tai-Pan, eh? Robb.' Gorth spat neatly. 'We can eat up Robb. Afore the land sale I'd say we could chew Culum like salt pork. Now I baint sure. But if Tess were his wife – then it's Brock-Struan and Company. After Robb, Culum's Tai-Pan.'

'Dirk be never leaving. Never. Thee's crazy in thy head. Just because Culum be dancin' with her doan mean—'

'Get it through thy head, Da',' Gorth interrupted. 'One day Struan be leaving. Common knowledge he wants in t' Parliament. Like thee'll want to retire. One day.'

'There be time enough for that, by God.'

'Yes. But one day thee'll retire, eh? Then I'm Tai-Pan.' Gorth's voice was not harsh, but calm and final. 'I be Tai-Pan of Noble House, by God, not the second house. Culum-Tess'd fix it clever.'

'Dirk'll never leave,' Brock said, hating Gorth for implying that where he had failed Gorth would succeed.

'I be thinking of us'n, Da'! An' our house. An' how you and me beed working day and night to beat him. An' about the future. Culum-Tess be perfect,' Gorth added inflexibly.

Brock bristled at the challenge. He knew that in time he would have to pass over the reins. But not soon, by God. For without the house, and without being Tai-Pan of Brock's, he would shrivel and die. 'Wot makes thee think it be Brock-Struan? Why not Struan-Brock and he be Tai-Pan and thee out?'

'Doan thee worry, Da'. With thee an' devil Struan it be like the fight today. Thee's both equal matched. Both equal strong, equal cunning. But me an' Culum? That be different.'

'I be thinking about wot thee says. Then I decides.'

'Of course, Da'. You be Tai-Pan. With joss, you'd be Tai-Pan o' The Noble House afore me.' Gorth smiled and walked towards Culum and Horatio.

Brock eased the patch over his eye and watched his son, so tall and dynamic and strong, and young. He looked at Culum, then glanced around, seeking Struan. He saw the Tai-Pan standing alone, down by the shore, looking out into the harbour. Brock's love for Tess and his wish for her happiness was balanced against the truth of what Gorth had said. And he knew with equal truth that Gorth would eat up Culum if conflict was joined between them – and that Gorth would force the issue in time. Beed that right? To let Gorth eat up the husband that mayhaps Tess loved?

He wondered what he would really do if the love blossomed – what Struan would do. It be solving us'n, he told himself. An' that baint a wrong thing, eh? Yus. But you knowed old Dirk be never leaving Cathay – nor thee – and there'll be a settling 'twixt thee and him.

He hardened his heart, loathing Gorth for making him feel old.

Knowing that even so he must settle the Tai-Pan. For Gorth against Culum with Struan alive was no contest.

When the ladies came back, there were more dancing, but the Kankana was not repeated. Struan danced first with Mary and she enjoyed it greatly; his strength calmed her and cleaned her and gave her courage.

Next he chose Shevaun. She pressed close enough to him to be exciting, but not close enough to be indelicate. Her warmth and perfume surrounded him. He half noticed Mary being led off the floor by Horatio, and when he turned again, he saw that they were strolling down to the shore. Then he heard the ship's bells. Half past eleven. Time to see May-may.

When the dance ended he escorted Shevaun back to the table. 'Would you excuse me a moment, Shevaun?'

'Of course, Dirk. Hurry back.'

'I will,' he said.

'It's a beautiful night,' Mary said awkwardly.

'Yes.' Horatio held her arm lightly. 'I wanted to tell you something amusing. George drew me aside and asked, formally, for your hand in marriage.'

'You're astonished that anyone would want to marry me?' she asked coldly.

'Of course not, Mary. I meant it's preposterous for him to think you'd consider such a pompous ass as himself, that's all.'

She examined her fan and then stared into the night, troubled.

'I said that I thought he—'

'I know what you said, Horatio.' She cut him off sharply. 'You were sweet and sloughed him off with "time" and "my dear only sister". I think I'm going to marry George.'

'You can't! You can't possibly like that bore enough to consider him for even a moment.'

'I think I'm going to marry George. At Christmas. If there is a Christmas.'

'What do you mean – if there is a Christmas?'

'Nothing, Horatio. I like him enough to marry him, and I'm – well, I think it's time to leave.'

'I don't believe it.'

'I don't believe it myself.' Her voice trembled. 'But if George wants to marry me – I've decided George is a good choice for me.'

'But, Mary, I need you with me. I love you and you know—'

Her eyes flashed suddenly, and all the pent-up bitterness and agony of years choked her. 'Don't talk about love to me!'

His face became deadly white and his lips trembled. 'I've asked God to forgive us a million times.'

'Asking God to forgive "us" is a little late, isn't it?'

It had begun after a flogging when he was young and she was very young. They had crept into bed together, clutching each other to black out the horror and pain. She was comforted by the heat of their bodies, and she felt a new pain which made her forget the beating. There were other times, happy times – she too young to understand, but not Horatio; then he had left for school in England. When he returned they had never referred to what had happened. For by then both knew what it meant.

'I swear by God I've begged forgiveness.'

'I'm so glad, brother. But there is no God,' she said, her voice flat and cruel. 'I forgive you. But that won't make me virgin, will it?'

'Mary, I beg you, please, for the love of God, please—'

'I forgive you everything, brother dear. Except your rotten hypocrisy. We didn't sin – you did. Pray for your own soul, not mine.'

'I pray for yours more than mine. We sinned, God help us. But the Lord will forgive. He will, Mary.'

'This year, with joss, I'll marry George and forget you and forget Asia.'

'You're not the age of consent. You can't go. I'm your legal guardian. I can't let you go. In time you'll see how wise it is. It's best for you. I forbid you to leave. That scum's not good enough for you, you hear? You're not leaving!'

'When I decide to marry Glessing,' she hissed, her voice clawing him, 'you'd better give your fornicating "approval" in a hurry, because if you don't I'll tell everyone – no, I'll tell the Tai-Pan first and he'll come after you with a lash. I've nothing to lose – nothing. And all your godrotting praying to your non-existent God and to Father's sweet Christ won't help you a bit. Because there's no God and never was and never will be, and Christ was only a man – a saint but still a man!'

'You're not Mary; you're – his voice cracked – 'you're evil. Of course God exists. Of course we've souls. You're a heretic. You're a fiend! It was you, not me! Oh Lord God, give us Thy Mercy—'

Mary struck him with the flat of her hand. 'Stop it, brother dear. I'm sick of your useless praying. You hear? You've made my flesh crawl for years. Because I know from the lust in your eyes that you still want to bed me. Even though you understand incest, and you understood it before you began.' She laughed, a terrifying laugh. 'You're worse than Father. He was mad with belief, but you – you only pretend to believe. I hope your God exists, because you'll burn in hellfire for ever. And good riddance.'

She left. Her brother stared after her, then ran blindly into the night.

XXIII

'Heya, Mass'er!' Lim Din said, throwing open the door with a flourish.

'Heya, Lim Din,' Struan said, checking the barometer. Fair weather, 29.8 inches. Excellent.

He began to walk down the corridor, but Lim Din stood in the way and motioned importantly to the living-room. 'Missee say here-ah can. Can?'

Struan grunted, 'Can.'

Lim Din gave him the brandy that was already poured and bowed him into the high-back leather chair and hurried away. Struan put his feet on the ottoman. The chair smelled tangy and old and comfortable and mixed nicely with Shevaun's perfume that still seemed to surround him.

The clock on the mantel read twenty minutes to twelve.

Struan began to hum a sea chanty. He heard a door open, and the approaching rustle of silk. Waiting for May-may to appear in the doorway, he again compared her and Shevaun. He had been comparing them all evening, trying to weigh them dispassionately. Shevaun was a beautiful toy, dynamic certainly, and vital. A woman he would like to tame, aye. And as a wife Shevaun would be a superb hostess – assured, clever, and the opener of many doors. May-may would be an extreme gamble in England – as a wife. As mistress, nay. Aye, he told himself. Even so I'm going to marry her. With the power of The Noble House behind me, and an exclusive Russian licence in my pocket, I can risk thumbing my nose at convention and break an almost insurmountable barrier between Occident and Orient. May-may'll prove, beyond all doubt – for all time – among the people that really count in society, that the Oriental is completely worthy and worthwhile. May-may hersel' will hasten the day of equality. And it'll be in my own lifetime.

Aye, he exulted to himself. May-may's a marvellous gamble. Together we can do it. For all time. With joss, the whole of London will be at her feet.

Then his joy shattered.

May-may was standing in the doorway, a radiant smile on her face as she twirled. Her European dress was violently multi-coloured, bejewelled, its skirt huge and bustled. Her hair hung in curled ringlets on her bare shoulders and a feathered hat was on her head. She looked hideous. A nightmare.

'God's blood!'

There was an awful silence as they stared at each other.

'It's – it's very . . . nice,' he said, unconvincingly, crushed by the pain in May-may's eyes.

May-may was eerily pale now, except for two crimson splotches high on her cheeks. She knew she had lost face terribly before Struan. She swayed, near fainting. Then she whimpered and fled.

Struan rushed after her down the corridor. He tore through her private quarters. But the bedroom was bolted against him.

'May-may, lass. Open the door.'

There was no answer, and he was conscious of Lim Din and Ah Sam behind him. When he turned they vanished, petrified.

'May-may! Open the door!'

Still no answer. He was furious with himself for having been unable to mask his feelings, and for having been so stupid and unprepared. Of course May-may would want to be part of the ball and of course all her questions should have warned him, and of course she'd have a ball gown made and – oh Jesus Christ!

'Open the door!'

Again no answer. He crashed his foot against the door. It burst open and hung precariously on its shattered hinges.

May-may was standing beside the bed, looking at the floor.

'You shouldn't have bolted the door, lass. You – well, you – the dress and you just stunned me for a moment.' He knew that he must give her back her face or she would die. Die from misery or die by her own hand. 'Come on,' he said. 'We're going to the ball.'

As she fell to her knees to kowtow to him and beg his forgiveness, the dress got in her way and made her stumble. May-may opened her mouth to speak, but no sound came out. The feathered hat slid off.

Struan hurried over to her and began to pick her up. 'Come on, May-may lass, you mustn't do that.'

But she would not be helped up. She buried her face deeper in the carpet and tried to claw it with her nails.

He lifted her awkwardly and held her. She would not look at him. He took her hand firmly. 'Come on.'

'Wat?' she said dully.

'We're going to the ball.' He knew that it would be a disaster for himself and for her. He knew he would be socially destroyed and she would be ridiculed. Even so he knew that he must take her or her spirit would die. 'Come on,' he repeated, a scarred edge to his voice. But she continued to stare at the floor, trembling.

He pulled her gently but she almost fell. Then he grimly picked her up and she lay in his arms, a dead weight. He began to carry her out. 'We're going, and that's the end of it.'

'Wait,' she croaked. 'I – I – I must, the – the hat.'

He put her down and she went back into the bedroom, her swaying gait made ugly by the dress. Struan knew that nothing would ever be quite the same again between them. She had made a horrible mistake. He should have anticipated it, aye, but—

He saw her darting for the razor-sharp stiletto that she used for embroidery. He reached her just as she was starting to turn it into herself, and grabbed the haft of the knife. The point glanced off the whale bone of May-may's corset. He hurled the knife aside and tried to hold her, but, raving in Chinese, she pushed him away and clawed at the dress, mutilating it. Struan quickly turned her around and undid the hooks and eyes. May-may ripped the front apart and fought out of the gown and out of the corset and slashed the pantaloons. When she was free, she stamped on the dress, screaming.

'Stop it!' he shouted, and caught her, but she shoved him away, berserk. '*Stop it!*'

He smashed her flat-handed across the face. She reeled away drunkenly and fell across the bed. Her eyes fluttered, and she lost consciousness.

It took Struan a moment to overcome the hammering in his ears. He pulled the bedclothes off and covered May-may.

'Ah Sam! Lim Din!'

The two petrified faces were at the broken doorway.

'Tea – quick-quick! No. Get brandy.'

Lim Din returned with the bottle. Struan lifted May-may gently and helped her to drink. She choked a little. Then her eyes trembled and opened. They stared at him without recognition.

'You all right, lass? You all right, May-may?'

She made no sign that she had heard him. Her frightening gaze fell on the mutilated dress and she cringed piteously. A moan escaped her and she mumbled something in Chinese. Ah Sam came forward reluctantly, consumed with terror. She knelt and began to scoop up the clothes.

'What did she say? Wat Missee say-ah?' Struan kept his eyes unwaveringly on May-may.

'Devil clotheses fire, Mass'er.'

'No fire, Ah Sam. Put my room. Hide. Hide. Savvy?'

'Savvy, Mass'er.'

'Then come back.'

'Savvy, Mass'er.'

Struan waved his hand in dismissal at Lim Din, who scurried away.

'Come on, lassie,' he said gently, terrified by the fixity – and the madness – of her stare. 'Let's get you dressed your usual clothes. You have to come to the ball. I want you to meet my friends.'

He took a step towards her and she backed away abruptly like a snake at bay. He stopped. Her face twitched and her fingers were like talons. A wisp of saliva gathered in a corner of her mouth. Her eyes were terrifying.

Fear for her swept him. He had seen the same look in other eyes. In the eyes of the marine, just before his brain had blown apart, on the first day of Hong Kong.

He sped a silent prayer to the Infinite and gathered all his will. 'I love you, May-may,' he said softly, again and again, as he walked slowly across the room. Closer. Slowly, so slowly. He towered over her now, and saw the talons ready to strike. He raised his hands and gently touched her face. 'I love you,' he repeated. His eyes, dangerously unprotected, willed her with the vastness of their power. 'I need you, lassie, I need you.'

The madness in her eyes changed to agony, and she fell sobbing into his arms. He held her and thanked God weakly.

'I'm – I – sorry,' she whimpered.

'Dinna be sorry, lassie. There, there.'

He carried her to the bed and sat with her in his arms, rocking her like a child. 'There, there.'

'Leave . . . me, now. All . . . all right now.'

'I'll do nae such thing,' he said. 'First gather your strength, then we'll dress and we'll go to the ball.'

She shook her head through her tears. 'No . . . can't. I – please . . .' She stopped weeping and, easing herself out of his arms, stood up, swaying. Struan caught her and guided her into bed, helping to pull off the tattered clothes. He settled the bedclothes over her. She lay limp in the bed and closed her eyes, exhausted.

'Please. All right now. Must . . . sleep. You go.'

He stroked her head gently, pushing the obscene ringlets out of her face.

Later he was conscious that Ah Sam was standing in the doorway. The girl came into the room, tears streaking her cheeks. 'You goa, Mass'er,' she whispered. 'Ah Sam watchee, nev' mind. No fraid. Can.'

He nodded wearily. May-may was deep asleep. Ah Sam knelt beside the bed and softly, tenderly, stroked May-may's head. 'No fraid, Mass'er. Ah Sam watchee werry wen Mass'er come by.'

Struan tiptoed out of the room.

XXIV

Culum was the first to greet Struan when he returned to the ball.

'Can we start the judging?' he asked brusquely. Nothing could destroy his euphoria over his new-found love, and her brother, his new-found friend. But he still played the game.

'You should na have waited,' Struan harshly replied. 'Where's Robb? God's blood, do I have to do everything?'

'He had to leave. Word came that Aunt Sarah's labour pains have started. There seems to be some trouble.'

'What?'

'I don't know. But Mrs Brock went with him to see if she could help.'

Culum walked off. Struan hardly noticed his going. His worry for May-may returned, and now it was overlaid with concern for Sarah and Robb. But Liza Brock was the best midwife in Asia, and if any help were needed, Sarah would get it.

Shevaun approached, bringing him a brandy. She handed him the glass without a word, and put her arm lightly in his. She knew there was no need for conversation. At such a time it was best to say nothing: think as much as you like, but no questions. For even the most powerful person, she knew, needed a silent, understanding, patient warmth at times. So she waited and let her presence surround him.

Struan drank the brandy slowly. His eyes flickered over the throng and saw that all was well: merriment here and there, fans fluttering, swords glinting. He watched Brock in private conversation with the archduke. Brock was listening and nodding occasionally and totally concentrated. Was Zergeyev offering him the licence? Mary was fanning herself beside Glessing. Something amiss there, he told himself. Tess and Culum and Gorth were laughing with one another. Good.

And when Struan had finished the brandy and was whole, he looked down at Shevaun. 'Thank you,' he said, contrasting the grotesqueness of May-may in European dress and hair style with the perfection of Shevaun. 'You're very beautiful and very understanding.'

His voice was morose, and she knew that it must have something to do with his mistress. No matter, she thought, and held his arm compassionately.

'I'm fine now,' he said.

'Mr Quance is coming over,' she cautioned him softly. 'It's time for the judging.'

The light green of his eyes darkened. 'You're very wise, Shevaun, apart from being beautiful.'

It was on the tip of her tongue to thank him but she said nothing, only moved her fan a trifle. She sensed that the brandy and silence and understanding – and above all no questions – had done much to bring him to the brink of a decision.

'Ah, Tai-Pan, my dear fellow,' Quance said as he came up, his eyes merry, an alcoholic flush enveloping him. 'It's time for the judging!'

'Very good, Aristotle.'

'Then make the announcement and let's have at it!'

'*Mr Quance!*' Like a roll of thunder the words tore through the night. Everyone turned, startled.

Quance groaned mightily.

Maureen Quance was standing there, her eyes grinding him to dust. She was a tall, big-boned Irishwoman with a face like a piece of leather and a large nose and legs planted like oaks. She was of an age with Quance but strong as an ox, her iron-grey hair in an untidy bun. When she was young she had been attractive, but now with the girth created by potatoes and beer she was overpowering. 'The top of the evening to you, Mr Quance, me fine boy,' she said. ''Tis herself, glory be to God!'

She plodded across the dance floor oblivious of the stares and the embarrassed silence and stood in front of her husband. 'I've been after looking for you, me fine boy.'

'Oh?' he said in a trembling falsetto.

'Oh it is.' She turned her head. 'Top the night, Mr Struan, and I'll be thanking you for the lodgings and vittles. Glory be to God, herself has caught the wretch.'

'You're, er, looking fine, Mrs Quance.'

'Indeed I feel as fine as a body can feel. 'Twas a blessed miracle from St Patrick himself that sent a native boat to herself and guided her footsteps to this immortal spot.' She turned her lugubrious eyes on Aristotle and he quavered. 'We'll be saying good night now, me darlin' man!'

'But, Mrs Quance,' Struan said quickly, remembering the judging, 'Mr Quance has something that—'

'We'll be saying good night,' she growled. 'Say good night, me boy.'

'Good night, Tai-Pan,' Aristotle squeaked. Meekly he allowed Maureen to take him by the arm and lead him away.

After they had gone, the place erupted in laughter.

'God's death,' Struan said. 'Poor old Aristotle.'

'What's happened to Mr Quance?' Zergeyev asked.

Struan explained Aristotle's domestic tribulations.

'Perhaps we should rescue him,' Zergeyev said. 'I took a distinct liking to him.'

'We can hardly interfere between husband and wife, can we?'

'I suppose not. But who's going to judge the contest?'

'I suppose I'll have to.'

Zergeyev's eyes crinkled. 'May I volunteer? As a friend?'

Struan studied him. Then he turned on his heel and strode to the centre of the floor. The bands played a loud chord.

'Your Excellency, Your Highness, ladies and gentlemen. There is a contest to be judged for the best-dressed lady of the evening. I'm afraid our immortal Quance is otherwise engaged. But His Highness Archduke Zergeyev has volunteered to make the choice.' Struan looked at Zergeyev and began to clap. His applause was taken up, and there was a roar of approval as Zergeyev came forward.

Zergeyev took the bag with the thousand guineas. 'Who shall I choose, Tai-Pan?' he asked out of the corner of his mouth. 'The Tillman for you, the Vargas for me, the Sinclair because she's the most intriguing? Choose who's to win.'

'It's your choice, my friend,' Struan said, and with a calm smile he walked away.

Zergeyev waited a moment, enjoying the thrill of choosing. He knew that he must pick whom the Tai-Pan wanted. He made up his mind and walked across the floor, bowed and put the bag of gold at her feet. 'I believe this belongs to you, Miss Brock.'

Tess stared at the archduke blankly. Then she flushed as the silence broke.

There was loud applause, and those who had backed Tess at long odds screamed with delight.

Shevaun clapped with the crowd and contained her resentment. She knew it was a wise choice. 'The ideal political choice, Tai-Pan,' she whispered calmly. 'You're very clever.'

'It was the archduke's decision, na mine.'

'Another reason I like you, Tai-Pan. You're a huge gambler and your joss is unbelievable.'

'And you're a woman among women.'

'Yes,' she said without vanity. 'I understand politics very well. My father – or one of my brothers – will be President of the United States one day.'

'You should be in Europe,' he said. 'You're wasted out here.'

'Am I?' Her eyes challenged him.

XXV

Struan entered the house quietly. It was almost dawn. Lim Din was
sleeping beside the door and he awoke with a start.

'Tea, Mass'er? Breakfas'?' he asked sleepily.

'Lim Din bed,' Struan said kindly.

'Yes, Mass'er.' He padded away.

As Struan walked down the corridor, he glanced into the living-room
and stopped. May-may, pale and motionless, was sitting in the leather
chair, watching him.

When he came into the room, she got up and bowed gracefully. Her
hair was piled on her head and pulled back, her sloe eyes delicate, her
eyebrows arched. She wore a long and flowing Chinese robe.

'How are you, lass?' he asked.

'Thank you, this slave is well now.' The pallor and the cool green of
her silken gown added to the immensity of her dignity. 'Would you
brandy have?'

'No thanks.'

'Tea?'

He shook his head, awed by her majesty. 'I'm glad you're better. You
should be in bed.'

'This slave begs you to forgive her. This slave—'

'You're na a slave and never have been. Now, there's nothing to
forgive, lass, so off to bed.'

She waited patiently until he had finished. 'This slave begs you listen.
She must say in own what must be said. Please sit.'

A tear slipped from the corner of each eye and skidded down the
whiteness of her cheeks.

He sat, almost mesmerized by her.

'This slave begs her master to sell her.'

'You're na a slave, and you canna be sold or bought.'

'Please to sell. To anyone. To whorehouse or to another slave.'

'You're na for sale.'

'This slave offended you beyond bearing. Please to sell.'

'You have na offended me.' He got up and his voice was metallic. 'Now, off to bed.'

She fell on to her knees and kowtowed. 'This slave has nae face before her lord and owner. She cannot live here. Please to sell!'

'Get up!' Struan's face tightened.

She rose. Her face was shadowed and ethereal.

'You're na for sale because no one owns you. You will stay here. You have na offended me. You surprised me, that's all. European clothes do na suit you. The clothes you wear I like. And I like you as you are. But if you dinna want to stay, you're free to leave.'

'Please to sell. This is your slave. Until an owner sells, a slave cannot go.'

Struan was near exploding. Control yoursel', he told himself desperately. If you lose your temper now, you lose her for ever. 'Go to bed.'

'You must sell this slave. Sell this slave or order her to go.'

Struan realized that it was useless to argue or reason with May-may. You canna treat her as a European, he told himself. Deal with her as though you're Chinese. But how's that? I dinna ken. Treat her as a woman, he ordered himself, deciding on a tactic.

He exploded with pretended rage. 'You are a miserable slave, by God! And I've a mind to sell you into the Street of the Blue Lanterns,' he shouted, naming the worst of the seamen's streets in Macao, 'though who'd want to buy a dirty baggage slave like you I dinna ken. You're nothing but trouble and I've a mind to give you to the lepers. Aye, by God! I paid eight thousand taels of good silver for you, and how dare you make me angry? I was cheated, by God! You're worthless! Dirty slave – how I've put up with you these years I dinna ken!' He shook his fist in her face, and she recoiled. 'Am I na good to you? Eh? Generous? *Eh? Eh?*' he roared, and was pleased to detect fear in her eyes. '*Well?*'

'Yes, lord,' she whispered, biting her lips.

'You dare to get clothes made behind my back and dare to wear them wi'out my approval, by God? Well, *do you?*'

'Yes, lord.'

'I'll sell you tomorrow. I've a mind to throw you out now, you miserable motherless whore! Kowtow! Go on, kowtow, by God!'

She blanched at his fury and kowtowed quickly.

'Now keep kowtowing until I come back!'

He stormed out of the room, and went into the garden. He jerked out his knife and selected a thin bamboo from a newly planted grove. He cut it and slashed the air and rushed back into the living-room.

401

'Take your clothes off, you miserable slave! I'm going to flog you till my arm hurts!'

Trembling, she stripped. He seized the dress from her hand and threw it aside.

'Lie down there.' He pointed at the ottoman.

She did as he ordered. 'Please no to whip me too hard – I'm two months with child.' She buried her head in the ottoman.

Struan wanted to take her in his arms, but he knew that this would make him lose face in front of her. And a whipping was the only way to give her back her dignity.

So he slashed her buttocks with the bamboo. Hard enough to hurt, but not to damage. Soon she was crying out and weeping and squirming, but he kept on. Twice he deliberately missed her and slashed the leather violently, so that the noise was terrifying, for the benefit of Lim Din and Ah Sam who he knew would be listening.

After ten blows he paused and told her to stay where she was, and went over to the brandy bottle. He drank deeply, hurled the bottle against the wall, and resumed the whipping. But always with great care.

Finally he stopped and dragged her up by the hair. 'Put on your clothes, you miserable slave!' When she was dressed, he bellowed, '*Lim Din! Ah Sam!*'

They were trembling at the door in an instant.

'Wat for nae tea nae food, you miserable slaves! Get food!'

He hurled the bamboo at the side of the door and turned back to May-may.

'Kowtow, you motherless wreck!'

Aghast at the limitlessness of his fury, she hastily complied.

'Clean yoursel' and come back here. Thirty seconds or I'll start all over again!'

Lim Din served the tea and though it was just right, Struan said it was too cold and threw the teapot against the wall. May-may and Lim Din and Ah Sam rushed away and hurried back with more.

The food came with incredible speed also, and Struan allowed himself to be served by May-may. She whimpered with pain and he shouted, 'Shut up or I'll whip you for ever!'

Then he fell silent, ominously, and ate, letting the quiet torture them.

'Pick the bamboo up!' he screamed as he finished.

May-may fetched the bamboo and handed it to him. He prodded her in the stomach. 'Bed!' he ordered harshly, and Lim Din and Ah Sam fled, secure in the knowledge that the Tai-Pan had forgiven his Tai-tai, who had gained limitless face by enduring his righteous fury.

May-may turned around tearfully and went along the corridor towards her quarters, but he snarled, 'My bed, by God!'

She ran into his room. He followed and crashed the door shut, and bolted it.

'So, you're with child. Whose child?'

'Yours, lord,' she whimpered.

He sat down and extended a booted foot. 'Come on, hurry up.'

She fell on her knees and pulled off the boots and then stood beside the bed.

'How dare you think I'd want you to meet my friends? When I want to take you out of the house, I'll tell you, by God.'

'Yes, lord.'

'A woman's place is in the home. *Here!*'

'Yes, lord.'

He allowed his face to soften a trace. 'That's better, by God.'

'I did na want to go to ball,' she said in a tiny whisper. 'Only to dress like . . . I never want ball. How for go ball – never never want. Only to please. Sorry. Very sorry.'

'Why should I forgive you, eh?' He began to undress. 'Eh?'

'No reason – none.' Now she was crying piteously, silently. But he knew that now was too soon to relent completely.

'Perhaps, as you're with child, I may give you another chance. But it better be a son, not a worthless girl.'

'Oh yes – please, please. Please forgive.' She kowtowed and knocked her head on the floor.

Her crying was tearing at him, but he continued to undress sullenly. Then he blew the lantern out and got into bed.

He left her standing.

After a minute or two he said curtly, 'Get into bed. I'm cold.'

Later, when he could stand her weeping no more, he put his arms around her tenderly and kissed her. 'You're forgiven, lass.'

She cried herself to sleep in his arms.

BOOK FOUR

With the passing weeks spring became early summer. The sun gathered strength and the air became heavy with moisture. The Europeans in their regular clothes and long woollen underwear – and bustled dresses and whalebone corsets – suffered intensely. Sweat dried in the armpits and groin, and festering sores erupted. The usual summer sickness began – the Canton gutrot, the Macao flux, the Asian distemper. Those who died were mourned. The living stoically endured their torments as unavoidable tribulations sent by the good Lord to plague mankind, and continued to close their windows against the air which all believed carried the noxious gases that the earth emanated in summer; they continued to allow their doctors to purge them and leech them, for all knew that that was the only real cure for sickness; they continued to drink fly-touched water and eat flyblown meats; they continued to avoid bathing, which all knew was dangerous to health; and they continued to pray for the cool of winter, which would once more clean the earth of its more deadly poisons.

By June the distemper had decimated the ranks of the soldiers. The trading season was almost over. This year huge fortunes would be made. With joss. For never had the buying and the selling been so extravagant at the Canton Settlement. The traders and their Portuguese clerks and their Chinese compradors, and the Co-hong merchants, were all exhausted by the heat but more by the weeks of frantic activity. All were ready to relax until the winter's buying could begin.

And this year at long last, unlike any previous year, the Europeans were looking forward to summering in their own homes, on their own soil of Hong Kong.

Their families at Hong Kong had already moved from the cramped shipboard quarters to Happy Valley. Construction had boomed. Queen's Town was already taking shape: streets, warehouses, jail, wharves, two hotels, taverns, and houses.

The taverns that catered to the soldiers were nesting near the tents by Glessing's Point. Those that served the sailors were opposite the dockyard on Queen's Road. Some of these were tents, crude, temporary structures. Others were more permanent.

Ships arrived from home bringing supplies and relatives and friends, and many strangers. And each tide brought more people from Macao – Portuguese, Chinese, Eurasian, European – sail-makers, weavers, tailors, clerks, servants, businessmen, sellers and buyers, coolies, job seekers or those whose job now forced them to Hong Kong: all who served the China trade, all who lived upon it, or fed off it. Those who came included madams, girls, opium users, gin makers, gamblers and smugglers and pickpockets and kidnappers and thieves and beggars and pirates – the dross of all nations. These too found dwellings, or began to build dwellings and places of business. Gin shops, brothels, opium cellars began to infest Queen's Town and spot Queen's Road. Crime increased violently, and the police force, such as it was, was engulfed. Wednesday became whipping day. To the enjoyment of the righteous, convicted felons were publicly flogged outside the jail as a warning to the evil.

British justice, though quick and harsh, did not seem cruel to the Chinese. Public torture, and beatings to death, thumb-screws and mutilation and loss of eye or eyes or hand or hands or foot or feet, branding, flesh slicing, garroting, blinding, tongue ripping, genital crushing – all were conventional Chinese punishments. The Chinese had no trial by jury. Since Hong Kong was beyond the pale of Chinese justice, all criminals on the mainland who could escape fled to the safety of Tai Ping Shan and scoffed at the weakness of barbarian law.

And as civilization flourished on the island, refuse began to collect. With the refuse came the flies.

Water began to stagnate in discarded barrels, in broken pots and pans. It was cupped in bamboo scaffoldings, in the beginnings of gardens, and in the thin marsh of the valley basin. These small putrid waters began to seethe with life: larvae, which became mosquitoes. They were tiny, fragile and very special – and so delicate that they flew only when the sun was down: the Anopheles.

And the people in Happy Valley began to die.

XXVI

'For God's sake, Culum, I dinna ken any more than you do. There's a killer fever down in Queen's Town. No one knows what causes it and now little Karen's got it.' Struan was miserable. He had not heard from May-may for a week. He had been gone from Hong Kong for almost two months, except for a hurried visit of two days, some weeks ago, when his need to see May-may overpowered him. She was blossoming, her pregnancy was without sickness, and they were more content with each other than they had ever been. 'Thank the Lord our last ship's gone and we're leaving the Settlement tomorrow!'

'Uncle Robb says it's malaria,' Culum said heatedly, brandishing Robb's letter that had just arrived. He was frantic with worry over Tess. Only yesterday he had received a letter from her saying that she and her sister and mother had moved off the ship into Brock's partially completed factory. But no mention had been made of malaria. 'What's the cure for malaria?'

'There is na one that I know. I'm no doctor. And Robb says only a few of the doctors think it's malaria.' Struan waved the fly whisk irritably. '"Malaria" is Latin for "bad air". That's all I know – anyone knows. Mother of God, if the air of Happy Valley's bad, we're ruined!'

'I told you not to build there,' Culum raged. 'I hated that valley the first time I saw it!'

'By the blood of Christ, are you saying you knew in advance the air was rotten?'

'No. I didn't mean that. I mean – well, I hated the place, that's all.'

Struan slammed the window shut against the stench from the Settlement square and fanned more flies away. He prayed that the fever wasn't malaria. If it was, the plague could touch anyone who slept in Happy Valley. It was common knowledge that the earth in certain areas in the world was malaria-poisoned and for some reason gave off lethal gases by night.

According to Robb, the fever had begun mysteriously four weeks ago. First it had struck the Chinese labourers. Then it had afflicted others – European trader here, a child there. But only in Happy Valley. Nowhere else on Hong Kong. Now four or five hundred Chinese were infected, and twenty or thirty Europeans. The Chinese were superstitiously afraid, certain that the gods were punishing them for working on Hong Kong against the emperor's decree. Only increased wages had persuaded them to return.

And now little Karen was smitten. Robb had ended the letter: 'Sarah and I are desperate. The course of the sickness is insidious. First a ghastly fever for half a day, then a recovery, then a more severe recurrence of the fever in two or three days. The cycle is repeated again and again, each attack worse than before. The doctors have given Karen as strong a calomel purgative as they dare. They've bled the poor child but we don't hope for much. The coolies have been dying after the third or fourth attack. And Karen is so weak after the purgative and leeching, so very weak. God help us, I think Karen's lost.'

Struan strode for the door. Good God, first the baby, now Karen! Sarah had given birth to a son, Lochlin Ross, the day after the ball, but the child had been born sickly, his left arm damaged. Her labour had been very hard and she had almost died. But she had escaped the dreaded childbirth sickness, and though her milk had turned sour and her hair had greyed, her strength had gradually returned. When Struan had gone back to see May-may, he had visited Sarah. The lines of anguish and bitterness had etched themselves deep into her face, and she looked like an old woman. Struan had been further saddened when he had seen the babe: useless left arm, sickly, crying piteously, not expected to live. I wonder if babe's dead, Struan thought as he jerked the door open; Robb does na mention him.

'Vargas!'

'Yes, senhor?'

'Have you ever had malaria in Macao?'

'No, senhor.' Vargas whitened. His son and nephew worked for The Noble House and now they lived on Hong Kong. 'Are they sure it's malaria?'

'No. Only some of the doctors think so. Na all of them. Find Mauss. Tell him I want to see Jin-qua right smartly. With him.'

'Yes, senhor. His Excellency wants you to dine with him and the archduke tonight at nine o'clock.'

'Accept for me.'

'Yes, senhor.'

Struan closed the door and grimly sat down. He wore a light shirt without cravat, and light trousers and light boots. The other Europeans thought him mad to risk the devilish chills that all knew were borne by the summer winds.

'It canna be malaria,' he said. 'Na malaria. Something else.'

'The island's accursed.'

'Now you're talking like a woman,' Struan said.

'The fever wasn't there before the coolies. Get rid of the coolies and you'll be rid of the plague. They're carrying it with them. *They're* doing it.'

'How do we know that, Culum? I'll admit it started in the coolie lines. And I'll agree they live in the low-lying parts. And I'll agree that as far as we know you can only get malaria by breathing the poisoned night air. But why is there fever only in the valley? Is it only Happy Valley that's got bad air? Air's air, for the love of Christ, and there's a fine breeze blowing there most of the day and night. It does na make sense.'

'It makes very good sense. It's the will of God.'

'The pox on that for an answer!'

Culum was on his feet. 'I'll thank you not to blaspheme.'

'And I'll thank you to remember that not so many years ago men were burned at the stake just for saying the earth went round the sun! It's na the will of God!'

'Whatever *you* think, God has a vital and continuing say in our lives. The fact that the fever's in the one place we choose in Asia to live in is, I think, the will of God. You can't deny it because you can't prove otherwise, any more than I can prove it's true. But I believe it is – most do – and I believe we should abandon Happy Valley.'

'If we do that, we abandon Hong Kong.'

'We could build on the ground near Glessing's Point.'

'Do you know how much money we and all the traders've invested in Happy Valley?'

'Do you know how much money you can enjoy when you're six feet underground?'

Struan coldly appraised his son. For weeks now he had come to know that Culum's hostility was increasingly real. But he did not mind that. He knew that the more Culum learned, the more he would seek to put his own ideas into effect and the more he would crave power. That's fair, he thought and was greatly satisfied with Culum's development. At the same time he was worried for Culum's safety. Culum was spending too much time in Gorth's company, his mind dangerously open.

411

Ten days ago there had been a cruel, inconclusive row. Culum had been spouting some theories about steamships – obviously Gorth's opinions – and Struan had disagreed. Then Culum had brought up the feud between Brock and Struan, and he had said that the younger generation would not make the mistakes of the older. That Gorth knew it wasn't necessary for the younger generation to be trapped by the older. That Gorth and he had agreed to bury any enmity, and that both would try to bring peace between their fathers. And when Struan had begun to argue, Culum had refused to listen and had stormed off.

Then, too, there was the problem of Tess Brock.

Culum had never mentioned her to Struan. Nor had he to him. But he knew that Culum was desperate with longing for her and this fogged his thinking. Struan recalled his own youth and how he had yearned for Ronalda. Everything had seemed so clear and so important and so clean at that age.

'Ah, Culum lad, dinna fash yoursel',' he said, not wishing to argue with Culum. 'It's a hot day and all tempers are short. Sit down and rest your head. Little Karen's sick and many of our friends. I heard Tillman's got the fever, who knows how many more?'

'Miss Tillman?'

'I dinna think so.'

'Gorth said that they're closing their factory tomorrow. He's going to summer in Macao. All the Brocks are.'

'We'll be going to Hong Kong. The factory here stays open.'

'Gorth said it would be better to summer in Macao. He has a house there. We still have property there, haven't we?'

Struan stirred in his chair. 'Aye. Take a week or so, if you wish. Spend it in Macao, but I want you in Queen's Town. And I'll tell you again, watch your back. Gorth's na your friend.'

'And I must tell you again, I think he is.'

'He's trying to get you off balance, and one day he'll cut you to pieces.'

'You're wrong, I understand him. I like him. We get on very well. I find I can talk to him and I enjoy his company. We both know it's difficult for you – and for his father – to understand, but, well, it's hard to explain.'

'I understand Gorth too well, by God!'

'Let's not discuss it,' Culum said.

'I think we should. You're under Gorth's spell. That's deadly for a Struan.'

'You see Gorth through other eyes. He's my friend.'

Struan opened a box and selected a Havana cheroot and decided that the time had come. 'Do you think Brock'll approve your marrying Tess?'

Culum flushed and he said impulsively, 'I don't see why not. Gorth's in favour.'

'You've discussed it with Gorth?'

'I haven't discussed it with you. Or with anyone. So why should I talk about it with Gorth?'

'Then how do you know he approves?'

'I don't. It's just that he's always saying how well Miss Brock and I seemed to be getting on together, how she enjoyed my company, encouraging me to write to her, that sort of thing.'

'You think I've no right to ask your intentions towards Tess Brock?'

'You've the right, certainly. It's just – well yes, I have thought about marrying her. But I've never said so to Gorth.' Culum stopped uncomfortably and mopped his brow. He had been shaken by the suddenness with which the Tai-Pan had touched on what was foremost in his own mind, and though he had wanted to talk about it he did not want his love defiled. Damn it, I should have been prepared, he thought, and he heard himself rush on, unable to stop. 'But I don't think my – my affection for Miss Brock is anyone's concern at the moment. Nothing's been said, and there's nothing – well, what I feel for Miss Brock's my own affair.'

'I realize that's your opinion,' Struan said, 'but that does na mean you're correct. Have you considered that you might be being used?'

'By Miss Brock?'

'By Gorth. And by Brock.'

'Have you considered that your hatred of them tinges all your judgments?' Culum was furious.

'Aye. I've considered that. But you, Culum? Have you thought they might be using you?'

'Let's say you're correct. Let's say I did marry Miss Brock. Isn't that to your business advantage?'

Struan was glad that the problem was out in the open. 'Nay. Because Gorth will eat you up when you're Tai-Pan. He'll take all we have and destroy you – to become The Noble House.'

'Why should he destroy his sister's husband? Why shouldn't we join our companies – Brock and Struan? I run the business, he runs the ships.'

'And who's Tai-Pan?'

'We could share that – Gorth and I.'

'There can only be one Tai-Pan. That's what it means. That's the law.'

'But your law is not necessarily my law. Or Gorth's. We can learn by others' mistakes. Merging our companies would give us immense advantages.'

'That's what Gorth has in mind?' Struan wondered if he had made a mistake about Culum. His son's fascination for Tess and his trust in Gorth would be the key to destroy The Noble House and give Brock and Gorth all that they wanted. Only three months left and then I leave for England. Good sweet Christ! 'Is it?' he asked.

'We've never discussed it. We've talked about trading and shipping and companies, that sort of thing. And how to bring peace between you two. But a merger would be advantageous, wouldn't it?'

'Na with those two. You're na in the same class. Yet.'

'But one day I will be?'

'Maybe.' Struan lit the cheroot. 'You really think you could control Gorth?'

'Perhaps I wouldn't need to control him. Any more than he'd need to control me. Say I do marry Miss Brock. Gorth has his company, we have ours. Separate. We can still compete. But amiably. Without hate.' Culum's tone hardened. 'Let's think like a Tai-Pan for a moment. Brock has a beloved daughter. I ingratiate myself with her and with Gorth. By marrying her I'll merely be softening Brock's animosity to me while I gain experience. Always holding out the bait of a merger of the companies. Then I can savage them when *I'm* ready. A safe and beautiful ploy. The pox on the girl. Just use her – to the greater glory of The Noble House.'

Struan said nothing.

'Haven't you considered these possibilities dispassionately?' Culum went on. 'I'd forgotten you're much too clever not to have noticed that I'm in love with her.'

'Aye,' Struan said. He carefully knocked the ash off his cheroot into a silver ashtray. 'I've considered you – and Tess – "dispassionately" .'

'And what was your conclusion?'

'That the dangers, for you, outweigh the advantages.'

'Then you totally disapprove of my marrying her?'

'I disapprove of your loving her. But the fact is you do love her, or think you do. And another fact is that you'll marry her, if you can.' Struan took a long draw on the cheroot. 'Do you think Brock will approve?'

'I don't know. I don't think he will, God help me!'

'I think he will, God help you.'

'But you won't?'

'I told you once before: I'm the only man on this earth you can completely trust. Provided you dinna, with calculation, go against the house.'

'But you think such a marriage is against the interests of the company?'

'I did na say that. I said you dinna understand the dangers.' Struan put out the cheroot and stood up. 'She's under age. Will you wait five years for her?'

'Yes,' he said, appalled by the length of time. 'Yes, by God. You don't know what she means to me. 'She's – well, she's the only girl I could ever really love. I won't change and you don't understand, you can't. Yes, I'll wait five years. I'm in love with her.'

'Is she in love with you?'

'I don't know. I – she seems to like me. I pray she will. Oh God in heaven, what am I going to do?'

Thank God, I'm na that young again, Struan thought with compassion. Now I know that love is like the sea, sometimes calm and sometimes stormy; it's dangerous, beautiful, death-dealing, life-giving. But never permanent, ever-changing. And unique only for a short span in the eyes of time.

'You'll do nothing, lad. But I'll talk to Brock tonight.'

'No,' Culum said anxiously. 'This is my life. I don't want you to—'

'What you want to do crosses my life and Brock's,' Struan interrupted. 'I'll talk to Brock.'

'Then you'll help me?'

Struan fanned a fly away from his face. 'What about the twenty guineas, Culum?'

'What?'

'My coffin money. The twenty golden coins Brock gave me, and you kept. Had you forgotten?'

Culum opened his mouth to say no but changed his mind. 'Yes, I'd forgotten them. At least they'd slipped my mind.' His anguish showed in the depths of his eyes. 'Why should I want to lie to you? I almost lied. That's terrible.'

'Aye,' Struan said, pleased that Culum had passed another test and learned another lesson.

'What about the coins?'

'Nothing. Except you should remember them. That's Brock. Gorth's worse because he's na even got his father's generosity.'

*   *   *

It was almost midnight.

'Sit thee down, Dirk,' Brock said, rubbing his beard. 'Grog, beer or brandy.'

'Brandy.'

'Brandy-ah,' Brock ordered the servant, then motioned to the food on the table in the glittering candlelight. 'Help thyself to vittles, Dirk.' He scratched his armpits which were thick with the sores called 'prickly heat.' 'Godrotting weather! Why the devil baint thee suffering along with the rest of us'n?'

'I live right,' Struan said, and stuck his legs out comfortably. 'I've told you a million times. If you bathe four times a day you will na get prickly heat. Lice'll vanish and—'

'That be having nothing to do with it,' Brock said. 'That be foolishness. Against nature, by God.' He laughed. 'Them wot says thee's shipmate o' the devil mayhaps've put the finger on why thee's as thee are. Eh?' He shoved his empty half-gallon silver tankard at the servant, who immediately filled it from the small barrel of beer that was set against a wall. Muskets and cutlasses were on racks nearby. 'But thee'll get thy reward soon enough, eh, Dirk?' Brock pointed a blunt thumb downward.

Struan took the large balloon-shaped crystal glass and sniffed the brandy. 'We all get our rewards, Tyler.' Struan kept the brandy close to his nose to counteract the stench of the room. He wondered if Tess stank like her father and mother, and if Brock knew the reason for his visit. The windows were tight shut against the night and the monstrous hum from the square below.

Brock grunted and lifted the full tankard and drank thirstily. He was wearing his usual woollen frock coat and heavy underwear and high cravat and waistcoat. He studied Struan bleakly. Struan appeared cool and strong in his light shirt and white trousers and half boots, the red-gold hairs on his vast chest catching the candlelight. 'Thee looks right proper naked, lad. Proper disgusting.'

'It's the coming fashion, Tyler. Health!' Struan raised his glass and they drank.

'Talking of devil, I heared Maureen Quance be bending poor old Aristotle more'n maybe. Rumour sayed they be going home on next tide.'

'He'll escape, or cut his throat before he does that.'

Brock guffawed. 'When she come up sudden-like at ball, I baint laughing so much since Ma catched tits in't mangle.' He waved a hand in dismissal and the servant left. 'I heared all thy ships be off.'

'Aye. A great season eh?'

'Yus. And it be better when *Blue Witch* berth first in London Town. I heard she be a day ahead.' Brock drank deeply of the beer and sweated copiously. 'Jeff Cooper sayed his last boat be gone so Whampoa be clear.'

'Are you staying in Canton?'

Brock shook his head. 'We be going tomorrer. To Queen's Town, then Macao. But we be keeping this place open, not like afore.'

'Longstaff's staying. Negotiations'll be going on, I suppose.' Struan felt tension in the air and his disquiet increased.

'Thee knowed there be no concluding here.' Brock was fiddling with the patch over his eye. He half lifted it and rubbed the jagged, scarred socket. The string that had held the patch over the years had worn a neat red channel in his forehead. 'Gorth sayed that Robb's youngest beed with fever.'

'Aye. I suppose Culum told him?'

'Yus.' Brock marked the sharpness of Struan's voice. He drank heavily of the beer and wiped the froth off his whiskers with the back of his hand. 'I be sorry to hear that. Bad joss.' He drank again. 'Yor boy'n mine be just like old shipmates.'

'I'll be glad to be afloat again.' Struan ignored the taunt. 'I had a long talk with Jin-qua this afternoon. About the fever. They've never had it in Kwangtung, so far as he knows.'

'If it be truly malaria, then we's a passel of troubles on our'n hand.' Brock reached over and took a breast of chicken. 'Help thyself. I heard price on coolies be up. Costs is soaring terrible in Hong Kong.'

'Na enough to hurt. The fever'll pass.'

Brock moved his girth painfully and drained the tankard. 'Thee wanted to see me, private? To talk about fever?'

'No,' Struan said, feeling tainted by the stench and the perfume Brock wore and the smell of stale beer. 'It was about a long-standing promise I made to come after thee with a cat-o'-nine-tails.'

Brock picked up the handbell on the table and rang it vehemently. The sound splintered off the walls. When the door didn't open immediately, he rang it again.

'That cursed monkey,' he said. 'He be needin' a right proper kick in the arse.' He went over to the barrel of beer and, after refilling his tankard, sat down again and watched Struan. And waited.

'Wot about it?' Brock said at length.

'Tess Brock.'

'Eh?' Brock was astonished that Struan wanted to precipitate the decision over which he himself – and undoubtedly Struan, too – had fretted for so many nights.

'My son's in love with her.'

Brock gulped some more beer and wiped his mouth again. 'They's met but once. At the ball. Then there were afternoon walks with Liza and Lillibet. Three.'

'Aye. But he's in love with her. He's sure in love with her.'

'Are thee sure?'

'Aye.'

'Wot's thy feeling?'

'That we'd better talk this out. In the open.'

'Why now?' Brock said suspiciously, his mind trying to find the real answer. 'She be very young, as thee knowed.'

'Aye. But old enough to wed.'

Brock thoughtfully toyed with the tankard, looking at his reflection in the polished silver. He wondered if he had guessed Struan correctly. 'Is thee asking, formal, Tess's hand for thy son?'

'That's his duty, na mine – to ask formal. But we've to talk informal. First.'

'Wot's thy feeling?' Brock asked again. 'About the match?'

'You know it already. I'm against it. I dinna trust you. I dinna trust Gorth. But Culum's got a mind of his own and he's forced my hand, and a father canna always get a son to do what he wants.'

Brock thought about Gorth. His voice was brittled when he spoke. 'If thee's so strong against him, beat some sense into him or send him home, pack him off. Easy to rid of that young spark.'

'You know I'm trapped,' Struan said bitterly. 'You've three sons – Gorth, Morgan, Tom. I've only Culum now. So whatever I want, he's the one that's got to follow me.'

'There's Robb and his three sons,' Brock said, happy that he had read Struan's mind correctly, playing him now like a fish.

'You know the answer to that. I made The Noble House, na Robb. What's your feeling, eh?'

Brock drained the tankard thoughtfully. Again he rang the bell. Again no answer. 'I'll have that monkey's guts for garters!' He got up and began to refill his tankard. 'I'm equal against the match,' Brock said roughly. He saw a flash of surprise on Struan's face. 'Even so,' Brock added, 'I be accepting yor son when he be asking me.'

'I thought you would, by God!' Struan got up, his fists clenched.

'Her dowry'll be the richest in Asia. They be married next year.'

'I'll see you in hell first.'

The two men squared up to each other ominously.

Brock saw the same chiselled face he had seen thirty years ago, the same vitality permeating it. The same indefinable quality that caused his whole being to react so violently. By Lord God, he swore, I baint understanding why Thee put this devil in my path. I only knowed Thee put him there to be broken, regular, not with knife in't back and more's the pity.

'That be later, Dirk,' he said. 'First they be amarrying, fair and square. Thee's trapped right enough. Not o' my doing and more's the pity, and I baint driving thy bad joss in thy face. But I beed thinking muchly – like thee – about they two and us'n, and I thinks it be best for they and best for us'n.'

'I know what's in your mind. And Gorth's.'

'Who knowed wot's to be, Dirk? Mayhaps there be a joining in the future.'

'Na while I'm alive.'

'On the other hand, mayhaps there baint a joining and thee keeps thine an' we our'n.'

'You'll na take and break The Noble House through a girl's skirts!'

'Now you be alistening to me, by God! Thee brung this'n up! Thee sayed to talk open and I baint finished. So thee'll listen, by God! 'Less thee's lost thy guts like thee's lost thy manners an' lost thy brains.'

'All right, Tyler.' Struan poured another brandy. 'Say your mind.'

Brock relaxed slightly and sat down again and quaffed his beer. 'I hate thy guts and I always will. I doan trust thee either. I be mortal tired of killing, but I swear by Jesus Christ I be killing thee the day I see thee again' me with a cat in thy hand. But I baint starting that fight. No. I doan want to kill thee, just crush thee regirlar. But I beed athinking that mayhaps that young'uns be puttin' at rights wot we – wot bain't possible for us'n. So I says, let wot's to be, be. If there be a joining, then there be a joining. That be up to they – not t' thee and me. If there baint a joining – likewise that be up to they. Wotever they do be up to they. Not us'n. So I says the match be good.'

Struan drained his glass and shoved it on the table. 'I never thought you'd be so gutless as to use Tess when you're as opposed as I am.'

Brock stared back at him without anger now. 'I baint using Tess, Dirk. That be God's truth. She be loving Culum and that be mortal truth. That be only reason I be talking like this'n. We both be trapped. Let's be talking obvious. She be like Juliet to his Romeo, yus, by God, and that's wot I be afeared of. An' you too if truth be knowed. I baint wanting my Tess to end on marble slab' cause I hate thy guts. She love him. I be thinking of her!'

'I dinna believe it.'

'Nor I, by God! But Liza's rit half a dozen time about Tess. She sayed Tess be mooning and sighing and talking about ball but only about Culum. An' Tess's ritted sixteen time or more about wot Culum sayed and wot Culum baint saying and wot she sayed to Culum and how Culum be looking and wot Culum be asaying back till I be fit to bust. Oh yus, she love him right enough.'

'It's puppy love. It means nothing.'

'By the Lord God, you be a terrible hard man to talk sense to. Yo're wrong, Dirk.' Brock suddenly felt very tired and very old. He wanted to be done with this. 'Weren't for ball it baint never happening. Thee picked her to lead dance. Thee picked her to win prize. Thee—'

'I di'na! That was Zergeyev's choice, na mine!'

'That be truth, by God?'

'Aye.'

Brock looked at Struan deeply. 'Then mayhaps there be hand o' God in this'n. Tess baint best-dressed in't ball. I knowed it, all knowed it, 'cepting Culum and Tess.' He finished his tankard and set it down. 'I makes thee offer: thee doan love thy Culum like I be loving Tess, but give they two a fair wind and an open sea and a safe harbour and I be doing likewise. The boy deserve it – he saved thy neck over the knoll 'cause I swear by Christ I'd've strangled thee with it. If it's a fight thee wants, thee's got it. If I gets a lever to break thee, regilar, I swear by Christ I still be adoing it. But not to they two. Give 'em fair wind, open sea and safe harbour afore God, eh?'

Brock stuck out his hand.

Struan's voice grated. 'I'll shake on Culum and Tess. But na on Gorth.'

The way Struan said 'Gorth' chilled Brock. But he did not withdraw his hand even though he knew the agreement was fraught with danger.

They shook hands firmly.

'We be having one more drink to fix it proper,' Brock said, 'then thee can get t'hell out of my house.' He picked up the bell and rang it a third time and when no one appeared he hurled it against the wall. 'Lee Tang!' he roared.

His voice echoed strangely.

There was the sound of footsteps scurrying up the huge staircase, and the frightened face of a Portuguese clerk appeared.

420

'The servants have all disappeared, senhor. I can't find them any-where.'

Struan raced to the window. The hawkers and stall sellers and bystanders and beggars were streaming silently from the square. Groups of traders in the English garden were standing stock-still, listening and watching.

Struan turned and ran for the muskets, and he and Brock were at the rack in the same instant. 'Get everyone below!' Brock shouted at the clerk.

'My factory, Tyler. Sound the alarm,' Struan said, and then he was gone.

Within the hour all the traders and their clerks were crammed into the Struan factory, and into the English Garden which was its forecourt. The detachment of fifty soldiers was armed, in battle order, beside the gate. Their officer, Captain Oxford, was barely twenty, a lithe, smart man with a wisp of fair moustache.

Struan and Brock and Longstaff were in the centre of the garden. Jeff Cooper and Zergeyev were nearby. The night was wet and hot and brooding.

'You'd better order an immediate evacuation, Your Excellency,' Struan said.

'Yus,' Brock agreed.

'No need to be precipitate, gentlemen,' Longstaff said. 'This has happened before, what?'

'Aye. But we've always had some sort of warning from the Co-hong or from the mandarins. It's never been this sudden.' Struan was listening intently to the night, but his eyes were counting the lorchas moored alongside the wharves. Enough for everyone, he thought. 'I dinna like the feel of the night.'

'Nor I, by God.' Brock spat furiously. 'Afloat it be, says I.'

'Surely you don't think there's any danger?' Longstaff said.

'I dinna ken, Your Excellency. But something tells me to get out of here,' Struan said. 'Or at least get afloat. Trade's finished for the season, so we can go or stay at our pleasure.'

'But they wouldn't dare attack us,' Longstaff scoffed. 'Why should they? What do they gain? The negotiations are going so well. Ridicu-lous.'

'I'm just suggesting we put into effect what you're always saying, Your Excellency: that it's better to be prepared for any eventuality.'

Longstaff motioned queasily to the officer. 'Split your men into three parties. Guard the east and west entrances, and Hog Street. Deny access to the square until further orders.'

'Yes, sir.'

Struan saw Culum and Horatio and Gorth together near a lantern. Gorth was explaining the loading of a musket to Culum, who was listening attentively. Gorth seemed strong and vital and powerful alongside Culum. Struan looked away and glimpsed Mauss in the shadows talking to a tall Chinese whom Struan had never seen before. Curious, Struan walked over to them. 'Have you heard anything, Wolfgang?'

'No, Tai-Pan. No rumours, nothing. Nor has Horatio. *Gott im Himmel*, I don't understand it.'

Struan was studying the Chinese. The man was wearing filthy peasant clothes and appeared to be in his early thirties. His eyes were heavy-lidded, and piercing, and he was studying Struan with equal curiosity. 'Who's he?'

'Hung Hsiu-ch'uan,' Wolfgang said, very proudly. 'He's a Hakka. He's baptized, Tai-Pan. I baptized him. He's the best I've ever had, Tai-Pan. Brilliant mind, studious, and yet a peasant. At long last I've a convert who will spread God's word – and help me in His work.'

'You'd better tell him to leave. If there's trouble and the mandarins catch him with us, you'll have one convert less.'

'I've already told him, but he said, "The ways of the Lord are strange and men of God don't turn their back on the heathen." Don't worry. God will guard him and I'll watch him with my own life.'

Struan nodded briefly to the man and went back to Longstaff and to Brock.

'I be going aboard,' Brock said, 'and that be that!'

'Tyler, send Gorth and his men to reinforce the soldiers there.' Struan pointed to the maw of Hog Street. 'I'll take the east and cover you if there's trouble. You can fall back here.'

'You look after you'n,' Brock said. 'I be looking after mine. You baint commander-in-chief, by God.' He beckoned to Gorth. 'You come along with me. Almeida, you and the rest of the clerks get books and aboard.' He and his party marched out of the garden and headed across the square.

'Culum!'

'Yes, Tai-Pan?'

'Clean out the safe and get aboard the lorcha.'

'Very well.' Culum lowered his voice. 'Did you talk to Brock?'

'Aye. Na now, lad. Hurry. We'll talk later.'

'Was it yes or no?'

Struan felt others watching him, and although he wanted very much to tell Culum what had been said, the garden was not the place to do it. 'God's death, will you na do as you're told!'

'I want to know,' Culum said, eyes blazing.

'And I'm na prepared to discuss your problems now! *Do as you're told!*' Struan stamped off towards the front door.

Jeff Cooper stopped him. 'Why evacuate? What's all the hurry, Tai-Pan?' he asked.

'Just cautious, Jeff. Have you a lorcha?'

'Yes.'

'I'd be glad to give any of your people space who dinna have berths.' Struan glanced at Zergeyev. 'The view from the river's quite pleasant, Your Highness, if you'd care to join us.'

'Do you always run away when the square empties and the servants disappear?'

'Only when it pleases me.' Struan shoved back through the press of men. 'Vargas, get the books aboard and all the clerks. Armed.'

'Yes, senhor.'

When the other traders saw that Struan and Brock were in truth preparing for a quick withdrawal, they hastily returned to their own factories and collected their books and bills of lading and everything that represented proof of their season's trading – and thus their future – and began to pack them in their boats. There was little treasure to worry about, since most of the trading was done with bills of exchange – and Brock and Struan had already sent their bullion back to Hong Kong.

Longstaff cleared out his private desk and put his cipher book and secret papers into his dispatch box and joined Zergeyev in the garden. 'Are you all packed, Your Highness?'

'There is nothing of importance. I find all this extraordinary. Either there is danger or there isn't. If there's danger, why aren't your troops here? If there's none, why run away?'

Longstaff laughed. 'The heathen mind, my dear sir, is very different from a civilized one. Her Majesty's Government has been dealing directly with it for more than a century. So we've come to learn how to cope with Chinese affairs. Of course,' he added dryly, 'we're not concerned with conquest, only with peaceful trade. Though we do consider this area a totally British sphere of influence.'

* * *

423

Struan was going through his safe, ascertaining that all their vital papers were aboard.

'I've already done that,' Culum said as he barged into the room and slammed the door. 'Now, what was the answer, by God?'

'You're engaged to be married,' Struan said mildly, 'by God.' Culum was too stupefied to speak.

'Brock's delighted to have you as a son-in-law. You can get married next year.'

'Brock said yes?'

'Aye. Congratulations.' Struan calmly checked his desk drawer, and locked it, pleased that his talk with Brock had gone as planned.

'You mean he says yes? And you say yes?'

'Aye. You have to ask him formally, but he said he'd accept you. We have to discuss dowry and details, but he said you can be married next year.'

Culum threw his arms around Struan's shoulders. 'Oh, Father, thank you, thank you.' He did not hear himself say 'Father'. But Struan did.

A burst of firing shattered the night. Struan and Culum ran to the window in time to see the front ranks of a mob at the western entrance to the square reeling under the fusillade. The hundreds in the rear shoved those in front forward, and the soldiers were pathetically engulfed as the screaming torrent of Chinese poured into the far end of the square.

The mob carried torches and axes and spears – and Triad banners. They swarmed over the westernmost factory, which belonged to the Americans. A torch was thrown through a window and the doors were rushed. The mob began to loot and fire and rape the building.

Struan grabbed his musket. 'Nae word of Tess – keep it very private till you've seen Brock.' They charged out into the hall. 'To hell with those, Vargas,' he shouted as he saw him staggering under an armload of duplicate invoices. 'Get aboard!'

Vargas took to his heels.

The square in front of Struan's factory and the garden was filled with traders in full flight to the lorchas. Some of the soldiers were stationed on the garden wall ready for a last-ditch stand, and Struan joined them to help cover the retreat. Out of the corner of his eye he saw Culum run back into the factory, but he was distracted when the van of the second mob surged down Hog Street. The soldiers protecting this entrance fired a volley and retreated in good order towards the English garden, where they took up their positions with the other soldiers to defend the last of the traders who were running for the boats. Those already on the ships had muskets ready, but the mob concentrated solely on the factories on the far side of the square and, astonishingly, paid little attention to the traders.

Struan was relieved to see Cooper and the Americans aboard one of the lorchas. He had thought that they were still in their factory.

''Pon me word, look at those scallawags,' Longstaff said to no one in particular as he stood outside the garden and watched the mob, walking stick in hand. He knew that this meant the end of negotiations, that war was inevitable. 'Her Majesty's forces will soon put a stop to this nonsense.' He stamped back into the garden and found Zergeyev observing the havoc, his two liveried servants armed and nervous beside him.

'Perhaps you'd care to join me aboard, Your Highness,' he said above the noise. Longstaff knew that if Zergeyev were injured there would be an international incident, which would give the tsar a perfect opening to send reprisal warships and armies into Chinese waters. And that's not going to happen, God-damme, he told himself.

'There's only one way to deal with these carrion. You think your democracy will work with them?'

'Of course. Have to give them time, what?' Longstaff replied easily. 'Let's board now. We're fortunate it's a pleasant evening.'

One of the Russian servants said something to Zergeyev, who simply looked at him. The servant blanched and was silent.

'If you wish, Your Excellency,' Zergeyev said, not to be outdone by Longstaff's obvious contempt for the mob. 'But I think I'd rather wait for the Tai-Pan.' He took out his snuff box and offered it, and was pleased to see his fingers were not shaking.

'Thank you.' Longstaff took some snuff. 'Damnable business, what!' He strolled over to Struan. 'What the devil started them off, Dirk?'

'The mandarins, that's certain. There's never been a mob like this before. Never. Best get aboard.' Struan was watching the square. The last of the traders boarded the ships. Only Brock was not accounted for. Gorth and his men were still guarding the door to their factory on the east side, and Struan was infuriated to see Gorth fire into the looting mob, which was not threatening them directly.

He was tempted to order an immediate retreat; then, in the confusion, to raise his musket and kill Gorth. He knew that no one would notice in the mêlée. It would save him a killing in the future. But Struan did not fire. He wanted the pleasure of seeing the terror in Gorth's eyes when he did kill him.

Those on the lorchas cast off hastily, and many of the boats eased into midstream. Queerly the mob still ignored them.

Smoke was billowing from the Cooper-Tillman factory. The whole building caught as a squall of tinder wind hit it, and flames licked the night.

Struan saw Brock storm out of his factory, a musket in one hand, a cutlass in the other, his pockets bulging with papers. His chief clerk Almeida ran ahead towards the boat under the weight of the books, Brock, Gorth and his men guarding, and then another mob hit the east entrance, swamping the soldiers, and Struan knew it was time to run.

'Get aboard!' he roared, turning for the garden gate. He stopped in his tracks. Zergeyev was leaning on the garden wall, a pistol in one hand, his rapier in the other. Longstaff was beside him.

'Time to run!' he yelled above the tumult.

Zergeyev laughed. 'Which way?'

There was a violent explosion as the flames reached the American arsenal, and the building shattered, spilling burning debris into the mob, killing some, mutilating others. The Triad banners crossed Hog Street, and the berserk, pillaging mob followed, systematically tearing into the eastern factories. Struan was through the gate when he remembered Culum. He shouted to his men to cover and rushed back.

'Culum! Culum!'

Culum came charging down the stairs. 'I forgot something,' he said, and tore for the lorcha.

Zergeyev and Longstaff were still waiting with the men beside the gate. Their escape was blocked by a third mob which gushed across the square and fell on the factory next to theirs. Struan pointed to the wall and they shinned over it. Culum fell, but Struan grabbed him up and together they ran for the boats, Zergeyev and Longstaff close alongside.

The mob let them pass, but once they had started across the square, leaving the path to the factory clear, the leaders charged into the garden. Many had torches. And then fell on The Noble House.

Now flames poured from most of the factories, and a roof fell with a vast sigh and more flames showered the thousands in the square.

Brock was on the main deck of his lorcha, profanely exhorting the crew. They all were armed and their guns pointed landward.

Standing on the poop, Gorth saw the fore and aft hawsers cast off. As the lorcha began to fall away from the wharf, Gorth seized a musket, aimed at the Chinese who were jammed into the doorway of their factory, and pulled the trigger. He saw a man fall and grinned

426

devilishly. He picked up another musket; then noticed Struan and the others charging for their lorcha – milling Chinese ahead of and behind them. He made certain no one was watching him and aimed carefully. Struan was between Culum and Zergeyev, Longstaff alongside. Gorth pulled the trigger.

Zergeyev spun around and smashed into the ground.

Gorth took another musket but Brock rushed up to the poop. 'Get for'ard and man the fore cannon!' he shouted. 'No firing till I says!' He shoved Gorth along, roaring at his men, 'Get thy helm over, by God! Let go the reefs an' all sail ho!' He glanced shoreward and saw Struan and Longstaff bending over Zergeyev, Culum beside him, the mob surging towards them. He grabbed the musket that Gorth had dropped, aimed and fired. A leader fell and the mob hesitated.

Struan hoisted Zergeyev on to his shoulder. 'Fire over their heads!' he ordered. His men spun out protectively and fired a volley at point-blank range. The Chinese in front shrank back and those behind pressed forward. The hysterical mêlée which ensued gave Struan and his men enough time to make their boat.

Mauss was waiting on the dock beside the lorcha, the strange Chinese convert nearby. Both were armed. Mauss had a Bible in one hand and a cutlass in the other and he was shouting, 'Blessed be the Lord, forgive these poor sinners.' He hacked at the air with the blade and the mob avoided him.

When they were all aboard and the lorcha in midstream, they looked back.

The whole Settlement was ablaze. Dancing flames and billowing smoke and fiendish screaming all blended into an inferno.

Longstaff was on his knees beside Zergeyev, who lay on the quarter-deck. Struan hurried towards them.

'Get for'ard!' he roared at Mauss. 'Be lookout!'

Zergeyev was white with shock and was holding the right side of his groin. Blood was oozing from under his hand. The servant guards were moaning with terror. Struan pushed them out of the way and ripped open the front flap of Zergeyev's trousers. He cut away the trouser leg. The musket ball had scored the stomach deeply, low and obliquely, a fraction of an inch above his sex, and then had entered the right thigh. Blood seeped heavily but it was not spurting. Struan thanked God that the ball had not entered the stomach as he had expected. He turned Zergeyev over and the Russian choked back a groan. The back of his thigh was torn and bloody where the ball had come out. Struan gingerly probed the wound and took out a small piece of shattered bone.

'Get the blankets and brandy and a brazier,' Struan snapped at a seaman. 'Your Highness, can you move your right leg?'

Zergeyev shifted it slightly and winced with pain, but his leg moved. 'Your hip's all right, I think, laddie. Stay still, now.'

When the blankets were brought, he wrapped Zergeyev in them and propped him more comfortably on the seat behind the helmsman, and gave him brandy.

When the brazier came, Struan opened the wound to the air and doused it heavily with the brandy. He heated his knife in the coals of the brazier.

'Hold him, Will! Culum, give us a hand.' They knelt down, Longstaff at his feet, Culum at his head.

Struan put the red-hot knife into the fore wound and the brandy caught and Zergeyev passed out. Struan cauterized the wound in front and probed deeply and quickly, wanting to do it fast now that Zergeyev was unconscious. He turned him over; and probed again. The smell of burning flesh filled the air. Longstaff turned aside and vomited, but Culum held on and helped, and Longstaff turned back once more.

Struan reheated the knife and poured more brandy over the back wound and cauterized it deeply and thoroughly. His head ached from the stench, and sweat was dripping off his chin, but his hands were steady and he knew that if he did not do the burning carefully, the wound would rot and Zergeyev would certainly die. With such a wound nine men in ten would die.

Then he was finished.

He bandaged Zergeyev, and he rinsed his own mouth with brandy; its fumes cleared away the smell of blood and burning flesh. Then he gulped heavily and studied Zergeyev. The face was grey and bloodless.

'Now he's in the hands of his own joss,' he said. 'You all right, Culum?'

'Yes. Yes, I think so.'

'Get below. Organize hot rum for all hands. Check stores. You're Number Two aboard now. Get everyone sorted out.'

Culum left the poop.

The two Russian servants were kneeling beside Zergeyev. One of them touched Struan and spoke brokenly, obviously thanking him. Struan motioned them to stay beside their master.

He stretched wearily and put his hand on Longstaff's shoulder and drew him aside and bent low to Longstaff's ear. 'Did you see muskets among the Chinese?'

Longstaff shook his head. 'None.'

'Nor did I,' Struan said.

'There were guns going off all over the place.' Longstaff was white-faced and greatly concerned. 'One of those unlucky accidents.'

Struan said nothing for a moment. 'If he dies, there'll be very large trouble, eh?'

'Let's hope he doesn't, Dirk.' Longstaff bit his lip. 'I'll have to advise the Foreign Secretary of the accident at once. I'll have to hold an inquiry.'

'Aye.'

Longstaff looked across at the grey, corpse-like face. Zergeyev's breathing was shallow. 'Damned annoying, what?'

'From the position of the wound, and from where he was standing when he was felled, there's nae doubt that it was one of our bullets.'

'It was one of those unfortunate accidents.'

'Aye. But the bullet could have been aimed.'

'Impossible. Who'd want to kill him?'

'Who'd want to kill you? Or Culum? Or perhaps me? We were all very close together.'

'Who?'

'I've a dozen enemies.'

'Brock wouldn't murder you in cold blood.'

'I never said he would. Offer a reward for information. Someone may have seen something.'

Together they watched the Settlement. It was far astern now: only flames and smoke over the rooftops of Canton. 'Madness to loot like that. Hasn't happened ever before. Why would they do that? Why?' Longstaff said.

'I dinna ken.'

'As soon as we get to Hong Kong, we go north – this time to the gates of Peking, by God. The emperor's going to be very sorry he ordered this.'

'Aye. But first mount an immediate attack against Canton.'

'But that's a waste of time, what?'

'Mount an attack within the week. You'll na have to press it home. Ransom Canton again. Six millions of taels.'

'Why?'

'You need a month or more to get the fleet ready to stab north. The weather's na right yet. You'll have to wait till the reinforcements arrive. They're due when?'

'Month, six weeks.'

'Good.' Struan's face hardened. 'In the meantime the Cohong'll have to find six million taels. That'll teach them na to warn us, by God. You have to show the flag here, before you go north, or we'll lose face. If they get away with burning the Settlement, we'll never be safe in the future. Order *Nemesis* to stand off the city. A twelve-hour ultimatum or you'll lay waste Canton.'

Zergeyev moaned, and Struan went over to him. The Russian was still in shock and almost unconscious.

Then Struan noticed Mauss's Chinese convert watching him. The man was standing on the main deck beside the starboard gunnel. He made the sign of the cross over Struan and closed his eyes and, silently, began to pray.

XXVII

Struan jumped out of the cutter on to their new wharf at Queen's Town and hurried along its length towards the vast, nearly completed three-storey building. His limp was more pronounced today under a white-hot sky. The Lion and the Dragon fluttered atop the flagpole.

He noted that many smaller buildings and dwellings were completed all over Happy Valley and that a start had been made on the church on the knoll; that Brock's wharf on the far side of the bay was completed and the factory adjoining it almost ready. Other buildings and residences were still encased in soaring sheaths of bamboo scaffoldings. Queen's Road was rock-surfaced.

But there were very few coolies working, although it was only early afternoon. The day was hot and very humid. A pleasant easterly wind had begun to touch the valley lightly.

He strode into the main foyer, his shirt sticking to his back. A perspiring Portuguese clerk looked up, startled.

'*Madre de Deus*, Mr Struan! Good day, senhor. We did not expect you.'

'Where's Mr Robb?'

'Upstairs, senhor, but there—'

But Struan was already running up the staircase. The first-landing hallway led off north and east and west into the depths of the building. Many windows watched seaward and landward. The fleet was silently at anchor and his lorcha had been the first home from Canton.

He turned east and passed the half-completed dining-room, his footsteps a brittle echo on the uncarpeted stone. He knocked on a door and opened it.

The door let into a spacious suite. It was half furnished: chairs and sofas and stone floor and Quance paintings on the wall, rich carpets, an empty fireplace. Sarah was sitting in a high-backed chair beside one of the windows, a bamboo latticed fan in her hand. She was staring at him.

'Hello, Sarah.'

'Hello, Dirk.'

'How's Karen?'

'Karen's dead.'

Sarah's eyes were pale blue and unwavering, her face pink and greasy with sweat. Her hair was streaked with white, her face aged.

'I'm sorry. I'm so sorry,' he said.

Sarah fanned herself abstractedly. The slight breeze made by the fan wafted a limp strand of hair into her face but she did not brush it away.

'When did it happen?' he asked.

'Three days ago. Perhaps two,' she said, her voice flat. 'I don't know.'

The fan kept moving back and forth, seemingly of its own volition.

'How's the bairn?'

'Still alive. Lochlin's still alive.'

Struan wiped a droplet of sweat off his chin with his fingers. 'We're the first back from Canton. They burned the Settlement. We got Robb's letter just before we left. I've just arrived.'

'I watched your cutter come ashore,' she said.

'Where's Robb?' he asked.

She motioned with the fan at a door, and he saw the thinness of her blue-veined wrists.

Struan went into the bedroom. The room was large, and the canopied four-poster had been made from a pattern of his own.

Robb was lying in the bed, his eyes closed, his face grey and gaunt against the sweat-stained pillow.

'Robb?' Struan said. But the eyes did not open and the lips were slightly parted. Struan's soul twisted.

He touched his brother's face. Coldness. Death-coldness.

A dog barked close by, and a fly battered the window.

Struan turned and walked out of the room, and closed the door quietly.

Sarah was still sitting in the high-backed chair. The fan moved slowly. Back and forth. Back and forth.

He loathed her for not telling him.

'Robb died an hour ago,' she said. 'Two or three hours, or an hour. I don't remember. Before he died he gave me a message for you. It was this morning, I think. Maybe it was in the night. I think it was this morning. Robb said, "Tell Dirk I never wanted to be Tai-Pan." '

'I'll make the necessary arrangements, Sarah. Best you and the bairns get aboard *Resting Cloud*.'

'I closed his eyes. And I closed Karen's eyes. Who'll close your eyes, Tai-Pan? Who'll close mine?'

*   *   *

432

He made the arrangements and then walked up the small rise towards his house. He was thinking about the first day Robb had arrived in Macao.

'Dirk! All your troubles are over, I've arrived!' Robb had said with his wonderful smile. 'We'll smash the East India Company and obliterate Brock. We'll be like lairds and start a dynasty that will rule Asia for ever! There's a girl I'm going to marry! Sarah McGlenn. She's fifteen now and we're betrothed and we'll marry in two years.'

Tell me, God, Struan asked, where do we go wrong? How? Why do people change? How do quarrel and violence and hatred and hurt come from sweetness and youth and tenderness and love? And why? Because they always do. With Sarah. With Ronalda. And it'll be the same with Culum and Tess. Why?

He was at the gate in the high wall that surrounded his house. He opened it and looked at the house. All was quiet: ominously quiet. The word 'malaria' flooded his brain. A slight wind waved the tall bamboos. The garden was well planted now: flowers, shrubs, bees foraging.

He walked up the steps and opened his door. But he did not enter at once. He listened from the doorstep. There was no welcome laughter, no muted chattering singsong from the servants. The house felt empty.

He looked at the barometer: 29.8 inches, fair weather.

He walked slowly down the passageway, the air strangely incense-laden. He noticed dust where there had been none before.

He opened the door of May-may's bedroom. The bed was made and empty and the room abnormally neat and tidy.

The children's room was empty. No cot or toys.

Then he saw her through the windows. She came from the hidden side of the garden with cut flowers in her hand and an orange sunshade shielding her face. Then he was outside and she was in his arms.

'God's blood, Tai-Pan, you've crushed my flowers.' May-may put the flowers down and threw her arms around his neck. 'Where you come from, heya? Tai-Pan, you crush me too tight! Please. Wat for your face so strange?'

He lifted her and sat on a bench in the sun. She stayed contentedly in his arms, warmed by his strength and his relief at seeing her.

She smiled up at him. 'So. You miss me fantastical, heya?'

'I missed you fantastical, heya.'

'Good. Why for you unhappy? And wat for when I see you, you are like ghosted?'

'Troubles, May-may. And I thought I'd lost you. Where're the children?'

'In Macao. I sent them into house of Chen Sheng into the keeping of Elder Sister. When fever sickness began, I thought it terrifical wise. I sent them with Ma-ree Sin-clair. Wat for you think you lost me, heya?'

'Nothing. When did the children go?'

'A week ago. Ma-ree would watch them safe. She returns tomorrow.'

'Where's Ah Sam and Lim Din?'

'I sent them for foods. When we spy your lorcha, I think ayeee yah, the house she is terrifical dirty and no foods, so I make them hurry clean house and send off to get foods, never mind.' She tossed her head. 'Those lazy good-for-nothing whores needs a beating. I'm terrible glad you're back, Tai-Pan, oh yes indeed. Housekeepings have soared and I have no moneys, so you'll have to give me more because we support Lim Din's whole clan and Ah Sam's. Huh, na that I mind their immediate family, that's of course fair squeeze, never mind, but their whole clans? A thousand times no, by God! We're rich, yes, but na that rich, and we must hold on to our wealth or soon we'll be penniless!' She frowned as she watched him. 'Wat for troubles?'

'Robb's dead. And little Karen.'

Her eyes widened and her happiness fled. 'I knew about little girl. But na Brother Robb. I hear he has fever – three, four days ago. But na he's deaded. When this happen?'

'A few hours ago.'

'That's terrible joss. Better we leaving this cursed valley.'

'It's na cursed, lass. But it does have fever.'

'Aye. But forgive me for mentioning it again, dinna forget we live on the dragon's eyeball.' Her eyes turned up and she loosed a stream of Cantonese and Mandarin supplications. When she was calm again she said, 'Dinna forget our fêng shui here is dreadful terrible bad.'

Struan had to come to grips with the quandary that had racked him for weeks. If he left the valley, everyone would leave; if he stayed, May-may might catch the fever and die, and he could never risk that. If he stayed and she went to Macao, others would die that need not die. How to keep everyone safe from the fever, and at the same time preserve Queen's Town and Hong Kong?

'Tai-Pan, we hear you had bad troubles in Canton?'

He told her what had happened.

'Fantastical crazy. Why for loot, heya?'

'Aye.'

'But terrifical wise for all na to fire Settlement until trade is finished. Very wise. What will happen now? You go against Peking?'

'First we crush Canton. Then Peking.'

434

'Why Canton, Tai-Pan? It was the emperor, na them. They do orders only.'

'Aye. But they should have warned us of trouble. They'll pay six millions of ransom and pay it quickly or they'll have nae city, by God. First Canton, and then north.'

May-may's frown deepened. She knew that she must send word to her grandfather, Jin-qua, to forewarn him. Because the Co-hong would have to find all the ransom, and if Jin-qua was not prepared he would be ruined. She had never sent information to her grandfather before, and had never used her position of knowledge clandestinely. But this time she felt she must. And the thought that she would be part of an intrigue excited her greatly. After all, she told herself, without intrigue and secrets a huge part of the joy of life is missing. I wonder why the mobs pillaged when there was no need to pillage. Stupid.

'Will we mourn a hundred days for your brother?' she asked.

'I canna mourn more than I have, lass,' he said, drained of strength.

'A hundred days is custom. I will arrange Chinese funeral with Gordon Chen. Fifty professional mourners. With drums and rattles and banners. Uncle Robb will have a funeral remembered for years. In this we spare no expense. Then you will be pleased as the gods will be pleased.'

'We canna have such a thing,' he said, shocked. 'This is na a Chinese funeral. We canna have professional mourners!'

'Then how for do you public honour your loved brother, and give him face before the real people of Hong Kong? Of course there must be mourners. Are we na The Noble House? Can we lose face afore the meanest coolie? Apart from being disordinary bad manners and bad joss, you simply canna do it!'

'It's na our custom, May-may. We do things differently.'

'Of course,' she said cheerfully. 'My whole point, Tai-Pan. You look over your face with barbarians, but I will do same with my people. I will mourn private one hundred days, for of course I canna go in public to your funeral or Chinese funeral. I will dress in white clotheses, which is colour of mourning. I will have a tablet made, as always, and we'll kowtow nightly to it. Then, at the end of hundred days, we burn the tablet as always and his soul will be reborn safely as always. It is joss, Tai-Pan. The gods had need for him, never mind.'

But he was not listening to her. He was racking his brain for an answer: how to fight the fever and how to save the valley and how to protect Hong Kong?

XXVIII

Three days later Robb was buried, beside Karen's grave. Wolf-gang Mauss said the service in the roofless church under a cloudless sky.

All the tai-pans were present except Wilf Tillman, who still lay on the Cooper-Tillman hulk more dead than alive with Happy Valley fever. Longstaff was not at the service. He and the general and the admiral had already sailed for Canton – with the fleet and troopships and all the soldiers who were fit. The distemper – dysentery – had decimated their ranks. HMS *Nemesis* had been sent ahead.

Sarah sat in the first rough-hewn pew. She wore black clothes and her veil was black. Shevaun was also in black. And Mary and Liza, Tess and the others. The men too were dressed sombrely and they sweated profusely.

Struan got up to read the lesson, and Shevaun watched him intently. She had given him her condolences yesterday and knew that there was nothing more to be done now. In a week or two all would be well again. Now that Robb had died, she would have to revise her plans. She had planned to marry Struan quickly and then take him away: first to Washington to meet those of great importance, thence to London and to Parliament – but with the added strength of close American ties. Later, back to Washington, Ambassador. But now the plan would be delayed, for she knew he could not leave until Culum was ready to take over.

Simultaneously with the silent, sombre, black-clothed funeral in Happy Valley and the cortège along Queen's Road to the cemetery, a deafening white-clothed Chinese funeral procession wove through the narrow alleys of Tai Ping Shan and cried to the gods about the great loss of The Noble House, shrieking and moaning and groaning and tearing their raiment and banging drums.

And the people of Tai Ping Shan were greatly impressed with the manners of the Tai-Pan and with the largess of his house. The stature of

436

Gordon Chen increased with the gained face of his father, for none of the dwellers on the hill would have guessed that the Tai-Pan would so honour their gods and their customs. Not that Gordon Chen needed an increase of face. Was he not already the greatest landlord in Hong Kong and did not his business tentacles extend in all directions? Did he not own most of the buildings? And the sedan chair business? And three laundries? Fourteen fishing sampans? Two apothecary shops? Six restaurants? Nineteen shoeshine stands? And clothes shops and shoe-making shops and knife-making shop? And did he not own fifty-one per cent of the first jewellery-making shop with expert Kwangtung carvers, both of jewels and of wood?

All this apart from his vast moneylending business. Ayeeee yah, and what a moneylender! Incredible to believe, he was so rich he loaned money at one and a half per cent less than was customary and monopolized the industry. And it was rumoured that he was in partnership with the Tai-Pan himself, and that with the death of his barbarian uncle new huge riches would come to him.

Among the Triads Gordon Chen needed nothing to improve his position. They knew who he was and he was obeyed without question. Even so, the Triads in the building trade and the stevedore trade and cleaning trade and night-soil-collecting trade, and in the fishing, cooking, and hawking trades, in the laundry, servant, and coolie trades – they too needed to borrow money from time to time and needed houses to live in; consequently they too were filled with great sorrow that their leader's barbarian uncle had died, and they happily gave the extra week of squeeze. They knew that it was wise to be on the side of the Tai-Pan of the Tai Ping Shan; they knew that part of the squeeze would pay for the offerings to the gods – roast suckling pigs and pastries and sweet meats and cooked meats without number, and lobsters and prawns and fish and crabs by sampan load, and breads and mountains of rice; they knew that once the gods had benignly looked upon such magnificence, these offerings would be distributed and that they themselves would feast upon them to the satisfaction of even the hungriest.

So all the people groaned aloud with the mourners, enjoying the drama of death hugely, blessing their joss that they were alive to mourn, to eat, to make love, to make money, to become perhaps – with joss – as rich, and thus have so colossal a face in death before all their neighbours.

Gordon Chen followed the cortège. He was very solemn and rent his garments – but with great dignity – and cried aloud to the gods of the huge loss he had suffered. The King of the Beggars followed him and thus both gained face. And the gods smiled.

When the grave was filled with the dry, sterile earth, Struan accompanied Sarah to the cutter.

'I'll come aboard this evening,' he said.

Without answering him, Sarah sat in the stern of the boat and turned her back on the island.

When the cutter was seaborne, Struan headed towards Happy Valley.

Beggars and sedan-chair coolies were infesting the roadway. But they did not bother the Tai-Pan; he had continued to pay the monthly squeeze to the King of the Beggars.

Struan saw Culum standing beside Tess in the midst of the entire Brock clan. He approached the group and raised his hat politely to the ladies. He glanced at Culum. 'Would you walk with me, Culum?'

'Certainly,' Culum said. He had not talked to his father since their return – not about important things, like how Uncle Robb's death would affect their plans, or when the engagement could be official. It was no secret that he had asked Brock formally for Tess at Whampoa on the retreat from Canton, and had been gruffly accepted. It was also no secret that because of the sudden tragedy, plans for the announcement had been held in abeyance.

Struan raised his hat again and walked off, Culum beside him.

They strolled the road silently. Others who had seen them with the Brocks shook their heads in renewed amazement that Brock had agreed to a marriage that surely was the Tai-Pan's brainchild.

'Morning, Mary,' Struan said as Mary Sinclair came up to him, Glessing and Horatio with her. She looked drained and unwell.

'Morning, Tai-Pan. Could I drop by this afternoon?' she asked. 'Perhaps I could have a few moments of your time?'

'Aye, of course. Around sunset? At my house?'

'Thank you. I can't tell you how sorry I am about – about your loss.'

'Yes,' Glessing said. 'Terrible luck.' Over the weeks he had become more and more impressed with Struan. Dammit, anyone who was Royal Navy, who was a powder monkey at Trafalgar, was worthy of the greatest respect, by God. When Culum had told him, he had immediately asked, 'What ship?' and had been astonished when Culum said, 'I don't know, I didn't ask.' He wondered if the Tai-Pan had served with his father. It was on the tip of his tongue to ask, but he could not, for Culum had told him privately. 'Damned sorry, Tai-Pan.'

438

'Thank you. How're things with you?'

'Fine, thank you. Damned lot of work to do, that's certain.'

'Might be a good idea to put deepwater storm anchors out for the capital ships.'

Glessing was abruptly attentive. 'You can smell a storm coming?'

'Nay. But this is typhoon season. Sometimes they come early, sometimes late.'

'Thanks for the suggestion. I'll have them begin this afternoon.' Damn wise, Glessing told himself. The man bears so much tragedy well. And he's as canny a seaman as ever sailed the seas. Mary thinks the world of him, and her opinion's valuable, by Jove. And because of him the fleet's slamming against Canton, by God, within a couple of days of those devils daring to fire the Settlement. Damn the admiral's eyes! Why the devil won't that stupid bugger give me back my ship? Wonder if I dare ask the Tai-Pan to put in a word for me? 'Are you going to join the fleet?'

'I dinna ken.' Struan glanced at Horatio. 'When did you get back, lad?'

'Last night, Tai-Pan. His Excellency sent me back to represent him at the funeral. I'm glad to pay my respects. I'll be going back with the tide.'

'It was kind of him, and kind of you. Please give him my regards.'

'He was most anxious to find out how His Highness was.'

'Na so bad. He's aboard *China Cloud*. Why do you na pay him a visit? I think his hip's damaged, but you can never tell this early. See you later, Mary.' He raised his hat again, and he and Culum took their leave. Struan wondered about Mary. I suppose she wants to tell me about the children. Hope nothing's amiss. What's the matter with Horatio and Glessing? They seem so tense and ruffled.

'May I see you to the hotel, Miss Sinclair?' Glessing was saying. 'Perhaps you'd both care to lunch with me at the dockyard?'

'I'd like that, George dear,' Mary said, 'but Horatio won't be able to join us.' Before Horatio could say anything she added quietly, 'My dear brother told me you asked formally for my hand in marriage.'

Glessing was startled. 'Yes, er – yes, I did. I hope – well, yes.'

'I would like to tell you that I accept.'

'By Jove!' Glessing took her hand and kissed it. 'I swear to God, Mary, by the Lord Harry, by Jove! I swear –' He turned to thank Horatio. His joy vanished. 'God's death, what's the matter?'

Horatio's eyes were fixed malevolently on Mary. He forced a twisted smile but did not look away from her. 'Nothing.'

'You don't approve?' Glessing's voice was tight.

'Oh yes, he does, don't you, dear brother?' Mary broke in.

'It's – you're very . . . very young and—'

'But you do approve, don't you? And we'll be married three days before Christmas. If that would suit you, George?'

Glessing was chilled by the blatant animosity between sister and brother. 'Is that satisfactory, Horatio?'

'I'm sure that Tai-Pan would appreciate your approval Horatio.' Mary was glad that she had decided to marry George. Now she would have to get rid of the baby. If May-may could not help, then she would have to ask the Tai-Pan for the favour that he owed her. 'I'm accepting George,' she said defiantly, hiding her fear.

'Be damned to both of you!' Horatio stalked off.

'What in God's name's the matter with him? Does that mean he approves? Or that he doesn't?' Glessing asked irately.

'He approves, George dear. Don't worry. And please forgive me for being so abrupt, but I wanted it said now.'

'No, Mary. I'm sorry. I had no idea that your brother was so bitterly against it. If I'd thought for a moment – well, I wouldn't have been so precipitate.' His joy at being accepted was twisted by the pain he saw in Mary's face. And by his ever-present fury at not being with the fleet. God damn the admiral! The pox on this cursed shore berth and the pox on Sinclair. How the devil could I ever have liked that bastard! How dared he be so rude?

'I'm so glad you're here, George,' he heard her say.

He saw her brush away some tears and his happiness returned. Without the shore job he would never be able to spend so much time with Mary. He blessed his luck! She'd accepted him and that was all that counted. He put his arm in hers. 'No more tears,' he said. 'This is the best day in my life and we're going to have lunch and celebrate. We'll dine together tonight – and every lunch and every dinner from now on. We'll make the announcement next month. From now on I'll look after you. If anyone troubles you, he'll have to answer to me, by God!'

Struan and Culum were having brandy in the factory office. The room was vast, stone-floored. In it were a polished teak desk and ships' lanterns, a barometer in gimbals near the teak door, Quance paintings on the walls, well-oiled leather chairs and sofa, sweetly smelling.

Struan stood at the window and stared at the harbour. The calm expanse seemed empty without the fleet and troopships. Of the clippers, only *China Cloud* and the *White Witch* remained. There were a few merchantmen which had not yet found full cargoes for home, and several incoming ships that had just arrived with stores ordered last year.

Culum was studying that painting that hung over the mantel. It was the portrait of a Chinese boat girl wearing a cloak; she was startlingly beautiful. She carried a basket under her arm, and was smiling.

Culum wondered if the rumour were true – that this was his father's mistress who lived in his house a few hundred yards away.

'I canna leave now as we planned. I've decided to stay,' Struan said, without turning from the window.

Culum felt a shaft of disappointment. 'I could manage. I'm sure I could.'

'Aye. In time.'

Culum marvelled again at the wisdom of his friend Gorth. Last night on the quarterdeck of the *White Witch*, Gorth had said, 'You mark my words, old friend. He'll never leave now. I'll wager wots you like, but he'll be acalling you in and he'll say he'll not be leaving. It be a terrible thing to say, but you and me's to wait for dead men's shoes.'

'But I couldn't manage, Gorth, by myself. Not as Tai-Pan, not alone.'

'O' course you could. Why, if you needs help, which you won't, I'd help you all you needs. And so will Da'. After all, Culum, you be family now. Of course you could manage, by God. But if you says that, the Tai-Pan'll say, "Sure you can, Culum. *In time*." '

'You really think I could?'

'No doubt on God's green earth. Wot's so hard, eh? You buys and sells, and yor comprador takes most of the risk. Ships is ships and tea's tea and opium's opium. A Tai-Pan makes decisions, that be all. Just common sense mostly. Why, look wot you did over the knoll! You decided right clever. *You* did, no one else. And you forced him to talk to Da' about Tess, and Da' forced him to give you and Tess a safe harbour.'

'Perhaps I could manage the house if all was quiet. But not Longstaff and a war and Jin-qua.'

'Them's unimportant. The war be out of our'n hands, howsomever your Da' would like to pretend otherwise. An' as for that old fox Jin-qua, I can helps you keep that monkey in place. No, Culum, we's to wait till they dies, and that be terrible when we's young with new ideas

441

and wot not. An' even if they gives us reins now, wot's so wrong with that? Our Da's protects our back at home and we seeks their help at the drop of a bowler. Not like we was casting they out. It be their house, o' course. But they'd never believe that. They both be having salt water for brain. They've to keep all to theyselves, and then and only then'll they be happy. He'll sluff you off with "You be needin' experience – two or three years," but that mean for ever . . .'

Culum stared at his father's back. 'I could manage, Tai-Pan.'

Struan turned to him. 'Longstaff? Jin-qua and the war?'

'The war's not in your hands, is it?'

'No. But without guidance Longstaff would have wrecked us years ago.'

'If you were to leave, well, it's not like you'd be washing your hands of the house, would it? If there was anything I couldn't handle, I'd ask you at the drop of a bowler.'

'When I leave, lad, you have to be in total charge. The mails take six months home and back. Too much could happen in that time. You need experience. You're na ready yet.'

'When will I be?'

'That depends on you.'

'You promised I'd be Tai-Pan a year after – well, a year after Uncle Robb.'

'Aye. If you were ready. And you're na ready for me to leave as planned. Brock and Gorth'll eat you up.'

Yes, Culum told himself, Gorth's right again. It's dead men's shoes. 'Very well. What can I do to prove I'm worthy?'

'Nothing more than you're doing, lad. You need more experience. Two years, three – I'll tell you when I'm sure.'

Culum knew that nothing could be gained by arguing at this time. 'Do you want me to take over Uncle Robb's departments?'

'Aye. But for the moment order nothing and sell nothing and sack naebody wi'out my approval. I'll give you a specific letter of instruction. Help Vargas to assess our loss in the Settlement and put the books in order.'

'When do you think it would be all right to announce our engagement?'

'Have you discussed this with Brock?'

'Only when I saw him at Whampoa. He suggested Midsummer Night.'

Struan suddenly remembered Scragger and what he had said about Wu Kwok: that Wu Kwok could be ambushed easily at Quemoy on

Midsummer Night. He knew that now he had no alternative but to gamble that Scragger had been speaking the truth and to go after Wu Kwok. Wu Kwok dead would mean one less hazard for Culum to worry about. What about the other three half coins? What Machiavellian 'favours' would they require? And when? He looked at the calendar that was on his desk. Today was June 15th. Midsummer Night was nine days off. 'Leave it for Midsummer Night. But only a small party. Just family,' he added with thin irony.

'We've thought about the wedding present we want you to give us. It was Tess's idea.' He handed a sheet of paper to Struan.

'What is it?'

'Just a solemn contract to forget the past and be friends. To be signed by the Brocks and the Struans.'

'I've already made the only bargain I'll make with those two,' Struan said, giving it back without reading it.

'Gorth's willing, and he said his father would be.'

'I'll bet Gorth is, by God. But Tyler will na sign any such paper.'

'If he's willing, will you sign it?'

'No.'

'Please.'

'No.'

'Our children will belong to both of you and—'

'I've considered the children carefully, Culum,' Struan interrupted. 'And a lot of other things. I doubt very much if your children will have an uncle and a grandfather on their mother's side by the time they're old enough to understand what those are.'

Culum stalked to the door.

'Wait, Culum!'

'Will you please give us the present we ask for, beg for?'

'I canna. They'll never honour that. Gorth and Brock are after your hide and—'

Culum slammed the door in his face.

Struan drank another brandy, then hurled the glass into the fireplace.

That night Struan lay awake in the four-poster beside May-may. The windows were open to the moon and to the breeze that carried a bracing salt tang. Outside the vast net which enclosed the bed a few mosquitoes relentlessly sought an entrance to the food within. Unlike most of the Europeans, Struan had always used a mosquito net. Jinqua had advised it as good for health, years upon years ago.

Struan was brooding about the malarial night gases, afraid that he and May-may were breathing them now.

And he was concerned about Sarah. When he had seen her a few hours ago, she had told him she was determined to leave by the first boat.

'You're na strong enough,' he had said. 'Nor is Lochlin.'

'Even so, we're leaving. Will you make the arrangements or shall I? You've a copy of Robb's will?'

'Aye.'

'I've just read it. Why should you be trustee for his share of the company, not me?'

'It's na a woman's job, Sarah! But you need na worry. You'll get every penny.'

'My lawyers will see to that, Tai-Pan.'

He had controlled his anger with an effort. 'This is typhoon season. It's a bad time to sail home. Wait till fall. You'll both be stronger then.'

'We leave at once.'

'Have it your own way.'

He had gone to see Zergeyev. The Russian's wound was inflamed but not gangrenous. So there was hope. Next he had returned to his office and had written a dispatch for Longstaff, telling him that he had heard the pirate Wu Kwok would be at Quemoy on Midsummer Night, that frigates should lie in wait for him, that he knew these waters well and would be glad to lead the expedition if the admiral wished. He had sent the dispatch to Horatio. And just before he left for home, the army doctors had come to see him. They told him there was no doubt any more. The fever of Happy Valley was malaria . . .

He twisted fitfully in the bed.

'You like to play backgammon?' May-may asked, as tired as he was, and as restless.

'No, thank you, lass. Can you na sleep either?'

'No. Never mind,' she replied. She was worried about the Tai-Pan. He had been strange this day. And she was worried about Mary Sinclair. This afternoon Mary had arrived early, before Struan had returned. Mary had told her about the baby, and about her secret life in Macao. Even about Horatio. And Glessing. 'I'm sorry,' Mary had said in tears. They were speaking Mandarin, which they both preferred to Cantonese. 'I had to tell someone. There's no one I can ask for help. No one.'

'There, Ma-ree, my dear,' May-may had said. 'Don't cry. First we'll have some tea and then we'll decide what to do.'

So they had had tea, and May-may had been astonished at the

barbarians and the way they looked at life and sex. 'What help do you need?'

'Help to – to get rid of the child. My God, it's already beginning to show.'

'But why didn't you ask me weeks ago?'

'I hadn't the courage. If I hadn't forced the issue with Horatio, I'd still not have the courage. But now . . . what can I do?'

'How long is it in your womb?'

'Almost three months, less a week.'

'That's not good. Ma-ree. It may be very dangerous after two months.' May-may had considered the practicability of Mary's problem, and the dangers that it entailed. 'I will send Ah Sam to Tai Ping Shan. I've heard there's a herbalist who may be able to help you. You understand it may be very dangerous?'

'Yes. If you can help me, I'll do anything. Anything.'

'You're my friend. Friends must help each other. But you must never, never tell anyone.'

'I promise, before God.'

'When I've got the herbs, I'll send Ah Sam to your servant, Ah Tat. Can you trust her?'

'Yes.'

'When's your birthday, Ma-ree?'

'Why?'

'The astrologer will have to find an auspicious day to take the medicine, of course.'

Mary had told her the day and the hour.

'Where will you take the medicine? You can't at the hotel – or here. It may take days for you to recover.'

'Macao. I'll go to Macao. To my – my private house. It'll be safe there. Yes, I'll be safe there.'

'These medicines do not always work, my dear. And they are never easy.'

'I'm not afraid. It will work. It must work,' Mary had said.

May-may shifted in the bed.

'What's amiss?' Struan asked.

'Nothing. Just the baby moving.'

Struan put his hand on the slight roundness of her belly. 'We'd better get a doctor to look at you.'

'Nay, thank you, Tai-Pan, never mind. None of those barbarian devils, thank you. In this I will be as always, Chinese.'

445

May-may lay back smoothly, content with her child, sad for Mary. 'Mar-ee did na look well, did she?' she said tentatively.

'No. And that lass has something on her mind. Did she tell you what it was?'

May-may did not want to lie, but she was reluctant to tell Struan that which might not really concern him. 'I think she's just worried about her brother.'

'What about him?'

'She said she wants to marry the man Glessing.'

'Oh, I see.' Struan had known that Mary had mainly come to see May-may and not to see him. He had hardly spoken to her other than to thank her for taking the children to Macao. 'I suppose Horatio does na approve and she wants me to talk to him? Is that what she came about?'

'Nay. Her brother approves,' May-may said.

'That's surprising.'

'Why? This Glessing is bad man?'

'Nay, lassie. It's just that Mary and Horatio have been very close for years. He'll find it very lonely without her here.' Struan wondered what May-may would say if she knew about Mary's secret house in Macao. 'She's probably poorly because she's worried over him.'

May-may said nothing and shook her head sadly at the troubles of man and woman. 'How is it with the young lovers?' she asked, trying to find out what was truly bothering him.

'All right.' He had never told her what he and Brock had said to each other.

'Have you decided what to do about devil fever?'

'Na yet. I think you should go back to Macao.'

'Yes, please, Tai-Pan. But na before you decide about Hong Kong.'

'It's dangerous here. I dinna want aught to happen to you.'

'Joss,' she said with a shrug. 'Of course, our fêng shui is very gracious bad.' She put her hand on his chest and smoothed him, then kissed him gently. 'Once you said me that were three things you had to do before you would decide about a Tai-tai. Two I know. Wat was the third?'

'To pass over The Noble House into safe hands,' he said. Then he told her what Brock had said, and about his argument with Culum today.

She was silent a long time, thinking through the problem of the third thing. And because the solution was so easy, she hid it deep in her heart and said innocently, 'I said I would help you with the first two, that I would think about the third. This third is too much to me. I canna help, much as I would like.'

'Aye,' Struan said. 'I dinna ken what to do. At least,' he added, 'there's only one answer.'

'The killing answer is unwisdom,' she said firmly. 'Very unwisdomly dangerous. The Brocks will be expect it. Everyone. And you risk vengeance of your terrible law wat stupidly demands eye for eye whoever has eye which is crazy mad. Why else be riches, heya? You must na do it, Tai-Pan. And I further counsel you give your son and new daughter the present they desire.'

'I canna do that, by God. That'd be like cutting Culum's throat mysel'!'

'Even so, that is my counsel. And I further counsel a fantastical immediate marriage.'

'That's out of the question,' he exploded. 'That'd be in very bad taste, an insult to the memory of Robb, and ridiculous.'

'I agree very heartedly Tai-Pan,' May-may said. 'But I seems to memory that following barbarian custom – which for once follows wise Chinese custom – the girl comes into the house of the husband. Na the opposite, heya? So the immediater the Brock girl gets from under the Gorth's thumb, the sooner the Brocks lose controls over your son.'

'What?'

'Aye wat! What for is your son sick crazy in the head? He needs to bed her fantastical bad.' Her voice rose as Struan sat up in the bed. 'Now, dinna give me arguments, by God, but listen and then I will listen dutifully. That's wat's making him crazy sick – because the poor boy's cold and weary and unbedded by night. That is fact. Why for you na say open, heya? I say open. He's frantic hot. So he listen with tongue hanging up to all that Gorth crazy talk. Me, if I was him, I'd do likewise because brother has power over sister! But let son Culum have the girl, and then will your Culum spend hour after godrot hour listening to brother Gorth? By God, nay! He spends every minute in bed playing busums and exhausting himself and making babies and he detest interruptions from you, from Brock or from Gorth.' She looked at him sweetly. 'Nay?'

'Aye,' he said. 'I love you for your shrewdness.'

'You love me 'cause I drive you crazy mad but sleep you, sleep you till you busted.' She laughed, greatly satisfied with herself. 'Next: start *them* building *their* house. Tomorrow. Put their minds on that and away from fan-quai Gorth. She is young, eh? So thought of own house will fantastical occupation her mind. This will anger the Brocks and they will begin to decide wat sort of home and so on, which will anger her and bring her closer to you wat gave her home. Gorth must absolute oppose quick marriage – thusly turn Culum against him, because he loses his – wat you call it? – his jack in the hole.'

'Ace in the hole.' He hugged her delightedly. 'You're fantastical! I should have thought of that mysel'. There's another land sale next week. I'll buy you a marine lot. Because you're wise.'

'Huh!' she said crossly. 'You think I protect my man for filthy Hong Kong land? A single miseration suburban lot? For taels of silver? For jades? Wat for you think this priceless T'Chung May-may is, heya? A dirty lump of dogmeat whore?'

She rattled on and on and reluctantly allowed him to gentle her, proud that he understood the value of land to a civilized person, and grateful that he had given her such face by pretending not to know how pleased she was.

The room was quiet now, except for the soft drone of the mosquitoes.

May-may curled up against Struan and turned her mind to the solution of the third thing. She decided to think about it in Mandarin and not in English because she did not know enough words with the correct shades of meaning. Like 'nuance', she thought. How would you say that in barbarian? Or 'finesse'? The solution of the third thing required true Chinese nuance and perfect finesse.

The solution is so delightfully simple, she told herself gleefully. Assassinate Gorth. Have him assassinated in such a way that no one suspects that the assassins are anything other than robbers or pirates. If it's done clandestinely in this fashion, one danger to my Tai-Pan is removed; Culum is protected from an obvious future hazard; and the father Brock can do nothing because he still is bound by the astounding and unbelievable finality the barbarians put into such a 'holy' oath. So simple. But fraught with danger. I must be very careful. If my Tai-Pan ever found out, he would bring me before one of the barbarian judges – that revolting Mauss probably! My Tai-Pan would charge me – even me, his adored concubine. And I would be hanged. How ridiculous!

After all this time, and all my studying – learning their tongue and assiduously trying to comprehend them – certain barbarian attitudes are still absolutely beyond me. How ridiculous to have one law for all – for rich or for poor. What else is the point of working and sweating to become rich and powerful?

448

Now, what is the best way? she asked herself. I know so little about assassination. How to do it? Where? When?

May-may was awake the whole night. With the coming of dawn she had decided on the best procedure. Then she slept sweetly.

XXIX

By Midsummer Day Happy Valley was in complete despair. The malaria had continued to spread but there was no pattern to the epidemic. Not everyone in the same house was infected. Not every house in the same area was touched.

Coolies would not come into Happy Valley until the sun was high, and they returned to Tai Ping Shan before dark. Struan and Brock and all the traders were at their wits' end. There was nothing they could do – except move, and moving meant disaster. Staying could mean worse disaster. And though there were many who insisted it could not be the poisoned soil and polluted night air that brought malaria, only those who slept in the valley were afflicted. The God-fearing believed as Culum had believed, that the fever was the will of God, and they redoubled their petitions to the Almighty to protect them; the godless shrugged, though equally frightened, and said, 'Joss.' The trickle of families back to the ships developed into a flood, and Queen's Town became a ghost town.

But this despair did not grip Longstaff. He had returned from Canton last night in the flagship, flushed with success, and as he lived aboard her and had no intention of residing in Happy Valley, he knew he was out of reach of the poisonous night gases.

He had gained everything he had set out to get – and more.

The day after the investing of Canton had been launched the six million taels of ransom he had demanded were paid in full, and he had called off the attack. But he had ordered immediate preparations for full-scale war to the north. And this time there would be no stopping – not until the treaty was ratified. Within a few weeks the promised reinforcements from India would arrive. And then the armada would sail north once more to the Pei Ho – to Peking – and the Orient would be opened up once and for all.

'Yes, absolutely,' Longstaff chuckled. He was alone in his quarters in

450

HMS *Vengeance*, admiring himself in a mirror. 'You're really quite clever, my dear fellow,' he told himself aloud. 'Yes indeed. Much more clever than the Tai-Pan and he's the personification of cleverness.' He put down the mirror and rubbed cologne on his face, then glanced at his fob watch. Struan was due in a few minutes. 'Even so, no need to let your right hand know what your left's doing, eh?' he chortled.

Longstaff could hardly believe that he had arranged the acquisition of the tea seeds so easily. At least, he reminded himself contentedly, *Horatio* had arranged it. I wonder why the man's so distraught over his sister's wanting to marry Glessing. I would have thought that it was an excellent match. After all, she *is* rather drab and mousy – though she did look stunning at the ball. But a damned good piece of luck he hates Glessing, what? And damned good piece of luck that he's always hated the opium trade. And damned clever the way I put the idea into his mind – the hook baited with Glessing's removal.

' 'Pon me word, Horatio,' he had said a week ago at Canton, 'damnable business all this opium trade, what? And all because we have to pay bullion for tea. Pity British India doesn't *grow* it, what? Then there'd be no need for opium. We'd simply outlaw it, save the heathen for better things, what? *Plant seeds* of goodness among them instead of that damnable drug. Then the fleet could go home and we'd live in peace and quiet forevermore.'

Within two days Horatio had drawn him aside and had excitedly expounded the idea of getting tea seed from the Chinese and sending them to India. He had been suitably astonished, but he had allowed Horatio to convince him of the idea's potential.

'But, good Lord, Horatio,' he had said, 'how on earth could you get the tea seeds?'

'This was my plan: I'll speak privately to Viceroy Ching-so, Your Excellency. I'll say that you're a keen gardener, that you have the idea of turning Hong Kong into a garden. I'll ask for fifty pounds each of mulberry seeds, cotton seeds, spring rice, camelias and other flowers as well as assorted teas. That will throw him off tea specifically.'

'But Horatio, he's a very clever man. He must know that few, if any, of these plants will grow in Hong Kong.'

'Of course. He'll just put it down to barbarian stupidity.' Horatio had been beside himself with excitement.

'But how would you get him to keep this secret? Ching-so would tell the mandarins – or the Co-hong – and they would surely tell the traders. You know how those damned pirates would move heaven and earth to prevent what you propose. They would surely see through your purpose. What about the Tai-Pan? Surely you see what you propose would put him out of business.'

'He's rich enough now, Your Excellency. We have to stamp out the opium evil. It's our duty.'

'Yes. But both Chinese and Europeans would be implacably against the plan. And when Ching-so realizes what you really have in mind, as he must – well, you'd never get the seeds then.'

Horatio had thought a moment. Then he had said, 'Yes. But if I were to say that in return for the favour to me – for I just want you, my employer, to be happy with a surprise gift – I, who have to count the chests of silver and sign for them, well, I might not miss one chest – then he would be sure to keep it secret from everyone.'

'What's the value of a chest?'

'Forty thousand taels of silver.'

'But the bullion belongs to Her Majesty's Government, Horatio.'

'Of course. In your negotiations you could "privately" ensure that there is one extra chest which could not be official so the Crown would not lose. The seeds would be your gift to Her Majesty's Government, sir. I would be honoured if you would say that it was your idea. I'm sure it was. Something you said triggered it in my mind. And rightfully you should have the credit. After all, you are the plenipotentiary.'

'But if your plan succeeds, then you're not only destroying the China traders, you're destroying yourself. That doesn't make sense.'

'Opium is a terrible vice, sir. Any risk we'd take is justified. But my job depends on your success, not on opium.'

'If this succeeds then too, you're undermining the very foundations of Hong Kong.'

'But it will take many years for tea to thrive elsewhere. Hong Kong is safe in your time, sir. Hong Kong will still be the emporium of Asian trade. Who knows what will happen over the years?'

'Then I take it you want me to investigate the tea-growing possibilities with the Viceroy of India?'

'Who but you, Your Excellency, could bring the idea – your idea – to a perfect conclusion?'

He had reluctantly allowed himself to be persuaded and had cautioned Horatio about the need for extreme secrecy.

The very next day Horatio had reported happily, 'Ching-so agreed! He said that within six weeks to two months the chests of seeds would be delivered to Hong Kong, Your Excellency. Now all that remains to make everything perfect, for me, is for Glessing to be sent home immediately. I believe Mary's just infatuated. Pity she can't be given a year or so to make absolutely sure she knows what she'd doing, out of reach of his everyday influence . . .'

Longstaff chuckled again at youth's transparent attempt at subtlety. He brushed his hair and opened the cabin door and went into the chart room. He searched through the papers in his safe and found the letter that Horatio had translated for him weeks ago. 'No more need for this,' he said aloud. He tore up the paper, leaned out of a porthole, threw the pieces into the sea, and watched them float away.

Perhaps Glessing should be sent home. The girl is under age and Horatio's in a very difficult position. Well, I'll think about it. After the seeds are *en route* to India.

He saw Struan's longboat approaching. Struan was sitting disconsolately amidships. The Tai-Pan's gravity reminded Longstaff about the malaria. What the devil are we going to do about that, eh? Ruins the whole strategy of Hong Kong, what?

Struan was staring out the stern windows waiting patiently for Longstaff to finish.

' 'Pon me word, Dirk, it was almost as though Ching-so knew we were going to demand six million taels. The ransom was instantly ready. To the penny. He was most apologetic for the raping of the Settlement. He said it was those damned anarchists – the Triads. He's ordered a thorough investigation and hopes to be able to crush them once and for all. It seems that one of their leaders has fallen into his hands. If he can't get anything out of the man, no one can. He promised to tell me at once the names of the Triads here.'

Struan turned from the windows and sat in a deep leather chair. 'That's very good, Will. I'd say you've done a remarkable job. Remarkable.'

Longstaff felt very pleased. 'I must say things went according to plan. Oh, by the way. The information you sent about the pirate Wu Kwok. I would have preferred you to lead the flotilla, but the admiral was adamant. He went himself.'

'That's his privilege. Let's hope he does a good job tonight. I'll rest a lot easier if that devil's sunk.'

'Quite right.'

'Now all you have to do is to save Hong Kong, Will. Only you can do it,' Struan said, praying that once more he would make Longstaff put into effect the plan he had eventually devised as the only way to save the necks of all of them. 'I think it advisable for you to order an immediate abandonment of Happy Valley.'

'Bless my soul, Dirk,' Longstaff cried, 'if I do that, well – that's tantamount to abandoning Hong Kong!'

'Queen's Town's malarial. At least Happy Valley is. So it has to be abandoned.'

Longstaff shakily took some snuff. 'I can't order the abandonment. That'd make me responsible for all losses.'

'Aye. You've decided to use the six million taels to reimburse everyone.'

'Good God. I can't do that!' Longstaff burst out. 'The bullion belongs to the Crown. The Crown – only the Crown – can decide what to do with it!'

'You've decided that Hong Kong's too valuable to risk. You know you've got to move quickly. It's a gesture worthy of a governor.'

'I absolutely can't, Dirk! Not at all. Impossible!'

Struan went over to the sideboard and poured two glasses of sherry. 'Your entire future depends on it.'

'Eh? It does? How?'

Struan gave him a glass. 'Your reputation at court is tied to Hong Kong. Your whole Asian policy – and that means the Crown's Asian policy – is focused on Hong Kong. Rightly. Without Hong Kong safe the governor, on Her Majesty's behalf, will na be able to dominate Asia as he should. Without a town built there's nae safety for you or for the Crown. Happy Valley's dead. So a new town must be built and quickly.' Struan drank the sherry and savoured it. 'If you immediately reimburse those who've built, you'll restore confidence at once. All the traders will rally to your support – which you'll need in the future. Dinna forget, Will, many have considerable influence at court. It's a grand gesture, one worthy of you. Besides, the reimbursement is really being paid for by the Chinese anyway.'

'I don't understand.'

'Within three months you'll be at the gates of Peking, commander-in-chief of an invincible force. The cost of the expedition will be, say, four million. Add six million for the damage to the Settlement. Ten million. But you ask fourteen million, which would be fair indemnity. The extra four million will be the basis of your Hong Kong government treasury – and thus one of the richest colonial treasuries in the Empire. Actually, instead of fourteen you will demand twenty million: The extra six repays the six you – in your shrewdness – "invested" in Hong Kong on the Crown's behalf. Dinna forget, without a safe base you *canna dare* make the attack north. Without Hong Kong safe, England's dead in Asia. Without Hong Kong safe you're dead. You're thinking of the whole future of England, Will. It's that simple!'

Struan could sense Longstaff's mind churning the possibilities. This was the only possible solution. The only way everyone could save face and save the island. And the instant he saw Longstaff open his mouth to speak he said, 'A last thing, Will. You get the money back at once, most of it.'

'Eh?'

'You hold a land sale immediately. The bidding will be furious for the new lots. Where does the money go? Back into your government treasury. You gain all ways. The land you're selling costs you nothing. You know how desperately you need money for all the problems of government – salaries, police, the governor's palace, roads, law courts, harbour vessels and a thousand other things, and you certainly canna use the ransom money as such. I'd say that it would be a statesmanlike master-stroke. You *have* to make the decision now because it's impossible for you to wait six months for a dispatch to go to England and the obvious approval to arrive back here. You save Hong Kong at no cost. But most of all you show Zergeyev very bluntly that England plans to stay in Asia permanently. I'd say, Will, your astuteness would impress the entire Cabinet. And certainly Her Majesty the Queen. And permanent honours go with such approval.'

Eight bells sounded. Longstaff took out his fob watch. It was slow, and he turned the hands to noon as his mind tried to find a flaw in Struan's reasoning. There was none, he told himself. He felt queasy at the realization that but for the Tai-Pan he would have done nothing about the fever. Except stay out of the valley, hoping that a cure would turn up. He, too, had been perturbed by the epidemic, but, well, it was more important to win the Canton war first.

Yes. There's no flaw. Damn it, you almost jeopardized a brilliant future. Certainly it's exceeding instructions, but then governors and plenipotentiaries have unwritten powers and therefore it's only an expedient extension of necessity. We can't wait till next year to implant Her Majesty's will on the heathen. Absolutely not. And the scheme about the tea seeds fits neatly into the design and shows foresight on a scale that even surpasses the Tai-Pan's.

Longstaff had an overpowering impulse to tell Struan about the seeds. But he controlled himself. 'I think you're right. I'll make the announcement right away.'

'Why do you na call a meeting of the Tai-Pans tomorrow? Give them two days to present construction and land bills to your treasurer. Set the new land sale for a week hence. That'll give you time to get the lots surveyed. I suppose you'll want the new townsite to be near Glessing's Point.'

'Yes. My thought entirely. That will be the best spot. After all, it was one we considered a long time back.' Longstaff got up and poured more sherry, then tugged the bellpull. 'As always, I'm pleased to have your counsel, Dirk. You'll lunch, of course.'

'I'd better be getting along. Sarah's leaving for home with the tide tomorrow, aboard *Calcutta Maharajah*, and there's a great deal to do.'

'Very bad luck. About Robb and your niece.'

The door opened. 'Yes, sorr?' the master-at-arms asked.

'Ask the general if he'll join me for lunch.'

'Yes, sorr. Beggin' yor pardon, sorr, but Mrs Quance is waiting to see you. And Mr Quance. Then there's all these' – he gave Longstaff a long list of names – 'wot've come by to ask for appointments. Shall I say yo're busy to Mrs Quance?'

'No. I'd better see her now. Please don't go yet, Dirk. I'm afraid I may need moral support.'

Maureen Quance strode in. Aristotle Quance followed her. There were dark rings under his lifeless eyes. Now he was simply a drab little man. Even his clothes were untidy and colourless.

'Morning, Mrs Quance,' Longstaff said.

'The saints preserve Your Excellency on this foin day.'

'Morning, Your Excellency' Aristotle said, his voice barely audible, his eyes on the deck of the cabin.

'Good day to you, Tai-Pan,' Maureen said. 'There'll be a settlin' of yor bill with the grace of St Patrick himself, in a few days.'

'There's nae hurry. Morning, Aristotle.'

Aristotle Quance slowly looked up at Struan. His eyes filled with tears as he read the warmth on Struan's face. 'She broke all my brushes, Dirk,' he choked out. 'This morning. All of them. And my – she threw my paints in the sea.'

'It's about that we're acoming to see you, Yor Excellency,' Maureen said thickly. 'Mr Quance's decided to give up all that painting folderol at long last. He wants to settle down to a nice steady job. And it's about a job we've come to see Yor Excellency.' She looked back at her husband and her face wearied. 'Anything at all. So long as it's steady and pays a fair wage.' She turned back to Longstaff. 'A nice clerking job, perhaps. Poor Mr Quance hasn't much experience.'

'Is, er, that what you want, Aristotle?'

456

'She broke my brushes,' Quance said helplessly. 'That's all I had. My paints and brushes.'

'We agreed, me foin boy, didn't we now? By all that's holy? Eh? No more painting. A nice steady job and stand up to yor responsibilities to yor family, and no more galavanting.'

'Yes,' Aristotle said numbly.

'I'd be glad to offer a post, Mrs Quance,' Struan broke in. 'I need a clerk. Pay's fifteen shillings a week. I'll throw in your lodgings on the hulk for one year. After that you're on your own.'

'May the saints preserve you, Tai-Pan. Done. Now thank the Tai-Pan,' Maureen said.

'Thank you, Tai-Pan.'

'Be at the office at seven o'clock tomorrow morning, Aristotle. Sharp, now.'

'He'll be there, Tai-Pan, don't you be after worrying. May the blessings of St Peter be on you in these troubled times for looking after a poor wife and her starving children. Good day to you both.'

They left. Longstaff poured himself a stiff drink. 'Good God. I'd never've believed it. Poor, poor Aristotle. You're really going to make Aristotle Quance a clerk?'

'Aye. Better me than some other. I'm shorthanded.' Struan put on his hat, very satisfied with himself. 'I'm na one to interfere 'twixt husband and wife. But anyone who'd do that to old Aristotle's nae right to the title "wife", by God!'

Longstaff smiled suddenly. 'I'll detach a capital ship if it'll help. The total resources of Her Majesty's Government are at your disposal.'

Struan hurried ashore. He hailed a closed sedan chair and directed the coolies.

'Wait-ah, savvy?' he said as it arrived at its destination.

'Savvy, Mass'er.'

He walked past the surprised doorman into the parlour of the house. The room was carpeted – large sofas, chintz curtains, mirrors and bric-à-brac. There was a rustle from the back and then approaching footsteps. A small old lady came through the bead curtains. She was neat and starched and grey-haired, with big eyes and spectacles.

'Hello, Mrs Fortheringill,' Struan said politely.

'Well, Tai-Pan, how nice to see you,' she said. 'We haven't had the pleasure of your company in many a long year. It's a little early for callers, but the young ladies are making themselves presentable.' She smiled and revealed her yellowed false teeth.

'Well, you see, Mrs Fortheringill—'

'I quite understand, Tai-Pan,' she said knowingly. 'There comes a time in every man's life when he—'

'It's about a friend of mine.'

'Don't you worry, Tai-Pan, mum's the word in this establishment. No need to worry. We'll have you fixed in a jiffy.' She got up hastily. 'Girls!' she called out.

'Sit down and listen to me! It's about Aristotle!'

'Oh! That poor bleeder's got himself in a proper mess.'

Struan told her what he wanted, and the girls were sad for him to leave.

As soon as he got home, May-may said, 'Wat for you go whore-house, heya?'

He sighed, and told her.

'You think I believe that, heya?' Her eyes were spiteful.

'Aye. You'd better.'

'I believe you, Tai-Pan.'

'Then stop looking like a dragon!' He went into his room.

'Good,' May-may said as she closed the door behind them. 'Now we see if you tell truth. We make love at once. I'm madly desiring you, Tai-Pan.'

'Thank you, but I'm busy,' he said, finding it difficult to keep from laughing.

'Ayee yah on your busy,' she said, beginning to unbutton her honey-coloured pyjamas. 'We make love immediate. I soon see if some mealymouthed whore's took your strength, by God. And then your old mother'll deal with you, by God.'

'You're busy too,' Struan said.

'I'm very busy.' She stepped out of her silk trousers. Her ear-rings jingled like bells. 'And you better have busy plenty very quick.'

He studied her and allowed none of his happiness to show. Her stomach was curved nicely with the child four months in her womb. He took her quickly in his arms and kissed her violently and lay on the bed and let his weight crush her a little.

'Be careful, Tai-Pan,' she said breathlessly, 'I'm na one of your busum-boned barbarian giants! Kissing does na prove nothing. Off with clotheses, then we see for truth!'

He kissed her again. Then she said in a different voice, 'Take off clotheses.'

He leaned on his elbows and looked down at her, then rubbed his nose against hers, no longer teasing. 'There's nae time now. I've got to go to an engagement party and you've got to pack.'

'Wat for pack?' she asked startled.

'You're moving to *Resting Cloud*.'

'Why?'

'Our fêng shui's bad here, lassie.'

'Oh good, oh very terrifical good!' She flung her arms around him. 'Truly go from here? For always?'

'Aye.'

She kissed him and quickly slid from under his arms and began to dress.

'I thought you wanted to make love,' he said.

'Huh! Wat for is that proof? I know you too much. Even if you had whore one hour past you're bull enough to pretend and pull cotton over eyes of your poor old mother.' She laughed and flung her arms around him again. 'Oh, good to leave bad fêng shui. I pack hurriedly.'

She ran for the door, and shrieked 'Ah Sam-ahhhh!' Ah Sam hurried up anxiously, followed by Lim Din, and after a tumult of shouting and jabbering Ah Sam and Lim Din scurried away, beseeching the gods in vast, noisy excitement. May-may came back and sat on the bed and fanned herself. 'I'm packing,' she said cheerfully. 'Now I help you dress.'

'Thank you, but I'm capable of doing that.'

'Then I watch. And scrub your back. The bath is waiting. I am very gracious glad you decided to leave.' She chattered on exuberantly as he changed. He bathed and she shrieked for hot towels, and when they were brought, she dried his back. And all the time she was wondering if he had had a whore after he had arranged about the funny little artist who had painted her portrait so beautifully. Not that I mind, she told herself, rubbing him vigorously. It's just that he shouldn't go into one of those places. Absolutely not. Very bad for his face. And very bad for my face. Very bad. Soon those dirty dogmeat servants will begin spreading rumours that I can't take care of my man. Oh gods, protect me from dirty gossips, and him from dirty doxies of all kinds.

It was dusk before she and Ah Sam and Lim Din were ready, and they were all exhausted with the drama and excitement of leaving. Coolies took the luggage away. Others waited patiently beside the closed sedan chair that would carry her to the cutter.

May-may was heavily veiled. She stood momentarily at the gateway of the garden with Struan and looked back at her first house on Hong Kong. But for the bad fêng shui – and the fever that was part of the fêng shui – she would have been loath to depart.

The twilight was pleasant. A few mosquitoes whined about them. One settled on her ankle but she did not notice it.

The mosquito drank its fill, then flew away.

Struan went into the great cabin of the *White Witch*. The Brocks were all waiting for him, except Lillibet who had already gone to bed. Culum was beside Tess.

'Evening,' Struan said. 'Sarah sends her apologies. She's na feeling well.'

'Welcome aboard,' Brock said, his voice rough and charged with worry, his face brooding.

'Well,' Struan said with a laugh, 'this is nae way to start a happy occasion.'

'Baint the occasion, by God, as thee well knowed. We all be bankrupted – at least hurt terrible by godrotting malaria.'

'Aye,' Struan said. He smiled at Culum and Tess and, noting their disquiet, decided to tell them all the good news now. 'I hear Longstaff's ordering an abandonment of Queen's Town,' he said nonchalantly.

'By blood of Christ!' Gorth exploded. 'We can't abandon. We be putting too much brass into land and buildings. We can't abandon. Weren't for thy godrotting picking of that cursed valley, we wouldn't—'

'Hold thy tongue,' Brock said. He turned to Struan. 'Thee stands to lose more'n us'n, by God, yet there thee be with smile on thy face. Why?'

'Father,' Tess said, terrified that anger would spoil their evening and the unbelievable acceptance of Culum, 'can we have a drink? The champagne's chilled and ready.'

'Yus, of course, Tess luv,' Brock said. 'But dost thee understand wot Dirk's sayed? We stand to lose a turr'ble sum of brass. If we've to abandon, then our future be black as pitch. And his too, by God.'

'The future of The Noble House's white as the cliffs of Dover,' Struan said evenly. 'Na only ours but yours too. Longstaff's going to reimburse all of us for the money we laid out in Happy Valley. Every penny. In cash.'

'That baint possible!' Brock exclaimed.

'That's a lie, by God!' Gorth said.

Struan turned on him. 'A piece of advice, Gorth. Dinna call me a liar more than once.' Then he told them what Longstaff intended to do.

Culum was awed by the beauty of the arrangement. He saw clearly that though his father had never implied that he had influenced

Longstaff's decision, he must have been instrumental in arranging it so delicately. He remembered his first meeting with Longstaff and how his father had manipulated the man like a puppet. Culum's faith in himself was shaken. He realized that what Gorth had said was not completely true, that he could never dominate Longstaff as his father had done – to save them again.

'That's almost like a miracle,' he said, and held Tess's hand.

'By all that be holy, Tai-Pan,' Gorth said. 'I takes back wot I sayed. Apologies – it were sayed in shock. Yus, I've to hand it to you.'

'Dirk,' Brock began with grim good humour, 'I be glad – right glad – to have thee as relation. Thee saved our'n necks and that be God's truth.'

'I've done nae such thing. It was Longstaff's idea.'

'Quite right,' Brock said sardonically. 'More power to him. Liza, drinks, by God. Dirk, thee's given us'n powerful reason to celebrate this evening. Thee's made the whole night, by God. So let's drink and make merry.' He took a glass of champagne, and when they all had their glasses, he raised his in a toast. 'To Tess 'n' Culum, and may they be always having a calm sea an' a safe harbour all their days.'

They all drank. Then Brock shook hands with Culum, and Struan hugged Tess, and there was friendship among them all.

But only temporarily. They all knew it. But tonight they were prepared to forget. Only Tess and Culum felt safe.

They all sat down to dinner. Tess was wearing a gown that showed her ripening figure to advantage, and Culum was almost helpless with adoration. More wine was poured, and there was more laughter and more toasts. In a lull Struan took out a stiff envelope and handed it to Culum. 'A small gift for the two of you.'

'What is it?' Culum asked. He opened the envelope. Tess craned to look too. The envelope contained a sheaf of papers, one heavy with Chinese characters.

'It's a deed to some land just above Glessing's Point.'

'But there never beed land for sale there,' Brock said suspiciously.

'His Excellency approved certain deeds of the village Chinese who owned land before we took over Hong Kong. This is one of them. Culum, you and Tess now own an acre jointly. The view's fine. Oh yes, and along with the deed there's enough building material for a house with seven bedrooms, a garden and a summer house.'

'Oh, Tai-Pan,' Tess said, her smile glorious, 'thank you! Thank you!'

'Our own land? And our own house? You really mean it?' Culum asked, dazed by his father's magnanimity.

461

'Aye, lad. I thought you'd like to begin building immediately. I've made an appointment for both of you with our architect tomorrow at noon. To start the plans.'

'We all be leaving tomorrow for Macao,' Gorth said sharply.

'But, Gorth, you won't mind delaying for a day or two, will you?' Culum said. 'After all, this is very important—'

'Oh yes,' Tess said.

'– and with the solution to Queen's Town and the land sale –' Culum stopped and turned excitedly to his fiancée. 'Sousa's the best architect in the East.'

'Our man Remedios be better, I be thinking,' Brock said, furious with himself that he had not thought of letting them build themselves a house. He had planned to give them one of the company houses in Macao as a wedding present, well away from Struan's influence.

'Oh yes, he's very good, Mr Brock,' Culum said quickly, sensing the jealousy. 'If we're not satisfied with Sousa, then perhaps we could talk to him.' Then to Tess, 'You agree?' and then to Struan, 'I can't thank you enough.'

'Nae thanks, Culum. Young people should have a good start in life and a place of their own.' Struan was delighted with the way he had aroused Gorth and Brock.

'Yes,' Liza said complacently. 'By gum, a right proper truth.'

Brock picked up the deed and studied it. 'Thee be sure the deed be proper?' he asked. 'It baint regirar.'

'Aye. Longstaff confirmed it. Officially. His chop's on the last page.'

Brock frowned at Gorth, his tufted brows a black bar on his weathered face. 'I be thinking that mayhaps we better be alooking into these native deeds.'

'Yes,' Gorth said. He looked directly at Struan. 'Mayhaps there baint any left for sale, Da'.'

'I imagine there're others, Gorth,' Struan said easily, 'if you're prepared to track them down. By the way, Tyler, as soon as the new land lots are surveyed, perhaps we'd better discuss our position.'

'My thort too,' Brock said. 'As before, Dirk. But thee pick first this time.' He passed the deed back to Tess, who caressed it.

'Culum, be thee still deputy colonial secretary?'

'I think so.' Culum laughed. 'Though my duties have never been specified. Why?'

'Nothing.'

Struan finished his wine and decided that it was time. 'Now that

Happy Valley's abandoned and solved, and the new town's to go up at the Crown's cost, Hong Kong's future's assured.'

'Yus,' Brock said expansively, some of his humour returning, 'now that the Crown be risking along o' us'n.'

'So I think there's nae need to delay the marriage. I propose Tess and Culum marry next month.'

There was a shocked silence.

Time seemed to be standing still for all of them. Culum wondered what was behind the smile that Gorth wore so badly, and why the Tai-Pan chose next month, and – oh God, let it be next month.

Gorth knew that next month would obliterate his hold over Culum and that, by God, this must not come to pass. Whatever Da' says, he swore, no marriage soon. Next year perhaps. Yes, perhaps. Wot's in that devil's mind?

Brock too was trying to divine Struan's purpose – for Struan must have a purpose and it boded no good for him or for Gorth. His instinct immediately told him to delay the marriage. But he had sworn before God to give them safe harbour – as Struan had – and he knew that such an oath would bind Struan as it would bind him.

'We could have the first banns read next Sunday,' Struan said, deliberately breaking the tension. 'I think next Sunday would be fine.' He smiled at Tess. 'Eh, lass?'

'Oh yes. Yes,' she said, and held Culum's hand.

'No,' Brock said.

'It's too fast,' Gorth snapped.

'Why?' Culum asked.

'I was just thinking of you, Culum,' Gorth said placatingly, 'and your uncle's sad loss. It'd be unseemly haste, very unseemly.'

'Liza, luv,' Brock said throatily, 'you an' Tess be excused. We be joining thee after port.' Tess threw her arms around his neck and whispered, 'Oh please, Da',' and the four men were left alone.

Brock got up heavily and found the bottle of port. He poured four glasses and handed them around.

Struan sipped the wine appreciatively. 'Very good port, Tyler.'

'It be the year of '31.'

'A great year for port.'

Another silence fell.

'Will it be convenient to postpone your leaving for a few days Mr Brock?' Culum said uncomfortably. 'I mean if it's not possible – but I'd certainly like Tess to see the land and the architect.'

'With abandonment and land sale and all, we baint leaving now.

Least,' Brock said, 'Gorth and me baint. Liza and Tess and Lillibet should, soon as possible. Macao be healthful this time of year. And cooler. Baint it, Dirk?'

'Aye. Macao's fine now,' Struan said, lighting a cheroot. 'I hear the inquiry in the archduke's accident will be next week.' He looked searchingly at Gorth.

'That were bad joss,' Brock said.

'Yes,' Gorth echoed. 'Guns be going off all over.'

'Aye,' Struan said. 'Just after he was hit, someone shot the leader of the mob.'

'I did that,' Brock said.

'Thank you, Tyler,' Struan said. 'Were you firing too, Gorth?'

'I was for'ard getting afloat.'

'Yus,' Brock said. He tried to remember if he had seen anyone firing. He recalled only sending Gorth forward. 'Bad joss. Mobs be terrible, and at a time like that who knowed wot might happen.'

'Aye,' Struan said. He knew that if the bullet had been aimed, Gorth was the culprit. Not Brock. 'Just one of those things.'

The oil lamps that hung from the rafter swung gently to the heel of the ship as the wind backed slightly. The seamen, Gorth, Brock and Struan, were suddenly alert. Brock opened a porthole and sniffed the breeze. Gorth was peering out the stern windows at the sea, and Struan listened to the spirit of the ship.

'Baint nothing,' Brock said. 'Wind's backed a few degrees, that be all.'

Struan went out into the passageway where a barometer was hanging. It read 29.8 steady. The air pressure had varied but a fraction in weeks.

'It's bonny steady,' he said.

'Yus,' Brock replied. 'But soon it baint steady and then we be battening down. I see thee's set storm buoys off thy wharf in deep water.'

'Aye.' Struan poured more port and offered the bottle to Gorth. 'You want some more?'

'Thankee,' Gorth said.

'Dost smell storm soon, Dirk?'

'Nay, Tyler. But I like to have the buoys ready just in case. Glessing's ordered them set out for the fleet, though.'

'Thy suggestion?'

'Aye.'

'I hear rumours he be marrying young Sinclair's sister.'

464

'Seems that marrying's in the air.'

'I think they'll be very happy,' Culum said. 'George idolizes her.'

'Be right hard on Horatio,' Gorth said, 'her leaving him abrupt-like. She be all the kin he has. An' she's young, under age.'

'How old is she?' Culum asked.

'Nineteen,' Struan said.

The tension increased in the cabin.

'Tess is very young,' Culum said, his voice anguished. 'I wouldn't want her hurt in any way. Even though – well, can we . . . what do you think, Mr Brock? About the marriage? Next month? Whatever's best for Tess is right for me.'

'She be very young, lad,' Brock said, fogged with the wine, 'but I be glad that you be asaying what you be saying.'

Gorth kept his voice kind and steady. 'A few months baint troubling you two, eh, Culum? Next year's hardly half a year away.'

'January's seven months away, Gorth,' Culum said impatiently.

'It baint up to me. Wot's good for the two of you is good for me, says I.' Gorth drained his glass and poured some more. 'Wot say you, Da'?' he said, deliberately putting Brock on the spot.

'I be thinking about that,' Brock said, examining his glass carefully. 'She be very young. Haste be unseemly. You knowed each other bare three month and—'

'But I love her, Mr Brock,' Culum persisted. 'Three months or three years won't make any difference.'

'I knowed, lad,' Brock said, not unkindly. He remembered the joy that had bloomed in Tess when he had told her that he would accept Culum. 'I just be thinking for thy good, for her good. I needs time to think.' To figure what's in thy mind, Dirk, he said to himself.

'I think it would be very good for them and for us.' Struan could feel the warmth that radiated from Culum. 'Tess is young, yes. But Liza was young too, and so was Culum's mother. Marrying young's the fashion. They've money to spare. And a rich future. With joss. So I say that it would be good.'

Brock rubbed his forehead with the back of his hand. 'I be thinking. Then I'll tell thee, Culum. It be a sudden idea, that be why I needs time.'

Culum smiled, touched by the sincerity in Brock's voice. For the first time he liked and trusted him. 'Of course,' he said.

'How much time do you think you'll need, Tyler?' Struan asked bluntly. He saw that Culum was softening in the face of their false amiability, and he felt that pressure would make them show their true colours. 'We should na keep the youngsters like hooked fish, and

465

there'll be a lot to plan. We have to make this the greatest wedding Asia has ever seen.'

'As I recalls it,' Brock said curtly, 'it be bride's Da' wot gives wedding. An' I be quite compitent in knowing wot be right and wot be not.' He knew that Struan had him hooked and was playing him. 'So any plan for wedding be our'n.'

'Of course,' Struan said. 'When will you let Culum know?'

'Soon.' Brock got up. 'We be joining the ladies.'

'How soon, Tyler?'

'Now, you heared Da',' Gorth said hotly. 'Why rile him, eh?'

But Struan ignored him, and continued to stare at Tyler.

Culum feared that there would be a fight, and that this would change Brock's mind about their marrying at all. At the same time he wanted to know how long he would have to wait and was glad that Struan was pressing Brock. 'Please,' he said. 'I'm sure Mr Brock won't – will consider the idea carefully. Let's leave it for the present.'

'What you want to do is your own affair, Culum!' Struan said with pretended rage. 'But *I* want to know now. I want to know if you're being used or if they're cat-and-mousing you, by God.'

'That's a terrible thing to say,' Culum said.

'Aye. But I've finished with you for the moment, so hold your tongue.' Struan whirled back on Brock, knowing that his rebuking Culum had pleased both Brock and Gorth. 'How much time, Tyler?'

'A week. A week, no more, no less.' Brock looked at Culum and again his voice was kind. 'No harm in asking for time, lad, and no harm in asking for answer man to man. That be proper. A week, Dirk. Do that satisfy thy godrotting bad manners?'

'Aye. Thank you, Tyler.' Struan walked to the door and opened it wide.

'After thee, Dirk.'

Safe in the privacy of his quarters aboard *Resting Cloud*, Struan told May-may all that had happened.

She listened attentively and delightedly. 'Oh good, Tai-Pan. Oh very good.'

He took off his coat and she hung it in the wardrobe for him. A scroll fell out of the sleeve of her tunic gown. He picked it up and glanced at it.

The scroll was a delicate Chinese water-colour painting with many characters. It was a fine sea-landscape and there was a tiny man bowing before a tiny woman below vast misted mountains. A sampan floated off the rocky shore.

'Where'd this come from?'

'Ah Sam got it in Tai Ping Shan,' she cried.

'It's pretty,' he said.

'Yes,' May-may said calmly, awed again by the marvellous subtlety of her grandfather. He had sent the scroll to one of his minions in Tai Ping Shan from whom May-may bought jade from time to time. Ah Sam had accepted it unsuspectingly as a casual gift for her mistress. And though May-may was sure that Ah Sam and Lim Din had examined the picture and the characters very carefully, she knew that they would never know that it contained a secret message. It was too well concealed. Even her grandfather's private family chop was cleverly overlaid with another. And the verse – 'Six nests smile at the eagles, Greenfire is part of the sunrise, and the arrow harbingers nestlings of hope' – was so simple and beautiful. Now, who but she could know that he was thanking her for the information of the six million taels; that 'greenfire' meant the Tai-Pan; and that he would be sending her a messenger, bearing some form of arrow as identification to help her in any way possible.

'What do the characters mean?' Struan was asking.

'Difficult to transtalk, Tai-Pan. I dinna know all the words, but it says, "Six bird houses smile at great birds, green fire is in the sunup, arrow brings" ' – she frowned, seeking the English word – ' "brings little hope birds" .'

'That's gibberish, by God,' Struan laughed.

She sighed happily. 'I adore you, Tai-Pan.'

'I adore you, May-may.'

'This next time we build our house, first a fêng-shui gentlemans, please?'

467

XXX

At dawn Struan went aboard the *Calcutta Maharajah*, the merchant-man that was taking Sarah home. The ship belonged to the East India Company. She was to sail with the tide in three hours, and seamen were making last-minute preparations.

Struan went below and knocked on the door of Sarah's stateroom. 'Come in,' he heard her say.

'Morning, Sarah.' He closed the door behind him. The cabin was large and commodious. Toys and clothes and bags and shoes were scattered about. Lochlin was querulously half asleep in a tiny crib near the porthole.

'You all set, Sarah?'

'Yes.'

He took out an envelope. 'This is a sight draft for five thousand guineas. You'll get one every two months.'

'You're very generous.'

'It's your money – at least, it's Robb's money, na mine.' He put the envelope on the oak table. 'I'm just following his will. I've written to arrange the trust fund that he wanted, and you'll be getting the papers on that. Also I've asked Father to meet the ship. Would you like to have my Glasgow house until you find one you like?'

'I want nothing of yours.'

'I've written our bankers to honour your signature – again according to Robb's instructions – up to the amount of five thousand guineas once a year in excess of your allotment. You must realize that you're an heiress, and I must advise you to be careful, for many'll try to take your wealth away. You're young and there's life ahead—'

'I want none of your advice, Dirk,' Sarah said witheringly. 'As to taking what's mine, I can look after myself. I always have. And as to my youth, I've looked into the mirror. I'm old and ugly. I know it and you know it. I'm used up! And you sit nicely on your godrotting fence and play man against man and woman against woman. You're

468

glad Ronalda's dead – she'd more than served her stint. And that clears the way nicely for the next. Who's it to be? Shevaun? Mary Sinclair? The daughter of a duke, perhaps? You always set your sights high. But whoever it is, she'll be young and rich and you'll suck her dry like everyone else. You feed off others and give nothing in return. I curse you before God, and I pray that I live to spit on your grave.'

The child began to wail pathetically, but neither heard the cries as they stared at each other.

'You forgot one truth, Sarah. All your bitterness comes from your belief that you picked the wrong brother. And you made Robb's life a hell because of it.'

Struan opened the door and left.

'I hate the truth,' Sarah cried to the emptiness that surrounded her.

Struan was slumped morosely at his desk in the factory office, hating Sarah but understanding her, and tormented by her curse. 'Do I feed on others?' he unwittingly said aloud. He looked at May-may's portrait. 'Aye, I suppose I do. Is that wrong? Do they na feed off me? All the time? Who's wrong, May-may? Who's right?'

He remembered Aristotle Quance. 'Vargas!'

'Yes, senhor.'

'How's Mr Quance doing?'

'It's very sad, senhor. Very sad.'

'Send him here, please.'

Quance appeared at the door shortly.

'Come in, Aristotle,' Struan said. 'Close the door.'

Quance did as he was ordered and then came and stood unhappily in front of the desk.

Struan spoke rapidly. 'Aristotle, you've nae time to lose. Sneak out of the factory and get down to the wharf. There's a sampan waiting for you. Get aboard *Calcutta Maharajah* – she sails in a few minutes.'

'What, Tai-Pan?'

'Help is at hand, laddie. Make a huge scene as you get aboard *Calcutta Maharajah* – wave and shout as you sail out of harbour. Let everyone know you're aboard.'

'God bless you, Tai-Pan.' A flicker of light returned to the eyes. 'But I don't want to leave Asia. I can't leave.'

'There're coolie clothes in the sampan. You can sneak aboard the pilot's lorcha outside the harbour. I've bribed the crew but not the pilot, so keep out of his way.'

'Great balls of fire!' Quance seemed to have grown inches. 'But – but where can I hide? Tai Ping Shan?'

'Mrs Fortheringill's expecting you. I've arranged a two-month visit. But you owe me the money I've laid out, by God!'

Quance threw his arms around Struan and let out a bellow which Struan cut short. 'God's blood, watch yoursel'. If Maureen has any suspicion, she'll make our lives a misery and she'll never leave.'

'Quite right,' Quance said in a hoarse whisper, and raced for the door. He stopped short. 'Money! I'll need money. Can you make a small loan, Tai-Pan?'

Struan was already holding up the small bag of gold. 'Here's a hundred guineas. I'll add it to your bill.'

The bag vanished into Quance's pocket. Aristotle embraced Struan again and blew a kiss at the portrait over the fireplace. 'Ten portraits of the most beauteous May-may. Ten guineas under my regular price, by God. Oh, immortal Quance, I adore you. Free! Free by God!'

He danced a Kankana, then threw himself into the air and was gone.

May-may stared at the jade bracelet. She took it closer to the sunlight that streamed through the open porthole and examined it meticulously. She had not mistaken the arrow that was delicately carved on it, or the characters that read: 'Nestlings of hope.'

'It's beautiful jade,' she said in Mandarin.

'Thank you, Supreme of the Supreme,' Gordon Chen replied in the same language.

'Yes, very beautiful,' May-may replied, and gave it back to him. He took the bracelet and enjoyed its touch for a moment, but he did not put it back on his wrist. Instead he threw it deftly out of the porthole and watched it until it had disappeared under the sea.

'I would be honoured if you would have accepted it as a gift, Supreme Lady. But certain gifts belong to the sea darkness.'

'You're very wise, my son,' she said. 'But I am not a Supreme Lady, Only concubine.'

'Father has no wife. Therefore you are his Supreme of the Supreme.'

May-may did not reply. She had been staggered when the messenger turned out to be Gordon Chen. And the jade bracelet notwithstanding, she decided to be very cautious and talk in riddles in case he had intercepted the bracelet – just as she knew that Gordon Chen would be equally cautious and talk in riddles.

'Will you take tea?'

'That would be too much trouble, Mother.'

'No trouble, my son,' she said. She went into the next cabin. Gordon Chen followed her and was awed by the beauty of her walk and her tiny feet, his head swimming with the delicacy of her perfume. You've loved her from the moment you saw her, he told himself. She's your creation in some ways, for it was you who gave her barbarian speech and barbarian thoughts.

He blessed his joss that the Tai-Pan was his father and that his respect for him was immense. He knew that without this respect his love for May-may could not remain filial. Tea was brought and May-may dismissed Lim Din. But for propriety she allowed Ah Sam to stay. She knew that Ah Sam would be unable to understand the Soochow dialect in which she resumed her conversation with Gordon.

'An arrow can be very dangerous.'

'Yes, Supreme Lady, in the wrong hands. Are you interested in archery?'

'When I was very small we used to fly kites, my brothers and I. Once I used a bow but it frightened me. But I suppose that sometimes an arrow could be a gift from the gods and not dangerous.'

Gordon Chen thought a moment. 'Yes. If it was in the hands of a starving man and he aimed at game and hit his prey.'

Her fan moved prettily. She was glad that she knew the way his mind worked; this made the transfer of information easier and more exciting. 'Such a man would needs be most careful if he had but one chance to hit the mark.'

'True, Supreme Lady. But a wise hunter has many arrows in his quiver.' What game has to be hunted? he asked himself.

'A poor woman can never experience the masculine joys of hunting,' she said calmly.

'Man is the yang principle – he is the hunter by choice of the gods. Woman is the yin principle – the one to whom the hunter brings food to be prepared.'

'The gods are very wise. Very. They teach the hunter what game is fit to eat and what is not.'

Gordon Chen sipped his tea delicately. Does she mean that she wants someone found? Or someone hunted and killed? Who could she want found? Uncle Robb's late mistress and his daughter, perhaps? Probably not, for there'd be little need of such secrecy – and certainly Jin-qua would never involve me. By all the gods, what hold has this woman over Jin-qua's head? What has she done for him that would force him to order me – and through me the full power of the Triads – to do whatever she wishes?

Then a rumour he had heard clicked into place: the rumour that Jin-qua knew before all others that the fleet was immediately returning to Canton, and not going north as all had presumed it would. She must have sent word privately to Jin-qua and thus put him into her debt! Ayeeee yah, such a debt! Such fore-knowledge certainly saved Jin-qua three to four millions of taels.

His respect for May-may increased. 'Sometimes a hunter has to use his weapons to protect himself against the wild beast of the forest,' he said, giving her a different opening.

'True, my son.' Her fan snapped close and she shuddered. 'The gods protect a poor woman against such evil things.'

So she wants someone killed, Gordon thought. He examined the porcelain teacup and wondered who. 'It's joss that evil walks in many places. High and low. On the mainland, on this island.'

'Yes, my son,' May-may said, and her fan fluttered and her lips trembled slightly. 'Even on the sea. Even among the highborn and the very rich. Terrible are the ways of the gods.'

Gordon Chen almost dropped his cup. He turned his back on May-may and tried to collect his scattered wits. 'Sea' and 'highborn' meant only two people. Longstaff or the Tai-Pan himself. Dragons of Death, to go against either would precipitate a holocaust! His stomach turned over. But why? And was it the Tai-Pan? Not my father, oh gods. Don't let it be my father!

'Yes, Supreme Lady,' he said with a trace of melancholy, for he knew that his oath bound him to do anything she ordered. 'The gods have terrible ways.'

May-may had marked the sudden change in Gordon Chen and she could not understand why. She hesitated, baffled. Then she got up and walked to the stern windows.

The flagship was gently at anchor in the harbour, sampans surrounding it in a sparkling sea. *China Cloud* was beyond at storm anchor, the *White Witch* nearby. 'The ships are so beautiful,' she said. 'Which do you find the most pleasing?'

He came close to the windows. He did not think that it could be Longstaff. There would be no purpose in that, not for her. For Jin-qua perhaps, but not for her. 'I think that one,' he said gravely, nodding at *China Cloud*.

May-may gasped and dropped her fan. 'God's blood,' she said in English. Ah Sam looked up briefly and May-may was instantly under control. Gordon Chen picked up the fan and bowed low as he returned it to her.

'Thank you,' she continued in Soochow dialect. 'But I prefer that ship.' She pointed with her fan at the *White Witch*. She was still shaky from the horrified realization that Gordon Chen thought she wanted her adored Tai-Pan dead. 'The other is priceless jade. Priceless, you hear? Inviolate, by all the gods. How dare you have the impertinence to think otherwise?'

His relief was palpable. 'Forgive me, Supreme Lady. I would kowtow a thousand times to show my abject apology here and now, but your slave might find it curious,' he said in a rushing mixture of deliberately intermingled Soochow and Mandarin words. 'For a moment a devil entered my foolish head and I did not understand you clearly. Of course I would never, never consider a balance of such ships, one against another.'

'Yes,' she said. 'If one thread of hempen rope, if one sliver of wood, were touched on the other, I would follow him who dared to defile such jade into the bowels of hell, and there I'd claw off his testicles and rip out his eyes and feed him them with his entrails!'

Gordon Chen winced, but kept his voice conversational. 'Never fear, Supreme Lady. Never fear. I will kowkow a hundred times as penitence for not understanding the difference between jade and wood. I would never imply – I would never wish you to think that I do not understand.'

'Good.'

'If you will excuse me now, Supreme Lady, I will be about my business.'

'Your business is unfinished,' she said curtly. 'And manners suggest that we should have more tea.' She clapped her hands regally to Ah Sam and ordered fresh tea. And hot towels. When Ah Sam returned, May-may talked in Cantonese. 'I hear many ships are leaving for Macao very soon,' she said, and Gordon Chen immediately understood that Brock was to be removed underground in Macao and at once.

Ah Sam brightened. 'Do you think we'll be going? Oh, I'd adore to see Macao again.' She smiled coyly at Gordon Chen. 'Do you know Macao, honoured sir?'

'Of course,' he said. Normally a slave would not have dared to address him. But he knew that Ah Sam was May-may's personal confidante and private slave, and as such had manifold privileges. Also he found her very pretty – for a Hoklo boat girl. He glanced back at May-may. 'Unfortunately I won't be able to go this year. Though many of my friends ply back and forth.'

May-may nodded. 'Have you heard that last night Father's barbarian son was engaged to be married? Can you imagine it? To the daughter of his enemy. Extraordinary people, these barbarians.'

'Yes,' Gordon Chen said, surprised that May-may thought it necessary to make the removal of Brock any clearer. Surely she doesn't want the whole family destroyed? 'Unbelievable.'

'Not that I mind the father – he's old, and if the gods are just, his joss will run out soon.' May-may tossed her head and set her jade and silver ornaments ajingling. 'As for the girl, well, I suppose she'll make good sons – though what any man could see in that thick-legged, cow-chested thing I really can't imagine.'

'Yes,' Gordon said agreeably. So Brock's not to be killed. Nor the daughter. That leaves the mother and the brother. The mother is most unlikely; therefore it is the brother. Gorth. But why only the brother, why only Gorth Brock? Why not father and brother? For obviously both are a danger to the Tai-Pan. Gordon's respect for his father increased immensely. How subtle to make it look as though May-may was the instigator of the stratagem! How devious to drop a hint to May-may, who went to Jin-qua, who came to me! How subtle! Of course, he told himself, that means the Tai-Pan knew May-may passed on secret information – he must have deliberately given her the information to put Jin-qua in her debt. But does he therefore know about the Triads? And me? Surely not.

He felt very tired. His mind was surfeited with so much excitement and danger. And he was greatly worried by the increased pressure the mandarins were exerting on the Triads in Kwangtung. And on the Triads in Macao. And even on Tai Ping Shan. The mandarins had many agents among the people on the hill, and though most were known and four already obliterated, the anxiety that their presence brought weighed heavily on him. If it became known that he was the Triad leader on Hong Kong, he could never return to Canton, and his life here would not be worth a sampan owner's faeces.

And, too, his senses were drowned by May-may's exquisite perfume and by Ah Sam's blatant sexuality. I'd like to bed the slave, he thought. But that's unwise, and dangerous. Unless Mother suggests it. Better hurry back to Tai Ping Shan to the arms of the most valuable concubine on the hill. By all the gods, she's almost worth the thousand taels she cost. We'll make love ten times tonight in ten different ways. He smiled to himself. Be honest, Gordon, it will be only thrice. And then thrice with joss – but how marvellous!

'I'm sad that I won't be able to go to Macao,' he said. 'I suppose all Father's relations by marriage will be going? Particularly the son?'

'Yes,' May-may said with a sweet sigh, knowing that her message was now clear, 'I suppose so.'

'Huh!' Ah Sam said contemptuously. 'There will be great happiness when the son leaves Hong Kong.'

'Why?' May-may asked attentively, and Gordon Chen was equally alert, his fatigue vanishing.

Ah Sam had been saving the rare information for such a dramatic time as this. 'This son is a real barbarian devil. He goes to one of the barbarian whorehouses two or three times a week.' She stopped and poured some tea.

'Well, go on, Ah Sam,' May-may said impatiently.

'He beats them,' she said importantly.

'Perhaps they displease him,' May-may said. 'A good beating could never hurt one of those barbarian whores.'

'Yes. But he flogs them and savages them before he lies with them.'

'You mean every time?' May-may asked incredulously.

'Every time,' Ah Sam said. 'He pays for the beating and then pays for the, well, the manipulation – for that's all the rest appears to be. *Pffff!* In and finished' – she snapped her fingers – 'just like that!'

'Huh! How do you know all this, eh?' May-may asked. 'I think you deserve a good pinching. I think you're making this all up, you weevil-mouthed slave!'

'I most certainly am not, Mother. That barbarian madam – the old witch, with the impossible name? The one with the glass eyes and the incredible self-moving teeth?'

'Fortheringill?' Gordon Chen asked.

'Quite right, honoured sir. Fortheringill. Well this madam has the biggest house in Queen's Town. Recently she bought six Hoklo girls and one Cantonese girl. One of the—'

'It was five Hoklo girls,' Gordon Chen said.

'Are you in that business, too?' May-may asked politely.

'Oh yes,' he replied. 'It's becoming quite profitable.'

'Go on, Ah Sam, my pet.'

'Well, Mother, as I was saying, one of the Hoklo girls is a relation of Ah Tat – who, as you know, is related to my mother – and this girl was assigned to be his partner for the night. Once was enough!' Ah Sam dropped her voice even more. 'He nearly killed her. He beat her belly and her buttocks till the blood flowed and then made her do peculiar things with his sex. Then—'

'What peculiar things?' Gordon Chen asked in an equal whisper, leaning closer.

'Yes,' May-may said, 'what things?'

'It's certainly not up to me to tell such weird and obscene practices, oh dear no, but she had to honour it with great facility with all parts of herself.'

'All?'

'All, Mother. What with the terrible beating and the way he bit her and kicked her and savaged her, the poor girl nearly died.'

'How extraordinary!' Then May-may told her sharply, 'I still think you're making it all up, Ah Sam. I thought you said that it was' – she snapped her fingers imperiously – '*pfft*, like that for him.'

'Quite right. It is. And he always blames the girl hideously, though it's never her fault. That's the main trouble. That and being so small and limp.' Ah Sam raised her hands to heaven and began to wail, 'May I never have children if I lied! May I die a withered spinster if I lied! May my ancestors be consumed by worms if I lied! May my ancestors' ancestors never rest in peace and never be reborn if I lied! May my—'

'Oh all right, Ah Sam,' May-may said testily. 'I believe you.'

Ah Sam huffily went back to sipping her tea. 'How would I dare to lie to my superb mother and her honoured relation? But I think the gods should surely punish such barbarian beast!'

'Yes,' Gordon Chen said.

And May-may smiled to herself.

BOOK FIVE

That afternoon Struan went aboard China Cloud. *He sent Captain Orlov to one of the lorchas and Zergeyev to spacious quarters in* Resting Cloud. *He ordered all sails set and the moorings let go and he fled the harbour into the deep.*

For three days he drove China Cloud *like an arrow southeast, her yards screeching with the fullness of canvas.*

He had gone to sea to cleanse himself. To cleanse away the dross and the words of Sarah and the loss of Robb and of Karen.

And to bless May-may and the joy of her.

He went to the bosom of the ocean as a lover who had been gone for an eternity, and the ocean welcomed him with squall and with storm, yet controlled, never endangering the ship or him who drove the ship. She sent her wealth sparingly, making him strong again, giving him life, giving him dignity, and blessing him as only the sea can bless a man, cleansing him as only the ocean can cleanse a man.

He drove himself as he drove the ship, not sleeping, testing the limit of strength. Watch after watch changed and still he walked the quarterdeck: sunrise to sunrise to sunrise, singing softly to himself and hardly eating. And never talking, except to force more speed, or to order a ripped shroud replaced or another sail set. He drove into the depths of the Pacific, into infinity.

On the fourth day he turned about and drove her for half the day northwest. Then he hove to and went below and shaved and bathed and slept for a day and a night, and the next dawn he ate a full meal. Then he went on deck.

'Morning, sorr,' *Cudahy said.*

'Set course for Hong Kong.'

'Yes, sorr.'

He stayed on the quarterdeck all day and part of the night, and once more he slept. At dawn he shot the sun and marked the chart and again ordered the ship hove to. Then he dived over the side and swam naked in the sea. The seamen crossed themselves superstitiously. There were sharks circling.

But the sharks kept their distance.

He climbed aboard and ordered the spotless ship cleaned and the decks holystoned – sand and broom and water – rigging replaced, sails tended, scuppers and cannon cleansed. All his own clothes and those of his men he cast overboard. He issued new gear to his men and took seamen's clothes for himself.

A double tot of rum was issued to all hands.

At dawn on the seventh day Hong Kong loomed on the horizon, dead ahead. The Peak was shrouded with mist. There was cirrus aloft and a lusty swell below.

He stood on the bowsprit, the spray billowing beneath him.

'Do your worst, Island!' he shouted into the wake of the east wind. 'I'm home!'

XXXI

China Cloud came back into harbour through the western channel. The rising sun was strong, the wind east and steady – and humid.

Struan was on the quarterdeck, naked to the waist, his skin deeply tanned and his red-gold hair sun-bleached. He trained his binoculars on the ships of the harbour. First *Resting Cloud*. Code flags fluttered on the mizzen: 'Zenith' – owner to come aboard immediately. Only to be expected, he thought. He remembered the last time – an eternity ago – that he had read 'Zenith' on *Thunder Cloud*, the time that had heralded the news of so many deaths, and Culum's arrival.

In the harbour there were more troopships than before. They were all flying the East India Company flags. Good. The first of the reinforcements. He saw a large three-masted brigantine near the flagship. The Russian flag flew aft and the tsarist pennant aloft the mainmast.

There were many more sampans and junks than usual scurrying over the waves.

After he had scanned the rest of the fleet meticulously, he turned to the shore, the sea tang mixing nicely with the smell of land. He could see activity near Glessing's Point and many Europeans and clusters of beggars walking Queen's Road. Tai Ping Shan seemed to have grown appreciably.

The Lion and the Dragon flew over the abandoned factory of The Noble House and the abandoned emptiness of Happy Valley.

'Four points t' starboard!'

'Aye, aye, sorr,' the helmsman sang.

Struan adroitly conned the lorcha alongside *Resting Cloud*. He pulled on a shirt and went aboard.

'Morning,' Captain Orlov said. He knew the Tai-Pan too well to ask where he had been.

'Morning. You're flying "Zenith". Why?'

'Your son's orders.'

'Where is he?'

'Ashore.'

'Please fetch him aboard.'

'He was sent for when you came into harbour.'

'Then why is he na here?'

'Can I have my ship back now? By Thor, Green Eyes, I'm mortal tired of being a captain-flunkey. Let me be a tea captain or an opium captain, or let me take her into Arctic waters. I know fifty places to get a cargo of furs – more bellygutting bullion for your coffers. That's not much to ask.'

'I need you here,' Struan grinned and years dropped from him.

'You can laugh, by Odin's foreskin!' Orlov's face twisted with his own smile. 'You've been to sea and I've been stuck on an anchored hulk. You look like a god, Green Eyes. Did you have storm? Typhoon? And why's my mains'l changed, and the fore-royal, crossjack, the flying jib? There're new halyards and stays and clew lines all over. Why, eh? Did you tear the heart out of my beauty just to clean your soul?'

'What kind of furs, Captain?'

'Seal, sable, mink – you name them and I'll find them – just so long as I can say to any, "Get to Hades off my ship," even you.'

'In October you sail north. Alone. Does that satisfy you? Furs for China, eh?'

Orlov peered up at Struan and knew at once that he would never sail north in October. A little shudder ran through him and he hated the second sight that plagued him. What's going to happen to me twixt June and October? 'Can I have my ship now? Yes or no, by God? October's a bad month and far off. Can I have my ship now, yes or no?'

'Aye.'

Orlov shinned over the side and stamped on to the quarterdeck. 'Let go the forehawser,' he shouted, then waved to Struan and laughed uproariously. *China Cloud* fell away from the mother ship and snaked daintily for her storm mooring off Happy Valley.

Struan went below to May-may's quarters. She was deeply asleep. He told Ah Sam not to awaken her; he would come back later. Then he went to the deck above, to his own private quarters, and bathed and shaved and put on fresh clothes. Lim Din brought him eggs and fruit and tea.

The cabin door opened and Culum hurried in. 'Where've you been?' he began with a rush. 'There're a thousand things that need to be done and the land sale's this afternoon. You might have told me before you disappeared. The whole place's in turmoil and—'

'Do you na knock on doors, Culum?'

'Of course, but I was in a hurry. I'm sorry.'

'Sit down. What thousand things?' Struan asked. 'I thought you could manage everything.'

'You're Tai-Pan, I'm not,' Culum said.

'Aye. But say I'd na come back today, what would you have done?'

Culum hesitated. 'Gone to the land sale. Bought land.'

'Did you make a deal with Brock on which lots we would na bid against each other?'

Culum was unsettled by his father's eyes. 'Well, in a way I made a tentative arrangement. Subject to your approval.' He took out a map and laid it on the desk. The site of the new town surrounded Glessing's Point, two miles west of Happy Valley. Level building space was cramped by the surrounding mountains and barely half a mile wide and half a mile deep from the shore. Tai Ping Shan overlooked the site and blocked expansion eastward. 'These are all the lots. I picked 8 and 9. Gorth said they wanted 14 and 21.'

'Did you check this with Tyler?'

'Yes.'

Struan glanced at the map. 'Why pick two lots next to each other?'

'Well, I don't know anything about land or factories or wharves, so I asked George Glessing. And Vargas. Then privately, Gordon Chen. And—'

'Why Gordon?'

'I don't know. Just that I thought it was a good idea. He seems to be very smart.'

'Go on.'

'Well, they all agreed 8, 9, 10, 14 and 21 were the best of the marine lots. Gordon suggested two together in case we wanted to expand, then one wharf would service two factories. At Glessing's suggestion I had Captain Orlov privately plumb the depth offshore. He said that's good rock bottom, but the shelf is shallow. We'll have to reclaim land from the sea and put our wharf well out.'

'Which suburban lots did you pick?'

Culum nervously pointed them out. 'Gordon thought we should bid on this property here. It's – well, it's a hill, and – well, I think it would be a fine place for the Great House.'

Struan got up and went to the stern windows and looked through the binoculars at the hill. It was west of Tai Ping Shan on the other side of the site. 'We'd have to build a road up there, eh?'

'Vargas said if we could buy suburban lots 9A and 15B we'd have an – I think he called it an "easement", something like that, and that

483

would protect our property. Later we could build on them and rent if we wished. Or resell later.'

'Have you discussed this with Brock?'

'No.'

'Gorth?'

'No.'

'Tess?'

'Yes.'

'Why?'

'No reason. I like talking to her. We talk about lots of things.'

'It's dangerous to talk to her about a matter like this. Like it or na, you've put her to a test.'

'What?'

'If Gorth or Brock bid for 9A and 15B, you know she canna be trusted. Without the smaller lots the hill's an extreme gamble.'

'She'd never say anything,' Culum said belligerently. 'It was private, between ourselves. Perhaps the Brocks have had the same idea. It won't prove anything if they do bid against us.'

Struan studied him. Then he said, 'Drink or tea?'

'Tea, thank you.' The palms of Culum's hands felt clammy. He wondered if Tess had indeed talked to Brock or to Gorth. 'Where did you go?'

'What other things need decisions?'

Culum collected his thoughts with an effort. 'There's a lot of mail, both for you and Uncle Robb. I didn't know what to do about it, so I put it all in the safe. Then Vargas and Chen Sheng estimated our Happy Valley costs and I – well – I signed for the bullion. Longstaff's paid everyone, like you said. I signed for it and counted it. And yesterday a man arrived from England on Zergeyev's ship. Roger Blore. He said he picked her up in Singapore. He wants to see you urgently. He won't tell me what he wants but, well – anyway I put him in the small hulk. Who is he?'

'I dinna ken, lad,' Struan said thoughtfully. He rang the bell on the desk and the steward came in. Struan ordered a cutter sent for Blore.

'What else, lad?'

'Orders for building materials and ships' supplies are piling up. We have to order new stocks of opium – a thousand things.'

Struan played with his mug of tea. 'Has Brock given you an answer yet?'

'Today's the last day. He asked me aboard the *White Witch* tonight.'

'Tess has na indicated her father's decision?'

'No.'

'Gorth?'

Again Culum shook his head. 'They're leaving for Macao tomorrow. Except Brock. I've been invited to go with them.'

'Are you going?'

'Now that you're back, I would like to. For a week – if he says we can marry soon.' Culum drank some tea. 'There'd be furniture to buy and – well, that sort of thing.'

'Did you see Sousa?'

'Oh yes, we did. The land is wonderful, and the plans are already drawn. We can't thank you enough. We were thinking – well, Sousa told us about the separate room for the bath and toilet you designed for your house. We – well, we asked him to build us one.'

Struan offered a cheroot, and lit it. 'How long would you have waited, Culum?'

'I don't understand.'

'For me to come back. The sea might have swallowed me.'

'Not you, Tai-Pan.'

'One day she might – one day she will.' Struan blew out a thread of smoke and watched it float. 'If I ever leave again without telling you where I'm going, wait forty days. Nae more. I'm either dead or never coming back.'

'Very well.' Culum wondered what his father was getting at. 'Why did you leave like that?'

'Why do you talk to Tess?'

'That's no answer.'

'What else has happened since I left?'

Culum was desperately trying to understand, but he could not. He had greater respect than before for his father, yet he still felt no filial love. He had talked for hours with Tess and had found an uncanny depth to her. And they had discussed their fathers, trying to fathom the two that they loved and feared and sometimes hated most on earth, yet ran to at the breath of danger. 'The frigates returned from Quemoy.'

'And?'

'They laid waste fifty to a hundred junks. Big and small. And three pirate nests ashore. Perhaps they sank Wu Kwok, perhaps they didn't.'

'I think we'll know soon enough.'

'The day before yesterday I checked your house in Happy Valley. The watchmen – well, you know no one will stay at night – I'm afraid it was broken into and looted badly.'

Struan wondered if the secret safe had been tampered with. 'Is there na any good news?'

'Aristotle Quance escaped from Hong Kong.'

'Oh?'

'Yes. Mrs Quance doesn't believe it, but everyone – at least almost everyone – saw him on the ship, the same that took Aunt Sarah home. The poor woman believes he's still in Hong Kong. Did you know about George and Mary Sinclair? They're going to be married. That's good, even though Horatio is terribly upset about it. But that's not all good either. We've just heard Mary's very sick.'

'Malaria?'

'No. A flux of some kind in Macao. It's very strange. George got a letter yesterday from the mother superior of the Catholic Nursing Order. Poor fellow's worried to death! You can never trust those Papists.'

'What did the mother superior say?'

'Only that she felt she should inform Mary's next of kin. And that Mary had said to write to George.'

Struan frowned. 'Why the devil did she na go to the Missionary Hospital? And why did she na inform Horatio?'

'I don't know.'

'Have you told Horatio?'

'No.'

'Would Glessing have told him?'

'I doubt it. They seem to hate each other now.'

'You'd better go with the Brocks and find out how she is.'

'I thought you'd want firsthand news, so I sent Vargas' nephew, Jesús, by lorcha yesterday. Poor George couldn't get leave of absence from Longstaff, and I wanted to help him as well.'

Struan poured more tea and then looked at Culum with new respect. 'Very good.'

'Well, I know she's almost like your ward.'

'Aye.'

'The only other thing is that the inquiry into the archduke's accident was held a few days ago. The jury found that it was just an accident.'

'Do you think it was?'

'Of course. Don't you?'

'Have you visited Zergeyev?'

'At least once a day. He was at the inquiry, of course, and he – he said many nice things about you. How you helped him, saved his life, things like that. Zergeyev attached blame to no one and said that he had informed the tsar to that effect. He said openly that he thought he owed his life to you. Skinner brought out a special edition of the *Oriental Times* covering the inquiry. I have it for you.' Culum handed him the paper. 'I wouldn't be surprised if you got a royal commendation from the tsar personally.'

'How is Zergeyev?'

'He's walking now, but his hip's very stiff. I think he's in great pain though he never mentions it. He says he'll never ride again.'

'But he's well?'

'As well as a man can be who lives to ride.'

Struan went to the sideboard and poured two sherries. The lad's changed, he thought. Aye, very much changed. I am proud of my son.

Culum accepted the glass and stared at it.

'Health, Culum. You've managed very well.'

'Health, Father.' Culum had chosen the word deliberately.

'Thank you.'

'Don't thank me. I want to be Tai-Pan of The Noble House. Very much. But I don't want a dead man's shoes.'

'I never thought you did,' Struan snapped.

'Yes, but I considered it. And I know in truth I don't like that idea.'

Struan asked himself how his son could say such a thing, so calmly. 'You've changed a lot in the last few weeks.'

'I'm learning about myself, perhaps. It's Tess mostly – and being alone for seven days. I found I'm not ready to be alone yet.'

'Does Gorth share your opinion of dead men's shoes?'

'I can't answer for Gorth, Tai-Pan. Only for myself. I know that you're mostly right, that I love Tess, that you're going against everything you believe to help me.'

Again Struan remembered Sarah's words.

He sipped his drink contemplatively.

Roger Blore was in his early twenties, his face as taut as his eyes. His clothes were expensive but threadbare, and his short frame spare and fatless. He had dark blond hair, and his blue eyes were deeply fatigued.

'Please sit down, Mr Blore,' Struan said. 'Now, what's all the mystery? And why must you see me alone?'

Blore remained standing. 'You're Dirk Lochlin Struan, sir?'

Struan was surprised. Very few people knew his middle name. 'Aye. And who might you be?' Neither the man's face nor his name meant anything to Struan. But his accent was cultured – Eton or Harrow or Charterhouse.

'May I see your left foot, sir?' the youth asked politely.

'God's death! You insolent puppy! Come to the point or get out!'

'You're perfectly correct to be irritated, Mr Struan. The odds that you're the Tai-Pan are fifty to one on. A hundred to one on. But I must be sure you're who you say you are.'

'Why?'

'Because I have information for Dirk Lochlin Struan, Tai-Pan of The Noble House, whose left foot is half shot away – information of the greatest importance.'

'From whom?'

'My father.'

'I dinna ken your name or your father and I've a long memory for names, by God!'

'My name's not Roger Blore, sir. That's just a pseudonym – for safety. My father's in Parliament. I'm almost sure you're the Tai-Pan. But before I pass the information, I have to be absolutely sure.'

Struan pulled the dirk out of his right boot and lifted the left boot. 'Take it off,' he said dangerously, 'And if the information's na "of the greatest importance", I'll carve my initials on your forehead.'

'Then I suppose I stake my life. A life for a life.'

He pulled the boot off, sighed with relief, and sat weakly. 'My name's Richard Crosse. My father's Sir Charles Crosse, member of Parliament for Chalfont St Giles.'

Struan had met Sir Charles twice, some years ago. At that time Sir Charles was a small country squire with no means, a vehement supporter of free trade and of the importance of Asian trade, and well liked in Parliament. Over the years Struan had supported him financially and had never regretted the investment. It must be about the ratification, he thought eagerly. 'Why did you na say so in the first place?'

Crosse rubbed his eyes tiredly. 'May I have a drink, please?'

'Grog, brandy, sherry – help yoursel'.'

'Thank you, sir.' Crosse poured himself some brandy. 'Thanks. Sorry, but I'm – well, a little tired. Father told me to be very careful – to use a pseudonym. To speak only to you – or if you were dead, to Robb Struan.' He undid his shirt and worked open a pouch that was strapped around his waist. 'He sent you this.' He handed Struan a soiled, heavily sealed envelope and sat down.

Struan took the envelope. It was addressed to him, dated London, April 29th. Abruptly he looked up and his voice grated. 'You're a liar! It's impossible for you to have got here so quickly. That's only sixty days ago.'

'Yes it is, sir,' Crosse said breezily. 'I've done the impossible.' He laughed nervously. 'Father will almost never forgive me.'

'No one's ever made the journey in sixty days. What's your game?'

'I left on Tuesday the 29th of April. Stagecoach London to Dover. I caught the mail ship to Calais by a nose. Stage to Paris and another to Marseilles. The French mail to Alexandria, by a hair. Overland to Suez through the good offices of Mehemet Ali – whom Father met once – and then the Bombay mail by a whisker. I rotted in Bombay for three days and then had a fabulous stroke of luck. I bought passage on an opium clipper for Calcutta. Then—'

'What clipper?'

'*Flying Witch*, belonging to Brock and Sons.'

'Go on,' Struan said, his eyebrows soaring.

'Then an East Indiaman to Singapore. The *Bombay Prince*. Then bad luck, no ship scheduled for Hong Kong for weeks. Then huge luck. I talked myself on to a Russian ship – that one,' Crosse said, pointing out the stern windows. 'She was the most dangerous gamble of all, but it was my last chance. I gave the captain every last guinea I had. In advance. I thought they'd be sure to cut my throat and throw me overboard once out to sea, but it was my last chance. Fifty-nine days, sir, actually – London to Hong Kong.'

Struan got up and poured another drink for Crosse and took a large one for himself. Aye, it's possible, he thought. Na probable but possible. 'Do you know what's in the letter?'

'No, sir. At least I know only the part that refers to me.'

'And what's that?'

'Father says that I'm a wastrel, a ne'er-do-well, gambler and horse-mad,' Crosse said with disarming frankness. 'That there's a debtor's warrant out for my arrest from Newgate Prison. That he commends me to your generosity and hopes you'll be able to find a use for my "talents" – anything to keep me out of England and away from him for the rest of his life. And he sets forth the stakes of the wager.'

'What wager?'

'I arrived yesterday, sir. June 28th. Your son and many others are witnesses. Perhaps you should read the letter, sir. I can assure you my father'd never wager with me unless it was news of the "utmost importance".'

Struan re-examined the seals and broke them. The letter read: 'Westminster, 11 o'clock the evening of April 28th, '41. My dear Mr Struan: I have just become secretly privy to a dispatch the Foreign Secretary, Lord Cunnington, sent yesterday to the Hon. William

Longstaff, her Majesty's plenipotentiary in Asia. The dispatch read in part: "You have disobeyed and neglected my directives and appear to consider them so much flatulence. You obviously seem determined to settle the affairs of Her Majesty's Government at your whim. You impertinently disregard instructions that five or six mainland Chinese ports are to be made accessible to British trading interests, and that full and diplomatic channels be permanently established therein; that this be done expeditiously, preferably by negotiation, but if negotiation be impossible, by use of the Force sent for this explicit purpose and at considerable cost. Instead you settle for a miserable rock with hardly a house on it, for an entirely unacceptable treaty, and at the same time – if naval and army dispatches are to be believed – continually misuse Her Majesty's Forces under your command. In no way can Hong Kong ever become the market emporium for Asia – any more than Macao has become one. The Treaty of Chuenpi is totally repudiated. Your successor, Sir Clyde Whalen, will be arriving imminently, my dear Sir. Perhaps you would be kind enough to hand over your duties to your deputy, Mr C. Monsey, on receipt of this dispatch, and leave Asia forthwith on a frigate which is hereby detached for this duty. Report to my office at your earliest convenience.'

'I am at my wits' end . . .'

Impossible! Impossible that they could make such a god-rotting-fornicating-stupid-Christforsaken-unbelievable mistake! Struan thought. He read on: 'I'm at my wits' end. There's nothing I can do until information is presented officially in the House. I daren't use this secret information openly. Cunnington would have my head and I'd be damned out of politics. Even putting it on paper to you in this fashion is giving my enemies – and who in politics has only a few? – an opportunity to destroy me and, with me, all those who support free trade and the position you've so zealously fought for all these years. I pray God my son puts it into your hands alone. (He knows nothing of the private contents of this letter, by the way.)

'As you know, the Foreign Secretary is an imperious man, a law unto himself, the bulwark of our Whig party. His attitude in the dispatch is perfectly clear. I'm afraid that Hong Kong is a dead issue. And unless the Government is defeated and Sir Robert Peel's Conservatives come into power – an impossibility, I would say, in the foreseeable future – Hong Kong is likely to remain a dead issue.

'The news of the failure of your bank spread through the inner circles in the City – greatly assisted by your rivals, headed by young Morgan Brock. "In great confidence" Morgan Brock judiciously dropped seeds

490

of distrust, along with the information that the Brocks now own most, if not all, of your outstanding paper, and this has immeasurably hurt your influence here. And, too, a letter from Mr Tyler Brock and certain other traders arrived, almost simultaneously with Longstaff's "Treaty of Chuenpi" dispatch, in violent opposition to the Hong Kong settlement and to Longstaff's conduct of hostilities. The letter was addressed to the Prime Minister, the Foreign Secretary, with copies to their enemies – of which, as you know, there are many.

'Knowing that you may have put the remainder of your resources, if any, into your cherished island, I write to give you the opportunity to extricate yourself and save something from the disaster. It may be that you have made some form of settlement with Brock – I pray you have – though if the arrogant Morgan Brock is to be believed, the only settlement that will please them is the obliteration of your house. (I have good reason to believe that Morgan Brock and a group of Continental banking interests – French and Russian, it is further rumoured – started the sudden run on the bank. The Continental group proposed the ploy when the news somehow leaked out about Mr Robb Struan's planned international structure. They broke your bank in return for fifty per cent of a similar plan which Morgan Brock is now trying to effect.)

'I'm sorry to bear such bad tidings. I do so in good faith, hoping that somehow the information will be of value and that you will be able to survive to fight again. I still believe your plan for Hong Kong is the correct one. And I intend to continue to try to put it into effect.

'I know little about Sir Clyde Whalen, the new Captain Superintendent of Trade. He served with distinction in India and has an excellent reputation as a soldier. He's no administrator, so I believe. I understand that he leaves tomorrow for Asia; thus his arrival would be imminent.

'Last: I commend my youngest son to you. He is a wastrel, black sheep, ne'er-do-well whose only purpose in life is to gamble, preferably on horses. There is a debtor's warrant out for him from Newgate Prison. I told him that I would – a last time – settle his debts here if he would forthwith undertake this dangerous journey. He agreed, wagering that if he achieved the impossible feat of arriving in Hong Kong in under sixty-five days – half the normal time – I would give him a thousand guineas to boot.

'To ensure as fast a delivery as possible, I said five thousand guineas if under sixty-five days; five hundred guineas less for every day over that stipulated period; all provided that he stayed out of England for the rest of my life – the money to be paid at five hundred guineas per year until finished. Enclosed is the first payment. Please advise me by return mail the date of his arrival.

'If there is any way you could use his "talents" and control him, you would earn a father's undying gratitude. I've tried, God help both me and him, and I've failed. Though I love him dearly.

'Please accept my sorrow at your bad luck. Give my best to Mr Robb, and I end on the hope that I will have the pleasure of meeting you personally under more favourable circumstances. I have the honour to be, Sir, your most obedient servant, Charles Crosse.'

Struan gazed out at the harbour and the island. He remembered the cross that he had burned on the first day. And Brock's twenty golden guineas. And Jin-qua's remaining three coins. And the lacs of bullion that were to be invested for someone who, one day, would come with a certain chop. Now all the sweat and all the work and all the planning and all the deaths were wasted. Through the stupid arrogance of one man: Lord Cunnington. *Good sweet Christ, what do I do now?*

Struan overcame the shock of the news and forced himself to think. The Foreign Secretary's a brilliant man. He would not repudiate Hong Kong lightly. There must be a reason. What can it be? And how am I to control Whalen? How to fit a 'soldier and no administrator' into the future?

Perhaps I should stop buying the land today. Let the rest of the traders buy and to hell with them. Brock'll be crushed along with the others, for Whalen and the news will na arrive for a month or more. By that time they'll be deep into desperate building. Aye, that's one way, and when the news is common knowledge, we all retire to Macao – or to one of the treaty ports that Whalen will get – and everyone else is smashed. Or hurt very badly. Aye. But if *I* can get this information, Brock can too. So perhaps he'll na be sucked. Perhaps.

Aye. But that way you lose the key to Asia: this miserable threadbare rock, without which all the open ports and the future will be meaningless.

The alternative is to buy and build and gamble that – like Longstaff – Whalen can be persuaded to exceed his directives, that Cunnington himself can be got at. To pour the wealth of The Noble House into the new town. Gamble. Make Hong Kong thrive. So that the Government will be forced to accept the colony.

That's mortal dangerous. You canna force the Crown to do that. The odds are terrible, terrible. Even so, you've nae choice. You have to gamble.

Odds reminded him of young Crosse. Now, here's a valuable lad. How can I use him? How can I keep his mouth shut tight about his fantastic journey? Aye, and how can I create a favourable impression on Whalen for Hong Kong? And get closer to Cunnington? How can I keep the treaty as I want it?

'Well, Mr Crosse, you did a remarkable voyage. Who knows how long it took you?'

'Only you, sir.'

'Then keep it to yoursel'.' Struan wrote something on a pad of paper. 'Give this to my chief clerk.'

Crosse read the note. 'You're giving me the whole five thousand guineas?'

'I've put it in the name of Roger Blore. I think you'd better keep that name – for the time, anyway.'

'Yes, sir. Now I'm Roger Blore.' He stood up. 'Are you finished with me now, Mr Struan?'

'Do you want a job, Mr Blore?'

'I'm afraid there's – well, Mr Struan, I've tried a dozen things but it never works. Father's tried everything and, well – I'm committed – perhaps it was preordained – to what I am. I'm sorry, but you'd be wasting good intentions.'

'I'll bet you five thousand guineas you'll accept the job I'll offer you.'

The youth knew that he'd win the wager. There was no job, none that the Tai-Pan could offer him, that he would accept.

But wait. This is no man to play with, no man to wager lightly with. Those devil calm eyes are flat. I'd have to see them across a poker table. Or at baccarat. Watch your step, Richard Crosse Roger Blore. This is one man who'll collect a debt.

'Well, Mr Blore? Where're your guts? Or are you na the gambler you pretend?'

'The five thousand guineas is my life, sir. The last stake I'll get.'

'So put up your life, by God.'

'You're not risking yours, sir. So the wager's uneven. That sum's contemptible to you. Give me odds. Hundred to one.'

Struan admired the youth's brashness. 'Very well – the truth, Mr Blore. Before God.' He shoved out his hand, and Blore reeled inside for he had gambled that asking for such odds would kill the wager. Don't do it, you fool, he told himself. Five hundred thousand guineas!

He took Struan's hand.

'Secretary of the Jockey Club of Hong Kong,' Struan said.

'What?'

'We've just formed the Jockey Club. You're secretary. Your job is to find horses. Lay out a racetrack. A clubhouse. Begin the richest, finest racing stable in Asia. As good as Aintree or any in the world. Who wins, lad?'

Blore desperately wanted to relieve himself. For the love of God, concentrate, he shouted to himself. 'A race track?'

'Aye. You start it, run it – horses, gambling, stands, odds, prizes, everything. Begin today.'

'But, Jesus Christ where're you going to get the horses?'

'Where will *you* get the horses?'

'Australia, by God,' Blore burst out. 'I've heard they've horses to spare down there!' He shoved the banker's draft back at Struan and let out an ecstatic bellow. 'Mr Struan, you'll never regret this.' He turned and rushed for the door.

'Where're you going?' Struan asked.

'Australia, of course.'

'Why do you na see the general first?'

'Eh?'

'I seem to remember they've some cavalry. Borrow some horses. I'd say you could arrange the first meet next Saturday.'

'I could?'

'Aye. Saturday's a good day for race day. And India's nearer than Australia. I'll send you by the first available ship.'

'You will?'

Struan smiled. 'Aye.' He handed back the slip of paper. 'Five hundred is a bonus on your first year's salary, Mr Blore, of five hundred a year. The rest is prize money for the first four or five meets. I'd say eight races, five horses each, every second Saturday.'

'God bless you, Mr Struan.'

Then Struan was alone. He struck a match and watched the letter burn. He ground the ashes to dust then went below. May-may was still in bed, but she was freshly groomed and looked beautiful.

'Heya, Tai-Pan,' May-may said. She kissed him briefly, then continued fanning herself. 'I'm gracious glad you're back. I want you to buy me a small piece of land because I've decided to go to bisness.'

'What sort of business?' he asked, slightly peeved at the off-hand welcome but pleased that she accepted his going and returning without question, and without fuss.

'You will see, never mind. But I want some taels to begin. I pay ten per cent interest, which is first-class. A hundred taels. You will be a sleep partner.'

He reached over and put his hand on her breast. 'Talking about sleeping, there's—'

She removed his hand. 'Bisness before sleepings. You buy me land and lend me taels?'

'Sleepings before business!'

'Ayeee yah, in this hot?' she said with a laugh. 'Very well. It's terrifical bad to tax yoursel' in this hot – your shirt sticks already to your back. Come long, never mind.' She obediently walked towards her bedroom door, but he caught her.

'I was just teasing. How are you? Has the baby given you any troubles?'

'Of course na. I am a very careful mother, and I eat only very special foods to build a fine son. And think warlike thoughts to make him Tai-Pan-brave.'

'How many taels do you want?'

'A hundred. I already said. Have you nae ears? You're terrifical strange today, Tai-Pan. Yes. Certainly very strange. You're na sick, are you? You have bad news? Or just tired?'

'Just tired. A hundred taels, certainly. What's the "bisness"?'

She clapped her hands excitedly and sat back at the table. 'Oh, you will see. I've thought much since you gone. What do I do for you? Make love and guide you – both terrifical good, to be sure, but that's na enough. So now I make taels too for you, and for my old age.' She laughed again and he delighted in her laugh. 'But only from the barbarians. I will make fortunes – oh, you will think I am cleveritious.'

'There's nae such word.'

'You know very well what I mean.' She hugged him. 'You want to make love now?'

'There's a land sale in an hour.'

'True. Then best you change clotheses and hurry back. A small lot on Queen's Road. But I pay no more than ten taels' rent a year! Did you bring me present?'

'What?'

'Well, it's a good custom,' she said, her eyes innocent, 'that when a man leaves his woman, he brings her present. Jades. Things like that.'

'Nae Jades. But next time. I'll be more attentive.'

She shrugged. 'Good custom. Your poor old mother's werry impoverish. We eat later, heya?'

'Aye.' Struan went to his own staterooms on the next deck above. Lim Din bowed. 'Bathe werry cold, all same, Mass'er. Wantshee?'

'Aye.'

Struan took off his limp clothes and lay in the bath and let his mind consider the implications of Sir Charles's news, his fury at Cunnington's stupidity almost overwhelming him. He dried himself and dressed in fresh clothes, and in a few moment his shirt was damp with sweat again.

Best I sit and think it out, he thought. Let Culum take care of the land. I'll bet my life Tess told her father about his plan for the hill. Maybe Culum'll be trapped into overbidding. The lad did well; I must trust him with this.

So he sent word to Culum to bid for The Noble House, and also told him to buy a small but good lot on Queen's Road. And he sent word to Horatio that Mary was poorly and arranged for a lorcha to take him immediately to Macao.

Then he sat in a deep leather chair and stared out of a porthole at the island and let his mind roam.

Culum bought the marine and suburban lots, proud to bid for The Noble House and to gain more face. He was asked by many where the Tai-Pan was – where he had been – but he answered curtly that he had no idea and continued to imply a hostility he no longer felt.

He bought the hill – and the lots that made the hill safe – and he was relieved that the Brocks did not bid against him, thus proving that Tess could be trusted. Even so, he decided to be more cautious in the future, and not put her in such a position again. It was dangerous to be too open with some knowledge, he thought. Dangerous for her and for himself. For example, the knowledge that the thought of her, the slightest touch of her, drove him almost frantic with desire. Knowledge that he could never discuss with her or his father but only with Gorth, who understood: 'Yes, Culum lad. I knows only too well. It be terrible pain, terrible. Thee can hardly walk. Yes – and it be terrible hard to control. But doan worry, lad. We be pals and I understands. It be right to be frank, thee and me. It be terrible dangerous for thee to be like monk. Yes. Worse'n that, it be storing up troubles in the future – and even worse, I heard tell it be making for sickly offspring. The pain in thy guts be the warning of God. Yes – that pain'll sicken a man all his life, and that be the mortal truth, so help me God! Doan thee worry – I knowed a place in Macao. Doan thee worry, old lad.'

And though Culum did not truly believe the superstitions that Gorth pronounced, the pains he endured day and night sapped his will to resist. He wanted relief. Even so, he swore, if Brock agrees to let us marry next month, then I won't go to a whore-house. I won't!

*   *   *

At sunset Culum and Struan went aboard the *White Witch*. Brock was waiting for them on the quarterdeck, Gorth beside him. The night was cool and pleasant.

'I be decided about thy marrying, Culum,' Brock said. 'Next month be unseemly. Next year be probable better. But the third month from now be Tess's seventeenth birthday, and on that day, the tenth, thee can marry.'

'Thank you, Mr Brock,' Culum said. 'Thank you.'

Brock grinned at Struan. 'Do that suit thee, Dirk?'

'It's your decision, Tyler, na mine. But I think three months or two's nae different to one. I still say next month.'

'September suit thee, Culum? Like I sayed? Be honest, lad.'

'Yes. Of course. I'd hoped, but – well, yes, Mr Brock.' Culum swore that he would wait the three months. But deep inside he knew that he could not.

'Then that be settled proper.'

'Aye,' Struan echoed. 'Three months it is then.' Aye, he told himself, three months it is. You've just signed a death warrant, Tyler. Maybe two.

'And, Dirk, mayhaps thee'll give me time tomorrer? We can fix dowry and wot not.'

'At noon?'

'Yus. At noon. And now I thinks we be joining the ladies below. You be staying for supper, Dirk?'

'Thank you, but there are some things. I have to attend to.'

'Like the races, eh? I've to hand it to you. Proper smart to bring that Blore fellow out from home. He be a proper young spark. The last race o' every meet be the Brock Stakes. We be putting prize money.'

'Aye. So I hear. It's fitting we have the best track in Asia.'

Blore had made the announcement at the land sale. Longstaff had agreed to be the first president of the Jockey Club. The annual membership fee was set at ten guineas, and every European on the island had immediately joined. Blore was besieged with volunteers to ride the cavalry mounts the general had agreed to provide.

'Thee can ride, Dirk?'

'Aye. But I've never raced.'

'Me likewise. But mayhaps we should try our hands, eh? You ride Culum?'

'Oh, yes. But I'm not an expert.'

Gorth clapped him on the back. 'We can get mounts in Macao, Culum, practise a little. Mayhaps we can take on our Da's, eh?'

Culum smiled uneasily.

'Aye, we might at that, Gorth,' Struan said. 'Well, good night. I'll see you at noon, Tyler.'

'Yus. Night, Dirk.'

Struan left.

During dinner Culum tried to heal the antagonism that existed between Gorth and Brock. He found it strange that he liked them both, could see through them both – could understand why Gorth wanted to be Tai-Pan and why Brock would not pass over control, not for a time. And strange why he felt wiser in this than Gorth. Not so strange, really, he thought. Gorth hadn't suddenly been left alone for seven long days with all the responsibility. The day I marry Tess I'm throwing away Brock's twenty sovereigns. Not right to keep them now. Whatever happens, we're starting afresh. Only three months. Oh God, thank you.

After dinner Culum and Tess went on deck by themselves. Both were breathless under the stars, holding hands and aching. Culum brushed her lips in a first tentative kiss, and Tess remembered the roughness of Nagrek's kiss and the fire that had followed his hands and the pain that he had caused – not pain really, but an agony-pleasure that in the remembrance always made her burn anew. She was glad that soon she would be able to quench the fire inside her. Only three months, then peace.

They returned to the fetid cabin below, and after Culum had left, she lay in her bunk. Her longing racked her and she wept. Because she knew that Nagrek had touched her in a way that only Culum should have touched her, knowing that this knowledge must be held secret from him for all eternity. But how? Oh, my love, my love.

'I tell thee, Da', that were a mistake,' Gorth was saying in the great cabin, keeping his voice low. 'A terrible mistake!'

Brock slammed the tankard down and beer slopped on to the table and the floor. 'It be my decision, Gorth, and that be the end of it. They be wed come September.'

'And it were mistake not to bid on the hill. That devil's stolen another march on us'n, by God.'

'Use thy brains, Gorth!' Brock hissed. 'If we'd done that, then young Culum'd knowed for sure that Tess be telling me innocent wot's sayed and wot baint. The hillock were unimportant. Mayhaps there be a time when she be saying somethin' wot'll gut Dirk, and that's wot I wants to know, naught else.' Brock despised himself for listening to Tess and for using her unknowingly to spy on Culum, and as a tool against Dirk Struan. But he loathed Gorth more, and distrusted him more than ever. Because he knew that Gorth was right. But he wanted Tess's happiness more than anything, and this knowledge made him dangerous. Now the fruit of Struan's godrotting loins would join with his adored Tess. 'I swear to Christ I'll kill Culum if he hurts a hair on her head,' he said, his voice terrible.

'Then why let Culum marry her fast, by all that's holy? 'Course he'll hurt her and use her against us'n now.'

'And wot's changed thy mind, eh?' Brock flared. 'Thee was for it – enthusiastical for it.'

'I still be, but not in three months, by God. That be the ruination of everything.'

'Why?'

'Course it ruin everything,' he said. 'When I were for it, Robb were alive, eh? Then the Tai-Pan were leaving this summer for good and passing over Tai-Pan to Robb – then to Culum in a year. It be the truth. They's marrying next year'd be perfect. But now the Tai-Pan be staying. And now that they agree to marrying in three month, the Tai-Pan'll take her away from thee and train Culum against us'n and now I thinks he be never leaving. And certainly never while yo're Tai-Pan of Brock and Sons!'

'He never be leaving Asia, wotever he sayed to Culum. Or Robb. I knows Dirk.'

'And I knows thee!'

'When he be leaving – or deaded – then I be leaving.'

'Then he better be deaded right smartly.'

'Thee better possess thyself with patience.'

'I be patient, Da'.' It was on the tip of Gorth's tongue to tell Brock the vengeance he had planned on Struan – through Culum – in Macao. But he did not. His father was more concerned with the happiness of Tess than with becoming Tai-Pan of The Noble House. His father no longer had the necessary consuming ruthlessness that Struan possessed in a measure that made being *the* Tai-Pan possible. 'Remember, Da' – he outsmarted thee with the bullion, on their house, the marriage, even on the ball. Tess's thy weakness,' he stormed. 'He knowed it, and thee beed set up with her as thy wrecker's beacon and thee's heading for disaster.'

'I baint. I baint! I knowed wot I be doing,' Brock said, trying to keep his voice low, the veins in his temples like the knots in a cat-o'-nine-tails. 'An' I warned thee afore. Doan go after that devil by thyself. He'll cut off thy balls and feed 'em to thee. I knowed that devil!'

'Yes, that you do, Da'!' Gorth could smell the age of his father, and knew for the first time that in truth he could crush him, man to man. 'So get thee out of the way and let a man do a man's job, by God!'

Brock slammed to his feet and the chair crashed over. Gorth was up and waiting for his father to snake for his knife, knowing that now and for evermore he could afford to wait, for he had the measure of him.

Brock saw clearly that this was his last chance to dominate Gorth. If he did not go for the knife, he was lost. If he went for the knife, he would have to kill Gorth. He knew that he could – but only by cunning, no longer by strength alone. Gorth be yor son, yor eldest son. He baint enemy, he told himself. 'Baint right,' he said, stifling his desire to kill. 'Baint right for thee – for thee 'n' me – like this'n. No, by God. I tell thee a last time, thee go after him, thee'll meet thy Maker.'

Gorth felt the thrill of victory. 'Only joss'll get us'n out of this mess.' He kicked his chair out of the way. 'I be going ashore.'

Brock was alone. He finished the tankard, and another, and another. Liza opened the door but he did not notice her and she left him to his drinking, and she went to bed and prayed for the happiness of the marriage. And for her man.

Gorth went ashore. To Mrs Fortheringill's house.

'I'm not wanting your business, Mr Brock,' she said. 'The last one were hurt brutal.'

'Wot's a monkey to you, you old witch? Here!' Gorth slammed twenty gold sovereigns on the table. 'An' here's the same to keep yor trap shut.'

She gave him a young Hakka girl and a cellar far to the back of the house.

Gorth abused the girl, flogged her brutally, and left her dying.

The next day he set out in the *White Witch* for Macao, forty miles southwest. All the Brocks were aboard except Brock himself. Culum also stood on the quarterdeck, his arm linked with Tess's.

XXXII

Five days days later was race day.

And during this time the foundations of the new town had been laid. Following the lead of The Noble House, the traders had harnessed all the labour and skills of Tai Ping Shan into digging and carrying and building. The traders poured back into the land all the bullion Longstaff had given them. The brickmakers in Macao and the timber makers in Kwangtung – and all those who were concerned with the building of houses or factories or wharves – began to work night and day to satisfy the frantic zeal of the traders to replace that which had been abandoned. Wages rose. Coolies began to be in short supply – The Noble House alone employed three thousand bricklayers, builders and artisans of all kinds – even though each tide brought more workers. These quickly found well-paid work. Tai Ping Shan swelled even more. The foreshore around Glessing's Point pulsated with energy.

And race day marked the fourteenth day since Struan and May-may had left their house in Happy Valley to move aboard *Resting Cloud*.

'You dinna look well, lassie,' Struan said. 'Best stay abed today.'

'I think I will,' she said. She had been restless all night and her head and neck and back had begun to ache. 'It's nothing, never mind. You look terrifical good.'

'Thank you.' Struan was wearing new clothes that he had had made in honour of the meet. Dark green riding coat of the finest, lightest wool. White drill pleated trousers thonged under his half boots, waistcoat of primrose cashmere, green cravat.

May-may eased the ache in her shoulders and Ah Sam settled the pillow more comfortably for her. 'It's just a summer devil. I send for doctor. You go ashore now?'

'Aye. The meet begins in an hour. I think I'll get our doctor, lass. He'll—'

'*I* will send for doctor. Chinese doctor. And that's the end of that.

501

Now, dinna forget, twenty taels on number-four horse in fourth race. The astrologer said it was absolute good winner.'

'I will na forget.' Struan patted her cheek. 'You rest yoursel'.'

'When I win, I feel fantastical better, heya? Go along, now.'

He tucked her up and saw that fresh tea was brought and an earthenware bottle filled with hot-water for her back. Then he went ashore.

The racetrack had been laid out to the west of Glessing's Point and was mobbed with people. Part of the foreshore, near the post that marked the starting and finishing lines, had been cordoned off for Europeans against the hordes of curious Chinese who swarmed around. Tents had been set up here and there. A paddock and betting stands had been constructed. Flags on bamboo poles marked the oval track.

The betting was heavy, and Henry Hardy Hibbs had the biggest book. 'Take yor pick, gents,' he shouted in his sonorous voice, thumping his blackboard upon which he chalked the odds. 'Major Trent, up on the black stallion, Satan, be favourite in the first. Even money. Three to one the field!'

'God rot you, Hibbs,' Glessing said testily, sweating in the heat of the day. 'Three to one the field and you're bound to win. Give me six to one on the grey mare. A guinea!'

Hibbs glanced at the blackboard and whispered hoarsely, 'For you, Capt'n, sir, five it is. One guinea it is. On Mary Jane.'

Glessing turned away. He was furious that he was not in Macao and that Culum's promised letter had not arrived. Oh God above, he thought, frantic with worry, I should have heard from him by this time. What the devil's the delay? What's that bugger Horatio doing? Is he hacking at her again?

He walked moodily down to the paddock and saw Struan and Zergeyev together, but Longstaff joined them so he did not stop.

'What's your choice, Your Highness?' Longstaff was saying jovially.

'The gelding,' Zergeyev replied, leaning on a stick. The excitement and the smell of the horses refreshed him and lessened much of his constant pain. He wished that he could be a rider, but blessed his luck that he had survived the wound. And blessed Struan. He knew that without Struan's operation he would have died.

'La, Your Highness,' Shevaun said as she strolled up on Jeff Cooper's arm. She was dressed in shimmering green and shaded by an orange parasol. 'Have you a tip for me?' She favoured all of them with a smile. Particularly Struan.

502

'The gelding's the best horse, but who the best rider is I don't know, Shevaun,' Zergeyev said.

Shevaun glanced at the big brown horse, its coat sleek and eyes full. 'La,' she said with a mischievous twinkle, 'Poor horse! If I were a horse and that'd been done to me, I swear I'd never run a foot. For no one! Barbaric!'

They laughed with her.

'Are you betting the gelding, Tai-Pan?'

'I dinna ken,' he said, worried about May-may. 'Somehow I favour the filly. But I think I'll make my final choice when they're at the starting gate.'

She studied him for an instant, wondering if he was speaking in parables.

'Let's take a closer look at the filly,' Jeff said, forcing a laugh.

'Why don't you, Jeff, my dear? I'll stay here and wait for you.'

'I'll come along,' Longstaff said, missing Cooper's flash of irritation. Cooper hesitated, then they walked off together.

Brock lifted his hat politely as he passed Shevaun and Struan and Zergeyev, but did not stop. He was glad that Struan had decided not to jockey one of the horses, for he was not fond of riding himself and his dig at Struan had been involuntary. God curse him, he thought.

'How is your wound, Your Highness?' Shevaun said.

'Fine. I'm almost whole again, thanks to the Tai-Pan.'

'I did nothing,' Struan said, embarrassed by Zergeyev's praise. He noticed Blore down by the paddock in private conversation with Skinner. I wonder if I gambled correctly on the lad, he thought.

'Modesty becomes you, sir,' Shevaun said to Struan and bobbed a graceful curtsy. 'Don't they say "*noblesse oblige*"?'

Struan marked Zergeyev's open admiration for the girl. 'You've a fine ship, Your Highness.' The Russian vessel was four-masted, eight hundred ton burden. Many cannon.

'I'd be honoured to have the captain show you over her,' Zergeyev said. 'Perhaps we could talk specifics with you. When you're ready.'

'Thank you. I'd like that.' Struan would have continued, but Blore rushed up to them, dusty and exhausted.

'Almost ready to begin, Tai-Pan – you look whizz-o, Miss Tillman – afternoon, Your Highness,' he said in a run. 'Everyone put your money on number four in the fourth, decided to ride her myself – oh yes, Tai-Pan, I checked the stallion last night. He took the bit, so we can use him in the next meet – Your Highness, best let me guide you to your position, you're starting the first race.'

503

'I am?'

'Didn't His Excellency mention it? Blast it – I mean would you care to?' Never had Blore worked so hard and never had he been so excited. 'Would you follow me, please?' He guided Zergeyev hastily through the crowd.

'Blore's a nice young man,' Shevaun said, glad to be alone with Struan at last. 'Where did you find him?'

'He found me,' Struan said. 'And I'm glad he did.' His attention was distracted by an altercation near one of the tents. A group of soldier-guards was hustling a Chinese out of the enclosure. The coolie's hat fell off – and with it the long queue. The man was Aristotle Quance. 'Excuse me a second,' Struan said. He hurried over and stood in front of the little man, shielding him with his bulk. 'That's all right, lads, he's friend of mine!' he said.

The soldiers shrugged and moved off.

'Great thundering cannon balls, Tai-Pan,' Quance choked out, adjusting his filthy clothes. 'Saved in the nick. Bless you!'

Struan hastily shoved the coolie hat back on Quance's head and pulled him behind a flap of the tent. 'What the devil are you doing here?' he whispered.

'Had to see the races, by God,' Quance said, settling the hat so that the queue fell down his back, 'and wanted to talk to you.'

'This is nae time! Maureen's in the crowd somewhere.'

Quance blanced. 'God protect me!'

'Aye, though why He should, I've nae idea. Be off with you while you're safe. I heard she's booked passage for home next week. If she suspects – well, be it on your own head!'

'Just the first race, Tai-Pan?' Quance begged. 'Please. And I've information for you.'

'What?'

To Struan's shock, Quance told him what Gorth had done to the prostitute. 'Ghastly! Poor girl's near death. Gorth's mad, Tai-Pan. Mad.'

'Send me word if the girl dies. Then we'll – well, I'll have to think about what to do. Thank you, Aristotle. Best you vanish while you can.'

'Just the first race? Please, for the love of God! You don't know what it means to a poor old man.'

Struan looked around. Shevaun was studiously ignoring them. Then he noticed Glessing walking by. 'Captain!'

When Glessing recognized Quance, his eyes soared to heaven. 'By Jove! I thought you were on the seas!'

'Do me a favour, would you?' Struan said quickly. 'Mrs Quance is over by the post. Would you keep Aristotle out of trouble and out of her way? Better, take him over there.' Struan pointed to where the Chinese were milling about. 'Let him watch the first race, then take him home.'

'Certainly. Good God, Aristotle, I'm glad to see you,' Glessing said, then to Struan. 'Have you heard from Culum? I'm terribly worried about Miss Sinclair.'

'No. But I told Culum to see her as soon as he arrived. We should hear any moment. I'm sure she's all right.'

'I hope so. Oh, where should I take Aristotle after the race?'

'Mrs Fortheringill's.'

'By Jove! What's it like, Aristotle?' Glessing asked, his curiosity getting the better of him.

'Terrifying, my boy, mortal terrifying.' Quance grasped his arm and his voice hoarsened. 'Can't get a wink of sleep and the food's hideous. Nothing but quent for breakfast, lunch, tea, dinner and supper. Can you lend me a few guineas, Tai-Pan?'

Struan grunted and walked off.

'What's quent, Aristotle?'

'It's, er, a kind of gruel.'

Struan rejoined Shevaun.

'A friend of yours, Tai-Pan?'

'It's na politic to notice some friends, Shevaun.'

She tapped him lightly on the arm with her fan. 'There's never a need to remind me about politics, Dirk. I've missed you,' she added gently.

'Aye,' he said, realizing that it would be easy and wise to marry Shevaun. But na possible. Because of May-may. 'Why do you want to be painted in the nude?' he asked suddenly, and he knew from the flash in her eyes that his hunch was correct.

'Aristotle said that?' Her voice was level.

'Great God, no. He'd never do that. But some months ago he was teasing us. Said he had a new commission. For a nude. Why?'

She blushed and fanned herself, and laughed. 'Goya painted the Duchess of Alba. Twice, I believe. She became the toast of the world.'

His eyes crinkled with amusement. 'You're a devil, Shevaun, 'Did you really let him – well, see the subject?'

'That was poetic licence on his part. We discussed the idea of two portraits. You don't approve?'

'I'd say your uncle – and your father – would hit the sky if they heard about it, or if the portraits fell into the wrong hands.'

'Would you buy them, Tai-Pan?'

'To hide?'

'To enjoy.'

'You're a strange girl, Shevaun.'

'Perhaps I despise hypocrisy.' She looked at him searchingly. 'Like you.'

'Aye. But you're a girl in a man's world, and certain things you canna do.'

'There's a lot of "certain" things I would like to do.' There were cheers and the horses began to parade. Shevaun made a final decision. 'I think I will leave Asia. Within two months.'

'That sounds like a threat.'

'No, Tai-Pan. It's just that I'm in love – and in love with life as well. And I agree with you. That the time to choose the winner is when they're at the starting gate.' She fanned herself, praying that her gamble would justify the risk. 'Who do you pick?'

He did not look at the horses. 'The filly, Shevaun,' he said quietly.

'What's her name?' she asked.

'May-may,' he said, the light in his eyes gentle.

Her fan hesitated and then continued as before. 'A race is never lost until the winner's judged and garlanded.' She smiled and walked away, head high, more beautiful than she had ever been.

The filly lost the race. Only by a nose. But she lost.

'Back so soon, Tai-Pan?' May-may said thinly.

'Aye. I tired of the meet, and I was worried over you.'

'Did I win?'

He shook his head.

She smiled and sighed. 'Oh well, never mind.' The whites of her eyes were pink, and her face was grey under the gold.

'Has the doctor been?' Struan asked.

'Na yet.' May-may curled on her side, but that did not ease her discomfort. She moved the pillow away, but that did not help either, so she replaced it again. 'Your poor old mother's just old,' she said with a forlorn grin.

'Where does it hurt?'

'Nowhere, everywhere. A good sleep will cure everything, never mind.'

He massaged her neck and her back and would not allow himself to think the unthinkable. He ordered fresh tea and light food and tried to persuade her to eat, but she had no appetite.

506

At sunset Ah Sam entered and spoke briefly to May-may.

'The doctor is come. And Gordon Chen,' May-may said to Struan.

'Good!' Struan got up and stretched.

Ah Sam walked over to a jewel cabinet and took out a small ivory statue of a nude woman lying on her side. To Struan's astonishment, May-may pointed to parts of the tiny statue and spoke at length to Ah Sam. Ah Sam nodded and went out, Struan followed, bewildered.

The doctor was an elderly man, his queue long and well oiled, his ancient black robes threadbare. His eyes were clear and a few long hairs grew from a wart in his cheek. He had long thin fingers and the backs of his slender hands were blue-veined.

'So sorry, Tai-Pan,' Gordon said, and he bowed with the doctor. 'This is Kee Fa Tan, the best doctor in Tai Ping Shan. We came as fast as we could.'

'Thank you. You'd better come this –' He stopped. Ah Sam had gone over to the doctor and had bowed deeply and shown him the statue, indicating parts of it in the same manner as May-may. And now she was answering questions volubly.

'What the devil's he doing?'

'Making a diagnosis,' Gordon Chen said, listening attentively to Ah Sam and to the doctor.

'With the statue?'

'Yes. It would be unseemly for him to see the Lady if it was not necessary, Tai-Pan. Ah Sam is explaining where the pains are. Please to be patient. I'm sure it's not serious.'

The doctor contemplated the statue in silence. Finally he looked up at Gordon and said something softly.

'He says it is not an easy diagnosis. With your permission, he would like to examine the Lady.'

Seething with impatience, Struan led the way into the bedroom. May-may had dropped the curtains surrounding the bed. She was only a discreet shadow behind them.

The doctor went to May-may's bedside and again fell silent. After a few minutes he spoke quietly. Obediently May-may's left hand came up from under the curtains. The doctor picked up her hand and examined it intently. Then he put his fingers on her pulse and closed his eyes. His fingers began tapping the skin gently.

The minutes passed. The fingers were tapping slowly as though seeking something impossible to find.

'What's he doing now?' Struan asked.

'Listening to her pulse, sir,' Gordon whispered. 'We must be very quiet. There are nine pulses in each wrist. Three on the surface and three a little lower and three deep down. These tell him the cause of the sickness. Please, Tai-Pan, be patient. It is most hard to listen with fingers.'

The finger tapping continued. It was the only sound in the cabin. Ah Sam and Gordon Chen watched spellbound. Struan shifted uneasily but made no sound. The doctor seemed to be in a mystical reverie. Then suddenly – as if falling on an elusive prey – the tapping ceased and the doctor pressed hard. For a minute he was like a statue. Then he let the wrist lie on the coverlet, and May-may silently gave him her right wrist and he repeated the procedure.

And again after many minutes the tapping abruptly ceased.

The doctor opened his eyes and sighed and put May-may's wrist on the coverlet. He beckoned to Gordon Chen and to Struan.

Gordon Chen closed the door behind them. The doctor laughed softly and nervously and began speaking quietly and rapidly.

Gordon's eyes widened.

'What's the matter?' Struan said sharply.

'I didn't know Mother was with child, Tai-Pan.' Gordon turned back to the doctor and asked a question and the doctor answered at length. Then silence.

'Well, what the devil did he say?'

Gordon looked at him and tried unsuccessfully to appear calm. 'He says Mother's very sick, Tai-Pan. That a poison has entered her bloodstream through her lower limbs. This poison has centred in her liver, and the liver is now' – he sought for the word – 'maladjusted. Soon there will be fever, bad fever. Very bad fever. Then three or four days of time and again fever. And again.'

'Malaria? Happy Valley fever?'

Gordon turned back and asked the question.

'He says yes.'

'Everyone knows it's the night gases – na poison through the skin, by God,' he slammed at Gordon. 'She's na been there for weeks!'

Gordon shrugged. 'I only tell you what he says, Tai-Pan. I'm no doctor. But this doctor I would trust – I think you should trust.'

'What's his cure?'

Gordon queried the doctor.

'He says, Tai-Pan: "I have treated some of those who suffered the Happy Valley poison. The successful recoveries were all strong men who took a certain medicine before the third fever attack. But this patient is a woman, and though in her twenty-first year and strong with

508

a fire spirit, all her strength is going into the child that is four months in her womb." ' Gordon stopped, uneasily. 'He fears for the Lady and the child.'

'Tell him to get the medicine and treat her now. Na after any attack.'

'That's the trouble. He can't, sir. He has none of the medicine left.'

'Then tell him to get some, by God!'

'There's none on Hong Kong, Tai-Pan. He's sure.'

Struan's face darkened. 'There must be some. Tell him to get it – whatever it costs.'

'But, Tai-Pan, he—'

'God's blood, tell him!'

Again there was chatter back and forth.

'He says there is none in Hong Kong. That there will be none in Macao, or in Canton. That the medicine is made from the bark of a very rare tree that grows somewhere in the South Seas, or in lands across the seas. The tiny quantity he had came from his father who was also a doctor, who got it from his father.' Gordon added helplessly, 'He says he's completely sure that there's no more.'

'Twenty thousand taels of silver if she's cured.'

Gordon's eyes widened. He thought a moment, then he spoke rapidly to the doctor. They both bowed and hurried away.

Struan took out his handkerchief, wiped the sweat off his face, and walked back into the bedroom.

'Heya, Tai-Pan,' May-may said, her voice even thinner. 'Wat for is my joss?'

'They've gone to get a special medicine which'll cure you. Nae anything to worry about.'

He settled her as best he could, his mind tormented. Then he hurried to the flagship and asked the chief naval doctor about the bark.

'Sorry, my dear Mr Struan, but that's an old wives' tale. There's a legend about Countess Cinchón, wife of the Spanish viceroy of Peru, who introduced a bark from South America into Europe in the seventeenth century. It was known as "Jesuit's bark", and sometimes as "cinchona bark". Powdered and taken with water, it was supposed to cure the fever. But when it was tried in India it failed completely. Worthless! Damned Papists would say anything to get converts.'

'Where the devil can I get some?'

'I really don't know, my dear sir. Peru, I suppose. But why your anxiety? Queen's Town is abandoned now. No need to be concerned if you don't breathe the night gas.'

'A friend's just come down with malaria.'

509

'Ah! Then heroic purging with calomel. As soon as possible. Can't promise anything, of course. We'll leech him immediately.'

Struan tried the chief army doctor next, and then, in the course of time, all the lesser doctors – both service and civilian – and they all told him the same thing.

Then Struan remembered that Wilf Tillman was still alive. He hastened to the Cooper-Tillman opium hulk.

And all the while Struan was questioning the doctors, Gordon Chen had returned to Tai Ping Shan and had sent for the ten Triad leaders under him. Then they had gone to their own headquarters and had sent for the ten leaders under them. Word spread with incredible speed that a certain bark of a certain tree was to be found. By sampan, by junk, word filtered out across the harbour to Kowloon, soon to reach hamlets and villages and towns and cities. Up the coast, down the coast, inland. Soon all the Chinese of Hong Kong – Triads and non-Triads – knew that a rare bark was being sought. They did not know by whom or for what reason: only that a great reward had been offered. And this knowledge fell into the ears of the anti-Triad agents of the mandarins. They too began to seek the bark, and not only for the reward; they knew that a portion of bark might perhaps be used as a lure to unmask the leaders of the Triad.

'Sorry to arrive uninvited, Wilf. I –' Struan stopped, alarmed by the sight of Tillman.

Tillman was propped on a sweat-stained pillow, his face skeletal – the colour of unwashed ancient linen – the whites of his eyes filth-yellowed. 'Come in,' he said, his voice hardly perceptible. And then Struan saw that Tillman, whose teeth had been fine and strong and white, was now toothless.

'What happened to your teeth?'

'The calomel. It affects some people . . .' Tillman's voice trailed off dully. And his eyes took on a curious lustre. 'I've been expecting you. The answer's no!'

'What?'

'No. A simple no.' Tillman's voice grew stronger. 'I'm her guardian and she'll never marry you.'

'I did na come here to ask for her. I just came to see how you were and how the malaria—'

'I don't believe you,' Tillman's voice rose hysterically. 'You're just hoping I'll die!'

'That's ridiculous! Why should I want you dead?'

510

Tillman weakly lifted the handbell that was on the rancid coverlet and rang it. The door opened and a big Negro, Tillman's slave, came in barefoot.

'Jebidiah, ask Mass'er Cooper and Missee to come here at once.'

Jebidiah nodded and closed the door.

'Still peddling humans, Wilf?'

'Jebidiah's content as he is, goddam you! You've your way and we've ours, you pox-ridden swine!'

'The pox on your ways, you damned blackbirder.' Struan's second ship was etched on his memory, and occasionally he still had nightmares that he was aboard again. With his share of Trafalgar's prize money he had bought himself out of the navy and had signed as cabin boy on an English merchantman that plied the Atlantic. It was only when far out at sea that he discovered she was an illicit slave trader, sailing down to Dakar for slaves and then across the lower Atlantic and the doldrums to Savannah, the men, women and children crushed belowdecks like maggots. Their dying cries and whimpers filling his ears, the stench choking him, week after week after week. He was a lad of eight, and helpless. He had deserted at Savannah. This was the only ship that he had deserted in his life.

'You're worse than the slavers,' he said, his voice raw. 'You just buy the flesh and put 'em on the block and take the profit. I've seen a slave market.'

'We treat them well!' Tillman shrieked. 'They're only savages and we give them a good life. We do!' His face twitched as he lay back and fought for strength, desperate with envy of Struan's vitality and health, and feeling near death. 'You'll not benefit by my death, God curse you for eternity!'

Struan turned for the door.

'You'd better wait. What I have to say concerns you.'

'Nothing you could say would concern me!'

'You call me blackbirder? How'd you get your mistress, you goddamn hypocrite?'

The door flung open and Cooper rushed in. 'Oh, hello, Tai-Pan! I didn't know you were aboard.'

'Hello, Jeff,' Struan said, hardly able to control his temper.

Cooper glanced at Tillman. 'What's up, Wilf?'

'Nothing. I wanted to see you and my niece.'

Shevaun came in, and stopped in surprise. 'Hello, Tai-Pan. Are you all right, Uncle?'

'No, child, I feel very bad.'

'What's the matter, Wilf?' Cooper asked.

Tillman coughed weakly. 'The Tai-Pan came "visiting". I thought this a perfect time to settle an important matter. I'm due for another fever attack tomorrow and I think . . . well,' – the limp eyes turned on Shevaun – 'I'm proud to tell you that Jeff has formally asked for your hand in marriage and I have accepted gladly.'

Shevaun blanched. 'I don't want to marry yet.'

'I've considered everything very carefully—'

'I *won't*!'

Tillman pulled himself up on one elbow with a great effort.

'Now, will you listen to me!' he shrieked, strengthened by his anger. 'I'm your legal guardian. For months I've been corresponding with your father. My brother has formally approved the match if I formally decided that it's to your advantage. And I've decided it is. So—'

'Well, I haven't, Uncle. It's the nineteenth century, not the Middle Ages. I don't want to marry yet.'

'I'm not concerned with your wishes, and you're quite right, it is the nineteenth century. You *are* betrothed. You *will be* married. Your father's hope and mine was that during your visit here Jeff would favour you. He has.' Tillman lay back exhausted. 'It is a most pleasing match. And that's the end to it.'

Cooper walked over to Shevaun. 'Shevaun darling. You know how I feel. I had no idea that Wilf was . . . I'd hoped that, well . . .'

She backed away from him and her eyes found Struan. 'Tai-Pan! Tell my uncle. Tell him he can't do this – he can't betroth me – tell him he can't!'

'How old are you, Shevaun?' Struan asked.

'Nineteen.'

'If your father approves and your uncle approves, you've nae option.' He looked at Tillman. 'I suppose you have it in writing?'

Tillman motioned at a desk. 'The letter's there. Though it's none of your goddam business.'

'That's the law, Shevaun. You're a minor and bound to do what your father wants.' Struan sadly turned for the door but Shevaun stopped him.

'Do you know why I'm being sold?' she burst out.

'Hold your tongue, girl!' Tillman cried. 'You've been nothing but trouble since you got here, and it's time you learned manners and respect for your elders and betters.'

'I'm sold for shares,' she said bitterly. 'In Cooper-Tillman.'

'That's not so!' Tillman said, his face ghastly.

512

'Shevaun, you're overwrought,' Cooper began unhappily. 'It's just the suddenness and—'

Struan started to pass her, but she held on to him. 'Wait. Tai-Pan. It's a deal. I know how a politician's mind works. Politics is an expensive business.'

'*Hold your tongue*,' Tillman shouted, then whimpered with pain and collapsed back into the bed.

'Without income from here,' she rushed on shakily, 'Father can't afford to be a senator. Uncle's the oldest brother, and if Uncle dies, Jeff can buy out the Tillman interests at a nominal sum and then—'

'Come on, Shevaun,' Cooper interrupted sharply. 'That has nothing to do with my love for you. What do you think I am?'

'Be honest, Jeff. It is true, isn't it? About the nominal sum?'

'Yes,' Cooper replied after a grim pause. 'I can buy out the Tillman interests under those circumstances. But I haven't made such a deal. I'm not buying a chattel. I love you. I want you to be my wife.'

'And if not, will you *not* buy Uncle out?'

'I don't know. I'll decide that when the time comes. Your uncle could buy my shares if I were to die before him.'

Shevaun turned back to Struan. 'Please buy me, Tai-Pan.'

'I canna, lass. But I dinna think Jeff's buying you either. I know he's in love with you.'

'Please buy me,' she said brokenly.

'I canna, lassie. It's against the law.'

'It's not. It's not.' She wept uncontrollably.

Cooper put his arms around her, tormented.

When Struan returned to *Resting Cloud*, May-may was still sleeping fitfully.

As he watched over her he wondered dully what to do about Gorth and about Culum. He knew that he should go to Macao at once. But na until May-may's cured – oh God, let her be cured. Do I send *China Cloud* and Orlov – perhaps Mauss? Or do I wait? I've told Culum to guard himsel' – but will he? Oh Jesus Christ, help May-may.

At midnight there was a knock on the door.

'Aye?'

Lim Din came in softly. He glanced at May-may and sighed. 'Big Fat mass'er come Tai-Pan see, can? Heya?'

Struan's back and shoulders ached and his head felt heavy as he climbed the gangway to his quarters on the next deck.

'Sorry to come uninvited and so late, Tai-Pan,' Morley Skinner said, heaving his greasy, sweating bulk out of a chair. 'It's a little important.'

513

'Always pleased to see the press, Mr Skinner. Take a seat. Drink?' He tried to turn his mind off May-may and forced himself to concentrate, knowing this was no casual visit.

'Thank you. Whisky.' Skinner took in the rich interior of the large cabin: green Chinese carpets on well-scrubbed decks; chairs and sofas and the fragrance of clean oiled leather, salt and hemp; and the faint sweet oily smell of opium from the holds below. Well-trimmed oil lamps gave a warm pure light and shadowed the main-deck beams. He contrasted it with the hovel he had on Hong Kong – a threadbare and dirty and stench-ridden room over the large room that housed the printing press. 'It's nice of you to see me so late,' he said.

Struan raised his glass. 'Health!'

'Yes, "health". That's a good toast in these evil days. What with the malaria and all.' The little pig eyes sharpened. 'I hear you've a friend who's got malaria.'

'Do you know where to find cinchona?'

Skinner shook his head. 'No, Tai-Pan. Everything I've read says that that's a will-o'-the-wisp. Legend.' He pulled out a proof copy of the weekly *Oriental Times* and handed it to Struan. 'Thought you'd like to see the editorial about today's races. I'm putting out a special edition tomorrow.'

'Thank you. Is that what you wanted to see me about?'

'No, sir.' Skinner gulped whisky thirstily and looked at the empty glass.

'Help yoursel' if you'd like another.'

'Thank you,' Skinner lumbered to the decanter, his elephantine buttocks jiggling. 'Wisht I had your figure, Mr Struan.'

'Then dinna eat so much.'

Skinner laughed. 'Eating's nothing to do with fatness. You're fat or you aren't. One of those things that the good Lord fixes at birth. I've always been heavy.' He filled his glass and walked back. 'A piece of information came into my hands last night. I can't reveal the source, but I wanted to discuss it with you before I print it.'

Which skeleton have you smelled out, my fine friend? Struan thought. There're so many to choose from. I only hope it's the right one. 'I own the *Oriental Times*, aye. As far as I know, only you and I are the ones that know. But I've never told you what to print or what na to print. You're editor and publisher. You're totally responsible, and if what you print's libellous, then you'll be sued. By whoever's libelled.'

'Yes, Mr Struan. And I appreciate the freedom you give me,' The eyes seemed to sink farther into the rolls of jelly. 'Freedom necessitates

514

responsibility – to oneself, to the paper, to society. Not necessarily in that order. But this is different, the – how shall I put it? – the "potentials" are far-reaching.' He pulled out a scrap of paper. It was covered with speed-written hieroglyphics which only he could read. He looked up. 'The Treaty of Chuenpi's been repudiated by the Crown, and Hong Kong along with it.'

'Is this a funny story, Mr Skinner?' Struan wondered how convincing Blore had been. Did you gamble correctly, laddie? he asked himself. The lad's a fine sense of humour: *The stallion took the bit.* Cart horse would be more apt.

'No, sir,' Skinner said. 'Perhaps I'd better read it.' And he read out, almost word for word, what Sir Charles Crosse had written, what Struan had told Blore to whisper secretly in Skinner's ear. Struan had decided that Skinner was the one to stir up the traders into a complex of fury so that they would all, in their individual ways, refuse to allow Hong Kong to perish; so that they would agitate as they had agitated so many years ago and had at length dominated the East India Company.

'I dinna believe it.'

'I think perhaps you should, Tai-Pan.' Skinner drained his glass. 'May I?'

'Of course. Bring back the decanter. It'll save you going back and forth. Who gave you the information?'

'I can't tell you.'

'And if I insist?'

'I still won't tell you. That would destroy my future as a newspaperman. There are very important ethics involved.'

Struan tested him. 'A newspaperman must have a newspaper,' he said bluntly.

'True. That's the gamble I'm taking – talking to you. But if you put it that way, I still won't tell you.'

'Are you sure it's true?'

'No. But I believe it is.'

'What's the date of the dispatch?' Struan asked.

'April 27th.'

'You seriously believe that it could get here so fast? Ridiculous!'

'I said the same. I still think it's true information.'

'If it's true, then we're all ruined.'

'Probably,' Skinner said.

'Na probably – certainly.'

'You forget the power of the press and the collective power of the traders.'

'We've nae power against the Foreign Secretary. And time's against us. Are you going to print it?'

'Yes. At the correct time.'

Struan moved the glass and watched the lights flickering from its bevelled edges. 'I'd say when you do there'll be a monumental panic. And Longstaff will carpet you right smartly.'

'I'm not worried about that, Mr Struan.' Skinner was perplexed: Struan was not reacting as he had expected. Unless the Tai-Pan already knew, he told himself for the hundredth time. But it makes no sense for him to have sent Blore to me. Blore arrived a week ago – and in that week the Tai-Pan's invested countless thousands of taels in Hong Kong. That would be the act of a maniac. So whom did Blore courier for? Brock? Unlikely. Because he's spending as lavishly as Struan. It must be the admiral – or the general – or Monsey. Monsey! Who but Monsey has the high-level connections? Who but Monsey hates Longstaff and wants his job? Who but Monsey is vitally concerned that Hong Kong succeeds? For without a successful Hong Kong, Monsey has no future in the Diplomatic Corps. 'It looks as though Hong Kong's dead. All the money and effort you've put in – we've all put in – is tossed aside.'

'Hong Kong canna be finished. Wi'out the island all the future mainland ports we'll have are so much dross.'

'I know, sir. We all do.'

'Aye. But the Foreign Secretary feels otherwise. Why? I wonder why. And what could we possibly do? How to convince him, eh? How?'

Skinner was as strong for Hong Kong as Struan was. Without Hong Kong there was no Noble House. And without The Noble House there was no weekly *Oriental Times* and no job.

'Maybe we won't have to convince that bugger,' he said shortly, eyes icy.

'Eh?'

'That bugger won't always be in power.'

Struan's interest heightened. This was a new slant, and unexpected. Skinner was a voracious reader of all newspapers and periodicals and a most well-informed man on 'published' parliamentary affairs. At the same time – with an extraordinary memory and a vital interest in people – Skinner had sources of information that were manifold. 'You think there's a chance for a change in Government?'

'I'll bet money that Sir Robert Peel and the Conservatives will topple the Whigs within the year.'

'That'd be a devilish dangerous gamble. I'd put money against you mysel'.'

'Would you gamble the *Oriental Times* against the fall of the Whigs within the year – and a retention of Hong Kong by the Crown?'

Struan was aware that such a wager would put Skinner totally on his side and the paper would be a small price to pay. But a quick agreement would show his hand. 'You've nae chance in the world of winning that wager.'

'It's a very good one, Mr Struan. The winter at home last year was one of the worst ever – economically and industrially. Unemployment's incredible. Harvests have been terrible. Do you know the price of bread is up to a shilling and two-pence a loaf according to last week's mail? Lump sugar's costing eight-pence a pound; tea seven shillings and eightpence; soap nine-pence a cake; eggs four shillings a dozen. Potatoes a shilling a pound. Bacon three shillings and sixpence a pound. Now take wages – artisans of all sorts, bricklayers, plumbers, carpenters – at most seventeen shillings and sixpence a week for sixty-four hours' work; agricultural workers nine shillings a week for God knows how many hours; factory workers around fifteen shillings – all these *if* work can be found. Good God, Mr Struan, you live up in the mountains with incredible wealth where you can give a thousand guineas to a girl just because she's got a pretty dress, so you don't know, you can't know, but one out of every eleven people in England is a pauper. In Stockton nearly ten thousand persons earned less than two shillings a week last year. Thirty thousand in Leeds under a shilling. Most everyone's starving and we're the richest nation on earth. The Whigs have their heads up their arses and they won't face up to what anyone can see is outrageously unfair. They've done nothing about the Chartists except to pretend they're anarchists. They won't face up to the appalling conditions in the mills and the factories. Good Christ, children of six and seven are working a twelve-hour day, and women too, and they're cheap labour and they put the men out of work. Why should the Whigs do anything? They own most of the factories and mills. And money's their god – more and more and evermore and to hell with everyone. The Whigs won't face up to the Irish problem. My God, there was a famine last year, and if there's another this year, the whole of Ireland'll be in revolt again and it's about time. And the Whigs haven't lifted a finger to reform banking. Why should they – they own the banks too! Look at your own bad luck! If we'd had a rightful proper law to protect depositors from the cursed machinations of the cursed Whigs –' He stopped with an effort, his jowls shaking and his face florid. 'Sorry, didn't mean to make a speech. Of course the Whigs have got to go. I'd say if they don't go in the next six months, there'll be a

517

blood bath in England which'll make the French Revolution look like a picnic. The only man who can save us is Sir Robert Peel, by all that's holy.'

Struan remembered what Culum had said about conditions in England. He and Robb had discounted it as the ramblings of an idealistic university undergraduate. And he had discounted the things his own father had written as unimportant. 'If Lord Cunnington's out, who'll be the next Foreign Secretary?'

'Sir Robert himself. Failing him, Lord Aberdeen.'

'But both're against free trade.'

'Yes, but both are liberal and pacific. And once in power, they'll have to change. Free trade is the only way England can survive – you know that – so they'll have to support it. And they'll need all the support they can get from the powerful and the wealthy.'

'You're saying I should support them?'

'The *Oriental Times*, lock, stock and printing press, against a fall of the Whigs this year. And Hong Kong.'

'You think you can help that?'

'Hong Kong, yes. Oh, yes.'

Struan eased his left boot more comfortably and leaned back in his chair again. He let a silence hang. 'A fifty per cent interest, and you have a deal,' he said.

'All or nothing.'

'Perhaps I should throw you out and have done with it.'

'You should, perhaps. You've more than enough wealth to last you and yours for ever. I'm asking you how much you want Hong Kong – and the future of England. I think I've a key.'

Struan poured himself some more whisky and refilled Skinner's glass. 'Done. All or nothing. Would you care to join me in some supper? I'm feeling a little hungry.'

'Yes, indeed. Thank you. Talking's hungry work. Thank you kindly.'

Struan rang the bell and blessed his joss that he had gambled. Lim Din arrived and food was ordered.

Skinner swilled his whisky and thanked God that he had judged the Tai-Pan correctly. 'You'll not regret it, Tai-Pan. Now listen a moment. The loss of Longstaff – I know he's a friend of yours, but I'm talking politically – is a huge piece of luck for Hong Kong. First he's a highborn, second a Whig, and third he's a fool. Sir Clyde Whalen's a squire's son, second no fool, third a man of action. Fourth, he knows India – spent thirty years in service to the East India Company. Prior to

518

that he was Royal Navy. Last, and most important of all, even though he's a Whig outwardly, I'm sure he must secretly hate Cunnington and the present Government and would do anything in his power to cause their downfall.'

'Why?'

'He's an Irishman. Cunnington's been the spearhead of most of the Irish legislation for the past fifteen years, and directly responsible – all *Irishmen* feel – for our disastrous Irish policy. That's the key to Whalen – if we can find a way to exploit it.' Skinner chewed an ink-stained thumbnail.

Lim Din and another servant returned with plates of cold meats and picked sausages and sweetmeats and cold pies and cold tarts and huge tankards of chilled beer, and champagne in an ice bucket.

Skinner smiled greedily. 'A feast fit for a millowner!'

'Fit for a publisher-owner! Help yoursel'.' Struan's mind was racing. How to twist Whalen? Will the Whigs fall from power? Should I switch my power to the Conservatives now? Stop supporting men like Crosse? By now word will be back in England that The Noble House is still The Noble House and stronger than ever. Do I gamble on Sir Robert Peel?

'When you publish this dispatch, a panic will hit everyone,' he said, closing in for the kill.

'Yes, Mr Struan. If I wasn't utterly opposed to letting Hong Kong go, I've the future of my paper to think of.' Skinner stuffed more food into his mouth, and talked as he chewed. 'But there're ways of presenting news and other ways of presenting news. That's what makes newspaper work so exciting.' He laughed and some of the food dribbled down his chin. 'Oh yes – I've the future of *my* paper to think of.' He turned his full attention to the food and ate monstrously.

Struan ate sparingly, lost in thought. At last, when even Skinner was replete, he stood and thanked him for the information and advice.

'I'll inform you privately before I publish the dispatch,' Skinner said, bloated. 'It'll be in a few days, but I need time to plan. Thank you, Tai-Pan.' He left.

Struan went below. May-may was still tossing in her sleep. He had a bunk made up in her room and let himself drift into half sleep.

At dawn May-may began to shiver. Ice was in her veins, in her head, and in her womb. It was the fifteenth day.

XXXIII

May-may lay fragile and helpless as a baby under the weight of a dozen blankets. Her face was grey, her eyes ghastly. For four hours her teeth chattered. Then abruptly the chills changed to fever. Struan bathed her face with iced water but this brought no relief. May-may grew delirious. She thrashed in the bed, muttering and screaming in an incoherent mixture of Chinese and English, consumed by the terrible fire. Struan held her and tried to comfort her, but she didn't recognize him, didn't hear him.

The fever disappeared as suddenly as it had come. Sweat gushed from May-may, drenching her clothes and the sheets. Her lips parted slightly and she uttered an ecstatic moan of relief. Her eyes opened and gradually began to focus.

'I feel so good, so tired,' she said feebly.

Struan helped Ah Sam changed the soaking pillows and sheets and clothing.

Then May-may slept – as the dead sleep, inert. Struan sat in a chair and watched over her.

She awoke after six hours, serene but depleted. 'Hello, Tai-Pan. I have Happy Valley fever?'

'Aye. But your doctor's got medicine to cure it. He'll have it in a day or so.'

'Good. Very good. Dinna worry, never mind.'

'Why're you smiling, lassie?'

'Ah,' she said, and closed her eyes contentedly and settled deeper into clean sheets and pillows. 'How else can you dominate joss? If you smile when you lose, then you win in life.'

'You going to be fine,' he said. 'Fine. Dinna worry.'

'I have no worries for me. Only you.'

'What do you mean?' Struan was exhausted by his vigil, and anguished by the fact that she seemed thinner than before, wraithlike, her eyes deeply shadowed. And aged.

'Nothing. I would like some soup. Some chicken soup.'

'The doctor sent some medicine for you. To make you strong.'

'Good. I feel fantastical weak. I will have the medicine after soup.'

He ordered the soup and May-may sipped a little, then lay back again.

'Now you rest, Tai-Pan,' she said. She furrowed her brow. 'How many days before next fever?'

'Three or four,' he said miserably.

'Dinna worry, Tai-Pan. Four days is for ever, never-mind. Go and rest, please, and then later we will talk.'

He went into his own cabin and slept badly, waking every few moments, then sleeping and dreaming that he was awake, or almost asleep and getting no rest.

The dying sun was low on the horizon when he awakened. He bathed and shaved, his brain jumbled and unclean. He stared at his face in the mirror and did not like what he saw. For his eyes told him that May-may would never survive three such battles. Twelve days of life remained for her at most.

There was a knock at the door.

'Aye?'

'Tai-Pan?'

'Oh, hello, Gordon. What news?'

'None, I'm afraid. I'm doing everything I can. How is the Lady?'

'The first attack had come and gone. Nae good, lad.'

'Everything's being done. The doctor sent some medicine to keep her strength up and some special foods. Ah Sam knows what to do.'

'Thank you.'

Gordon left, and Struan turned again to his reflections. He groped agonizingly for a solution. Where do I get cinchona? There must be some somewhere. Where would Peruvian bark be in Asia? Na Peruvian bark – Jesuits' bark.

Then his vagrant thought exploded into an idea. 'For the love of God!' he shouted aloud, his hope quickening. 'If you want horseflies, go to a horse. If you want Jesuits' bark – where else, you stupid fool!'

Within two hours *China Cloud* was ripping out of the sunset-painted harbour like a Valkyrie, all sails set but tightly reefed against the thickening monsoon. When she broke through the west channel and hit the full force of the Pacific swell and the wind, she heeled over and rigging sang exultantly.

'Sou' by sou'east!' Struan roared over the wind.

'Sou' by sou'east it is, sorr,' the helmsman echoed.

Struan peered aloft at the shrouds, etched against the implacable coming of night, and was chagrined to see so much canvas reefed. But he knew that with this easterly and with this sea the reefs would have to stay.

China Cloud came on to the new course and gained way into the night but still fought the sea and the wind. Soon she would turn again and have the wind astern and then she could run free.

After an hour Struan shouted, 'All hands on deck – ready to ware ship!'

The men scurried from the fo'c'sle and stood ready in the darkness on the ropes and hawsers and halyards. 'West by sou' west,' he ordered, and the helmsman swung the tiller wheel to the new course and the clipper swung with the wind. The yards screeched and strained to leeward and the halyards howled and stretched and then she was on the new course and Struan shouted, 'Mains'l and top ta' gallants reefs let go!'

The ship tore through the waves, the wind well abaft the beam, the bow wave cascading.

'Steady as she goes,' Struan ordered.

'Aye, aye sorr,' the helmsman said, straining his eyes to see the flickering light of the binnacle and maintain a steady course, the wheel fighting him.

'Take over, Cap'n Orlov!'

'It's about time, Green Eyes.'

'Perhaps you can get more speed,' Struan said. 'I'd like to be in Macao forthwith!' He went below.

Orlov thanked God that he had been prepared, as always, for instant departure. He had known the moment he saw the Tai-Pan's face that *China Cloud* had better be out of harbour in record time or he would be without a ship. And though his seaman's caution told him so much sail at night in such shoal and rock-filled seas was dangerous, he shouted exultantly. 'Let go reefs fore-royal and upper top ta' gallants,' and revelled in the freedom of being at sea and in command again after so many days at anchor. He inched the ship a point starboard and let go more reefs and drove her relentlessly. 'Get the for'ard cutter ready, Mr Cudahy! God knows, it better be ready when he comes on deck – and get the pilot's lantern aloft!'

'Aye, aye, sorr.'

'Belay the pilot's lantern! We'll not get one at this time of night,' Orlov said, correcting himself. 'I'll not wait for dawn and any shark-guts pilot. I'll take her in myself. We've urgent cargo aboard.'

Cudahy bent down and put his lips near Orlov's ear. 'Is she the one, sir? The one that he was after buying for her weight in gold? Did you see her face?'

'Get for'ard or I'll have your guts for the belt of my trousers! And keep your mouth shut and spread that word, by the blood of Christ! Everyone's confined to ship when we reach Macao!'

'Aye, aye, me foine Captain sorr,' Cudahy said with a laugh and stood to his full height, towering over the little man he liked and admired. 'Our mouths are clams, by the beard of St Patrick. No fear of that!' He leaped down the quarterdeck gangway and went forward.

Orlov strode the quarterdeck, wondering what all the mystery was about, and what was amiss with the tiny, shrouded girl the Tai-Pan had brought aboard in his arms. He saw the thickset Chinese, Fong, following Cudahy like a patient dog, and he wondered again why the man had been sent aboard to be trained in the ways of a captain, and why the Tai-Pan had put one of the heathen aboard each of his clippers.

I'd like to have seen the girl's face, he told himself. Her weight in gold, yes, so the story goes. I wish – oh, how I wish I was not as I am, that I could look into a man's face or a woman's face and not see revulsion, and not have to prove that I'm a man like any, and better than any afloat. I'm tired of being Stride Orlov *the hunchback*. Is that why I was afeared when the Tai-Pan said, 'In October you'll go north, alone'?

He looked moodily over the gunnel, at the black waves rushing past. You are what you are and the sea's waiting. And you're captain of the finest ship in the world. And once in your life you looked into a face and saw the green eyes studying you just as *a man*. Ah, Green Eyes, he thought, his misery leaving him, I'll go into hell for the moment you gave me.

'Avast there, you swabs! Bend smartly on the top ta' gallants ho!' he shouted.

And his order sent the men scurrying aloft again to grasp more power from the wind. And then, when he saw the lights of Macao on the horizon, he ordered the sails reefed and eased his ship cautiously – but always with the maximum speed – into the shallow harbour of Macao, the leadsman calling the fathoms.

'Fine seamanship, Cap'n,' Struan said.

Orlov spun around, startled. 'Oh, didn't see you. You sneak up on a man like a ghost. Cutter's ready to go alongside.' Then he added nonchalantly, 'thought I might as well take her in as wait till dawn and a pilot.'

'You're a mind reader, Captain.' Struan looked at the lights and at the unseen city, low on the water but rising to a crest. 'Anchor at our usual mooring. Guard my cabin yoursel'. You're na to go in – or any. Everyone's confined to the ship. With a tight mouth.'

'I've already given those orders.'

'When the Portuguese authorities come aboard, apologize for not waiting for the pilot and pay the usual dues. And the squeeze to the Chinese. Say I'm ashore.'

Orlov knew better than to ask how long the Tai-Pan would be gone.

Dawn was nudging the horizon when *China Cloud* moored half a mile from the still indiscernible wharves on the southwest harbour. This was as close as she could safely come; the bay was dangerously shallow and therefore almost useless – another reason Hong Kong was an economic necessity. As he hastened the cutter to shore, Struan noticed the riding lights of another clipper to the south: *White Witch*. A few smaller European ships were at anchor, and hundreds of sampans and junks plied their silent way.

Struan hurried along the jetty still rented by The Noble House. He saw that there were no lights on in their vast company residence which was also leased from the Portuguese. It was a colonnaded mansion, four-storeyed, on the far side of the treelined *praia*. He turned north and walked along the *praia*, skirting the Chinese customshouse. He cut through a wide street and began climbing the slight hill towards the church of São Francisco.

He was glad to be back in Macao, back in civilization amid cobbled streets and stately cathedrals and gracious Mediterranean houses and fountained *praças* and spacious gardens – sweet-smelling with their abundance of flowers.

Hong Kong will one day be like this, he told himself . . . with joss. Then he recalled Skinner and Whalen and malaria, and May-may aboard *China Cloud*, so frail and so weak and another fever due in two or three days. And what about *Blue Cloud*? She should be home soon. Will she beat *Gray Witch*? Or is she a thousand miles astern at the bottom of the sea? What about all the other clippers? How many do I lose this season? Let *Blue Cloud* be first! How is Winifred? And is Culum all right, and where's Gorth, and will it be today that there will be a reckoning?

The city was still asleep in the dawn. But he could feel Chinese eyes watching him. He crested the hill and crossed the beautiful Praça de São Francisco.

Beyond the *praça* northward, at the highest point of the isthmus, were the battlements of the ancient fort of São Paulo de Monte. And beyond this was the Chinese section of Macao: narrow alleys, and hovels built on hovels, crusting the north slope of the hill and falling away.

For half a mile farther there was flat land and the isthmus narrowed to barely a hundred and fifty yards. There were gardens and walks and the emerald of the small racecourse and the cricket ground that the English had developed and sponsored over the centuries. The Portuguese did not approve of racing and did not play cricket.

A hundred yards beyond the cricket ground was the wall where Macao ended and China began.

The wall was twenty feet high and ten feet thick and stretched from shore to shore. Only after the wall was built three centuries ago had the emperor agreed to lease the isthmus to the Portuguese and allow them to settle on the land.

In the centre of the wall's length was a portalled guard tower and a single majestic gate. The gate to China was always open, but no European could set foot through it.

Struan's boots sounded loud as he hurried across the *praça* and opened the tall, wrought-iron gates of the bishop's palace and walked through the gardens that had been tended for three centuries. One day I'll have a garden like this, he promised himself.

He crossed the cobbled forecourt, his boots clattering, and went up to the huge door. He pulled the bell and heard it echo within and pulled it again and again, insistently.

At length a lantern flickered past the downstairs windows and he heard footsteps approaching and a stream of querulous Portuguese. The door opened.

'*Bom dia*. I want to see the bishop.'

The half-dressed, half-asleep servant stared at him without recognition and without comprehension, then spouted another stream of Portuguese and began to close the door. But Struan shoved his foot in the door, pushed it open, and walked into the house. He turned into the first room – an exquisite, book-tiered study – and sat in a carved-back chair. Then he let his eyes fall on the gaping servant. 'The bishop,' he repeated.

*　　*　　*

Half an hour later Falarian Guineppa, Bishop of Macao, General of the Church of Rome, strode imperiously into the room that Struan had commandeered. He was a tall patrician who carried his fifty years youthfully. His nose was Roman-beaked, his forehead high, his features well used. He wore a magenta skullcap and magenta robes, and around his taut neck hung a bejewelled crucifix. His black eyes were sleepy and hostile. But when they fell on Struan, the anger and the sleepiness vanished. The bishop stopped on the threshold, every fibre of his being alert.

Struan stood. 'Good morning, Your Grace. Sorry to come uninvited and so early.'

'Welcome in the name of God, senhor,' the bishop said pleasantly. He motioned to a chair. 'I think a little breakfast. Would you join me?'

'Thank you.'

The bishop spoke curtly in Portuguese to the servant, who bowed and hurried away. Then he strolled slowly to the window, his fingers on his crucifix, and stared out at the rising sun. He saw *China Cloud* and the clusters of sampans surrounding it in the bay far below at anchor. What emergency, he wondered, brings the Tai-Pan of the Noble House to me? The enemy I know so well but have never met. 'I thank you for an awakening. This dawn is very beautiful.'

'Aye.'

Each man assumed a civility that neither felt.

To the bishop, Struan represented the materialistic, evil, fanatic Protestant English who had broken the laws of God, who – to their everlasting damnation – had denied the Pope as the Jews had denied Christ; the man who was their leader, and the one who had, almost singlehanded, destroyed Macao, and with Macao, Catholic domination of the Asian heathen.

To Struan, the bishop represented all that he despised in the Catholics – the dogmatic fanaticism of self-castrated, power-seeking men who sucked riches from the poor in the name of a Catholic God, drop by bloody drop, and from the drops built mighty cathedrals to the glory of their version of Divinity, who had idolatrously set up a man in Rome as Pope and made the man an infallible arbiter of other men.

Liveried servants obsequiously brought silver trays and hot chocolate and feather-light croissants and fresh butter and the sweet kumquat jelly for which the monastery was famous.

The bishop said grace and the Latin increased Struan's discomfort, but he said nothing.

Both men ate in silence. The bells from the multitude of churches tolled matins, and the faint, deep-throated litany from the chorus of monks in the cathedral filled the silence.

After chocolate there was coffee from Portuguese Brazil; hot, sweet, powerful, delicious.

At a motion of the bishop's hand a servant opened the bejewelled cigar box and offered it to Struan. 'These are from Havana, if they please you. After breakfast, I enjoy Sir Walter Raleigh's "gift" to humanity.'

'Thank you.' Struan chose one. The servants lit the cigars, and at a sign from the bishop they left.

The bishop watched the smoke spiral. 'Why should the Tai-Pan of The Noble House seek my help? *Papist* help?' he added with a brittle smile.

'You wager, wi'out odds, Your Grace, that it's na sought lightly. Have you heard of cinchona bark? Jesuits' bark?'

'So. You have malaria. Happy Valley fever,' he said softly.

'Sorry to disappoint you. Nay, I've na malaria. But someone I cherish has. Does cinchona cure malaria?'

The bishop's fingers toyed with the huge ring on his middle finger, then touched his crucifix. 'Yes. If the malaria of Happy Valley is the same as the malaria that exists in South America.' His eyes were piercing. Struan felt their power but stared back as relentlessly. 'Many years ago I was a missionary in Brazil. I caught their malaria. But cinchona cured me.'

'Do you have cinchona here? In Macao?'

There was a silence, broken by the clicking of the fingernails tapping the cross, reminding Struan of the Chinese doctor tapping May-may's wrist. He wondered if he had judged correctly – about the bishop.

'I don't know, Senhor Struan.'

'If cinchona can cure our malaria, then I'm ready to pay. If you want money you have that. Power? I'll give you that. If you want my soul you can have that – I dinna subscribe to your views, so that would be a safe exchange. I'll even gladly go through the form of becoming a Catholic, but it would be meaningless, as you know and I know. Whatever you want I'll give you if it's in my power to give. But I want some of the bark. I want to cure one person of the fever. Name your price.'

'For one who comes as a supplicant, your manners are curious.'

'Aye. But I'm presuming that, irrespective of my manners – or what you think of me or I think of you – that we have the means of a trade. Do you have cinchona? If you have it, will it cure Happy Valley malaria? And if it does, what's your price?'

527

The room was very quiet, quiet overlaid with movements of minds and wills and thoughts.

'I can answer none of those questions now,' the bishop said.

Struan got up. 'I'll come back tonight.'

'There's no need for you to return, senhor.'

'You're saying you'll na trade?'

'I'm saying that tonight may be too soon. It will take time to send word to every healer of the sick and to get a reply. I will get in touch with you as soon as I have an answer. To all your questions. Where will you be? *China Cloud* or your residence?'

'I'll send a man to sit on your doorstep and wait.'

'There's no need. I will send word.' The bishop remained seated in his chair. Then, seeing the depths of Struan's concern, he added compassionately, 'Don't worry, senhor. I will send word to both places, in Christ's name.'

'Thank you.' As Struan was leaving, he heard the bishop say, 'Go with God,' but he did not stop. The front door clanged behind him.

In the stillness of the little room the bishop sighed deeply. His eyes saw the bejewelled crucifix that hung at his chest. He prayed silently. Then he sent for his secretary and ordered the search to begin. Then, alone once more, he split himself into the three persons that all generals of the Church must simultaneously be. First, the anointed Peter, first Bishop of Christ, with all that that spiritually implied. Second, the militant guardian of the Church temporal with all that that implied. And last, just a simple man who believed the teachings of a simple man who was the Son of God.

He settled back in his chair and let these facets of himself argue one with another. And he listened to them.

XXXIV

Struan walked up the marble stairs of the company residence, fatigued yet strangely at peace. I've done all I can he thought.

Before he could open the door it was flung wide with a flourish. Lo Chum, the majordomo of the servants of The Noble House in Macao, beamed at him toothlessly. He was a tiny old man with a face like ancient ivory and a pixie smile, and he had been in Struan's service ever since Struan could afford a servant. He wore a neat white smock, black trousers and rope sandals.

'Hallo-ah, Tai-Pan. Bath ready, brekfass ready, clothses ready, wat for Tai-Pan wantshee, can? Never mind.'

'Heya, Lo Chum.' Struan never ceased being wonder-struck at the rapidity with which news travelled. He knew that if, as soon as he had come ashore, he had run the length of the jetty and had gone directly to the mansion, the door would still have been flung open and Lo Chum would have been there as he was now.

'Bath, clothses can,' Struan said.

'Comprador Chen Sheng been have gone. Say come back nine o'clock, can?'

'Can,' Struan replied wearily.

Lo Chum closed the door and scuttled ahead of Struan up the marble staircase and opened the door of the master bedroom. The large, iron hip bath was filled with steaming water, as always, a glass of milk was on a small table as always, his shaving gear was laid out, fresh shirt and clothes were on the bed – as always. It's good to be home, Struan thought.

'Tai-Pan wantshee cow chillo in bath, heya?' A neigh of laughter.

'Ayee yah! Lo Chum. A'ways talkshee werry bad troubles, a'ways talkee jig-jig cow chillo in bath, wat never mind. Wake Mass'er Culum – say here can!' Struan said, getting out of his dirty clothes.

'Mass'er Culum no slep-slep.'

'Where Mass'er go-ah?' Struan asked.

529

Lo Chum picked up the clothes and shrugged. 'A'l night out, Mass'er.'

Struan frowned. 'All same, every night, heya?'

Lo Chum shook his head. 'No, Mass'er. One, two night slep-slep here.' He bustled out.

Struan immersed himself in the bath, disturbed by the report of Culum's absence. I hope to God Culum's sense enough na to go into Chinatown.

Promptly at nine o'clock, a rich sedan chair stopped outside the mansion. Chen Sheng, comprador of The Noble House lowered himself ponderously. His robes were crimson and his hat bejewelled and he was very conscious of his majesty.

He marched up the steps and the door was opened by Lo Chum personally – as always. This gave Chen Sheng great face; for Lo Chum opened the door personally only to the Tai-Pan and to him.

'He is expecting me?' he asked in a dialect of Cantonese.

'Of course, Excellency. I'm sorry to arrange your appointment so early but I felt you would want to be first.'

'I hear he left Hong Kong in frantic haste. Do you know what's the matter?'

'He went directly to the Tai-Pan of the longskirts and—'

'I know that,' Chen Sheng said petulantly. He could not fathom why Struan had rushed to the monastery. 'I really don't know why I'm so patient with you, Lo Chum, or why I continue to pay you monthly squeeze to keep me informed in these very hard times. I knew the ship was in the harbour before you sent word. Disgusting lack of interest in my affairs.'

'I'm really very sorry, Excellency,' Lo Chum said. 'Of course, the Tai-Pan did bring his concubine on the ship.'

'Ah!' Good, he thought. I'll be glad to pass back the children and have done with that responsibility. 'That's a little better, though I would have been told by others within the hour. What other pearls of information have you that merit so vast a retainer all these years?'

Lo Chum showed the whites of his eyes. 'What wisdom could I, a lowly slave, have for such a mandarin as yourself?' He spoke very sadly. 'These are hard times, Excellency. My wives harass me for money and my sons spill taels on gambling as though silver grew like paddy. Distressing. Only by preknowledge of great importance can one defend oneself against fate. It is terrible to think that such knowledge could fall into the incorrect ear.'

Chen Sheng played with his queue, instantly aware Lo Chum had very special information.

'I agree. In such hard times as these it is very important – the gods have decreed as much – to assist the impoverished,' he said gravely. 'I was thinking of sending you an unworthy gift on behalf of your illustrious ancestors – three roast pigs, fourteen laying hens, two bolts of Shantung silk, a pearl worth ten taels of the purest silver, a fine jade belt buckle of the early Ch'ing Dynasty worth fifty taels, and some incidental sweetmeats and pastries that are quite inadequate for your palate but perhaps you would care to give them to your own servants.'

'A gift of such magnificence I could hardly accept,' Lo Chum said with great deference. 'It would put me in your debt for ever.'

'If you refuse, then I can only presume that it is an inadequate offering to your illustrous ancestor and I shall lose face.'

At length Lo Chum allowed himself to be persuaded to accept, and Chen Sheng allowed himself to be persuaded that the gift was princely.

'I hear that the Tai-Pan seeks something,' Lo Chum whispered, 'because his concubine is very sick. Sick with the fever poison of Hong Kong.'

'What?' Chen Sheng was horrified by the news, but pleased that the amount of the gift had been well spent. 'Please go on!'

Lo Chum told him about the doctor and the strange medicine – and all that Ah Sam had whispered this morning to a sampan owner whom Lo Chum had sent to her.

'Rumour has it further that the Tai-Pan has offered twenty thousand taels' reward. His son, your third wife's illustrious son and your foster son, has instituted a frantic search for the drug in Hong Kong.'

Chen Sheng's mind swam with the implications. He motioned to Lo Chum and was guided into Struan's study.

'Hallo-ah, Tai-Pan,' he said expansively. 'Good you see-ah Macao, nev'r mind.'

'Hallo-ah, Chen Sheng,' Struan said. He motioned to a chair. 'Sitshee!'

'Boat-ah, *Blue Cloud*, come home number one, heya?'

'Doan knowa. Werry wen I say you plenty quickee. Chen Sheng wantshee see my, heya?'

Chen Sheng was worried. He, the leader of the Macao Triads, had been made personally responsible by Jin-qua for the safety of T'chung May-may and her children. Only he, of all Jin-qua's associates, knew that she was Jin-qua's granddaughter and that as the Tai-Pan's concubine her value to them personally was enormous, and her value to the

531

future Triad cause – which was the cause of China – inestimable. Word that the fleet was returning immediately to Canton instead of going directly to Peking had saved them nearly four millions of taels – a hundred times the cost of May-may's education. He blessed his joss for May-may; without her he would have had to find a substantial amount of that ransom himself.

And now the stupid, worthless woman has had the bad joss to catch the incurable. At least, he amended quickly, incurable unless we can track down the drug. And if we can, she'll get better and our investment in her – and the Tai-Pan – will be ensured and there'll be twenty thousand taels to boot. Then another scrap of information clicked into place and he thought, Ah, so that explains why Gordon Chen sent forty Triad members of the Hong Kong lodge secretly into Macao yesterday. There must be some of the drug here. He wondered what Gordon Chen would say if he told him that his secret 'Teacher' had been sent on Jin-qua's orders – that Jin-qua was the Triad leader of all Kwangtung, and that he, Chen Sheng, was second to Jin-qua. Ah, he told himself, it is very wise to keep secret many things; you never know when someone will slip.

'Tai-Pan chillo little in house my, werry good, werry happy,' he said jovially. 'You wantshee see-ah? Take back Hong Kong?'

'See today. Take back soon. I say werry wen.' Struan had been wondering if he should tell Chen Sheng about May-may.

'Tai-Pan. Your chillo littel good,' Chen Sheng began. 'Thinkee best you fetch cow chillo mama 'shore. Make chillo mama happy, can. Werry number-one doctor here can. Werry number-one medicine can. Doan troubles. Thinkee medicine here in Macao. Chen Sheng fix plentee werry good.'

'How'd you know she was here, and about the malaria?'

'Wat? No unnerstan'.'

'How can you knowa cowa chilla my bad sick hav?'

Chen Sheng chuckled to himself, and shrugged. 'Knowa all same, never mind.'

'Medicine here? Truth?'

'If here get. I send junk quick-quick to *China Cloud*. Bring cow chillo 'shore. Chen Sheng fix.'

He bowed politely and walked out.

Struan went aboard *China Cloud* and gave the crew shore leave by watches. Soon Chen Sheng's junk was alongside. May-may was carefully brought ashore, a Chinese doctor in attendance, and carried to her house that nestled in the hill of São Antonio.

532

The house was clean and staffed with servants, and tea was ready. Ah Sam rushed about officiously and hugged the children, who were waiting in the house with their personal amahs, and propped May-may in the huge bed and brought the children to her. There were tears of happiness and more rushing to and fro, and more shouting, and Ah Sam and May-may were gratified to be home at long last.

The doctor had brought special foods and medicines to increase May-may's strength and to maintain the strength of the child in her womb, and ordered her to stay in bed.

'I'll be back soon,' Struan said.

'Good. Thank you, Tai-Pan. Thank you.'

'I'm going to the residence – then perhaps to the Brock house.'

'They are in Macao?'

'Aye. All except Tyler. I thought I'd told you. Do you na remember? Culum and Tess's here too.'

'Oh yes,' she replied. She remembered what had been arranged with Gordon Chen. 'Sorry. I had forget. My head's all like sieve. Of course I remember now. I'm very gracious glad to be off ship and home. Thank you.'

He went back to the residence. Culum had not returned, so he walked along the *praia* to the Brock residence. But neither Tess nor Liza knew where Culum was. Gorth said that the two of them had gone gambling last night at the English Club but that he, Gorth, had left early.

'I'll see thee to door,' Gorth said. When they were alone by the door, he smiled sardonically, exulting in the sweetness of revenge. 'You know how it be – I were visiting a lady. Mayhaps he be visiting likewise. No harm in that, eh? He were winning at cards when I be leaving him, if that be wot's aworryin' thee.'

'Nay, Gorth. I'm na worried about that. You know there're good British laws about murder – a quick trial and a quick noose, whoever it is. Even a prostitute.'

Gorth whitened. 'Wot thee mean by that, eh?'

'If someone becomes gallows bait, I'll be hangman gladly.'

'Be thee threatening me? There be law against that too, by God.'

'If there's a death – then there'll be a charge of murder, by God.'

'Doan know wot thee means!' Gorth blustered. 'Thee be false accusing me!'

'I'm na accusing you of anything, Gorth. Just reminding you of facts. Aye. I hear that there are two possible witnesses to a possible death – who'd be prepared to talk in court.'

Gorth controlled his panic. That'll be that godrotting bitch Fortheringill, and that bugger Quance. She was paid enough to keep her tongue quiet. Well, I'll be dealing with they right smartly if necessary, but it won't be, 'cause the little bitch won't die anyways. 'I baint afeared of the likes of you – or they godrotting false accusations.'

'I'm na accusing you, Gorth,' Struan said. He was sorely tempted to provoke the inevitable fight now. But he knew that he would have to wait for Gorth to make the first mistake, to insult him unforgivably in public. Only then could he openly and freely send seconds with a formal challenge and kill him before an audience. Only that way could he avoid a breach of the Culum-Tess match and avoid giving Brock the means to destroy him in the courts of law. For May-may had been right – everyone in Asia knew that he was spoiling to slaughter Gorth. 'If you see Culum, please tell him I'm looking for him.'

'Do thy own messengering! I'm not thy lacky. Thee's Tai-Pan of The Noble House not much longer, by God.'

'Watch your step,' Struan said. 'I'm not afraid of you.'

Gorth gorged on the bait. 'Nor I, Dirk. I tells thee man to man – watch thy step or I'll be comin' after thee.'

Struan walked back to the residence, delighted with himself. Got you hooked, Gorth.

Culum still had not returned. And there was no word from the bishop. Struan told Lo Chum to try to find Culum. He went out on to the *praia* and turned up the hill towards the cathedral, thence into lesser known streets, past gracious sidewalk restaurants and colourful umbrellas. He crossed a wide *praça* and went through a huge doorway.

The nun at the desk looked up.

'Morning. Do you speak English?' Struan asked.

'A littel, senhor.'

'You have a patient. Miss Mary Sinclair. I'm a friend of hers.'

A long pause. 'You wish see?'

'Please.'

She motioned to a Chinese nun and talked rapidly to her in Portuguese. Struan followed the Chinese nun down a corridor and up some stairs into Mary's room.

It was small, filth-stained and rancid, its windows closed tight. A crucifix hung over the bed.

Mary's face was drained, her smile faint. And suffering had aged her.

'Hello, Tai-Pan.'

'What's the trouble, Mary?' he asked gently.

'Nothing I don't deserve.'

534

'I'll get you out of this damned place,' Struan said.

'I'm fine, Tai-Pan. They're very kind to me.'

'Aye, but this is nae place for a Protestant English girl.'

A gaunt, tonsured monk came in. He wore simple robes – stiff with ancient bloodstains and spilled medicaments – and a plain wooden crucifix.

'Good morning,' the monk said, his English cultured and accentless. 'I am Father Sebastian. The patient's doctor.'

'Good morning. I think I'll take her out of your care.'

'I wouldn't advise it, Mr Struan. She shouldn't be moved for a month at least.'

'What's the matter with her?'

'Her inside is disordered.'

'You're English?'

'Is that so strange, Mr Struan? There are many English – and also Scots – who acknowledge the true Church of Christ. But being Catholic doesn't make me any less a doctor.'

'Do you have any cinchona bark here?'

'What?'

'Cinchona bark. Jesuits' bark.'

'No. I've never used it. I've never seen any. Why?'

'Nothing. What's wrong with Miss Sinclair?'

'It's quite complicated. Miss Sinclair should not be moved for a month – better, two.'

'Do you feel well enough to be moved, lassie?'

'Her brother, Mr Sinclair, does not object to her staying here. And I believe Mr Culum Struan also approves of what I suggest.'

'Has Culum been here today?' Struan asked Mary.

She shook her head and spoke to the monk, her face tragic. 'Please tell the Tai-Pan. About – about me.'

Father Sebastian said gravely, 'I think you're wise. Someone should know. Miss Sinclair is very sick. She drank a potion of Chinese herbs – perhaps poison would be a better word – to cause an abortion. The poison dislodged the foetus but caused a haemorrhage which is now, by the Grace of God, almost under control.'

Struan felt a sudden sweat. 'Who else knows, Mary? Horatio? Culum?'

She shook her head.

Struan turned back to the monk. ' "Almost under control"? Does that mean the lass is all right? That in a month or so she'll be all right?'

'Physically, yes. If there is no gangrene. And if it is the will of God.'

'What do you mean, "physically"?'

'I mean, Mr Struan, that it is impossible to consider the physical without the spiritual. This lady has sinned terribly against the laws of God – against the laws of the Catholic Church and also your Church – so a peace, and a reckoning, must be made with God before there can be a healing. That's all I was trying to say.'

'How – how did she get here?'

'She was brought here by her amah, who is a Catholic. I obtained special dispensation to treat her and, well, we put her in here and treated her as best we could. The mother superior insisted that someone be informed because we felt she was failing. Word was sent to a Captain Glessing. We presumed he was the – the father, but Miss Sinclair swears he is not – was not. And she begged us not to reveal the cause of her illness.' Father Sebastian paused. 'That crisis, by the Grace of God, passed.'

'You'll keep this secret? What – what has happened to her?'

'Only you, I and the sisters know. We have oaths to God that may not be broken. You need have no fear from us. But I know there'll be no healing of this poor sinner without a peace and a reckoning. For He knows.'

Father Sebastian left them.

'The – the father was one of your "friends", Mary?'

'Yes. I don't – I don't regret my life, Tai-Pan. I don't – I can't. Or – or what I've done. It's joss.' Mary was looking out of the window. 'Joss,' she repeated. 'I was raped when I was very young – at least . . . that's not true. I didn't know what . . . I didn't understand, but I was a little forced the first time. Then I . . . then it wasn't necessary to force – I wanted.'

'Who was he?'

'One of the boys at school. He died. It was so long ago.'

Struan searched his mind but could remember no boy that had died. No boy that could have had the run of the Sinclair house.

'Then after that,' Mary continued haltingly, 'I had a need. Horatio . . . Horatio was in England, so I asked – I asked one of the amahs to find me a lover. She explained to me that I . . . that I could have a lover, many lovers, that if I was clever and she was clever I could have a secret life and pretty things. My real life had never been pleasant. You know the father I had. So the amah showed me how. She . . . procured for me. We – we grew . . . we grew rich together and I'm glad. I bought the two houses and she always brought only very rich men.' She stopped, and then after a long time she whimpered, 'Oh, Tai-Pan, I'm so afraid.'

Struan sat beside her. He remembered what he had said to her only a few months ago. And her confident reply.

XXXV

Struan was at the open window, moodily watching the crowed *praia* below. It was sunset. The Portuguese were all in evening dress and they strolled back and forth, bowing, conversing animatedly – the young *fidalgos* and the girls flirting cautiously under the watchful eyes of parents and duennas. A few sedan chairs and their coolies plodded in search of customers or deposited latecomers to the promenade. To-night there was a ball at the governor's palace and he had been invited but he did not know if he would go. Culum had not returned yet. And word had not come from the bishop.

He had seen Horatio this afternoon. Horatio had been furious because Ah Tat, Mary's amah, had disappeared. 'I'm sure she's the one who fed poor Mary the poison, Tai-Pan,' he had said. Mary had told him that she had by mistake drunk some herb tea she found in the kitchen – nothing more.

'That's nonsense, Horatio. Ah Tat's been with you both for years. Why should she do a thing like that? It was an accident.'

After Horatio had gone, Struan had searched for the men whom Culum and Gorth had been with last night. They were mostly cronies of Gorth and had all said that some hours after Gorth had left, Culum had left; that he had been drinking but was no drunker than the rest, than he usually was.

You stupid idiot, Culum, Struan thought. You ought to know better.

Suddenly he noticed an immaculate, bewigged liveried servant approaching, and he recognized the bishop's coat of arms instantly. The man came unhurriedly along the *praia*, but he passed the residence without stopping and disappeared down the *praia*.

The light was failing fast now, and the oil lights of the lanterned promenade began to dominate the gloaming. Struan saw a curtained sedan chair stop outside the house. Two half-seen coolies left it and lost themselves in an alley.

Struan rushed out of the room and down the stairs.

Culum was sprawled unconscious in the back of the chair, his clothes torn and vomit-stained. He stank of alcohol.

Struan was more amused than angry. He pulled Culum to his feet and threw him over his shoulder and, careless of the stares of the passers by, carried him into the house.

'Lo Chum! Bath, quick-quick!'

Struan laid Culum on the bed and stripped him. There were no bruises on his chest or back. He turned him over. Nail scratches on his stomach. And blotched love bites.

'You idiot,' he said examining him quickly but scrupulously. No broken bones. No teeth missing. Signet ring and watch gone. Pockets empty.

'You've been rolled, laddie. Perhaps for the first time, but surely na the last.' Struan knew that slipping a drug into a lad's drink was an old trick in whorehouses.

Servants brought pails of warm water and filled the iron bath. Struan lifted Culum into the bath and soaped and sponged him. Lo Chum supported the lolling head.

'Mass'er plentee terribel crazy drink, plentee terribel jig-jig, heya.'

'Ayee yah!' Struan said. As he lifted Culum out, a stabbing pain soared from his left ankle, and he knew that today's walking had tired his ankle more than he had realized. I'd better bandage it tight for a few days, he thought.

He dried Culum and put him into bed. He slapped him gently around the face but this did not bring him around, so he had dinner and waited. His concern increased with the hours, for he knew that by this time, however much Culum had drunk, he should be recovering.

Culum's breathing was deep and regular. The heartbeat was strong.

Struan got up and stretched. There was nothing to do but wait. 'I go-ah number-one Missee. You stay watchee werry good, heya?' he said.

'Lo Chum watchee like mummah!'

'Send word, savvy? Wat time Mass'er wake, never mind, send word. Savvy?'

'Wat for Tai-Pan say "savvy", heya? A'ways savvy werry wen, never mind. Heya?'

But Lo Chum did not send word that night.

At dawn Struan left May-may's house and returned to the residence. May-may had slept peacefully, but Struan had heard every passerby and every sedan chair – and many that were only wraiths of his imagination.

Lo Chum opened the front door. 'Wat for Tai-Pan early, heya? Brekfass ready, bath ready, wat for Tai-Pan wantshee can, heya?'

'Mass'er wake, heya?'

'Wat for ask? If wake send word. I savvy plenty werry good, Tai-Pan,' Lo Chum replied, his dignity offended.

Struan went upstairs. Culum was still heavily asleep.

'One, two time Mass'er make like –' and Lo Chum groaned and chomped his jaws and snuffled and yawned and groaned loudly.

After breakfast Struan sent word to Liz and Tess that Culum had returned, but he did not tell them how. Next he tried to apply his mind to business.

He signed papers and approved heavier spending on the Hong Kong buildings, indignant at the rising costs of lumber and brick and labour and all manner of ships' stores, ship repairs, ship equipment.

The pox on't! Costs are up fifty per cent – and no sign of them coming down. Do I lay keels for new clippers next year or gamble on what we have? Gamble that the sea will na sink any? You have to buy more.

So he ordered one new clipper. He would call her *Tessan Cloud* and she would be Culum's birthday present. But even the thought of a new, beautiful clipper did not thrill him as it should. It reminded him of *Lotus Cloud* soon to be abuilding in Glasgow, and the sea fight next year with Wu Kwok – if he was still alive – or Wu Fang Choi, the father, and his pirates. He wondered if Scragger's lads would get home safely. It would be another month at least before they were home – another three months for the news to come back.

He closed his office and went to the English Club and chatted to Horatio for a moment, then with some of the traders, and played a game of billiards, but got no enjoyment from the company or the game. The talk was all business, all anxiety about disaster signs on the international level and the extent of their huge trade gambles of the season.

He sat in the large, quiet reading room and picked up the last mail's newspapers of three months ago.

With effort, he concentrated on an editorial. It told of widespread industrial unrest in the Midlands and asserted that it was imperative to pay a fair wage for a fair day's work. Another article lamented that the huge industrial machine of England was operating at only half capacity and cried that greater new markets *must* be found for the productive wealth it could spew forth; more production meant cheaper goods, increased employment, higher wages.

There were news articles that told of tension and war clouds over France and Spain because of the succession to the Spanish throne; Prussia was spreading its tentacles into all the German states to dominate them and a Franco-Prussian confrontation was imminent; there were war clouds over Russia and the Hapsburg Holy Roman Empire; war clouds over the Italian States that wished to throw out the upstart French King of Naples and join together or not to join together, and the Pope, French-supported, was involved in the political arena; there were war clouds over South Africa because the Boers – who had over the last four years trekked out of the Cape Colony to established the Transvaal and the Orange Free State – were now threatening the English colony of Natal and war was expected by the next mail; there were anti-Semitic riots and pogroms throughout Europe; Catholic were fighting against Protestants, Mohammedans against Hindus, against Catholics, against Protestants, and they fighting among themselves; there were Red Indian wars in America, animosity between the Northern and Southern states, animosity between America and Britain over Canada, trouble in Ireland, Sweden, Finland, India, Egypt, the Balkans . . .

'Does na matter what you read!' Struan exploded to no one in particular. 'The whole world's mad, by God!'

'What's amiss, Tai-Pan?' Horatio asked, startled from his hate-filled reverie.

'The whole world's mad, that's what's amiss! Why the devil will people na stop hacking each other to pieces and live in peace?'

'Quite agree,' Masterson shouted from across the room. 'Absolutely. Terrible place to bring children into, by God. Whole world's going to the dogs. Gone to the dogs. Much better years ago, what? Disgusting.'

'Yes,' Roach said. 'World's going too fast. The cursed Government's got its head in its proverbial rectum – as usual. By God, you'd think they'd learn, but they never will. Every God-cursed day you read that the Prime Minister said, "We've all got to tighten our belts." For the love of God, have you ever heard anyone say we could loosen them a bit?'

'I hear the import tax on tea's being doubled,' Masterson said. 'And if that maniac Peel ever gets in, that bugger's sure to bring in income tax! That invention of the devil!'

There was a general outcry and venom was heaped on Peel's head.

'The man's a damned anarchist!' Masterson said.

'Nonsense,' Roach said. 'It's not taxes, it's just that there are too many people. Birth control's the thing.'

'What?' Masterson roared. 'Don't start on that blasphemous, disgusting idea! Are you anti-Christ, for God's sake?'

'No, by God. But we're being swamped by the lower classes. I'm not saying *we* should, but they should, by God! Gallows bait, most of the scum!'

Struan tossed the papers aside and went to the English Hotel. It was an imposing, colonnaded building like the Club.

In the barbershop he had his hair trimmed and shampooed. Later he sent for Svenson, the Swedish seaman masseur.

The gnarled old man pummelled him with hands of steel and rubbed ice all over him and dried him with a rough towel until his flesh tingled.

'By the lord Harry, Svenson, I'm a new man.'

Svenson laughed but said nothing. His tongue had been torn out by corsairs in the Mediterranean many years ago. He motioned for Struan to rest on the mattressed table and covered him tightly with blankets, then left him to slumber.

'Tai-Pan!' It was Lo Chum.

Struan was instantly awake. 'Mass'er Culum?'

Lo Chum shook his head and smiled toothlessly. 'Longskirt Mass'er!'

Struan followed the taciturn Jesuit monk along the cathedral cloisters surrounding the inner court and its beautiful garden.

The cathedral clock chimed four o'clock.

The monk turned at the end of the walk and led the way through a great teak door into a vast ante-room. Tapestries draped the walls. Carpets covered the well-worn marble floor.

He knocked deferentially on the far door, and entered the room. Regal and imposing, Falarian Guineppa was sitting on a high-backed chair which seemed like a throne. He gestured in dismissal at the monk, who bowed and went out.

'Please sit down, senhor.'

Struan sat down on the chair indicated. It was slightly lower than the bishop's chair, and he felt the strength of the man's will reaching out to dominate him.

'You sent for me?'

'I asked you to come to see me, yes. Cinchona. There is none in Macao, but I believe there is some at our mission at Lo Ting.'

'Where's that?'

'Inland.' The bishop straightened a crease in his magenta robe. 'About a hundred and fifty miles northwest.'

Struan got up. 'I'll send someone immediately.'

'I've already done that, senhor. Please sit down.' The bishop was solemn. 'Our courier left at dawn with orders to make record time. I think he will. He's Chinese and comes from that area.'

'How long do you think it will take him? Seven days? Six days?'

'That is also a reason for my concern. How many fever attacks has the girl had?'

Struan wanted to ask the bishop how he knew about May-may but held himself in check. He realized that the sources for secret information of the Catholics were legion, and that in any event 'girl' would be a simple deduction for so astute a man as the bishop. 'One. The sweat broke two days ago, about this time.'

'Then there'll be another bout tomorrow, certainly within forty-eight hours. It will take at least seven days for the courier to get to Lo Ting and back – if all goes well and there are no unforeseen difficulties.'

'I dinna think she'll be able to stand two more attacks.'

'I hear she's young and strong. She should be able to endure for eight days.'

'She's four months with child.'

'That's very bad.'

'Aye. Where's Lo Ting? Give me a map. Perhaps I can cut the time by a day.'

'In this journey my connections outweigh yours a thousandfold,' the bishop said. 'Perhaps it will be seven days. If it is the will of God.'

Aye. Struan thought. A thousandfold. I wish I had the knowledge that the Catholics have collected over the centuries from the constant probes into China. Which Lo Ting? There could be fifty within two hundred miles. 'Aye,' he said at length, 'if it is the will of God.'

'You're a strange man, senhor. I am glad that I have had the opportunity of meeting you. Would you care for a glass of Madeira?'

'What's the price of the bark? If it exists and if it's back in time and if it cures?'

'Would you care for a glass of Madeira?'

'Thank you.'

The bishop rang the bell and immediately a liveried servant was at the door with an engraved silver tray bearing decanter and glasses.

'To a better understanding of many things, senhor.'

They drank – and measured each other.

'The price, Your Grace?'

'There are too many ifs at present. That answer can wait. But two things cannot.' The bishop savoured his wine. 'Madeira is such a perfect apéritif.' He collected his thoughts. 'I am gravely worried about Senhorita Sinclair.'

'I also,' Struan said.

'Father Sebastian is a miraculous healer. But he leads me to believe that unless the senhorita is helped spiritually she may take her own life.'

'Na Mary! She's very strong. She'd na do that.'

Falarian Guineppa steepled his fine fingers. A shaft of sun turned the huge ruby ring molten. 'If she were to put herself totally in Father Sebastian's hands – and in the hands of the Church of Christ – we could turn her damnation into a blessing. That would be the best for her. I believe with all my heart that that is the only real solution. But if this is not possible, before she is released I must pass over the responsibility for her to someone who will accept it.'

'I'll accept that.'

'Very well, but I do not think you are wise, senhor. Even so, your life and soul – and hers – are also in the hands of God. I pray that you and she will be given the gift of understanding. Very well. Before she leaves I will do everything in my power to try to save her soul – but as soon as she is fit enough to leave, I will send word.'

The cathedral clock chimed five o'clock.

'How is Archduke Zergeyev's wound?'

Struan's eyebrows knotted. 'This is the second thing that cannot wait?'

'For you Britons, perhaps.'

Falarian Guineppa opened a drawer and pulled out a heavily sealed leather briefcase. 'I have been asked to give you this prudently. It seems that certain diplomatic authorities are most concerned with the arch-duke's presence in Asia.'

'The Church authorities?'

'No, senhor. I am asked to tell you that you can, if you wish, pass on the documents. I understand certain seals prove their validity.' A faint smile passed across his face. 'This case too is sealed.'

Struan recognized the seal of the governor-general's office. 'Why should I be given diplomatic secrets? There are diplomatic channels. Mr Monsey is within half a mile of here and His Excellency is in Hong Kong. Both are very well acquainted with protocol.'

'*I'm* giving you nothing. I'm merely doing what I was asked to do. Don't forget, senhor, as much as I personally detest what you stand for, you are a power at the Court of St James, and your trade connections are worldwide. We live in hazardous times and Portugal and Britain are ancient allies. Britain has been a good friend to

544

Portugal and it is wise for friends to help each other, no? Perhaps it is as simple as that.'

Struan took the proffered briefcase.

'I will send word as soon as the Lo Ting courier returns,' Falarian Guineppa said. 'At whatever hour that may be. Would you like Father Sebastian to examine the lady?'

'I dinna ken,' Struan said, rising. 'Perhaps. I'd like to think about that, Your Grace.'

'At your pleasure, senhor.' The bishop hesitated. 'Go with God.'

'Go with God, Your Grace,' Struan said.

'Hello, Tai-Pan,' Culum said, his head pounding and his tongue like dried dung.

'Hello, lad.' Struan put down the still-unopened briefcase which had been burning him all the way home. He went to the sideboard and poured a stiff brandy.

'Food, Mass'er Culum?' Lo Chum said brightly. 'Pig' Potats? Gravee? Heya?'

Culum shook his head weakly and Struan dismissed Lo Chum. 'Here,' he said, giving Culum the brandy.

'I couldn't,' Culum said, nauseated.

'Drink it.'

Culum swallowed it. He choked and quickly drank some more of the tea that was beside the bed. He lay back, his temples thundering.

'Would you like to talk? Tell me what happened?'

Culum's face was grey and the whites of his eyes dirty pink. 'I can't remember anything. God, I feel terrible.'

'Start from the beginning.'

'I was playing whist with Gorth and a few of our friends,' Culum said with an effort. 'I remember winning about a hundred guineas. We'd been drinking quite a bit. But I remember putting the winnings in my pocket. Then – well, the rest is blank.'

'Do you remember where you went?'

'No. Not exactly.' He drank more tea thirstily and wiped his face with his hands, trying to clean away the ache. 'Oh God, I feel like death!'

'Do you remember which whorehouse you went to?'

Culum shook his head.

'Do you have a regular one that you've been going to?'

'Good God, no!'

'Nae need to get on your high horse, laddie. You've been to one –

545

that's clear. You've been rolled, that's clear. Your liquor was drugged, that's clear.'

'I was drugged?'

'It's the oldest trick in the world. That's why I told you never to go to a house unrecommended by a man you could trust. Is this the first time you've been to a house in Macao?'

'Yes, yes. Good Lord, I was drugged?'

'Now use your head. Think, lad! Do you remember the house?'

'No – nothing. Everything's blank.'

'Who picked the house for you, eh?'

Culum sat up in the bed. 'We were drinking and gaming. I was, well, pretty drunk. Then, well, everyone was talking about – about girls. And houses. And, well' – he looked at Struan, his shame and torment open – 'I was just – well, with the liquor and – I felt, well, on fire for a girl. I just decided that I had – had to go to a house.'

'Nae harm in that, lad. Who gave you the address?'

'I think . . . I don't know – but I think they each gave me one. They wrote addresses – or told me addresses, I can't remember. I do remember going out of the Club. There was a chair waiting and I got into it. Wait a minute – I remember now! I told him to go to the F and E!'

'They'd never roll you there, laddie. Or put a drug in your drink. Or deliver you back like that. More than their reputation's worth.'

'No. I'm sure. That's what I told the man. Yes. I'm absolutely sure!'

'Which way did they take you? Into Chinatown?'

'I don't know. I seem to remember – I don't know.'

'You said you felt "on fire". What sort of fire?'

'Well, it was like . . . I remember being very hot and, well – God's death, I'm frantic with desire for Tess, and what with the liquor and everything . . . I've had no peace, so – so I went to the house . . .' The words trailed off. 'Oh God, my head's bursting. Please leave me alone.'

'Were you carrying protections?'

Culum shook his head.

'This fire. This urge. Was it different last night?'

Again Culum shook his head. 'No. It's been like it for weeks but – well in a way I suppose it was – well no, not exactly. I was hard as a piece of iron and my loins were on fire and I just had to have a girl and, oh, I don't know. Leave me alone! Please – I'm sorry, but please . . .'

Struan went to the door. 'Lo Chum-ahhh!'

'Yes, Mass'er?'

'Go-ah house Chen Sheng. Get number-one cow chillo sick doctor quick-quick here-ah! Savvy?'

546

'Savvy plentee good-ah!' Lo Chum said huffily. 'A'ready werry plenty good-ah doctor downstairs for head boom-boom sick and all sick-sick. Young Mass'er like Tai-Pan – all same, never mind!'

Downstairs, Struan talked to the doctor through Lo Chum. The doctor said that he would send the medicines and special foods promptly, and he accepted a generous fee.

Struan went back upstairs.

'Can you remember anything else, lad?'

'No – nothing. Sorry. I didn't mean to jump at you.'

'Listen to me, lad! Come on, Culum, it's important!'

'Please, Father, don't talk so loudly,' Culum said, opening his eyes forlornly. 'What?'

'It sounds as though you've been slipped an aphrodisiac.'

'What?'

'Aye, aphrodisiac. There's dozens that could be put into a drink.'

'Impossible. It was just the liquor and my – my need of . . . it's impossible!'

'There are only two explanations. First, that the coolies took you to a house – and it wasn't the Macao branch of the F and E – where'd they'd get more squeeze for a rich customer and a share of the robbery to boot. There the girl or girls drugged you, rolled you and delivered you back. For your sake, that's what I hope happened. The other possibility is that one of your friends gave you the aphrodisiac at the Club, arranged for the chair to be waiting for you – and for a particular house.'

'That's nonsense! Why'd someone do that? For a hundred guineas and a ring and watch? One of my friends? That's madness.'

'But say someone hated you, Culum. Say the plan was to put you with a diseased girl – one who has the pox!'

'What?'

'Aye. That's what I'm afraid's happened.'

Culum died for an instant. 'You're just trying to frighten me.'

'By the Lord God, my son, I am na. But it is one very definite possibility. I'd say it's more likely than the other because you were brought back.'

'Who'd do that to me?'

'You have to answer that one, laddie. But even if that's what happened, all's na lost. Yet. I've sent for Chinese medicines. You're to drink them all, wi'out fail.'

'But there's no cure for the pox!'

'Aye. Once the disease is settled. But the Chinese believe you can kill the pox poison or whatever causes it, if you take precautions at once to purify your blood. Years ago when I first came out here, the same thing happened to me. Aristotle found me in a gutter in the Chinese quarter and got a Chinese doctor and I was all right. That's how I met him – why he's been my friend for so long. I canna be sure the house – or the girl – was diseased or na, but I never got the pox.'

'Oh God help me.'

'Aye. We'll na know for certain for a week. If there's nae swelling or pain or discharge by then – you've escaped this time.' He saw the terror in his son's eyes, and his compassion went out to him. 'A week of hell's ahead of you, laddie. Waiting to find out. I know what it'll be like – so dinna fash yoursel'. I'll help all I can. Same way Aristotle helped me.'

'I'll kill myself. I'll kill myself if I . . . oh God, how could I have been so foolish? Tess! Oh God, I'd better tell—'

'You'll do nae such thing! You tell her you were jumped by robbers on your way home. We'll report it as such. You'll tell your friends the same. That you think you must have had too much to drink – after the girl. That you can na remember anything except you're sure you had a great time and woke up here. And for the week you'll act as you normally act.'

'But Tess! How can I—'

'That's what you'll do, laddie! That's what you'll do, by God.'

'I can't, Father, it's just imp—'

'And under no circumstances will you tell anyone about the Chinese medicines. Dinna go to a house until we know for certain, and dinna touch Tess until you're married.'

'I'm so ashamed.'

'Nae need for that, laddie. It's difficult being young. But in this world it's up to a man to watch his back. There're a lot of mad dogs around.'

'You're saying it was Gorth?'

'I'm saying nothing. Do you think that?'

'No, of course not. But that's what you're thinking, isn't it?'

'Dinna forget, you've got to act normally or you'll lose Tess.'

'Why?'

'You think Liza and Brock'd allow you to marry Tess if they find out you're so immature and stupid that you'll go whoring in Macao drunk – and to an unknown whorehouse and get filled with love potions and rolled? If I was Brock I'd say you had na enough sense to be my son-in-law!'

'Sorry.'

'You get some rest, laddie. I'll be back later.'

And all the way to May-may's house Struan was deciding on the way

548

to kill Gorth – if Culum had the pox. The cruellest way. Aye, he thought coldly, I can be very cruel. This will na be just a simple killing – or quick. By God!

'You look terrible, Culum darling,' Tess said. 'You really ought to have an early night.'

'Yes.'

They were promenading along the *praia* in the night quiet. It was after dinner, and his head was clearer but his agony almost unbearable.

'What's the matter?' she asked, sensing his torment.

'Nothing, darling. I just drank too much. And those highwaymen weren't very gentle. By the Lord God, I'm forswearing drink for a year.' Please God, don't let anything happen. Hurry the week – and let nothing happen.

'Let's go back,' she said, and taking his arm firmly, turned him towards the Brock residence. 'A good night's rest will do you the world of good.' She felt very maternal and couldn't help feeling happy that he was almost helpless. 'I'm glad you're forswearing drink, my dear. Father gets terrible drunk sometimes – and Gorth, my word, many's the time I seed him besotted.'

' "I've seen him," ' he said, correcting her.

'I've *seen* him besotted. Oh, I'm glad we'll soon be wed.'

What possible reason could Gorth have for doing that? Culum asked himself. The Tai-Pan must be exaggerating. He must be.

A servant opened the door and Culum took Tess into the parlour.

'Back so soon, luvs?' Liza said.

'I'm a little tired, Ma.'

'Well, I'll be off,' Culum said. 'See you tomorrow. Will you be going to the cricket match?'

'Oh yes, let's, Ma!'

'Mayhaps thee'll escort us, Culum lad?'

'Thank you. I'd like that. See you tomorrow.' Culum kissed Tess's hand. 'Good night, Mrs Brock.'

'Night, lad.'

Culum turned for the door just as Gorth was entering. 'Oh, hello, Gorth.'

'Hello, Culum. I were waiting for thee. Just going for a drink at the Club. Come along.'

'Not tonight, thanks. I'm all in. Too many late nights. And there's the cricket tomorrow.'

'A drink won't hurt thee. After thy beating it be best.'

'Not tonight, Gorth. Thanks, though. See you tomorrow.'

'As thee wish, old lad. Now, take care of thyself.' Gorth closed the front door behind him.

'Gorth, what happened last night?' Liza scrutinized him.

'Poor lad got in his cups. I be leaving Club as I told thee, afore him, so I doan know. Wot'd he sayed, Tess?'

'Just that he drank too much, and that the highwaymen fell on him.' She laughed. 'Poor Culum – I think he'll be cured of the demon drink for a long time.'

'Would thee get my cheroots, Tess luv?' Gorth said. 'They be in't dresser.'

'Certainly,' Tess said and ran out.

'I heared,' Gorth said, 'I heared our Culum lad's been kicking over the traces like.'

'Wot?' Liza stopped her sewing.

'Baint harmful,' Gorth said. 'Mayhaps I shouldn't've sayed it. Baint harmful if a man's careful, by God. Thee knowed wot a man's like.'

'But he be marrying our Tess! She baint marrying no rake.'

'Yes. I thinks I be havin' a talk with the lad. Best be careful in Macao and no doubt about that'n. If Da' were here'd be different. But I've to protect the family – and the poor lad – from weaknesses. Thee'll say na about this, now!'

'Of course not.' Liza hated that which made men masculine. Why baint they controlling theyselves? Mayhaps I better be rethinking this marriage. 'Tess baint marrying no rake. But Culum baint that way at all. Are thee sure wot thee's saying?'

'Yes,' Gorth said. 'At least that's what some of the lads sayed.'

'I wisht yor da' were here.'

'Yes,' Gorth said, then added as though making a sudden decision, 'I think I be visiting Hong Kong for a day or two. I'll talk to Da'. That be best. Then I be talking to Culum proper. I be leaving on the tide.'

XXXVI

Struan finished the last page of the English translation of the Russian documents. He slowly tidied the pages and put them back in the briefcase and let it rest on his lap.

'And?' May-may asked. 'Why for so fantastical silent, heya?' She was propped in bed, under a mosquito net, her gold silk gown making her skin whiter.

'Nothing, lass.'

'Put bisnesses away and talk to me. For one hour you are like scholar.'

'Let me think for five minutes. Then I'll talk to you, eh?'

'Huh,' she said. 'If I was na sicknesses, then you'd be bedding all time.'

'Och aye, lassie.' Straun went to the garden door and stared up at the night sky. The stars were brilliant and the heavens foretold good weather.

May-may settled into the bed and watched him. He's looking very tired, she thought. Poor Tai-Pan, so many troubles.

He had told her about Culum and his fears for him, but not about Gorth. He had also said that there was fever bark to be had, within a few days. And he had told her about Mary and had cursed Ah Tat.

'Damned murdering fool. She should have known better. If Mary'd told me, or you, we could have sent her away to have the baby safely and secretly. To America or somewhere. The baby could have been adopted and—'

'And her Glessing man?' she had asked. 'Would he have still married her? Nine months away?'

'That's finished, either way!'

'Who's the father?' May-may had asked.

'She would na tell me,' Struan had said, and May-may had smiled to herself.

'Poor Mary,' he had added. 'Now her life's finished.'

'Nonsense, Tai-Pan. The marriage can go forward – if the Glessing and the Horatio never know.'

'Have you taken leave of your senses? Of course it's ended – what you say's impossible. Dishonest, terribly dishonest.'

'Aye. But what is never known does na matter, and the reason for hiding is good and na evil, never mind.'

'How will he never know, by God? Eh? Of course he'll find out. He'll certainly know she's na a virgin.'

There are ways, Tai-Pan, May-may thought. Ways of deceiving. You men are so simple in some things. Women are so much cleverer in most things that are important.

And she resolved to send someone to Ma-ree who could explain that which was necessary and thus stop all this suicide nonsense. Who? Obviously Elder Sister, Chen Sheng's third wife, who once was in a house and would know such secrets. I'll send her tomorrow. She'll know what to tell Ma-ree. So Ma-ree is not a trouble any more. With joss. But Culum and Gorth and Tess? Not a trouble soon, for an assassination will take place. My fever trouble? That will be solved according to my joss. All things are solved according to joss, so why is there need to worry? Better to accept. I pity you, Tai-Pan. You think so much and plan so much and try to bend joss eternally to your whims – but that's not so, is it? she asked herself. Surely he does only what you do, what all Chinese do. He laughs at fate and joss and gods and tries to use men and women to advance his aims. And twist joss. Yes, surely that is right. In many ways, Tai-Pan, you are more Chinese than I.

She sank deeper into the sweet-smelling coverlet and waited for Struan to talk to her.

Struan, however, was concentrating totally on what he had learned from the briefcase.

The papers had included a translated copy of a secret report prepared for Tsar Nicholas I in July last year, 1840, and contained, incredibly, maps of the lands between Russia and China. The maps alone, the first that Struan had ever seen, were priceless. There was also an analysis of the implications of the documents.

The secret report had been prepared by Prince Tergin, Chief of the secret Foreign Affairs Planning Committee. It said:

'It is our considered opinion that within half a century the Tsar will rule from the Baltic to the Pacific, from the Ice North Seas to the Indian Ocean, and be in a position to dominate the world, *if* the following strategy is adopted within the next three years.

'The key to world dominance is Asia plus North America. North

America is almost in our hands. If Britain and the United States allow us ten years of freedom in Alaskan Russian-America, all North America is ours.

'Our position there is solid and friendly. The United States in no way considers our vast territorial expansion in the northern wastelands a threat. Consolidation from Alaska to our southernmost "trading fort" in Northern California – and from there inland to the Atlantic – can be accomplished by the usual method: immediate emigration on a vast scale. Most of the western United States, and all but a small proportion of eastern Canada, is presently almost empty of settlers. Therefore the extent of our emigration into the northern wilderness can be kept secret – as it must be. From there the emigrants, which would be our hardy Euro-Asian warlike tribes – Uzbeks, Turkmen, Siberians, Kirghiz, Tadzhiks and Uigurs – many of whom deliberately would be nomadic peoples, would fan out and claim the whole land almost at will.

'We must maintain cordial relations with Britain and the United States for the next ten years. By that time emigration will have made Russia the most virile American power and our tribes – who in ancient days made up the hordes of Tamerlane and Genghis Khan – armed with modern weapons and commanded by Russians, can at our whim sweep the Anglo-Saxon into the sea.

'But a thousand times more important: *Asia*. We could concede the Americas, never Asia.

'The key to Asia is China. And China lies at our feet. We share almost five thousand miles of continuous land border with the Chinese Empire. *We must control her or we will never be safe*. We can never allow her to become strong or dominated by another Great Power, or we would be trapped between East and West and might be forced to war on two fronts. Our Asian policy is axiomatic: China must be kept weak, vassal and a Russian sphere of influence.

'Only one power – Britain – stands between us and success. If she can be prevented, by guile or pressure, from acquiring and consolidating a permanent island fortress off China, Asia is ours.

'Of course, we dare not alienate our ally Britain at this time. France, Poland, Prussia and the Hapsburgs are in no way content with the Dardanelles détente, any more than Russia is, and we must be on constant guard against their continuous harassment. Without British support our sacred heartland would be open to invasion. Providing the British adhere to their stated position in China – that they "merely wish to establish trade relations and trading depots, which all Western nations may share equally" – we can move forward into Sinkiang,

Turkestan and Mongolia, and control the land route to China. (We already dominate invasion routes within easy reach of the Khyber Pass and Kashmir, thence into British India.) Should word leak out about our land conquests, our official position will be that "Russia is merely subduing hostile wild tribes in our hinterland." Within five years we should be poised on the threshold of China's heartland, northwest of Peking. Then, with simple diplomatic pressure, we will be in a position to force advisers on the Manchu Emperor and, through him, control the Chinese Empire until such time it may be conveniently partitioned into vassal states. The hostility between Manchu overlords and Chinese subjects is vastly to our advantage and we will, of course, continue to encourage this.

'At all cost, we should encourage and assist British trading interests to settle in the mainland ports of China, where they would be restrained by direct Chinese pressure which we would, in time, diplomatically control. And at all costs we must discourage England from fortifying and colonizing any island – as they have done at Singapore, Malta, Cyprus (or an impregnable position like Gibraltar) – which would not be subject to our pressure, and would serve as a permanent bastion for her military and naval might. It will be advantageous to initiate immediate and close trading relations with selected firms in that area.

'The keystone of our foreign policy must be "Let England rule the seas and the trade routes, and be the first industrial nation of the earth. But let Russia rule the land." For once the land is secured – and it is our sacred heritage, our God-given right, to civilize the land – the seas become Russian seas. And thus the Tsar of all the Russias will rule the world.'

Zergeyev could easily be a key to the plan, Struan thought. Is he the man sent to find out our strength in China? To settle 'trade relations with selected firms'? Is part of his mission to report, at first hand, on American attitudes to Russian Alaska? Is he the man sent to prepare Russian Alaska for the hordes? Remember he said to you, 'Ours is the land, yours the sea!'

The commentary on this report had been equally bold and penetrating: 'Based on this secret document and accompanying maps, the validity of which is to be unquestioned, certain conclusions of far-reaching importance may be drawn:

'First, concerning the North American strategy: it must be noted that although the United States is gravely concerned over the present United States-British Canadian border dispute, she does not seemingly wish to acquire more territory on the North American continent. And

554

because of the friendly relations that exist between the United States and Russia – carefully nurtured, it is believed, to fulfil this aim – the present general political feeling in Washington is that Russian involvement in Alaska and southward down the western coast does not infringe on her sovereignty. In short, the United States of America will not invoke the Monroe Doctrine against Russia and will therefore – astonishingly – leave their back door open to a foreign Power, contrary to their obvious best interest. Certainly contrary to the interests of British Canada. If five hundred thousand Euro-Asian tribesmen were to be introduced quietly in the north, as is perfectly possible, certainly the English and Americans would be in a completely untenable position.

'It must be noted further that, although the present Tsar is contemptuous of Russian America, this territory does present a Russian key to the continent. And if there should ever be a civil war in the United States over the slave issue, as indeed appears inevitable, these Russian tribes would be in a position to dominate that conflict. This would certainly bring England and France into the war. Russian nomadic hordes, with short lines of communication over the Bering Sea and a primitive ability to live off the land, would have a distinct advantage. And as most of the western and southwestern lands *are* sparsely populated, these settlers – or "warriors" – could sweep southward with relative ease.

'Thus, if Britain wishes to maintain her position as a world power and nullify Russia's never-ending search for world domination, she must first eliminate the Russian Alaska threat to Canada and the weakling United States. She must persuade the United States, by any means in her power, to invoke the Monroe Doctrine to expel the Russian threat. Or she must exert diplomatic pressure and purchase this territory, or take it by force. For unless Russia is eliminated quickly, the whole of North America, within half a century, *will* come under her sway.

'Second, England must maintain absolute dominance in China. It is necessary to trace Russian conquest thus far across the Urals, and see how far they have *already* penetrated into lands loosely under the historical overlordship of the Chinese Emperor.' With a series of maps and dates and places, translated copies of treaties, the whole panorama of the Russian move east was documented.

'For the last three hundred years (since 1552) Muscovite armies have steadily worked eastward in their search for a "final" border. By 1640 Okhotsk, on the Sea of Okhotsk – north of Manchuria on the Pacific

Ocean – was reached. Immediately these armies moved south and for the first time clashed with Manchu-Chinese hordes.

'The Treaty of Nerchinsk, in 1689, signed between Russia and China, settled the north border between the two countries along the Argun River and Stanovoi Mountains. The whole of Manchurian eastern Siberia was ceded to Russia. To date, this line was a "final" Russian border north of China.

'About this time, 1690, a Russian named Zaterev was sent by land to Peking as an ambassador. *En route* he surveyed ways for possible invasion of the incredibly rich heartland of China. The best route he found followed the natural corridor of the Selenga River which flowed into the plains north of Peking. The key to this route is the possession of Turkestan, Outer Mongolia and the Chinese province of Sinkiang.

'And, as Prince Tergin's report has stated, their armies already dominate Eurasia, north of Manchuria, to the Pacific, and are already on the borders of Sinkiang, Turkestan and Outer Mongolia. It is from this direction that Russian encroachment on China proper will come, and will continue to come for a long time.'

The report added: 'Unless Britain maintains a firm attitude that China and Asia is her sphere of influence, Russian advisers will be in Peking within a generation. Russian armies will control all the easy access routes from Turkestan, Afghanistan, Kashmir, into British India and the whole British Indian Empire can be invaded and swallowed at whim.

'If Britain wishes to continue as a world power it is vital that China be made a bulwark against Russia. It is vital that Russian advances be halted in the Sinkiang area. It is vital that a dominant British fortress be centred in China, for, by herself, China is helpless. If China is allowed to wither in her ancient ways and is not helped to emerge into the modern era, she will be conquered easily by Russia and the balance of Asia destroyed.

'In conclusion: it is a matter of great regret that Portugal is not strong enough to hold the land-seeking hunger of the Russians at bay. Our only hope is that our ancient ally, Britain, will by eminence and strength prevent that which seems *inevitable*.

'For this reason alone we have illegally prepared this dossier, entirely without official or unofficial permission. Prince Tergin's report and the maps were acquired in St Petersburg and found their way into un-official friendly hands in Portugal. From thence here.

'We have asked His Grace – who is not privy to any of this information – to place these papers in the hands of the Tai-Pan of

The Noble House, one who will, we believe, ensure that they reach their correct destination, so that action may be taken before it is too late. And as a measure of our sincerity we have signed our names, praying that our careers, perhaps our lives, will be in equally safe hands.'

The report was signed by two minor Portuguese foreign policy experts whom Struan knew slightly.

He threw the butt of his cheroot into the garden and watched it burn itself out. Aye, he said to himself, it's inevitable. But na if we keep Hong Kong. God damn Lord Cunnington.

How to use the information? That's easy. As soon as I get back to Hong Kong, a word in Longstaff's ear and Cooper's ear. But what do I gain by that? Why do I na go home mysel'? This type of knowledge is a chance in a lifetime. What about Zergeyev? Do we talk 'specifics' now? Do I bargain with him?

'Tai-Pan?'

'Aye, lass?'

'Would you close garden window-door? It's getting very gracious cold.'

The night was warm.

XXXVII

The chills convulsed May-may. The fires consumed her. During the delirium May-may felt her womb rip asunder and she screamed. The life-to-be passed out of her, and in the passing took all but the merest spark of her soul and strength. Then the fever broke and the sweat released her from the nightmare. Four hours she teetered on the brink of death. But her joss decreed that she was to come back.

'Hello, Tai-Pan.' She could feel the continuous seeping from her womb. 'Bad joss to lose baby,' she whispered.

'Dinna fash yoursel'. Just get yoursel' better. Any moment the cinchona bark'll arrive. I know it will.'

May-may summoned her strength and shrugged with a trace of her old imperiousness. 'Pox on the longskirts! How for can the man hurry in a skirt, heya?'

But the effort depleted her and she slipped into unconsciousness.

Two days later she seemed much stronger.

'Morning, lass. How do you feel today?'

'Fantastical good,' May-may said. 'It is a pretty day, heya? Did you seen Ma-ree?'

'Aye. She's looking much better. A tremendous change. Almost miraculous!'

'Why for so good change, heya?' she asked innocently, knowing that Elder Sister had gone to see her yesterday.

'I dinna ken,' he said. 'I saw Horatio just before I left. He brought her some flowers. By the way, she thanks you for the things you sent her. What did you send?'

'Mangoes and some herb tea my doctor recommended. Ah Sam went two, three days ago.' May-may rested a moment. Even talking was a great strain for her. She must be very strong today, she told herself firmly.

There is much to do today, and tomorrow there is fever again. Oh well, at least now no problem for Ma-ree – she's rescued. So easy now that Elder Sister has explained to her what all young girls in houses are taught – that with care and meticulous acting and tears of pretended pain and fear, and the final modest telltale stains cautiously placed, a girl can, if necessary, be virgin ten times for ten different men.

Ah Sam came in and kowtowed, and muttered something to her. May-may brightened. 'Oh, very good, Ah Sam! You may go.' Then to Struan, 'Tai-Pan, I need some taels of silver, please.'

'How many?'

'Lots. I am impoverished. Your old mother's very fond of you. Wat for you ask such things?'

'If you hurry up and get better, I'll give you all the taels you need.'

'You give me great face, Tai-Pan. Hugest face. Twenty thousand taels for medicine cure – ayeee yah, I am worth like an empress lady to you.'

'Gordon told you?'

'No. I was listen at door. Of course! Do you think your old mother likes not to know what doctor says and you say, heya?' She glanced at the doorway.

Struan turned to see a lovely young girl bowing gracefully. Her hair was coiled in a thick, dark snake atop her exquisite head and adorned with jade ornaments and flowers. Her almond-shaped face was like purest alabaster.

'This is Yin-hsi,' May-may said. 'She is my sister.'

'I did na ken you had one, lass. She's very pretty.'

'Yes, but, well, she's not really sister, Tai-Pan. Chinese ladies often call each other "sister". It's politeness. Yin-hsi's your birthday present.'

'What?'

'I bought her for birthday.'

'Have you taken leave of your senses?'

'Oh, Tai-Pan, you are very trying sometimes badly,' May-may said, beginning to cry. 'Your birthday is in four monthses. At that time I would have been heavy with child so I arranged search for a "sister". It has been difficult to decide bestest choice. She is bestest, and now because I am sick I give her now and na wait. You dinna like her?'

'Good God, lass! Dinna cry, May-may. Listen. Dinna cry . . . Of course I like your sister. But you dinna buy girls as birthday presents, for the love of God!'

'Why not?'

'Well, because you just dinna.'

'She's very nice – I want her for my sister. I was going to teach her for the four monthses, but now . . .' She broke out sobbing again.

Yin-hsi hurried from the doorway and knelt beside May-may and held her hand and dried her tears solicitously and helped her to drink a little tea. May-may had warned her that barbarians were sometimes strange and showed their happiness by shouting and cursing, but not to worry.

'Look, Tai-Pan, how pretty she is!' May-may said. 'You like her, surely?'

'That's na the point, May-may. Of course I like her.'

'Then that's settled, then.' May-may closed her eyes and lay back in her nest of pillows.

'It's na settled, then.'

She summoned a final broadside. 'It is, and I'll na argue with you any more, by God! I paid huge monies and she's bestest and I canna send her away for she'll lose all face and she'd have to hang herself.'

'Dinna be ridiculous!'

'I promise you she will, Tai-Pan. Everyone knows I was looking for a new sister, for me and for you, and if you send her away her face is finished. Fantastical finished. She'll hang herself, truly!'

'Dinna cry, lassie. Please.'

'But you dinna like my birthday present to you.'

'I like her and you need na send her away,' he said quickly – anything to stop the tears. 'Keep her here. She'll – she'll be a sister to you, and when you're well we'll – we'll find her a good husband. Eh? There's nae need to cry. Come on, lassie, now stop the tears.'

At length May-may stopped weeping and lay back again. Her outburst had sapped too much of her precious energy. But it was worth the price, she exulted. Now Yin-hsi will stay. If I die, he will be in good hands. If I live, she will be my sister and the second sister in his household, for of course he will want her. Of course he will want her, she told herself as she drifted away. She's so pretty.

Ah Sam came in. 'Mass'er. Young Mass'er outside. See can?'

Struan was alarmed by May-may's dreadful pallor. 'Get doctor plentee quick-quick, savvy?'

'Savvy, Mass'er.' Struan bleakly left the room. Ah Sam closed the door after him and knelt beside the bed and said to Yin-hsi, 'Second Mother, I should change Supreme Lady's dressings before the doctor comes.'

'Yes. I will help you, Ah Sam,' Yin-hsi said. 'Father certainly is a strange giant. If Supreme Lady and you hadn't warned me, I would have been very frightened.'

'Father's very nice. For a barbarian. Of course, Supreme Lady and I have been training him.' Ah Sam frowned at May-may, who was deep in sleep. 'She looks very bad indeed.'

'Yes. But my astrologer foretold good tidings, so we must be patient.'

'Hello, Culum,' Struan said as he came into the beautiful walled garden forecourt.

'Hello, Tai-Pan. I hope you don't mind my coming here,' Culum rose from the willow-shaded seat and took out a letter. 'This just arrived and – well, instead of sending Lo Chum I thought I'd like to see how you were. And find out how she is.'

Struan took the letter. It was marked 'Personal, Private and Urgent' and came from Morley Skinner.

'She lost the bairn the day before yesterday,' he said.

'How terrible!' Culum said. 'Has the cinchona come?'

Struan shook his head. 'Sit down, lad.' He tore open the letter. Morley Skinner wrote that he had intended to withhold the 'repudiation' news until Struan's return – he felt it dangerous to release it in his absence – but that now it was imperative to publish the report immediately: 'A frigate from England arrived this morning. My informant on the flagship said that the admiral was delighted with the private Admiralty dispatch he received and was heard to say, "It's about bloody time, by God. With any luck we'll be north within the month." This can only mean that he, too, is privy to the news and that Whalen's arrival is imminent. I cannot stress too highly the necessity of your return. By the way, I hear there's a curious private codicils to the Longstaff-Ching-so agreement over Canton's ransom. Last, I hope you have been able to prove, one way or another, the value of cinchona bark. I regret that, as far as I know, none is to be found here. I am, sir, your must humble servant, Morley Skinner.'

May-may'll na last another fever spell, Struan thought, anguished. That's the truth and you have to face it. Tomorrow she'll be dead – unless the cinchona arrives. And who knows if it really will cure her?

If she dies you must save Hong Kong. If she lives you must save Hong Kong. But why? Why na leave that cursed island as it was before? You may be wrong – Hong Kong may na be necessary to Britain. What do you prove by your mad crusade to open up China and bring her into the world on your terms, in your way? Leave China to her own joss and go home. With May-may if she lives. Let Culum find his own level as Tai-Pan. One day you'll die and then The Noble House will find its own level. That's law – God's law, nature's law, and the law of joss.

Go home and enjoy what you've sweated and sacrificed for. Release

561

Culum from his five-year servitude; there's more than enough to last you and him and his children's children. Let Culum decide if he wants to stay or does na want to stay. Go home and forget. You're rich and powerful and you can sit in the courts of kings if you wish. Aye. You're *the* Tai-Pan. Leave as *the* Tai-Pan, and to the devil with China. Give up China – she's a vampire mistress.

'More bad news?'

'Oh, sorry, Culum lad, I'd forgotten about you. What did you say?'

'More bad news?'

'Nay, but important.' Struan noticed that the last seven days had taken their toll on Culum. Nae youth to your face now, laddie. You're a man. Then he remembered Gorth and he knew that he could not leave Asia without a reckoning – with Gorth and with Brock.

'Today's your seventh day, lad, the last, is it na?'

'Yes,' Culum said. Oh God, he thought, protect me from such a week again. Twice he had been frightened to death. Once it had hurt to pass water and once it seemed that there had been a swelling and rash. But the Tai-Pan had succoured him and father and son had grown closer together. Struan had told him about May-may.

And in the watches of the night Struan had talked to his son as a father can sometimes talk, when grief – or sometimes happiness – has unlocked the doors. Plans for the future, problems of the past. How very difficult it is to love someone and live with someone over years.

Struan got up. 'I want you to go to Hong Kong at once,' he told Culum. 'You'll go in *China Cloud*, with the tide. I'll put Captain Orlov officially under your orders. For this voyage you'll be master of *China Cloud*.'

Culum liked the idea of being master of a real clipper. Yes.

'As soon as you get to Hong Kong, have Captain Orlov fetch Skinner aboard. Deliver to him personally a letter I'll give you. Then do the same with another for Gordon. Under no circumstances go ashore yoursel' or allow anyone else aboard. As soon as Skinner and Gordon have written their replies, send them back ashore and return here immediately. You be back tomorrow night. Leave on the noon tide.'

'Very well. I can't thank you enough for – well, for everything.'

'Who knows, lad? Mayhaps you never were within a league of the pox.'

'Yes. Even so – well, thanks.'

'I'll see you in the office in an hour.'

'Good. That'll give me time to say goodbye to Tess.'

'Have you ever considered taking your lives into your own hands. Na waiting for three months?'

'You mean, elope?'

'I asked if you've ever considered it, that's all. I'm na saying you should.'

'I wish I could – we could. That would solve . . . it's not possible, or I would. No one'd marry us.'

'Brock'd certainly be furious. And Gorth. I would na recommend that course. Is Gorth back yet?' he asked, knowing he was not.

'No. He's due tonight.'

'Send word to Cap'n Orlov to meet us in my office, in an hour.'

'You'll put him under my absolute orders?' Culum asked.

'Na as far as seamanship is concerned. But in all other matters, aye. Why?'

'Nothing, Tai-Pan,' Culum said. 'See you in an hour.'

'Evening, Dirk,' Liza said, striding into the residence dining-room. 'Sorry to interrupt thy supper.'

'That's all right, Liza,' Struan said, getting up. 'Please sit down. Would you join me?'

'No, thank you. Be the youngsters here?'

'Eh? How could they be here?'

'I be waiting more'n hour with their supper,' Liza said irritably. 'I thort they be dawdling again.' She turned for the door. 'Sorry to interrupt your supper.'

'I dinna understand. Culum left in *China Cloud* on the noon tide. How could you be expecting him for supper?'

'Wot?'

'He left Macao on the noon tide,' Struan repeated patiently.

'But Tess – I thort she were with him. At cricket match all afternoon.'

'I had to send him suddenly. This morning. The last I heard was that he was going to say goodbye to Tess. Oh, it must've been just before noon.'

'They never sayed he was leaving today, only that they'd be aseeing me later. Yes, it were afore noon! Then where be Tess? She baint been back all day.'

'That's nothing to worry about. She's probably wi' friends – you know how young people dinna notice the passing of time.'

Liza bit her lip anxiously. 'She never beed late afore. Not this late. She be a homebody, none of that there galavantin' around. Anything's happened to her, Tyler'll . . . If she went with Culum on't ship, there'll be the devil to pay.'

'Why should they do that, Mrs Brock?' Struan asked.

'God help 'em if they has. An' you if you've ahelped 'em.'

After Liza had gone, Struan poured himself a glass of brandy, and went to the window to watch the *praia* and the harbour. When he saw the *White Witch* almost at her moorings he went downstairs.

'I go-ah Club, Lo Chum.'

'Yes, Mass'er.'

XXXVIII

Gorth came charging into the foyer of the Club like a wild bull, a cat-o'-nine-tails in his hands. He shoved startled servants and guests out of the way and crashed into the gaming room.

'Where be Struan?'

'I believe he's in the bar, Gorth,' Horatio said, shocked by Gorth's face and the cat that twitched maliciously.

Gorth whirled around and bolted across the foyer and into the bar. He saw Struan at a table with a group of traders. Everyone moved out of the way as Gorth strode up to Struan.

'Where be Tess, you son of a bitch?'

There was dead silence in the room. Horatio and the others crowded the doorway.

'I dinna ken, and if you call me that again I'll kill you.'

Gorth jerked Struan to his feet. 'Be she on *China Cloud*?'

Struan freed himself from Gorth's grip. 'I dinna ken. And if she is, what does it matter? Nae harm in a couple of youngsters—'

'You be planning it! You planned it, you scum! You tol' Orlov t'marry 'em!'

'If they eloped, what does it matter? If they're married now, what does it matter?'

Gorth slashed at Struan with the cat. One of the iron-tipped tails sliced Struan's face neatly. 'Our Tess wedded to that poxridden rake?' he shouted. 'You stinking son of a bitch!'

So I was right, Struan thought. You *are* the one! He lunged at Gorth and grabbed the handle of the cat, but others in the room fell on the two of them and pulled them apart. In the mêlée a candelabrum on one of the tables crashed to the floor, and Horatio stamped out the flames which caught the fluffy carpet.

Struan ripped himself free and glared at Gorth.

'I'll send seconds to call on you tonight.'

'I baint needin' seconds, by God. Now. Choose yor godrotting weapons. Come on! And after you, Culum. I swear to God!'

'Why provoke me, Gorth, eh? And why threaten Culum?'

'You knowed, you son of a bitch. He be poxed, by God!'

'You're mad!'

'You baint covering up, by God.' Gorth tried to fight loose from the grasp of four men but could not. 'Let me go, for Christ sake!'

'Culum's na poxed! Why say he is?'

'Everyone knowed. He beed t' Chinatown. You knowed it and that be why they's gone – afore it be showing terrible.'

Struan picked up the cat in his right hand. 'Let him go, lads.'

Everyone backed off. Gorth went for his knife and readied for a charge, and a knife seemed to appear in Struan's left hand as if by magic.

Gorth feinted but Struan remained rock-still and let Gorth see for an instant all the primeval murder lust that was consuming him. And his pleasure. Gorth stopped in his tracks, his senses screaming danger.

'This is nae place to fight,' Struan said. 'This duel's na of my choosing. But there's nae anything I can do. Horatio, would you be a second?'

'Yes. Yes, of course,' Horatio replied, conscience-stricken over the tea seeds he had arranged for Longstaff. Is this the way to repay a lifetime of help and friendship? The Tai-Pan sent you word about Mary and gave you a lorcha to come to Macao. He's been like a father to you and her, and now you knife him in the back. Yes – but you're nothing to him. You're only destroying a great evil. If you can do that, then that will make up for your own evil when you face God, as you will.

'I'd be honoured to be your other second, Tai-Pan,' Masterson was saying.

'Then perhaps you'll come with me, gentlemen.' Struan wiped the trickle of blood from his chin and threw the cat over the bar and headed for the door.

'You be a dead man!' Gorth shouted after him, confident again. 'Hurry it up, you bastard-whorebitch-whelp!'

Struan did not stop until he was outside the club and safely on the *praia*. 'I choose fighting irons.'

'Good Lord, Tai-Pan, that's not – not usual,' Horatio said. 'He's very strong and, well, you've . . . you're . . . the last week's taken more out of you than you realize.'

'I quite agree,' Masterson said. 'A bullet between the eyes is wiser. Oh yes, Tai-Pan.'

'Go back and tell him now. Dinna argue. My mind's firm!'

'Where – where will you . . . well, surely this must be kept quiet. Perhaps the Portuguese'll try to stop you.'

'Aye. Hire a junk. You two, me, Gorth and his seconds'll leave at sunup. I want witnesses and a fair duel. There'll be more than enough room on the deck of a junk.'

I'm na going to kill you, Gorth, Struan exulted to himself. Oh, no, that's too easy. But by the Lord God, from tomorrow on you'll never walk again, you'll never feed yoursel' again, you'll never see again, you'll never bed again. I'll show you what vengeance is.

By nightfall the news of the duel had flown mouth to mouth, and with the news the betting began. Many favoured Gorth: he was in the full flush of strength and, after all, had good reason to challenge the Tai-Pan if there was truth to the rumour that Culum was poxed and that, knowing this, the Tai-Pan had sent Tess and Culum to sea with a captain who could marry them beyond the three-mile limit.

Those who put money on the Tai-Pan did so because they hoped, not believed, he would win. Everyone knew of his frantic anxiety over the cinchona and that his legendary mistress was dying. And everyone could see the havoc this had caused in him. Only Lo Chum, Chen Sheng, Ah Sam and Yin-hsi borrowed every penny they could and bet on the Tai-Pan confidently and petitioned the gods to watch over them. Without the Tai-Pan they were lost anyway.

No one mentioned the duel to May-may. Struan left her early and went back to his residence. He wanted to sleep soundly. The duel did not trouble him; he was sure that he could handle Gorth. But in the process he did not care to be mutilated, and he knew that he would have to be very strong and very fast.

Calmly he walked the quiet streets in the warmth of another beautiful, starlit night.

Lo Chum opened the door. 'Night, Mass'er.' He motioned blandly to the ante-room. Liza Brock was waiting.

'Evening,' Struan said.

'Be Culum poxed?'

'Of course he's na poxed! God's blood, we dinna even know if they're married yet. Perhaps they just went for a secret trip.'

'But he beed to house – who knowed where? That night with the highwaymen.'

'Culum's na got the pox, Liza.'

'Then why dost others sayed it?'

'Ask Gorth.'

567

'I did an' he sayed he were told it.'

'I'll say it again, Liza. Culum does na have the pox.'

Liza's huge shoulders shook with sobs. 'Oh, God, wot've we done?' She wished that she could stop the duel. She liked Gorth even though he was not her own son. She knew that her hands also were guilty with the blood that would be spilled – Gorth's or the Tai-Pan's or Culum's or her man's. If she hadn't forced Tyler to let Tess go to the ball, then all this might never have happened.

'Dinna worry, Liza,' Struan said kindly. 'Tess's all right, I'm sure. If they're wed, then you've na anything to fear.'

'When be *China Cloud* comin' back?'

'Tomorrow night.'

'Thee be letting our'n doctor examine him?'

'That's up to Culum. But I'll na forbid him. He does na have the pox, Liza. If he had, you think I'd allow the marriage?'

'Yes, I do,' Liza said, tormented. 'You be a devil and only the Devil knowed wot be in thy mind, Dirk Struan. But I swear to God, if thee be lying, I be killing thee if my men doan.'

She groped for the door. Lo Chum opened it and closed it after her.

'Mass'er, best slep-slep,' Lo Chum said cheerfully. 'Tomollow soon, heya?'

'Go to hell.'

The iron front door knocker sent a dull reverberation through the sleeping residence. Struan listened keenly in the warm, airy darkness of his bedroom and then heard Lo Chum's soft footsteps. He slipped out of bed, knife in hand, and grabbed his silk robe. He went out to the landing quickly and silently, and peered over the balustrade. Two floors below, Lo Chum put down the lantern and unbolted the door. The grandfather clock chimed 1.15.

Father Sebastian stood on the threshold.

'Tai-Pan see me can?'

Lo Chum nodded and put away the cleaver that he had been carrying behind his back. He started up the staircase but stopped as Struan called out:

'Aye?'

Father Sebastian craned up into the darkness, the hackles of his neck crawling from the suddenness of the cry. 'Mr Struan?'

'Aye?' Struan said, his voice strangled.

'His Grace sent me. We've got the cinchona bark.'

'Where is it?'

The monk held up a small, soiled bag. 'Here. His Grace said you'd be expecting someone.'

'And the price?'

'I know nothing about that, Mr Struan,' Father Sebastian called out weakly. 'His Grace simply said to treat whomsoever you'd take me to. That's all.'

'I'll be there in a second,' Struan shouted, charging back into the room.

He threw on his clothes, fought into his boots, rushed for the door and stopped. After thinking a second, he picked up the fighting iron and came down the stairs four at a time.

Father Sebastian saw the fighting iron and flinched.

'Morning, Father,' Struan said. He hid his disgust at the monk's filthy habit, and hated all doctors anew. 'Lo Chum, wen Mass'er Sinclair here – you fetch, savvy?'

'Savvy, Mass'er.'

'Come on, Father Sebastian!'

'Just a moment, Mr Struan! Before we go I must explain something. I've never used cinchona before – none of us have.'

'Well, that does na matter, does it?'

'Of course it matters!' the gaunt monk exclaimed. 'All I know is that I've to make a "tea" of this bark by boiling it. The trouble is we don't know for certain how long to boil it or how strong to make it. Or how much the patient should have. Or how often the patient should be dosed. The only medical treatise we have on cinchona is archaic Latin – and vague!'

'The bishop said he'd had the malaria. How much did he take?'

'His Grace doesn't remember. Only that it tasted very bitter and revolted him. He drank it for four days, he thinks. His Grace told me to make it quite clear that we treat her at your own risk.'

'Aye. I understand very well. Come on!'

Struan dashed out of the door, Father Sebastian beside him. They followed the *praia* for a little way and started up a silent, tree-lined avenue.

'Please, Mr Struan, not so fast,' Father Sebastian said, out of breath.

'A fever's due tomorrow. We've to hurry.' Struan crossed the Praça de São Paulo and headed impatiently into another street. Suddenly his instincts warned him and he stopped and darted to one side. A musket ball smashed into the wall beside him. He pulled down the terrified priest. Another shot. The ball nicked Struan's shoulder, and he cursed himself for not bringing pistols.

'Run for your life!' He pulled the monk up and shoved him across the road into the safety of a doorway. Lights were going on in the houses.

'This way!' he hissed, and rushed out. Abruptly he changed direction and another shot missed by a fraction of an inch as he reached the safety of an alley, Father Sebastian panting alongside.

'You've still the cinchona?' Struan asked.

'Yes. For the love of God, what's going on?'

'Highwaymen!' Struan took the frightened monk's arm and ran through the depths of the alley and up on to the open space of the fort of São Paulo do Monte.

In the shadows of the fort he took a breather. 'Where's the cinchona?'

Father Sebastian held up the bag limply. The moonlight touched the livid whip scar on Struan's chin and flickered in the eyes and seemed to make him more huge and more devilish. 'Who was that? Who was firing at us?' he asked.

'Highwaymen,' Struan repeated. He knew that actually Gorth's men – or Gorth – must have been in ambush. He wondered for a moment if Father Sebastian had been sent as a decoy. Unlikely – na by the bishop and na wi' cinchona. Well, I'll know soon enough, he thought. And if he is, I'll cut a few Papist throats.

He studied the darkness warily. He slipped his knife out of his boot and eased the fighting-iron thong around his wrist. When Father Sebastian was breathing less heavily, he led the way across the crest, past the Church of São Antonio and down the hill a street to the outer wall of May-may's house. A door was set into the high, thick granite wall.

He rapped harshly with the knocker. In a few moments Lim Din peered through the spy hole. The door swung open. They went into the forecourt and the door was bolted behind them.

'We're safe now,' Struan said. 'Lim Din, tea – drink plentee quick-quick!' He motioned Father Sebastian to a seat and laid the fighting-iron on the table. 'Catch your breath first.'

The monk took his hand off the crucifix he had been clutching and mopped his brow. 'Was someone really trying to kill us?'

'It felt that way to me,' Struan said. He took off his coat and looked at his shoulder. The ball had burned the flesh.

'Let me look at that,' the monk said.

'It's nothing.' Struan put his coat on. 'Dinna worry, Father. You treat her at my risk. You're all right?'

'Yes.' The monk's lips were parched and his mouth tasted rancid. 'First I'll prepare the cinchona tea.'

570

'Good. But before we begin, swear by the cross that you'll never talk to anyone about this house or who's in it or what happens here.'

'That's not necessary, surely. There's nothing that—'

'Aye, there is! I like my privacy! If you'll na swear, then I'll treat her mysel'. Seems that I know as much as you about how to use cinchona. Make up your mind.'

The monk was distressed by his lack of knowledge, and longed desperately to heal in the name of God. 'Very well. I swear by the cross my lips are sealed.'

'Thank you.' Struan led the way through the front door and down a corridor. Ah Sam came out of her room and bowed tentatively, pulling her green pyjamas closer to her. Her hair was tousled and her face still puffed with sleep. She followed them into the kitchen with the lantern.

The cooking room was small, with a fireplace and a charcoal brazier, and adjoined the cluttered back garden. It was filled with pots and pans and tea-kettles. Hundreds of bunches of dried herbs and mushrooms, vegetables, entrails, sausages, hung on the smoke-grimed walls. Rattan sacks of rice littered the filth-stained floor.

Two sleep-doped cook amahs were half upright in untidy bunks, staring groggily at Struan. But when he carelessly swept a mass of pans and dirty plates off the table to make a space, they leaped out of their beds and fled out of the house.

'Tea, Mass'er?' Ah Sam asked, bewildered.

Struan shook his head. He took the sweat-stained cloth bag from the nervous monk and opened it. The bark was brown and ordinary and broken into tiny pieces. He sniffed it but it had no odour. 'What now?'

'We'll need something to cook the brew in.' Father Sebastian picked up a fairly clean pan.

'First, will you please wash your hands?' Struan pointed to a small barrel and the nearby soap.

'What?'

'First wash your hands. Please.' Struan dipped water into the barrel and offered the soap. 'You'll na do anything till you've washed your hands.'

'Why is that necessary?'

'I dinna ken. An old Chinese superstition. Please – go on, Father, please.'

While Struan washed out the pan and put it on the table. Ah Sam watched, bright-eyed, as Father Sebastian scrubbed his hands with soap, rinsed them off, and dried them on a clean towel.

Then he closed his eyes and steepled his hands and breathed a silent

571

prayer. 'Now something to measure with,' he said, coming back to earth, and selecting a small cup at random, filled it to the brim with cinchona. He tipped the bark into the pan, and then, slowly and methodically, added ten equal measures of water. He set the pan to cook on the charcoal brazier. 'Ten to one to start with,' he said in a parched voice. He wiped his hands nervously on the sides of his habit. 'Now I'd like to see the patient.'

Struan beckoned to Ah Sam and indicated the pan. 'No touchee!'

'No touchee, Mass'er!' Ah Sam said vigorously. Now that she was over her initial shock of the sudden awakening she was beginning to enjoy all these strange proceedings. 'No touchee, Mass'er, never mind!'

Struan and the monk left the kitchen, and went into May-may's bedroom. Ah Sam followed.

A lantern splashed pockets of light in the darkness. Yin-hsi was brushing her tousled hair in front of the mirror. She stopped and bowed hastily. Her mattress bed was on the floor to one side of May-may's vast four-poster.

May-may was shivering feebly under the weight of blankets.

'Hello, lassie. We've the cinchona,' Struan said, coming close to her. 'At long last. All's well now!'

'I'm so cold, Tai-Pan,' she said helplessly. 'I'm so cold. What have you done to your face?'

'Nothing, lass.'

'You've cut yourself.' She shivered and closed her eyes and fell back into the blizzard that was engulfing her. 'It's so cold.'

Struan turned and looked at Father Sebastian. He saw the shock on his stretched face. 'What's amiss?'

'Nothing. Nothing.' The monk, set a tiny sand-timer on a table, and kneeling beside the bed, took May-may's wrist and began to count her heartbeats. How can a Chinese girl speak English? he asked himself. Is the other girl a second mistress? Am I in a harem of the devil? Oh God, protect me, and give me the power of Thy healing and let me by Thy instrument this night.

May-may's pulse was so slow and soft that he had great difficulty in feeling it. With extreme gentleness he turned her face around and peered into her eyes. 'Do not be afraid,' he said. 'There's nothing to be afraid of. You're in God's hands. I must look at your eyes. Don't be afraid, you're in His hands.'

Defenceless, and petrified. May-may did as she was told. Yin-hsi and Ah Sam stood in the background and watched apprehensively.

'What's he doing? Who is he?' Yin-hsi whispered.

'A barbarian devil witch doctor,' Ah Sam whispered back. 'He's a monk. One of the longskirt priests of the naked Godman they nailed to a cross.'

'Oh!' Yin-hsi shuddered. 'I've heard about them. How absolutely dreadful to do such a thing! They really are devils! Why don't you bring Father some tea? That's always good for anxiety.'

'Lim Din's getting it, Second Mother,' Ah Sam whispered; swearing that not for anything would she move, for then she might miss something of great import. 'I wish I could understand their dreadful tongue.'

The monk put May-may's wrist on the coverlet, and looked up at Struan. 'His Grace said the malaria caused an abortion. I must examine her.'

'Go on, then.'

When the monk moved the blankets and sheets aside, May-may tried to stop him and Yin-hsi and Ah Sam anxiously hurried to help her.

'No!' Struan snapped. 'Stay-ah!' He sat beside, May-may and held her hands. 'It's all right, m' lassie. Go on,' he said to the priest.

Father Sebastian examined May-may, and then settled her comfortably again. 'The haemorrhage has almost stopped. That is very good.'

He put his long fingers on the base of her skull and probed carefully.

May-may felt the fingers smooth away some of her pain. But the ice was forming in her again and her teeth began chattering. 'Tai-Pan. I'm so cold. Can I have a warm bottle or blankets? Please. I'm so cold.'

'Aye, lass, just a moment.' There was a hot bottle at her back. She lay under four down quilts.

'Have you a watch, Mr Struan?' Father Sebastian asked.

'Aye.'

'Please go to the kitchen. As soon as the water boils, note the time. When it has simmered one hour . . .' Father Sebastian's eyes mirrored his awful desperation. 'Two? Half an hour? How much? Oh God, please help me in this hour of need.'

'One hour,' Struan said firmly, confidently. 'We'll set the same amount to simmer for two hours. If the first's nae good we'll try the second lot.'

'Yes. Yes.'

Struan checked his watch under the lantern's light in the kitchen. He took the brew off the brazier and set it to cool in a bucket of water. The second pan was already simmering.

'How is she?' he asked as the priest came in, Ah Sam and Yin-hsi close behind.

'The chills are severe. Her heart is very weak. Can you remember how long she shivered before the heat came?'

'Four hours, perhaps five. I dinna ken.' Struan poured some of the hot liquor into a tiny teacup, and tasted it. 'God's blood, it's horribly bitter!'

The priest took a sip, and he grimaced too. 'Well. Let's begin. I only hope she can keep it down. A teacupful every hour.' He selected a cup at random from a smoke-stained shelf, and picked up a dirty scrap of rag from the table.'

'What's that for?' Struan asked.

'I'll have to strain the bark out of the brew. This'll be fine. The mesh is coarse enough.'

'I'll do it,' Struan said. He took out the silver tea strainer that he had ready and wiped it clean again with a clean handkerchief.

'Why're you doing that?'

'The Chinese are always very careful to keep the teapot and cups clean. They say it makes the tea more wholesome.' He began to pour the foul-smelling bark tea into an immaculate porcelain teapot. He willed the strength of the liquor to be correct. 'Why na the same with this, eh?'

He carried the pot and the cup into the bedroom.

May-may vomited the first cup. And the second.

In spite of her pathetic pleadings. Struan forced her to drink again. May-may held it down – anything not to have to swallow another.

Still nothing happened. Except that her chills grew more severe.

An hour later Struan made her drink again. She retained this cupful, but the chills continued to worsen.

'We'll make it two cups,' Struan said, fighting his panic. And he forced her to consume the double measure.

Hour after hour the process was repeated. Now it was dawn.

Struan looked at his watch. Six o'clock. No improvement. The rigors made May-may flutter like a twig in a fall wind.

'For the love of Christ,' Struan burst out, 'It's got to work!'

'With the love of Christ, it is working, Mr Struan,' Father Sebastian said. He was holding May-may's wrist. 'The fever heat was due two hours ago. If it doesn't begin, she has a chance. Her pulse is imperceptible, yes, but the cinchona is working.'

'Hold on, lassie,' Struan said, gripping May-may's hand. 'A few more hours. Hold on!'

Later there was a knock on the gate in the garden wall.

Struan walked blearily out of the house and unbolted the door. 'Hello, Horatio. Heya, Lo Chum.'

'Is she dead?'

'Nay, lad. I think she's cured, by the grace of God.'

'You got the cinchona?'

'Aye.'

'Masterson's at the junk. It's time for Gorth. I'll ask them – his seconds – to postpone until tomorrow. You're in no state to fight anyone.'

'There's nae need for you to worry. There're more ways of killing a snake than stamping its godrotting head off. I'll be there in an hour.'

'All right, Tai-Pan.' Horatio left in a hurry, Lo Chum with him.

Struan bolted the door and returned to May-may.

She was lying perfectly still in bed.

And Father Sebastian was taking her pulse. His face was stiff with anxiety. He bent down and listened to her heartbeat. Seconds passed. He raised his head and looked searchingly at Struan. 'For a moment I thought . . . but she's all right. Her heartbeat is terribly slow, but, well, she's young. With the grace of God . . . the fever's dead, Mr Struan. Peruvian cinchona will cure the fever of Happy Valley. How marvellous are the ways of God!'

Struan felt weirdly detached. 'Will the fever return?' he asked.

'Perhaps. From time to time. But more cinchona will arrest it – there's nothing to worry about now. This fever's *dead*. Don't you understand? She's cured of malaria.'

'Will she live? You say her heart's very weak. Will she live?'

'God willing, the chance is good. Very good. But I don't know for certain.'

'I've got to go now,' Struan said, rising. 'Would you please stay here till I get back?'

'Yes.' Father Sebastian was going to make the sign of the cross over him, but decided against it. 'I cannot bless your departure, Mr Struan. You're going to a killing, aren't you?'

'Man is born to die, Father. I just try to protect mysel' and mine as best I know how and to choose the time of my dying, that's all.'

He picked up the fighting-iron and tied it to his wrist, then left the house.

As he walked the streets, he felt eyes watching him but paid them no heed. He drew strength from the morning and from the sun, and from the sight and smell of the sea.

It's a good day to stamp out a snake, he thought. But you're the one that's dead. You've na the strength to go against Gorth with a fighting iron. Na today.

XXXIX

There was a large crowd near the junk. Traders, a detachment of Portuguese soldiers under a young officer, seamen. The junk was moored to a jetty off the *praia*. When Struan appeared, those who had wagered on him were dismayed. And those who had wagered on Gorth were exultant.

The Portuguese officer politely interrupted Struan. 'Good morning, senhor.'

'Morning, Captain Machado,' Struan replied.

'The governor-general wishes you to know that duels are forbidden in Macao.'

'I realize that,' Struan said. 'Perhaps you'll thank him for me and tell him I'd be the last to break Portuguese laws. I know we're all guests and guests have responsibilities to their hosts.' He shifted the thong of his fighting iron and walked towards the junk. The crowd parted and he saw the animosity on the faces of Gorth's men and on those who wished him dead. There were many.

Lo Chum was waiting on the high quarterdeck beside Horatio. 'Morning, Mass'er.' He held up the shaving gear. 'You wantshee?'

'Where's Gorth, Horatio?'

'His seconds are looking for him.'

Struan prayed that Gorth was flat on his back in a whorehouse, drunk as a fiddler's bitch. Oh God, let us fight tomorrow!

He began to shave. The crowed watched silently and many crossed themselves, awed by the serenity of the Tai-Pan.

When he had shaved he felt somewhat better. He looked at the sky. Threads of cirrus touched the heavens and the sea was calm as a lake. He called to Cudahy, whom he had taken off *China Cloud*. 'Guard my back.'

'Yes, sorr.'

Struan stretched out on a hatch and fell asleep at once.

'Good Lord,' Roach said, 'he's inhuman.'

'Yes,' Vivien said, 'he's the Devil, all right.'

'Double the wager, eh, if you're so confident?'

'No. Not unless Gorth arrives drunk.'

'Say he was to kill Gorth – what about Tyler?'

'They'll fight to a death, I'm thinking.'

'What'll Culum do, eh? If Gorth be victor today.'

'Nothing. What can he do? Except hate, maybe. Poor lad, I rather like him. He hates the Tai-Pan anyway – so maybe he'll bless Gorth, eh? He becomes Tai-Pan, right enough. Where the devil's Gorth?'

The sun rose relentlessly in the sky. A Portuguese soldier raced out of an adjacent street and spoke animatedly to the officer, who immediately began to march his men at quick time up the *praia*. Bystanders began to follow.

Struan awoke to aching reality, every fibre shrieking the need for sleep. He groped leadenly to his feet. Horatio was looking at him strangely.

Gorth's brutally savaged body was lying in the filth of an alley near the wharves of Chinatown and around the corpse were the bodies of three Chinese. Another Chinese, more dead than alive with the haft of a broken spear in his groin, was lying moaning at the feet of a patrol of Portuguese soldiers.

Traders and Portuguese were crowding for a closer look. Those who could see Gorth turned away sickened.

'The patrol says they heard screaming and fighting,' the Portuguese officer told Struan and others who were near. 'When they rushed down here, they saw Senhor Brock on the ground, as he is now. Three or four Chinese were spearing him. When the murdering devils saw our men, they vanished up there.' He pointed at a silent cluster of hovels and twisting alleys and passageways. 'The soldiers gave chase but . . .' He shrugged.

Struan knew that he had been saved by the assassins. 'I'll offer a reward for the one who escaped,' Struan said. 'A hundred taels dead, five hundred if alive.'

'Save your "dead" money, senhor. The heathen will merely produce three corpses – the first they can find. As to "alive" ' – the officer jerked a disdainful thumb at the prisoner – 'unless that *bastardo degenerado* tells us who the others are, your money is quite safe. On second thoughts, I think the Chinese authorities would be – shall we say – more deft in interrogation.' He spoke sharply in Portuguese and the soldiers put the man on a broken door and carried him away.

The officer flicked a smudge of dirt off his uniform. 'A stupid and unnecessary death. Senhor Brock should have known better than to be in this area. It seems that no honour has been satisfied.'

'You be right lucky, Tai-Pan,' one of Gorth's friends sneered. 'Right lucky.'

'Aye. I'm glad his blood's na on my hands.'

Struan turned his back on the corpse and slowly walked away.

He broke out of the alley and climbed the hill to the ancient fort. Once on the crest, surrounded by sea and sky, he sat on a bench and thanked the Infinite for the blessing of the night and the blessing of the day.

He was oblivious of passers-by, of the soldiers at the gate of the fort, of the song of the church bells. Of birds calling or the gentle wind or the healing sun. Or of time.

Later he tried to decide what to do, but his mind wouldn't function. 'Get hold of yoursel',' he said aloud.

He walked down the hill to the bishop's residence but the bishop was not in. He went to the cathedral and asked for him. A monk told him to wait in the cloistered garden.

Struan sat on a shaded bench and listened to the fountains bubbling. The flowers seemed more brilliant than ever to him, their perfume more exquisite. The beating of his heart and strength of his limbs and even the constant ache of his ankle – these were not a dream but reality.

Oh God, thank you for life.

The bishop was regarding him from the cloistered walk.

'Oh, hello, Your Grace,' Struan said, exquisitely refreshed. 'I came to thank you.'

The bishop pursed his thin lips. 'What were you seeing, senhor?'

'I dinna ken,' Struan replied. 'I was just looking at the garden. Enjoying it. Enjoying life. I dinna ken exactly.'

'I believe you were very close to God, senhor. You may not think so, but I know you were.'

Struan shook his head. 'Nay, Your Grace. Just happy on a glorious day in a lovely garden. That's all.'

But Falarian Guineppa's mien did not change. His lean fingers touched his crucifix. 'I was watching you for a long time. I could feel that you were close. *You!* Surely that's wrong.' He sighed. 'Yet how can we poor sinners know the ways of God? I envy you, senhor. You wished to see me?'

'Aye, your Grace. The cinchona cured the fever.'

579

'*Deo gratias!* But that is wonderful! How marvellous are the ways of God!'

'I'm going to charter a vessel immediately for Peru, with orders to load cinchona,' Struan said. 'With your permission I'd like to send Father Sebastian, to find out how they harvest the bark, where it comes from, how they treat their malaria – everything. We share the cargo and the knowledge equally when he returns. I'd like him, under your authority, to write a medical paper immediately and send it to the *Lancet* in England – and to *The Times* – about your successful treatment of malaria with cinchona.'

'Such an official medical treatise would have to be sent through official Vatican channels. But I will order him to do so. As to sending *him* – that I will have to consider. However, I shall send someone with the vessel. When will it leave?'

'Three days.'

'Very well. We will share the knowledge and cargo equally. That is very generous.'

'We did na fix a price for the cure. She's cured. So now will you please tell me the price?'

'Nothing, senhor.'

'I dinna understand.'

'There is no price on a handful of cinchona that saved the life of one girl.'

'Of course there's a price. I said whatever you wanted! I'm ready to pay. Twenty thousand taels were offered in Hong Kong. I'll send you a sight draft.'

'No, senhor,' the tall priest replied patiently. 'If you do I will only tear it up. I want no payment for the bark.'

'I'll endow a Catholic church on Hong Kong,' Struan said. 'A monastery if you wish. Dinna play with me, Your Grace. A trade is a trade. Name your price.'

'You owe me nothing, senhor. You owe the Church nothing. But you owe God very much.' He raised his hand and made the sign of the cross. '*In nomine Patris, et Filii, et Spiritus Sancti*,' he said quietly, and left.

XL

May-may found herself awakening, Struan's arms supporting her, and the cup at her lips. She vaguely heard Struan talking quietly to Father Sebastian, but she did not make the effort to understand the English words. Obediently she swallowed the cinchona and let herself slide back into semi-consciousness.

She heard the monk leave and felt the alien presence gone, and this pleased her. She felt Struan lift her again and she swallowed the second cup, the foulness of the taste still nauseating her.

Through the comfortable mist she heard Struan sit in the bamboo chair, and soon came his heavy, regular breathing and she knew that he was asleep. This made her feel very safe.

The sounds of the amahs chattering in the kitchen, and Ah Sam's brittle caustic humour, and the perfume of Yin-hsi were so enjoyable that May-may would not let sleep embrace her wholly.

She lay quiet and gathered strength by the minute. And she knew that she would live.

I will burn incense to the gods of my joss. Perhaps a candle to the longskirt god. After all, the monk brought the bark, didn't he? – however foul it tastes. Perhaps I should become a longskirt Christian. That would give the monk great face. But my Tai-Pan wouldn't approve of that. Even so, I might as well. For if there's no longskirt God, no harm is done, and if there is – then I will have been very clever. I wonder if the barbarian God is like our Chinese gods. Who, if you think about it, are very stupid. But not really. They're like human beings with all our weaknesses and strengths. That's so much more sensible than pretending, as the barbarians do, that their God is perfect and sees all and hears all and judges all and punishes all.

I'm glad I'm not one of them.

She heard the sibilance of Yin-hsi's clothes and breathed her perfumed presence. She opened her eyes.

'You look better, Supreme Lady,' Yin-hsi whispered, kneeling close to her. 'Look, I've brought you some flowers.'

The tiny bouquet was very pretty. May-may nodded weakly, but felt her strength coursing. Struan was sprawled in the reclining chair, heavily asleep, his face young in repose, dark shadows under his eyes and raw red of a weal on his chin.

'Father's been there for an hour or more,' Yin-hsi said. She was wearing pale blue silk trousers and a knee-length double-breasted silk tunic of ocean green, and there were flowers in her hair.

May-may smiled and moved her head and saw that it was dusk.

'How many days is it since this fever began, Sister?'

'It was last night. Father came with a longskirt monk. They brought the magic drink, don't you remember? I sent that miserable slave Ah Sam to the joss house early this morning to give thanks to the gods. Why don't you let me wash you? Let me arrange your hair. You'll feel so much better.'

'Oh, yes, please, Sister,' May-may said. 'I must look dreadful.'

'Yes, Supreme Lady, but that's only because you almost died. Ten minutes and you'll be as beautiful as you always are – I promise!'

'Be as quiet as a butterfly, Sister,' May-may said. 'Don't wake Father, whatever you do, and tell those turtledung slaves if Father wakes before I'm presentable you'll personally – on my orders – put the thumbscrews on them.'

Yin-hsi delightedly shuffled away. A vast silence fell on the house.

Yin-hsi and Ah Sam tiptoed back into the room and bathed May-may with perfumed water and brought sun-fresh trousers of finest crimson shantung and a crimson tunic, and helped her to dress. They bathed her feet and changed her bandages, then propped her while she brushed her teeth and rinsed her mouth out with baby urine. Finally, May-may chewed fragrant tea leaves and felt greatly purified.

They combed and brushed her hair, braided it and dressed it elegantly with fresh, sweet-smelling flowers, and changed the sheets and the pillows and sprinkled them with perfume and put aromatic herbs under the pillow.

And even though the moving and changing had sapped much of her strength, May-may felt reborn.

'Now some broth, Supreme Lady. And then a fresh mango,' Yin-hsi said.

'And then,' Ah Sam said importantly, her silver ear-rings jingling, 'we have marvellous news for you.'

'What?'

'Only after you've eaten, Mother,' Ah Sam said. When May-may began to protest, Ah Sam shook her head firmly. 'We have to look after you, you're still a patient. Second Mother and I know that good news is marvellous for digestion. But first you must have something to digest.'

May-may drank some broth and ate a little of the sliced mango. They encouraged her to eat more. 'You must build up your strength, Supreme Lady.'

'I'll finish the mango if you tell me the news now,' May-may said.

Yin-hsi frowned. Then she nodded to Ah Sam. 'Go on, Ah Sam. But begin with what Lo Chum told you – how it all started.'

'Not so loud!' May-may said warningly. 'Don't wake Father.'

'Well,' Ah Sam began, 'the night before we arrived – seven dreadful days ago – Father's barbarian son fell into the clutches of the devil incarnate, a barbarian. This monstrous barbarian laid a plot so foul, so fiendish – to destroy Father's beloved son – that I almost cannot describe it. And last night and today, while the devil magic drink was wrecking your fever sickness, things came to their terrible doom-filled climax. We spent the vigil of the night on our knees begging the gods. But to no avail. Father was lost, you were lost, and worse – the enemy had won the game.' Ah Sam paused and with studied faintness tottered to the table, picked up the tiny glass filled with the wine that Yin-hsi had brought as a present to May-may and sipped it, overcome with emotion.

When she was refreshed she told the entire story with harrowing pauses and unbelievable sighs and mighty gesticulations.

'And there, on the filth-filled ground,' Ah Sam ended with a sobbing whisper, stabbing the floor with her fingers, 'hacked into forty pieces, surrounded by the bodies of fifteen assassins, lay the corpse of the devil barbarian. Gorth! And thus was our Father saved!'

May-may clapped her hands gleefully, and congratulated herself for her foresight. The gods are certainly looking over us! Thank goodness I talked to Gordon Chen when I did. But for him . . . 'Oh, how wonderful! Oh, Ah Sam, you told it brilliantly. I nearly died when you came to the part about Father leaving the house this morning. If you hadn't said before you began that the news was marvellous I would *really* have died.'

'Heya, lassie!' Struan was awake, roused by May-may's clapping.

Yin-hsi and Ah Sam got up hastily and bowed.

'I feel fantastical better, Tai-Pan,' May-may said.

'You look fantastical better.'

'You need food, Tai-Pan,' May-may said. 'You probably have no eaten all day.'

'Thank you, lass, but I'm na hungry. I'll get something at the residence later.' Struan stood and stretched.

'Please eat here,' May-may said. 'Stay here tonight. Please. I dinna want to – well, please stay. That would make me very happy.'

'Of course, lassie,' Struan said. 'You've got to take the cinchona for the next four days. Three times a day.'

'But, Tai-Pan, I feel very gracious good. Please, no more.'

'Three times a day, May-may. For the next four days.'

'God's blood, it tastes like birds' droppings mixed with vinegar and snake's bile.'

A table laden with food was brought into the bedroom. Yin-hsi served them, then left them alone. May-may picked daintily at a few quick-fried shrimps. 'What did you do today?' she asked.

'Nae anything of import. But one problem's settled. Gorth's dead.'

'Oh? How?' May-may asked, and was suitably surprised and shocked as he told her the news. 'You're very clever, Tai-Pan. But your joss is fantastical good.'

Struan pushed his plate away and stifled a yawn and thought about joss. 'Aye.'

'Will Brock be terrible angry?'

'Gorth's death's na on my hands. Even if it was, he deserved to die. In some ways I'm sorry he died like that.' Gorth's death and the elopement will break Brock's temper, he thought. I'd best be ready with a gun or knife. Will he come after me like an assassin in the night? Or openly? I'll worry about that tomorrow. 'Culum should be back soon.'

'Why do you na go to bed? You look very tired. When Lo Chum brings word, Ah Sam will wake you, heya? I think I'd like to sleep now too.'

'I think I will, lassie,' Struan kissed her tenderly and held her in his arms. 'Ah, lassie, lassie. I was so afraid for you.'

'Thank you, Tai-Pan. Go to sleep now, and tomorrow I'll be much better and so will you.'

'I have to go to Hong Kong, lassie. As soon as possible. For a few days.'

Her chest tightened. 'When do you go, Tai-Pan?'

'Tomorrow, if you're well.'

'Will you do something for me, Tai-Pan?'

'Of course.'

'Take me with you. I dinna want to – to be alone here if you're there.'

'You're na well enough to move and I have to go, lass.'

'Oh, but I will be tomorrow. I promise. I'll stay in bed on the ship and we can live on *Resting Cloud* as we did before. Please.'

'I'll only be a few days, lass, and it would be better for you to stay here. Much better.'

But May-may nestled closer to him, needing him. 'Please. I'll be very good and take all the cups without troubles and stay in bed and get well and eat and eat and eat and be fantastical very good. I promise. Please dinna leave me until I'm truly better.'

'Well, you sleep now and we'll decide tomorrow.'

She kissed him. 'No decides tomorrow. If you go off, I will na eat and na take the cups, by God! There!' she said, aping his gruffness. 'Your old mother's put her feets in the deck and she'll na budge!'

Struan held her very close. Minute by minute he could feel her growing stronger. God bless the cinchona.

'All right, but we'll na go tomorrow. The next day, at dawn. If you're well enough. If you—'

'Oh, thank you, Tai-Pan. I'll be very well.'

He held her away from him and appraised her closely. He knew that it would take months for her to recover her former beauty. But it's na just a face that makes a person exquisite, he told himself. It's what's underneath, in the eyes and in the heart. 'Ah, lassie, you're so beautiful. I love you.'

She touched his nose with a tiny finger. 'Wat for you say such things to your old mother?' She pressed into his arms. 'I think you're terrifical beautiful too.'

Then he gave her the two cups and she held her nose and drank them. She put some fragrant tea leaves in her mouth to take the taste away. He tucked her up like a child, kissed her again, and went to his room.

He threw off his clothes and got into the bed and lay blissfully in the cool sheets. Sleep came quickly.

And while he slept the Chinese assassin continued to be questioned. His torturers were very patient – and very skilled in the art of extracting information.

XLI

China Cloud returned to Macao harbour just after dawn. By the time she approached her moorings, Struan was hurrying down the jetty. His cutter was waiting.

'Dirk!'

He looked up, startled. 'Morning, Liza.'

Liza Brock was sallow and drawn. 'I be going with thee.'

'Of course.' Struan held out his hand to help her in, but she refused it.

'Cast off!' he ordered.

The oarsmen pulled strongly. The day was glorious and the sea calm. Struan saw the small figure of Captain Orlov on the quarterdeck of the ship and knew that he had been observed. Good, he thought.

'I be taking Gorth's body back t' Hong Kong tomorrow,' Liza said.

Struan made no reply. He merely nodded and looked at his ship.

When they reached the gangway, he let Liza go on deck first.

'Morning,' Captain Orlov said.

'Is Miss Brock aboard?' Struan asked.

'Aye.'

'Be you – be you marrying they? Culum and my Tess?' Liza asked.

'Aye.' Orlov turned to Struan. 'You put me under his orders. He ordered me to marry them. The master is the master and that's your law. I followed orders.'

'I quite agree,' Struan said mildly. 'You were na responsible except in matters of seamanship. I made that clear to Culum.'

Liza whirled on Struan furiously. 'Then it were deliberate. Thee arranged this'n. Thee knowed they were eloping!'

'No, he didn't, Mrs Brock.' Culum was emerging from the gangway, confident but tense. 'It was my idea. Hello, Tai-Pan. I ordered Orlov to marry us. It's my responsibility.'

'Aye, Let's below, lad.'

Liza, her face ashen, took Culum by the shoulder. 'Be thee poxed?'

586

'Of course not. What put that in your head? Do you think I'd marry Tess if I were?'

'I pray t' God you be telling truth! Where be Tess?'

'In the cabin. We're . . . come below.'

'Be – be she all right?'

'Of course, Mrs Brock!'

'This is nae place for family matters,' Struan said. He went down the gangway, and Liza followed.

'Hello,' Tess said shyly, coming out of the main cabin. 'Hello, Mumma.'

'Be you all right, luv?'

'Oh yes, oh yes.'

Then mother and daughter were in each other's arms.

Struan motioned Culum out of the cabin.

'I'm sorry, Tai-Pan, but we decided it was best.'

'Listen lad. There was trouble while you were away.' He told Culum about Gorth. 'There's nae doubt it was him. He set you up like we thought.'

'There's no – no chance that after seven days . . . is there?'

'Nay. But best to go to Brock's doctor. It'll set Liza's mind at rest.'

'You were right again. You warned me. God in heaven, you warned me. Why would Gorth do that?' How could any man do that to another, he asked himself.

'I dinna ken. Is everything all right, 'twixt you and Tess?'

'Oh, yes. Damn Gorth! He's ruined everything.' He took two letters from his pocket. 'Here are the replies from Skinner and Gordon.'

'Thank you, lad. Dinna worry about—'

'We be going ashore,' Liza said, standing formidably in the doorway. 'I be taking Tess, and then—'

Culum interrupted her. 'You won't take my wife anywhere, Mrs Brock. As to the rumours about the pox, we'll see your doctor instantly and settle that right now.'

'Tyler'll have marriage broke. It were without permission.'

'We're married before God, legally, and that's the end to that.' Culum was saying what he and Tess had planned to say. But his boldness seemed hollow now, because of Gorth. 'I'm sorry we eloped – no, not sorry. We're married and I'll do everything in my power to be a good son-in-law, but Tess stays with me and does what I say.'

'Tyler'll horsewhip you!'

'Oh Mumma, no,' Tess burst out, running to Culum. 'We be wed and

587

it be the same as three month and that's over. Tell her, Tai-Pan, tell her that she's wrong.'

'I'm sure your father will be angry, Tess. Rightly so. But I'm also sure he'll forgive you both. Liza, can you na forgive them here and now?'

'It's not me, Dirk Struan, who's to forgive.'

'Come on, Mumma,' Tess said. Nothing can happen now, she told herself. Now that we're husband and wife and he's loved me and it hurt like afore but different. And he's satisfied and so gentle and wonderful. She had cast Nagrek away for ever. 'Let's all have breakfast together.'

Liza wiped her sweat-beaded lips. 'You'd best move into house. I'll send word to thy Da'.'

'We'll be staying at the English Hotel,' Culum said.

'Nae need for that, Culum,' Struan said. 'There's suite for you in our residence.'

'Thank you, but we've decided it's best. We think we should go back to Hong Kong immediately and see Mr Brock and ask his forgiveness. Please, Mrs Brock, let's be friends. Father told me about what happened to Gorth . . . It wasn't of his choosing.'

'I think it were, lad. And thee can't leave immediate. We've to take coffin back tomorrow.'

'What?' Tess asked.

'Gorth was killed, darling,' said Culum. 'Yesterday.'

'What?'

'He were foully murdered by assassins!' Liza screamed.

'Oh God, no!'

Struan told her everything. Except what Gorth had tried to do to Culum. 'I had nae option but to challenge him,' Struan ended. 'But his blood is na on my hands. I think it best we all go ashore.'

Tess was sobbing quietly. Culum kept his arm around her. 'Come on, love, dry your eyes. It was none of our doing – or Father's doing.' He led her out of the cabin.

Struan broke the silence. 'They're married and happy, Liza. Why na leave it at that?'

'If it were me, I'd say yes. If wot Culum says be truth. But Tyler won't – thee knowed him as he knowed thee. I knowed thee planned this'n, Dirk. He'll know it. He'll kill thee – or try t'kill thee, and I think thee's planned it that way. Tyler an' thee'll kill each other once he starts on thee or thee on him. Why baint thee leaving it be – three month were not much to wait. But now – oh, God!'

*   *   *

Struan looked up from the letters as Culum came dejectedly into the office and sat down.

'All's well?'

'Yes. The doctor said I was clean.'

'Have you had lunch?'

'No. Neither of us felt like eating. Oh, God – everything had been going so well. God damn Gorth and his goddamned madness.'

'How's Mrs Brock?'

'As well as can be expected – as the papers would say. How's – did the cinchona arrive?'

'Aye. She's fine now.'

'Oh, that's wonderful!'

'Aye.' But in spite of his feeling of well-being, Struan was troubled by a vague, yet piercing apprehension. It was nothing that he could articulate, just an awareness of danger somewhere. The letters had given no hint of what it might be. Gordon Chen had written that he still had hopes of finding the cinchona. And Skinner had said that he would release the news immediately and expect Struan today.

But it canna be today now. I wish to God I'd been firm and told May-may she'll stay.

'I'll be returning to Hong Kong tomorrow. You two'd best come with me.'

'I think we'd better go in *White Witch* with Mrs Brock and Lillibet,' Culum said. 'Mrs Brock sent word to Brock by lorcha this morning. About us – and about Gorth.'

'Dinna worry, lad. Liza Brock'll come around and Tyler will na trouble you either. He swore an oath, remember?'

Culum studied the Tai-Pan for a moment. 'Did you know I was going to take Tess on *China Cloud*?'

'Well, lad, when she was missing, I hoped you had,' Struan said circumspectly.

Culum picked up a paperweight that was on the desk. It was white jade and heavy. 'I've been very stupid.'

'I dinna think so. Best thing you could have done. You're settled now.'

'I've been very stupid because again I've been a puppet.'

'Eh?'

'I think you put the idea of eloping into my head. I think you deliberately put Orlov under my command knowing that I would order him to marry us. I think you sent me and Tess off knowing that this would drive Gorth berserk, and make him publicly attack you and give you the opportunity to kill him openly. Did you?'

Struan sat motionless in the chair. His eyes did not waver from Culum's. 'I dinna quite know how to answer you, Culum. I dinna know for certain if you want an answer. The fact is that you wanted to marry Tess quickly and you *are* married. The fact is that Gorth did try to murder you in the foulest way a man could conceive. The fact is that he's dead. The fact is I regret na having the pleasure of killing him, but the fact is that his blood's na on my hands. The fact is that because he is dead, you're alive – you and Tess. The fact is that whatever Brock wants to do about it, he swore a holy oath to give you a safe berth in a safe harbour. And a last fact is that soon now you can take over. As Tai-Pan.'

Culum put down the paperweight. 'I'm not ready to be Tai-Pan.'

'I know. But you soon will be. I'm going home in a few months,' Struan said. 'I'll bring *Lotus Cloud* back next year and deal with Wu Kwok. But everything else will be your problem.'

Culum thought about being Tai-Pan, about being on his own. But he knew that now he was not on his own. Now he had Tess. 'I think I can make peace with Brock – if you don't try to do it for me,' he said. 'Did you plan all this? Can I have a "yes" or a "no"?' He waited, desperately wanting a 'no'.

'Aye,' Struan said deliberately. 'I used certain facts to achieve a calculated end.'

'When I'm Tai-Pan I'm joining Struan and Company with Brock and Sons,' Culum said. 'Brock'll be the first Tai-Pan and I'll be after him!'

Struan was on his feet. 'That bastard'll na be Tai-Pan of The Noble House. He'll na run my ships!'

'They're not *your* ships. They're the company's. Isn't Brock just another pawn to be used or abused at whim?'

'I swear to God, Culum, I dinna understand you. Your whole life's put into your hands and now you'll do that one thing to destroy it.'

Culum suddenly saw his father clearly – as a man. He saw the size and strength and the hard, weathered face, the red-gold hair and the startling green of the eyes. And he knew that he would always be this man's tool. He knew he could never battle with him, or persuade him that the only way he could survive alone as Tai-Pan would be to join with Brock and gamble that Brock would leave him and Tess in peace. 'I can never be *the* Tai-Pan of *the* Noble House. I'm not like you,' he said with calm finality. 'I don't want to be, and I never will.'

There was a knock.

'Aye?' Struan grated.

Lo Chum opened the door. 'So'dger mass'er see, can?'

'I will na be a minute.'

Culum got up. 'I think I'll go and—'

'Just a minute, Culum.' Struan turned back to Lo Chum. 'See now, savvy?'

Lo Chum huffed irritably and opened the door wider.

The young Portuguese officer entered. 'Good afternoon, senhor.'

'Please sit down, Captain Machado. Do you know my son Culum?'

They shook hands and the officer sat down.

'As leader of the English nationals, my superiors have asked me to tell you officially the result of our investigation into the murder of Senhor Brock,' he began.

'Have you caught the others?' Struan interrupted.

The officer smiled and shook his head. 'No, senhor. I doubt if we ever will. We passed the assassin over to the Chinese authorities as we are bound to do. They investigated him in their inimitable way. He admitted he was a member of a secret society. The Hung Mun. Triads, I believe you call them. It seems he came here from Hong Kong a few days ago. According to him, there is a thriving lodge in Tai Ping Shan.' The officer smiled again. 'It seems, too, that you have many enemies, Senhor Struan. That *Cabrão* claimed your – your natural son, Gordon Chen, was the leader.'

'That's the best joke I've heard in years,' Struan said, outwardly amused. But he was considering very carefully the possibility that it was true. And if it is? he asked himself. I dinna ken. But you'd better find out fast, one way or another.

'The mandarins were amused too, so they said,' Machado told him. 'In any event, unfortunately the heathen devil died before they could get the real leader's name.' He added disdainfully, 'He claimed he had been sent here to assassinate Senhor Brock on the leader's orders. Of course he gave names of his associates but these are as meaningless as the rest of his story. It was a simple robbery. These damned Triads are nothing but highwaymen. Or perhaps,' he said pointedly, 'a matter of vengeance.'

'Eh?'

'Well, senhor. The young Senhor Brock was – how shall I put it – not exactly admired in certain quarters of ill repute. It seems that he frequented a house near where he was found. He brutally attacked a prostitute a week or so ago. She died the day before yesterday. We have just received a complaint against him from the mandarins. Who knows? Perhaps the mandarins decided a tooth for a tooth, and this is all a diversion. You know how devious they are. Perhaps it's just as well he is dead, for we would have to have taken action and that would have embarrassed everyone.' He got up. 'My superiors will, of course, send an official report to His Excellency, as one of your nationals is involved.'

Struan offered his hand. 'Will you thank them for me? And I wonder if this could be hushed up? The part about the prostitute. My son's married to his sister, and I'd like to guard the Brock name. Tyler Brock is an old associate.'

'So I understand,' the officer said, faintly ironic. He glanced at Culum. 'My congratulations, senhor.'

'Thank you.'

'I will mention your suggestion to my superiors, Senhor Struan. I'm sure they would appreciate the delicacy of the position.'

'Thank you,' Struan said. 'If you catch the others, the reward still stands.'

The officer saluted and left.

'Thank you for suggesting that,' Culum said. 'What would have happened to Gorth?'

'He would have hanged. There are good English laws about murder.'

'It would be ironic if that story were true.'

'Eh?'

'Gordon Chen and the secret society. If in actual fact you hadn't planned Gorth's challenge because you'd already secretly arranged for him to be assassinated.'

'That's a terrible accusation. Terrible.'

'I'm not accusing you,' Culum said. 'I merely said it would be ironic. I know that you're what you are; any killing you do would have to be in the open, man to man. That's the way *the* Tai-Pan's mind would have to work. But mine won't. It never will. I'm tired to trapping people and using them. I'm not you and I never will be. You have to put up with me the best you can. And if your Noble House dies in my hands – well, to use your own words, that's joss. Your face is safe. You'll leave as *the* Tai-Pan, whatever happens afterwards. I'll never understand you and know you'll never understand me, but we can be friends even so.'

'Of course we're friends,' Struan said. 'One thing – promise you'll never join with Brock.'

'When I'm Tai-Pan I have to do what *I* think is best. It's no longer your decision. That's the law you set up, the law I swore to obey.'

There were the sounds from the *praia*. Somewhere in the distance church bells began chiming.

'Will you have dinner with us tonight? At the Club?'

'Aye.'

Culum departed. Struan remained at his desk. How can I put fire into Culum? he asked himself.

He could not think of an answer. He sent for his secretary and arranged for all company business to be completed before he returned to Hong Kong. He left the office, and on the way to May-may's house he thought about Brock. Will he come storming into the Club tonight, like Gorth did?

Struan stopped for a moment and gazed out to sea. The *White Witch* and *China Cloud* looked beautiful in the afternoon sun. His eyes strayed over Macao and he saw the cathedral. Why did that devil bishop na put a fair price on the bark? Be fair yoursel', Dirk. He's nae devil. Aye, but he trapped you. Now you'll never forget him for the rest of your life – and you'll be doing all sorts of favours for the Church. And for the devil Catholics. Are they devils though? The truth, now.

Nay.

The only devil you know is Gorth, and Gorth's dead – finished. Thank God!

Aye. Gorth's dead. But na forgotten.

BOOK SIX

XLII

China Cloud slipped her moorings at dawn. The sea was calm and the wind east and firm. But two hours out to sea the breeze freshened, and Struan left May-may in the great cabin and went on deck.

Orlov was scanning the sky. It was clear to the horizon, but far off a few cumulus clouds were gathering. 'No danger there,' he said.

'Nothing amiss there either,' Struan said, gesturing towards the sea. He strolled along the deck and then swung into the foremast shrouds. He climbed easily, the wind tugging him pleasantly, and he did not stop until he was braced on the topgallant halyards at the pinnacle of the foremast.

He searched the sea and the sky, meticulously seeking the squall or storm that might be lurking, or the hidden reef or uncharted shoal. But there were no danger signs as far as the horizon.

For a moment he let himself enjoy the speed and the wind and the limitlessness, blessing his joss for life and for May-may. She was much better – still quite weak, but strong compared to yesterday.

He examined all the rigging in sight, checking for damage or weakness, then climbed down and went back to the quarterdeck. An hour later the wind freshened again and the clipper heeled over more, spray digging into the lower sails.

'I'll be glad to be in harbour tonight,' Orlov said uneasily.

'Aye. You feel it too?'

'I feel nothing. Only that I'll be happy to be in harbour tonight.' Orlov spat to leeward and shifted his tobacco quid. 'Sea's fair, wind's fair, sky's clean – even so, there's devilment abrewing.'

'It's always brewing in these waters.'

'With your permission we'll reef down and I'll get the leadsman acalling the fathoms. Mayhaps it's just a shoal or stinking, belly-gutting rock out there somewhere.' Orlov shivered and pulled his sea jacket closer, even though the day was warm and the wind safe.

'Aye.'

So the leadsman was sent forward, and he tolled the fathoms. And the crew shinned aloft and *China Cloud*'s press of canvas was eased off.

Late that afternoon she was safe in the neck of the west channel. Hong Kong Island was to port, the mainland to starboard. It had been a perfect voyage with no mishap.

'Perhaps we're just getting old,' Struan said with a short laugh.

'The older you get, the more the sea wants to suck you down,' Orlov said without rancour, looking at the ocean aft. 'Weren't for my beautiful ship I'd sign off today.'

Struan walked to the wheel. 'I'll spell you a turn, helmsman. Go for'ard.'

'Aye, aye, sir.' The seaman left them alone on the quarterdeck.

'Why?' Struan asked Orlov.

'I can feel the sea watching me. She's always watching a seaman, testing him. But there comes a time when she watches different – jealous, aye, jealous like the woman she is. And as dangerous.' Orlov spat the tobacco quid overboard and rinsed his mouth with the cold tea that was in the canvas bag near the binnacle. 'I've never acted a priest and married anyone before. That was mortal strange – strange, Green Eyes, looking at those two, so young and eager and confident. And listening to the echo of you, puffed like a peacock, "By God, Orlov, you'll marry us, by God. I'm master of *China Cloud*, by God. You know the Tai-Pan's law, by God." And there's me, aranting and araving and terrible reluctant so as to give him *face*, knowing all the time old Green Eyes is the puppeteer.' Orlov chuckled and peered up at Struan. 'But I acted very well and let him command me – as you wanted me to be commanded. It was like, well, like my marriage present to the lad. Did he tell you our deal?'

'Nay.'

' "Marry us and you'll keep your ship, by God. Don't, and I'll hound you out of seas, by God." ' Orlov grinned. 'I'd've married them anyway.'

'I was thinking of taking away your ship mysel'.'

Orlov's grin vanished. 'Eh?'

'I'm thinking of reorganizing the company – putting the fleet under one man. Would you like the job?'

'Ashore?'

'Of course ashore. Can you run a fleet from the quarterdeck of one clipper?'

Orlov bunched his fist and shook it towards Struan's face.

598

'You're a devil from hell! You tempt me with power beyond my dreams, to take the only thing I love on earth. On a quarterdeck I forget what I am – by God, you know that. Ashore what am I, eh? Stride Orlov the hunchback!'

'You could be Stride Orlov, Tai-pan of the noblest fleet on earth. I'd say that's a man's job.' Struan's eyes did not waver from the dwarf's face.

Orlov spun around and went to the windward gunnel and began a paroxysm of Norwegian and Russian obscenities that went on for minutes.

He stamped back. 'When would this be?'

'The end of this year. Maybe later.'

'And my trip north? For furs? Have you forgotten that?'

'You'd want to cancel it, eh?'

'What gives you the right to puppetize the world? Eh?'

'Helmsman! Come aft!' Struan gave the wheel back to the seaman as *China Cloud* broke out of the channel into the calm waters of the harbour. Ahead a mile was the jutting Kowloon Peninsula. The land on either side of the ship was barren and parched and fell away rapidly. To port, a mile or so ahead, was the rocky island promontory that had been called North Point. Beyond North Point, unseen from this position, were Happy Valley and Glessing's Point and the small part of the harbour that was being used.

'Nor' by nor'west,' Struan ordered.

'Nor' by nor'west, sorr,' the helmsman echoed.

'Steady as she goes.' He looked over his shoulder at Orlov.

'Well?'

'I've no option. I know when your mind's set. You'd beach me without a second thought. But there're conditions.'

'Well?'

'First I want *China Cloud*. For six months I want to go home. A last time.' Either your wife and sons will come back with you or they'll stay, Orlov told himself. They'll stay, and they'll spit in your face and damn you to hell and you waste six months of a ship's life.

'Agreed. As soon as I've another clipper here, *China Cloud's* yours. You'll bring back a cargo of furs. Next?'

'Next, Green Eyes, your law: that when you're aboard, you're captain. That for me.'

'Agreed. Next?'

'There's no "next".'

'We have na discussed money.'

'The pox on money! I'll be tai-pan of the fleet of The Noble House. What more could a man desire?'

Struan knew the answer. *May-may*. But he said nothing. They shook hands on the deal, and when the ship was a quarter mile off Kowloon, Struan ordered *China Cloud* on to a south-west-by-south tack and headed into the harbour proper.

'All hands on deck! Lay for'ard! Take over, Captain. Lie alongside *Resting Cloud*. Our passengers'll transship first. Then the storm anchorage.'

'Thank you, *Captain*,' Orlov grunted. 'It's good to be in harbour, by God!'

Struan surveyed the shore with the binoculars. Now he could see into the depths of Happy Valley: buildings abandoned, no movement. He moved the glasses slightly and adjusted the focus, and the building sites of the new Queen's Town around Glessing's Point sharpened. The scaffolding of his new, huge factory was already up, and he could see coolies swarming like ants: carrying, building, digging. Scaffoldings were up, too, on the knoll where he had ordered the Great House to be built. And he could see the thin, lean cut of the road that now snaked up the hill.

Tai Ping Shan had grown appreciably. Where there had been a few hundred sampans plying back and forth to the mainland, now there were a thousand.

More warships and transports were swinging at anchor, and a few more merchantmen. Houses and hovels and temporary shelters were sprawling the ribbon of Queen's Road that skirted the shore. And the whole foreshore was pulsating with activity.

China Cloud saluted the flagship as she rounded the headland, and there was an answering cannon.

'Signal from the flagship, sorr!' the lookout called.

Struan and Orlov swung their binoculars on the flags, which read: 'Captain requested to report aboard immediately.'

'Shall I lay alongside her?' Orlov asked.

'Nay. Put the cutter over the side when we're within two chains. You're responsible for seeing my passengers aboard *Resting Cloud* safely. Wi'out any alien eyes sniffing around.'

'Leave it to me.'

Struan went below and told May-may that he would see her soon and got her and Ah Sam and Yin-hsi ready to transship.

Orlov's eyes darted around the ship. A shore job, eh? Well, we'll see. There's many a league to travel yet, he told himself. Devil take him.

Yes, but I'd go against the Devil himself for Green Eyes – Odin's whelp. He needs a man like me. But he's right again. That would be a *man*'s job.

His thought warmed him very much.

'Look lively!' he roared at the crew, knowing that many glasses would be trained on them, and he kept full sail and ripped carelessly towards the flagship. His heart sang with the rigging, and then at the last second he shouted. 'Helm, alee!' and the ship spun around and pointed as breathlessly as a hound at a covey of partridges.

The cutter was lowered over the side and Struan shinned down the boarding ropes. The cutter cast off and *China Cloud* fell off a few points and eased perfectly alongside *Resting Cloud*.

'All hands below!' Orlov ordered. 'Clear decks, Mr Cudahy. Our and theirs. We're transhipping a cargo that's not about to be counted, by God!'

Struan opened the door to the flagship's main cabin.

'By God, Dirk! We're all ruined!' Longstaff said agitatedly, coming over to him and waving a copy of the *Oriental Times* in his face. 'Have you seen this? Ruined! Ruined!'

Struan took the paper. The headlines on the inside editorial page were glaring: FOREIGN SECRETARY REPUDIATES CHINA TRADERS.

'Nay, Will,' he said.

'By all that's holy, how dare he do such a stupid thing, what? Damned fool! What are we going to do?'

'Let me read it, Will. Then I'll see what it's all about.'

'Idiot Cunnington's repudiated our treaty. That's what it's about. And I'm sacked. Replaced! Me! How dare he?'

Struan raised his eyebrows and whistled. 'Have you na been informed by dispatch yet?'

'Of course not! Who the devil informs the plenipotentiary, what?'

'Perhaps it's false?'

'That Skinner fellow swears it's true. It better be or I'll have him for libel, by God!'

'When did it come out, Will?'

'Yesterday. How the devil did that obese stinking popinjay Skinner lay his fat, filthy hands on a secret dispatch that I haven't even received yet? He ought to be horsewhipped!' He poured a glass of port, drained it and poured another. 'Didn't sleep a wink last night, worried to death over our future in Asia. Read it. God damn Cunnington!'

As Struan read, he found himself beginning to smoulder. Although the article ostensibly presented the broad facts and documented the dispatch word for word, as Crosse had written to him, Skinner's editorial implied that Cunnington, well known for his imperious handling of foreign affairs, had totally repudiated not merely the treaty itself but the whole experience of the trading community, the Royal Navy and Army as well: 'Lord Cunnington, who has never been east of Suez, is setting himself up as an expert on the value of Hong Kong. More than likely, he does not know whether Hong Kong is north or south of Macao, east or west of Peking. How dare he imply that the Admiral of our glorious Fleet is a bag of wind and knows nothing about seamanship and the historic value of the greatest harbour in Asia? Where would we be without the Royal Navy? Or the Army, who are equally discounted – nay, insulted – by the stupid mishandling of our affairs? Without Hong Kong where will soldiers find a haven, or our ships sanctuary? How dare this man who has been in office far too long say that the experience of all the traders, who have rightly invested their future and their wealth in Hong Kong, are fools? How dare he imply that those who have spent their life in China for the glory of England know nothing about affairs Chinese, the huge value of a free port, a trade emporium, and island fortress . . .' And the article evaluated the island and described how, at great risk to themselves, the traders had developed Happy Valley and, when it had to be abandoned, had dauntlessly begun the new town, for the glory of Britain. It was a masterly piece of news slanting.

Struan hid his delight. He knew that if he – who had planted the story – could be aroused by the editorial, others would be violent.

'I'm shocked! That he would dare! Cunnington should be impeached!'

'My thought entirely!' Longstaff drained his glass again and slammed it down. 'Well, now I'm sacked. All the work and sweating and talking and warring – all down the spout because of that imperious, jumped-up maniac who thinks that he's master of the earth.'

'Damned if he'll get away with it, Will! We have to do something about him! He'll no get awa' with it!'

'He has, by God!' Longstaff got up and paced the cabin, and Struan felt a tinge of pity for him. 'What's going to happen? My career's ruined – we're all ruined!'

'What have you done about this, Will?'

'Nothing.' Longstaff glared out of the cabin windows. 'That cursed island's at the root of all my troubles. That hell-spawned rock's destroyed me. Destroyed all of us!' He sat down morosely. 'There was damn nearly a riot yesterday. A deputation of traders came here and demanded I refuse to leave. Another under Brock demanded I leave Asia immediately with the fleet and present myself to London to demand Cunnington's impeachment, and if necessary blockade the Port of London.' He pillowed his chin with his hands. 'Well, it's my own fault. I should have followed my instructions to the letter. But that wouldn't have been right. I'm not a power-hungry, land-grabbing conqueror. The pox on everything!' He looked up, his face twisted with humiliation. 'The admiral and general are delighted, of course. Have a drink?'

'Thanks.' Struan poured a brandy. 'All's not lost, Will. On the contrary. Once at home, you can put your power to work.'

'Eh?'

'What you did here is right. You'll be able to convince Cunnington if he's still in office. Face to face you're in a very strong position. You have right on your side. Definitely.'

'Have you ever met Cunnington?' Longstaff asked bitterly. 'You don't argue with that monster.'

'True. But I have a few friends. Say you had a key to prove you were right and he was wrong?'

Longstaff's eyes gleamed. If Struan was not worried by the terrible news, all was not lost. 'What key, my dear fellow?' he asked.

Struan sipped his brandy, relishing it. 'Diplomats are permanent; governments change. Before you get home, Peel'll be Prime Minister.'

'Impossible!'

'Probable. Say you brought with you news of the highest importance, that proved Cunnington an idiot. How would Peel and the Conservatives view you?'

'Admirable. 'Pon me word! What news, Dirk my friend?'

There was a commotion outside the door, and Brock crashed in, a hapless sentry trying futilely to restrain him. Struan was up in a split second, ready to go for his knife.

Brock's face was swollen with malice. 'Be they wed?'

'Aye.'

'Be Gorth murdered?'

'Aye.'

'When be *White Witch* due?'

'Before nightfall, I'd say. She was scheduled to leave midmorning.'

'First I be talking with Liza. Then they two. Then, by the Lord God, I be talking with thee.' He stormed out.

'Ill-mannered sod!' Longstaff huffed. 'He might have at least knocked!'

Struan relaxed as a cat will relax after a danger has passed – the muscles unlocking fluidly, ready to tighten again at the next threat, but the eyes not changing, still watching where the danger was.

'You've nothing to fear from Cunnington, Will. He's finished.'

'Yes, of course, Dirk. And damn good riddance!' He looked at the door and remembered the prizefight, and knew that the fight between Dirk and Brock would be equally vicious. 'What's in Brock's mind, eh? Is he going to challenge you? Of course we heard about your fracas with Gorth. Bad news has a habit of travelling fast, hasn't it? Terrible business! Damned good luck he was killed by others.'

'Aye,' Struan said. Now that the danger had passed, he felt slightly sick and weak.

'What possessed those two young idiots to elope? Stands to reason Brock would go berserk. Stupid!'

'Na stupid, Will. Best thing for them to do.'

'Of course. If you say so.' And Longstaff wondered if the rumours were true: that the Tai-Pan had deliberately precipitated the marriage and the duel. The Tai-Pan was much too smart not to plan that, he told himself. So – Tai-Pan versus Brock. 'What about Peel, Dirk?'

'You're a diplomat, Will. Diplomats should na have specific party associations. At least they should be well thought of by all parties.'

'My views entirely.' Longstaff's eyes widened. 'You mean become a Conservative – support Peel?'

'Support Whig and Conservative equally. Hong Kong's correct for England. You're Hong Kong, Will. Perhaps this' – Struan waved the paper – 'is a huge stroke of luck for you. It proves Cunnington's na only a fool but also a blabber-mouth. It's shocking to read a private dispatch in the paper.' Then he told him about the briefcase, but only enough to set Longstaff's head reeling.

'Good God!' If, as the Tai-Pan indicated, there was a copy of the actual secret report with maps of the Russia-China border areas and hinterland, bless my soul, they'd be a passport to an ambassadorship and a peerage. 'Where'd you get it?'

'From a source of undoubted trust.' Struan got up. 'I'll put it into your hands before you go. Use it how you like. It'll certainly prove that you're right and Cunnington wrong, apart from anything else.'

'Will you dine with me, Dirk?' Longstaff felt better than he had in years. 'We can chat about old times.'

'Na tonight, if you'll excuse me. Perhaps tomorrow?'

'Fine. Thank you. And I'm so glad our judgment's vindicated.'

'Last – there's something else that needs immediate attention. The Triads.'

'Eh?'

'Gorth Brock was murdered by Triads from Hong Kong. From Tai Ping Shan.'

''Pon me word! Why?'

'I dinna ken.' Struan related what the Portuguese officer had told him about the Triads. And about Gordon Chen. He knew that he had to give Longstaff this information, else it would seem as if he were trying to protect his son when it came out officially. If Gordon was involved with them, this would flush him out. If he was not, then nae harm done.

'Bless my breeches,' Longstaff said with a laugh. 'A ridiculous story.'

'Aye, spread by my enemies, nae doubt about it. But issue a proclamation about Triads and order Major Trent to crush them. Else we'll have the cursed mandarins on our necks.'

'Good idea. Excellent, by Jove. I'll get Horatio – damn it, I gave him Macao leave for two weeks. Can I borrow Mauss?'

'Certainly. I'll send him to you.'

When Struan had gone, Longstaff sat down elatedly at his desk. 'My dear Sir William,' he said to his glass. 'I feel wonderful. If the truth be known, I'm damned glad to be leaving this malodorous island. I couldn't care a tinker's cuss what happens to it – to the traders, the Chinese or the poxy Triads.' He went to the window and began to chuckle. 'We'll see what the briefcase contains. And when we get back to England we'll decide. If Cunnington's out, we can safely back Hong Kong to advantage. If Cunnington's still in, I can agree he's right and dump the island as one of those things. Because I'll have the papers, a key to any Foreign Secretary's bedchamber, and also lots of tea.' He roared with laughter. A few days ago a private emissary had come from Ching-so to tell him the seeds that Horatio had requested would be shipped within two weeks. 'I'd say you've done a fine day's work, Your Excellency!'

Aboard *Resting Cloud*, Struan found May-may already in bed in her own quarters, looking very well and even stronger.

'I'm very gracious happy to be home, Tai-Pan. There, you see! Your old mother obeys like seaman. I've had two cups of cinchona and am prepared for three more.'

'Eh?' he said, his suspicions rising.

'Why, absolute yes. And dinna look like that. I am truth speaking! Am I a Hoklo whore? A dogmeat beggar? Do I lie in my face? A promise is a promise, and dinna forget it. Of course,' she added sweetly, 'now I take dungtasting poison magic with mango juice, which any normal womans would think of immediate but nae mans, oh dear no – that's much too simple.' She tossed her head with her old imperiousness. 'Mans!'

Struan hid his smile, and his pleasure that she was more her own self. 'I'll be back later. And you stay in bed.'

'Huh! Do I break promises? Am I a good-for-nothing turtle dropping?' She held out her hand like an empress. 'Tai-Pan!'

He kissed her hand gallantly and she burst into laughter and hugged him. 'Run along, my son, and no dirty whore-houses!'

Struan left her and went to his own cabin. He unlocked his safe and took out one of the two copies of the briefcase papers and maps that he had meticulously made. He put them in his pocket, with the small sack which contained the remains of the cinchona bark.

He boarded his cutter again.

'*Boston Princess*,' he ordered, naming the Cooper-Tillman hulk.

The sun was teetering on the horizon, but it glowed dully as though a veil had been drawn across the heavens.

'What do you make of that, Bosun?'

'Doan know, sorr. I seed it like that in the South Seas, afore good weather an' bad. If moon be ringed tonight, then mayhaps we be getting a spell of rain.'

Or worse, Struan added to himself. He stood up and looked to the west channel. There was no sign of the *White Witch*. Well, he thought, maybe they'll stand off and come in at dawn. I will na think about you yet, Tyler.

The cutter swung alongside the *Boston Princess*. She was a huge three-decked, converted merchantman, permanently at anchor.

Struan ran up the gangplank. 'Permission to come aboard,' he said to the American officer on deck. 'Perhaps Mr Cooper would see me. It's urgent.'

'Just a minute, Mr Struan.' The officer went below.

Struan lit a cheroot and threw the match overboard. *China Cloud* was bearing off towards her moorings that lay in deep water abreast of Happy Valley.

'Hello, Tai-Pan,' Jeff Cooper said, briskly coming on deck. 'I suppose you heard what that stupid son-of-a-bitch Cunnington's done? We were terribly sorry to hear about the duel and everything. Did those two young fools elope?'

'Aye. How's Wilf?'

'He's dead.'

'Damnation! When did he die?'

'Three days ago.'

'Let's below, eh?'

'All right. What about Longstaff being sacked and the treaty repudiated?'

'Means nothing. Just a stupid political blunder. I'm sure it'll be corrected.'

Cooper led the way below. The main cabin was luxurious. 'Brandy?'

'Thanks.' Struan accepted the drink. 'Health!'

'Health.'

Struan opened the small bag and took out some of the cinchona. 'See this, Jeff? It's a bark. Cinchona bark. Sometimes called Jesuits' bark. Make a tea out of it and it'll cure malaria.'

'Are you sure?'

'Aye. It cured my mistress. That part's private – but it cures for certain.'

Cooper picked up a piece of the bark, his fingers trembling. 'Oh my God, Tai-Pan, do you realize what you've done? Do you realize what you're saying?'

'Aye. Malaria's worldwide – you've got it in the States all over Florida and the Louisiana Purchase. I know a cure and how to get the bark. What does that lead you to?'

'A service to mankind – and a fortune to whoever gets in first.'

'Aye, laddie. I'm proposing a partnership.' Struan put the bark back in the bag, suddenly sad. 'Ironic, is it na? A few weeks ago this could have saved Robb and little Karen. All the others – and even Wilf, though I despised him.'

'He died badly,' Cooper said.

'I'm sorry for that.' Struan tasted the brandy and dismissed what was past. 'My proposal is simple. We form a new company to specialize in the bark. We put up equal money. Four directors – you and your appointee, mysel' and Culum. You run the company. I supply the where and the how and the what immediately and you start planning tomorrow.'

Cooper put out his hand. 'You've a deal.'

Struan told him how he had got the bark and from whom, and about the ship that he had chartered that was leaving Macao tomorrow for Peru. 'The bishop sent word Father Sebastian will go with her. I propose we double up and na take chances. The company'll be debited the costs of this vessel, and we send another ship – but direct from America. We hire two doctors and two businessmen to go with the ship and find out everything they can about cinchona. The day the US ship leaves, we release the news in the States through your connections. We'll be one step ahead of our competitors and we'll cover my bet with the bishop. We release the news instantly here to take the curse off Happy Valley. And as soon as we can in Europe. By the time our ships are back, doctors throughout the world will be screaming for cinchona. My ships will freight to the British Empire – you take care of the American continent – and we split the rest of the world. We could sell it by the ton in southern Italy alone.'

'Who else knows about it?'

'Only you. Today. I'm giving Skinner a story tonight if I can find him. So, business's over. Now, how's Shevaun?'

'Good and bad. She's accepted the fact that she's betrothed. But I have to admit, however much I love her, she doesn't love me.'

'Will you buy out Tillman's interests?'

'Not if Shevaun marries me. If she hadn't agreed – well, it would be bad business not to. Now that Wilf's dead, I'll have to find another partner. That will mean giving a stock interest – you know very well the problems.'

'Aye. What's Zergeyev up to?'

'Oh, he's still here. His hip doesn't trouble him very much. We see quite a lot of him. Dine with him two or three times a week.' Cooper smiled wanly. 'He's very much attached to Shevaun and she seems to like him. She's visiting on his ship now.'

Struan rubbed his chin speculatively. 'Then I've another gamble for you. More dangerous than cinchona.'

'What?'

'Send Shevaun home for a year. Give her her head – she's a thoroughbred. If she wants to come back at the end of a year, you'll marry her happily. If she decides against you, you give her her freedom. In any event tell her you'll continue to pay her father his "share" for his lifetime. Her brothers can rot. Dinna forget, we can make good use of Senator Tillman's connections on our cinchona venture. The money you give him will more than repay itself.'

Cooper walked over to his desk to fetch the cigars and to give himself time. Why was the Tai-Pan suggesting this? Did he plan to go after Shevaun himself? No, there was no need for him to be so devious: if he beckoned, Shevaun would go running.

'I'd have to think about that, Tai-Pan,' he said. 'Cigar?'

608

'Nay, thanks. And while you're considering it, add a further gamble. Ask Zergeyev to offer her passage home on his ship – chaperoned, of course.'

'You're out of your head!'

'Nay, laddie.' Struan produced the copy of the papers, neatly bound with green ribbon. 'Read these.'

Cooper picked it up. 'What is it?'

'Read. Take your time.'

Cooper sat at his desk and undid the ribbon.

Well, Struan was telling himself, cinchona's launched. Now what about Culum? Perhaps the lad's right, he does need a partner. Jeff's the answer. Struan-Cooper-Tillman. At least, Struan-Cooper: we can forget Tillman now. Why na? It's a huge advantage to Jeff. We gain an advantage with the Americas. Jeff's canny and straight. Think about it very carefully. It's a good solution. Longstaff? Longstaff's taken care of as much as he can ever be. Once out of your sight, he'll only do what the next strong man tells him to do. How about Skinner? Thus far he's done well. Blore? Must check on him. Mauss too. What next? Home and May-may. Perhaps Orlov was right. Perhaps all you felt was the sea watching you – you've had a fair run for your money. Dinna put aside such feelings lightly.

Inexorably his mind bore down on Brock. Aye. There's a killing to be done. And Liza was right. Once it starts, perhaps it'll never end. Or it will end with both of you.

'How true is that?' Cooper had finished with the dossier.

'The source would be called "beyond question". What's your feeling about it?'

'It's diabolical. Zergeyev's obviously the man – certainly one of them – sent to investigate the "British sphere of influence" in Asia, and to study the means of emigration into Russian Alaska.' Cooper collected his thoughts a moment. Then he said, 'What to do about it? Well, following your thought: Shevaun. Zergeyev would be delighted to escort her to America. She beguiles him either deliberately or unknowingly and takes him to Washington. Her father, who is the obvious one to give all this to, tells Zergeyev privately that the United States is distressed with Russia and wants them out. Monroe Doctrine and all that. Is this what you had in mind?'

'You're a smart man, Jeff.'

'This information makes Lord Cunnington look like a fool.'

'It does that.'

609

'And absolutely makes the need – and vital importance – of Hong Kong obvious.'

'Aye.'

'Now what we have to decide is how to get this information immediately and safely into the senator's hands. This will raise his stock in political circles enormously, so he'll play it for all he's worth. Should we risk letting Shevaun in on all this, or just give her a copy of the dossier to take to her father?'

'I'd na let her read the dossier or even tell her what's in it. After all, she's a woman. Women are likely to do the unpredictable. She might fall in love with Zergeyev. Then she'd dump the United States of America, because female logic says that she must protect the mate, irrespective of heritage or whatever. It'd be disastrous if Zergeyev knew we were aware of all that's in the dossier.'

'I'd like to think about all this,' Cooper said. He tied up the folder and handed it back. 'It sounds pompous, Tai-Pan, but my country'll learn to thank you.'

'I want nae thanks, Jeff. It might help, perhaps, if Senator Tillman and other diplomats began to ridicule Lord Cunnington's stupid mishandling of our area.'

'Yes. Take it as done. By the way, you owe me twenty guineas.'

'For what?'

'Don't you remember our bet? Over who was the nude? The first day, Dirk. Aristotle's painting of the ceding of the island was part of the bet, don't you remember?'

'Aye. Who was she?' Struan asked. Twenty guineas is na much against a lady's honour, he thought. Aye, but dammit, I liked that painting.

'Shevaun. She told me two days ago – said she was going to have the paintings done of herself. Like the Duchess of Alba.'

'Are you going to let her?'

'I don't know.' Cooper's face crinkled with a wan smile and lost, momentarily, its usual anguish. 'The sea voyage would stop that, wouldn't it?'

'Na with that lassie. I'll send the purse aboard tomorrow. As I remember, the loser was to have Aristotle paint the winner in to boot. Take it as done.'

'Perhaps you'd accept the painting. As a gift. I'll have Aristotle paint both of us in, eh?'

'Well, thank you. I've always fancied that painting.'

Cooper motioned at the papers. 'Let's talk some more about these tomorrow. I'll decide overnight about sending Shevaun.'

Struan thought about tomorrow. He handed the papers back to Cooper. 'Put this in your safe. For safety.'

'Thanks. Thanks for trusting me, Tai-Pan.'

Struan went ashore to the temporary office he had had erected on their new marine site. Vargas was waiting for him.

'Let's have all the bad news first, Vargas.'

'There's a report from our agents, senhor, in Calcutta. It seems that *Grey Witch* was three days ahead of *Blue Cloud*, according to last reports.'

'Next?'

'Building costs are huge, senhor. With yesterday's editorial, well, I've held up all work. Perhaps we should cut our losses.'

'Continue work immediately and double our labour force tomorrow.'

'Yes, senhor. The stock-market news from England is bad. The market is very jittery. The budget has not balanced again and financial troubles are expected.'

'That's normal. Have you na some special disaster to relate?'

'None, senhor. Of course robberies are incredibly frequent. There have been three piracies since you left and a dozen were attempted. Two pirate junks were captured and all the crew were publicly hanged. Forty to fifty thieves, robbers, cut-throats are whipped every Wednesday. Hardly a night goes by without a home being burglarized. Distressing. Oh, by the way, Major Trent has ordered a curfew for all Chinese at sunset. That seems to be the only way to control them.'

'Where's Mrs Quance?'

'Still on the small hulk, senhor. She cancelled her passage for England. Apparently there's rumour that Senhor Quance is still on Hong Kong.'

'Is he?'

'I would not like to feel we've lost the immortal Quance, senhor.'

'What's Mr Blore been up to?'

'He's spending money as if the rocks of Hong Kong were made of gold. Of course, it's not our money,' Vargas said, trying not to show his disapproval, 'but "Jockey Club funds". I understand the Club is to be non-profit-making, any profits going to benefit the racecourse, horses, and so on.' He dried his hands on a handkerchief. The day was very humid. 'I hear Senhor Blore has arranged a cockfight. Under Jockey Club auspices.'

Struan brightened. 'Good. When's it to be?'

'I don't know, senhor.'

'What's Glessing doing?'

'Everything a harbour master should. But I hear he's furious with Longstaff for not allowing him to go to Macao. There's a rumour he's going to be sent home.'

'Mauss?'

'Ah, the Reverend Mauss. He's returned from Canton and has rooms in the hotel.'

'Why the "ah", Vargas?'

'Nothing, senhor. Just another rumour,' Vargas replied, annoyed that he had been loose-tongued. 'Well, it seems – of course we Catholics disapprove of him and are sad that all Protestants do not believe as we do, for the salvation of their own souls. In any event, he has a cherished follower, a baptized Hakka called Hung Hsiu-ch'uan.'

'Would Hung Hsiu-ch'uan have anything to do with Hung Mun – the Triads?'

'Oh no, senhor. The name is a common one.'

'Aye, I remember him. A tall curious-looking man. Go on.'

'Well, there's not much to tell. It's just that he's begun preaching among the Chinese at Canton, unbeknownst to the Reverend Mauss, calling himself the brother of Jesus Christ, saying that he talks to his father – God – nightly. That he's the new Messiah, that he's going to clean out the temples like his brother did, and a lot of garbled idolatrous nonsense. Obviously he's mad. If it weren't so sacrilegious, it would be very amusing.'

Struan thought about Mauss. He liked him as a man and pitied him. Then he remembered Sarah's words again. Aye, he told himself, you've used Wolfgang in many ways. But in return you gave him what *he* wanted – the chance to convert the heathen. Without you he'd have been dead long ago. Without you . . . let it rest. Mauss has his own salvation to find. The ways of God are passing strange. 'Who knows, Vargas? Perhaps Hung Hsiu-ch'uan is what he claims. In any event,' he added seeing Vargas bridle, 'I agree. It is na amusing. I'll talk to Wolfgang. Thank you for telling me.'

Vargas cleared his throat. 'Do you think I could have next week off? This heat and – well, it would be nice to see my family.'

'Aye. Take two weeks, Vargas. And I think it would be good for the Portuguese community to have its own club. I'm starting a subscription. You're appointed temporary treasurer and secretary.' He scribbled on a pad and tore off the sheet. 'You can cash this at once.' It was a sight draft for a thousand guineas.

Vargas was overwhelmed. 'Thank you, senhor.'

'Nae thanks,' Struan said. 'Wi'out the support of the Portuguese community we'd na have any community.'

'But surely, senhor, this news – this editorial! Hong Kong is finished. The Crown has repudiated the treaty. Double the labour force? A thousand guineas? I don't understand.'

'Hong Kong's alive as long as one trader stands on it, and one naval vessel is in the harbour. Dinna worry. Any message for me?'

'Mr Skinner left word. He'd like to see you at your convenience. Mr Gordon Chen too.'

'Send word to Skinner that I'll stop by the newspaper this evening. And to Gordon that I'll meet him aboard *Resting Cloud* at eight o'clock.'

'Yes, senhor. Oh, by the way, one other thing. You remember Ramsey? The sailor who deserted? Well, he's been living in the hills all this time in a cave, like a hermit. On the Peak. He survived by stealing food from the fishing village at Aberdeen. It seems he raped several women there and the Chinese tied him up and gave him to the authorities. Yesterday he was tried. A hundred lashes and two years penal servitude.'

'They might as well have hanged him,' Struan said. 'He'll never last two years.' Jails were death traps, indescribably brutal.

'Yes. Terrible. Thank you again, senhor. Our community will be most appreciative,' Vargas said.

He left, but returned almost instantly. 'Excuse me, Tai-Pan. One of your seamen's here. The Chinese, Fong.'

'Send him in.'

Fong bowed himself in silently.

Struan studied the thickset, pockmarked Chinese. In the three months that he had been aboard he had changed in many ways. Now he wore European seaman's clothes easily, his queue coiled neatly under a knitted cap. His English was passable. An excellent sailor. Obedient, soft-spoken, quick to learn.

'What are you doing off ship?'

'Captain say can go shore, Tai-Pan. My watch go shore.'

'What do you want, Fong?'

Fong offered a crumpled piece of paper. The writing on it was childlike. 'Aberdeen. Same place, matey. Eight bells, midwatch. Come alone.' It was signed 'Bert and Fred's Dad.'

'Where'd you get this?'

'Coolie stop me. Give me.'

613

'Do you know what it says?'

'I read, yes. Not read easy. Very hard, never mind.'

Struan considered the scrap of paper. 'The sky. Have you seen it?'

'Yes, Tai-Pan.'

'What did it tell you?'

Fong knew that he was being tested. 'Tai-fung,' he said.

'How long?'

'Doan knowah. Three day, four day – more, less. Tai-fung, never mind.'

The sun was already below the horizon, the light dying fast. Lanterns were dotting the foreshore and the building sites.

The veil over the sky had thickened. A gigantic bloody moon sat ten degrees above the clear horizon.

'I think you've a good nose, Fong.'

'Thank you, Tai-Pan.'

Struan held up the paper. 'What does your nose say about this?'

'Not go alone,' Fong said.

XLIII

With the coming of darkness the sky began to cloud over and the humidity intensified. The China traders who were old in the ways of wind and sea knew that rain would come soon. The clouds heralded merely the first of the season's rains, which would alleviate the constant mugginess for a time and lay the dust. Just a shower if joss was with them. If joss was against them, there would be a storm. And only joss would decide if the storm was to become a typhoon.

'I'm hot, Tai-Pan,' May-may said, fanning herself in the bed.

'So am I,' Struan said. He was changing out of a limp, dank shirt into a fresh one. 'I told you you should stay in Macao. It's much cooler there.'

'That may be, but then I'd na have the pleasure of telling you that I'm hot, by God.'

'I preferred you when you were sick. Nae cheek then and nae vulgar swearing.'

'Huh!' she snorted. 'Dinna be mendacious with me!'

'What with you?'

'Mendacious, Tai-Pan. Do you na ken the English? While you're out all day, na worrying about your poor old mother, I've been terrifical busy reading your Dr Johnson word book, improving my mind with the barbarian tongue. Everyone knows "mendacious". It means "lying". That's wat you are, by God.' She forced a pout and this made her even prettier. 'You dinna adore me any more!'

'I've a good mind to mendacious your bottom.'

May-may forced a long-suffering groan. 'Tai-Pan wantshee cow chillo jig-jig, heya, Mass'er? Can, oh ko, never mind.'

Struan approached the bed and May-may backed off. 'Now, Tai-Pan, that was joke!'

He held her tight. 'Ah, lassie, you get yoursel' well, that's the important thing to do.'

She was wearing a soft blue silk tunic and her hair was done elegantly, her perfume intoxicating. 'Don't you dare to go to whore-houses, eh?'

'Dinna be silly.' He kissed her and finished dressing. He put his knife in its back holster and the small dirk in his left boot, and retied his hair neatly with ribbon at the nape of his neck.

'Why for you cut your hair, Tai-Pan? Grow it into a queue like a civilized person. Very pretty.'

Lim Din knocked and came in. 'Mass'er. Mass'er Chen here-ah. Can?'

'See-ah cabin topside.'

'You come back, Tai-Pan?'

'Nay, lassie. I'll go straight ashore.'

'Ask Gordon to see me – yes?'

'Aye, lassie.'

'Where you go?'

'Out, by God. And you better behave yoursel' while I'm away. I'll na be back till after midnight. But I'll look in as soon as I'm aboard.'

'Good,' she purred. 'But wake me if I'm sleepings. Your old mother would like to know her mendaciousical son's safe.'

He patted her fondly and went to the cabin on the next deck. 'Hello, Gordon.'

Gordon Chen was wearing a long robe of blue silk and light silk trousers. He was hot and greatly worried. 'Good evening, Tai-Pan. Welcome back. I'm so happy to hear about the cinchona. How is the Lady T'chung?'

'Very well, thank you.'

'I'm sorry my inadequate efforts were fruitless.'

'Thank you for trying.'

Gordon Chen was again vexed because he had had to lay out a substantial number of taels on the quest, but his vexation was nothing compared to his anxiety over Hong Kong. The whole Kwangtung hierarchy of the Triads was in an uproar over the news from England. He had been summoned by Jin-qua and ordered to sound out the Tai-Pan, to use the total power of the Triad, and whatever means were necessary – bullion, squeeze, increased trade – to prevent the barbarians from leaving the island and to encourage them to stay. 'There's a matter of grave importance, Tai-Pan; otherwise I would not have intruded. Hong Kong. This editorial. Is it true? If it is, we're lost – ruined.'

'I hear you're Tai-Pan of the Hong Kong Triads.'

'What?'

'Tai-Pan of the Hong Kong Triads,' Struan repeated blandly, and told him what the Portuguese officer had said. 'Stupid story, eh?'

'Not stupid, Tai-Pan, terrible indeed! A shocking lie!' If Gordon had been alone he would have torn his hair and clothes and screamed with rage.

'Why should Triads murder Gorth?'

'I don't know. How should I know what those anarchists do? Tai-Pan of the Triads? Me! What a foul accusation!' My life's not worth the price of a coolie's droppings, he was shouting to himself. That turtle-dung traitor! How dare he divulge secrets! Get your wits about you. The Tai-Pan of the barbarians is staring at you and you'd better give him a clever answer! 'I simply have no idea. Good heavens. Triads in Tai Ping Shan, under my very nose? Ghastly.'

'Have you enemies who'd spread such a story?'

'I must have, Tai-Pan. Great heaven! I wonder if –' The whites of his eyes showed.

'If what?'

'Well, I am – well, you are my father. Could it be that someone is trying to attack you, through me?'

'It could be, Gordon. It could be you *are* chief of the Triads.'

'An anarchist? Me?' Oh gods, why have you forsaken me? I spent fifty taels on incense and offerings, and on having prayers said only last week. Am I not the most lavish supporter of all your temples without favour? Have I not personally endowed three temples and four burial grounds, and have I not a retinue of forty-three Buddhist priests on my personal payroll? 'Why should I mix with those felons? Through you I am becoming rich. I've no need to steal or rob.'

'But you'd like the Manchus off the throne of China?'

'Manchus or Chinese, it's all the same to me, Tai-Pan. Why should I care? Nothing to do with me.' Oh gods, close your ears for a moment. 'I'm not Chinese – I'm English. I'd think the last person any Chinese secret society would trust is me. That would be dangerous, don't you think?'

'Perhaps. I dinna ken. Perhaps you should spend some taels, Gordon. Start a spy system. Find out who these men are, who their leaders are.'

'At once, Tai-Pan.'

'Three months should be enough for a man of your astuteness to produce the leaders.'

'Six months,' Gordon Chen said automatically, desperately trying to think of a way out of the trap. Now he had an inspiration. Of course.

Let the barbarians be the ones to deal with the anti-Triad turtledung. We'll recruit spies from among them and arrange for them to join a sub-lodge and initiate them with false ceremonies. Excellent! Then . . . let me see. We let drop that the real Triad leader is – is who? I'll think of some enemy when the time comes. Then we reveal them to the barbarians as actual Triads and off come their heads. 'Oh yes, Tai-Pan, I'll get on to it at once.'

'I think you should. Because one way or another, I'm going to smash the Triads.'

'And I'll assist you to the limit of my being,' Gordon said fervently. Ten heads should satisfy even you, Tai-Pan. Pity Chen Sheng is family, otherwise he'd be the perfect one to set up as the 'head Triad'. With any joss at all I'd be next in line to be comprador of The Noble House. Don't worry, Jin-qua will assist you to find the right decoy. 'Tai-Pan. To more important things. What about this editorial? Is Hong Kong finished? We stand to lose a fortune. It would be disastrous if we lost the island.'

'There are a few minor problems. But they'll be settled. Hong Kong's permanent. This Government will be out of office soon. Dinna worry. The Noble House and Hong Kong are one.'

Gordon Chen's anxiety disappeared. 'Are you sure? This Cunning-ton will be removed?'

'One way or another. Aye.'

He looked at his father with admiration. Ah, he thought, even by assassination. Excellent. He would have liked to tell the Tai-Pan that he had eliminated Gorth and thus saved his life. But this could wait until a more important time, he said to himself, filled with delight. 'Excellent, Tai-Pan. You've reassured me marvellously. I agree. The Noble House and Hong Kong *are* one.' If they're not, you're a dead duckling, he thought. But you'd better not set foot on the mainland ever again. Not with this Triad story set in motion. No. You're committed to Hong Kong. It's your palace or your tomb. 'Then we'd better expand, gamble heavily. I will work to make Hong Kong very strong. Oh yes. You can depend on me! Thank you, Tai-Pan, for reassuring me.'

'My Lady wished to say hello. Go below, eh?'

'Thank you. And thank you for warning me about that ridiculous but dangerous story.' Gordon Chen bowed and left.

Struan had watched his son very carefully. Is he or is he na? he asked himself. The surprise could have been real, and what he said makes a lot of sense. I dinna ken. But if Gordon *is*, you'll have to be very clever to catch him. And what then?

* * *

Struan found Skinner in the printing-press room of the *Oriental Times*. It was stifling and noisy. He complimented the newspaperman on the way he had handled the release.

'Don't worry, Tai-Pan,' Skinner said. 'There's a follow-up issue tomorrow.' He handed the proof sheet to Struan. 'I'll be glad when this cursed summer's over.' He was wearing his usual black broadcloth frockcoat and heavy trousers.

Struan read the article. It was filled with invective and sarcasm and emphasized that all traders should band together to bombard Parliament and destroy Cunnington.

'I'd say this would make a few of the lads break out in a rash,' Struan said approvingly.

'I certainly hope so.' Skinner held his arms away from his sides to relieve the fiery itch in his armpits. 'Cursed heat! You take your life in your hands, Tai-Pan, walking out in the night like that,' he said.

Struan wore only a light shirt and linen trousers and thin boots. 'You should try it. You'll sweat less – and no prickly heat.'

'Don't mention that cursed plague. Nothing to do with heat, it's a summer flux. Man was born to sweat.'

'Aye, and to be curious. You mentioned something in your note about a strange codicil to Longstaff's agreement with Viceroy Ching-so. What was it?'

'Just one of those strange bits of information a newspaperman collects.' Skinner wiped his face with a rag, which left ink stains in its wake, and sat back on the high stool. He told Struan about the seeds. 'Mulberries, camellias, rice, tea, all sorts of flowers.'

Struan brooded awhile, 'Aye, that's curious, right enough.'

'Longstaff's no gardener that I know of. Perhaps it was Sinclair's idea – he's a bent for gardening. At least his sister has.' Skinner watched the Chinese coolies working at the printing press. 'I hear she's quite sick.'

'The lass is recovering, I'm happy to say. The doctor said it was a stomach flux.'

'I hear Brock was aboard the flagship this afternoon.'

'Your information's very good.'

'I was wondering whether I should be preparing an obituary.'

'Sometimes I dinna find your humour amusing.'

The sweat ran down Skinner's jowls and dropped on to his soiled shirt. 'That wasn't meant as a pleasantry, Tai-Pan.'

'Well, I'm taking it as such,' Struan said easily. 'Bad joss to talk about obituaries.' He watched the press spewing out tomorrow's paper.

'I had a thought about Whalen. Longstaff named the old town Queen's Town. Now we have a new town. Perhaps Whalen should have the honour of choosing another name.'

Skinner chuckled. 'That would involve him nicely. What name have you decided on, Tai-Pan?'

'Victoria.'

'I like it. Victoria, eh? In one simple stroke Longstaff's obliterated. Take it as "suggested", Tai-Pan. Leave that to me. Whalen will never realize it wasn't his own idea – I guarantee.' Skinner scratched his belly contentedly. 'When do I own the paper?'

'The day Hong Kong's accepted by the Crown and the Treaty's ratified by both governments.' Struan gave him a document. 'It's all down here. My chop's on it. Of course, provided the *Oriental Times* is still a going concern at that time.'

'Have you any doubt, Tai-Pan?' Skinner asked happily. He could see the future clearly. Ten years, he told himself. Then I'll be rich. Then I'll go home and marry a squire's daughter and buy a small manor house in Kent and start a paper in London. Yes, Morley, old lad, he thought, you've come a long way from the alleys of Limehouse and that pox-ridden orphanage and gutter scavenging. God curse those devils who birthed me and left me. 'Thank you, Tai-Pan. I won't fail, never fear.'

'By the way, you might like an exclusive story. Cinchona cures the malaria of Happy Valley.'

Skinner was momentarily speechless. 'Oh my God, Tai-Pan, that's not a story – that's immortality,' he finally blurted. 'Exclusive, did you say? This is the greatest story in the world! Of course,' he added craftily, 'the peg to that story is the "she" – or "he" – who was cured.'

'Write what you like – but dinna involve me or mine.'

'No one'll ever believe it unless they've seen the cure with their own eyes. The doctors will say it's hogwash.'

'Let 'em. Their patients will die. Say so!' Struan told him bluntly. '*I* believe the story so much that I'm putting a substantial investment into it. Cooper and I are now partners in the cinchona business. We'll have stocks available in six months.'

'Can I print that?'

Struan laughed shortly. 'I'd na tell you if it was secret.'

On Queen's Road, Struan was blasted by the heat of the night. The moon was high and misted in a sky almost completely cloud-locked. But as yet there was no nimbus.

He set off down the road and did not stop until he had reached the dockyard. There he turned inland slightly, down a shabby potholed street. He went up a short flight of stairs and into a house.

'Bless my soul,' Mrs Fortheringill said, her false teeth making her smile grotesque. She was in the parlour having supper – kippers and brown bread and a flagon of ale. 'Ladies,' she called out, and rang a bell that was attached to her belt. 'Nothing like a good frolic on a hot night, I always say.' She noticed Struan was in shirt-sleeves. 'No wasted time undressing, is that the idea, Tai-Pan?'

'I just came to see – er, your guest.'

She smiled sweetly. 'That old bugger's outstayed his welcome.'

Four girls ambled in. Their feathered woollen kimonos were stained and they stank of perfume and stale sweat. They were barely twenty – hard, rough, and used to the life they led. They waited for Struan to choose.

'Nelly's the one for you, Tai-Pan,' Mrs Fortheringill said. 'Eighteen and sound in limb and vigorous.'

'Thank you, ma'am.' Nelly bobbed a curtsy and her full breasts swayed out of the kimono. She was heavy and blonde, her eyes ancient and frosted. 'You wanta come with me, Tai-Pan luv?'

Struan gave them each a guinea and sent them away. 'Where is Mr Quance?'

'Second floor back, left. The Blue Room.' Mrs Fortheringill peered over her spectacles at him. 'Times is very hard, Tai-Pan. Your Mr Quance eats like a horse and swears something terrible. Shocking for the young ladies. His bill's long overdue.'

'Where d'you get the girls, eh?'

A stony glint came into the old woman's eyes. 'Where there's a market there's always ladies to service it, eh? From England. Some from Australia. Here and there. Why?'

'How much does one cost you?'

'Trade secret, Tai-Pan. You've yours, we've ours.' She nodded to the table and changed the subject. 'You'd like to sup? The kippers is special from home. This week's mail ship.'

'Thank you, but I've already eaten.'

'Who's to pay dear Mr Quance's bill?'

'How much is it?'

'He has the reckoning. I hear Mrs Quance is right proper upset with him.'

'I'll discuss the reckoning with him.'

'Your credit's never in question, Tai-Pan.'

'Did Gorth's girl die?' Struan asked abruptly.

The old woman was again a model of gentility. 'What? I don't know what you mean. There ain't any bad goings-on in my establishment!'

Struan's knife was in his hand, the point touching the withered folds of skin that hung from Mrs Fortheringill's neck. 'Did she?'

'Not here she didn't. She were took away. For the love of God, don't—'

'Did she or did she na die?'

'I hear she did, but it weren't nothing to do with me—'

'How much did Gorth pay, to keep your mouth shut?'

'Two hundred guineas.'

'What happened to the girl?'

'I don't know. That's God's mortal truth, so help me! Relations came for her. He paid 'em hundred nicker and they were satisfied. They took her away. She were only a heathen.'

Struan put the knife away. 'You may have to repeat that in a court of law.'

'That bugger's dead, I hear, so there's naught to be said, I'd be thinking. And how can I say anything? Don't know her name and there's no corpse that I knows of. You know how it is, Tai-Pan. But I'll swear on a Bible to Brock, if that's wot's in yor mind.'

'Thank you, Mrs Fortheringill.'

He climbed the stairs to the Blue Room. Its whitewashed walls with a dirty grey, and wind blew through cracks. There was a huge mirror on one wall, and crimson-frilled curtains were draped around the great four-poster. Paintings were stacked on the floor and hung on the walls, and the floor was speckled with oil- and water-colour paints. In the centre of the room was an easel, and scattered around it were dozens of pots of paints and paintbrushes.

Aristotle Quance was snoring in bed. Only his nose and nightcap were visible.

Struan picked up a broken pitcher and flung it against the wall. It exploded into tiny pieces, but Quance just snuggled down deeper under the covers. Struan picked up a larger pitcher and crashed it against the wall.

Quance eased himself up and opened his eyes. 'Bless my soul! The Devil himself, by all that's holy!'

He bounded out of the bed and embraced Struan. 'Tai-Pan, my beloved patron! I worship you! When did you arrive?'

'Get away with you,' Struan said. 'Just got in today!'

'I hear Gorth's dead.'

'Aye.'

'Thank the Lord for that. Three days ago that dung-eater came here and swore he'd cut me throat if I told a soul about the girl.'

'How much did he give you na to tell?'

'Not a penny, dirty miser! Great balls of fire, I only asked a hundred.'

'How're things with you?'

'Terrible sad, my dear fellow. Herself is still here. Oh God, protect me! So I have to still hole up here. Can't move – daren't. Quance hopped back into bed and, picking up a huge stick, thumped the floor three times. 'Ordering breakfast,' he volunteered. 'Care to join me? Now tell me all your news!'

'You eat breakfast at nine at night?'

'Well, my dear fellow, when you're in a whorehouse you act like a whore!' he roared with laughter, then grabbed his chest. 'God's blood, Tai-Pan, I'm faint. You see before you a shadow of a man – a veritable ghost of the immortal Quance.'

Struan sat on the bed. 'Mrs Fortheringill said something about a bill. I gave you a bag of gold, by God!'

'Bill?' Quance rummaged under the pillow and shoved a half-eaten sandwich, two books, a few paintbrushes and several articles of female underwear out of the way and found the paper. He pressed it into Struan's hands breathlessly. 'Look what that usurer's charging you.'

'Charging *you*, you mean,' Struan said. He read the total. 'Good God Almighty!' The bill came to four hundred and sixteen pounds four shillings and fourpence and a farthing. Seven and sixpence per day, board and lodging. One hundred and seven pounds for paints, brushes, canvas. The balance was headed 'Miscellaneous charges.' 'What the devil's this figure?'

Quance pursed his lips. ' 'Pon me word, that's what I've tried to get out of the old cat.'

Struan went to the door and bellowed downstairs. 'Mrs Fortheringill!'

'Did you call me, Tai-Pan?' she asked sweetly from the well of the stairs.

'Aye. Would you kindly step this way?'

'You wanted me?' she asked even more sweetly as she came into the room.

'What the devil's this?' Struan stabbed the bill viciously with a finger. ' "Miscellaneous" – nearly three hundred and twenty pounds!'

'Ah,' she replied archly. 'Trade, Tai-Pan.'

'Eh?'

'Mr Quance likes company at all hours, and that's the amount of his

623

trade since he's been in our care.' She sniffed disdainfully. 'We keep proper books here. It's correct to the minute.'

'Lies!' Quance howled. 'She's cooked the books, Tai-Pan. It's blackmail!'

'Blackmail?' Mrs Fortheringill shrieked. 'Why you – you – and here's me and my ladies saving you from worse than death and the second time to boot!'

'But three hundred-odd pounds?' Struan said.

'Correct to the minute, by God. He likes to paint 'em as well as . . . my book-keeper's the best in Asia. Has to be!'

'It's impossible,' Struan insisted.

Quance stood on the bed and put one hand over his heart and with the other pointed at the woman. 'I refuse the entire bill on your behalf, Tai-Pan!' He was puffed up like a peacock. 'It's usury!'

'Oh, it is, is it? Well, I'll tell you, you blathering old fart-dungheap right to your face – out you go! And I'll send word to that woman tonight!' The little woman spun around and screeched, 'Ladies!'

'Now, Mrs Fortheringill, there's no need for temper,' Quance said tentatively.

The girls came running. Eight of them.

'Take them out and put 'em in me room,' she ordered, waving at the paints and brushes and paintings. 'No more credit, and them's mine until the bill's paid to the penny!' And she huffed out.

Quance scrambled out of bed, his nightshirt flaring. 'Ladies! You'll touch nothing, by God!'

'Now, be a good boy,' Nelly said calmly. 'If Ma'am says they's to go, if the Lord Himself was standing there, they's to go!'

'Oh yes, funnybunny darling,' another said. 'Our Nelly's said it proper.'

'Just a minute, ladies,' Struan said. 'Mr Quance's been given a bill. That's the reason for all the trouble. Miss Nelly, er, have you, well, spent time with him?'

Nelly stared at Struan. ' "Time" you say Tai-Pan? Our dear Mr Quance has an appetite for time the like of which ain't even in the Bible.'

'Oh yes, Tai-Pan,' another said with a chuckle. 'Sometimes he likes two of us together. Oh, he is a one!'

'To paint, by God!' Quance shouted.

'Oh, go on with you, Mr Quance,' Nelly said. 'We's friends together.'

'He paints us some of the time,' another said agreeably.

'When?' another asked. 'I ain't ever beed painted.'

624

'Lies, by God!' Quance protested to Struan, and when he saw the Tai-Pan's expression, he winced and shrank back into the bed. 'Come now, Tai-Pan,' he implored. 'No need to be precipitate. A fellow can't help it if he's – popular.'

'If you think I'm paying for your quent, you're sick in the head!'

'What's "quent"?' Nelly asked, indignant. 'We're respectable ladies, that's wot. We bleedin' well are and we don't like dirty words!'

'It's Latin for "time", my dear Miss Nelly,' Quance said hoarsely.

'Oh,' she said, and bobbed a curtsy. 'Beggin' your pardon, Tai-Pan!'

Quance clutched his heart and rolled his eyeballs. 'Tai-Pan, if you forsake me, I'm finished. Debtors' prison! I beg you' – he clambered out of bed and knelt supplicatingly – 'don't turn your back on an old friend!'

'I'll settle this bill and take all your paintings against your loan. But this is the last penny. Understand, Aristotle? I'm paying no more!'

'Bless you, Tai-Pan. You're a prince.'

'Oh yes,' Nelly said and sidled up to Struan. 'Come on, luv. You pay Ma'am's bill and it'll be on the house.'

'Wot about me?' another asked. 'Course, Nelly's got more trickeries.'

They all nodded amiably and waited.

'I'd recommend,' Quance started, but Struan's glare cut him short. 'Every time you look at me like that, Tai-Pan, I feel near death. Forlorn. Lost. Forsaken.'

In spite of his irritation Struan laughed. 'Devil take you!' And he strode for the door. But a sudden thought stopped him. 'Why's this room called the Blue Room?'

Nelly leaned down and picked up the chamber pot from under the bed. It was blue. 'Ma'am started a new fashion, Tai-Pan. Each room have a different colour, Tai-Pan. Mine's green.'

'I've got the old cracked gold one,' another said with a sniff. 'Ain't lady-like at all!'

Struan shook his head hopelessly and disappeared.

'Now, ladies!' Quance said in an exultant whisper, and there was an expectant hush. 'As the slate's clean, after breakfast I propose a modest celebration.'

'Oh good,' they said, and clustered around the bed.

XLIV

At midnight the lorcha nosed the beach at Aberdeen, and Struan jumped into the shallows, Fong beside him. Earlier he had landed his men secretly just to the west and positioned them around the well. He tramped up the beach towards the well and the fork in the path. Fong carried a lantern and was very nervous.

The moon was hidden by the low overcast, but a trace of its glow filtered through. The air was heavy with the stench of low tide, and the hundreds of sampans in the narrow inlet were like so many hibernating wood bugs. No lantern except Fong's cut the darkness. There were no sounds but for the inevitable foraging of dogs.

The village was equally ominous.

As Struan broke out on to the fork in the path, he searched the night. He could feel many eyes watching him from the sampans.

He loosened the pistols in his belt and stood carefully out of the light of the lantern that Fong had placed on the lip of the well.

The silence intensified. Suddenly Fong stiffened and pointed shakily. Just beyond the fork, lying across the path, was a sack. It looked like a rice sack. His pistols ready, Struan motioned Fong ahead, not trusting him. Fong advanced, panic-stricken.

When they reached the sack, Struan tossed Fong a dirk, haft first. 'Cut it open.'

Fong knelt down and slit the hempen sacking. He let out a terrified whimper and backed off.

Scragger was in the sack. He had no arms or legs or eyes or tongue, and the stumps of his limbs were cauterized with tar.

'Top o' the evening, matey!' Wu Kwok's malignant laughter echoed harrowingly out of the night and Struan jerked to his feet.

The laugh seemed to come from the sampans.

'What do you want, you devil from hell?' Struan shouted back.

There was a guttural stream of Chinese, and Fong blanched. He shouted something back, his voice constricted.

'What did he say?'

'He . . . Wu Kwok says I'm to go – there.'

'You stay where you are,' Struan said. 'What do you want, Kwok?' he yelled at the sampans.

'You alive! For Quemoy, by God! You an' yor muckpissed frigates!'

Figures swarmed from the sampans and raged up the hill with spears and cutlasses. Struan waited until he could see the first of the pirates clearly, then dropped him with a shot. Immediately muskets blazed from Struan's ambushing crew. There were screams, and the first wave of twenty or thirty pirates was annihilated.

Another wave of shouting cut-throats hurtled up the path. Again the muskets blasted them to pieces, but four gained the well. Struan cut one down, Fong another, and musket balls killed the other two.

Again a quietness.

'The pox on you matey!'

'And you, Wu Kwok!' Struan bellowed.

'My fleets be goin' again' the Lion and Dragon!'

'Come out of your rat hole and face me and I'll kill you now. Scum!'

'When I catched you, that be yor way o'dying, matey. A limb a week. That scum live five, six week, but you be a year adying, I'll be bound. We meets face t' face in a year, if not afore!' Again the evil laugh and then silence. Struan was tempted to fire the sampans, but he knew that hundreds of men and women and children were aboard.

He stared down at the half-opened sack. 'Pick it up, Fong.' And he called to his men in the surrounding darkness: 'Fall back on the lorcha, lads!'

He covered Fong and they withdrew. When he was well out to sea, he put a chain around the sack and read a service over it and cast it into the deep. He watched it disappear in a tiny circle of sea froth.

Struan would have liked to tell Scragger about the farewell he had had with his sons.

He had put them into the hands of the captain at Whampoa, with letters tó The Noble House's agents in London whom he had made responsible for the boys and their schooling.

'Well, good luck, lads. When I get home I'll come to see you.'

'Can I be seeing you, Yor Worship, privy?' little Fred had asked, trying not to cry.

'Aye, laddie. Come along.' Struan had taken him into a cabin and Bert, the Eurasian, had been uneasy to be left alone and Wu Pak had held on to Bert's hand.

'Aye, Fred?' he had asked when they were alone.

'Me dad sayed we was t' have a proper name afore we be leaving home waters, Yor Worship.'

'Aye, lad. It's on your papers. I told you last night. Do you na remember?'

'Beggin' yor pardon, no, Yor Worship. I forgets. Can we be knowing it again, please?'

'You're Frederick MacStruan,' he had said, for he had taken a liking to the boy and the clan name was a good one. 'And Bert's Bert Chen.'

'Oh,' the little boy had said. 'Yus, now I remembers. But why's we different? Me and my bruvver?'

'Well,' Struan had said as he tousled the boy's head, remembering with frantic pain the loss of his own sons, 'you've different mothers, have you na? That's the reason.'

'Yus. But we be bruvvers, Yor Honour,' Fred had said, his tears brimming. 'Beggin' yor pardon, can we be having the same name? Chen's a proper nice name. Frederick Chen's nice, Tai-Pan.'

So Struan had changed the papers and the captain had witnessed his signature. 'There, lads, now you're both MacStruan. Albert and Frederick MacStruan.'

Then they had both wept happily and had put their arms around him.

Struan went below and tried to sleep. But sleep would not come. Scragger's end had sickened him. He knew it was a favourite torture of Wu Fang Choi, Wu Kwok's father and little Wu Pak's grandfather. The victim who was to be dismembered was given three days' time to choose which limb was to come off first. And on the third night a friend of the man would be sent to him secretly to whisper that help was on the way. So the man chose the limb he felt he could most do without until help came. After the tar had healed the stump, the man was forced to choose yet another limb, and again there was the promise of imminent help which would never come. Only the very strong could survive two amputations.

Struan got off the bunk and went on deck. There was a slight swell and the cloud cover had thickened: no moon glow now. The sea was high but safe enough.

'Rain tomorrow, Mr Struan,' Cudahy said.

'Aye,' he replied. He peered east, into the wind. He could feel the sea watching him.

'Supreme Lady,' Ah Sam said, touching May-may awake. 'Father's cutter's approaching.'

628

'Has Lim Din drawn his bath?'

'Yes, Mother. He's gone upstairs to welcome Father.'

'You can go back to bed, Ah Sam.'

'Shall I wake Second Mother?' Yin-hsi was curled up in a bed at one side of the cabin.

'No. Go back to bed. But first give me my brush and comb, and make sure Lim Din has breakfast ready if Father wants it.'

May-may lay back for a moment, remembering what Gordon Chen had told her. That dirty turtledung assassin! Fancy his accusing my son of being connected with a secret society! He was paid more than enough to keep his mouth shut and die quietly. How foolish!

She eased out of bed cautiously. For the first few seconds her legs felt weak and wobbly. Then she stopped reeling and stood erect.

'Oh,' she said aloud, 'that feels better.' She walked to the mirror and studied herself critically. 'You look old,' she said to her reflection.

'You don't at all. And you shouldn't be out of bed,' Yin-hsi said, sitting up in her bed. 'Let me brush your hair. Is Father back? I'm so pleased you're better. You look really very good.'

'Thank you, Sister. His boat's just approaching.' May-may allowed Yin-hsi to brush her hair and braid it. 'Thank you, dear.'

She perfumed herself and got back into bed feeling refreshed.

The door opened and Struan tiptoed in. 'What're you doing awake?' he asked.

'I wanted to see you back safe. Your bath's ready. And breakfast. I'm very glad you're back safe and sound!'

'I think I'll turn in for a few hours. You go back to sleep, lassie, and we'll have breakfast when I wake up. I've told Lim Din to let me sleep unless there's something urgent.'

He kissed her briefly, a trifle embarrassed by Yin-hsi's presence. May-may noticed this and smiled to herself. How curious barbarians were!

Struan nodded vaguely to Yin-hsi and left the room.

'Listen, dear Sister,' May-may said, when she was certain Struan was out of earshot. 'Bathe with perfumed water, and when Father is heavily asleep go into his bed and sleep with him.'

'But, Supreme Lady, I'm sure that Father did not indicate in any way that he wanted me to go to him. I was watching very carefully. If I went uninvited, I – he might be very angry and send me away, and then I'd lose much face before you and before him.'

'You just have to understand barbarians are very different from us, Yin-hsi. They've no idea of face as we have. Now, do as I say. He'll

629

have a bath and go to bed. Wait an hour. Then join him. If he wakes up and orders you out, just be patient and say' – she changed to English – ' "Supreme Lady sent me." '

Yin-hsi repeated the English words and memorized them.

'If that's no use, come back here,' May-may continued. 'No face is lost, I promise you. Don't be afraid. I know a lot about Father and how he views face. We certainly can't have him visiting those dirty whore-houses. The naughty man went straight to one of them last night.'

'No!' Yin-hsi said. 'We have terribly lost face. Oh dear. I must disgust Father. Perhaps you'd better sell me to a gravedigger.'

'Huh!' May-may said. 'I'd give him what-for if I was well. Don't worry, Yin-hsi. He hasn't even seen you yet. I keep telling you. He's a barbarian. Disgusting to go to a whorehouse when you're here, and even Ah Sam.'

'I quite agree. Oh, the bad man!'

'They're all bad, dear,' May-may said. 'I'm hoping that he's so tired he won't send you away as I expect him to. Just sleep in his bed. With Father, we have to work up to things. Even at his age he's still very shy about love.'

'Does he know that I'm not a virgin?' Yin-hsi was caressing May-may's head.

'He's much too young yet to need virgins to excite him, dear sister. And much too old to have the patience yet to teach a virgin in the ways of love again. Just say to him, "Supreme Lady sent me." '

Yin-hsi repeated the English words again.

'You're very pretty, Sister. Run along, now. Wait an hour, then go to him.'

May-may closed her eyes and settled contentedly in the bed.

Yin-hsi gazed down at Struan. One of his arms lay carelessly across the pillow and he was sound asleep. The curtains on the cabin portholes were drawn tightly against the morning. It was very quiet.

Yin-hsi took off her pyjamas and slid gingerly under the covers beside Struan.

The warmth of the bed excited her.

She waited breathlessly, but he did not awaken. She moved closer and gently put a hand on his arm and waited. Still he did not awaken. She moved even closer and put her arm across his chest and let it rest there. And waited.

Through the mist of his dreams Struan knew that May-may was beside him. He could smell her perfume and feel her close, and he was content that the fever was in the past and that she was well again. They were together in the sun and he could sense her well-being. He asked her what she would like for her birthday and she just laughed and pressed close in the sun, which was dark and curious and unreal but beautiful. Then they were very close and he listened to her chattering and then they were swimming together and he found this strange for he knew that she could not swim and he wondered when she had learned. Then they were lying naked on the beach, side by side, the length of her touching him. Then she began shivering and he was terrified that she had fever again and there was the monk with his bloodstained robes and the cup, and the cup took May-may's fever away and then there was darkness. But the clouds were above and it was dark when it should have been day and Fong was shouting from the waves, 'Tai-fung!' Then they ran from the clouds and were in bed, safe together.

He stirred in his sleep and half awoke and felt the warm, tender body touching him, and his hand strayed and he cupped her breast and felt the shiver run through her and through him.

He lay in the gloaming of the room on the threshold of awakening. Her breast was soft in his hand and he felt the hardness of the nipple.

Then he opened his eyes.

Yin-hsi smiled demurely.

Struan braced himself on an elbow. 'God's blood, what the devil are you doing here?'

Yin-hsi blinked at him uncomprehendingly. 'Sup-reem – Lady – sen' – me.'

'Eh?' Struan tried to clear his head.

'Sup-reem Lady sen' me, Tai-Pan.'

'Eh? May-may? May-may? Is she out of her head?' He pointed to the door. 'Off you go.'

Yin-hsi shook her head. 'Sup-reem Lady sen' me.'

'I dinna care if you've been sent by the queen of England! Off you go!'

Yin-hsi pouted. 'Sup-r'm Lady sen' me!' And she planted her head firmly on the pillow and glared at him.

Struan began to laugh.

Yin-hsi was bewildered. My goodness, Supreme Lady was right. Barbarians are astounding. But I'm not moving from this bed! How dare you go to a whorehouse and make me lose face in front of Tai-tai? Am I a rotten old hag, for goodness sake? Oh no Tai-Pan! I'm not moving! I'm very nice and I'm Second Sister and Second Lady in your house and that's that!

'By the gods,' Struan said, pulling himself together. 'I'm going to marry May-may if it's the last thing I do. And the pox on everyone!'

He lay back and mulled what he and May-may would do at home in England. She'll be the toast of London . . . so long as she never wears any European clothes. Together we'll rock the society of England. Now I have to hurry home. Perhaps I can destroy the Foreign Secretary mysel'! Or block Whalen. Aye. Now the key to Hong Kong's in London. So home – and the sooner the better.

He turned his head on the pillow and looked at Yin-hsi, and really saw her for the first time. She was very desirable. Her perfume was as exquisite as her skin.

'Ah lassie, I'm sorely tempted,' he said.

She nestled closer to him.

XLV

The *White Witch* staggered into harbour just before noon. Her foremast was gone and there was a tangle of broken spars and twisted rigging on the main deck.

Brock came alongside in a cutter as she nosed for her moorings.

'By God, someone's to pay!' he roared as he came on deck, knowing instinctively from the shattered unreefed sails that were strewn among the halyards that the ship had been carrying too much canvas. 'Wot be happened?'

'Day, sir,' Michaelmas said. He was a hard, pockmarked first mate. 'I took over for Mr Gorth. Till I knowed wot was in your mind.' There was a lash in his huge fist. 'We run into squall two hour out've Macao. Godrotting squall almost turned us in our beam end. Carried mast away, and blew us'n off course for fifty league.'

Brock bunched a fist and shook it in the man's face. 'Doan thee knowed enough to see squall? Doan thee knowed enough to reef in this season?'

'Yus, Mr Brock,' Michaelmas said without fear. 'But the squall came up alee. Doan curse me for squall, by God!'

Brock's fist smashed him against the gunnel and he collapsed to the deck unconscious.

'Pennyworth!' Brock bellowed to the second mate, a thick-set burly young man. 'You be captain till further orders! Get storm anchors out. We be in for dirty weather.' Then he saw Culum on the quarterdeck. The seamen scattered as he climbed over the rigging and walked up the short gangway. He loomed over Culum.

'Morning, Mr Brock. I wanted—'

'Where be Mrs Brock?'

'Below, sir. It wasn't Mr Michaelmas' fault. And I wanted—'

'Shut thy face!' Brock snarled and then contemptuously turned his back on Culum. Culum boiled at the insult; Brock would never turn his back on the Tai-Pan.

'No one be allowed ashore!' Brock shouted. 'Get this mess cleaned

633

up, Pennyworth, or you'll be beached like that bugger Michaelmas. Get him off my ship!' He whirled back on Culum. 'I be talking to thee right smartly.'

'I'd like to talk now.'

'One more word afore I'm ready and I'll grind thee to dust.'

Culum followed Brock below and wished that the Tai-Pan were there. Oh God, how can I handle Brock? Why did we have to run into that cursed squall?

Tess was standing at the door to her cabin. She smiled tentatively and curtsied, but Brock shoved past and opened the main cabin door and slammed it behind him.

'Oh, God help us, darling,' Tess cried to Culum.

'Don't worry. We'll be all right.' Culum tried to level his voice and he desperately wished he had a pistol. He went to a rack and pulled out a belaying pin and motioned Tess into the cabin. 'Don't worry. He made a holy oath. He promised.'

'Let's run while we've the chance,' she begged.

'Can't run now, darling,' Culum said. 'Don't worry. It's best to have it out now. We must.'

'So you let Tess slip out and that bugger pull wool over thy face, eh?' Brock was saying.

'Yus.' Liza said, and she was trying to contain her panic. 'I were watching careful an' I never thort, but they did an' I be at fault. But they's married, lad, and there baint naught we—'

'I be deciding that, by God! Wot happened with Gorth?'

She told him all she knew. 'It were Gorth wot challenged Dirk Struan,' she said. She was terrified, not only for herself but even more for Tess and Culum and her man. If Tyler be going after that devil like this'n, he be a goner. 'It were Gorth, Tyler. He called the Tai-Pan terrible names. An' hit him with lash. In public he did. I tol' Gorth to wait – to come here and get thee – but he hit me and left.'

'Wot?'

She pulled her hair away from her right ear. It was puffed and black, and inside was caked with dried blood. 'It still hurt something terrible.' She undid her blouse. Her chest was hideously bruised. 'He did this. Yor son. He be a right devil and thee knowed it.'

'By God, Liza. If he . . . if I knowed . . . it be best he be dead. But not by assassins and not without honour, by God.' His face terrible, he drew a mug of ale from the barrel and Liza thanked God that she'd had the foresight to have a fresh keg ready.

'The doctor be sure about the pox? That young bugger?'

'He has no pox and he baint a bugger. He's thy son-in-law!'

'I knowed that. God curse him!'

'Tyler, forgive they two. I be beggin' thee. He be a good boy and he be terrible in love with Tess and she be happy and—'

'Hold thy tongue!' Brock gulped the beer and slammed the tankard down. 'Dirk be planning all this'n. I knowed it. T' spite me! First he be out to destroy my eldest son – and then takes away me marrying my girl proper. God curse Struan! He even tooked that from me!' He hurled the tankard against the bulkhead. 'We be burying Gorth at sea today.'

'Tyler, luv,' Liza began. She touched his arm. 'Tyler, luv, there be somethin' else. It must be sayed. Thee's got to forgive – thee's a lot to forgive. About Nagrek.'

'Eh?'

'Gorth tol' me what thee and him did to Nagrek. That be terrible – but he be deserving it. 'Cause he laid with Tess. He did. But Culum doan know, it seem. So thy girl be saved from a terrible fate.'

The muscles around Brock's eye socket began twitching fiercely. 'Wot be thee sayin'?'

'It be truth. I hid it from thee 'cause I were afeared for thee. I hid it from her – least I persuaded her Nagrek baint . . . it weren't lovin', true lovin' – and it were no harm.'

'Wot is thee saying?'

'It be true, Tyler,' Liza said, and then her torment broke. 'At least give they a chance. It were thy oath, afore God. And God helped us'n with Tess, lad. Forgive they.' She buried her head in her arms and sobbed convulsively.

Brock's lips moved but no sound came out. He lumbered to his feet, crossed the corridor, and then he was standing before Culum and Tess.

He saw the terror in Tess's eyes. This hurt him and made him cruel. 'Thee choosed to go again' my wish. Three month, I sayed. But thee—'

'Oh, Da' – oh, Da'—'

'Mr Brock. Can I—'

'Shut thy face. Thee'll get thy say soon enough! And thee, Tess, thee choosed to run off like a cheap doxy. Very well. Go say goodbye to thy ma. Then thee's out of our life and ashore with thy man.'

'Oh, Da', please listen—'

'Go on! I wan' t'talk to him.'

'I baint leaving!' Tess shouted hysterically. She picked up the belaying pin. 'Thee'll not touch 'im. I'll kill thee!'

He snatched the belaying pin out of her hands before she knew he had moved. 'Out you go and ashore.' Brock was watching himself as though in a nightmare; he wanted to forgive and he wanted her arms around him, but some depraved other self was driving him and he could not resist. 'Out, by God!'

'It's all right, darling,' Culum said. 'Go along and pack your bags.'

She backed out of the cabin, then scurried away.

Brock kicked the door to. 'I swore to give thee berth and safe harbour. But that were when you be wedding proper.'

'Listen, Mr Brock—'

'You listen, by God, or I'll crush thee like bedbug.' A thread of saliva trickled from a corner of his mouth. 'I sayed to thee fair, man t'man, if three month were agreeable. Thee sayed yes. But thee broke thy word. I sayed, "Be honest, lad." '

Culum said nothing. He prayed for strength and knew that he was beaten. But he would try, by God.

'Did thee or didn't thee?'

'Yes.'

'Then I be thinkin' I be absolved from oath.'

'Can I speak now?'

'I baint finished. But even though thee cheated, thee's wed. Will thee answer question? Afore God? Then we be even.'

'Of course.' Culum wanted to tell Brock about the pox and the whorehouse and the why of it.

'Afore God?'

'Yes. I've nothing to hide and—'

Brock cut him short, 'Did thy father plan all this'n? Put elopement into thy head? Knowing it be making Gorth mad? Knowing this'n'd make Gorth so mad he be challenging him in public so thy Da' be able to fight him fair and square? Did thee go t'whorehouse drunken, not knowing where thee be, with whom thee be? Thee doan have to answer. It's writ in thy face.'

'Yes – but you must listen. There's a lot—'

'Thee's got thy safe harbour from me. But I'll tell thee square, I'm after thy Da'. I'm after Noble House. I be never resting till they's broke. Now thy only harbour be in Brock and Sons. Only there, Culum godrotting Struan! And till that day thee's dead afore my face. Thee and Tess.'

He hurled the door open.

'You haven't heard my side!' Culum shouted. 'That's not fair!'

'Doan thee talk about "fair",' Brock said. 'I asked thee to thy face.

636

Three month! I sayed "Be honest, lad". But thee still broke thy word. Thee's no honour afore me, by God!'

He strode away and Culum stared after him, his anguish and relief and shame and hate wrenching him. 'You're not fair,' he said, his voice hurting him.

Brock came on deck and the crew kept their distance.

'Pennyworth!'

The second mate turned away from supervising the sorting out of spars and broken rigging and clambered warily over towards Brock.

'Find Struan,' Brock said. 'Tell him I be waiting for he at Happy Valley. Twixt his wharf and mine.' He stopped, and his face twisted into a mirthless smile. 'No. At knoll in Happy Valley. Yus. His knoll wot were. Tell him I be waiting for he at the knoll in Happy Valley – like he wanted to go again' Gorth. Understand?'

'Yes, sir.' Pennyworth bit his lip. 'Yes, sir.'

'And if you whisper this to any man but he, by the Lord God, I'll cut thy balls off.' Brock started down the gangway.

'Who's to get the ship squared away sir?'

'Thee. Yo're cap'n o' the *White Witch*. After thee delivers message.'

Struan was contemplating Yin-hsi. She was still asleep beside him. He compared her with May-may. And May-may with his Chinese mistress of years ago. And the three of them with Ronalda, his only wife. So different. Yet so much the same in so many ways. And he wondered why the three Orientals excited him more than Ronalda who was his love – until he knew May-may. And he asked himself what love was.

He knew that the three Chinese had much in common: an unbelievable silkiness of skin and a humour and a belongingness and a worldliness beyond anything that he had experienced. But May-may far excelled the other two. She was perfect.

He touched Yin-hsi affectionately. She stirred but did not awaken. He carefully slid out of bed and looked out of the portholes to check the sky. The overcast was heavier. He dressed and went below.

'So,' May-may said. She was sitting up in bed, exquisite.

'So,' he said.

'Where's my sister?'

' "Sup-reem Lady sen' me." '

'Huh!' May-may said and tossed her head. 'You're just lustful mendacity and you do na adore your old mother any more.'

'True,' Struan said, teasing her. She looked more beautiful than ever, and the gauntness of her face seemed to suit her. 'I think I'll pack you off!'

'Ayeee yah! See if I care!'

He laughed and lifted her up in his arms.

'Be careful, Tai-Pan,' she said. 'Did you enjoy Yin-hsi? I'm so pleased you did. I can tell.'

'How would you like to be Tai-tai?'

'Wat?'

'Well, if you're na interested, that's the last we'll say about it.'

'Oh no, Tai-Pan! You mean Tai-tai? Real Tai-tai, according to customs? Oh, you're na teasing me? Please dinna tease about so important thing.'

'I'm na teasing, May-may.' He sat on the chair with her in his arms. 'We're going home. Together. We'll take the first clipper available and be married on the way home. In a few months.'

'Oh, wonderful.' She hugged him. 'Let me go a minute.'

He released her, and wobbling slightly, she walked over to the bed. 'There. I am almost well again.'

'You get into bed now,' he said.

'You really mean marry? According to your customs? And to mine?'

'Aye. Both, if you wish.'

She knelt gracefully in front of him and touched her forehead to the carpet and kowtowed. 'I swear I will be worthy to be Tai-tai.'

He raised her up quickly and put her into the bed. 'Dinna do that, lassie.'

'I kowtow because you give me the hugest fantastical great face on earth.' She hugged him again and then pushed him away a little and laughed. 'How you like birthday present, heya? Is that why you marry your poor old mother?'

'Nay and aye. It's just the thought.'

'She's nice. I like her very gracious much. I'm glad you like her too.'

'Where did you find her?'

'She was a concubine in a house of a mandarin who died six months ago. Did I tell you she was eighteen? His house fell on bad times, so Tai-tai asked a marriage broker to find a good match for her. I heard about her and interviewed her.'

'When? In Macao?'

'Oh no. Two, three months ago.' May-may snuggled closer. 'I talk to her in Canton. Jin-qua's Tai-tai tol' me about her. When I became with child I thought, Ah, very good, so I sent for her. Because my man is lustful and instead of staying home perhaps goes to whorehouse. You promise na to go, but last night you go whorehouse. Dirty turtle droppings!'

'I did na go with one of the girls. Just to see Aristotle.'

'Huh!' May-may shook a finger in his face. 'That your story. I dinna mind whores but na those ones. Oh very well, this time I'll believe you.'

'Thank you kindly.'

'Yin-hsi is special nice, so no need for whorehouses. Oh, I feel so happy. She sings beautiful and plays many instruments and sews nicely and very quick to learn. I teach her the English. She will come to England with us. And Ah Sam and Lim Din.' A slight frown. 'But we come back home to China? Very often?'

'Aye. Maybe.'

'Good. We come back of course.' Again a little smile. 'Yin-hsi is very accomplished. She is nice in bed?'

Struan's eyes crinkled with amusement. 'I did na make love, if that's what you're asking.'

'Wat?'

'I like to choose who's in my bed and when.'

'She's in your bed and you dinna make love?'

'Aye.'

'I swear to God, Tai-Pan I never understand you. You do na desire her?'

'Of course. But I decided today was na the time. Tonight maybe yes. Or tomorrow. When I choose. Na before. But I appreciate your thoughtfulness.'

'I swear to God you're peculiar. Or maybe you were just so exhausted with a dirty whore you could na respond. Eh?'

'Go on with you.'

There was a knock on the door.

'Aye?'

Lim Din padded in. 'Tai-Pan, Mass'er here. See Tai-Pan. Can?'

'Mass'er wat?'

'Mass'er Penneewort.'

XLVI

Brock watched Struan climb the path that led up the knoll from the shadow of the roofless abandoned church. He saw the bunched fighting iron and felt somewhat nauseated. Yet he was glad that at long last there was to be a showdown.

He shifted the thong of his fighting iron, stood up, and moved into the open. He grasped his knife with his left hand.

Struan saw Brock the instant he moved from the cover of the church and momentarily forgot the plan that he had decided upon. He stopped. All he could remember was that this was his enemy whom he must destroy. With an effort Struan cleared his head and continued to climb the path, his muscles quivering with the anxiety to begin.

At last the two men confronted each other.

'Thee planned elopement and duel, didn't thee?' Brock snarled.

'Aye,' Struan let the bunched fighting iron fall. It jingled hatefully. Again he had to strain to recall what he had decided to say.

Brock gripped the haft of his fighting iron and eased forward a step and readied.

Only Struan's eyes moved. 'I'm sorry Gorth died the way he died,' Struan said. 'I'd have enjoyed killing him.'

Brock made no answer. But he shifted his weight imperceptibly, the east wind ruffled his hair.

Struan's dirk appeared in his left hand and he crouched slightly. 'Tess be poxed.'

Brock stopped in his tracks. 'She baint. Doctor sayed Culum were clean.'

'Doctors can be bought,' Struan said, feeling the blood lust swamping him. 'She was poxed deliberately!'

'Why, you –' Brock swung the fighting iron viciously and lunged at Struan. The metal barb missed Struan's eyes by only a fraction of an inch. Struan swayed back and hacked, but Brock sidestepped and they began to circle each other like two animals.

'By Gorth! That's what Gorth planned,' Struan said. He wanted to have done with talking. 'You hear? That was Gorth's doing.'

Brock's head was pounding. All he could think of was to close with the enemy and kill.

Again there was a violent skirmish, and again they flailed at each other with the fighting irons. Brock parried a knife slash by Struan, who twisted out of range and knew that he could not contain himself and back off much longer. 'Gorth planned the pox!'

'God curse thy lies!' Brock stalked Struan slowly.

'Gorth gave Culum spiked liquor. And an aphrodisiac. Gorth paid a whorehouse to put him with a poxed woman. He wanted Culum poxed! That's your cursed son. Understand?'

'Liar!'

'But by the grace of God, Culum's na poxed – I only said it to make you understand why I wanted to kill Gorth. Culum's na poxed. Tess neither.'

'Wot?'

'Aye. That's the truth, before God.'

'Devil! Blasphemer! You lie afore God!'

Struan feinted and Brock backed and readied menacingly. But Struan did not hack with the weapon. He went through the open door of the derelict church and stood in front of the altar.

'Before God I swear that's the truth!'

He turned, and his control snapped. All sound seemed to cease, and the whole world was Brock and the frantic urge to kill. He began to come back down the aisle, slowly. 'Gorth murdered a whore in Macao and another here,' he hissed. 'That's more truth. His blood is na on my hands, but yours will be.'

Brock backed out of the doorway, his gaze never wavering from Struan's. The wind had dropped and he knew it to be strange, untoward strange. But he paid it no heed.

'Then – then thee . . . had cause,' Brock said. 'I – takes back wot I sayed. Thee had cause, by God.' Now he was outside on the ground and he stopped at bay. 'I takes it all back about Gorth. But that baint the settling 'twixt thee an' me.' His rage at Gorth and at Struan and at all the years scorched him, and he knew only that now he must fight and hack and kill. To stay alive.

Then he felt the new wind on his cheek.

Abruptly his head cleared. He stared at the mainland.

Struan was momentarily put off balance by the suddenness of Brock's movement, and he hesitated.

'Wind be changed,' Brock croaked.

'Eh?' Struan made an effort to concentrate and backed away, not trusting Brock.

Now they were both staring over mainland China, listening intently, tasting the wind.

It was coming from the north.

Gently but unmistakably.

'It be squall, mayhaps,' Brock said, his voice wounding him, his heart thundering; all strength was gone from him.

'Na from the north!' Struan said, feeling equally depleted. Oh God, for a moment I was an animal. But for the wind changing—

'Typhoon!'

They looked at the harbour. The junks and sampans were scurrying for shore.

'Aye,' Struan said. 'But that was the truth. About Gorth.'

Brock tasted the bile in his mouth and he spat it out. 'I be apologizing for Gorth. Yus. That were provoked and he be dead an' more's the pity.' Where be I goin' wrong? he asked himself. Where? 'Wot be done, be done. I sayed my piece to thee at Settlement. Yus, I were wrong to call thee out today, but I sayed my piece in Canton and I baint changing. I baint changing any more than thee. But the day thee come again' me with cat in thy hand be the day there baint a stopping 'twixt us'n. Thee choose that day, as I sayed afore. Agreed?'

Struan felt curiously faint. 'Agreed.' He backed off and unfastened his fighting iron and sheathed his knife, watching Brock, distrusting him.

Brock also put away his weapons.

'And you'll forgive Culum and Tess?'

'They's dead afore my face, like I sayed. Till Culum be part of Brock and Sons and Brock and Sons be Noble House and I be Tai-Pan o' Noble House.'

Struan dropped his metal whip on the ground and Brock dropped his.

Both men swiftly left the hill by different paths.

XLVII

All that day the north wind increased. By nightfall Queen's Town was as prepared as it would ever be. Windows were shuttered and doors jammed and those who had had the foresight to dig cellars blessed their joss. Those with makeshift or temporary habitations sought stronger buildings. But few buildings were strong – except in Happy Valley. And few men were prepared to risk the night gases even though they had read today's *Oriental Times* about a cure for malaria. Today there was no cinchona to be had.

All ships battened down and every available anchor was bedded deeply. The ships were eased as far apart as possible to give maximum swinging room when the wind would back or veer.

But there were some who said that because this wind was constant from the north, it could not possibly herald a typhoon. Never had anyone known the typhoon to blow from the north alone. A typhoon wind veered or backed constantly.

Even Struan was inclined to agree. Never had the barometer stayed so high. And never had there been a typhoon without the barometer's dropping.

Drizzle came at nightfall from a lowering ceiling and brought relief from the heat.

Struan had weighed the dangers carefully. If he had had only himself to worry about, he would have put to sea in *China Cloud* and run south until the wind backed or veered. Then he would have taken the safest course and escaped. But some instinct he did not understand told him not to risk the sea. Instead, he moved May-may and Yin-hsi and Ah Sam and Lim Din to the vast abandoned factory in Happy Valley and put them in his quarters on the third floor. He felt that the rain and the wind would blow away the night gases. May-may would be safer protected by brick and stone than on the sea or in a hole in the ground, and that was all that counted.

Culum had thanked Struan for the offer of a berth in the factory but had said that he preferred to bring Tess into the harbour master's office. It was a low, granite building, and Glessing had set aside space for Culum and Tess in the quarters that were part of the building.

Struan had told them what had happened on the knoll and that a peace of sorts had been made. And all day while he was preparing against a typhoon that might never come, he brooded over the violence of man.

'What's the matter, Husband?' May-may had asked.

'I dinna ken. Brock, mysel', typhoon – I dinna ken. Maybe the cloud ceiling's too low.'

'I'll tell you wat's wrong. You think too much about wat happened – and worse, you worry about wat could possible have happened. Huh! Foolishness! Be Chinese! I order you! Past is past. A peace is made with Brock! Dinna waste time moping like constipate hen. Eat some foods and drink some tea and make love to Yin-hsi.'

She laughed and called Yin-hsi, who hurried across the huge bedroom and sat on the bed and held her hand. 'Look at her, by God! I've already give her a good talking-to.'

He grinned and felt easier.

'That's better,' she said. 'I think of you all time, never mind. Yin-hsi is in the room next door alone. She waits dutifully all night.'

'Get on with you, lassie.' He chuckled, and May-may spoke rapidly in Chinese to Yin-hsi. Yin-hsi was all attention and then she clapped her hands elatedly and beamed at Struan, then hurried out.

'What did you say, May-may?' he asked suspiciously.

'I tell her how you make love. And how to make you fantastical excited. And na to be afraid when you cry out at the ending.'

'Devil take you! Have I nae privacy at all?'

'Tai-tai knows wat's best for her losing-temper little boy. Yin-hsi's waiting for you now.'

'What?'

'Yin-hsi. I told her to get ready. Love in the evening is pleasant, never mind. Have you forgotten?'

Struan grunted and walked for the door. 'Thank you kindly, but I'm busy.' He went downstairs and suddenly found that he was feeling much better. Aye, it was nonsense to worry about the past. And again he blessed his joss for May-may.

Brock had had the broken foremast of the *White Witch* unstepped and lashed alongside for safety. All the broken spars and twisted rigging had been sorted out and the ship battened down. He had put three anchors forward and a canvas storm anchor aft to keep her head to wind.

All day he had felt dulled. His head and chest ached, and he knew that his dreams would be bad tonight. He would have liked to get drunk, to lose himself. But he knew that there was danger coming. He took a last turn around the rain-swept deck with a lantern, then went below to check on Liza and Lillibet.

'Here's thy tea, luv,' Liza said. 'Best get into dry clothes. They be ready for thee.' She pointed at the bunk and at the sea coat and trousers and sea hat and boots.

'Thanks, luv.' He sat at the table and drank the tea.

'Da',' Lillibet said, 'will you play game with me?' And when Brock did not answer, for he had not heard her, she tugged at his wet coat. 'Da', will you please play a game with me?'

'Leave thy father be,' Liza said. 'I be playin' with thee.'

She took Lillibet into the next cabin and thanked God that there was peace between her man and Struan. Brock had told her what had occurred, and she thanked God for answering her prayers. The wind be miracle, she told herself. Now all that he needed be patience. He be comin' round to bless Tess. Liza asked God to guard Tess and Culum and the ship and all of them, then sat down and began to play a game of noughts and crosses with Lillibet.

This afternoon Gorth's coffin had been put into a cutter. Liza and Brock had gone into deep water and Brock had said the funeral service. When he finished, he had cursed his son and cast the coffin into the deep. They had returned to the *White Witch* and Brock had gone into his sea cabin and bolted the door, and he had wept for his son and for his daughter. He wept for the first time as a man, and the joy of life had gone out of him.

All night the wind and the rain gradually worsened. With the coming of dawn the downpour was strong but not fearsome and the sea high but not threatening.

Brock had slept in his clothes, and he came on deck blear-eyed. He checked the barometer. Still 29.8 inches, steady. He rapped it with a knuckle but the reading did not change.

'Morning, sir,' Pennyworth said.

Brock nodded apathetically.

'It just be a rainstorm, I'm thinking,' Pennyworth said, perturbed by Brock's lack-lustre manner.

Brock peered at the sea and sky. The cloud blanket was only a few

645

hundred feet away and hid the mountains of the island and the Peak, but this too was not unusual.

Brock forced himself to walk forward and check the anchor hawsers. They were firm: three anchors and three hawsers as thick as a man's thigh. Enough to hold in any storm, he thought. But this did not please him. He felt nothing.

China Cloud was riding neat and sleek in the harbour, the watch cowering in the lee of the quarterdeck. All the other ships were riding without trouble, the huge flagship dominating the harbour. A few late-coming sampans and junks were searching for moorings beside the floating village in the lee shore of a small cove near Glessing's Point.

Brock went below, and Pennyworth and the rest of the watch were greatly relieved to have him gone.

'He's aged since yesterday,' Pennyworth said. 'He looks like he's dying on his feet.'

In the dawn light, Struan was checking the rough shutters on the first floor. He went downstairs to the main floor and checked the others. He read the barometer: 29.8 and steady.

'By the gods!' he said, and his voice rattled around the buildings. 'Either begin to drop or finish the godrotting rain and let's have done with it.'

'Wat, Tai-Pan?' May-may called down from the landing.

She looked minute and lovely. 'Nothing, lassie. Go back to bed,' he said.

May-may was listening to the rain pattering and wished she was in Macao where the sound of the rain on the roof would be sweet. 'I dinna like this rain,' she said. 'I hope the children are all right. I miss them very much.'

'Aye. Go back to bed, there's a good lassie. I'm going outside for a while.'

She waved jauntily. 'You be careful, now.'

Struan pulled on his heavy sea coat and went outside.

Now the rain was slanting. It had not increased in the last hour. In fact, he thought, it seemed to be lessening. The clouds were very low. He studied the lie of *China Cloud*. She's pretty and safe, he told himself.

He went back and checked the barometer. No change.

He ate a good breakfast and prepared to leave again.

'Up! Down! Why so unpatient? Where you go now, heya?' May-may asked.

'The harbour master's office. I want to see if Culum's all right. Dinna on any account go out or open any of the windows or doors, Supreme Lady Tai-tai or nae Supreme Lady Tai-tai.'

'Yes, Husband.' May-may kissed him.

Queen's Road was deeply puddled and almost empty. But the wind and the rain felt bracing, and it was better than being shut up in the box of the factory. It was just like a spring nor'easter in England, he thought; nae, na as strong as that.

He entered the harbour master's office and shook the rain off.

Glessing got up from his desk. 'Morning. Strange storm, isn't it? Care for tea?' He motioned to a chair. 'Suppose you're looking for Culum and Mrs Struan. They've gone to early service.'

'Eh?'

'They'll be back any minute. It's Sunday.'

'Oh. I'd forgotten.'

Glessing poured the tea from a huge pot, then put it back on the side of the brazier. The room was large and filled with charts. A mast came through the raftered ceiling, and beside it was a hatch. Signal flags were in neat cubicles, muskets in racks, and the whole room was tidy and shipshape. 'What's your opinion of the storm?'

'If it's a typhoon, then we're dead in its path. That's the only answer. If the wind does na back or veer, then the vortex'll pass over us.'

'God help us if you're right.'

'Aye.'

'Once I got caught in a typhoon off Formosa. Never want to be in a sea like that again, and we weren't anywhere near the vortex. If there is such a thing.'

A gust of rain-heavy wind rattled the storm shutters. They watched the wind indicator. Still inexorably north.

Glessing put down his teacup. 'I'm in your debt, Mr Struan. I got a letter the day before yesterday from Mary. She told me how kind you were – you and Culum. Particularly you. She sounds very much better.'

'I saw her just before I left. She was certainly ten times better than the first time I saw her.'

'She says she'll be released in two months. That you told the Papists you'd accept responsibility for her. Of course, that's up to me now.'

'As you wish. It's only a formality.' Struan wondered what Glessing would do when he found out the truth about Mary. Of course he had to find out; how could May-may believe that he would na?

'Did the doctor say what her trouble was?'

'A stomach disorder.'

'That's what she wrote. Again, thanks.' Glessing moved a chart on his desk and wiped a tea stain off the teak. 'Culum mentioned that you were Royal Navy as a lad. At Trafalgar. Hope you don't mind my asking, but my father had the honour of serving there too. I was wondering what ship you were in. He was flag lieutenant to Admiral Lord Collingwood, in—'

'In *Royal Sovereign*,' Struan said for him. 'Aye. I was aboard.'

'By Jove!' was all that Glessing could splutter.

Struan had kept this private from Glessing deliberately, always knowing that he had another ace to play should he need it to bring him to his side. 'Aye. Of course, I dinna remember your father – I was a powder monkey and scared out of my wits. But the admiral was aboard and I was in *Royal Sovereign*.'

'By Jove,' Glessing repeated. He had seen the 110-gun ship of the line off Spithead once as a boy. 'A ship's company of eight hundred and thirty-six and the future Tai-Pan of The Noble House. No wonder we won, by God!'

'Thank you,' Struan said. 'But I had little to do with the battle.'

'By gad, Tai-Pan – if I may call you that – I think this is wonderful. I'm very glad. Yes, I am. My word! Used to hate your guts, as you know. Don't any more. I still think my decision was right at the Battle of Chuenpi, but I realize now that that nitheaded misbegotten sod Longstaff was right when he said if I'd been you or you'd been me our attitudes would have been the same.'

'What're you riled at Longstaff for?'

Glessing's face lost its warmth. 'Bloody sod had the impertinence to interfere in naval affairs! He "suggested" to the admiral that I be sent home! Thank God the admiral's Royal Navy and the bugger's sacked! And while we're on the subject of fools, I'm sure you've read last night's paper. That stupid bastard Cunnington! How dare he say Hong Kong's a godforsaken rock with hardly a house on't! Absolute bloody nerve! Best harbour on earth! How dare he say we don't know anything about the sea?'

Struan remembered the first day – good Lord, was that only six-odd months ago? – and he knew that he had been right. Glessing might go down with Hong Kong, but he would fight to the death to protect Glessing's Point. 'Perhaps the new man, Whalen, will agree with Cunnington.'

'Not if I have anything to do with it. Or the admiral. He nearly had apoplexy when he read it. Stands to reason. Look at the fleet. Riding snug and safe as in Portsmouth harbour. Where the devil'd we be a day like today without Hong Kong? Good sweet God! I'd be frightened to

648

death if I was anchored at Macao. Got to have Hong Kong and that's the end to it. Even that idiot general's seen the light for once and agrees absolutely,' and he ranted on, damning Cunnington and Longstaff to Struan's amusement.

The door opened and a flurry of wind and rain rustled the charts. Culum and Tess came in, their spirits high in spite of the weather. 'Oh, hello, Tai-Pan,' Culum said. 'Can we have tea, Glessing old boy? We said a prayer in your honour!'

'Thanks.' Glessing motioned at the iron pot on the coal stove. 'Help yourself.'

Tess curtsied to Struan and took off her sodden cloak. 'Morning, Tai-Pan.'

'You're lovely today, Mrs Struan,' he said.

She blushed and busied herself pouring the tea.

'You two look happy enough,' Struan said.

'Yes, we are,' Culum said. 'We've given thanks to God. And for sending the change of wind.'

'Will you na change your mind, lad? Come over to the residence?'

'No, thanks, we're quite safe here.'

Struan noticed a small jewelled silver box dangling from Culum's watch chain. 'What's that, Culum?'

'A keepsake. Tess gave it to me.' The little box contained Brock's twenty sovereigns now, and Culum felt guilty again that he had never told Tess of their significance. He had put them into the box after he and Tess had come ashore off *White Witch* the last time: to remind him about Tyler Brock – that Brock hadn't been fair, hadn't given him the chance to tell his side.

'It was my grandma's. It's not much of a wedding gift,' Tess told Struan. 'But with no dowry and all, beggars can't be pickers.'

'Dinna worry about that, lass. You're part of The Noble House. When do you move into *your* house?'

'In three weeks,' Culum and Tess said together, and they laughed, happy again.

'Good. We'll do the day proud. Well, see you all later.'

'Look at that fool, Tai-Pan!' Glessing said. He was training his telescope through a porthole at a lorcha barrelling into the east channel, sails reefed.

'What the devil's he doing? Nae day to be out there,' Struan said.

'With your permission, Mr Struan, I'll signal her to tie up to your wharf in Happy Valley. She'll have trouble anchoring in the Roads. And your wharf's clear.'

649

'Aye, with pleasure. Who is she?'

'Naval lorcha. Flying the deputy captain superintendent's pennant.' He snapped his telescope shut. 'Her captain needs his head examined to leave Macao in this weather. Or Mr Monsey's in a devil of a hurry. What's your evaluation of that?'

Struan grinned. 'I'm no crystal gazer, Captain Glessing.'

Glessing gave the necessary orders to a seaman, who promptly bound the signal flags to the halyard. He opened the ceiling hatch. Rain sprinkled them as the flags were run up.

'Where's Longstaff?' Struan asked.

'Aboard the flagship,' Glessing said. 'Must confess I'd be happier afloat myself.'

'I wouldn't,' Culum said.

'Oh dear, no,' Tess added.

Struan finished his tea. 'Well, I'll be off. You know where I am if I'm needed.'

'Baint – I mean isn't that dangerous, Tai-Pan?' Tess asked. 'The Happy Valley fever and all? Staying there?'

'The wind and the rain'll beat down any poison gases,' Struan said with a confidence he did not feel.

'Don't forget, Tess, there's some cinchona left, and we'll soon have plenty,' Culum said. 'Tai-Pan, I think the new venture is wonderful. A service to all mankind.'

Struan had told Culum about his arrangement with Cooper before it had been printed. He had also encouraged Culum to spend time with the American; the more he thought about a joining of Cooper and Culum, the more he liked the idea. 'Jeff's very smart, lad. You'll like working with him.' He pulled on his rain cloak. 'Well, I'll be off. Listen, you two. Dinna worry about Brock. Dinna worry about your father, lass. I'm sure he'll come around if you give him time. Just give him time.'

'I hope so,' Tess said. 'Oh, I hope so.'

On his way out, Struan stopped at the barometer. 'Good sweet Jesus! It's down to 29.5 inches!'

Glessing looked at the time anxiously. It was almost ten o'clock. 'That's damn near half an inch in half an hour.' He made a notation on a pressure chart and followed Struan, who had run outside.

A quarter of the eastern horizon was black, and there seemed to be no division between sea and sky. The wind was fiercer, gusty, still dead-north, and the rain was heavier.

'There she is, all right,' Struan said tensely. 'Batten down for your life.' He began sprinting along Queen's Road towards Happy Valley.

650

'Inside! Culum! Tess!' Glessing ordered. He slammed the door and bolted it. 'Whatever you do, don't open any doors until further orders.' He pulled the porthole covers over the storm windows and checked all the fastenings, and he realized that Struan was right. The vortex was going to pass directly over them. 'I'm very glad you've made peace with your father, Culum. Now, I think, some breakfast,' he said calming them: 'Mrs Struan, perhaps you'd supervise?'

XLVIII

Struan ran hard. A few Chinese sedan-chair coolies were hurrying for
Tai Ping Shan, and a few stray Europeans were scurrying for cover.
Through the rain Struan could see the naval lorcha abreast of him in
the harbour, scudding fast for Happy Valley under many reefs. The
churning sea was dull grey-green. The dark line of a squall raced at
incredible speed across the harbour; its edge caught the lorcha, tore off
her mainsail and heeled her over. Struan braced himself and was
enveloped by the squall. It lasted only a few seconds, but he felt the
lash of the blinding, wind-whipped rain and was almost thrown off his
feet. When he could open his eyes, he looked seaward. Amazingly the
lorcha was still afloat, limping ahead with a mizzen sail, her decks
awash, the tatters of the mainsail streaming aft.

Once more Struan began running. He arrived on his wharf at Happy
Valley just in time to see the white-capped swell catch the lorcha and
fling her against the pilings. A sailor jumped from the gunnel with the
fore hawser, but he slipped and fell between the wharf and ship. His
hands caught the edge of the wharf and he shrieked as the ship slammed
into the jetty and cut him in half. When the sea pulled the ship away, the
sailor had disappeared.

Struan shouted to the frightened deckhands and raced forward. One
seaman threw him the line and he made it fast around a stanchion.
Another, taking his life in his hands, jumped and made the wharf safely
with the aft hawser.

The sea was rising and the lorcha and the wharf pilings screamed,
and then the lorcha was fast and men began jumping ashore.

'Make for the factory!' Struan motioned them to follow and he ran
for the front door. He yanked it open, the wind tugging at him. The
crew of eight men ran in, cursing and blessing their luck.

Struan pulled off his soaking clothes, then noticed Horatio and Monsey. 'Great God, what are you doing here, Horatio? Hell, Mr Monsey!'

'Never thought we'd see land again,' Monsey wheezed.

Horatio leaned against a wall, his chest heaving, and vomited.

The door opened, and in a flurry of wind and rain the captain – a young lieutenant – strode in angrily and shook himself like a dog. Struan walked over and slammed the door.

'By the Lord God of Moses!' the man said to Struan. 'Have you seen the sky?'

'What the devil were you doing at sea on a day like this? Did you na have sense enough to use your eyes in Macao?'

'Yes, by God! But I was ordered to Hong Kong, so I came to Hong Kong. We're in the hands of a maniac!'

'Eh?'

'That blood-mucked Captain Superintendent of Trade, Sir Clyde Blood-mucking Whalen, by God! That stupid Irish bugger damn near sank my ship with all hands. I told him there was bad weather and he just looked at the sky and said, "Plenty of time to get there. You're ordered to sea!" Thank God for Hong Kong.'

'What's the sea outside like?'

'One more hour and we'd never have made it. Twenty, thirty-foot waves. But that cursed wind! It won't veer and it won't back – it's impossible! Is it a typhoon or isn't it? How's that possible?'

'Because the storm's due east of us and we're dead in its path, lad.'

'Oh God, protect us!'

'Make yourself at home. I'll see about some tea and grog for all hands.'

'Thank you,' the young man said. 'Sorry for the outburst.'

Struan went across the room to Monsey and Horatio. 'Can you make it upstairs, Mr Monsey?'

'Yes. Thank you, Tai-Pan. You're very thoughtful.'

'Give me a hand with Horatio.'

'Of course. Don't know what's got into the poor lad. He's been moaning incoherently ever since we left Macao. Most peculiar.'

'It's fright,' Struan said.

They helped Horatio out of his rain-sodden coat. His face was dirty grey now and he was almost helpless with nausea. Together they half carried him up the stairs and laid him on a couch in the west wing in the quarters that once belonged to Robb.

Struan went to the sideboard and poured brandies. Monsey took one, his hands trembling, and drained it. He accepted a refill. 'Thanks.'

'Give Horatio some,' Struan said. 'I'll be back in a minute.'

He walked along the corridor on to the landing and then down the east-wing corridor. His suite occupied the south end of this floor.

May-may, Yin-hsi, Ah Sam and Lim Din were playing mah-jongg at a small table in the expanse of the living-room. Lanterns were lit and the flames danced cheerily.

'Hello, Tai-Pan,' May-may said. She picked up another of the bamboo-ivory tiles and slammed it down with a curse. 'Oh stinky day, Tai-Pan!' she said. 'My joss is terrifical bad. I have na won a single game. I've lost four hundred cash, and we've been playing for hours. Woe, woe, woe! I'm glad to see you, never mind.'

The rain battered the shutters and the wind was rising.

'Cursed noise! Can you lend me some taels? I'm impoverished!'

'I'll take it out of your allowance. Go back to your game, lassie.' Struan grinned. 'We've company downstairs and all around, so dinna go out.'

'Wat for go out?'

He returned to Robb's quarters.

Monsey was looking better. He had taken off his soaked clothes and had wrapped himself in a blanket. Horatio was sleeping restlessly.

'God saved us this time, Tai-Pan,' Monsey said.

'Why the devil did you leave Macao? Asking for trouble. You must have seen the weather.'

'Official business, Tai-Pan,' Monsey sneered. 'His Imperial Excellency Whalen arrived by frigate last night. He ordered me to Hong Kong with an official dispatch for the ex-plenipotentiary. In this weather, if you please! As if a day or two matters! I hadn't the heart to tell him the "big news" had already been printed in the paper.'

'What's he like?'

'I'd say he's rather trying. He sailed into Macao about midnight, aboard a frigate, unannounced. Within four minutes I was summoned aboard. He presented his credentials, gave me the Foreign Secretary's dispatch to read – it's word for word with Skinner's story; how do these damned newsmen get secret documents? – and ordered me to leave with the dawn to deliver the dispatch to Longstaff immediately. Said that he would be arriving in Hong Kong forthwith, that Longstaff was to leave at once. That I was to see the admiral and general and tell them that everything must be ready for an immediate departure north.' Monsey plopped into a chair. 'An Irishman. What more can I say?'

'Why did he na come direct?'

'Can't have two plenipotentiaries here at once – distinctly against the rules, Mr Struan. There's such a thing as protocol, thank heavens. I have to take over from Longstaff right away. As soon as he's left harbour I can inform His Excellency. Then *he* will arrive.'

A gust of wind slammed against the shutters and rattled them.

'Blast the man. Nearly killed me. Things are going to buzz in Asia with him in control. The first thing he said was "That cursed rock can sink as far as I'm concerned." Oh, my word! If you don't mind, I'll turn in for a few minutes. I'm not feeling myself.'

Horatio began moaning again and then he vomited.

'Give him some more brandy,' Struan said. 'There's a bedroom next door.'

He went below to see how the lorcha's crew was faring. They had already found the stores and liquor. Those who were not drinking or eating were sleeping or trying to sleep.

The barometer read 29.1, still falling.

'Good God, that's more than three tenths of an inch in an hour,' the young lieutenant said. He was tall and fair. 'Oh, by the way, Mr Struan, I'm Lieutenant Vasserly-Smythe, RN.'

Struan shook the offered hand.

'Thanks for giving us a berth.'

A north window burst open and rain and wind poured into the foyer. Three of the seamen slammed the window shut and relocked the shutters.

'I think I'll take a look at my ship,' the lieutenant said.

'Better come this way.' Struan led him along a corridor to a side window that was heavily shuttered but in the lee of the north wind. He opened it warily and peered out.

He saw that *China Cloud* and *Resting Cloud* were riding easily. The lieutenant's lorcha was rising and falling with the waves, creaking and grinding against the pilings, and to the east there was no horizon. Just blackness. And the blackness was bearing down on them.

'Your ship's as safe as she'll ever be, Lieutenant.'

'Yes.' The young man took a last frightened look at the eastern sky and bolted the shutters. 'She's my first command. I've only been in these waters a few months. What happens in a typhoon?'

'The Supreme Winds come out of the gale against you.'

'What're they?'

'Gusts. Squalls. Sometimes they're called the Devil Winds.'

XLIX

The first of the Supreme Winds swooped across the harbour an hour later and fell on *Resting Cloud.* Her hawsers snapped and she was adrift and helpless in the darkness. Mauss, in one of the cabins, looked up from his Bible and thanked God for His mercies and for Hung Hsiuch'uan. The gale heeled *Resting Cloud* over, slamming Mauss unconscious against the bulkhead, and the ship was driven, almost on her beam end, towards the shore. In her path was *Boston Princess*, the Cooper-Tillman vessel. The two ships collided violently and *Resting Cloud*'s bowsprit tore away part of the other vessel's upperworks before it snapped off, and she careened away, stern towards the shore. The tempest flung her into the floating village of sampans, swamping scores of the tiny boats, and grounded her viciously. Hundreds of Chinese were drowning, and those still secure in the sampans cowered under their flimsy bamboo coverings. But the next Supreme Wind snatched up the coverings and with them many families.

Aboard *Boston Princess*, Jeff Cooper dragged himself off the deck of the main cabin and helped Shevaun to her feet. The gale rose in violence and battered the vessel, but her hawsers held.

'Are you all right?' Cooper shouted above the tumult.

'I think so. Oh God help us!'

'Stay here!' 'Cooper opened the cabin door and fought his way towards the deck, pandemonium surrounding him. But the gale and horizontal rain drove him below. He went down three decks and along a corridor and into the hold. He peered around with a lantern. Where *Resting Cloud* had hit, the timbers were crushed and the seams starting to go. Cooper went back to Shevaun.

'It's all right,' he lied. 'So long as we don't break our moorings.'

A Supreme Wind struck Glessing's Point and snapped the flagpole, throwing it like a javelin at the harbour master's office.

The flagpole smashed through the granite wall and chopped Glessing's arm off at the elbow. It punched its way through the other side of the building, throwing Culum aside and cascading bricks and debris and burning coals on Tess before coming to rest.

The rain and gale howled through the broken walls, and Tess's dress was ablaze. Culum groped to his feet and beat at the flaming clothes with his hands.

When he had extinguished the fire, he held Tess in his arms. She was unconscious. Her face was white, and her hair was partially singed. He ripped off her dress and examined her carefully. There were burns on her back.

Culum heard screaming. Turning around, he saw Glessing, blood spurting from his stump. And across the room he saw the disjoined arm. Culum stood up, but his legs would not move.

'Do something, Culum!' he shouted against the wind.

His muscles obeyed and he grabbed a flag halyard and bound a tourniquet around the stump and stopped the bleeding. He tried to decide what he should do next, and then he remembered what his father had done when Zergeyev was shot.

'Clean the wound,' he said aloud. 'That's what you've got to do. Then cauterize it.'

He found the tea-kettle. There was still water in it, so he knelt beside Glessing and began to daub the stump. 'Hold on, old boy,' he muttered, Glessing's agony tearing his guts.

Tess whimpered as she regained consciousness. She groped to her feet, the wind churning the papers and flags and dust, half blinding her. Her eyes cleared and she screamed.

Culum spun around in panic and saw her staring at the severed arm.

'Help me! Find the fire tongs!' he yelled above the storm.

She shook her head and backed away hysterically, and then she was very sick.

'Get the godrotting tongs!' Culum shouted, his hands on fire. 'You can be sick later!'

Tess forced herself upright, shocked by the venom in Culum's voice. She began searching for the tongs.

'For God's sake, hurry up!'

She found them and through her nightmare handed them to Culum.

Culum picked up a burning coal with the tongs and held it against the stump. Glessing screamed and fainted again. The stench from the

657

burning flesh was overpowering. Culum fought his nausea down until the stump was thoroughly cauterized.

Then he turned his head and retched violently.

Brock looked up from the barometer, the whole ship vibrating and timbers howling. '28.2 inches, Liza! It's never beed that low!'

Liza held Lillibet and tried to contain her fear. 'I wonder where Tess be. Oh God, protect her.'

'Yus,' Brock said.

Then there was a shrieking of timbers and the whole ship reeled, but she corrected herself.

'I be going on deck!'

'Stay here! For luv of God, lad, doan risk –' But she stopped, for he had already gone.

'When's it going to stop, Mumma?' Lillibet sobbed.

'Any minute now, luv.'

Brock poked his head cautiously out of the leeward quarterdeck gangway. He craned to look at the masts. They were bent like twigs. There was a monstrous crack as the main topmast stay parted.

'Belay there!' Brock shouted down the gangway. 'Port watch on deck!'

A Supreme Wind shrieked out of the north and another halyard parted, and another, and the mainmast sheared off just above the deck and slammed into the mizzen, and both masts and spars and rigging pounded on to the deck, crushing the quarterdeck gangway. *White Witch* heeled dreadfully.

Brock freed himself from the debris and railed at the petrified crew. 'On deck, you scum! For your lives! Cut masts adrift or we be lost!'

He spurred the men on deck, and, hanging on with one hand, the gale wrenching him and the rain blinding, he slashed frantically with an axe at the main halyards and remembered the other typhoon that had cost him an eye, and he prayed that he would keep his remaining eye and that Tess was safe and Liza and Lillibet would not drown.

The scaffoldings of the new town had long since been torn away. A Supreme Wind rushed at the shore, demolishing the remains of the soldiers' tents and wrecking the dockyard. It snuffed out the gin shops and pubs and whorehouses near the dockyard and flattened Mrs Fotheringill's establishment, pulverizing the paintings and entombing Aristotle Quance in the rubble. Then it tore an arrow-straight swath through the hovels of Tai Ping Shan, obliterating a hundred families, and swept the remnants of the debris a mile away on the breast of the Peak.

Deep below ground on the Tai Ping Shan hillside, Gordon Chen crouched in the secret cellar he had constructed and congratulated himself on his prudence. The cellar was rocklined and very strong, and though he knew that his house above had vanished, he cheerfully reminded himself that all his valuable possessions were safe here, and the house could quickly be replaced. His eyes ranged over his sets of ledgers, the files of land deeds, promissory notes, outstanding debts and mortgages, over the chests of bullion, boxes of jades, bolts of expensive silks and kegs of the finest wine. And over his concubine, Precious Blossom. She was propped comfortably, under the finest down coverlets, in the bed that was set against one of the walls. He poured himself another tiny cup of tea and got in beside her.

You're a very clever fellow, he told himself.

The wind and the rain were pounding the north side of Struan's factory in Happy Valley, and from time to time one of the Devil Winds would pull at it. But apart from an occasional tremor, and the raging noise, the building stood firm.

Struan was lighting a cheroot. He hated being inside the house and doing nothing.

'You smoke too much,' May-may shouted above the tempest.

'Smoking's good for the nerves.'

'Dirty habit. Stinky.'

He said nothing, but checked the barometer again.

'Wat for you keep looking at that every ten minutes?'

'It tells me where the storm is. When it stops dropping, the centre'll be over us. Then it'll rise. I think.'

'I'm na very pleasurably happy we're here, Tai-Pan. It would be much better at Macao.'

'I dinna think so.'

'Wat?'

'I dinna think so!'

'Oh! Do we have to sleep here again tonight?' she asked, tired of shouting. 'I would na want you or Yin-hsi or even that turtle-dung Ah Sam to get the fever.'

'I think we're safe enough.'

'Wat?'

'We're safe enough!' He glanced at his watch. The time was twenty past two. But when he peered through a crack in the shutter, he could see nothing. Only a vague movement in the darkness and horizontal streaks of rain on the windowpanes. He was thankful that they were in the lee of the wind. This corner of the residence faced east and west and south and was protected from the violence. And Struan was thankful to be ashore. Nae ship can live through this, he told himself. Nae harbour on earth can protect the fleets from such an act of God for long. I'll wager Macao's catching it. No protection there. I'll wager half her shipping's wrecked and ten thousand junks and sampans for five hundred miles up and down the coast. Aye. And the ship sent to Peru? I'll wager she was caught and she's gone. Father Sebastian with her.

'I'm going to look in on the others.'

'Dinna be long, Tai-Pan.'

He went along the corridor and checked the shutter fastenings. Then he walked across the landing and absently straightened a Quance painting and entered Robb's quarters.

Horatio was sitting – half shadowed – on the bamboo chair in which Sarah had been seated long ago, and in the frail, flickering light of the lanterns Struan thought for a moment that it *was* Sarah.

'Hello, Horatio. Where's Monsey?'

Horatio looked at Struan without recognizing him. 'I found Ah Tat,' Horatio said, his voice weird.

'I canna hear, lad. You'll have to shout.'

'Ah Tat. Oh yes, I found her.'

'Eh?'

Horatio began to laugh hideously, as though Struan were not in the room. 'Mary's had an abortion. She's a filthy whore for stinking heathens and has been for years.'

'Nonsense. That's nonsense, lad. Dinna believe it,' Struan said.

'I found Ah Tat and lashed the truth out of her. Mary's a devil whore of Chinese and she carried a half-caste bastard in her. But Ah Tat gave her the poison to murder it.' Again a shriek of laughter. 'But I caught Ah Tat and beat her till she told me the truth. She was Mary's pimp. Mary sold herself to heathens.' His eyes went back to the lantern's core. 'Glessing'll never marry a whore of Chinese. So she'll be mine again. All mine. I'll forgive her if she crawls and begs.'

'Horatio. Horatio!'

'She'll be all mine. Like when we were young. She'll be all mine again. I'll forgive her.'

Another devil gust rocked the building, and another, and a third, and it seemed as though they were in the middle of ten thousand raging maelstroms, and Struan heard windows and shutters blowing apart. He took to his heels and rushed along the corridor to his suite. May-may and Yin-hsi were quailing in the bed, and Ah Sam was moaning, petrified. Struan charged over to the bed and took May-may in his arms. The roaring screaming violence crescendoed.

Abruptly the storm vanished.

There was silence.

Light began seeping through the cracks in the shutters, growing in intensity with the seconds.

'Wat's happened?' May-may asked, her voice sounding unreal in the overpowering hush. Struan put May-may down and walked over to the window. He peered through one of the cracks, then cautiously opened the window and unbolted the shutters. He winced as hot, dry air swarmed into the room.

He stared incredulously into the harbour.

China Cloud was still at her moorings. *White Witch* was dismasted, the ends of her halyards drooping over the side. *Resting Cloud* was grounded at Glessing's Point. The lorcha was still tied up at the company wharf. He saw one frigate aground, heeled over, high above the surf. But the rest of the fleet and troopships and merchantmen were still at anchor, untouched.

Above were feathers of clouds and blue sky and sunshine. But in the harbour the sea had gone mad. Pyramidal waves rose out of the surface and clashed into each other, and he saw *China Cloud* take water over both gunnels and stern and bow at the same time. Beyond, in the distance, an encircling screen of gigantic thunderclouds grew out of the sea and towered, peerless, to sixty thousand feet.

And over all, but for the slopping of the waves against one another, the unearthly silence.

'We're in the vortex!'

'Wat?'

'The eye of the storm. This is it. The centre!'

May-may and Yin-hsi and Ah Sam hurried over.

'The fleet's safe, by all that's holy!' Struan said exultantly. 'The ships are safe. They're safe.' Abruptly his joy vanished and he slammed the shutters and windows and bolted them.

'Come on,' he said urgently, flinging the door open, and they followed, astonished. He ran the length of the corridor across the landing into the opposite wing of the building and opened the door of the northmost suite.

The shutters were partially broken and one window was smashed and glass was everywhere.

'Stay here,' he said.

'Wat's the matter, Tai-Pan? The storm's gone.'

'Do as I say.' He hurried out. May-may shrugged and sat on a broken chair.

'What's the matter with Father?' Yin-hsi asked.

'I don't know. I really don't understand him sometimes. Thank heaven the noise is finished. Isn't it quiet? It's so quiet it almost hurts.'

Yin-hsi went over to a window and opened it. 'Oh, look!' she said. 'Isn't it beautiful? I'm so glad the storm's gone.'

May-may and Ah Sam crowded around her.

Brock was standing on deck, paralysed. He saw waves coming at him from all directions, but here in the lee of the shore the waves were small. The sun was warm and dry. Water dripped loudly. The encircling thunderclouds were like the walls of a mighty cathedral, five miles wide. But the walls were moving: The eastern quadrant was closing on them.

'What be happening, luv?' Liza said, coming on deck with Lillibet, 'Oh, how beautiful!'

'Oh, it's so pretty,' Lillibet said.

'We be in't eye of storm. In't vortex!' Brock burst out. Seamen coming on deck turned and looked at him.

'Oh, look!' Lillibet said. She pointed to the island. 'Isn't that funny!'

The trees that dotted the island were white against the brown earth; their limbs had been stripped clean of leaves. Now Queen's Town had almost vanished and Tai Ping Shan was a shambles. Tiny figures were beginning to move over the foreshore.

'Get thee below,' Brock said, his voice grating.

Bewildered, they did as he ordered.

'Cap'n Pennyworth!'

'Yes, sir?'

'Best make peace with thy Maker,' Brock said. 'Only He knowed wot be t'other side of them devil clouds. Get thee all below!'

He picked up his telescope and trained it on the residence of The Noble House. He could see Struan standing in the midst of a group outside the front door. There were a few heads peeking out of third-storey windows.

He snapped the telescope closed. 'Best get thee inside, Dirk,' he said quietly.

He jammed the remnants of the gangway hatch into place and battened it down as best he could and went below.

'I thinks we be sayin' prayers,' he said breezily.

'Oh good,' Lillibet said. 'Can I say mine first? Like at bedtime?'

*   *   *

Culum had his arm around Tess.

'If we get out alive, I'm damned if I'm staying here,' he said. 'We're off home, and to the devil with this place.'

'Yes,' Tess said, sickened by the destruction. She looked in terror at the gradually approaching cloud screen. It swallowed Kowloon Peninsula. 'We'd better get inside,' she said.

Culum closed the door after her, and the pain from his burned hands was excruciating. But he bolted the door.

She picked her way over the debris, and knelt beside Glessing. His face was cadaverous but his heart was beating. 'Poor George.'

Struan was gauging the distance from the wharf to *China Cloud* and to the eastmost thunderclouds. He knew there was no time to get a cutter, so he ran down to the end of the wharf and cupped his hands.

'Orlov!' he roared. 'Ahoy, *China Cloud*!' His voice echoed eerily over the Happy Valley harbour, and he saw Orlov wave to him and heard him call back faintly, 'Aye?'

'Point her south! The winds'll come from the south now! Head her south!'

'Aye,' he heard Orlov answer, and in a moment he saw seamen scurrying forward, and a cutter was over the side and the men began to pull feverishly and shove the bow around.

Struan hurried back to the group of men at the front door.

'Get inside!'

Some of them moved, but the young lieutenant still stared at his lorcha and at the harbour with disbelief. 'Great God on high, she's still afloat! And look at the fleet – look at the ships! I thought they'd all be blown to hell by now, but only one frigate's aground, and that clipper's lost its masts. Incredible, by god! South, did you say? Why?'

'Come on,' Struan said, tugging his arm. 'Get inside – and get your men inside.'

'What's the matter?'

'For God's sake, we'll be out of the vortex in a few minutes. And then the gale'll reverse – I think it'll reverse and blow from the south. Get your men—'

He was almost bowled over as Horatio rushed past and bolted up Queen's Road towards the dockyard.

'Come back, you fool, you'll be killed!' Struan shouted, but Horatio paid no attention. Struan chased after him.

'Horatio! What the devil's the matter with you?' he said, catching up with him and grabbing him by the shoulders.

'I've got to tell Glessing. Finish all this marriage filth,' Horatio screamed. 'Get away from me – murderer! You and your filthy murdering whore! I'll see you both hanged!' He tore himself loose and rushed away.

Struan charged after him again, but rain began spattering and he stopped. The thundercloud wall was already halfway across the harbour, the sea boiling at its feet. He saw the cutter's crew scramble aboard *China Cloud* and vanish below decks. Orlov waved a final time, then he too was gone.

Struan turned and raced for the shelter of the residence. A gust clawed at him and he redoubled his efforts. He gained the threshold in driving downpour and looked back.

Horatio was running out of Happy Valley along the shore. The cloud wall covered the dockyard and Horatio began to disappear into the mist. Struan saw him stop and look up, and then the tiny figure was wafted away like a leaf.

Struan hurled the door open and shoved it closed, but before he could bar it, darkness came and a Supreme Wind burst in and tossed him deep into the foyer. It blew out all the ground-floor windows and killed three seamen. And was gone.

Struan picked himself up, astonished that he was still alive. He rushed the door, and with all his huge strength closed and barred it. The maelstrom passed the windows, sucking debris and papers and lanterns out of the residence – everything that was not nailed down.

As Struan ran for the stairs, he came across the crushed body of the young lieutenant. He stopped, but another gust drove him back and snatched the body away, and then Struan was fighting out of the suction up the stairs to safety.

As the gale hit from the south, the *White Witch* pitched drunkenly. She heeled on her beam ends and swung on the fore hawsers, by some miracle righted herself, and, trembling, pointed into the wind. Brock picked up Lillibet and Liza and put them back in the bunk. He shouted encouragement, but they could not hear, and all of them held on desperately for their lives.

Water sluiced down the gangway and began crashing against the barred cabin door, seeping under it. A Devil Wind slammed into the ship. There was a thundercrack and the ship shuddered, and Brock knew that an anchor hawser had parted.

*   *   *

Aboard *Boston Princess*, Shevaun was holding her hands over her ears to try to shut out the shrieking of the winds as they assaulted the ship. Cooper felt the last hawser go. He shouted to Shevaun to hold on, but she did not hear him. He reeled over to her and held her against a stanchion with the limit of his strength.

The vessel lurched. Her port gunnel gasped out of the sea and took more water, and she began to drown. The storm gloated over her and flung her into the Russian ship.

In the main cabin of the huge brigantine a glass-fronted cabinet shattered, scattering bottles, crystal and cutlery, and Zergeyev hung on and cursed and said a prayer. As his ship settled back, her nose to wind, he kicked the debris from under his feet, said another prayer and poured another brandy.

A pox on Asia, he thought. I wish I were home. The pox on the devil storm. The pox on the British. The pox on this foul island. The pox on everything. The pox on Prince Tergin for sending me out here. The pox on Alaska – and on emigration. And on the Americas and Americans. But bless Shevaun.

Yes, he told himself as the ship reeled again and shrieked under the tempest's violence. And bless Mother Russia and her sanctity, and her place in history. Prince Tergin's plan is marvellous and correct, of course it is, and I'll help it come to pass. Yes. Curse that damned bullet and the damned pain. No more riding over the limitless plains. That's finished. Now I'm forced to forget the playing. Face yourself, Alexi! The bullet was luck – what's the word the Tai-Pan uses? – ah yes, joss. The bullet was joss. Good joss. Now I can turn all my energies to the service of Russia.

What to do? Leave Hong Kong now. It's finished. The stupid Lord Cunnington has throttled Britain and given us the key to Asia. Good. Make a trade deal with the Tai-Pan or with Brock, and then leave as soon as possible and go on to Alaska. Make arrangements for the tribes. Then go home. No, better – go on to Washington. Look and listen and think, and do what you were born to do – serve mother Russia to the ends of the earth. Her earth.

Zergeyev felt the pain in his hip and for the first time enjoyed it. Very good joss, he thought. So it's decided. We leave if we survive.

But what about Shevaun? Ah, there's a girl worth thinking about, by the cross. Valuable politically, eh? And physically. But not good enough to marry even though her father's a senator. But perhaps she is. Perhaps that would be a very wise move. Consider it, Alexi.

We're going to need leaders for Russian America. The continent will be split into principalities. Intermarriage has always been a form of conquest, eh? Perhaps you could hurry the day.

By St Peter, I'd like her for a mistress. How could I arrange that? Would she? Why not? Stupid fool, Cooper. Damned annoying that she's betrothed. Pity. She said she didn't love him.

The typhoon was at its height, but the ring of mountains still deflected most of its violence from the harbour.

Boston Princess was floundering in mid-harbour, one gunnel awash, taking the seas heavily. Cooper knew that the end was near, and he held Shevaun and shouted that all would be well.

The ship sank deeper in the water and rushed at Kowloon. Then she beached heavily. The rocks gutted her, and the waves rushed into her holds, and then a Supreme Wind lifted her out of the havoc and thrust her on her side above the surf.

Now that the gale blew from the south, it soared over the mountain range towards the mainland. And in the funnel that Happy Valley formed it increased its impossible force. It bore down on The Noble House, seeking its weak spot.

Struan was cradling May-may in his arms in the relatively safe suite on the north side. A lantern flickered nervously and cast bizarre, dancing shadows. Beyond the shattered windows, in the lee of the shrieking rain-soaked gale, there was only darkness. Ah Sam was kneeling on the floor and Yin-hsi nestled close to Struan for protection.

May-may turned and put her lips near Struan's ear and shouted, 'Tai-Pan, I'm displeasurably unhappy with all this noise.'

He laughed and held her tighter and she put her arms around his neck. He knew that nothing would touch them now. The worst was past.

'Three or four more hours, and it'll be gone, lassie.'

'Stinky storm. Did I tell you it was a dragon? A sea-monster dragon?'

'Aye.'

'God's blood!'

'What's the matter?'

'I forgot to take the last dungtasting-poison-cinchona cup. Today's the last day, never mind.'

'You'll take it in a few hours, never mind!'

'Yes, Husband!' May-may felt very happy and very healthy. She played with the long hair at the nape of Struan's neck. 'I hope the children are all right.'

'Aye. Dinna worry, Chen Sheng will look after them.'

'When we go, heya? I'm fantastical urgent about marriage.'

'Three months. Definitely before Christmas.'

'I think you should take another barbarian wife as Third Sister.'

He laughed.

'Very important have lots of sons. Dinna laugh, by God!'

'Maybe you've a good thought, lassie,' he said. 'Perhaps I should have three barbarians. Then there's you and Yin-hsi. I think it's terrifical important we should get another Chinese sister before we leave.'

'Huh! If your activity thus far with Second Sister's any signal, we take lovers, by God!' Then she kissed his ear and shouted, 'I'm very gracious pleased my joss gave me you, Tai-Pan!'

A cannonade of Supreme Winds blew the windows in on the south side and the whole building shifted as though in an earthquake. The nails in the roof screamed against an untoward pull, and then a devil gust peeled off the roof and hurled it into the sea.

Struan felt Yin-hsi surge away into the maelstrom above. He grabbed for her, but she had vanished.

Struan and May-may held each other tightly.

'Dinna give up, Tai-tai!'

'Never! I love you, Husband.'

And the Supreme Winds fell on them.

L

The sun rose bravely and spread warmth over the shattered town and the safe harbour.

Culum found his father in the havoc of the residence. Struan was crumpled in a corner of the north suite, and in his arms was a small, gaunt Chinese girl. Culum wondered how his father could have loved her, for to him she was not beautiful.

But they were not made obscene by death. Their faces were calm, as if they were asleep.

Culum left the room and went down the broken staircase, and outside into the gentle east breeze.

Tess was waiting. And when she saw him shake his head helplessly, her eyes too filled with tears and she held his hand. They walked out of Happy Valley by Queen's Road, seeing nothing.

The new township was in ruins, with debris scattered everywhere. But, here and there, buildings were still standing, some mere shells, others damaged only slightly. The foreshore was alive with people hurrying to and fro, or standing still in groups surveying the wreckage of their dwellings or business houses. Many were supervising gangs of coolies, salvaging their sodden possessions or making repairs. Sedan-chair coolies were plying their trade. So were the beggars. Patrols of soldiers had been placed at strategic points against the inevitable looting. But, strangely, there were very few looters.

Sampans and junks were fishing in the calm harbour among the flotsam of broken boats. Others were arriving, bringing new settlers. And the procession of Chinese from the shore up to Tai Ping Shan had begun again.

Smoke hung over the hillside. There were a few fires amid the wreckage of hovels. But beneath the smoke was the hum of industry. Restaurants, tea and food shops and street vendors were doing business again while the inhabitants – hammering, sawing, digging, chattering –

patched up their homes or began to rebuild, blessing their joss they were alive.

'Look, Culum luv,' Tess said. They were near the dockyard.

Culum was numb, his brain hardly functioning. He looked where she was pointing. On a slight hillside their almost-finished home was roofless and tilted off the foundations.

'Oh dear,' she said. 'What're we going to do?'

He did not answer. Her fear magnified as she sensed his panic. 'Come on, luv. Let's – let's go to the hotel, then – then aboard *White Witch*. Come on, luv.'

Skinner hurried up to them. His face was grimy, his clothes ripped and filthy.

'Excuse me, Mr Culum. Where's the Tai-Pan?'

'What?'

'The Tai-Pan. Do you know where he is? I've got to see him immediately.'

Culum did not answer, so Tess said, 'He's – he's dead.'

'Eh?'

'He's dead, Mr Skinner. We – my – Culum saw him. He's dead. In't factory.'

'Oh God, no!' Skinner said, his voice thick. Just my cursed joss!

He mumbled condolences and went back to his printing shop and his demolished press. 'You're publisher-owner!' he shouted. 'Of what? You've no press and no money to buy another, and now the Tai-Pan's dead, so you can't borrow from him, so you own nothing and you're busted! Busted! What the hell're you going to do?' He kicked the rubble, careless of his coolies who stood to one side, waiting patiently. 'Why the hell did he have to die at a time like this?'

He ranted on for a few minutes and then sat on a high stool. 'What're you going to do? Get yourself together! Think!'

Well, he told himself, the first thing is to bring out the paper. Special edition. How? Handpress. 'Yes, handpress,' he repeated aloud. 'You've the labour and you can do that. Then what?'

He noticed the coolies watching him. Then you keep your mouth shut, he cautioned himself. You get out a paper and then go to that helpless young idiot Culum and talk him into putting up money for the new press. You can twist him easily. Yes. And you keep your mouth shut.

Blore came in. His face was lifeless.

'Morning,' he said. 'What a bloody mess! The stands've vanished,

669

and the paddock. Everything. Lost four horses – the gelding too, dammit to hell!'

'The Tai-Pan's dead.'

'Oh God!' Blore leaned against the shattered doorway. 'That tears it. Oh well, thought it was too good to last.'

'Eh?'

'Hong Kong – the Jockey Club – everything. This puts the coffin on everything. Stands to reason. The colony's a disaster. This new bugger Whalen'll take one look and laugh himself silly. No hope now, without the Tai-Pan. Dammit, I liked him.'

'He put you up to seeing me, didn't he? Giving me the dispatch?'

'No,' Blore said. The Tai-Pan had sworn him to secrecy. A secret was a secret. 'Poor chap. Glad in a way he didn't live to see the end of the colony.'

Skinner took him by the arm and pointed to the harbour. 'What's out there?'

'Eh? The harbour, for God's sake.'

'That's the trouble with people. They don't use their heads or their eyes. The fleet's safe – all the merchantmen! We lost one frigate aground, and she'll be repaired and floated in a week. *Resting Cloud* the same. *Bostom Princess* gutted on Kowloon. But that's all. Don't you understand? The worst typhoon in history put Hong Kong to the test – and she came out of it with all flags flying, by God. The typhoon was huge joss. You think the admiral won't understand? You think even that clot-headed Cunnington doesn't know our might rests with the fleet – whatever that dumb-brained general thinks? *Sea power*, by God!'

'Good Lord. You really think so?'

Skinner had already gone back inside and was shoving debris out of his way. He sat down and found a quill and ink and paper and began scribbling.

'You really think so?

'If I were you, I'd start making plans for the new stands. You want me to print that you're having a meet as scheduled?'

'Absolutely. Oh, jolly good! Yes.' Blore thought a moment. 'We ought to start a custom – I know, we'll have a special race. Biggest prize money of the year – last race of the season. We'll call it the Tai-Pan Stakes.'

'Good. You'll read it tonight!'

Blore watched Skinner writing. 'Are you doing his obituary?'

Skinner opened a drawer and pushed a sheaf of papers towards him. 'Wrote it a few days ago. Read it. Then you can help me on handpress.'

Culum and Tess were still standing where Skinner had left them.

'Come on, luv,' Tess said, tugging his arm, anguished.

With an effort Culum concentrated. 'Why don't you go aboard *White Witch*? I'm – I'm sure they're anxious to – to know you're safe. I'll come aboard later. Let me alone for a while, will you, dear? I've – well, just let me alone.'

'Oh Culum, what're we going to do?'

'I don't know. I don't know.'

He saw her looking up at him and then she had gone. He walked on towards Glessing's Point, not hearing and not seeing, time ceasing to exist for him. Oh God in heaven, what do I do?

'Mr Struan?'

Culum felt a tug on his arm and came out of his daze. He noticed that the sun was high in the sky and that he was leaning against the shattered flagpole at Glessing's Point. The master-at-arms was looking down at him.

'His Excellency's compliments, Mr Struan. Would you kindly step aboard?'

'Yes. Yes, of course,' Culum said, feeling drained and dull-witted.

He allowed the master-at-arms to guide him to the waiting cutter. He climbed the gangway on the flagship and then went below.

'My dear Culum,' Longstaff said, 'Terrible news. Terrible. Port?'

'No. No, thank you, Your Excellency.'

'Sit down. Yes, terrible. Shocking. As soon as I heard the news I sent for you to give you my condolences.'

'Thank you.'

'I'm leaving with the tide tommorow. The new plenipotentiary sent word by Monsey that he's in Macao.' Damn Whalen! Why the devil didn't he wait? Damn the typhoon! Damn Dirk! Damn everything! 'You've met Monsey, haven't you?'

'No – no, sir.'

'No matter. 'Pon my word, damned annoying. Monsey was in the residence and not a scratch. Yes, terrible. No accounting for joss.' He took snuff and sneezed. 'Did you hear that Horatio was killed too?'

'No – no, sir. The last – I thought he was at Macao.'

Damned fool, what did he have to get killed for? Complicates everything. 'Oh, by the way, your father had some documents for me. Have to have them before I leave.'

Culum searched his memory. Then effort exhausted him even more. 'He didn't mention them to me, Your Excellency. I don't know anything about them.'

'Well, I'm sure he kept them in a safe place,' Longstaff said, delighted that Culum was not privy to them. 'A safe, Culum, that's where they'd be. Where's his private safe?'

'I – I don't know, sir. I'll ask Vargas.'

'Come on, Culum, pull yourself together. Life goes on. The dead must bury their dead and all that sort of thing. Mustn't give up, what? Where's his safe? Think! In the residence? Aboard *Resting Cloud?*'

'I don't know.'

'Then I suggest you look, and very quickly.' Longstaff's voice sharpened. 'This is of paramount importance. And keep this entirely to yourself. You understand the punishment for treason?'

'Yes – yes, of course,' Culum answered, frightened by Longstaff.

'Good. And don't forget you're stil deputy colonial secretary and under a solemn oath to the Crown. I put the papers in your father's hands for safe-keeping. Highly secret diplomatic documents concerning a "friendly power". Maps, documents in Russian with English translations. Find them. Report back aboard the instant you have them. Report back aboard at sunset in any event. If you can't do the job, I'll do it myself. Oh yes, and I'll be consigning some seeds to you. They'll be arriving in a few days. You will redirect them to me and treat the matter with equal secrecy. Orderly!' he called out.

The door opened instantly. 'Yessir!'

'Show Mr Culum ashore!'

Culum went back to the longboat in panic. He hurried to *Resting Cloud.* She was in the middle of the sampan village, almost upright. Soldiers had been posted against looters. He clambered aboard and went below.

Lim Din was standing guard with a cleaver, outside Struan's quarters.

'Mass'er dead?' he asked.

'Yes.'

Lim Din made no reply. Nor did his expression change.

'When Tai-Pan hav paper – important paper – where putshee?' Culum asked.

'Heya?'

'Paper – put safe. Safe hav? Safe box?'

Lim Din motioned him inside and showed him the safe set in the bulkhead of Struan's bedroom. 'This piece?'

'Key-ah?'

'Key-ah no hav. Tai-Pan have, never mind.'

Where would he have the key? Culum asked himself in desperation. On him! On him, of course! I'll have to . . . would Vargas have a duplicate? Oh God in heaven, help me. There'll be – well, a funeral and a coffin. Where do I – and . . . and what about the girl, the Chinese girl? Can she be buried with him? No, that's not right. Does he have a family by her? Didn't he say that he had? Where are they? In the ruins? Think, Culum! Wake up, for God's sake! What about the ships? And money? Did he leave a will? Forget that, that's not important now – none of it is. You've got to find the secret papers. What did Longstaff say? Maps and a Russian document?

Brock walked, unnoticed, into the cabin. He saw the fear and help-lessness in the youth's face, and the bloodstains on his hands and clothes. 'Morning, lad,' he said kindly. 'I comed as soon as I heared. I be sorry, lad, but doan thee fret. I be doing everything for thee.'

'Oh, thank you, Mr Brock,' Culum said, his relief apparent. 'It's just that I . . .' He sat down weakly.

'Tess sayed without you, she beed deaded an' Glessing too. It be bad joss about thy Da', but doan thee fret. I been to residence, lad, and I be making all arrangements proper. I ordered Orlov t'put Lion and Dragon at half-mast and be getting *Resting Cloud* afloat in no time. Thee just catch thy breath. I be looking after all.'

'Oh, thank you, Mr Brock. Did you see his key? I need to get –' Culum was on the point of explaining about the documents, and then he remembered what Longstaff had said about treason and he stopped himself in time. 'I just thought,' he said lamely, 'well, I suppose I ought to go through his papers.'

'I baint going through his pockets,' Brock said, his voice cold, 'Just laid him out proper and put woman outa sight.' Ah, Dirk, he told himself, I baint never forgetting how thee looked, thee and the heathen. Together. But for thy own sake, and sake of kids, thee be buried Christian alone. 'I be making arrangements for her quiet.'

'Yes, of course,' Culum said.

'We be joining, Culum. Brock's and Struan's. It be best for all. Noble House be Brock-Struan. I be drawing up papers immediate and all's done.' Yus, he told himself. I baint rubbing thy joss in thy face, Dirk, but I be *the* Tai-Pan now. At long last. Culum be following, if he be good enough, after Morgan and Tom. 'All's forgot 'twixt thee and Tess'n me, lad. Best thee go aboard *White Witch*. Tess be needing comfort.'

'Yes. All right, Mr Brock. Thank you. But – well, if you don't mind, I'd like to – to go to the residence first.'

'Be aboard come sundown.' Brock walked out.

Culum wiped his face with his hands. That's best. Joining. That's best. You always said you would. Get yourself together, Culum. *Go and get the key!*

'Mass'er?' Lim Din beckoned him to follow, and led the way into another cabin. Mauss was lying on the floor. He was ugly in death.

'Joss. Never mind,' Lim Din said, and he laughed nervously.

Culum groped his way off the ship, his heart hurting him, and along the plank alleyways of the sampan village, and then he was near Glessing's Point. He walked along Queen's Road, picking his way around rubble and broken possessions, mumbling incoherent thanks to the many who came up to him offering their sympathy. There was only one thought in his shattered mind: you have to go through his pockets.

'Culum!'

Through his daze he saw Cooper, Shevaun beside him, in a group of traders near the hotel. He would have gone on, but they came up to him.

'We've just heard, Culum. I'm so sorry,' Cooper said. 'Is there anything we can do to help? It's terrible joss.'

'Yes,' Shevaun said, her face badly bruised and her clothes in tatters. 'Terrible. We've just got back from Kowloon. I think it's just awful, so unfair.'

'I – I . . . well – I'm sorry I can't talk now. I've – I've . . .'

They watched him hurry away.

'Poor young devil,' Cooper said.

'He looks frightened out of his wits.'

'I don't wonder. What with the Tai-Pan and Glessing.'

'Is he going to be all right? Glessing?'

'I don't know. Hope so.' Cooper looked across the harbour. He could see the wreckage of *Boston Princess* and he thanked God again for their lives. 'If I were him I'd be, too.' That poor lad's going to need all the help he can get, Cooper told himself. Thank God the Tai-Pan lived to give me the papers. I wonder if he had a premonition. No, surely not. What about Culum? What's he going to do? He's as helpless as a babe. Perhaps I could watch over him – I owe that to the Tai-Pan and more. We've the cinchona business together now. We'll cancel the other two directors, so it'll just be Culum and me. Why not join forces? Totally merge the companies? The new Noble House – Cooper-Struan. No! Struan-Cooper. You'll be fair with Culum. He'll be next. There are gigantic possibilities in a merger, of course there are. But you'd better move fast or Brock'll have the poor lad eating out of his hand. Tai-Pan of the Noble House. *The* Tai-Pan. Why not?

'What're you smiling about?' Shevaun asked.

'A passing thought,' he said, and put his arm in hers. You were very wise, Dirk, my friend. Both gambles. Yes. It'll take me a year to consolidate. 'I'm so very glad to be alive. Let's go to the jetty. We should see if Zergeyev's all right. Listen, Shevaun, I've decided to send you home for a year, by the next ship.'

'What?' Shevaun said, and stopped.

'Yes. At the end of that time, if you decide you love me and want to marry me, I'll be the happiest man alive. No, don't say anything,' Cooper added as she began to speak. 'Let me finish. If you decide you don't, then you have your freedom and my blessing with it. Either way I won't buy out the Tillman interests. Your father will receive, during his lifetime . . .'

Shevaun turned away and they began to walk again, arm in arm, as he continued. But she wasn't listening now. A year, she exulted, hiding her joy. Free in a year. Free of this cursed place! And father still has his shares! Oh God, you've answered my prayers. Thank you, thank you, thank you. Poor Dirk, my love. Now I'm free and now you're dead.

She looked at the Russian brigantine. Yes, she thought, the Tai-Pan's dead. But you're free and the archduke would be the perfect choice.

'I'm sorry, Jeff. What did you say?'

'Just that I want you to deliver some private documents to your father.'

'Of course, my dear. And thank you, thank you. The year will pass quickly.'

Gordon Chen bowed before the Buddha in the shattered temple and lit a final joss stick. He had wept for his father and for May-may.

But now is not the time for weeping, he told himself. Joss is joss. Now is the time for thinking.

The Noble House is dead.

Culum hasn't the strength to carry on. Brock will dominate him and join the companies together. Brock I cannot handle. If Culum joins with Brock, Culum is finished. So either way, he cannot help me. Can I help him? Yes. But I can't help him with the barbarians, and I can't help him to be *the* Tai-Pan. That is something a man gets for himself alone.

The thread of incense smoke curled delicately in the air and he watched it, the perfume pleasing.

Only my father knew about our arrangement. I have the lac of silver and it will become fifty, a hundred lacs in time. I am the richest Chinese on Hong Kong. And the most powerful. *The* Tai-Pan of the Chinese.

Let me be honest – I'm not Chinese, not English. No. But I am content with my joss and more Chinese than English. I will marry a Chinese and so will my children and my children's children, never mind.

Hong Kong? I will help the island grow strong. I stopped the looters today. Labour will be plentiful and obedient in the future.

I believe what my father said: the British Government will fall. It has to fall. Oh gods, I demand that it fall for the future of China! You're Chinese – think of China. I will endow the largest temple in south China . . . well, at least – a temple fit for the headquarters of the Triads and for Tai Ping Shan: as soon as the government falls and Hong Kong is absolutely British.

He kowtowed and touched his forehead on the floor in front of the statue to confirm the bargain.

Yes, only Father knew how rich we were to become. Even so, half will be Culum's. Each month I will account to him and we will split equally just so long as he fulfils Father's side of the bargain: that I control everything, and few, if any, questions asked; and everything private – just between the two of us.

Go and find him now. Pay your respects.

Pity Culum married the Brock girl. That's his downfall. Pity he hasn't the strength to go alone. I wish he and I could trade places. I'd show the barbarians how to run The Noble House. And the emperor, for that matter. If Culum had even a little strength and was prepared to take counsel. Chen Shang and I could hold the Brocks and all the other jackals at bay.

Well, never mind. I will give my father and his Tai-tai a funeral which will be legend for a hundred years. I will make him a tablet and his Tai-tai a tablet and mourn a hundred days. Then I'll burn the tablets for their safe rebirth.

I will fetch Duncan and the babe and bring them up as my own. And I will start a dynasty.

It was near sunset. Culum was sitting on the steps of the derelict church on the knoll in Happy Valley, his head propped in his hands. He was staring into the distance. You've got to get the key, he told himself

676

again and again. There's nothing to be afraid of. You've got to get the key and then the papers. Come on, Culum.

He was over his panic now. But now he was consumed with self-disgust – and loneliness. He looked at the residence below. Vargas and Orlov were still standing by the doorway. He remembered vaguely coming into the valley, hours ago, and seeing them there and then turning away to avoid them, then shrieking 'Leave me alone' when they came after him. He noticed that Gordon Chen was with them now. Gordon wasn't there before, he reminded himself. What does he want? To sneer? To pity me like all the others? Longstaff . . . Brock . . . Cooper . . . Shevaun . . . Skinner . . . Vargas . . . Orlov. Even Tess. Yes, I even saw it in your face when we stopped on Queen's Road. Even yours. And you're right. You're all right.

What do I do? What can I do? I'm not my father. I told him that I wasn't. I was honest with him.

Get the key. Get the key and get the papers. You've got to deliver the papers. Longstaff ordered you aboard. It's almost time. Oh God. Oh God.

He watched the shadows lengthen.

Do I tell Brock about Jin-qua's coins? About the remaining three half coins and the three favours and the holy oath and about *Lotus Cloud*? I'll have to. Oh God, what about Wu Kwok? And the Chinese apprentice-captains and the boys, Father's wards? Brock won't honour my oath, I know he won't. I don't care. What's the difference?

'Hello.'

'Oh hello, Mr Quance.' Culum dully squinted at the shadows. 'Please leave me alone. Please.'

Aristotle Quance ached in every limb. Only an hour ago he had been dug out of the wreckage. His hair and face were caked with blood and rubble dust, and his clothes were ripped.

'I'm sorry,' he said. 'It was joss. Just joss.'

'I hate that word. Please, please leave me alone.'

Quance saw the helplessness and agony and self-hatred in the face that vaguely resembled the one he knew so well. He remembered the first time he had seen Struan. In a back alley in Macao, lying unconscious in the dirt. Just as helpless, just the same, he told himself. No, not the same, never the same. Dirk was like a god even though he lay in the filth. Ah, Dirk, you always had the face of a god and the power of a god – awake, asleep. Yes, and even in death, I'll wager. *Face.* That's what you had.

So different from your son.

Yes, but not so different. Culum stood up to you over the knoll. And stood by you against Brock. And shooks hands with Gordon Chen in front of you. And eloped with the girl, damning the consequences. And saved Glessing's life. The spark's there.

Remember what you said when you regained consciousness? 'I dinna ken who you are, but thanks for giving me back my face.'

You'd never lost it, Dirk, my friend.

'*Aye. But give my son back his.*'

Isn't that what you'd say if you were here? Are you here? I miss you, laddie.

Aristotle Quance put away his own sadness and sat on the step beside Culum. 'I know this isn't the time to bring it up, Tai-Pan, but could you lend me four hundred and fifty guineas?'

'What? What did you say?'

'Could you lend me four hundred and fifty guineas, Tai-Pan? I know it's a terrible moment, but the old witch Fortheringill's alive – no typhoon'd dare touch her, by God! She's threatening to put me in debtor's prison. I've no one to turn to but you.'

'You said "Tai-Pan". You called me *Tai-Pan*.'

'Well, you are aren't you?'

Then Culum remembered what his father had said. About the joy and the hurt of being Tai-Pan; about being a man; about standing alone; about life and the battle thereof.

His loneliness vanished. He looked at the three men below. His anxiety returned. Simple enough for Aristotle to say 'Tai-Pan' he thought. But what about them? You've got to win them to your side. How? What was it Father said? 'You rule men by your brain and by magic.'

He stood up shakily. 'I – I'll try. By the Lord God, I'll really try. I'll never forget you, Aristotle. Never.'

He walked down the hill, his stomach fluttering uneasily. The master-at-arms was approaching from the cutter and they met at the front door.

'His Excellency wants you aboard right smartly.'

'Please tell him I'll see him as soon as possible,' Culum said with a calmness he did not feel.

'He wants you now.'

'I'm busy. Tell him I'm busy!'

The man reddened, saluted, then stamped away.

What's in those papers, anyway? Culum asked himself. He gathered his will and faced Orlov, Vargas and Gordon Chen.

'Brock sent *orders* aboard my ship,' Orlov said. He saw the bloodstains on Culum's hands and sleeves and shuddered. 'Orders to lower the flag, by Odin! I'd've done it anyway as I heard. Do I take orders from him now? Eh?'

'Brock will destroy us Mr Culum. What are we going to do?' Vargas said, wringing his hands.

'Vargas, go and make arrangements for the funeral. My father and his lady will be buried together.'

'What?'

'Yes. Together. She's a Christian and will be buried with him. Gordon, wait for me. I want to talk to you. Orlov, go aboard your ship and raise the flag. Fly it at the masthead. Then go aboard *White Witch* and fetch my wife ashore.'

'*Fetch* her, did you say?'

'Yes. And here.' He took out the twenty sovereigns. 'Give these to Brock with my compliments. Tell him I said to buy himself a coffin.'

The three men looked at Culum strangely.

Then they said, 'Yes, Tai-Pan,' and obeyed.